Sara's Garden

by

Linda Marie

DORRANCE PUBLISHING CO., INC.
PITTSBURGH, PENNSYLVANIA 15222

ISBN # 0-8059-5097-4
Printed in the United States of America

First Printing

For information or to order additional books, please write:
Dorrance Publishing Co., Inc.
643 Smithfield Street
Pittsburgh, Pennsylvania 15222
U.S.A.
1-800-788-7654
Or visit our web site and on-line catalog at
www.dorrancepublishing.com.

Dedication

Thank you Spike, for sharing my dream.
Thank you Michael, for helping me sift through it all.
I love both of you.

Preface

WE ALL SAY THINGS WE DON'T MEAN. WE ALL DO THINGS WE DON'T WANT We do it because we're human; we have faults. If we could take back our words or the stupid things we do, this would be a perfect world.

We can't do this, so we try to learn from our mistakes. Sometimes it takes us several tries to sink in, but that's our human side. After a while we all get it.

Everything you say and do is like a seed thrown into the wind. Some seeds will fall on stone, wither, and die. Others will fall on soil and grow. Some will be weeds; some will be beautiful flowers.

Anyway you look at it, some will get hurt. Some won't. It's our nature to only try and plant flowers, but it's also our nature to plant weeds. Just as a can has two sides, so does mankind.

We try to be good people. Things happen that change our lives forever.

We all grow up with sayings passed down from generation to generation. Some are strange and make us laugh. Others are good, sound advice. And we take notice of them.

Sometimes we wonder if the world will ever know we were here. Did we make our mark in life? We all make our mark in life: some weeds, some flowers. But the world knows you were here.

A garden can be many things. But the only things you need are one seed, soil, water, and love. Love is the most important ingredient; without it nothing grows.

In today's world we hear, "What's in it for me?" What would happen if there was nothing in it for you? No money, no acknowledgments that you did something for someone. Would you still do it? Probably not. It's in our nature to seek some kind of fame, just to prove we were here.

What would happen if you were granted a wish, a chance to change something you knew was wrong? Would you do it?

Sara was granted her only wish in life: to live in a time when life wasn't so hectic; a simple, meaningful life. Only Sara finds life isn't as easy as it seems.

A childhood friend Sean embarks on this journey with Sara.

Together they have to find out what happened, meeting people along the way and trying to find they're way back to the twentieth century.

Sara and Sean make friends with the Oneida Indians. Together they embark on a journey which, in time, will change the life of the Oneida Indians forever.

Sara finds that life is tough. Racism is rampant. Wars are everywhere. Everyone wants something.

For the first time in her life, she falls in love. Sara has to choose to stay in the 1800s with the man she loves or return to her other life, the one at which she worked so hard. If she stayed, she'd never see her children again. If she returned, she'd never know love. Which is more important, to love or be loved?

There is an actual garden planted by Sean and Sara in the 1800s, although this story is fiction. I hope to take you on a journey through time where there are no rewards for the seeds planted. Yet, one hundred years later, the garden still grows, entouched by time and still there for the world to see. All you have to do is look.

Chapter 1

KNOCK, KNOCK!

"What the —"

Whack!

"Shit!" cried Sean, reaching for his head. He opened his eyes slowly.

"Stove? Covered wagon? Where the hell was I?" thought Sean.

Knock, knock!

"Mr. Huntington it's Mr. Farley!"

"Who?" thought Sean, looking around.

He stopped looking when his eyes saw Sara.

"Who's she?" thought Sean. "She is pretty, but she doesn't look too healthy."

Knock, knock! "Mr. Huntington are you all right in there?" asked Mr. Farley.

"Yes!" yelled Sean. "Just banged my head!"

"Bam, damn," cried Sean, "these covered wagons weren't very big.

Mr. Farley laughed, "Takes some getting used to. They're not very big."

"I just found that out," Sean smiled, as he pulled back the flap on the back of the wagon.

Sean closed his eyes and held up his hand to shield the bright light. "Now this makes sense," thought Sean. "Go into the light." He knew he was dead; he felt the bullet go through his body this morning. He remembered falling to the ground. He remembered the pain as the bullet tore through the flesh and muscle. He remembered stepping in front of Sara to protect her.

As coldness slapped his face, he realized that Mr. Farley was talking.

"What?" asked Sean, confused.

"Pretty tough night?" asked Farley. "You've probably been up with Sara all night and just fell asleep when I woke you."

"Sara's here, too?" thought Sean. He was really confused. "Were they both dead?"

Sean shook his head. Farley thought Sean was shaking his head "no," but Sean was trying to shake some sense into his brain to wake up or something.

Cough…cough…cough.

"Sara don't sound too good," said Farley.

"No," said Sean, "I don't like the sound of her cough."

"Well," said Farley, kicking at the newly fallen snow, "that's why I'm here."

"Here?" Sean asked, looking at Farley and, for the first time, seeing a second man standing behind him.

Cough…cough…cough.

Farley looked toward the covered wagon, then back down at his feet. James Farley wasn't a tall man. You could never guess his age; his face was weather worn, leathery looking. But Sean guessed he couldn't be too old. There was no gray in his red hair or beard.

What concerned Sean was that man standing behind Mr. Farley.

"Tell me what's on your mind," Sean said, crossing his arms. Sean was tall, well muscled with black, curly hair and blue eyes. Crossing his arms only gave him a stronger look.

"I-I-I have to do something I've never had to do before in my life," stammered Farley.

"What's that?" asked Sean.

"I have to give you your money back for signing on. I know I promised to take you to the West, but I can't do that now," said Farley.

"Why not?" asked Sean. "I think I could understand this whole thing better if you would explain the whole thing to me right from the beginning," Sean added, thinking along the line maybe he could make sense out of this.

Farley cleared his throat, "Look, I know you've only been married, what, a week?"

Sean nodded. Now he knew the woman in the wagon was his wife.

"But three days ago when we left Rome, Sara was sick then. I know you stayed behind and away from us, but last night the families came to me concerned. Sara's not getting any better. They're afraid she has influenza. I can't take the chance she doesn't. It could kill all of us. So we sat down and talked it through. We wouldn't leave you behind unless it wasn't really for the good of everybody."

"Your right," said Sean. "Sara would never forgive herself if she made people die."

"She's too good a person," smiled Sean. Well, now Sean knew where he was.

"Well, I put up one hell of a fight," smiled Farley. "And we came up with a food plan for you."

"What's that?" asked Sean.

"The man behind me is Ely Smith. He owns the land we're standing on. He's willing to sell to you for fifty dollars," said Farley. "I know that probably sounds like a lot of money, but if I give you back the two hundred dollars you gave me to sign on, you could afford the land. The families in the wagon are willing to sell you enough supplies to get you through the winter. We even have offers of cows, sheep, pigs, and chicken. The men are willing to stay here a couple of days to build a small barn for you."

Well, now a lot of things made sense to him. Sean leaned to his right to get a good look at Mr. Ely Smith. He was the weasel, just like Sara said. Small man, big nose, black, beady eyes with tuffs of brown, thin hair sticking out of his hat. Sean stood back up straight. "Mole" was what he was thinking when he looked at Farley. Sean thought for a minute. This is one thing he did know about; this was a major land deal. It was one that created a lot of problems in the future. "Why would Mr. Smith want to sell me land?" asked Sean. Sean knew one story that was told a thousand times, but he knew it wasn't the real reason.

"Mr. Smith wants to go to California," smiled Farley. "And he's fifty dollars short. He's tried to sell his land, but nobody wants to buy it. Seems that everybody wants to live in the city these days," Farley laughed with a deep, burly laugh. "Still afraid of Indians?" "The Oneida Indians are the nicest people I've met. Very intelligent people. Better than a lot of folks I've met. And in my line of business, I've met a lot of people," Farley smiled and shook his head. "Sure have met a lot of people."

Sean uncrossed his arms and stuck his hands in his coat pockets. They were freezing. In his right pocket he felt the $3000.00 he took out of the bank this morning. In the left pocket he felt the pill bottles. The very pill bottles he went to Sara's to pick up this morning for Laura. Laura was his wife. Sara was the woman he really wanted to married but was afraid to ask. She married Thomas.

Sean cleared his throat.

"Tell you what, Mr. Farley. I will buy this land from Mr. Smith not for fifty dollars but one hundred dollars under two conditions," said Sean.

Mr. Smith stepped from behind Mr. Farley. "One hundred dollars he asked."

"Yes, one hundred dollars and two conditions," said Sean.

"Which might be?" asked Mr. Smith.

"Definitely a mole," though Sean. "One, I want four copies of this land deal drawn up; two for you, two for me," said Sean.

"Why?" asked Mr. Smith.

"Well, this way if anything happens, like, say, no papers being filed at the clerk's office or lost, we always have another copy," said Sean.

"That sounds fair," said Mr. Smith. "And the second request?"

"Well, that's the tricky one. I want you to attach a sheet of paper to each of the four copies stating that I legally bought the land for one hundred dollars from you. I did not steal it, I didn't win it in a poker game, or buy it from you while you were drunk. And the reason you sold it to me. Then I want everyone in the wagon train who can write to sign it as a witness that what is written on the paper is the truth."

"Why?" asked Mr. Smith.

"Well, I will do the same so that neither of us can say we were tricked into something, and we can't back out," said Sean.

Ely Smith looked at Sean for a couple of minutes.

"That sounds fair." Anything else he asked cagily.

"Yes, I would like Mr. Farley to go with you to the registers' office and get a bill laden. That will prove it was turned it. Better make two so you have a copy," said Sean.

Cough…cough…cough.

Sean's hands tightened around the pill bottles in his pocket.

"What for?" asked Mr. Smith.

"This is to protect you and I in case the registers' office loses our paperwork, then we have proof of who took the paperwork and the year, date, and time," smiled Sean.

"Now that's a good idea," said Farley.

"Yes," smiled Mr. Smith. "We must protect ourselves."

Cough…cough…cough.

"Well I have to tend Sara," said a saddened Sean.

"When this is done, Mr. Farley will give you one hundred dollars out of the two hundred he has of my money. This will be done in front of everyone in the wagon train. Mr. Farley will take the rest of the one hundred dollars and buy from everyone who has offered to give me something and leave some money for the men who have offered to help me build a small barn. I trust Mr. Farley to be fair. Now I must tend to Sara, then I will mark a spot for a small barn," said Sean.

Cough...cough...cough.

"Yes," said Farley, "you tend to Sara. Oh God, I forgot Mrs. Fergensen sent over some coffee and a meal for breakfast. It's probably cold now."

"Tell Mrs. Fergensen I said thank you."

Mr. Smith and Mr. Farley turned and walked toward the other wagons.

"Righteous man," said Mr. Smith "he didn't have to give me a hundred dollars, I'd taken fifty."

"Ah, but Sean was thinking!" smiled Farley.

"What do you mean 'thinkin?'" asked Mr. Smith.

"He was thinking of your welfare. He made sure you had money to get to California. Everything he did back there was for the welfare of everyone on the wagon train," said Farley.

"What do you mean?" asked Mr. Smith.

"Well, if your wife lay dying, would you be able to think as clearly as he did?" Farley, shaking his head, said, "That man just saved your ass on a land deal and probably saved everyone's life here. He put everyone else before himself. Now that's a just, good man," smiled Farley.

"You're right," said Mr. Smith.

"You get the paperwork drawn up, and I'll tell everyone what Sean has said," said Farley as they walked into camp.

"Sure," smiled Mr. Smith as he walked to his wagon.

"Sucker! Fool!" thought Mr. Smith as he climbed into his wagon. "I only paid ten dollars for this land, and now I sell it for one hundred. What made Sean think I would go along with his conditions at such as profit? He's going to die right along with his wife. The flu kills everything in its path." Mr. Smith wore a big smile as he wrote up his paperwork. "I'm out of here!" he thought.

Farley looked at the sea of faces, the worried eyes that looked back at him. Farley smiled and watched the relief wash over their faces. He brought everyone together and told them what Sean said.

There was relief among the families, but shock took over when Farley explained about the money and the land deal. Everyone knew that Sean had no more money. He used every penny he had to get married and join the wagon train. There was some murmuring among the people.

"What's wrong now?" said Farley. "The man has given you everything he has!"

"That's the problem," Ely Jones said, stepping forward. "Don't you think we feel bad enough leaving him behind as it is? We don't want his money, too."

"Yeah!" came a cry from the crowd.

"Well what do you suggest I do? He doesn't want you to feel guilty for your choice, and he won't take charity. He thinks he has made the right choice," said Farley.

"I know!" said Susan.

Everyone turned and looked at Susan. Susan was a small, petite, blond woman who didn't speak much, so when she did speak you listened.

"We can pretend to take the money," said Susan.

"Pretend?!" asked Farley, confused.

Susan worked her way up front. "Yes. The men will be building the barn, and us women will be making the meals and tending to the children. You and Mr. Smith have to go to Rome."

"Yes, your point being?" said Farley.

"Well you could take the one hundred dollars and buy some supplies. Us women can make up a list of what they would need. We could say they were wedding presents from us. We can still donate what we said we would, and everyone is happy," said Susan.

"Now that's a good plan," said Laura.

"Yes!" said Farley. "One that would work. They can't refuse wedding presents. Well men, we have a barn to build."

"I know this sounds stupid," said Laura, "but why a barn and not a house?"

Everyone looked at each other, you are right. If Sara was so sick then why weren't they building a house instead of a barn?

"Because," said Sean, walking into camp, "if we do it right, we can build a small room off the end that Sara and I can stay in until we build a house. After we build our house, we can use that room for a chicken coop," smiled Sean.

"That's a pretty good idea as long as you can stand the smell!" said Farley.

Everyone laughed. It was a good, hardy laugh; a laugh that was needed for a long time and one that relieved the tension. Everyone had a job, and they knew what to do. The women left first, and the men gathered around Farley.

"How is Sara?" asked Farley.

"She's resting now. The coughing has stopped, and her fever broke, so the only thing we can do now is pray," said Sean. "I drew up the paperwork as I said I would. See, there are four copies. Two for me and two for Mr. Smith. I also drew up a sketch of the barn. Like I said, it doesn't have to be very big. This is the room I was talking about. The wood stove I keep hitting my head on should keep it pretty warm all winter," smiled Sean.

"It's not very big, looking at it," said Farley.

"How big does it have to be? A couple of cows, a couple of horses, a couple of chickens, and a pig. What more do you need?" asked Sean.

"I don't know," said Farley, scratching his head. "It just seems small."

"Let's see," said Jacob. "This is small. Are you sure about this?"

"Yes. We can probably do this in a day. There are enough men here," smiled Sean.

"Mr. Huntington, here are your two copies," said Mr. Farley handing him Sean's copies.

Sean read his copies. Everything was in order. Mr. Smith and his family couldn't screw he or Sara out of the land. Sean looked up at Mr. Smith. Now all we have to do is get the lovely people of this wagon train to sign the papers and it's a done deal. Those that could write came forward and signed, and Mr. Farley gave Mr. Smith his one hundred dollars in front of everyone. They shook hands, and the deal was done. Mr. Farley and Mr. Smith got ready to go to Rome, and the rest of the men went to cut down trees.

Jacob worried about the size of the barn. It was true that the man didn't have much, but he never would if he didn't think bigger.

Sean's thoughts were running wild as he worked. He needed the fresh air and hard work while he thought things through. First Sara was on his mind. She was really sick! It looked like pneumonia to him. It also looked like he was back in the 1800s. That part didn't make sense to him at all. The pills he had in his pocket were the pills Sara gave him for Laura. Tylenol, penicillin, cough syrup, and flu medication. They were in his pocket but they weren't invented yet. He didn't know if this was even the Sara he thought he knew. Hell, he last knew, he was dead. He had no idea what this place was, though. Sean wished every time he swung the ax that its sudden stop would knock some sense into his brain. The only thing he was certain of was that he wanted these people out of here as soon as possible.

"Hey, Sean," yelled Jacob. "What are you, Paul Bunyon?"

"What?" asked Sean.

"It looks like you are trying to cut down the whole forest by yourself," laughed Jacob. "Take a break. It's lunch time."

Sean stopped. "I have to go check on Sara. I'll be right back." Sean set the ax down and set off for his wagon.

Susan ran up to Sean. "Here, give this soup broth to Sara. It will give her strength," smiled Susan.

"Thank you. Sara will love this," smiled Sean. "I'm afraid my cooking isn't very good."

It was time to give Sara more medication. He didn't hear her coughing as he approached the wagon and that was a good sign. Or was it! The thought scared him, so he set the soup down and jumped into the wagon, hitting his head as usual.

Damn!" cried Sean, rubbing his head.

He checked Sara, and she looked 100 percent better. She still looked weak, and he knew he would have to feed her, so he reached for the soup. He poured the broth into a cup, being careful not to spill any. Even he knew Sara needed this soup to get her strength back. He took a couple of Tylenol and a penicillin out and slid them into Sara's mouth. He held up the cup so that she could drink out of it. She was so fragile. He hoped that if this was his Sara that she would like her new looks.

A soft, fragile hand touched Sean's rough ones. "No more," she said softly.

Sean jumped. Her voice was so beautiful, soft and sweet. Sean could have swore he spilled some broth. "Y-Y-You'll be okay" stammered Sean. "You need to sleep."

"Sleep," whispered Sara as she closed her soft, green eyes.

Sean covered her with a quilt. He felt relieved Sara would pull through. But was it his Sara? Only time would tell. He picked up the bowl, climbed out of the wagon and then walked toward the smell of food. Sean hunted Susan down. "Here's your bowl. I made sure that it didn't go into the wagon so there's no germs on it. Sara loved it! She ate it all and told me to tell you thank you and that it was delicious," smiled Sean.

"She must be feeling better if she is talking and eating good," said Susan, surprised.

"Well, she's very weak and needs a lot of sleep, but the fever and cough are both gone. That make me feel a lot better and it gives me hope that she will make it through this," smiled Sean.

Susan didn't realize how much Sean loved Sara, but to hear him say her name you could feel the love he had for her. Underneath you could hear the concern he had for her welfare.

"Well, I'm glad she's feeling better. It looks like this winter is going to be a tough one. Who would have thought we would have snow in September?!" said Susan, smiling. "I was told that winters in New York could be bad."

"Yes they can be bad if you are ready for them they can be beautiful," said Sean. "September is the earliest I have ever heard of snow falling."

"That's right, you grew up in New York," smiled Susan.

"Hey, Sean! Are you going to eat yet?" yelled Jacob.

"Yes I'm coming," yelled Sean.

"Yes, I grew up in New York," smiled Sean. "I have to go now."

He walked away thinking he almost screwed up. At least he knew that he was in New York and it was September. He had to get everyone out of here now, but they were insistent on building the barn. He decided to let them build the barn. It would keep them busy until Farley got back. Sean smiled as he reached for a plate. He just had to keep his mouth shut and get them on their way. Then he would think this through.

"We should have the wood cut and trimmed by tonight," smiled Jacob.

"Well, if we split the work now we could have it all cut and built today," smirked Sean.

"Sounds like you are trying to get rid of us," said Jacob.

Sean laughed. "I am. I don't want you to get stuck in one of our New York storms. Even though you have to admit that September is a little early for snow storms. We got one, though."

"Yeah, that snow yesterday was really scary. I thought we would get stuck here," said Jacob. "I don't think I could stand another New York winter. These central New York winters are awful! I want warm weather all year, and no more freezing. You are right, though. We could split up the men. Half could get the logs split, and the other half could start putting it together. Farley and Smith should be back tonight, and we could leave tomorrow morning."

"Jacob," yelled Seth, "Susan's trying to get your attention."

Jacob leaned toward Susan then toward Sean. Seth always has his eye on Susan. "I think he carries his brotherly protection too far," smiled Jacob.

Sean smiled as he ate. Jacob, Seth, and Susan—three more names to remember. Sean knew wagon trains often carried families. He just didn't know if this was one whole family and whether he was a part of it or not. Jacob got up and walked toward Susan.

"What's wrong Susan?" asked Jacob.

"Sean. He seems different," Susan said, concerned.

"Susan, Sean has a lot on his mind right now, and he's very worried about Sara. Believe me, he's my best friend. If he had any problems, he would talk to me. It's tough on him, but if you would like I will talk to him," said Jacob.

Susan smiled. "Would you?"

"How much of these feelings you have are because you feel bad about leaving Sean and Sara behind?" asked Jacob.

Susan looked down. "Probably all of them," she replied.

"I know that you and Sara are best friends, and we did agree to go out West together, but things change," said Jacob.

Sean had walked around the back of the wagon to eavesdrop. It was the only way he could tell if he screwed things up or not. Now he needed to think fast. He pretended to walk toward his wagon, then turned around and walked toward Jacob and Susan.

"Suzy, I was just going over to check and see if Sara was sleeping okay. Would you like to go along with me?" asked Sean.

Susan looked up with a big smile on her face. "Could I?" she asked.

"Cover your nose and mouth with this hanky. I wouldn't want my best friend's wife getting sick," said Sean.

Susan took the hanky and covered her face.

"Sara may be confused because she has been very sick. She is coming back strong though. You'll see," Sean said as they walked toward his wagon.

"Sara snores," Susan laughed.

Sean laughed. "She doesn't snore all the time, but she sure has been snoring a lot today. I think it is a good sign, though, because that means she is in a deep sleep. Am I wrong?" asked Sean.

"Oh, my God!" cried Susan as she climbed into the wagon.

"What? Is something wrong?" asked Sean, climbing into the wagon and hitting his head once again. "Damn, I'll never learn," he murmured under his breath.

"Sean Huntington, I should kick you in the pants. What were you thinking?" said Susan.

"What?" asked Sean, rubbing a new bump. "Is Sara okay?"

"Sean, what were you thinking when you packed this wagon?" asked Susan.

"What? I packed wrong?" asked Sean, looking around.

"I told Jacob he should have helped you. I can see why you ended up having no money left: a new cooking stove, a fancy bed. These things don't belong on a wagon train. What's this?" asked Susan, pulling on a quilt. "You bought Sara a sewing machine?" Susan asked, turning toward Sean.

Sean shrugged. "Sara wanted it, and maybe there wouldn't be any out West," said Sean, weakly.

"I hope you realize this stuff would have ended up being left behind and you would have been out all that money. Where's the food?" asked Susan.

"I don't know. I started looking, but the only things I could find was clothes and blankets. I haven't looked everywhere yet though," said Sean.

"Has Sara had a bath?" shaking her head as she looked around the wagon.

"No. I didn't dare because I was afraid she would get sicker," said Sean.

"Men!" said Susan. "I'll give her a bath. Where is her night shirt?"

"Here in the hope chest. Let me unlock it for you," said Sean.

"Why is it locked?" asked Susan.

"I didn't want to lose things along the way," said Sean as he pulled out the night shirt and then a bathrobe. "I have been using my socks to cover her feet. Was that wrong?" asked Sean.

"No. That's probably the only thing you did right," laughed Susan.

"Sean, Sean," Sara said weakly.

"I am right here, babe. Susan is here," smiled Sean as he kneeled down beside Sara.

"Susan?" Sara looked at Sean worried.

"Oh, God!" This is his Sara. "Yes honey, Susan is your best friend. She made the broth you ate earlier," said Sean. "Please God let her pick up on what I'm saying," thought Sean.

Sara saw Sean close his eyes like he was praying. She was confused, but she knew she had to play along. She knew Sean would explain it all later. She'd always felt safe around Sean. Her body ached all over. It ached in places she didn't even know she had, but she sill sat up. "If Susan is here then why am I looking at you?" asked Sara.

Sean smiled. "Because I'm the one kneeling next to you," Sean said.

"Well, let Susan over here," said Sara.

"Yeah. You two ladies talk. I have to go help the guys," smiled Sean as he kissed Sara's head. "The fever is all gone," smiled Sean.

"Go!" said Susan. "I'm taking over now."

"Okay. I'm leaving," smiled Sean. "You ladies talk or do whatever you do." Sean walked out with a brief wink at Sara.

Sara was a very protective woman. She knew that wink meant that Sean was as confused as she was, and they both needed to find out what was going on.

Sean left being careful not to bang his head again.

"Sara I was so worried about you," said Susan.

"Worried?" smiled Sara. "Not as worried as me. I'm so scared right now."

"Scared, You? You've never been afraid of anything in your entire life," smiled Susan. "What do you have to be scared of?"

"Oh, Susan," cried Sara, letting some crocodile tears fall down her cheek.

"Sara what's wrong? Did Sean hurt you?" asked Susan.

"Sean hurt me? Never!" sobbed Sara. "I'm confused. I don't remember anything about my life at all. It's like the fever took it all away from me. I don't even know why I'm here in this covered wagon."

Susan kneeled down next to Sara. "Don't worry, I'll tell you everything. First I have to go get some water so that we can get you cleaned up. Then we will talk," said Susan.

"Thank you," smiled Sara.

"I'll be right back," smiled Susan. She left and returned with two buckets of water. One hot and one cold. She found Sara's clothes and some towels that Sean had left out for her. Susan found a wash basin and filled it with water as Sara took her clothes off. Susan handed her a wash cloth and some lilac soap.

"Oh, this feels like heaven," said Sara.

"I knew you would feel better getting washed up," said Susan. "Now we'll start the story here and work backwards. You are in a covered wagon, and we are headed west."

"We?" asked Sara.

"Yes we. We have no certain place in mind, just a place that looked good. But then you got sick at your wedding," said Susan.

"Wedding?" said Sara, looking at Susan confused.

"Boy, you don't remember anything do you?" asked Susan.

"No," smiled Sara.

"You and Sean were married August 28 in Rome, New York. Jacob and I stood up with you. Jacob is my husband, and he also is Sean's best friend. You all grew up in Boonville, New York. I grew up out West. My parents died, and I was sent to live with my aunt Jane in Boonville. There Jacob and I met, and we got married. After that you and Sean got married, and we all agreed to go out West. We took all our money and bought these wagons," said Susan.

"Why didn't I get married in Boonville?" asked Sara.

"Because your parents died, and you were sent to live with your uncle, whom I might add was a total bastard!" said Susan.

"Why do you say that he was a bastard?" asked Sara.

"Well, what else would you call someone who took everything your parents had and kept it for himself? I see he let you keep the hope chest that your father made for you. That was very big of him," Susan said sarcastically.

"Well, I guess I did get one thing," said Sara, smiling.

"Sean was so mad at your uncle for what he did that he threatened him," said Susan.

"Threatened? Sean?!" said Sara.

"Okay, he punched the bastard out and then married you. We're only a couple of hours out of Rome. We have been here for three days now. We had to stop because you were so sick, and we thought you were going to die. Sean was worried sick over you and never left your side. It snowed all last night, and we thought we would have to stay here the winter. Then the people of the wagon train got worried about staying here for the winter and went to Farley. They said that we had to move on and leave you and Sean here," sobbed Susan.

"Who's Farley?" asked Sara as she started getting dressed.

"Wait, don't get dressed. I'll wash your hair for you," said Susan.

"Okay," said Sara, noticing that she now had red hair.

Susan stood up and had Sara lean over one of the buckets that she emptied. She wet down her hair and started to wash it.

"Farley's the wagon master. He was very upset with everyone for suggesting such a thing. Then Ely Smith came forward and said that he would sell you two his land if you would stay back."

"Ely Smith is a rat," said Sara filled with hate.

"You remember Mr. Smith?" said Susan.

"No, but his name makes my skin crawl. Sean didn't buy the land did he?" asked Sara.

"Yes, but not without a couple of attachments, smiled Susan as she rinsed Sara's hair. "Sean knows that Mr. Smith is a weasel. Sean made sure to cover everything, so Mr. Smith couldn't take him for a ride. I'm sure that Sean will tell you all about that, though. Anyway, the men are all building a barn with a room attached to it for you to live in. The barn should be done today. The men cut the trees, the boys are stripping the bark, and the women are gathering the clay. Now the men are splitting the work, and you should have a roof over your head tonight," said Susan with a bent smile.

"What's my uncle's name?" asked Sara.

Susan took a deep breath. "Brian Starr with two Rs. He was your father's brother. Your parents, John and Rachel, never got along with him. Brian hated your father because he married an Irish woman," said Susan.

"Well, that's a stupid reason to fight," said Sara as she toweled off her hair. "I feel much better now. Thank you."

"I'm glad to hear you say that," said Susan.

"What? Why?" asked Sara.

"I always thought you were mad at me for marrying Jacob because he's Scottish," said Susan.

"Me hate Jacob or you? Never!" smiled Sara. "You're my best friend, and I worry about you. All I want for you is whatever makes you happy. If Jacob makes you happy, that's good enough for me."

Susan started to cry.

"What's wrong? Isn't Jacob good to you?" asked Sara.

"Jacob is perfect. The problem now is that I don't want to leave. I want to stay here with you. I thought everyone hated us and going out West would change things. But now I'm leaving my best friend," sobbed Susan.

Sara kneeled down in front of Susan. "Then don't leave. Stay here, and we will build another room for you and Jacob to stay in. Then we can build homes, share farming, and our children can grow up together."

"I don't know if Jacob would go for it or if Farley would give us our money back," said Susan.

"Let me talk to Sean. I bet he could talk to Jacob and Farley and they would understand," smiled Sara.

"I don't know. We are supposed to leave in the morning," sobbed Susan.

"Maybe not," said Sara, standing up.

"What do you mean?" asked Susan.

"Well if Farley and Jacob were convinced that Sean couldn't take care of me by himself..."

"I see," said Susan, standing up with a smile of her face. "Then Jacob and I would volunteer to stay behind and help, and Farley would give us our money back."

"Yes!" said Sara.

"Well, I better do some laundry," said Susan. "I'll show Sean how much he can't take care of you. I'll cook a meal, which Sean hasn't done since we left. He said he couldn't find the food. Do you remember where you put it?" asked Susan.

"Yes. I do now. I remember because when Sean had the wagon built I put up a fuss because I wanted one extra thing added," explained Sara.

"I remember that. What was that all about?" asked Susan.

"I had storage built in under the wagon for food. It runs the whole length of the wagon. It's not deep but it keeps the jars from breaking," smiled Sara. "This is the hatch. There's a rope you pull and that lets you see the food you have," Sara said as she pulled open the trap door.

"Well look at that! You thought of that all by yourself!" laughed Susan.

"No, Daddy did. When they moved here from California they brought a lot with them and needed extra space. He built the bottom storage and gave him just enough room for his food as he traveled across country," smiled Sara.

"Well, at least you remembered something good," said Susan.

"I remembered one thing, but with your help I could remember it all," smiled Sara. Sara knew that if Jacob and Susan stayed behind, some of this would fall into place."

But why was she here? "Sean would have a lot of explaining to do," thought Sara as she was closing the trap door.

"I'll strip the bed. You get some fresh bed linen from the hope chest," said Susan as she grabbed the corners of the sheets and quilt.

"Sure," smiled Sara. She lifted the top to the hope chest and there lay the pills she gave Sean for Laura, and some money with them. Sara closed the lid gently thinking of how she could have died if it weren't for those pills. "You know, maybe we should just put those sheets back on after they are washed. They will smell fresh, and the germs on them will be washed away and killed," Sara said, turning around.

"Of course. You're right," smiled Susan. "I'll be right back. I'm going to get some more hot water."

"Yes, that's a good idea," smiled Sara.

Susan climbed out of the wagon with dirty clothes tied in a bundle. After she left, Sara opened the chest again, pulled back the linen and found a hiding place. She put the pills and money in there and rearranged the linen. She was about to close the lid when Susan popped in.

"Change your mind?" asked Susan.

"Ahh!" screamed Sara. "You scared me half to death!" laughed Sara. "I was looking for something we could use for rags to clean with," said Sara, holding her chest.

"I'm sorry, I didn't mean to scare you," laughed Susan. "I have got some rags. If I know you, you have only got the best of linen in there. Or should I say Sean," laughed Susan.

"Are you saying that Sean spoils me?" asked Sara.

"Nooooo! Would I say that?" asked Susan. "Are you up to washing this stuff down? If not I'll do it. I've got the laundry boiling in a pot. I figured it would kill all the germs."

"No, I can help. I'm feeling really good. Sean pulled me through," said Sara. "With the help of those pills, she thought.

"Let's open the back flap and let some air in. It smells awful in here. While we are cleaning you can tell me more about my life, Sean and me."

"I would love to," said Susan as she pulled back the flap.

Susan and Sara talked as they cleaned. Susan was willing to talk about everything.

"It sure smells better in here!" thought Sara.

Chapter 2

"SEAN, WHAT THE HELL WERE YOU THINKING?" SAID JACOB, WALKING UP TO Sean.

"What? Did I do something wrong?" asked Sean.

"Wrong, damn it. Sean, you took Susan to see Sara. Now what do I do when Susan gets sick? She could die! She's pregnant! Her and the baby could both die!" exclaimed Jacob.

"Sara's not sick anymore. Do you think I would be stupid enough to put Susan in harm's way?" asked Sean.

"Sara's not sick?" asked Jacob.

"No. She's up and talking about old times with Susan. Go see for yourself. Don't take my word for it, old pal," said Sean.

"Well, I'm going to do just that!" yelled Jacob as he threw his ax down and stormed toward Sean's wagon.

"What was that all about?" asked Seth.

"Susan went into our wagon to take care of Sara, and Jacob blames me. Susan wanted to go, and I told Jacob about it. He's in a rage now because she's pregnant and now I'm at fault," said Sean.

"It looks like we better add another room to your barn," said Seth. "Farley will not let her come along now. That flu is probably running right through her now."

"That's not a bad idea, Seth. We'll add on another room on the other end of the barn. We've got enough wood cut," said Sean.

He had Seth figured right. The big trouble maker of the whole wagon, and he'd have everyone all worked up by the time Farley got back with the mole.

"Damn women! You can't figure them out. The next thing they will be wanting to do is vote and go to the saloons like men."

Sean looked at Seth and smiled. "If you only knew," he thought.

"You're right. Women are getting out of hand. I'll finish up here. Go and make sure we have enough wood to add on an extra room. If we do, then we'll help the other guys," said Sean.

As Seth walked away, Sean knew that he couldn't wait to tell everybody how stupid Susan was. Seth was the type of man that loved trouble. Sandy brown hair, brown eyes, short, and stocky, if you watched Seth walk you would almost see the word trouble fall off him. He lived, ate, and breathed trouble. Sean felt sorry for Seth's wife.

As Sean returned to work, he knew that keeping Jacob and Susan here with them was the right thing to do. He didn't know how he knew. He just knew.

"Susan are you…Sara?" asked Jacob confused.

"Hi Jacob," said Sara. Sara and Susan were sitting on the hope chest talking."

"You don't look sick," said Jacob.

"Oh, I was sick, but I'm better now. Do you think Sean would let Susan in here if I was still sick?" asked Sara.

"I don't know. I would like to think he wouldn't. Sean said you were feeling better, but I didn't think you were feeling this good," said Jacob. "What's going on?"

"You and Susan are staying here with me and Sean," smiled Sara.

"We are? But we don't have any money left. It is all tied up in this trip," said Jacob.

"Well, now that Susan is exposed to my flu, Farley won't let you go on the trip, and he will also give you your money back," said Sara.

"You make it sound so easy. Did it ever occur to you that Farley would be so mad at us that he would just leave us here and keep our money?" said Jacob.

"Don't worry, Jacob. If he wants your money, let him keep it. We've been in worse situations than this before," said Sara. "I just have a gut feeling that this is where we all belong."

Jacob closed his eyes. "Women," he whispered.

"I heard that Jacob," said Susan.

"Why can't women ever make up their minds?" asked Jacob.

Susan got up and walked over to Jacob. "Look, I know you don't understand any of this but, for once in your lie, trust me. Do you want our baby born on a trail somewhere? There's lots of talk about

Indians on the rise again. Do you want to take the chance that our baby or one of us will die along the way? You know what will be going through our minds: if only we had stayed where we were. So for now, accept this. If Farley keeps our money, so be it. Farley is a fair man, though, and, I think he will return our money just so that he could get out of here with a clean conscience," said Susan.

"You're probably right. I didn't want to leave in the first place," said Jacob.

"I know. I talked you into this, but now I know it was wrong. I wanted to leave for all the wrong reasons. Before we go too far and realize it was a mistake, let's stop here," pleaded Susan.

"Sure," said Jacob. "I just yelled at Sean. He might not let us stay now."

"Sean is your best friend," said Sara. "I doubt very highly he would leave you out in the cold."

"Well I better go help the men and talk to Sean," said Jacob.

"I have some laundry boiling, so I better tend to it before it boils away," smiled Susan. "Jacob, could you do me one itty-bitty favor before you go?" asked Susan, bashing her eyelashes at him.

"One itty-bitty favor? That sounds like a lot of work," teased Jacob.

Susan smiled. "I could find a lot of work for you, but all I wanted was for you to flip over Sara's mattress for me."

"Mattress? You have a mattress? We sleep on hay, and you have a mattress?" teased Jacob.

"Well, they packed all wrong for the trip. It's all your fault. I told you to help Sean pack, but you said that he was a big boy and he could do it all by himself," said Susan.

"Okay. I'll flip the mattress," said Jacob.

"Thank you. I have laundry to hang."

Jacob flipped the mattress and left to find Sean. He wanted to apologize and tell him what the women had cooked up.

As Susan walked toward the kettle of laundry boiling near her wagon, she noticed women and children moving out of her way rather quickly. Bad news travels fast, she thought. She used a wooden stick to pull the sheets out of the boiling water and put them in the cold water. She took her scrub board and lye soup out of her wagon and started to scrub Sara's clothes. She let them set for awhile and put Sara's nightgown in the boiling water. She sneezed. Lye soap always made her sneeze. What Susan didn't see was women running away from her. They all thought she was infected with the virus. Susan kept sneezing, laughing at how lye soap always made her sneeze, but she still kept on using it. Worried women kept staring at Susan, thinking she was delirious with fever because she was laughing so much.

For the first time in her life, Susan was happy, really happy. She hummed a little tune as she hung laundry up. Today had really turned into a nice day. A soft, warm, gentle breeze came up, and the snow had almost all melted away. There were a few patches here and there that just refused to melt, but it wouldn't take long with this warm September breeze. Susan stopped and looked around. Today was just one of those days that you were just happy to be alive. Susan drew in a long breath of fresh air. Even that felt right. She walked to her wagon and got out food for supper. Some days she hated to cook. This wasn't one of those days. This was the type of day that someone would bake a pie and put it in the window to cool. There was no stove or windows, so Johnny cake would have to do. Susan carefully went through her canned goods: sweet potatoes, ham slices, and some corn. "Ah, applesauce," said Susan to herself. She had the choice between ham slices and beef. Jacob loved the ham slices. "Ham slices it is. He was so sweet earlier, it didn't seem right not to cook his favorite meal for dinner." Susan hummed as she cooked. Her stomach grumbled. She was very hungry. This baby was going to be huge if she kept on eating the way she has been, Susan thought as she checked the clothes on the line. They were dry, so she folded them, checked the food, and walked the basket of clothes over to Sara's wagon.

Sara was still sitting on the chest. She had brushed her hair dry in the gentle breeze that came in the back of the wagon. Now it shined on the fall sun and fell in curls around her tiny waist.

"As many times as I see you, your hair gets me every time. The red with gold highlights. It's so beautiful. I'm so jealous," smiled Susan.

"There's nothing wrong with your beautiful, blond hair," smiled Sara.

"I love the color of my hair. It's just straight, and yours is so full of curls. What I wouldn't give for just one curl," said Susan.

"I don't think curls are that great. I just got done brushing my hair, and those curls get stuck in my brush. I was about to cut it all off, I was so disgusted," said Sara.

"Never cut your hair. It is so warm in the winter," laughed Susan, setting the basket on the floor and taking the sheets out to make the bed.

"Susan, I can't thank you enough for what you have done for me," said Sara.

"Me? What did I do? I sent a little broth over and washed some clothes. That's nothing compared to what you have done for me," smiled Susan.

"How did I help you?" asked Sara.

"You made me realize what a mistake it would have been to go out West. I've been so happy since we decided not to go. The other women think I'd delirious because I have been laughing and smiling. I haven't done that once since we planned this trip. In my heart I knew it was wrong, but I couldn't stop the feeling that we had to run away," said Susan.

Sara had gotten up to help Susan. "I guess we are even then. You gave me my life back by giving me my memory back. I know we didn't cover everything, but what you have told me has helped a lot. Sean would have been beside himself if I didn't remember marrying him," said Sara.

"You get back in bed and get some more sleep. We can talk more later. I'm making us all some supper right now," smiled Susan. "I have some of the canned applies that you like so well. They're in the storage area. Take some to go with supper. They were the last thing Mama canned."

Yawn. "I guess I am still a little tired. Thank you for being such a good friend," said Sara as she closed her eyes.

Susan took out two cans of apples. "This will go good with Johnny cake," she thought as she climbed out of the wagon. Susan walked slowly toward her wagon. She wanted to make sure all the other women could see that she was coming from Sara's wagon yet another time. Their mouths will be flapping soon. They sure like to gossip. The only thing that gossip did was hurt people. Susan knew gossip first hand. When she first moved, when her parents died, that's all everyone did was gossip about her. None of it was true. Sara came up to her one day while she was sitting on her porch. Susan laughed as she remembered that day. She was bold as daylight. "It looks like you need a friend. Would you like to come over and stay the night at my house sometime?" Susan smiled. She cooked, and her memories came back.

"Aren't you afraid of me, like everybody else?" asked a younger Susan.

"What? The gossip, right? I don't listen to gossip" smiled Sara. "I've found gossip is for idle-minded people. If you want to know someone, then you should go right up to them and talk to them."

Susan smiled, remembering how on that day a dark cloud was lifted from her heart. It was replaced with sunshine and warmth. They talked for a long time until Rachel, Sara's mother, came looking for her.

"I thought I would find you here," Rachel said. "Hi, I'm Sara's mother, Rachel." Susan knew that Sara looked just like her—right down to the red hair.

"Mom, I asked Susan to stay overnight sometime. When can she come over?" asked Sara.

"Well, school is out, so she can come and stay all summer if her aunt will let her," said Rachel.

Susan remembered how she held her breath when Sara was asking her mother. Never in a million years did she think she would say "Yes," let alone the whole summer.

"Rachel is that you?" said Susan's aunt Beth.

"Yes, Beth. Sara wants Susan to spend the summer with us. I don't mind if it is all right with you. It would be good for Sara," said Rachel.

Susan remembered her Aunt Beth looking shocked. Beth invited her in to have some lemonade. She only invited the most elite people in for her lemonade. Susan didn't even get to drink it, and on a hot day like this it would have tasted good.

"You have time for a glass while Susan packs," smiled Aunt Beth.

Susan remembered staring at her aunt in shock. She was actually going to let her spend the summer at Sara's house.

"Yea!" yelled Sara.

"Well, don't dawdle," said Aunt Beth. "Go pack. You must not keep them waiting."

Susan moved in a numb state. She wasn't allowed off the front porch, let alone go away for the whole summer.

"Thank you!" smiled Rachel. "It's been so hard on Sara not having anyone to play with."

Sara helped Susan pack. When they came downstairs, Rachel was sitting in the front parlor sipping lemonade. Susan drank a glass of water, kissed her aunt goodbye and headed for the unknown. Unknown, laughed Susan. She had the time of her life! A train ride to Boonville, lots of lemonade, and her own rooms. Yes her own rooms. Her bedroom had its own parlor, a walk-in closet, and maids. This was a whole other world, a world she felt she belonged in. She turned sixteen that summer, met Jacob and fell in love. When Susan returned to her aunt's house, she was a whole new person. Jacob and her kept in touch by post. Then one day he showed up and asked Beth and Ron for Susan's hand in marriage. Susan's stomach did a flip-flop just like it did that day. She hid in the hallway while Aunt Beth, Uncle Ron, and Jacob talked behind closed doors about her fate. It seemed like they talked for hours before she was summoned to come in. They agreed to let Susan marry Jacob. The wedding would be in July at Sara's house. Susan smiled gently as she stood before her aunt. Most of the things that her uncle spoke about she didn't hear. Only a couple of words slipped in, like living in Boonville and wedding at Rachel's in July. What was really on her mind was that Jacob was her soon-to-be husband. Nothing else mattered, Susan owed Sara her life. If Sara hadn't stopped that day, Susan would have ended up an old maid.

Susan heard the men working in the background. Somehow it seemed right on such a lovely day.

Sara felt guilty sleeping. She hurt all over, the bed felt good, the fresh clean smell of sheets always made her sleepy, the bath just washed away all her resolve. Now all she wanted was to sleep.

She should be up doing her fair share, Susan's pregnant, she shouldn't have everything dumped on her. Susan was great about filling her in on her life, but that didn't tell her why she was here. Only Sean knew this. The last thing she remembered was that man shooting Sean, the look on Sean's face as the bullet entered his body. That bullet was meant for her, Sean jumped in front of her, and the bullet went into Sean instead of her. She grabbed Sean as he fell. A look of shock on his face. Everything seemed like slow motion, like it took years for them to fall to the cement. Sara heard a second shot being fired, did that shot hit her? Now Sean and Sara laid dead on the cold concrete for Thomas to find. Was this heaven, hell, or purgatory? What was she doing here? Maybe Sean knew. Sara's head hurt. She didn't know if it was because she was sick or all this other stuff she had to learn. Soon Sara was asleep again. In and out of sleep was how Sara rested until Sean came home; he carried two plates of food with him.

"I'm not even washed up and Susan's pushing food at me," said Sean, setting the plates down.

"Don't give me that smile, Sean Mark. What is going on here?" asked Sara, scared.

"I don't know," said Sean. "I was hoping you could tell me. You're the one with the brains and Bible smarts. I've been trying to figure out if we're dead or alive all day. I feel alive but that don't mean anything. I've never been dead, so I can't tell you what dead feels like."

"We can't be dead, we're talking, breathing, eating, and sick. I don't think you get sick when you're dead," said Sara.

"How do you know, you ever been dead before?" asked Sean.

Sara starting laughing, "Can't say I have."

"This whole thing feels weird. I've been trying to avoid people all day, and they keep coming up and wanting to talk to me. I've done my best to keep my mouth shut, but I can't help thinking this place has a lot to do with that diary you found," smiled Sean.

"I got the same impression. Pass some food, please, I'm starved," said Sara.

"You better take a penicillin first. You need to take them with food. I've got all the pills you gave me for Laura. How or why, I don't know. The three thousand dollars I took out of the bank to go Christmas shopping wasn't the only funny-looking paper," said Sean. "That funny-looking paper is today's currency, so you still have three thousand dollars plus what I have stashed away. God, I don't know if it came with me," said Sara.

"What money?" asked Sean.

"Well, I've been putting money away each week for a rainy day. And this looks like a rainy day," said Sara.

"The pills are gone," said Sean. "I put them right here with the funny paper."

"Oh, I put them in my hiding place," said Sara, getting up and walking over to the chest.

"Hiding place?" asked Sean.

"I found a little cubbyhole in the chest. That's where I found the diary," said Sara.

Sean looked at Sara, "How much money is there?" Sean looked shocked at the pile of money Sara held out.

"Well, back home there was ten thousand dollars, but you know that's not much money for a rainy day. It would get you through maybe a half year, but here we could be millionaires with our knowledge of the future," said Sara.

"Ten thousand dollars," said Sean.

"Don't say it like that. A woman has to protect herself. What if Thomas died? I'm stuck with bills until the insurance is paid off. God knows how long that would take. They're eager to get their money but when they have to pay off that's another matter. It takes years to fill out all the paperwork they want, then ten years after that for them to pay off. In the meantime, I could lose everything I owned. I'd be in the streets, no roof over my head, no clothes to cover my behind, and no food. You die waiting for what is rightfully yours. Remember, I went through it with my mother when dad died. She ended up dying and never seeing any of the money from the insurance company. If Mom had gotten that money, she'd be alive today," sobbed Sara.

Sean felt bad.

"You're right, forgive me," said Sean. "Here, let's put this away before someone comes. Here's the pills." Sara took the pills. Sean put the money and pills back in their hiding spot.

Sara took the pills and washed them down with water. "God, what I wouldn't give for a Pepsi right now," laughed Sara.

"Or a decent cup of coffee," smiled Sean.

"Well, I understand you've had a busy day. Let's see a land deal and building a barn with homes attached," laughed Sara.

"Well, they're not what we would call homes. They're more like lean-tos, but it will get us through this winter.

"I figure if I cut logs all winter, come spring we could build a couple log homes. Nothing too big, we don't want to be noticed," said

Sean. "Hell, I don't even know if we get to stay here," said Sean, now picking up a cold supper.

Sara sat down, picked up her plate. "Well, we stick as close to what the diary says, or what I remember," smiled Sara.

"Did you find out anything about us from Susan?" asked Sean.

"Yes, she walked me through my life, from the time we met. I'll tell you later tonight when no one's around, but what we can talk about now is your dealings with weasel," said Sara.

"He's more like a mole," said Sean. "But I remembered all the problems you had buying your land because of that man, and we took care of that today. The poor bastard thought I was doing it for his best interest."

"Well I hope it wasn't too drastic. They say that if you change the future too much, some kind of momentum is lost or added. I'm not sure which but, then again, that's theory," smiled Sara.

Knock, knock.

"Mr. Huntington, it's Mr. Farley and Mr. Smith, could you come out here please."

"Something wrong, Mr. Farley?" asked Sean, stepping out of the wagon.

"No, nothing's wrong. We wanted to give you your signed papers, and I had some money left over, so I bought you some stove pipe so you could hook up your stove," said Mr. Farley. "And to tell you to move your wagon over to the barn. Jacob said he'd be along to help you take things off the wagon. Sure the hell surprised me to see the barn all up, but you were right, smaller was better. Well we'll say good bye now, we're pulling out early in the morning, so when you get up, we'll be gone," said Farley.

"Thank you for everything you've done for me; thank everyone for me. I'm sorry for holding you up like this," said Sean.

"Don't be, you may have saved our lives," laughed Farley.

"What do you mean?" Sean asked puzzled.

"Stopped in to see if there was any mail for me, and there was a telegram telling me not to go a certain route; it was flooded out. Now if you hadn't held us up, those couple of days we would have been caught in that flood. We all would have been killed. So things worked out for the best. There's always a reason for something. This time it was for the best," smiled Farley.

"Well, I should feel a little better," smiled Sean. "I felt bad holding everyone up here."

"Don't feel bad, their people got together and did something good for a good man," smiled Farley. "It gave them time to learn to work together; now they're ready to travel. What they learned here today would have taken them weeks on the trail, and lives would have been lost along the way. Now they've already built what it takes to make a good wagon train. I just know that this will be a good trip, this is my last trip West," said Farley.

"Why?" asked Sean.

"The trains are taking over," Farley said sadly. "Just as well. I'm getting too old to go running across country."

"Cough...cough...cough.

Sean's head turned toward the wagon.

"I wish you the best my son," said Farley, holding out his right hand.

Sean shook his hand. "Thank you," smiled Sean, then he held out his hand for Mr. Smith to shake.

Ely Smith seemed shocked that Sean would want to shake his hand, so he was slow in responding. "Thank you for helping me, Mr. Smith," smiled Sean.

"No problem," said Mr. Smith. "We really helped each other. Now I get my dream of going West. I hope your wife feels better."

"Yes, I must tend to her," smiled Sean.

Farley and Mr. Smith left. Sean wiped his hand on his pants. Mr. Smith's hand was like holding a dead fish in your hand.

"Are you all right?" asked Sean, climbing in the wagon.

"Yes, I had to cough to prove I was still sick," said Sara.

"Sara, this isn't our time. People here trust and believe in one another. They help one another, looking for nothing in return. These people genuinely love helping one another," said Sean.

"You make it sound like a utopia," said Sara.

"Maybe it is," said Sean. "There's just a sense of balance here. I've felt it all day, it's strange."

Sara stared at Sean. She'd known Sean all her life and knew that Sean wasn't someone who spoke stupid things. If Sean said it, it was true; it just was. Had she become so bitter toward the world that she became just what she didn't want to be?

"Sara, don't look back like that," said Sean.

"What? Oh, what if this is a dream state we're in, a place we go just before we die, a place where God gets to see into our hearts, to see if we're good people?" said Sara. "Ouch, you pinched me!"

"Well, then you're not dreaming," smiled Sean. "Don't you think I thought of that?"

Sean stood up, picked up the dirty plates. "We both can't be having the same dream. I have a theory. It's a stupid one, but it's a theory," said Sean.

"Stupid or not, let's hear it; it's better than nothing," smiled Sara.

"This is really stupid," said Sean, sitting on the bed. "Remember the other day, when I came down to the house? You were baking

Christmas cookies, you poured me coffee and asked me to sample the cookies and tell you which ones I liked and the ones I didn't," said Sean.

"Yes, you were no help," laughed Sara. "You liked them all."

"Well, you're a good cook," said Sean. "Anyway, somehow or other we got on the subject of Einstein, you said something about Einstein."

"Yes, I said Einstein said anyone could be a genius as long as he knew how to look up the answer," said Sara.

"That's it. Then Tom came in from work, he joked about me getting roped into cookie taster this year," laughed Sean.

"Yes, and he poured that mug of coffee and joined you," laughed Sara.

"Yes. And remember what Tom said about Einstein? We were quite taken back with his theory," said Sean.

Sara looked at Sean surprised. "Yes! Tom said he believed that Einstein was sent here from a future time to correct our mistakes, that life always had two roads, and if we screwed up, God always sent someone to correct our way," said Sara.

"Yes, what if that's what we're supposed to do," said Sean thinking about it. "Your brains, my brawn."

Sara crossed her legs. "Maybe that's not such a stupid idea," she said.

"But what are we supposed to change?"

"I don't know. Maybe all of it," said Sean. "Today, without trying, I changed that land deal, got Jacob and Susan to stay and saved a whole wagon train of people, and I tried not to do anything. You're the history nut. I thought you could tell me what needed changing," smiled Sean.

"God, the eighteenth century was a time of growth for America, a lot of stupid things happened," said Sara.

"Yes, but don't you find it strange that we're sitting on the very ground that your future home is sitting on? No, whatever it is involves this area," said Sean. "I can't believe we gather all this knowledge and not use it. Maybe if we use our knowledge for the better of mankind, then we go to heaven."

"Okay, let's say you're right. We change history as we know it now. I only have one question," said Sara.

"Believe it or not, I have an answer," said Sean. "I don't think we're dead, yet I think we're in comas."

"What makes you think that?" asked Sara.

"Think about it. We remember both present and future. We couldn't do that unless we were still alive in the future," said Sean.

"If what you say is true, then at any given moment we could change, we could go forward or backwards, forget everything we know or keep our knowledge and stay here," said Sara.

"Yup, scary ain't it?" said Sean.

Knock, knock. "Sean, it's Jacob. I've got the horses hooked up. I'm pulling the wagon over to the barn," yelled Jacob.

Sean pulled the back flap open. There was still sunlight, but it wouldn't be there long. Jacob lead the way. He grabbed hold of the reins and guided the horses toward the barn. He stopped them next to what was about to be their home, a room on the side of the barn that ran the whole length of the barn. First Sean and Jacob unloaded the bed, then Sean carried Sara over the threshold and laid her on the bed. He didn't do it for show, he did it because Sara had no shoes on. Next came the hope chest, the sewing machine, then the stove. Sean and Jacob connected the piping for the stove.

All we need is a table, and we have a home," laughed Sean.

"We'll build one tomorrow," said Jacob. "Right now let's try the stove out, make sure it's hooked up right," joked Jacob.

"Well, I thought maybe tomorrow we'd ride into Rome and buy you and Susan a stove," said Sean. "One just like this one."

Jacob looked at Sean and laughed. "You are joking."

"No, I'm not joking. Leave early, get back early, pick up a few things we need," said Sean. "I don't think we have any food, I haven't been able to find it, any way."

"There's food," said Sara. "There's a trap door on the wagon floor; and food's in there."

"You and your hiding places," laughed Sean.

Sara shrugged her shoulders and smiled. "I love this floor. Can I go tomorrow?"

"We'll see," said Sean. "We've got a lot to buy and bring back, and there may not be any room on the wagon. I want to get us set up first. If not tomorrow, maybe next week. You'll be stronger then," said Sean.

"Yes, you're right. Next week is fine," Sara said sadly.

Sean looked at Sara. "You're right, you can go tomorrow. We'll bring Susan."

Jacob shook his head, "I didn't think you would give in so easily," he said.

"Give in, the women can shop while we buy supplies for the farm. It cuts our time in half," smiled Sean. "Something tells me that we don't have a lot of time to waste before winter."

"You're right," said Jacob. "We all have to pull together on this if we're going to get through this winter. Well, the stove works, works real well," smiled Jacob. "It's warming up nicely in here."

"Nice and cozy," smiled Sara.

"Well, now that I know we have food, let's bring it in and bed the horses for the night," smiled Sean, looking at Sara. "Only you would hide the food."

Jacob and Sean brought in the food, bedded the horses down and took all the tools off the sides of the wagon and stored them in the barn. Sean said thank you and good night to Jacob as he closed the barn doors. Jacob went to his wagon. Sean to his new home.

"How's Sara?" asked Susan.

"Good, I guess. I'm supposed to tell you we're going into Rome in the morning. You and Sara are shopping while Sean and I shop for supplies for the farm," said Jacob.

"Shop? Shop for what, we don't have any money for anything. Farley refused to refund our money. Sean and Sara have no money."

"I know, maybe we're going to rob a bank along the way," said Jacob, "or Sean's mind is gone."

"Jacob! Neither one of those statements is funny," said Susan.

"It wasn't meant to be. Sean kept referring to Sara and her hiding places," said a saddened Jacob, wondering if staying here was a good idea.

"Hiding places," laughed Susan.

"Now you've got that stupid laugh Sean had. It don't make any sense."

Knock, knock. "Jacob, it's Mr. Farley."

Jacob threw back the flap on the back of the wagon. "Yes, Mr. Farley, may I help you?"

"I decided to give you your two hundred dollars back," said Farley.

"What changed your mind?" asked Jacob, climbing down.

"Mr. Smith showed me the error of my ways. I wasn't thinking right, so here's your money. I'm sorry, do you think you could help me put the Huntington's presents in the barn?" asked Farley.

"Yes sir," Jacob said sadly.

"What's the matter, son, you got problems?" asked Farley.

"I don't know how to explain it," said Jacob, opening the barn door. "It's like this sickness that's going around in making people mad."

"Mad?" asked Farley.

"Demented," said Jacob. "I feel like I'm the only sane person left in the world. I don't know, maybe I'm the crazy one. Mr. Smith's been nice; Mr. Smith has never been nice in his life," said Jacob, shaking his head.

"Well, son," said Farley, grabbing some packages, "even I have to admit Mr. Smith is different. He never went near a saloon today while we were in town. He even bought the Misses a present," laughed Farley. "But for everyone else, they have mixed feelings about the trip West. When I told them how Sean and Sara saved our lives, they gave a little more to them."

"Saved everyone's life?" Jacob puzzled.

"You didn't hear?" asked Farley.

"Hear what?" asked Jacob.

So Farley told Jacob about the telegram and what happened. Jacob stood frozen, listening to Farley talk.

"Any hoot, the way I see it, if there's a God, he's acting through those two right now. I ain't no religious man. Don't get me wrong, I believe in God, but I don't go to church every week like some folks. But those two people in that room are blessed."

Jacob led a very pregnant cow into the barn. Farley carried in a cage with chickens. Jacob thought over what Mr. Farley said. Maybe he was right. Jacob led another cow in the barn. Farley carried in some grain.

"I talked to John Little Feather in town today. He's a good man. Told him about Sean and Sara. He seems to think the gods have sent them. So if you see Indians, don't shoot, they're just watching out for them," said Farley. "Well, that's the last of it. Good luck, son."

"Thank you, Mr. Farley," said Jacob, closing the barn door. Farley walked toward his wagon; Jacob toward his. Somehow what Farley said made sense out of the madness. As Jacob walked, he felt a heavy weight lifting off him. By the time he climbed in the wagon, he felt like a new man, like something was suddenly all right; it was hard to explain, so he didn't. He slept instead.

Sean stood there over the stove, banking the coals. He didn't know where to sleep; there was only one bed up till now. He'd slept on the floor of the wagon. This floor didn't appeal to him.

"Which side of the bed do you want?" asked Sara.

"Don't look like that. I said 'sleep,' not 'sex.' I know that we're married to someone else, even if it is in another time. But we do need to sleep. If you keep John Henry tied up, we can make it work," smiled Sara.

"John Henry!" laughed Sean. "Where did you come up with that one?"

"The English. Now which side of the bed do you want?" asked Sara.

"The right," laughed Sean. "Have you got something I can put water in to get cleaned up in?" asked Sean.

"Yes, in the chest is a bowl and pitcher," said Sara, crawling under the covers.

Sean smiled as he took the bowl out of the chest. Leave it to Sara to face a situation head on. What did she call it, grab the bull by the horns. He looked at Sara. She was fast asleep.

Sean washed, put on clean longjohns and went to bed. It wasn't like his bed at home, but it was a bed and it beat the other option—

the floor. It was a wood floor, but it just didn't look like a wood floor. Stumps of trees driven in the ground wasn't his idea of a hardwood floor.

But a lot of things were different here: no cars, no roads, no electricity, no phones, no TV, no radios, no malls, no crazy people. "God, it is utopia," smiled Sean as he rolled over to sleep.

"Early to bed, early to rise," thought Sean. When he woke up, he said, "well, I'm still me, so we take another day by the horns." Sean was amazed at how well he slept; he hadn't slept that good since he was a child. Sean had stoked the fire in the stove. Now he was cooking breakfast; coffee going, bacon frying, eggs cooking, God this is the life.

"God, something smells good," said Sara, sitting up.

"Well, how do you feel today?" asked Sean.

"Like a million bucks," said Sara, stretching.

"Same old Sara, I see," laughed Sean. "Better get dressed. Jacob and Susan will be here shortly," said Sean. "I put your clothes on the end of the bed," Sean said, laughing.

"What's this suppose to mean?" asked Sara.

"You'll see," laughed Sean.

Sara sat up. "What's this shit?" asked Sara.

"Your clothes," laughed Sean.

"That's not funny, Sean. Where are my jeans and flannel shirt?" asked Sara.

"Sorry, there's only one pair of jeans and one flannel shirt and I'm wearing them," laughed Sean. "But you do have another dress if you don't like that one."

Sara looked at Sean with pure horror on her face. "A corset, pantaloons, slips, stockings, a dress, what else?" asked Sara.

"Wait till you see your lovely foot wear," said Sean.

"Do I have to?" asked Sara.

"Well, if you want to leave the house," yes!" laughed Sean.

Sara leaned off the side of the bed, grabbed a black thing. "Oh God, no. What is it?" cried Sara, falling back on the bed pillow.

"I think they call it a lady's boot," said Sean. "I've got a cow to milk."

Sara got up and struggled into her clothes, using a few choice words along the way. She measured her waist, wrote down the size. She looked at the boots; they would have to wait. "No, I better put them on," thought Sara.

Sean came back in carrying a note and a pail of milk. He looked at Sara and whistled, "we have some wedding presents in the barn."

"Don't talk to me, don't whistle at me. I'm in a bad mood," said Sara.

"PMS?" said Sean.

"Oh God, don't wish that on me on top of this," whined Sara.

"I can't walk in these things. I feel like I have a corn cob stuck up my ass when I walk. This is horrible," cried Sara.

Sean stopped teasing Sara when he saw she was really having problems. "There are no other shoes," said Sean.

"Shoes! These aren't shoes, this is torture," cried Sara.

"What's wrong?" asked Susan, running in. "I thought I heard Sara crying."

"She is. Boots don't fit her, feet are swollen," said Sean.

"Don't tell me you tried to put those black boots on again," laughed Susan.

"That she has," said Sean.

"Wait, take them off. I'll be right back," said Susan.

"Gladly," said Sara.

Instant relief came to her face; a sigh of relief escaped from her throat. "Oh God, that's a relief," said Sara.

"Here," said Susan. "They're not fancy like yours, but my feet are bigger. They're cheaply made, so they stretch more. Here, let me help."

Sara held out her foot. Susan looked at it, then at Sara.

"What, something wrong with my foot?" asked Sara.

"They're really swollen," whispered Susan. "Are you pregnant?"

"No, I don't think so, Sean and I haven't, you know. I've been too sick," said Sara.

"Well then, it's the curse," said Susan.

"Curse! What curse? Someone curse me?" asked Sara.

Susan laughed. "Boy when you forget things you really forget them. There, how's that feel?" asked Susan.

"Better, thank you," smiled Sara.

Susan stood up. "I think it will go down once the curse has passed," said Susan.

Sara looked confused.

"The monthly curse," said Susan, whispering in Sara's ear.

"Oh not that, I wouldn't know what to do, so I decided it ain't going to happen," said Sara.

Susan laughed. "I wish it was that easy."

"Well, it will have to be. I wouldn't know where to buy plugs around here," said Sara, seriously looking at her feet.

"Plugs?!" asked Susan. "Are you feeling good enough to go shopping?"

"Oh, I'm going shopping. There's going to be some changes made," said Sara.

"You girls will have to eat over there. We have no chairs to sit on," said Sean.

"We'll have them when we get back tonight," said Sara.

"Sara, you can't buy just anything," said Susan. "We don't have a lot of money. You have to be careful."

"I will," smiled Sara, "but some things are necessary, and I'm sure a table and chairs fall in that category."

"You're probably right, but I think a bed is more important. Sleeping on hay while you're pregnant isn't easy," laughed Susan.

"What size waist to you think Sean is?" asked Sara.

"Why?" asked Susan.

"Well, he owns one pair of jeans. That's not going to last him very long," said Sara.

"One pair of jeans should last him a couple of years," said Susan. "I don't think they go by waist size. I think you try them on; if they fit you buy them."

Sara froze and stared at Susan. Maybe this wasn't going to be so easy after all. Sara thought about it. No, this is going to be a nightmare. This wasn't a hop over-to-the-mall type thing.

"Are you all right? You look; I don't know how you look. Sean something's wrong with Sara," yelled Susan.

Sean looked over toward the girls. Sara looked awful. He ran over to his Sara. "Sara." He picked her up and carried her outside. "Come on Sara, breath," yelled Sean.

"Ahhh," said Sara.

"What, talk to me," said Sean.

"I-I-I," stammered Sara.

"Okay, you got 'I' out, but for me to understand you have to put other words with that," said Sean.

"I--m-- I'm going shopping a wagon," said Sara, taking in a deep breath.

"Yes, so that's how we get there," said Sean.

"There's no mall," said Sara.

"No, but there are stores. Just pretend they're a mall," said Sean.

"You don't understand. My life was always planned and organized. You make a list, you go to the mall, you know exactly where everything is; in, out, home in a couple of hours. It's going to take us four to get there," said Sara.

"What? Do you have to be home because you're expecting a phone call? Maybe you'll miss your favorite TV program?" said Sean. "If it's that important to you, tape your program and bring your cell phone with you."

Sara started laughing.

"What did I say now?" asked Sean.

"Well, you know I don't watch TV and refuse to own a cell phone. Well, even if I did they haven't been invented yet. Maybe in a hundred years or so," said Sara. "People are always saying they wish they were back in these times because life was simple. Well I'm here, and I have a chance to see how America grew, and all I can think about is all the nice things of our times. Why do we always hate what we have and want what we don't have?" asked Sara.

"Maybe we don't know what we want," said Sean. "As for myself, I love it here. There's something virginal about it. Don't get me wrong, yesterday building the barn I longed for power tools, but even with power tools I don't think we could have built that barn as fast as we did. There's just something about the way everyone works together that we don't have in our time," said Sean, putting his hands in his pant pockets.

"I know what you're talking about," said Sara. "Well, we better go shopping. I'd like to get Susan and Jacob a bed. She's sleeping on hay; that can't be good for the baby."

"Yeah, I want to get them a wood stove. They really don't have much. I've got a feeling we're in for a tough winter, and we don't have real nice homes to settle into, but we should try to be somewhat comfortable," smiled Sean. "Get to know one another."

"Is everything okay?" asked Jacob.

"Yes, we're ready to go," smiled Sean.

"Maybe you are, but I have to get my purse," said Sara, "and a bed that needs to be made."

"I made the bed and picked up the dishes," smiled Susan.

"Susan, I love you dearly. You don't have to do my work, I'm fine. I will hold my own around here, does everyone understand?" said Sara.

Everyone nodded.

"I'll get my purse, and we'll be on our way," said Sara.

Sara walked into her home, took some money out of hiding and put it in her purse. "Two thousand dollars should make a good shopping day," thought Sara. Sara looked around the room. It was quaint, but it gave her a strange sense of security and well-being. Sean was right in a strange sort of way; they belonged here. Then Sara walked back outside. Susan was sitting on the wagon waiting to help Sara up. It seemed late to Sara, but the sun suggested early morning. The wagon train was gone just like the wagon covering. Now it looked just like a plain old buckboard. Sean winked at Sara as he helped her up. She smiled sweetly and said thank you. Jacob lead the way. Sean followed on horse.

Sara and Susan talked on the way to town. Susan agreed to help Sara recognize people and fill her in on who they were. Susan wasn't sure Sara should be going to town. But Sara told Susan she'd be fine; her memory would come back soon. Sean just enjoyed the view and the silence. This place was beautiful without roads and signs sticking up all over, no roadside trash or clumping, no pollution of gas smells in the air, just fresh, clean air. Sean looked up. No planes, just what God wanted us to see: the clouds and blue sky.

"I thought yesterday was beautiful," said Susan. "I think today is going to be an even more beautiful day. The breeze is so warm and gentle," smiled Susan.

"I was just thinking the same thing," said Sara. "All the money in the world couldn't buy this."

Sara giggled lightly. "No, but Sean did," she said.

"Sean did what?" asked Sara.

"Bought all this," said Susan.

Sara looked around. "Yes, he did didn't he?" said Sara. "You know we'll have to ride around and find you a good spot to build a home on, somewhere that would be perfect for your children and then build you a home this spring, a nice home," smiled Sara.

"Sara, why are you doing all this for me and Jacob?" asked Susan.

"Susan, you and Jacob are Sean and my best friends. It's what friends do," said Sara.

"Sara, Jacob and I can never repay you for everything you've done for us already," said Susan.

"Susan, we don't want you to pay us back. We don't want anything from you two. Well, maybe you can let me play with the baby from time to time," said Sara.

Susan looked at Sara strangely. You say that like you and Sean will never have children."

"There's town," said Jacob.

"Already?" cried Sara.

"Already," said Susan. "Sara, sometimes you scare me."

"I'm all right. I just meant that you and I were talking so much that the trip to town felt like a short walk," laughed Sara.

"For you, maybe; for me it was torture. The baby bounced all over the place," laughed Susan.

"Well ladies, what do we do first?" asked Sean, coming up alongside the wagon.

"Eat!" said Sara. "Susan bounced the baby around so much, he's hungry."

"Sounds more like you're hungry," laughed Sean. "You must be feeling better. Let's go."

"Yes, I'm feeling better, but we must think of the baby. If you think it's easy riding in a wagon pregnant, you are sadly mistaken," said Sara. "Maybe you would like to carry the baby for awhile."

"Not made to do so, so I guess we feed the baby," smiled Sean. Jacob lead the way.

Jacob started toward Rome. In a half hour they were sitting in a restaurant ordering lunch, talking about what stores they wanted to shop in. Of course the men wanted tools and farm things, and women wanted household things. Susan pointed people out to Sara, explaining who they were and how she knew them. Lunch came; they ate. Sean tended to the bill. The women went one way, men another. Sara went nuts over the prices. She didn't say anything or do anything to bring attention to herself.

"Susan, look at the flannel nightgowns, feel how heavy," smiled Sara.

"Yeah, look at the prices. Five dollars, that's terrible. You can't afford to live these days," said Susan.

Sara smiled and thought, "in my time one nightgown like this is sixty dollars. Now that's highway robbery."

"I don't know. I like them a lot. I know five dollars is a lot, but it looks so warm," said Sara.

Susan stopped and felt the material. "You're right, it would be warm this winter. But five dollars could be put to good use elsewhere," said Susan.

"You're right," said Sara.

Susan walked away, looking at other things, things that would be useful.

Sara took eight nightgowns; four for her, four for Susan plus two chenille robes. This was going to be the cheapest she'd ever spent on clothes. Sara sat them on the counter. "You do have jeans for a young man? He's about my size, my nephew. I just don't know about those things," smiled Sara weakly. "Yes ma'am, this way," said the young man. "Do you know his waist size?" he asked.

"Yes. I have it written down here. Yes, this is it," smiled Sara. "The larger waist is my husband's." Sara tried to act like a poor, helpless woman. It wasn't easy. In her time, women weren't ladies. You bothered them, they maced you, shot you or just ran you over with the car. If you were still alive after that, they would stab you, call the police and say that man tried to hurt me, then his ass would be sitting in jail.

"Is your nephew very tall?" asked the young man.

"Oh, my no. Someday he'll be a tall man, but he's only ten now and about as tall as me. I know he should be in nickers, but I made a bet with him when he was young. I lost, now I must buy him some jeans."

"My sister-in-law is beside herself, says I spoil him, but a bet is a bet," smiled Sara.

"Yes ma'am," smiled the young man. He turned away and rolled his eyes. He hated waiting on women, they were so stupid. "This is what you want."

Sara looked at the sign, "One dollar Levi's. One dollar, yeah, right. Is this sign right, one dollar?" asked Sara.

"Yes ma'am, we have cheaper ones, but these are of the best quality."

Sara smiled, "Honey if only you knew. I'll take five pairs." The young man looked at Sara shocked, "Not enough, I'll take seven pairs. A bet is a bet."

"Yes ma'am. Is your husband tall?" asked the young man.

"Yes, what's your name?" asked Sara.

"Blaine Mckensy, why?" asked the young man.

"Well, Mr. Mckensy, I have a lot of shopping to do and since you will be helping me, I thought it only proper I call you by your given name," smiled Sara.

"Yes ma'am!" thought Blaine, "now to get you out of my sight would be good.

"This is your husband's size. How many would you like?"

"Fourteen pairs," smiled Sara.

"Four-four-fourteen. I don't know if we got that many," said Blaine.

"What you buying?" asked Susan. "I thought I'd buy the boys some jeans. Sean and Jacob are the same size, aren't they?" asked Sara.

"No, Jacob is smaller, but you don't have to buy Jacob anything," said Susan.

"Birthday present," Sara said quickly.

"Oh, God! Today is his birthday; I almost forgot," said Susan.

"I only have six pairs in this size," said Blaine.

"I'll take six that size and six the next size down," smiled Sara.

"Yes ma'am," said Blaine.

"I need T-shirts, longjohns, flannel shirts, and boots," smiled Sara.

"You look over there. I'll put these on the shelf with your other things, then I'll come back and help you," said Blaine.

"Thank you," smiled Sara.

Blaine left. "Sara, have you lost your mind? You're wasting a lot of money here," said Susan.

"No, I'm trying to think ahead. How many trips do you think you can make to town being pregnant?" asked Sara. "If we get this stuff now, then we won't have to worry about the baby."

"Oh," said Susan. "It makes sense, I guess."

"Let's see...socks, T-shirts, longjohns, underwear...ah! Flannel shirts," smiled Sara.

"Actually, they're wool," said Susan.

"Better yet, they're warmer," said Sara. Sara had a pile of clothing set aside when Blaine returned.

Blaine, only fourteen with brown hair, brown eyes, thought he had seen it all. But this lady was out of her mind. "You want this stuff, too?" asked Blaine.

"Yes, and these hankies, boots…let's see," said Sara, looking around.

"Boot are over there," said Blaine as he started carrying Sara's shopping to the front of the store.

"This lady is trying to buy the store out," he thought.

Sara and Susan walked over to the boot section. Sara looked until she found what she was looking for, then tried on some until she found a pair that fit. "Now this is a boot," smiled Sara.

"You're not buying yourself men's boots," said Susan.

"Why not. If I'm helping Sean in the barn, do you think I'd want to wear pretty slippers in the barn?" asked Sara.

"You plan on working on the farm?" asked Susan.

"Yes, while the men work the field, I can milk, feed the chickens, slop the hogs. Sean and I are in this together," said Sara.

"Oh, look at this coat. Now that looks warm." Sara tried one on and chose four. "Well, I guess we're done in the men's department. Now let's hit the women's section," smiled Sara.

"Sara, I'm worried about you," said Susan.

"Don't be, you'll see, this will all make sense, trust me," said Sara.

"I suppose you're right," said Susan, doubtfully.

"We'll shop till we drop," smiled Sara. "Women's department, here we come." Sara pulled a reluctant Susan into the women's fashion department. Sara found a lot of nice things for Susan. At first Susan was a little hesitant, but Sara got her in the swing of things. Blaine just kept picking up Sara's neat little pile of clothes and run them to the front of the store for them. He was getting tired. Sara went crazy on flannel sheets she found. That just about cleaned out the baby department. Blaine followed in an exhausted state. He'd never seen anyone shop like this. Now they were in the fabric department buying things.

"Well, I don't see anything more to buy," smiled Sara. "Ah! Blaine do you sell beds, tables, chairs, that kind of stuff?" asked Sara.

"Yes, over there," sighed Blaine. "I'll set these down and be right over to help you." Blaine couldn't help thinking how quiet it had been in here all month. Mr. Smithers went home, told Blaine to close up. He was about to when these two ladies walked in. Mr. Smithers' policy was you never closed shop on a lady. Blaine thought he'd sell one, maybe two things, nothing like this. Mr. Smithers will die when he sees that he sold today. Blaine, although young, worked to help his mother. Blaine begged for this job. Mr. Smithers wasn't sure. He said he'd pay Blaine five dollars a week. But he wasn't going to get paid until his mother's bill at the store was paid. Blaine's mother owned the store one hundred dollars, and at five dollars a week, he'd spent his youth paying off his mother's debt. He couldn't blame his mother. His father had got the sickness. Mom took care of him until he passed on. Now she worked at the restaurant trying to clear up all her debts. So why should Blaine complain about helping her? Mr. Smithers. could have set the coat aside that Blaine wanted. Now there was one left; it was his size. Maybe Mr. Smithers would be grateful for all he sold today and let him set it aside. "Never happen," thought Blaine, as he walked up to Sara.

"We want these two tables, these two cupboards, that bed, and those two armoires, and for my best friend in the world, that sewing machine."

"Oh, Sara, that's too much," said Susan.

"No it's not. How else do you propose to mend all the clothes the baby will destroy?" laughed Sara.

"I don't think Sean will like this?" said Susan.

"Guess what? This was Sean's idea and Sean's list," smiled Sara. "Now let's see, oh dishes and silverware," smiled Sara. "This way," smiled Blaine. For the first time Mr. Smithers said he'd never be able to sell this stuff. It's been sitting there for years. Three months on the job, and Blaine sold it.

"Okay, these two dish sets, these two pan sets, and these two sets of silverware, and I guess we're done," smiled Sara.

Blaine kept an ongoing receipt and choked when he told Sara $750.

"That ain't right, something is missing."

Susan put her hand on her chest, grabbed hold of a nearby table.

Blaine's mouth dropped open. She didn't give it a second thought.

"Well, I knew I forgot something. Those two rocking chairs and that stove, and whatever gizmos that go to hook it up," said Sara.

"Th—th—that's $870 ma'am," stammered Blaine. Blaine didn't think they sold that much all year.

Sara reached in her purse, counted out one thousand dollars and handed it to Blaine, who counted it and said he'd be back with the change.

"No! This is your tip for me being such a pain. I know I must have driven you nuts, and you probably think I'm nuts like my friend Susan," said Sara. "But I'm not."

"Did you get everything you needed?" asked Sean as walked in, the little bell above the door ringing as Sean and Jacob arrived.

"Everything on the list you gave me," said Sara.

"Did you need boots. And how did your shopping go?" asked Sara.

"No, I found boots at the hardware store. Had a hell of a time getting a pair, birthday or no birthday," said Sean.

"Same here. Susan fought me all the way, too," said Sara. "I think she's in shock."

"Jacob, too. He stopped talking about an hour ago. Well, pay the man, and you and Susan can go to the next store and buy all our food supplies while Jacob and I load up the wagon," said Sean.

"I already paid him and tipped him for helping me," said Sara.

"Well, I'll get the receipt and load the wagon," said Sean.

"Okay. Come on Susan, we have some shopping to do," said Sara.

"More shopping?" asked Susan.

"Yes, come on," said Sara, pulling Susan by the hand.

"Show me what they bought, and we'll move it out for you," said Sean.

"Yes, sir," said Blaine, handing Sean the receipt. "Put that stove, those two rockers, those four cabinets, these two table sets. I'll wrap the rest of the stuff at the counter," said Blaine, picking up two dish sets.

"Thank you," said Sean. He pointed Jacob toward the stove. Jacob moved in a stiff manner, his sense of conscience was lost a long time ago at the hardware store. Blaine put the money in the cash register, then walked back and got the pan sets and silverware. By the time Sean and Jacob had all the furniture moved out, Blaine had all the parcels wrapped and tied. He looked around the store, it looked empty. Jacob and Sean were carrying the wrapped packages out to the wagon, when Mr. Smithers came running in. Blaine was sweeping the floors in the bare spots, his thirty dollars neatly folded in his pocket, ten dollars in his shirt pocket, twenty dollars in his pant's pockets. He whistled as he swept. By the looks of the floor, Mr. Smithers never swept it.

"Blaine, what's going on here?" yelled Mr. Smithers.

"Figures that nosey, old man would see something going on and think he'd done something wrong. Well this time he couldn't say a word," Blain thought.

"Sold a few things," said Blaine, looking down at the floor he was sweeping.

Mr. Smithers looked around the store. A—a—a few things. How much of a few things? asked Mr. Smithers. Blaine stopped sweeping the floor and looked up. He wasn't going to miss this for nothing. "Eight hundred and seventy dollars," Blaine said, smiling.

Mr. Smithers grabbed his chest with his left hand and the counter with his right. Blaine watched as Mr. Smithers went from red to purple in color. Blaine didn't move; he just watched. After a while his color slowly returned to normal color.

"Th—th—that's impossible," sputtered Mr. Smithers.

"Well, look around, most everything is gone," smiled Blaine. "Since you're here, I would like to buy that coat. You wouldn't let me set it aside. It's the only one left," Blaine said calmly.

"You sold the coats out, too?" asked Mr. Smithers.

"Will when I buy mine," smiled Blaine. "I wrote everything down, go check it," said Blaine.

Mr. Smithers walked to the cash register, went over the receipts. "Looks to me you can't buy the coat," smiled Mr. Smithers. "Your ten dollars short."

Blaine walked calmly to the front of the store. "I always knew you were a crook, but you know what, I worked my behind off for you. I've been waiting for you to fire me because my mother's debt is paid, and this week you would have had to pay me. You had no intentions of doing so. All you want is a nigger to work for you. Well guess what? Here's twenty dollars. I'll buy the coat, and you get your ten bucks and you don't have to pay me," said Blaine. "I quit!" Blaine walked over and picked up his coat. "I'm calling the law. You're stealing the coat," yelled Mr. Smithers.

"I don't think so," said Sean, stepping around the corner. "Blaine, take your coat and go son. Get the sheriff for me."

"Yes sir," said Blaine.

"I heard the whole thing. I have a bill here in my hand that has the right total. You sir are up shit's creek without a paddle," said Sean.

"The boy was only trouble sir," smiled Mr. Smithers.

Sheriff Miller walked in the store with Blaine following. "Is there a problem here?" he asked looking, at Mr. Smithers and Sean.

"Yes," said Sean. "Mr. Smithers here has extracted money from this young man, then when Blaine bought the coat, Mr. Smithers threatened to call the police and say he stole it. And on top of that, he called him a nigger, which pissed me off," said Sean.

"The man is mistaken," said Mr. Smithers.

"Am I? Sheriff, check the till. I know for a fact that there was no money in it. I have a receipt for $870. Blaine bought a coat for ten dollars, that comes to $880. If I'm wrong, I will apologize to the man. But I'm not. Also, Blaine has worked in this store with no wages to pay off his mom's debt. How much was that, Blaine?" asked Sean.

"One hundred dollars. There's a black book in the till. I've worked here six months at five dollars a week. It's all gone on mom's bill. I had to sign the book," said Blaine.

"Mr. Smithers, step away from the cash register," said Sheriff Miller. "Hands in the air." Sheriff Miller walked over to the register.

There was the black book and money. The sheriff counted out $890. He checked Sean's bill. It totaled $870.

"There's ten dollars extra in here." Sheriff Miller picked up the black book. Blaine had indeed worked here six months at five dollars a week to pay his mom's debt. The sheriff looked at Mr. Smithers. "Seems you have some explaining to do," said Sheriff Miller.

"This man is crazy. He don't know what he's talking about," said Mr. Smithers. "He's lying. It's his word against mine," said Mr. Smithers.

"I don't think so," said Jacob, stepping around the corner. "I heard it all. What Sean said is true. You going to call me a liar?" asked Jacob.

"Seems to me that it's two-to-one now," said Sheriff Miller. "Come here, son. Is what these men talking about true?

"Yes sir," said Blaine.

"I see. Now it's three-to-one," said Sheriff Miller. "Seems to me that you don't stand a chance here, Mr. Smithers."

"Well, who are you going to believe here? Me, the businessman, someone you've known all your life or them whom you never met?"

"Well, seems to be a problem all right, but I don't know what," said Sheriff Miller.

Sara and Susan stepped around the corner. "Well, you bloody well believe me," said Sara, staring at Sheriff Miller.

"Sara!" cried Mr. Smithers.

"Miss Sara?" asked Sheriff Miller.

"Mrs. Sean Huntington," smiled Sara. "This is my husband Sean."

"Mr. Huntington, Mr. Farley told me all about you. Fine, upstanding young man," he said. "Mr. Smith said you were the most fairest, honest man on God's green earth. I figured if Mr. Smith has anything nice to say about a man, that man has to be a decent man. Mr. Smithers, on the other hand, has had numerous complaints filed against him. This I guess you could say is the last one."

"What do you mean?" asked Mr. Smithers.

"Well, the way I see it, you owe Blaine twenty dollars, the ten dollars you extracted from him and ten dollars you overcharged him on his Mom's bill. That's extortion and you are officially closed. Here, son this is your twenty dollars. But now I'm afraid you're out of a job," said Sheriff Miller.

"That's all right, I already quit," smiled Blaine. "Thank you, sir."

"That's my money!" yelled Mr. Smithers.

"No, Mr. Smithers. What I've done is paid your debts. This is your money, and the last you'll be making in this town. This is a good, honest Christian town. There's no room for liars or cheats. We respect all mankind here. You're not Rome's type. I recommend you leave," said Sheriff Miller. "I'd hate to see a man get run out of town. It ain't pretty, the choice is yours. However, I can guarantee you if you get run out of town, wherever you go, the rumor of what you did to the good people of this town will arrive before you do."

Mr. Smithers looked grief-strickened. He knew what rumors could do to a man. "I'll leave," said Mr. Smithers.

"Good choice," said Sheriff Miller.

"Well, I'm going next door," said Sara. "I started shopping and came to get Sean when all this started happening."

"My friend Susan grows tired. She'd with child and it has been a very long day for her. We need to finish shopping, eat, and be on our way," smiled Sara.

"Yes ma'am," said Sheriff Miller, tipping his hat toward Sara and Susan. "I hope Sean and Jacob will stay here and help me close this store."

"Yes sir!" said Sean.

Mr. Smithers muttered something under his breath.

"Sorry, did you say something, Mr. Smithers?" said Sheriff Miller.

"Just trying to figure out how long it will take to pack everything up," said Mr. Smithers.

"Oh, don't you worry. I'll get some good men of this town together. You'll be on your way tomorrow, " smiled Sheriff Miller.

"Yes, sir," said Mr. Smithers, handing Sheriff Miller the key to the store.

Sheriff Miller was a young man, tall, good-looking with black hair, brown eyes, very muscular and strong, not a man you messed with. When he spoke, you listened, then said, "sir." He was a good man; a fair, just man. He kept Rome a good town, a town you wanted to live in. He got respect from everyone in town because he earned it.

"How you two doing?" asked Sean, walking up to Sara and Susan.

"Just about done," said Sara. "Found something that looks like soda. Susan's getting tired. We should eat and head home. We want to get set up before dark," said Sara.

"Okay. Jacob and I will load the wagon," said Sean.

"Look, yarn!" said Sara. She handed some to Susan, and she took some, picked out a couple crochet hooks and knitting needles. They walked up front to set them on the counter. We need a couple of oil lamps and some oil, matches, and candles," said Sara.

"Yes, ma'am," said the clerk.

Sara signed. "Let's see...cotton, cheese cloth, soaps, coffee, must have coffee."

"The coffee's over there," said the clerk.

"Thank you," said Sara. Sara had to admit she was getting tired. It was a long day. Great, the coffee was in bean form. Ah, a grinder.

"Is this the only size coffee you have?" asked Sara. "Do you have them in bigger bags. We live outside of town, and Susan is expecting, so we don't know if we can get back into town before snow falls," said Sara.

"I've got burlap bags of coffee out back," said the clerk.

"I'll take four bags if you have them, and two of these grinders." Sara took two coffee pots off the shelf, blue enamel ones. Flour, sugar, and salt. Pepper, Sean loves pepper. Susan stood by the counter in silence. She stopped thinking a while back; only numbness was what she felt. This was a shocking day, far more than she could handle. Sara picked out some meats, hams for the holidays, brown sugar, baking powder, confectionery sugar, cocoa chocolate squares. She bought chocolates, then she remembered she needed tea. She paid the clerk, and Sean and Jacob loaded the last of the goods on the wagon. It was eight o'clock P.M. Jacob drove to the restaurant; they ate. Sara had a cake brought to the table for Jacob in honor of his birthday. Sean paid the bill and set a tip on the table.

"Sir, thank you for what you've done for my son, Blaine."

"The pleasure was all mine. He's a good boy, he didn't need such bad treatment," said Sara.

"Thank you," smiled Mary. "He's a good boy, he's watching your wagon. He didn't know how else to thank you. He wanted that coat for so long. I know Mr. Smithers didn't want to sell it to him. Mr. Smithers was upset with my husband for dying and owing him all that money. One night, Mr. Smithers showed up at my home thinking I should do certain favors for him to clear my husband's debts. He worked Blaine hard, long hours. I'm glad it's over now," said Mary.

"What I don't understand is why Mr. Smithers called him nigger," said Sean.

"Because we're Irish. A lot of people think Irish people are black men turned inside out," said Mary. "We moved here during the great potato famine; we lost much. Then Richard died. It was a lot all at once; too much for a young boy to handle. He had to grow old too soon," said Mary.

"We all here have our little stories. We don't talk about them. We would rather put all the hurt behind us. As adults I think we hide our sorrows better than a child. A child hasn't lived long enough to learn how to hide his feelings. No, their feelings they wear on their sleeves for everyone to see. And what I saw today was a happy, young man. He hasn't smiled like that since his father died. You gave him his life back, and I just wanted to say thank you," smiled Mary, wiping her hands on her apron.

Sean didn't know what to say, so he nodded his head, smiled, and left. When he went outside, Blaine was gone. Susan, Jacob, and Sara were in the wagon. Sean mounted his horse and followed Jacob home. Sean thought about what Mary said. He tried to think of one race of mankind that wasn't persecuted in one way or another. He couldn't be sure the Jews would say they were the most persecuted by God, then Hitler. But everyone has made their sacrifices. So that gave every man the right to live; live where he wanted, how he wanted. So why couldn't man let it go, live in peace? This world had so much to offer to man if he'd stop and take a long, hard look around. Why did mankind have to complicate things? "We really fucked things up," thought Sean. At 5:00 P.M. Jacob pulled the wagon to a halt in front of the barn.

Sara and Susan looked beat. Jacob helped them down. Sean watched Jacob as he dismounted his horse. Men, the protector of women and children. God did we ever screw up. The future was a mess: Women being forced to take over the role of the male and still be the mother and homemaker and man's plaything when he wanted. We fucked everything up, we took the woman's right away to be a lady.

"Sean, I'm taking Susan in our home while you and Jacob set up their home. I'll make some coffee. I think everyone is a little whipped, emotionally and physically," said Sara.

Sean smiled and nodded. Sara was always a thoughtful, caring person; everyone else first. She was a good woman. Tom never deserved her. He never treated her the way she deserved, but Sara had too much class to complain. She would never leave Tom; she took her vows too seriously."

"We'll set a table and chairs in your house first. I think the girls need to rest," said Jacob.

Sean laughed, "we're all exhausted. Sara can shop."

"You called that shopping? I thought Sara was trying to buy the town," laughed Jacob , handing chairs down to Sean. Sean laughed setting the chairs aside, grabbing the table Jacob slid over. Jacob jumped down, took one end of the table and helped Sean carry it inside, then they went back and grabbed two chairs a piece and put them in Sean's house. Sara sat Susan down. Jacob and Sean unloaded the furniture first and set it up in Jacob and Susan's new home. Jacob looked around. He never dreamed he would own all this stuff.

"Well, as much as we hate to," said Sean, "we better bring that stove in here and hook it up while we have some strength left, then have a coffee break."

"I'm with you," smiled Jacob.

While they hooked the stove up, Sara talked to Susan. She seemed down.

"What's wrong?" asked Sara.

"Where'd you and Sean get all that money? asked Susan.

"What, you think we stole it?" asked Sara.

"The thought crossed my mind," said Susan.

"Well, I wouldn't have known I had any money if it wasn't for you."

"Me? what have I got to do with this?" asked Susan.

"Remember that day you came to the wagon" You said you were happy that my uncle let me keep my hope chest, then asked me if we had any food."

"Yes, but what has one thing got to do with the other, let alone the money?" asked Susan.

"To make it simple, Dad made my hope chest, Dad liked hiding places. I found a hiding place, and it was full of money and a note from Mom, 'Don't trust your uncle. I won't tell you how much is there, but it's enough to last my lifetime," said Sara.

Susan gave a sigh of relief, "that sounds like your mother," laughed Susan. "She always could see into the future."

"Do you feel better now?" asked Sara. "You know my mother would have done the same thing I did today, and if I didn't, she would have haunted me," laughed Sara.

"You're right. I shouldn't have doubted you," said Susan.

"The men didn't bring in the dishes, so we have the whole pleasure of drinking out of tin cups," said Sara.

"That's fine," said Susan.

Sara had water boiling on the stove. She took the last of the coffee, wrapped it in cheese cloth a couple of times, and placed it in a colander that sat on top of a bowl. Sara poured boiling water over the coffee.

"What are you doing?" asked Susan.

"Making coffee, you can see that," smiled Sara.

"I hate to tell you this, but that's not how you make coffee," said Susan.

"If you like good coffee, coffee without grounds, it is," said Sara.

"Coffee without grounds? Impossible," said Susan.

"No it isn't," said Sara. "This also keeps the sediment out, and it's not bitter this way. They call it drip coffee."

"Drip coffee?" asked Susan.

"Yes, see how it's dripping slowly down through," said Sara, lifting the colander.

"If you say so," said Susan. "Seems like a lot of work to me."

"Maybe, but it's worth it once you taste it," smiled Sara. "You use less coffee, and you can use the grounds twice. Then set them aside to use as fertilizer in the garden. "Here, taste," said Sara, pouring Susan a cup. "Here's sugar and cream."

"Hey, this is good. How did you learn that?" asked Susan.

"Sean," said Sara, pouring the coffee in the coffee pot.

"Don't I smell coffee?" asked Sean as he walked in. "I hope drip coffee."

"Yes, it's drip coffee," smiled Sara.

"Drip coffee?" Jacob asked, puzzled.

"Wait till you taste this," said Susan. "It tastes good even in a tin cup."

"I get it, no dishes," smiled Sean, "be right back."

"Sean, you don't have to get the dishes now," said Sara, take a break, we'll be fine."

"I don't mind," said Sean.

"Sit, take a break," said Sara, "you've earned it."

"Okay," said Sean. "It would feel good to sit."

"Then sit. we can have the rest of Jacob's birthday cake. How much have you got done over there?" asked Sara.

"Everything but the bed made," snarled Jacob, "and I'd sleep on it even if it wasn't made."

"Jacob, you're bad," laughed Susan. "I wouldn't let you sleep on a bed that's not made up."

"I've got to admit Sean's plan of adding a room on the end of the barn was very smart. By putting the door inside the barn you're protected, you always have access to the barn, and you walk across the barn to your friend's house. This is very smart. At first I thought Sean was crazy, but it's very smart. Tomorrow we're building more things. By the time winter hits, we should be self-contained here."

"Well if we don't get the wagon unloaded tonight, we won't be doing anything tomorrow," said Sean.

"I was hoping you would forget," said Jacob as he stood up.

"I'll help," said Sara. "I'll show you which packages go where. It will save you time."

"Well, Jacob and I will bring the two blue things. Just show where you want them," said Sean.

"Blue there, green there," said Sara.

"Done," smiled Sean.

Susan cleared the dishes. "What do I do?" asked Susan.

"Rest!" said Sara. "This won't be long."

"Okay," said Susan.

Sara climbed into the wagon and started going through the packages, marking two piles, one for each home. When she was done, she took the package with the bed linen for Jacob and Susan and made her bed for her and set out a new nightgown for her. Sara couldn't wait to put her nightgown on. She could hear it calling her, but it was early, 6:30 P.M.; Too early for bed. It was still light out. Sara went to her home and put her stuff away, washed dishes, and dried them while she talked to Susan.

Susan wanted to go home but was afraid Sara would feel hurt for leaving her alone. Susan had to make the bed and everything. "Sara would you feel hurt if I went home. I know it sounds stupid, but I've got work to do, too," said Susan.

Sara smiled, "Susan, you owe me nothing. You don't have to sit here and baby sit me. You have a life, too. I realize this. You do what you have to. If something is on your mind, say so. I will understand," said Sara.

"You're right. I want to see my home. It sounds strange, 'my home.'"

"I think you'll like it," smiled Sara. "Go, get settled into your home; sleep well tonight."

Susan laughed. "That, I will have no problem with. It's been a long day. Just the thought of sleeping in a bed, I can't tell you."

"You don't have to. I swear I hear my nightgown calling me," laughed Sara. "I think I'm going to bed early."

"Well, I'll see you tomorrow," yawned Susan. "Hear that? My nightgown just called me, too, so I'm leaving."

"See you in the morning," said Sara.

Susan left Sara put on her nightgown. God, was it good to get out of those clothes. Sara was putting the canned goods in the cupboard she bought when Sean walked in.

"It's all unloaded, horses bedded, I milked the cow and gave Jacob and Susan the milk, fed our little critters, so we're set for the night."

"Well, I've got hot water cooking for you to get washed up. I'm going to bed right after I'm done here. I couldn't wait to get out of those clothes. I put your new clothes in the closet. They're on the left, mine on the right. There's coffee left."

"Thanks," said Sean. "I'm exhausted. I found some windows. "We'll put them in tomorrow. The hardware store made them while we shopped. They made them the size I wanted."

"Real windows, not shutters," laughed Sara. "That's what Jacob meant when he said we'd be ready for winter."

Sean shook his head, "Jacob thinks I'm a genius. I'm not. What I've thought of would be diddly back home. I've got a coupe of wagons coming tomorrow. Jacob's all excited now. I got some tin for the roof. The roof on here is good, but it might not handle snow and ice. I think it might leak, so I got a few rolls of what they call tar paper and some tin. I've got wood coming. I think I might be able to make a pump to have running water. I don't know how to make hot water yet, but it sure beats the hell out of lugging milk cans of water up from the creek," said Sean.

"What's the wood for?" said Sara, sitting down, her task done.

"Well, I bought two sinks. Thought I'd make a couple of cupboards. We need outhouses. I would really like to put in a bathroom of sorts, but I don't know how to get enough pressure to push it. This floor is good, but a wood floor would be better. I've been writing all this down, so if we go back or whatever, Jacob will know what I'm doing," laughed Sean.

"I know, I've been doing the same thing. Where would you put a bathroom in here?" asked Sara.

"I know this place isn't big, but I thought the back wall of the bedroom. The sink of the front of the kitchen wall. I'd run the pipes under the new floor," said Sean.

"Huh, north and south," said Sara, looking from one end to the other.

"That's it," said Sean.

"What's it?" said Sara.

"North and south, opposites attract," said Sean.

"What are we talking about, I'm lost here. Can you fill me in so we can have a conversation instead of you talking to air?" said Sara.

"For every action, there has to be a reaction, so if we want to pump water without an electric pump, what we do is use air," said Sean.

"Air?" asked Sara, confused.

"Yes, two pumps, one to use air to force the water to rise, one to suck the water out. It will create a vacuum to force the water up. That builds pressure. It should build enough pressure to flush the toilet. Now all I have to do is figure out how to make hot water!" said Sean.

"I don't know if this will help you any," said Sara, hesitantly. "but my father-in-law never paid for hot water, he had a holding tank that water went into first. Then had copper tubing that he wrapped around. I don't know, it looked like a wood stove to me. He would heat this wood stove, and the copper tubing would heat the water. The holding tank kept the water warmer than groundwater. I don't know how or why, but it worked for him. He refused to pay nimo for hot water," said Sara.

"Smart man," smiled Sean. "Do you know how much money we waste keeping water hot until we want to use it? How did he keep the fire going?" asked Sean.

"Trash, mostly. Sometimes wood. He said it didn't take much, something about copper heating up quickly. I never really paid much attention. I probably never would have known about it if I hadn't complained about how high my nimo bill was," Sara laughed, remembering. "He jumped right up and said hot water. He wanted to run it under the floor to keep the floors warm, but my mother-in-law wouldn't let him," laughed Sara.

"M—m—m," said Sean, he was thinking, "this coffee is good. What did you think seeing Rome today?" asked Sean.

"It was strange. Some of the buildings of our time were there. I kept thinking how it would look in the future. I think I like it this way better. Shopping was different, so many things in one store, like each store was a mini-mall," Sara laughed. "Susan was worried about prices, fifty cents for this nightgown. Hell, I'd pay fifty five dollars for a nightgown in our time, and it's not half as warm or heavy. Jeans one dollar. I found some bras that weren't corsets; they didn't look too bad. I'll find out tomorrow," smiled Sara. "Did you get me a washtub?"

"Yeah, it's in the barn. You know we haven't looked at our wedding presents yet," said Sean.

"What wedding presents?" asked Sara.

"Seems you were too upset this morning to hear me," said Sean. "The people of the wagon train left us some wedding presents."

"Oh, we'll go through them tomorrow. Right now I'm going to bed. I've had it," said Sara.

"I'll be along shortly, I need to get cleaned up. See ya in the morning," smiled Sean.

As Sean bathed, he thought about hot water, and Sara's father-in-law was right, it would work. So now he had pressure and hot water.

"Jacob, do you regret us not going with the wagon train?" asked Susan.

"Nope, this is where we belong. I know what you're thinking," said Jacob.

"What?" asked Susan.

"You think we're leaching off of Sean and Sara, but we're not," said Jacob.

"Now, you sound like them!" said Susan. "Just like them."

"No, Sean and I are partners," said Jacob.

"Partners, partners of what, his barn?" said Susan.

"No, partners of a farm. This can be a good farm with Sean's ideas, something to pass on to our children and their children," said Jacob.

"Sean's ideas and Sara's money," Susan said bitterly.

"No, we make the farm pay for itself," said Jacob.

"How do you make a farm pay for itself?" asked Susan.

"You grow things; you sell things," said Jacob.

"Grow what?" asked Susan.

"Food. No matter what, man has to eat," said Jacob.

"Oh," said Susan.

"Sara invested some money in a future, she'll get it back, plus Sara's smart," said Jacob.

"And I'm not?" said Susan.

Jacob signed, "yes you are, but you're smart in the areas that Sara's not, just like I'm smart in the areas Sean's not. You put the four of us together and we can conquer just about anything. That's why we're here," said Jacob.

"Oh!" said Susan. She knew Jacob was right, but lately she'd been blue. Sara said being pregnant did that; not all the time, just some of the time.

"Sean and I unloaded our wagon, too. That's why theirs looks like there's a lot here," smiled Jacob. Jacob stood up stretched. "Well, I'm getting washed up and going to bed, have to get up early."

Susan washed up earlier and put on her nightgown Sara set out for her. Susan had to admit it was cozy, but it felt good just rocking in the rocker, back and forth. It seemed to calm the baby. He was moving all over today. Her back ached, her ribs hurt where he kicked her. "Who ever said it was a joy being pregnant wasn't a woman," thought Susan. Tomorrow the doctor was coming out to check her over. Sara insisted the doctor come out after showing her who the doctor was, just to be safe, Sara said. One checkup; so Susan agreed to one checkup. No more, just one. Susan started to fall asleep rocking. So Jacob picked her up and carried her to bed, covered her up, got in bed and fell asleep by the time his head hit the pillow.

Chapter 3

SEAN'S SNORING WOKE SARA. THE SUN WAS JUST STARTING TO COME UP, SO she got up and got dressed. The new bra wasn't too bad, but the jeans and T-shirt were what made her feel comfortable. She put on socks and her boots, took out a flannel shirt, put it on, brushed her hair, walked outside. It was going to be a beautiful day. She needed to work off some energy. She couldn't jog in boots. So she decided to chop wood. She knew everyone would think this stupid on her part, but she needed to do something. While she chopped wood, she saw someone watching her. She tried to pretend he wasn't there. That didn't work, so she turned around. "You don't have to hide, you can come out. I've got coffee on. I don't bite, only on Thursdays," laughed Sara.

"Well I better not come out," John said laughing. "Today is Thursday."

Sara heard his laughter as he stepped into view.

"Well, since you're bigger than me I'll make an exception," laughed Sara. "Coffee?"

"Sure!" smiled John. "Why is it you're not afraid of me when everyone else runs when they see an Indian?" asked John, picking up some wood.

Sara picked some wood up. "Must be the red hair. It makes me a little more stubborn than most people," laughed Sara as she led the way into her little home. "Sit, I'll pour you some coffee. I was about to cook breakfast, would you like some?" asked Sara.

"No thank you, this is nice. I've been watching you. Pretty smart the way you set this up," said John.

"Well I'd like to take the credit, but Sean did this. Me, I'm just a woman," said Sara.

"Somehow I get the feeling that's not true. You were swinging that ax pretty good out there. Never seen a woman chop wood before. Well, a white woman, anyway," laughed John.

Sara set coffee on the table for her and John, then sat down. Sean heard voices and looked to see Sara talking to an Indian in their house. He forgot Sara's one fault: she trusted everyone, that's how they ended up being shot. There's good in everyone, she'd say as the fog left his brain. Sean realized that this must be John Red Feather that Farley told Jacob about.

"I'm not your type of woman," said Sara. "I don't believe in sitting around sipping drinks and getting fat."

"You don't like dresses either," laughed John.

"Hate dresses and shoes. I had to settle for boots, but I prefer moccasins or sneaks, but we can't get either. So boots will have to do," said Sara sipping coffee.

"You must be John," said Sean, walking up to John, his hand held out to shake John's. "I'm Sean, this is Sara. She's a bit too trusting for her own good," laughed Sean.

"I noticed. I figured if I didn't come out of the woods, she'd come up there and drag me out," laughed John, shaking his hand.

"She probably would have," laughed Sean.

"I was surprised she even knew I was there," said John.

"Well, you were there yesterday. And to keep hidden is stupid. Just come right out and say or do what has to be done," said Sara.

Sean shook his head, "she's also bold," said Sean. "I'm glad we get to talk' said Sean sitting down. As you know, I just bought this land from one Mr. Smith. There's a lot of land here, some I'm sure runs with yours. I would like to farm here, but before I do that I need to know how much land your people need and where they need it," said Sean.

John raised an eyebrow. "Your concern is for my people?" asked John.

"Yes, of course, shouldn't it be?" asked Sean. "That's why I bought it. I'm sure Mr. Smith would have had you run off or killed. I couldn't let that happen."

John was quite surprised. A white man that made sense. Farley said he was a good man, but where he sat right now he looked like a God. The chief counsel would be surprised.

"If you would like, we could draw up legal documents so there are no disputes now or in the future. I know there's over a thousand acres here, and I don't want to see the land destroyed," said Sean. "It's to beautiful."

"Yes," said Sara. "If we don't protect it now, everything will be lost."

"Both of you agree to this?" asked John.

"Well, actually, there's four of us, and we all agree," said Sean. "Let's say that Sara and I know things we shouldn't know, and we're here to right a wrong before it becomes a wrong," said Sean.

John was confused but he understood, because his people have seen what white men could do. Yet here sat a white man telling him what his people had said for years. "Don't get me wrong when I say this," said John. "But I want to make sure I understand you correctly. It's like you two can see into the future, and you don't like what you see, so you want to prevent it from happening," said John.

"Yes!" said Sean.

"Can all four of you do this?" asked John.

"No, we're the only two crazy ones here. I don't even know why we're able to do this or for how long we'll be able to do it," said Sean. "We've been writing things down in case we lost this gift."

"We have people like you," said John.

"Crazy people," Sara said sadly.

"We don't think they're crazy. We base our life on what they see," said John. "Can you tell me some of the things you see?" asked John.

Sara looked at Sean. Sean sighed.

"I see," said John. "Your friends, nobody knows you know this stuff. You're afraid people will think you're loco. You don't know who to trust, do you?"

"No, we don't," said Sara. "I think if we could talk to someone other than each other, it would help, but we don't know who to trust other than each other."

"That makes sense, more sense than you know," said John. "I will talk to my chief. He will want to talk to you. I'll set up a meeting. I'm sure that we can come up with something. But I have a gut feeling that this is right, and my gut feelings are never wrong. Your secret is safe with me," said John. "I watched you and Sara. You did things different than other white men. So I thought you were smart. Now you tell me you're crazy?" laughed John.

Knock, knock.

"Come in," called Sara.

Jacob and Susan walked in. "Hi, John," said Jacob.

"She is trusting, too trusting," smiled John.

"I know, it's her only fault," laughed Sean.

Susan was taken back. John thought her reaction was to him until she spoke. "Sara? Why are you dressed like that?" asked Susan.

"I'm a lady. I hate dresses, and I'm comfortable and would like something better for my feet," said Sara, getting up to cook breakfast.

Jacob and Susan sat down and talked to Sean and John. Everyone acted like they knew John for years and didn't care if he was an Indian. *These people were different,* thought John.

Sara poured more coffee, then set plates of food in front of everyone. Bacon, eggs, hash browns, and toast. Sara took out some butter and jelly and set them on the table. John ate. He didn't want to be rude, but he felt right eating with them. "More coffee?" asked Sara. Everyone said "yes," so she poured fresh coffee.

"This coffee is really good," said John. "What kind is it?" "Drip," said Sara.

"Drip?" John asked puzzled.

Susan explained how and why while Sara made coffee.

John was impressed. He watched Sara and knew she wouldn't be right for a dress.

"John, are there any places around here we can get berries or apples?" asked Sara.

"We have one spot that the snow didn't ruin," said John.

"By the sulfur springs?" asked Sara, knowing the minute she said it, it was the wrong thing to say.

John knew right then and there that Sara could see into the future. No white man know of the sulfur springs.

"Sara!" said Susan. "John you must forgive her, every now and then she says silly things. She was sick, now she's better. Well, almost. Running around in men's clothes isn't normal," smiled Susan.

"Yes, Susan keeps me going in the right direction. I get confused," said Sara. "The men's clothes stay."

John looked at Sean when Sara mentioned sulfur springs. He froze. He knew about them, too. These two knew a lot, and it would affect their nation for years to come. He would finish breakfast and go to his chief. They would meet tomorrow. "I'll show you where if you would like," said John.

"Thank you," Sara said blushing. As she cleared dishes, she put them in one pan to wash, one to rinse, then she dried them and put them away. Susan excused herself and went to her home to straighten up. She felt better and much stronger sleeping in a real bed.

Sara grabbed two berry buckets and a work hankie. "I'm ready, John," smiled Sara.

John stood, he said goodbye to Sean and Jacob and started out the door with Sara following. Then he stopped. "I'll see you later today and will have some answers." Sara almost ran into him.

"That would be great John, thank you," said Sean.

"Come on Red," said John, "I'll show you some good berries. Real big juicy berries."

"Great, I've been dying for pie," said Sara, walking ahead of John. John ended up following Sara. Somehow she knew exactly where she was going, like she walked it a thousand times. She seemed comfortable here, so John walked away toward his village. Sara didn't need him, only his permission to pick the berries. While Sara picked berries, Sean and Jacob unloaded the wagons that came from town and started work. Susan had picked up the house, rearranging this and that. Putting things in order seemed to give Susan a sense of security. Sara found some elderberries. She hadn't had elderberry pie in years. Everyone of her time thought she was crazy, talking about elderberry pie. A lot of people thought elderberries were grapes because of elderberry wine. "People are stupid," thought Sara, as she unfolded the hankie, laid it on the ground and gently laid elderberries on the hankie. "You can come out," said Sara. "I won't hurt you."

"How do you do that?" asked John, stepping forward.

"Well, I don't know, and I was talking to the person with you, you can bring him out, I won't hurt him," said Sara.

"How do you know it's a him?" "By his steps, they're heavy," smiled Sara.

"I told the chief about you and Sean. He was as surprised as I was at your proposal. He wanted to see you. I told him you were here. So he's been watching you," said John.

"I know," said Sara. "I wouldn't expect no less. He must watch me, to learn me, to see if I can be trusted. What did he think?" asked Sara.

"Our chief, Ben Green, is very wise, but you confuse him," said John.

"Believe me, nobody is more confused than me. I don't know if I'm dead or alive, if I'm dreaming or awake. I feel trapped somewhere, but I don't know where," said Sara.

"Well, that's not what's got my chief confused," said John. "He is a very wise man, very wise," said John, crossing his arms. "There is something about you that confuses him. He cannot come out until he believes you can be trusted. I don't understand why he thinks what he thinks."

"Well, what bothers him? He can ask me anything. I will answer as truthfully as I can," said Sara.

"Well, the chief will know if it's the truth," said John. "I told the old man he was confused. He says you're a virgin, yet married and wants to know if what he says is true."

Sara blushed lightly, then a deep red with purple hue. "I—I—I am a virgin," said Sara, "and Sean is my husband. It's complicated," said Sara.

John stared at Sara. The old man was right.

"I'm always right son, when are you going to learn this?" said Ben, walking into view, standing next to John. "Something tells me that you have something to tell me. We must talk. You have something important to tell me," said Ben.

"God, I don't know where to begin," said Sara. "I keep going over it in my head, and it confuses me, so I try not to think about it."

"Well, if you trust me, maybe we can sort this out together," said Ben. "We will start at the beginning," smiled Ben. "Let's sit here."

Sara sat down. "This is strange, believe me, I 'm not nuts. I keep thinking this whole thing is my fault. This all started December 1st, 1997. It was what I call a perfect winter day, snowing. The kind of snow that glitters as it falls and glitters in the moonlight. I love snow. There's something virginal about it, something pure. I had the house all decorated for Christmas. I'd been baking since October. I had breads, cookies, and candy made and frozen. Presents were all wrapped. I had the movie, "Miracle on 34th Street" on TV and was watching it. I sat in the chair in my living room with a cup of coffee. The phone rang; it was Sean. His wife, Laura, was deathly ill with the flu. He asked me if I had anything he could give her. I said "yes." And he said he'd be right over. So I paused the movie, went into the kitchen, unlocked the front door so Sean could come in. Then I walked into the bathroom, got some pills and cough syrup, put them in a plastic bag. I sat them on the counter for Sean. Well, Sean didn't come right over. I heard the door open, but I didn't think anything of it. I just thought it was Sean, but it was burglars. They hid when Sean pulled his truck in the driveway. Sean came in. I gave him the medication, he put them in his coat pocket. We were talking when two men jumped out of the closet waving guns in our faces. They demanded money. We didn't have money; they beat on us for awhile. Then they tied us up. One watched us while the other ransacked the house. I cried, all my work for Christmas ruined. Then when they found nothing, they shot us. Sean jumped in front of me, and I fell. But when I hit the floor I felt cold cement. I think they may have thrown us in the garage. I know it was cold, very cold. When Sean and I woke up we were here, I guess the same spot where my house sits in 1997. It's like we were sent here for a reason."

Sara stood up. "Hell, this could be a dream. Oh, the hope chest I bought in a garage sale is here with me, and the medication I gave Sean. I know it doesn't make sense. It drives me nuts if I think about it. That's why I'm still a virgin. I'm married in another time to someone else. Sean feels the same as I do, so we don't. God, I don't even know if we'll ever be able to go forward. I miss my children and grandchildren. I can't have children here, then go forward in time. I would be committing adultery. I know it doesn't sound sane, even saying it out loud. So Sean and I feel we're sent here to change something, but we don't know what, so we take it one day at a time."

Ben stood up, put his arm around Sara. "I believe you," he said.

"See, that's the problem. You would agree with me if this was a dream," cried Sara.

"But even dreams have a purpose. I would like to ask you a question," said Ben.

"What's that?" asked Sara, wiping the tears with her hands.

"If you had a chance to change things in your life, would you?" asked Ben.

"Sure, who wouldn't?" laughed Sara. "But the changes wouldn't be for me, they would be for my family."

"Isn't there something that you would like for yourself?" asked Ben.

"Me, I never wanted much from life. I was more a giver than a taker. And in my time they call that a sucker because people can bleed you dry."

"This future doesn't sound too good," said Ben. "You sound like you weren't happy there. Let's say you and Sean were sent here to change your future, then you would have been given a precious gift. Wouldn't you say that?" smiled Ben.

"Don't get me going on the future. There's so much wrong that nothing I could do here would change it that much. Happy? I guess I'm as happy as the next guy. Sent here to change my future? I don't know what I'm supposed to change," said Sara. "As for a precious gift, any time someone finds happiness, it's a precious gift."

"Well, if we work together maybe we can figure this out," smiled Ben. "I know you have a pure heart; it seems Sean has, too. I will speak to him next. We'll get through this," said Ben.

"Thank you, I feel so much better," said Sara. "Talking to someone other than Sean about this seems to make this whole thing seem more real and less strange. It's still strange, but somehow it puts it in some kind of order," said Sara, waving her hand in the air.

Sara looked at John, who was still standing with his arms crossed watching her. He had blue jeans and a flannel shirt on. "You look just like your father," smiled Sara.

Ben laughed, "much doesn't get by you, does it?" asked Ben.

"Not much. You need a sixth sense to live in my time. You have to be aware of what's around you or you're in trouble. Hell, I let my guard down once. Look where it got me," laughed Sara.

"You don't like it here?" asked Ben.

"That's the problem, I love it here. The only problem I found so far is there's no good shoes. I settled for men's boots, but back home

I either went barefoot or sneakers when I went out. Me, I like to feel the ground I walk on," said Sara.

Ben and John looked at Sara's feet. She indeed did have boots on. "I must say, your future must be very different if you don't like women's finery," smiled Ben.

"If only you knew," laughed Sara. "May I have your permission to pick some more berries tomorrow? I'd like to make some jellies for the winter. I promise to leave some," said Sara.

"Leave some," thought Ben, that's a strange thing to say. Most people wouldn't think to leave some. They would take all and leave none for life to go on. This woman was wise, very wise. She knew that there had to be a balance in nature. "Yes, you may. John tells me you are looking for apples?" said Ben.

"Yes, I love to can, put food up for the winter. Susan is pregnant, and I don't think she should do too much right now. She's carrying the baby too low. I think she should rest, see if the baby goes up where it should be. I was going to give her some rose hip tea to help with the delivery, but it could prove to be dangerous to her right now. I have a doctor coming today to check on her. He said he'd try to make it around supper time."

"I will ask the women of my nation to make something up for you to give her," said Ben.

"Thank you," said Sara. She hugged Ben.

John stepped forward; Ben held up his hand.

"I wasn't supposed to do that, was I?" asked Sara.

Ben laughed. "No! I'll stop by later, and I'll talk to Sean. How would you like some peaches and pears to can?" asked Ben.

"Really? I'd love that," smiled Sara.

"Tomorrow John will show you," smiled Ben.

"Thank you. Sorry about the hug. I'm known for hugging people. Another bad thing in my time: you don't care for people," Sara said sadly.

Ben shook his head, "you don't belong there then. You care too much for people. Your heart is good. Your soul is pure. You need sunshine," said Ben.

Sara looked at Ben, "that's a sweet thing to say; thank you for the berries. I must go now and bake pies. We'll talk later," smiled Sara. She tied the hankie over her arm and picked up her berry buckets then walked away.

Ben and John watched Sara walk away. When she was out of sight, Ben turned to John, "Well chief, how did I do?" John laughed. "I don't think we fooled her, but she does make sense. What do you think?"

"I think what she says is the truth. Why it happened I don't know, unless our forefathers sent her to protect us," said John.

Ben looked at John, "She couldn't do that, unless—" Ben stopped.

"I know, I think they both are," said John. "The white buffalo has been born."

Ben looked at John with pure shock on his face.

"We will take this proposal that Sean has offered us. The story as our forefathers have told us is here. The white buffalo will not be born for another one hundred and fifty years. By then all our people could be gone," said John. "I have much respect for Sean. Of one thing I am certain: Those two married wrong. They belong together. The sad part is they don't know it. Two lifetimes, and they don't know that they love each other."

"We could change that!" smiled Ben.

"No! They must find their love on their own. We don't do nothing," John said sternly.

"Why do you respect Sean so much? You only met him today," asked Ben.

"Let's say I have my reasons. Now would you mind telling me why you offered to send me to help Sara get apples?" asked John.

Ben smiled. "Your young and wise, you could learn a lot from Sara. Find out about the future so we can pass it on, then you will be the wisest chief we ever had," said Ben.

"Don't you think that's a little unfair to our people?" asked John.

"No, not if it saves us," said Ben.

"Perhaps you're right," said John. "I don't know why you stepped down as chief. You should still be chief, not me."

"Too many changes, too fast for me. I think this future is going to be for the young, not the old," said Ben.

"Did you stop to think that that's maybe the reason the future is so bad?" asked John.

"It could be, but if what Sara says is true, I don't think any one thing is at fault. I think it's a lot of little things," said Ben.

"We'll see," said John. "We'll see."

John put his arms in the air. "Why her?" he cried.

As Sara approached her home, she heard hammering. The new roof looked nice and shiny. Too bad by spring it would look old and rusty like it had been there for years. Time, thought Sara, sometimes it was kind, sometimes it wasn't. "Looks nice guys," Sara called out.

Sean looked down, blocking their sun with his hand. "Those berries for pies?" he asked.

"Sure are. I'm going to bake them now. Where's Susan?" said Sara.

"Well, we put her roof on first. She was tired, so we came over here to work, so she could sleep," called Sean.

"Okay, I won't bother her. Would you two like some lunch?" asked Sara.

"In a little bit, we're just about done here," said Sean.

"Okay, when your ready," said Sara. Sara left and went into the house, put the berries on the table, put her apron on and started cooking.

Sara was always at her best when she cooked. She'd made a beef stew from some beef she had canned. She made biscuits, washed the berries, checked them, made two pies, two for Susan and Jacob, two for them. There were some berries left so she made some tarts for lunch. Sara didn't hear anymore hammering, so Sean and Jacob must be done. Now they must be down by the creek washing up. Sara was setting the table when Susan walked in. Sara had the door open. She liked the breeze that came through the house with the door open. The only problem was Sean had to make a screen door because the chickens kept coming in.

"Something smells good," said Susan, walking up behind Sara.

"Screech!" yelled Sara, grabbing her chest. "You scared me to death," laughed Sara.

"Sorry," said Susan, "you cooked lunch."

"Yes, and some pies, two of them are yours," smiled Sara. "I picked berries and we have blackberry and elderberry pies. Those are for supper, but I made some tarts for lunch."

"You made us pies," said Susan. "You didn't have to do that. I could have made pies."

"I know, but I want you to rest you're so big with child. You'll need all the rest you can get for delivery. I know you don't like me pampering you," Sara said softly. "But I figure if I get pregnant some day I'll let you do the cooking," smiled Sara. "Now sit."

Susan smiled. "Okay, I'll sit if you promise I can cook for you when you're pregnant."

"Promise," said Sara. "Oh, those chickens," cried Sara. "Shoo," said Sara, waving her apron at them. "If you don't get out, you'll be supper." One chicken flew up on the bed. Susan laughed.

Sean and Jacob came in. Sean carried some soda or what was supposed to be the soda—root beer they kept in the creek to keep it cold. "Something smells good," said Sean, laughing when he saw Sara fighting with a chicken.

"It's not funny. I catch him, he's supper," said Sara.

Sean ran over, grabbed the chicken, "saved your life little buddy. You better be thankful," laughed Sean as he put the chicken in the barn and closed the door. "After lunch I'll build you a screen," said Sean.

"Thank you," said Sara, dishing lunch. "You don't know how close I was to killing him. All I want is the warm breeze that comes through here with the door open. And that chicken has to bother me. I tried putting things on the bottom, but that stupid bird flew over the top."

"We built you and Susan a clothes' line," said Jacob.

"Good, I'll do laundry after lunch," said Sara. "Susan has promised me she will rest, so I'll do the laundry. Yours and ours. The doctor will be here around supper time."

"Doctor?" asked Jacob. "Are you feeling okay?"

"Yes, Sara insisted Dr. Emerson check me over. I feel fine and I don't know what the fuss is about," said Susan. She took a bite of beef stew. "Oh God, this is good Sara."

"Thank you," said Sara.

The men agreed; it was excellent. They even had thirds. Susan and Sara were still on their first plate. The plate of biscuits was gone, the root beer soda wasn't too bad. Sara gave Susan a little more to eat, then got the pastries out, set them on the table, then poured coffee. Sara kept an eye on Susan. She looked pale. Why couldn't the men see what she saw. Well, they were busy working. "But didn't Jacob ever look at Susan?" thought Sara.

"These are great," said Sean.

Sara laughed. Sean always said that about her cookies. It made Sara feel good. It wasn't easy and baking on a wood stove. It wasn't the pot-belly type; it was an actual stove. You put wood in and hoped the oven part reached the right temperature. She wasn't getting too bad at it now. Yesterday was the worst. Susan showed her what to do. Banking the wood was the trick.

Now the men were outside working. Sara was clearing the dishes away when she noticed the dirt all over.

"Those men, I'll kill them. Look at the dirt, they did this nailing the roof on," said Sara.

"I know," laughed Susan. "I had to sweep my place. But it was easy to clean it. Only took a couple of minutes. I figure a couple of minutes is nothing, knowing the roof won't leak at all, creating a bigger mess to clean."

"You're right," said Sara. "It just seems I get one mess cleaned up and those two make another one," laughed Sara.

"Yeah, I know. Jacob says they want to get as much as they can done in case it snows again. Seems Sean's got this thing about getting everything secure for winter. He wants to cut hay for the animals. I think the two of them are crazy," said Susan.

"Maybe, but if they fix everything now they won't have to go in cold weather to try and fix it. We can feel secure knowing it will be warm and dry in here," said Sara as she finished sweeping, the dishes done, everything wiped down and dishes put away. She took the hot water off the stove, went outside and dumped it in a wash bucket. She put the clothes in to soak then went back inside to talk to Susan. Susan was crying. Sara ran over to her. "Are you all right?" asked Sara.

"I feel bad because you wouldn't let me do anything," sobbed Susan.

"Okay, I'm worried your carrying the baby to low. I think you're carrying twins. If you are you could deliver too early, harming the babies and yourself. That's why the doctor is going to check you," said Sara.

"Twins! Twins are on my side of the family," said Susan. "I just never thought about it. If it's twins, I do have to be careful. I thought you were doing this stuff, the cooking and cleaning, to make yourself look better than me, but you really were worried about me. Now I feel awful," said Susan.

Sara never looked at it from Susan's side, and she could see where Susan could think like she was. "You know what we need?" said Sara.

"What?" asked Susan.

"We need a huge pool of warm water to swim and bath in," said Sara. "I found just a spot today. The water will stop your backaches. It will take the pressure off your stomach, too. Let me hang up the laundry, then we'll go," smiled Sara, standing up.

"I thought pregnant women shouldn't swim," said Susan.

"That's an old wife's tale. Some old bitty probably couldn't find anything to wear in the water, so she made up that lie. Some cultures give birth in the water and let the baby swim to the top," said Sara.

Susan laughed. "I know you're joking."

"No, it's true. Now you get soap, towel, clean clothes. I'll hang up the laundry, and we'll go. You'll see how good it will feel. I think we both need it," said Sara.

"It does sound good," said Susan.

"Not half as good as it will feel. It will stop those stretch marks from itching," said Sara.

"That alone is worth it," smiled Susan. "I'll get my stuff."

"Good girl. I'll hang the laundry and we'll have fun," said Sara, going out the door. "I don't know why I didn't think of it sooner," Sara thought. "I know the water is warm there. It always is, even in her time. If Susan could take some of the weight off her belly, the baby could go back where it belonged, and the walk would help her. Susan sure was moody, nothing helps moods like fun," thought Sara as she finished the laundry.

She left the water. When they got back she'd do some more. Tonight they would sleep on the new flannel sheets they bought yesterday. "Money talks and bullshit walks no matter what generation it was,' thought Sara, getting her stuff together to go swimming. Sean and Jacob made two screen doors and were about to put Sara's on when she walked out.

"We're going to the quarry," Sara told Sean. "We're going swimming and taking in a hot bath. Nice screen door," said Sara.

"Well, it will keep the chickens out," said Sean. "It's chicken wire. Jacob suggested we build a section over there, enclose it with chicken wire and make it a chicken coop, then we don't have to hunt all over for eggs," laughed Sean.

"Afraid I'll kill the chickens, Jacob?" laughed Sara.

Jacob laughed. "Yes!" was his only reply.

"Smart idea," said Sara. "We're going swimming, thanks for the door."

It wasn't a fancy door. Four boards and chicken wire, but it would keep the animals out. The hinges were leather, but it worked. That's all that mattered. Sean and Jacob went from screens to windows, then to the chicken coop.

"God Sara, this feels great. It's like all the aches and pains are gone. It's like I'm not even pregnant. I could stay here forever," said Susan.

"Well, you can't, you would get all wrinkled up and old looking," laughed Sara. Sara picked up the wash cloth and soap and started washing herself. This sure beats washing up in a bowl of water. Sara washed her hair, then rinsed.

Susan had already washed and was floating around. Sometimes she just walked around. The water was only four feet deep with a sandy bottom. Why they called it a quarry, nobody knew.

"I can't believe my legs have stopped aching," smiled Susan. "This is great. Strange being here with no clothes on. I look down and see a huge belly. I think you're right. I've got twins. I'm rather large and all that movement couldn't be from one baby. Look, the baby's moving. He likes the water, too," smiled Susan.

"Well, if he moves up, we've got it made," thought Sara. "See, I told you babies could swim," laughed Sara.

"Well, this one or two can. Look, my belly is going up,' laughed Susan. "I think we should do this every day."

"Okay," said Sara. "Now if the little tyke stays where he belongs, we've got it made," thought Sara. "If not, we have problems." Sara swam, walked some. They were there about an hour and a half before they got out and dried off. Then they walked back feeling fresh and clean. The wind dried their hair as they walked.

"Now I'm sleepy," said Susan.

"So am I," smiled Sara. "It just kind of relieves you. I think I'll take a nap when we get back home."

"Me too," said Susan.

Susan went in and laid down. Sara did up their laundry and hung it on the line. Jacob and Sean had the four windows in and were working on the chicken coop. It looked pretty good. Then Sara looked at it; it looked like two chicken coops. "Why two chicken coops?" asked Sara.

"Thought we'd get some turkeys," smiled Sean.

"You two are thinking all the time," smiled Sara. "Just working right along aren't you?" Then Sara went inside. "Sean Huntington, I'll kill you. Not only did you make another mess," yelled Sara walking into the barn, "but you ate some pie!" Sara stood looking at Sean with her hands on her hips.

Sean smiled. "We took a coffee break. The pie just went with the coffee; it was good."

"Oh, what am I going to do with you?" said Sara. She walked over to Susan, who was getting a broom ready to sweep. "You lie down, I'll sweep," said Sara. She cleaned up Susan's mess then went home and cleaned up her mess, finished the laundry and hung it up to dry. She was too upset to lie down, so she looked around to see what to have for supper. Right now the only thing that sounded good was a roast: Sean with a big apple stuffed in his mouth. Seems like they lived on salt pork and beans around here, not much in assortment of meats were canned. Canned beef or chicken. They had beef for lunch. So chicken would be supper. Chicken in a gravy over biscuits. I guess you could make a lot and save it for the next day. There was no refrigerator, so each meal had to be freshly made. Whoever canned all the food that was in the cupboard had sense enough to can meat. Beef or chicken. At least it was meat enough to get them by until the farm was functional. But pork chops or a good pork roast right now sounded good, even a turkey. But you worked with what you had. So Sara started cooking. Sara didn't hear any hammering and wondered what other task the men went to do. Then she heard a strange sound. A dull thump, thump, like a hammering sound, but dull. So she went to investigate. Now Sean and Jacob were driving a metal pipe in the ground by the barn. They were using chucks of wood on a wooded handle. When the wooden chucks split they would put in on the wood pile. This was different.

"We're killing two birds with one stone," smiled Sean.

"Seems so," laughed Sara. "This is our water?" asked Sara.

"Yes, and if I remember right, the water table is high here, so we don't have to go far," said Sean.

"Yeah, eight feet was how deep my—" Sara stopped, Jacob was staring at her, "my father had to go with his," said Sara.

"Yeah, my Dad went six, had more water than he knew what to do with," smiled Sean. "We're down four feet now."

Jacob looked at Sean. "I think my dad went down fifteen feet, but he was on a hill. This is flat land, so we should have water soon," smiled Jacob.

"Well, you're the men, you have the brains and brawn of this whole thing," said Sara. "All I can do is act like a woman and complain about the mess," laughed Sara.

Sara left Jacob and Sean to their work and checked the clothes on the line to see what was dry. The dry clothes she took down and folded, then walked back inside. She took the iron out, set it on the wood stove to warm so she could press the clothes. The sheets she put in the closet. Sara looked around. Soon Sean and Jacob would have this whole place torn apart putting water in. That would end up a royal mess, but if you wanted running water and hot water, you had to put up with the mess. In the long run, it was worth it. Sara finished the ironing, took Susan's over to her. Sara checked Susan; she was sleeping. Good, so Sara left her. She looked like she was resting nicely. Sara was really wound up, so she decided to go for a walk. She went to tell Sean and Jacob that she was going for a walk. As she walked outside, she saw Sean and Jacob dancing in a mud puddle; they found water. On top of the pipe sat a hand pump.

"Congratulations," smiled Sara. "I'm going for a walk. I won't be long." She didn't know if they heard her or not, but she left anyway. She needed to walk off the stress she felt. She walked in the direction of the quarry. If she had sneakers she'd jog, but there was no jogging in boots. The air was warm. The sun bright, the air was crisp with the smell of fall. Sara loved it. Outdoors she always did. That's why she lived in the country. Sara looked around, but this was unbelievable. This is what God gave us, green grass, fresh water, clean air, and fields of wild flowers.

Sara heard a low thumping sound, she looked to her left, the direction of the sound. She saw something move. Sara walked carefully to her left until she saw the deer, its front leg caught in some rocks. He was trying his best to pull his leg free. Both front legs had blood on them. He looked scared and frightened. Sara felt his fear, his fear of dying there, and now his fear of her. Sara knew she'd have to move slowly. His fear could make him lunge at her with his antlers, and by the size of his rack, he could kill her.

"Shhh, baby," Sara spoke softly as she sat down. "If she talked to him and let him smell her scent, everything would be fine," she thought. "Well, I will help you. I can see you have yourself in a royal mess, but you see, you're afraid of me. I'm afraid of you," Sara said softly. "I wouldn't hurt you in a million years, but you don't know that, so you might hurt me not knowing. I'm only trying to help you, then we both could lie here and bleed to death. Sara moved slowly toward the deer. The deer was tiring from his struggle. Sara slowly held out her hand, she held it steady so the deer could smell it, so he could see Sara wouldn't hurt him. He seemed to accept this, so she gently rubbed his nose. "Well my friend." Now she knew why it was called a quarry, stones everywhere. They were heavy. Soon Sara had enough stones moved that the deer could get his leg free. She helped him. He tried walking, but limped, "Oh no, you didn't break it, did you?" asked Sara. "Come over here next to the water." Sara led the deer near the water. They were only a couple feet from the water. It took fifteen minutes to get the deer there. He lay down like he wanted to die there. "Oh no you don't," said Sara. "You ain't dying here and stinking the place up." Sara took off her T-shirt, went to the water's edge and soaked it in water, then walked over and rung the shirt out into the deer's mouth. He seemed to perk up some. So Sara did this a few times, putting water on the deer's leg. She carefully felt the leg, it wasn't broken. "How long were you there?" asked Sara. "Yeah, like you could tell me. What do you eat? I know you eat apples, but I don't know where the apples are. I don't know what else to do."

"Here," said John, handing Sara some apples. "I watched you. You have a way with animals."

"Thank you," said Sara, taking the apples. "As for having a way with animals, I don't know. I've always loved them. I just could never see taking an animal out of its habitat, putting it on a chain or locking it in a cage. I know I wouldn't like my freedom taken away, so why should I take theirs?" Sara fed the deer another apple. "Nature has a balance, and the balance shouldn't be interfered with."

"I can see you love freedom. You are different than anyone I know. You're open and honest; that's unusual," said John.

Sara petted the deer, who seemed grateful now. She fed him another apple. "Well, fella, you have to get up. You can't stay like this." The deer acted like he understood her and sat up. "There, see how good you feel? Here, this is the last apple, so you'll have to go get your own."

Sara put her T-shirt in the water, then realized she had no top on. She froze. "My God, what should I do? I can't turn around and face him," she thought. John took off his shirt and laid it on Sara's shoulder.

"You better put this on. You can get sunburned easily. It may be too big, but your skin is so white," said John.

"Thank you," Sara said, not looking up. She slipped the shirt on. It was huge, but it smelled so good. Sara carefully picked up her T-shirt full of water and rang it out in the deer's mouth. Sara avoided looking at John until the redness left her cheeks. She knew she was bright red; she felt the heat.

"There you go, little guy. Now you have to stand. Come on," Sara cooed softly as she stood up.

John laughed. "I think he likes your pampering him."

"He's a typical male then," said Sara. "Shooo. No more, all gone." Sara threw her arms in the air. "Men! All alike, no matter the spices."

John thought this an unusual statement. "Well, if we leave then he'll have to get up," said John.

"Yes, it's getting close to suppertime anyway," said Sara, turning around. "Whoa," cried Sara. She'd never seen a man built like that. His skin was soft and tan, muscle on muscle, his long black hair shined in the sun. Sara took two steps back.

"Something wrong?" asked John.

"Head rush, must be the sun," said Sara. Sara's senses were playing tricks on her, thought Sara. Nobody looked that good.

"Let's get you home," said John, "get you out of the sun. You've been here awhile."

"Sure," said Sara, walking slowly. John's shirt felt soft on her skin. It was long, very long, but the smell sent her senses reeling. The sun beat on her fair skin. Sara turned around. "John, I don't feel good." John caught Sara just as she passed out. John carried her home. Sean saw John carrying her, ran over and took her from his arms.

"What?" asked Sean. "Sara looked sunburned bad."

"I'll tell you once we get her out of the sun," said John.

"Yes, come inside. We'll talk there," said Sean.

"Doesn't she realize that she has fair skin and the sun will bother her?" asked John.

Jacob brought in some water then left. He heard John telling about the deer, and what Sara did for him.

"I'll check on Susan," said Jacob. He left.

"This is not what Sara looked like in her other life. Sara was half-Indian. Black hair, brown eyes, dark complexion; so she used to be. The way it was, it will take her some getting use too. How did you ever find her?" asked Sean.

"I was checking on things for the chief. I think he will take your offer, but I wanted to draw up some kind of map so we could discuss this fairly," said John. "What were you like in your other life?" asked John.

"That's the strange part. I look almost the same. I'm a half-breed: half-Indian, half-Irish. The only one who changed was Sara. But she'd always wished to look just like that. She never felt beautiful in her other life, but she was. She was the most beautiful thing I've ever seen. Long, beautiful black hair, huge, brown eyes with really long eyelashes, built like a brick shithouse."

"A what?" asked John.

"It's a saying in the future to describe a woman, meaning she had everything," laughed Sean.

"You use shithouse to describe a woman?" asked John.

"I told you, the future is strange," said Sean.

"I guess so. What nation are you two from?" asked John.

"Oneida, Bear clan; Greenfield was Sara's side. Light hall was my side," said Sean, wetting a washcloth and rubbing Sara's face. He looked over to John. "What I'm about to do you didn't see," said Sean.

Sean took out two aspirins, gave them to Sara with water. "The medicine from the future you talked about?" asked John.

"Yes, it will lower the body temperature. She'll be fine in a few minutes." Sean washed off Sara's face and neck again, rinsed the cloth and laid it on her head.

"Was Sara ashamed of being a half-breed?" asked John.

"No, God no. She loved being an Indian," said Sean.

"Then why did she wish to look like this?" asked John.

"The future is a cruel place. All her life she was made to feel ashamed and useless. She only had one wish and that was to see how it felt to feel beautiful like everyone else," said Sean.

"Didn't her husband make her feel beautiful?" asked John.

"Her husband didn't deserve Sara. Don't get me going on that worthless piece of shit," said Sean.

"Jacob and Susan are coming," said John.

Sean took the clue and shut up and tended to Sara.

"How is she?" asked Susan.

"I think it's sunstroke," said Sean.

"Pick her up, carry her to the creek, now," said Susan.

"The creek?" asked Sean.

"Yes, we're putting her in it. Her body needs fluids from the outside in. Do it," said Susan.

Sean grabbed a towel and some clothes. "That water is very cold," said Sean.

"Do it. If I wasn't pregnant, I'd carry her myself. Now go," said Susan.

"Yes, ma'am," smiled Sean, picking up Sara and heading to the creek. "Just lay her in the water," said Susan.

"Yes, take the shirt off, lay her in the water," said Susan.

"Okay, but if Sara's pissed, I'm sicking her on you," laughed Sean. He took off the shirt and laid Sara in the cold water.

"Wet her hair, everything," said Susan.

God, she was beautiful, even in this lifetime. Sean laid Sara's head gently in the cold water; her skin wasn't red but a soft pink.

"Rub water on her chest, get her wet," said Susan.

Sean panicked. "Touch Sara's body? Oh God," Sean splashed water over Sara's chest.

"Sean, take the water and rub it gently on her body."

"Think man, think," Sean said to myself. Then he turned to Susan. Susan, I don't want to do that. If she's burned worst than we think, it could hurt the skin," said Sean.

"Yeah, you're right. Turn her over," said Susan. "Keep her head out of the water."

Now that he could do. "Do you want me to keep her head wet?" asked Sean. "Oh God, she's coming around," cried Sean.

"C—c—cold," cried Sara.

Sean left her there a little longer.

Jacob stayed at the house and showed John what Sean and he were doing.

John was impressed. "Must be Sara's okay. I can hear her yelling at Sean," laughed John.

Jacob laughed. "She sure does light into him. She's always on him for something or other. I told him he wasn't doing sex the right way. She acts high strung," said Jacob.

"What'd Sean say?" asked John.

"Well, he became real quiet, like he was thinking, then said, 'No they liked things the way they were,' that Sara's a redhead, and redheads do that," said Jacob.

"He's probably right," laughed John.

"Men! Of all the hare brained ideas. The stupid fool tried to drown me," yelled Sara, walking in.

"Sean didn't do it; Susan made him do it. She was going to carry you down herself," said Jacob. "At least you're not red anymore."

"Do you have any idea how cold that water is?" yelled Sara.

"Where's Sean and Susan?" asked John.

"They're coming," Sara said, starting to calm down. She had clean clothes on, so she walked over to the stove and put the finishing touches on supper. "Men," she whispered under her breath as she took plates out of the cupboard.

"I'll take our dinner home," said Jacob. "The doctor will be here soon. Susan's been doing better since you two took a walk."

"That's good," said Sara. "Here's your supper, take some soda with you. The pies are all really at your house. Send the doctor over here when he's done looking at Susan," said Sara.

"Sure," said Jacob, puzzled. "Don't you feel good?"

"No. I'm fine," said Sara. "I just need to talk to him."

"Okay," said Jacob, taking supper and going home.

"Sara, you can't keep this up," said John. "You are a woman, and you have a woman's needs and wants," said John.

"You don't have to tell me that. When I saw you today, my heart went crazy. Then Sean's tender touch in the water," said Sara, pacing back and forth.

"Me! What have I got to do with anything? You're the one in love with Sean," said John.

Sean stopped outside the door when he heard his name mentioned.

"Don't you think I know that, too? I've loved Sean since we were kids, but I'm not his type. He's never been interested in me. He's always been my friend, and I his, nothing more or less. I've kept my feelings buried my whole life. Now I've got to do it again," said Sara, throwing her arms in the air. "Then when I saw you standing there with no shirt, the sun behind you, the wind blowing your beautiful hair, I felt doomed, trapped like I was losing my mind. Like my mind hasn't got enough to handle, dealing with all the shit that's happened. How much can one person take? I'm standing in my kitchen telling a man I've only known a couple days my whole life. What's wrong with this picture?" said Sara.

"If you loved Sean, why did you marry your husband?" asked John.

Sara sighed, "you haven't heard anything I said. It's like this. Sean is one of the beautiful people. God looked at him, he's perfect. He wouldn't want someone like me. My mother arranged for me to marry Thomas. She said I was lucky anyone even wanted me. So I married Tom as I was ordered, and took my place in life, did what I was told. End of story."

"Did you love Tom?" asked John.

"What does love have to do with anything? Love is for the beautiful people, people who have the right love. People like me, we get what's left and be damn grateful for what we have," said Sara.

"Is this what you meant earlier when the chief asked you if there was anything you would change in your life? You couldn't think of anything for yourself because you didn't think you deserved it?" asked John.

"Now you understand. I had a roof over my head, clothes on my back, and food on my table. What else is there?" asked Sara.

John stared at Sara. "You're the deer."

"What?" Sara asked, staring at John. "What makes you think I'm a deer?"

"You think about it. I'm going to leave and return later with the chief. We will talk later," said John.

"Oh no you don't. You sit right there. There is no way I can have anything else dumped on me. You are the one thing I can control," said Sara.

"How do you think you control me?" laughed John.

"Because I'm the one with the brains, the one who knows the future, the one who had nothing better to do with her life but learn, learn all the stupid things that nobody cared about. Because as far as everyone was concerned, it meant nothing. Well buster, it meant something to someone because I've been sent back in time to try and figure out what I could do to change the future. There's so much wrong with the future, I can't see how I can change it. The only thing I know for sure is it involves you, me, and Sean. I don't know how you two men see it, but there's two of you, one of me. So I guess that makes me the key because I'm the only woman. Now you try and figure it out; I'm sick of trying to."

Sara returned to the stove. She dished up some supper. "Here, eat. I'm sick and tired of living everyone's life for them. People need to stop coming to me for answers. I don't have them."

John leaned back in his chair, watching Sara. "I hope you know you're making no sense at all, and I don't know what you're talking about or who you're talking to."

"Yes, I know that," said Sara. "I don't know what I'm saying, what I'm doing. My emotions are running all over the place." Sara started crying.

"Sara, you love Sean. Tell him and a lot of your problems will be ended," said John.

"Easy for you. Everything for men is simple. I confess my love for Sean, go back to the future, and the life I had. How can I love here and not there? Answer me that, Mr. It's So Simple," said Sara.

"You know the answer to that. Look into your heart. I'm leaving," said John. "I suggest you get some rest. Thanks for supper." John got up and walked out the door. He stopped when he saw Sean leaning on the wall next to the door. The look on his face said it all. John just walked away; he wasn't responsible for them.

Sara got up, walked over to the bed. "Maybe John was right. Maybe she was tired. Maybe that's why she didn't make sense anymore and she rambled so. What was it Ben said? If she could change one thing, what would she change?" thought Sara as she sat down on the bed taking off her boots and lying down. Change one thing, what would it be, the family structure, the national debt, pollution? America had problems, lots of them. What would be the one thing that could change it all? "Look into your heart, you know, was what John said," thought Sara as she closed her eyes. "My heart says I should have married Sean, but that doesn't help anyone else but me."

Sean felt sick to his stomach. He was no different than everyone else. He made Sara feel undeserving of loving him.

"How could I be so blind. I'm no different than them," he thought. "What did she call them, the beautiful people. God, nobody could be more beautiful than Sara. She was beautiful inside and out."

Sean went in the house, he got something to eat and sat at the table. All those years with Thomas never feeling love. A lot made sense to him now. "What was it she said?" thought Sean as he cleared the dishes and washed them. "'Why can't people live there own lives?' That one was like a knife to the heart. Maybe John didn't know what Sara was talking about, but he did. God, everyone he knew relied on Sara. They dumped all their problems on her, and she helped them sort things out. No one came around if things were going good for them; they only came around to bitch and complain. Everyone dumped on Sara. Somehow it seemed right. She was always there to help. If she had problems, nobody knew, she never said a word.

"A roof over my head, clothes on my back, food on the table, what else is there" were the words that leaped into Sean's thought. He walked over to Sara, covered her with a quilt. "There's a lot more Sara, more than you ever imagined, love and happiness being the two most important," thought Sean.

"How's she doing?" asked Jacob, walking in carrying dishes.

"She's resting now. She lost her temper with John but that's Sara," smiled Sean. No, that's not Sara, not his Sara. The Sara he knew never would have yelled, let alone not make sense. Sean took the dishes from Jacob, washed then, and put them away. Sean tried to think of a time when Sara flared up to home. Only once, and it was at him. That memory he wanted buried forever. But memories haunt you. "Let's get some work done," said Sean.

Sean and Jacob went back outside. They were digging holes for septic tanks for the toilets. Sean thought of Sara and their fight. It was September 1, 1962. He remembered it because that was the day he got drafted. Vietnam War was going. Sara begged him not to go. She wanted him to run away to Canada; he refused. "Get yourself killed then. No good will come of the war," cried Sara. "You'll be lost to me forever."

He should have realized then that Sara loved him as much as he loved her. They wrote each other, but when he returned, Sara had married Tom. Now he knew why. Sara's mother was a strange woman. She blamed all her problems on Sara. She had everyone convinced Sara was a liar, cheat, and troublemaker. She degraded Sara twenty-four hours a day. Sara fought to get one ounce of love from her. Yet everyone thought Sara's mom was the greatest thing in the world. Boy did she have people duped. Sean just kept digging and thinking it was easy to marry Tom. Sara never knew love, so she could set love aside. Damn, how could he be so blind?

"How far you going?" asked Jacob.

"Huh!" Sean looked. He was so angered by his thoughts he didn't pay attention to what he was doing. "China," smiled Sean.

"Looks like a good start," laughed Jacob.

"Think those blocks we made are dry yet?" asked Sean, climbing out.

"Should be. Want to make some more?" asked Jacob.

"Yeah, we can probably get a couple more batches done tonight," said Sean. "We'll mix up some cement and dump it in the bottom of the hole, and let it set all night. Then we can start laying blocks tomorrow."

"Whatever you say, you're the brains here," said Jacob.

"Well, we'll pour some blocks, then dig out a leach field," said Sean.

"Now the leach is where all the rocks go we've been stacking, right?" said Jacob.

"Yup." We're not making bad time," said Sean.

"No, but we sure are a mess. Susan and Sara will be pissed," laughed Jacob. "Susan said that her and Sara went swimming at the quarry."

"Yeah, Sara told me where it was. We could take a nice, hot bath there until we get the bathrooms in," said Sean.

"Hard to believe there's warm water there this time of year." said Jacob.

"Not really, the rocks heat up with the sun and, in turn, heat up the water," said Sean.

"Something like our hot-water tanks, right?" asked Jacob as Sean and he walked through the barn.

"Exactly," smiled Sean as he squatted down to check on the blocks they made. "There, dry," said Sean as he lifted one out.

"Well, I've got to admit this was a stroke of genius on your part, making our own stones," laughed Jacob.

Sean laughed. Jacob called cement blocks "stones" because he had stones ground to a powder-like substone, which the mill grinder was happy to do. His work was slow right now, and the money looked good. Jacob thought he was nuts, but he was a good sport about it. He helped Sean mix cement, sand, and water. Then they built a form where they make fifty cement blocks at a time, so Jacob called it "making stones." Jacob mixed cement while Sean took the dried blocks and stacked them.

Sara woke up; the nap helped a lot. She wasn't so confused. Her skin burned a little but not bad, just enough to let her know she'd done something stupid. She still wasn't hungry, but she got up to do dishes. She put her boots on, walked over to the kitchen. It was spotless. "Oh God, Sean cleaned up. He didn't have to do that," thought Sara. She went outside to thank him. She froze. Sean had removed his shirt. Sweat glistened his body, his hair wet with sweat now, rested on curls around his forehead. Wet jeans clung to his masculine body. She loved him, really loved him.

Sean looked up and smiled, showing beautiful, white teeth as he smiled. "Feel better?" he asked.

"Y—y—yes," stammered Sara, wanting to run away. "You didn't have to do the dishes, I would have."

Sean stood up from his bent position. He had removed the blocks from their forms. "It's okay, I had nothing better to do at the moment," smiled Sean.

"Thank you," smiled Sara. "I'm sorry for being such a bitch earlier," Sara said softly. "I'm going to see if that deer is okay. I won't be long. I don't want to miss the doctor."

"Okay," smiled Sean. "Good to see my Sara back! Not the redhead."

Sara smiled. She knew what he meant. Sean leaned over to remove the last of the cement blocks. Sara walked by and gave him a swat on the butt. "Nice butt," she whispered.

"I heard that," laughed Sean.

Jacob shook his head. "It's like she's two people," said Jacob. "One so nice you can't help but love her; one such a tyrant you want to take her over your knee and spank her."

"Yeah, but I love them both," laughed Sean.

"I heard that," called Sara.

Sean shook his head. "How's the rock mixture?" asked Sean.

"Looks done," said Jacob.

Sean and Jacob had made a wheelbarrow. It was crude, but it got the job done. Jacob wheeled it over and poured it in the platform. Sean smoothed it out with the back of the rake, hitting the platform from time to time to make sure the cement settled right. It may look crude but it worked; that's all that mattered. All the hole parts of the cement blocks were the stones they used for the leach field. Sean was throwing them in a pile as he worked. They would break in pieces, which Sean thought would be the right size. The cement poured and leveled, Sean was ready to dig some more. Jacob just finished rinsing out the wheelbarrow.

"Feel like digging some more?" asked Sean.

"Feel like it, no," Jacob said, laughing. "Will I do it, yes."

"Am I working you too hard," asked Sean. "I know I can be relentless sometimes."

"Relentless! Have you stopped to see how much we've done these past couple of days? You could say we built two homes and a barn, got ourselves a well, now running water. Well, we had help with the barn and houses. But we've done a lot. We keep going like this, we'll be building a town by next year." laughed Jacob.

"No, next year we build real homes, plant crops, and get this place going," said Sean, laughing as they walked through the barn. "Back to digging trenches," said Sean.

"Whatever," said Jacob. Sometimes he didn't understand what Sean was talking about, so he said, "whatever."

"This is the easy part," said Sean. "We don't have to dig down so far. That is until the end, then we go down a couple of feet," laughed Sean.

"That's all?" teased Jacob.

Sean laughed. Jacob had become quite the joker. He loosened up a lot around Sean; he seemed relaxed. They dug in silence.

When Sara got to the quarry, the deer was gone. She felt sorrow over this. The sorrow was an emptiness in her heart. She walked over and filled the hole in.

"He's gone," said John, walking up to her.

"Yes," said Sara looking up at John, tears glistening on her eyelids from the setting sun. "I'm sorry about earlier. I shouldn't have yelled at you. I didn't know what I was saying." The hole covered, Sara stood up. "I hope that my actions won't stop you from taking Sean's offer," said Sara.

"I want you to tell me why this is such a good offer," said John. "Why should my nation trust the white man and his word?"

"Because the white man is gong to come in here and destroy all of this. You will be forced to live in squalor; many will die. President Lincoln will have you driven off your land. He freed the slaves but imprisoned the Indians. You are stripped of everything, even your pride. The white man is led to believe he is bad and should be killed. Woman and children are raped; villages burned. The French give you money for the white man's scalp but give land to the white man for killing you. Your hunting grounds are ruined, lost forever. The streams and rivers are polluted, so there's no fish to eat. There are homes, roads, telephone poles, signs all over the place. People in a hurry to go nowhere. Trash dumped wherever people want to dump it. Noise from cars, trucks, radios, TVs, gun fights, children running around with guns and knives killing whoever they think needs killing, even their parents. One man hating another man because of skin color, religion. Would you like me to go on?" asked Sara tears running down her cheeks.

John stared at her in horror. Now he knew what she meant when she said there's too much wrong for one person to fix. He couldn't imagine more wrong. "There's worse than what you told me?" asked John.

"Yes, people kill one another for clothing; greed is at their hearts. Young children are beaten, raped, killed, just for the thrill of it. Prisons are built all over the place to hold bad people. All kinds of disease, starvation, a national debt in the trillions of dollars, drug abuse, suicide, wife beating, job loss, divorce is 90 percent."

"Divorce?" asked John.

"Divorce. When you marry someone then you decide you don't like them. You go to a judge, he grants a divorce so you're free to marry and divorce again. Some people do this a lot. It hurts a lot of people. Okay, let's say Sean and I confess we love each other. Now we've hurt my husband and children, his wife and children, then you hurt all the families involved in this; then you live a life of hell because you're constantly reminded that you hurt all these people. So rather than do this, you have an affair. Now if nobody finds out, you feel safe loving each other, but you go to hell because you committed adultery," said Sara.

"Hell?" asked John.

"It's a Bible thing," said Sara.

"Oh," said John.

"So if I confess my love for Sean here and have sex with him, am I committing adultery because here we are legally married, but in the future we're not? If we go back to the future knowing what we have down here, then we'd have lust in our hearts. And by the Bible's standard, we are still committing adultery. It's what we call a Catch 22," said Sara.

"But how do you feel?" asked John.

"Honestly, I don't know," said Sara, looking up at John. "Sex with Tom was 'wham, bam, thank you ma'am.' It's not the way other woman talk about it, I feel nothing. Yet all everyone talks about is the pleasure that sex gives. I've never had anyone take me in their arms and say 'I love you,' let alone kiss me senseless. I just think it's all lies," said Sara.

John stared at her. She really didn't know about the union of a man and a woman, not in this lifetime or her future life. No wonder his bare chest had such an effect on her. In both lifetimes she is still a virgin. Right then and there he wanted to take her in his arms and show her love. "Now I see your problems," said John.

"Well, I've got to go. The doctor should be coming for Susan, and I'd like to be there," said Sara.

"Yes," said John. He couldn't think of anything else to say. She had struck his heart with fear for his people, yet struck his heart with love for her and her tenderness.

"I'll see you and Ben in a little while," said Sara.

"Yes, we'll be there shortly," said John. He needed to talk to his father, tell him all that Sara had told him.

Sara got back just as the doctor was rolling in with his horse and carriage. Sara waved. "Dr. Emerson, I'm glad you made it." said Sara.

"Problems?" asked the doctor.

"No," smiled Sara, "just glad that it was a nice day for you to come out in. This way to Susan's house."

"I must admit, this is different," said Dr. Emerson, looking at the barn.

"Well, it was this or a covered wagon all winter," laughed Sara. "This seemed more logical."

Sara knocked on the door, then walked in. Dr. Emerson followed. He was medium height, reddish blond hair with blue eyes. Dressed in a modest black suit with white shirt, he was carrying a black bag. "Susan, Dr. Emerson's here," called Sara.

Susan was lying on the bed, trying to get up, but she couldn't bend in the middle for weight of the child. Dr. Emerson looked around the room; it was quite nice.

"Oh, you can stay there," said Dr. Emerson, walking over to the bed. "I'll check you out here."

"Thank God," Susan said, laughing.

"Well, I'll go home, it's right across the way," said Sara. "If you would stop in before you leave Dr Emerson."

Sure," said Dr. Emerson as he helped Susan lie flat on the bed.

Sara made some coffee. She'd offer the doctor coffee and pie. She felt total embarrassment about what she was about to ask him.

Knock, knock. "Come in," called Sara.

"How's Susan doing?" asked Sara.

"Good, she should deliver in a couple of days," said Dr. Emerson, closing the door. "Seems she's further along than she thought. Baby sounds good and healthy. Now what do you want to see me about?" asked Dr. Emerson.

"It's rather embarrassing," said Sara. "As you know, I was deathly sick, and I don't think that Sean and I, you know. Well, I was wondering if you could tell me if we did or not," asked Sara. "I think he's waiting until I'm strong enough in case I get pregnant. Phew," said Sara. "Got that out without dying of embarrassment; not too much anyway."

"Well, let's check you over and see how healthy you are. The rest, well, yes I can tell if you like to. Sit here, let's listen to your chest. Take a deep breath in, and let it out slowly again. Again." The doctor looked in Sara's eyes, down her throat and checked her ears.

The only thing that ran through Sara's mind is how he was doing it without one of those lights. He felt Sara's glands. "Mmm and ahhed" here and there.

"Lie on the bed, we'll check the rest of you," said Dr. Emerson. Sara took off her boots, walked to the bed, pulled down her jeans and bloomers, then laid on the bed. He poked around her stomach. "Ow," said Sara.

"That hurts?" asked Dr. Emerson.

"I wouldn't have said "ow" if it felt good," said Sara. "Ow."

When Dr. Emerson was through, he told her that she was a virgin and was getting ready to ovulate. Unless you want to get pregnant your first time, you had better wait. But you're healthy as a horse. I see you got sunburned. You know better. When you were young, you did it. Didn't you learn from that?" asked Dr. Emerson.

"Must be I didn't, or I wouldn't have done it again," said Sara, getting dressed. "I learned today."

"Well, stay out of the sun a couple of days. We don't want you dying of heat stroke."

"I was going to get apples tomorrow to can," said Sara.

"Then stay in the shade of the trees, but stay out of the sun," said Dr. Emerson.

"Here, you can wash your hands here. I made coffee and pie. I have blackberry and elderberry."

"If your cooking is at all like your mama's I'll have elderberry. Nobody could bake a pie like your mama," smiled Dr. Emerson.

"Oh, here before I forget. Here's your payment," Sara handed him twenty dollars from her purse.

Dr. Emerson looked shocked. "What makes you think I charge this much?"

"That's for Susan and me," smiled Sara.

"But what do I do with the extra? I only charge two dollars for a house call."

"Keep it. You'll be back out for Susan, then you'll probably want to check the baby. So instead of paying each time, it will be paid ahead," said Sara, pouring coffee.

"Boy, this pie is excellent. You beat your mama's good cooking. I didn't think that could be done," said Dr. Emerson.

Susan came walking in. Sara got up and helped her sit down. "Want some pie?" asked Sara.

"I need something. I'm still in shock over what Dr. Emerson said. Sometime this week?"

Sara poured Susan coffee, then sat in front of her. "Well, I'm not!" said Sara. "You drop any lower, the baby will fall out while you're walking!"

Dr. Emerson started choking. Sara patted him on the back. "Sorry, doc, but it's the truth," said Sara, putting pie in front of Susan.

"As long as I live, I'll never get used to your boldness," Sara Elizabeth," said Dr. Emerson.

"Well, the truth is the truth," said Sara.

"That is it my girl, and God knows you speak it," laughed Dr. Emerson. "That's why I'm not surprised to see you wearing men's pants. All you ever did was complain about dresses."

"Well, you can't work around here in a dress," said Sara.

"I must admit, this is a good setup. Who thought of this?" asked Dr. Emerson.

"Sean did," said Sara. "After we build our homes, he can use it as a chicken coop."

"Yeah," laughed Susan. "They tried it out yesterday. They like it."
"Well, like it or not, they ain't getting in here no more," said Sara.

Dr. Emerson laughed. "Is that why those doors are on, the ones with chicken wire?" he asked.

"Yup, they came in yesterday. Bold as ever, thought they owned the place. One nearly became supper," said Sara.

"The funny part is I can see you wanting to kill him," said Dr. Emerson.

"She almost did. I had to rescue the poor guy," said Sean, walking in.

"You better be clean walking in here," said Sara.

"Clean as I could get. We need a coffee break," said Sean. "What do you think of a woman who expects a man to work all day and night with no breaks? She's a slave driver," said Sean, kissing Sara's cheek. "Then yells at a man for eating fresh baked pies." Sean poured two cups of coffee and handed one to Jacob, who laughed.

Sara didn't say a word. Sean's kiss burned her cheek. It was soft and gentile.

"I don't know. Sounds like most the women I know," laughed Dr. Emerson.

Sean sat in the empty chair; Jacob leaned against the cupboard.

"Well, how's Susan?" asked Jacob.

"She's fine. She'll have the baby in the next couple of days. I'll come back and check on her," said Dr. Emerson.

"Couple of days?" said Jacob, shocked.

"Yes, she figured wrong. I showed her how to figure it, and she knows now," said Dr. Emerson.

"God, if we'd gone with the wagon train, she would never have made it to the fort. Something could have happened to either one of them," said Jacob.

"Why didn't you go with the wagon train?" asked Dr. Emerson.

"Because of me," said Sara. "I was too sick, and Mr. Farley didn't want everyone to get what I had, so here we are."

"Everything ends up working for the best," said Dr. Emerson, getting up. "Now I must leave before it gets too dark. Days are getting shorter and shorter. I'm afraid winter will be here soon."

"Well, if it holds off for about three weeks, we should be ready," said Sean.

"Well, what you've got done now looks good, real good. You planned this well. You used your brain on this one. Ain't never seen nothing like it," said Dr. Emerson as he walked out the door.

"He'll really be surprised when he comes back next time," laughed Jacob, sitting down. "Did he look at your sunburn, Sara?"

"Yes, he told me to be careful for a couple of days," said Sara. "He checked me all over, said I was healthy as a horse, so whatever I had couldn't have been much."

"Maybe it's God's way of saying we belong here," said Jacob. "Well, you ready to finish up for the night? We've got a pile of rocks to move," laughed Jacob.

"Now who's the slave driver," laughed Sean.

"Well, I'm going to be a daddy soon, so if we work hard now, I can be around for my baby," smiled Jacob.

"Let's get to it," said Sean, drinking the last of his coffee. They walked outside. The cement was poured in the bottom of the holes, and the ditch dug. Now they shoveled the stone in the wheelbarrow and would spread it out in the ditch. The horses and cows were out in a field behind the barn. Sean and Jacob had made a temporary area for them. After they were through with the septic tank area, they planned to make an area right behind the barn. The pigs and sheep had a separate area. Sean had made his mind up on what to do with them, yet Sean laughed as he looked around. "Jacob, sometimes I feel like Noah and his ark; two of this, two of that."

Jacob looked around. "I see what you mean. All the women are pregnant except Sara," laughed Jacob.

"Well, we've only been married a little over a week. You got to give it some time," laughed Sean.

"Now this is true, but you do realize once Sara sees our baby, she will want one. Women are like that," laughed Jacob.

Sean stopped shoveling and wiped his brow. Jacob was right, Sara was a good mother. Sara needed children. What if they stayed here forever? Sara couldn't be childless, not unless they already made love and she was already pregnant. He didn't know.

"You're right, Jacob," said Sean, who went back to work. It's strange how he didn't miss Laura and the kids. He didn't know if

Sara missed Tom. He knew she missed her kids. She was close to the kids and the grandchildren. Sara spoiled the grandchildren rotten. If only he had asked her to marry him. Why he didn't, he wasn't sure. Maybe he didn't think he was coming back from the war. Sean knew that if he died in the war, Sara would have never forgiven herself for telling him to go get killed.

"Want some help?" asked Susan.

"No, you stay put, there's only a couple of dishes. I can handle it," said Sara.

"Sara, don't you find it a little strange how your getting sick helped so many people? You saved a wagon train full of people. What were there, 102 people? Then you saved me and my baby, then that young man at the store. What's his name, Blaine. It seems you're always saving someone, then the deer today. It just seems a little odd to me," said Susan.

"What, you think I had something to do with this, like a guardian angle-type thing? If you remember, I was down sick. I couldn't do this. That was God's work, not mine," said Sara, drying her hands. "Don't go thinking God's working through me in some strange way. He doesn't need me to do his work, he does well all on his own. I'm a simple human being with flaws like everyone else. I don't like that religious mumbo-jumbo. I believe man has a right to his religion, but don't start in on me being some saint," said Sara.

"You always had strong opinions on religion, and I wasn't making you out to be a saint. I just find it odd that when you're around, only good things happen," said Susan.

"God, you make it sound like I walk on water," laughed Sara, sitting down. "Maybe I just see things differently than you do. Everyone has a different way of seeing things. I know people are always looking for signs from God to see if they're in favor with God. I don't need signs. All I have to do is look around. God's everywhere: the trees, the grass, the sun, the moon, the stars, the rain, the snow, life, that's God's work. That's what I see. I don't need statues or visions every day. I wake up, I feel God's love. The breeze is like a huge hug from God. He gives us what we need, if we take the time to say thank you," said Sara.

"That's what I mean. You have, I don't know, some kind of understanding of how it all works. You know when someone needs you. You know what has to be done; you do it. You don't care if someone else thinks it's right or not," said Susan.

"Look, I care what people think. It's just sometimes people think stupid things, and if I know that they're wrong, I will do what I think is right. I'm not saying I'm a genius. I'm doing what is right for me, not everyone else. I have no special understanding of anything, it's just the way I see things. I'm no angel of any kind, guardian or otherwise. I'm flesh and bone just like you, with faults, just like you. I'm not perfect, no one is," said Sara. "And anyone who thinks he is, is a fool."

"It just seems everything you do is perfect, flawless in every way," said Susan.

"Okay, if everything I do is perfect, then how come I got sunburned today? That was really stupid on my part, wasn't it?" said Sara.

Susan giggled. "Was it? Look who carried you home," said Susan.

"Yes, it was stupid. I passed out and didn't know what it felt like to be carried in his arms. Now if I had swooned, pretended to pass out, then I would have known how it felt for John to hold me, then I would have been smart. You should have smelled his shirt he gave me to put on. I thought I'd died and gone to heaven. I better stop there before I get myself in trouble," said Sara.

Susan giggled her little girl giggle.

John had heard enough, so he knocked on the door. So she felt what he had felt at the quarry.

"Come in," said Sara.

"John, Ben, please come in, sit down," said Sara. "Coffee?"

"Yes please," said Ben.

John shot Ben a look. He saw that twinkle in his eye. He heard everything John did and was busting at the seams to say something. Ben was built like John, looked like John but had white hair. Ben is what John would look like in years to come. John didn't speak; he couldn't think of anything but Sara admitting to Susan she found him, or, he couldn't remember.

"I was just telling Susan how foolish it was of me to get sunburned like I did. I missed out on the best part: John carrying me home in those big, strong arms. Pie?" asked Sara.

Ben's eyes twinkled like firecrackers on the Fourth of July. "So you think my son has big, strong arms?" asked Ben, smiling.

Sara giggled.

"I don't know what is stronger, the big shoulders, the massive chest, the big hands or strong arms. I don't know Ben, he's got a lot there," said Sara, winking at Ben. "Him be big, strong chief someday," said Sara in a deep voice.

Ben started laughing. "I don't know about chief. He's not too smart, you know. Keeps finding pretty ladies and returning them to where they belong. I keep telling him it's not the way we do things. We're supposed to be big, mean people, but he won't listen. Kids today have a mind of their own," laughed Ben.

"Are you two through taunting me?" asked John, his arms crossed.

"I don't know Ben, are we through or are we just getting started?" teased Sara.

"I just got the look, so I guess we are through," smiled Ben.

"Oh, the look," said Sara, jumping up. "What one, this one?" Sara crossed her arms and looked down. "No, this one," said Sara, furrowing her eyebrows, then looking at Ben who by now was laughing so hard he had tears running down his cheeks. John was trying not to laugh. Susan's was holding her belly, she was laughing so hard. "No, this one," said Sara as she leaned on the table and growled, "me bear clan." That's all John needed. He started laughing. Sara, waving her red hair in the air, hands clasped in claw fashion, growled. "That's the one," said Sara.

"What's going on?" asked Sean, walking in all fresh and clean from his bath at the quarry with Jacob behind him.

"Sara, ha ha, is impersonating John! Ha ha," said Ben.

"Be careful, she's good at it," said Sean.

"I can see," laughed Ben, standing up and extending his hand to Sean.

"Ben, this is Sean, my husband. This is Jacob, and this is Susan."

"How do you do," said Ben, shaking Sean and Jacob's hands and nodding to Sara. Jacob left to get two chairs.

"There's fresh coffee and these," said Sara, pulling a plate from the cupboard. Sara held a plate of chocolate chip cookies.

"Yes, and I hid them so you wouldn't eat them all," smiled Sara, setting the plate down on the table.

"Chocolate chip, what's chocolate chip?" asked Susan.

"It's a special cookie my wife made up for me," smiled Sean, putting his arm around Sara. "Nobody can have the recipe, it's just for me." Sean kissed Sara's cheek.

Sara froze. This was the second time today Sean had kissed her. Now his arm was around her. She felt uncomfortable and hoped it didn't show. She smiled softly.

John and Ben both picked up on Sara's feeling. John wondered how far Sean would go. There was something in the way he said my wife that put John ill at ease.

Susan reached for a cookie and took a bite. "God these are good," she said.

"Well, they're better with nuts, but I couldn't find any in the store," said Sara.

"No nuts?" said Sean. "I guess I could get through it," joked Sean, sitting down across from John. "Well, what do you think about my proposal?" Sean asked Ben.

"Well, I've thought about it. I had John draw me some rough maps. These maps are how we live our lives. I don't want you to think that we are greedy. Each area is marked according to its importance to us. Now if we can reach an agreement, I think we have a deal," said Ben.

Ben slid a piece of paper toward Sean. Sean opened it. Sean looked at it, nodded, then took a piece of paper out of his pocket. He looked at the two together, m-m-md," for a while. "Sara, could you get me a piece of paper?" Sara stood up, walked over to the cupboard, took out sheets of paper, a pen, and ink well and set them in front of Sean. Sean drew out the shape of the land, then drew out the map Ben had given him; then he drew out his map.

"Mmm," said Sean. No one said a word. "Jacob, how do you feel about owning this land here?" asked Sean.

Jacob leaned over. "Yeah, that would be okay." "Well, I was thinking of setting it up like this." Sean drew in a house, a barn, a garden, an orchard, and growing fields. He drew in a road. "That leaves a small piece here we can plant. We could put an orchard there, then we'd have three. Then this piece here we'll give to the nation. I think they need this." Sean drew everything out on his map. "Well, Ben, what do you think? You can have all you asked for plus this is what it would look like," said Sean, passing the map to Ben. "See where we added the extra land?" "Yes," said Ben. "What do you think John?" John studied the map. It was more than fair, more than what they needed.

"Why the extra land?" asked John.

"Well, I was thinking that we could build a village here, one with good homes, safe homes, a place for you to have pride in," said Sean.

John remembered Sara saying they were forced to live in squalor. If he didn't do this now, the future was bleak. There was a hidden message here. Deep in his soul his forefathers told him to do this. Soon the white buffalo would no longer be white. Everything he was ever taught in his world, and what the white man's world told him, he could do no better than this for his nation of people. "Who will build these homes?" asked John. "We all will, together. I can show you how. I can design the homes. First, Jacob gets the first home. He can't live in one room with a baby for too long. Children grow too fast. We have to create our own world here, become united and self-supporting. We must invest in our future," said Sean.

"You can keep us here?" asked John.

"I don't see why not; I own it. I will pay the taxes, I can have whoever I want to live on my land and in my homes, that's the law. The agreement between us will be for one hundred and thirty years. By then it will be turned over to you and your nation, when, at that time, you will live free and tax free," said Sean. "But you have to understand, this involves a lot of money. We can make the money. I know that the government will do everything it can to tax us to death trying to get us to fold, so they can take this land away from me and move you out, We will have to be united on this," said Sean.

"Money, where will we get money?" asked John.

"I've got a plan. I've written it down; it's called investment. I know how to do this. Sara has written a major guideline down for us, so that if anything should happen to us, the whole plan must be followed to a tee. I'll have papers drawn up by a lawyer. I will have five copies made, one for each of us, one for the lawyer, one for state files. It will state that all money and land will be passed down from generation to generation. Money will be set aside for the future, so any one of our generations can't lose money that's to pay taxes. No matter how careful we are, any one of our offspring could get greedy and try to take it all. That could ruin everything, so we have to make sure we cover everything. I've been thinking we should buy more land for our children and Jacob's children. Times change; we must allow for changes. The nation will grow. Everything must be considered. We will build a school, a church, things that the government cannot deny us. All our children will go to school, learning both cultures. They will not grow up feeling hate for one another. Money will be set aside for education of our children for college. We will make our own town. Does this sound fair to everyone?" asked Sean.

"Yes," everyone said at once.

"This will take a couple of weeks to draw up. This gives us time to buy more land. I will go over a larger map and see what we can do. I will make provisions in all our names, so we have money, but I will do all the investing and you be informed monthly on how we do. The name of the game is money. If we have more than them, we win," said Sean. "Money talks."

That night a treaty was made, one that would change the future forever; one they hoped would show mankind he could live together peacefully. Jacob and Susan would never know how Sean and Sara knew what they knew. Jacob and Susan went home. Sean helped Jacob carry the chairs home.

John and Ben left with a copy of all the important facts they would need for the future, just in case they couldn't pull it off. "Never trust your fellow man," said Sara. "The future is all about money. You can't make someone like you, but if you have money, he will love you, remember that."

After John and Ben left, Sara cleaned and straightened her house. Dishes were washed and put away. Sara walked outside. The moon was so big and bright it looked like daylight cast in a blue-white brightness. A soft, warm breeze slid over so gently through Sara's hair. She heard Jacob and Sean talking, so she walked inside, got some soap and a towel, her bathrobe and night-gown and walked up to the quarry and dove in. The water was so warm. She bathed, then swam, the moon reflecting on the water as Sara swam and created waves. The tips of the waves sparkled like diamonds. The water felt cool on Sara's sunburned skin, so she got out, dried herself off, patting her skin gently, put on her nightgown, sat down, and brushed her hair. She remembered swimming as a child, then someone bought this land, put up a double-wide trailer and banned everyone from swimming here. He was a very mean man. He wouldn't let Sara take pictures of the quarry. All she wanted was pictures to record the history of the town. Sara knocked on his trailer door seeking permission, and he yelled at her, threatening to call the police. Sara left shocked, so she told Sean about it. Rumors flew. Then one day his home caught on fire. The fire department responded, but refused to go on his land. It was posted, and the fire department didn't want a lawsuit against them. It was a volunteer unit; they couldn't afford to be sued. It would shut them down and then no one around here would have help when it was needed.

Sara smiled. "That grumpy, old man tried to sue, but he hung himself on his posted signs. He listed the fire department as one not allowed on his land, so he lost. He rebuilt on the same spot, then put up an ugly fence around his land to keep the world away. As far as the town was concerned, he could die there and rot there, his home being his coffin. Every town had one mean old man. How they handled it, she didn't know. She only knew how her own handled it.

"It's beautiful here in the moonlight," said John.

"Yes, it is," said Sara, still brushing her hair, not looking up at John. "Sorry about earlier, you're not mad at me, are you?" asked Sara.

"No! I know I came on strong, I always have," said John, sitting down.

"Can I ask you something personal?" asked Sara.

"How personal?" asked John.

"That smell on your shirt, what was it? I loved it," said Sara.

"Pine," said John, "but a special pine. I will show you. We mix it with flowers of luck and happiness. I will show you."

"Thank you," said Sara.

"Where's Sean?" asked John.

"Well when I left he was talking to Jacob. He might be in bed by now," said Sara.

"May I ask you something personal?" asked John.

"Yes," said Sara, putting her brush down.

"Do you love Sean? I noticed he kissed you, and you acted like you didn't like it," said John.

Sara sighed. "Sean has acted strange all day. I don't know if it's because he loves me, or his sex drive is on high gear. I've tried all day to figure out if I truly love Sean, or if I love what I could never have. I've never had to deal with love and it's feelings between a man and a woman. Please don't take this wrong, but what I thought was love for Sean could have been a fascination. I met you, and you have stirred feelings in me that I never knew women felt. I don't know if it's the savage in your blood, or the fact that you're different," said Sara.

John laughed. "Your honesty amazes me. How did you feel when Sean kissed you?" asked John.

"Well, his kiss was soft and gentle, but something deep inside said it wasn't right. I don't know if it's guilt because of my being married in the future," said Sara.

"Mmm," said John.

"Mmm what?" said Sara.

"Well, I wonder if I kissed you if you could tell if it was love or guilt," said John.

"This isn't one of those things where one kiss will lead to other things, and we'll get to the point we can't stop," said Sara.

John threw his head back and laughed. "It's one kiss, I can control myself. I know most men can't, but I can," said John. "But you must tell me what you feel, then we will talk about your feeling."

"Okay, that sounds fair," said Sara.

"Stand up," said John.

"Why?" asked Sara.

"Do you want me to lie beside you or on you for a kiss?" asked John.

"Oh, I see," said Sara, standing right up.

John laughed at Sara's swiftness when he mentioned a sexual position. Sara closed her eyes and puckered her lips. "What are you doing, preparing for a kiss?" said John. "No wonder you have problems telling your feelings. You don't prepare for a kiss. It should be natural, show, full of meaning."

"Meaning?" said Sara.

"A kiss can mean different things. A kiss on the cheek could mean hello, thank you, glad to see you. In time of sorrow it could show someone you feel his sorrow. A kiss on the forehead could mean good night, or I respect you, but a kiss on the lips between a man and a woman can show the strength of love. A kiss can bring forth deep desires in a woman, awaken her sexuality as a woman," said John.

"Oh yeah, right, one kiss can make me a woman," said Sara.

John grabbed Sara and kissed her soft and tender, then deep and probing. Her blood boiled, every nerve in her body sprung to life, a warmth grew in her, then John let go. He sat down. Sara stood, enjoying the feeling that ran through her body. John watched the water. He let her think about her feelings. She had to know that deep inside Sara kept a beautiful woman hidden.

Sara sat down, embarrassed at how she felt.

"How do you feel?" John asked, staring at the water.

"Embarrassed," said Sara.

"Why, because you were made to feel like a woman, because it brought forth feelings you didn't think you have a right to feel?" asked John.

Sara was silent. "I never felt like that," Sara said slowly. "I felt like I wanted you. It felt like I could never settle for one kiss, like there was something more, something I don't know. I talk foolish," said Sara.

"It's not foolish," said John. "I made you feel like the woman you are, the woman you keep hidden deep inside, the woman who needs and wants love, a love you've never felt before. That woman needs to be awakened. You've kept her hidden long enough. In order for you to find love peace and happiness, you must set her free," said John.

"You are telling me I've never known sex or love, but do you forget I'm married in my other life? I do know about sex and love," said Sara.

"I did not forget. Yes, you know of sex and love, but do you feel them with your heart? I don't think so. What you feel is duty; you don't feel passion, real passion," said John.

"Well, I think I do," said Sara.

"That kiss I just gave you, the feeling you had, do you feel it all the time? Does it burn as a fire deep within your soul, always wanting more?" asked John.

"No, I never felt anything like I just felt. But that doesn't mean that what I feel is wrong," said Sara.

"Yes it does. It means the woman in you has never been awakened and that is sad. You've never known true love and passion. You're still a virgin even though you're married," said John, standing up. "I will stop by tomorrow and show you where the fruit is."

"Okay. But the doctor wants me to stay out of the sun for a couple of days. He said it will be okay if I stay in the shade," said Sara, standing up. She looked up to see John watching her. "What?" asked Sara.

"The kiss was good for me," said John.

"Want another one?" smiled Sara, picking up her brush.

"No, I may be strong but not that strong," said John, and he was gone.

"What's that John?" Sara looked around, Did John desire her? "That's stupid," said Sara. She walked back home, more confused than ever. John's kiss was hot on her lips. Little squirreling waves of feelings ran through her body. Damn, something else to deal with. What if the feelings didn't go away? Shit!" Sara said out loud.

"Problems," asked Sean. He was standing outside looking at the moon.

"Don't start," said Sara. "I just got unwound, I don't need you to start in on me, then I'll never be able to sleep," said Sara. She started crying.

Sean walked over, picked her up and carried her into the house. He kicked the door shut with his foot. He laid her on the bed. "Okay, let's have it," said Sean, "all of it." We talk it out, right here, right now. I don't need you to lose it now."

"I saw John. We talked about you and my feelings for you. We talked about me never feeling passion or love. Then he kissed me. I've never felt like that. Tom and me, it never was or I don't think it was. Damn, I don't know. I always thought... I don't know what I thought," said Sara, hot tears running down her face.

"Why did John kiss you?" asked Sean, putting his arm around Sara.

"Because I wasn't sure how I felt about you, and he wanted to know if you made me feel like he did when he kissed me," said Sara.

"And?" said Sean.

"You never kissed me like he did," said Sara. "I've never been kissed like that," sobbed Sara, wiping her tears away.

"I have to tell you something," said Sean. "I love you; I've always loved you. I never asked you to marry me because I didn't think I was good enough for you. I felt you deserved better than me. When I came back from Vietnam, and you married Tom, I'd felt my choice was right. Then I met Tom, he treated you like shit, he didn't deserve you. You don't know how many times I wanted to kill him. I married Laura and moved in the neighborhood to watch over you. I always felt guilty. John is right, the woman in you has never come out. Only a man can bring it out, a man who loves you more than life itself. But you should love him the same way because if you don't, the magic won't happen," said Sean.

"Magic?" Sara asked puzzled.

"The magic is when a man takes a woman in his arms for the first time and makes her a woman. That first time will stay with her forever. She must be made to feel beautiful, not shameful. There are a lot of places on a woman that can make her feel aroused. Anyone can have sex; it's the beautiful that is hard to get. That beautiful is love, true love," said Sean. "I don't think we have that beautiful kind of love."

"How do you know that?" said Sara.

"By the look on your face. One kiss from John has made you glow," said Sean.

"But you never kissed me like he did, so how do you know?" said Sara.

"Okay," said Sean. "I can kiss you. I can kiss you until you're so hot and bothered you'll beg me to make love to you. But I won't touch you unless you feel better than that one kiss John gave you."

"Yeah right," said Sara, laughing.

"Okay, take the nightgown off," said Sean.

Fifteen minutes later Sean rolled off the bed, walked in the kitchen. Sara lay on the bed, reached for her robe and put it on. She was shaking. "Sean, why'd you walk away?"

"It's not me you want," said Sean.

"How do you know that?" said Sara.

"You would have given yourself to me just like you gave yourself to Tom. You felt obligated, not out of love," said Sean.

"But I love you," said Sara. "I've always loved you."

"There's different kinds of love, Sara. The kind of love you need, I can't give you. You're a very special woman, you deserve the best," said Sean.

"You're the one I want. I want your child: I want you, don't you understand?" said Sara, crying. "Fuck you!" Sara yelled and ran out.

"Go after her Sean, go after her. Don't have regrets a second time," Sean's brain cried. "Shit," yelled Sean. He ran after her, he thought that she ran toward the quarry, so he ran, calling her name. "Sara, Sara," called Sean.

"What's wrong?" asked John and Ben running up.

Sean fell to his knees. "Sara," cried Sean.

"What happened Sean?" asked Ben. John dove in the water thinking Sara was there.

"I sent Sara into the night crying because I wouldn't make love to her. She loves John, not me."

"You said what?" asked John. "Why did you tell her that?"

"Because it's true. You and her belong together, not me and her," said Sean.

"But you have no right to tell her that is what she wants. She has to make her own mind up, not you," said Ben.

"I know, I'm no better than her mother. She loves John and now I've driven her away. She's so confused, I ran after her to explain. Oh God, I ruined her life."

"Sean, what's wrong," asked Jacob, running up to the men.

"Jacob, take Sean home. Him and Sara had a fight. She ran off. I will find her and bring her home," said John. "Ben, you go back to camp. I'll handle it from now on."

"Come on, Sean," said Jacob, "let's make some coffee." They walked toward their home. Susan had a lamp on and coffee made. John walked back with them. He tracked Sara down. He'd seen which direction she went and tracked her down. This was a stupid move on her part, and it was time those two had a talk. This time she was going to listen to him. She couldn't keep running away; he couldn't keep saving her. This woman was more trouble than she was worth.

Sara ran blindly into the night, tears running wildly down her cheeks. Pain ran through her body. Nobody wanted her now; she was a beautiful person and still nobody wanted her. Her mother was right. Her right side ached, she fell. Sara lay on the ground, curled up in a ball sobbing. Years of hurt, pain, and humiliation flowed with the tears. Her chest hurt from the deep wrenching sobs. Her nose filled with the scents around her. Pine, John's pine, the scent soothing her. She wiped away the tears.

"To hell with them all. I don't need them, I'll do what I was sent here for then go back to my life," she thought. "It wasn't great, but it was my life, and I didn't have all these fucking problems."

Sara made her peace, she stood up, then fell down. "Oh, great." She felt her right ankle. "Well, it's not broken, must be sprained. Shit," cried Sara. "That's what I get. Do something stupid, something stupid will happen. Well I guess I'm not going anywhere. Sean won't look for me. He hates me, he sent me away. So tonight I sleep out; tomorrow I find a way home," Sara curled up in a ball, tucking her nightgown tight around her. She felt total exhaustion.

John followed Sara's tracks, his heart beating. He worried about Sara. She had this attitude that she didn't need anyone; she could handle everything on her own. She was so wrong. If anyone needed taking care of, it was Sara. She was so fragile, delicate, like a rose. It didn't take much to crush it, but you give it water and sunlight and it blossomed into beauty. Sara needed a chance to blossom. Sean didn't help, he crushed the rose. Now he didn't know what shape the rose was in.

John found her. He fell to his knees next to her. She looked so peaceful and delicate, like a small child. He hated to wake her up to yell at her, but this thing was getting settled here and now. John reached out his large hand and touched her face, gently. "Sara," said John.

"What?" asked Sara, sleepily. "John, you came looking for me?"

"Yes, I think we should talk. No, we have to talk," said John.

Sara sat up. "What's the use? I was supposed to get pregnant tonight, but nobody wanted me," said Sara, sadly.

"What are you talking about?" said John.

"Remember I told you I bought the chest in a garage sale?" said Sara.

"Yes," said John, sitting down.

"Well, I brought the chest home, started to clean it. I found a diary in a hidden spot in the bottom. Sara wrote it. She wrote about all this. I've tried my best to follow the diary the best I can, but everything is all screwed up. Jacob and Susan went with the wagon train, they were killed. The land deal with Sean and Mr. Smith got all screwed up. The house I live in in the future was affected by this deal. I nearly lost everything I had. Sean had gone and changed all this. What it's done to the future, I don't know. But there's a belief that time shouldn't be played with. Tonight I get pregnant, and I have to get pregnant tonight. The son I have will go on to fight for Indians' rights. Sean just seems to go around and do what he wants. He refused to make love to me tonight, he says I'm in love with you. In Sara's diary, she writes about you, so I don't know what to do. I can't give birth to the one person who fought for your right. Real great woman I make. I feel trapped.

"Do you love me, Sara?" asked John.

"The Sara that's here loves you very much. The other Sara I don't know," said Sara. "I wish we were married in the future. I'd love you to be my husband, but like my father always said, 'Wish in one hand, shit in the other, see which gets filled first,'" laughed Sara.

"Mmm. My father always told me to be careful of what you wish for, you might get it," laughed John.

"I like your father's better, so I wish you to be my husband," smiled Sara.

"What would we do with the one you have now?" laughed John.

"Mmm, I know, I'll write my whole life down and how to change it, then you can be my husband," said Sara.

"Okay, that sounds good to me. I may be a little old, but I'll be there," smiled John. "But you've got to stop running off." Sean's worried sick."

"John, do you love me?" asked Sara.

"Yes, but I can't have you. My duty is first to the nation," said John.

"John would you show me what it's like to be loved by you? I really need to know what love is. No ties. I won't bother you ever again. One night, you and me. I will be Sean's wife, but I want you to make me a woman," said Sara.

"You will bear my child," said John.

"Who better to fight for Indians' rights than one of their own?" said Sara. "Please John, teach me what being a woman is about. Let me have one good memory in my life."

"What if once isn't enough? What if our desires force us to need one another? What if passion takes over our senses?" said John.

"I will make love to you as long as I am here. I don't know about the other Sara, but this one needs you. I don't know how long I'm here for," said Sara.

"We, that's what I'm talking about. I can't do that. My people. I can't be there just for you. I have to put my people first. I can't put my needs before my people; it's not so simple. If it was, I would not have stopped earlier tonight," said John.

"You wanted me," said Sara, shocked.

"Yes, and still do, but what kind of chief would I make if I couldn't control my desires? The temptations of the flesh are what make a man weak. A chief must go beyond the temptations. If he doesn't, then the temptations will be his downfall, and the ruination of its people," said John.

"You're right," said Sara. "I'm being selfish. Everything is screwed up.

"Anyway, whatever made me think I could change it? I've failed miserably. I should be used to it by now."

"Are you ready to go home?" asked John.

"I can't walk, I sprained my ankle. You see, I did something foolish. I ran away only in a nightgown, no shoes, stepped in a hole, fell, end of story. One stupid thing. I give up, I'm trapped with my hands tied. All I can do is live my life here. I can't get apples and peaches and pears now, so our winter supply will be nothing. We'll starve and die anyway. You would think I'd get something right just once. Shit, I even had written instructions, and I couldn't do it right. How sad is that?" laughed Sara.

"Well you never know about life when you think it's worse. It could be the best. Now let's get you home," said John.

"I'd love that," smiled Sara.

John picked her up and carried her home. They talked on the way home; they stopped a couple times. Sara's foot throbbed so bad she couldn't let it hang down too long. John checked it. It didn't feel broken, but it was really swollen.

Sean paced back and forth, running his hands through his hair. "John will find her," said Susan. "So sit down, tell me what happened."

"I refused to make love to her. I told her to look elsewhere, so she ran away," said Sean. "How does that sound, Susan? Now do you understand why I choose not to talk about it? To make things worse, I sent the very man I told her to sleep with to go find her. How is that for lousing things up?"

"Oh Sean, Sara wouldn't, she loves you too much," said Susan.

"You know Sara, she stomps off and will do just what she wants, and she wants John. I can't believe I did this. She wanted my baby. Instead of me doing what I was supposed to, I sent her out to someone else. Stupid, stupid," said Sean.

"Sean, sit down!" yelled Susan.

Sean stopped, looked at Susan and sat down.

"Don't mess with me, drink the coffee. Sara will not sleep with John. I don't see how you could think such a thing. She's agreed to everything you've done here. She's chipped in and helped. She's been working her butt off right here for you. If you think for one second she would run out of here into the arms of another man, you're wrong. Sara has class. Sara ran out of here because you didn't want her. She's done everything she could for you, even made you cookies, and you refuse to sleep with your wife. I would have killed you," said Susan.

"Well, they're not back yet," said Sean.

"So you think that because they're not back yet, they're having sex? Did you ever stop to think that there's a lot of space out there? It's dark, and he has to find her on top of that, then calm her down and talk her into coming home. Even I know he can't do that in ten minutes," said Susan.

"You're right, I know you're right. But what if she's hurt?" said Sean. "I hurt her."

"If she's hurt, John will know what to do," said Susan.

John sat Sara down on a rocky bank. "This water will be cold. It's a runoff from the sulfur spring, but we have to get the swelling down. Putting it in the swirling water should help," said John.

"Like a spa?" said Sara.

"Spa?" said John.

Sara sighed, she was getting tired of explaining everything. "Ahh," said Sara. "That's like ice water."

"Ice water?" questioned John.

"Future stuff," said Sara.

"Why is money so important in the future?" asked John. "That's all Sean talked about."

Sara moved her foot in the water. It felt good. "Well, an average house cost between eighty-five thousand to one hundred thousand dollars. A good truck like a Ford Explorer costs thirty-eight thousand dollars, then you get taxes and insurances, then you have to have food to eat, cleaning products to keep the house clean, then clothes to wear, shoes for your feet. Sneakers can run from twenty dollars to two hundred dollars for one pair of shoes. Then you have personal care products to buy because you don't want to insult anyone with body odor or bad breath. Heaven for bid, if your hair is not clean, or if women have hair on their bodies; we have to shave it off. Then when you're through with all that stuff, you throw it out in plastic bags. The trash man comes and picks it up, takes it to a trash recycling center, where it's put in a big pile so everyone can fight over what to do with it," said Sara. "This all takes money."

"You people have this kind of money," asked John.

"No! They have what they call credit and plastic money. Plastic money is credit cards where you can buy things and pay monthly on it. This is one of America's downfalls, probably the major one because the national debt is in the trillions of dollars caused because people want everything now. Why wait? Slap down the plastic, take it home, then when you've extended your credit, you can't pay your bills, then you go bankrupt," said Sara.

"Bankrupt?" asked John.

"Bankruptcy is a process you can do that wipes out your bills. There's lots of reasons for it. I don't want to sound like everyone does this because they don't It's one way of helping someone so they don't lose everything. But if you go bankrupt, you can't have credit for a while," said Sara.

"Why does everything cost so much?" asked John.

"Well everyone you talk to has a different reason. Some say thief, others might say middleman, or wages. But, some people blame the companies themselves, saying they're greedy. Then you have logo names. If you buy a product with a name on it, you'll pay three to four times as much. We have what you call ads; these ads tell people that they can't live without this stuff, so people go to what we call malls, and we 'shop until we drop'—it's a saying. We bring all this stuff home and find a place to put all the stuff we can't live without. Most of it sits around and collects dust, then you get disgusted and have a garage sale, make some money, then go buy more stuff. It's an endless circle," said Sara.

"Sounds like people don't know what they want," said John.

"They know it's an electronic age; you buy something one week, the next week it's outdated. You either get rid of it or update it. Anyway you look at it, you have to spend the money to keep up. Anyway you look at it, it just adds up as more trash. I don't feel nothing on my foot anymore, is that good?" asked Sara.

"If the swelling's down, it's good; let's see," said John. "This plastic money, is that all you have?" asked John.

"No, we work, we get paid. We put our money in banks, then write a check. It's a piece of paper," said Sara, taking her foot out of the water for John to look at. "Then we take the piece of paper and sent it out in the mail to pay off the plastic money," said Sara. "I know it sounds strange, but it's easy."

"This paid money you get must be a lot of money," said John. "It's a little better, put your foot back in the water."

"Well we really don't make a lot of money. Well, some do, some don't. We have what we call a minimum wage," said Sara, putting her foot in the water. "This is the least amount an employer can pay an employee. Some people work for less, these people are usually illegal aliens. They work in sweatshops, another subject. Anyway, the minimum wage is so low that you can't support yourself, so a husband and wife both work. This is not good because now a woman has a job, she has children, plus the cooking, cleaning, and child-rearing. A lot of times parents can't afford a babysitter or day care, so the children sometimes get left home alone. This is not good because there's so much stuff kids can get into; mostly it's trouble. So without the mother home, there's no family structure. Without family structure, you have no security or control, so you have a bunch of people running around trying to grab hold of anything that looks solid to them. You have family fights, misunderstandings, so you have people running around trying to make sense of it. They use sex as love, which leads to divorce, and the whole thing boils down to money. When people say money won't change them, they're full of shit," said Sara. "Money's what runs this country; money will put a smile on your face faster than anything. You also have problems if you have too much money. But if your bills are paid, and you have a roof over your head, food on the table, and clothes on your back, you're a lot happier. Don't let anyone tell you any different."

"Why's too much money not good?" asked John.

"Well, if you have too much money, people think you don't deserve it. They come up with stupid ideas on how to sue you to take your money away. See, we have three kinds of people: poor, middle-class, and rich. The poor and middle-class hate the rich. They think they have too much money. The rich hate the poor and middle-class because they thinks they're supporting them. Both sides are right. The rich are usually people who have corporations, like movie stars, sports figures. Because they're rich, they think they pay too much in taxes, but the reason they pay more in taxes is because they make more than we do. But the rich wouldn't be rich without the poor and middle-class because we do the work that sells the products that make them rich," said Sara. Sara took her foot out of the water. "So as you can see, both sides are right, but neither side wants to see the other one's side, so they fight over it. While they do all this arguing, America is falling apart. Everyone is so wrapped up in their little world that they can't see what's really happening," said Sara.

"Why? What's happening?" said John, looking at Sara's foot. The swelling was just about down, so John put Sara's foot back in the water.

"Well, while America fights over these issues, the Japanese are coming over here and buying everything up: our banks, our corporations, so by the time America wakes up to what's happening, it will be too late; there will be no America. There's petty fighting going on that nobody sees the real picture," said Sara.

"Fighting?" asked John.

"Well, in my time, not all wars are with guns. Usually it's show of force. Amendments. God, there are so many amendments in the Constitution of the United States nobody know the true Constitution anymore," laughed Sara. Some things are good, some are plain stupid, but you have people we call agitators who will get groups of people going. Once they get going, it gets out of hand, people get hurt, people get killed. It's so stupid," sighed Sara. "Then you have some things that are two sided, where both sides are right. Okay, we have legal abortion. This is a major fight that people die for. One amendment put the responsibility in the lap of the woman, this way the government can stay out of it and not take sides. I, personally, don't believe in it. I look at a child as a gift from God. But if a child or woman is raped, did not ask to get pregnant and does not want a child, why should she have it? The child would never feel loved. It would constantly be a reminder of what happened. Everyone who's against abortion feels she should have the child and give it up for adoption. It's easy for them to say, they don't have to go through what that woman has to go through: the constant reminder of what happened, the pain she suffered getting raped, then the pain she suffered in giving birth. And when the child grows up, it will seek the natural mother and want to know why she gave the baby up at birth. So this woman suffers all her life. Is she wrong for her choice? I don't know. I can only speak for myself. We never know until judgment day. Then you have women who do not want children and get an abortion. Is this wrong? I don't think so if they know they don't want a child and birth control failed. Maybe an abortion is right for them. A lot of children are abused for years before they die from their abuse. Is it right these children should suffer this abuse? No, it's not. There's so many dead-beat dads out there it's awful, and it's always the children who suffer. Everyone says they're kids, they bounce back, they can take it. Well, they're wrong. They're little adults; they think and feel the same way we do. I wonder sometimes how these adults would like the abuse kids get, being slapped around, beaten, burned, humiliated, and raped. They wouldn't like it one bit. Divorce is just as bad for a child as an adult. Just think how they feel. They love both parents and the court chooses who is the better parent, usually the mother, and Dad's gone. They think it's their fault, wish they had been better, even wished they weren't born. People can't see what's wrong, the kids are so fucked up it's unreal. And parents have the nerve to say, 'Oh, it was a bad seed.' I'd like to punch them up side the head, see if it knocks any sense in them," Sara took her foot out of the water. "That's why I say everyone should stop trying to live everyone else's life for them and just live their own life. It's none of our business if some woman thinks it's best for her not to have a baby. It is of no concern to two thousand other people. It's her life, not theirs. They say the unborn needs protection, that somebody has to stand up for them. Well, nobody's standing up for the child that's already born. They figure once they saved the unborn child it's no longer their problem, the child lived. Sure the child lived to be tortured and killed, big fucking deal. The child still died," said Sara. "Sorry, I swore. I swear a lot in my other life."

John looked at Sara's foot. "I think I can get you home before it swells again. Are there a lot of these show-of-force groups?" asked John, picking up Sara.

"Yes," said Sara. "Gay rights, animal activists, all these groups try to live someone else's life. It's not our life to live. God gave us our life to live, not everyone else's. Jesus said, 'You without sin cast the first stone.' We can't, we're born sinners; everyone misses the point. We better start worrying about the world we live in, instead of the petty shit; the petty shit God handles, or he would if we let him, but man has always done stupid things," sighed Sara, "always will."

"Sounds like you don't like your other life," said John.

"It's a mixture, good and bad. You can't have one without the other. I must say, I became obsessed with the diary. The things Sara wrote about don't do this place justice. Each day I find something new that amazes me, it's so beautiful. But I worry about my family at home. I miss my children and grandchildren. God, I got three grandchildren," smiled Sara. "Here in this life I'll probably never have children." Sara started laughing.

"What's so funny?" asked John.

"Back in my times, if I looked like this and still was a virgin, there would be lines of men ready to deflower me. Here I can't give it away," laughed Sara.

"You love children don't you?" asked John.

"Yes, there's nothing like a baby to make you feel like a woman. Men can, but a child is always there to give you love for no reason other than you're mom, the different type of giggles that let you know it they're having fun or in something they shouldn't be. No, I feel a child is the most previous thing God can give you and should be treated as such," said Sara. "Little fingers, toes, don't get me going." John sat Sara down and rested.

"You sound different than the other people in your time," said John.

"Oh, there's probably other people who think like I do. I've just never met them. I'm a homebody. There's nothing out there that I want, so why waste my time looking?" laughed Sara. "People try to be good, they just don't know how. There's just so much bullcrap that by the time you sift through it all, you're too old to care anymore. I feel lucky though, I got to see the past and future. If I didn't have a family in the future, I'd stay here. I love it here. Why not, when I have big, strong men to carry me?" laughed Sara.

"Well, this big, strong man is tired of running after you. I need a break," said John, laughing.

"Spoiled sport," teased Sara. "I can't get over how warm these nightgowns are. Wish we had flannel like this in my time. Well not many women like flannel like I do. They wear these sexy nightwear. It's supposed to turn a man on," said Sara.

"Why don't you ever talk about your husband?" asked John.

"Tom? Tom's hard to describe: tall, bald, beer belly, always wears blue jeans, T-shirt and sneakers. He works for the state of New York, does channel surfing, bowls, golfs, lives in the past. He's an 'if only' person; if only this happened, if only that happened. He does not look into the future, lives for the day," Sara paused, choked back a sob. "Screws everybody but his wife."

"Your husband sleeps with other women?" asked John shocked.

"Yup, brags about it, too," said Sara. "End of story."

John learned when Sara said 'end of story' nothing else would be said, so he dropped it there. "Let me look at your foot," said John. The swelling was staying down, that was a good sign.

"When I get home, I can wrap it, put it up, take two aspirins and get the fruit tomorrow," said Sara.

"But I thought you didn't want to get the fruit," said John.

"Changed my mind. I need something to keep me busy or I'll go nuts. I can't just sit around, I'll go nuts," said Sara.

"I know where you can get nuts, all kinds," said John.

Sara was sitting with her legs straight out in front of her. Her arms propped on either side of her to hold her up in a sitting position. John was in a squatting position dressed in blue jeans, a blue flannel shirt, and boot moccasins. Staring ahead, his long, black hair flew in the breeze behind him.

"Do you think you father would let me get some?" asked Sara.

"Under one condition," said John.

"What's that?" asked Sara.

"You make more of those cookies, only with nuts," said John.

Sara pushed on John's arm, "those cookies are for you. I saw the way you ate those cookies," laughed Sara.

"Yeah, but I must ask my father's permission," laughed John.

Sara shook her head. "John Red Feather, you're bad," laughed Sara.

"Yeah, but do I get some cookies?" laughed John.

"Yes, I'll make you some cookies," laughed Sara.

John lay down on the ground and looked up to the sky. The moon is so full and bright," said John.

"That moon your looking at, Americans will send a rocket ship to on July 20, 1969. A man named Neil Armstrong will walk on the moon. He will be an American, and it will be a step for all mankind," said Sara.

"A man will walk on the moon?" asked John, surprised.

"Yup, makes us feel small and useless down here, if you stopped to think about it," said Sara.

"No man is small and useless," said John. "Every man has a purpose."

"Yeah, in the future it's to be an asshole," said Sara, lying down and staring into the sky. "You know in the future cities, big cities will have so many lights they can't see the stars," said Sara.

"What do they look at when the moon is out like this?" asked John.

"The moon, that's all they see. I live in the country, this country, and I sit on my porch at night and watch the sky; it's so beautiful," said Sara, yawning. "Boy, I'm tired. It's probably eleven o'clock, the latest I've been up since I've been here."

"A man walks on the moon," said John, staring at the moon.

"So many changes, who would believe. Well, look at the changes in your time, the great Oskanondonha, who came to be known as Skenandoah," said Sara.

"You know Oskanondonha?" asked John surprised.

"Yes, he was one of the Oneida Indian Nation's most important leaders. He was in the American Revolutionary War. He was the wampum keeper of his nation, and the originator of government to governments. He was a noble man, projecting a tall, intellectual, and dignified demeanor. He was a fierce enemy but a stalwart friend. Skendandoah prevented a massacre of settlers in German Flats and encouraged the Oneida Nation to fight on the side of the Americans during the Revolutionary War. His fellow Indians called him the white man's friend."

"Skenandoah signed two treaties with the federal government. The first treaty recognized the Oneida sacrifices and help during the Revolutionary War. The second was the 1794 Canadian treaty, which recognizes Oneida sovereignty land rights and tax freedoms. The treaty is celebrated by the nation each year in Canandaigua to celebrate the November 11, 1794 signing. The treaty remains in effect in my time. Oskanandoah's pipe is on exhibit at the Shakoiwi cultural center in Oneida. The pipe is an important part of the nation's culture, because Gov. Tompkins gave it to him. It was engraved, 'presented by Gov. Tompkins to Skenandoah.' Smoking tobacco was closely associated with public business, so a gift of a pipe is appropriate," said Sara.

John had rolled on his left side and was listening to Sara talk. "If those treaties are still honorable in your time, then why are we changing things now?" asked John.

"Well the problem isn't with all the government but some of the government and a lot of people," said Sara.

"Show-of-force people," asked John.

"Yes, these people are raising a stink because Indians live tax free. Our taxes are high. By the time you get through totaling it all up, we pay like 90 percent. The money you make is taxed before you get it, then everything you buy is taxed. But you see we wouldn't have to pay taxes if they legalized gambling, but you've got groups who complain about gambling, although the Indians have casinos and make tax-free millions, which ruffles a lot of people's feathers," said Sara.

"That is Catch-22 you were talking about?" asked John.

"Exactly," said Sara.

"You know a lot about our people," said John.

"Yeah, well, I was an ugly child, so I buried my face in books so I wouldn't have to see all the things that I was missing that was going on around me. I never had a date, never went to the prom, there was a lot of things I didn't get to do, so instead of saying, 'Wooh is me,' I decided to learn everything I could that didn't involve any contact with people. They call people like me loners. We're not loners, but outcast from society. Society doesn't want people like me around," said Sara.

"People like you?" asked John.

"Long story; another time," said Sara. "Now I want to go home and go to bed," said Sara.

John looked at Sara's foot, it was starting to swell again, so he picked her up and walked until they were home. Sara fell asleep.

"John's here; he has Sara," called out Susan.

Sean ran out and took Sara out of John's arms.

"She fell, hurt her foot, I carried her for five miles, give or take. I soaked her foot in cold water. It was worse, that's why it took so long," said John, following Sean in the house. "I'm sorry it took so long, but that foot was bad. I couldn't take any chances, I had to soak it."

"You did good, John," said Susan. "How about some coffee?"

"Give him some chocolate chip cookies," said Sara. "He loves them; he earned them."

Sean laid Sara on the bed and looked at her foot. "What I wouldn't give for an Ace bandage right now," whispered Sean. "We'll have to use cotton bandage; Tylenol would help a lot, but Jacob and Susan are here."

"I know," said Sara. "Sean I can wait until they leave. That cold water John soaked my foot in took the swelling down a lot. The swelling was starting to run up my leg, the pain was awful. The water was cold but felt so good," smiled Sara.

Sean wrapped Sara's foot in silence. He hurt physically and mentally. Could he ever forgive himself? He could only blame himself if she gave herself to John. When he screwed up, he screwed up big time. Sean did everything he could to avoid looking into her eyes to see if the look was there, so he just stared at her foot as he wrapped it.

"Thank you," said Sara.

Sean propped her foot up on a folded quilt. Sara slid down, her nightgown slid up. "Sara you cut your leg."

"I know, it hurts bad. I thought it was the ankle," said Sara.

"Let me see," said Susan as she walked over. "Sara, that's not good. You need stitches. I'll stitch it for you."

Sara's eyes flew open. "You'll what?" asked Sara.

"I'll take care of it Susan," said Sean. "I want to clean it good first so there's no infection. You can boil some water if you like."

"It needs stitches," said Susan.

"And I will give her stitches, but first I want to clean this out and sterilize everything I need," said Sean.

Okay, you do it," said Susan. "I was only trying to help."

"So am I. What would happen if Sara kicked you?" asked Sean.

"You're right, I wasn't thinking," smiled Susan. "I'm so sensitive these days. I think everyone's against me, when actually they're trying to help me. I can't wait to have the baby to be my old self again," laughed Susan, handing Sean a bowl of warm water and a small glass.

"Hold my hand, Susan?" asked Sara. Sara was scared. In this time they didn't have Novocaine, they just sewed. Sean flushed the cut gently. A leaf fell out.

"What the hell is that?" asked Sean. The leaf floated on top of the water. "Anybody ever see anything like this?" asked Sean as he walked over to the table and set the bowl down.

John looked and froze right there. The cup paused on his lips. This whole thing was getting stranger and stranger.

Ben walked in. "You found Sara," smiled Ben. "What's wrong?" asked Ben. "Sara okay?"

"Well, she fell, sprained her ankle," said Sean. "I saw a cut, washed it out, and this fell out. Do you know what it is?" asked Sean.

John's eyes followed the bowl as Sean carried it to Ben. Ben looked from the bowl to John, who hadn't moved, then back to the bowl. "You got this out of Sara's leg?" asked Ben.

"Yes, the damnest thing I ever seen," said Sean.

"Well, I don't care what it is. The pain is gone, the swelling is gone, I feel great," smiled Sara.

"May I see your leg," asked Ben.

"Sure," smiled Sara. "Seen one leg, you've seen them all."

"That is a moon flower leaf," said John. "May I see it?"

"You can have it if you want," Sean said, laughing.

"We call it moon flower for many reasons," said Ben. "But it's a very special flower for us, a very special flower." Ben looked at Sara's leg; it was fine. There was a crescent moon cut on her leg.

"Damn," said Sean. "I didn't see that. Look it has a small white flower on it."

John looked. "That flower wasn't there before." He looked at Ben who crossed the room and looked at the flower, then John. John shook his head; he was just as shocked as Ben. "The bud must have been there. The water probably made it blossom. They're sensitive plants, that's why they are so special to us," said Ben.

"Well, everything's fine here, so I'm taking Susan home," said Jacob. "Must get up early to start work."

"Sure," said John, puzzled as he looked at the flower.

"We're going too," said Ben.

"Don't forget about tomorrow and picking fruit," said Sara, walking over to the table. "Leg feels great."

John smiled, "Tomorrow then. I'll see you then." John looked at Sara and shook his head.

"What?" asked Sara.

"You just don't stop, do you?" asked John.

"Don't need to," smiled Sara.

"May I have the flower?" asked Ben.

"Sure, bring the bowl back tomorrow," said Sara.

"Thank you, now go to bed and rest," said Ben as John and Ben left.

"I didn't want to hear it, father," said John.

"The nation will have to see this when we get back," said Ben.

"Did you touch her?" asked Ben.

"No, the flower proves that; she asked me to. I put my duties first," said John. "I couldn't just love her once. She wanted me to. She wanted me to get her pregnant tonight, and I refused," said John.

"Why did she want to get pregnant tonight?" asked Ben.

John sat down. "Something about a diary she found in her time. She was supposed to get pregnant tonight. The son she bore was to fight for our rights. She knows about us, our leaders, our ways. I couldn't do it. You don't know how I wanted to. I couldn't love her once and leave her. I knew once wouldn't be enough; a lifetime wouldn't be enough," said John. "I love her; she's so honest and pure. I couldn't do it."

"Son, the signs: the white buffalo, the white moon, the virgin, the white moon flower. There's never been a white moon flower. She's our spirit guide. She's pure; the ground was white when she came."

"I know the signs. I try to understand the old ways. It was you who made me go to the white man's school, learn both ways, you said. Well, I did and right now it's confusing me," said John. "I will meet with counsel tonight. Show Sara where the fruit and nuts are, then I will go away for a while to think this through. You will be chief while I'm gone. I will talk to Sean in the morning," said John.

"What will you do if the prophecy is true?" asked Ben.

"I don't know," said John, standing up. "I just don't know. There never was one word about it being a woman," said John. "Never."

"A spirit guide can be anything, even a hawk," said Ben.

"I know," said John. "Half of me believes, half of me just can't believe it."

"John, if she comes to you tonight, you two must," said Ben.

"And if she doesn't come to me, then I won't worry about it," said John.

"But she will come one night, if not tonight, one night within a year," said Ben. "You two belong together forever. It's written in the stars. It's been told by our ancestors. We will call counsel now," said John.

"I'm going to bed," said Sara. "I just want you to know that John didn't touch me. I'm a virgin and will remain one until I return to where I belong. I understand your feelings. I forgive you."

Sean's shoulders sagged with relief. "I'll be to bed shortly," said Sean. Sean cleaned the dishes and put them away, then went to bed.

Sara's loins ached with want of John, but she would keep her word and not ask him to love her. She fell asleep. She dreamed of her and John in the field in the moonlight, how safe she felt in his arms. Tonight she had a memory, a good one. When she returned to her time, she would always remember the moon and the smells of the night. One special memory is all she asked of John, and he gave her that.

Sean's dreams were strange to him. He held a long list, and he was checking things off on the list as he went along. The last was to return home, so Sean knew that he would return home when everything here was done. This brought relief to Sean's soul. The only thing that he worried about now was Sara returning home to Tom. Sean hated Tom with every fiber of his body. Maybe if he talked to Ben, Ben could change their future like Sean changed theirs and have Sara marry Sean. The future. Sean sat up right in bed. He'd have to live through getting shot again! Their children would lose both their parents. Would he come back here again? Would this thing keep repeating itself, or did it end here? What if it kept happening over and over until they straightened out all the problems in the world? Would they end up in a perfect world? History could keep going in his life, where he got shot and came back here, over and over. God, how many times would I have to get shot to fix the world?" he thought. Sean's eyes flew open; he wasn't sitting up, he was sleeping. "No dreaming," said Sean. The sun was coming up.

"What?" asked Sara sleepy.

"Nothing, go to sleep," said Sean, relieved he spoke out loud. His body was soaked with sweat, so he gathered clothing and soaps and went to the quarry to bathe. John showed up the same time.

"I'm glad to see you," said Sean. "We need to talk."

"Yes we do," said John. "You first."

Sean talked, John listened.

Then John talked and Sean listened.

"I know you find what I say hard to believe, but it's been written and told for years," said John.

"No, I believe you," said Sean. "I really do. It all makes sense to me now. Before it was all crazy. Now I understand."

"Well, I wish you would explain it to me because I don't understand it at all," said John.

So Sean explained the whole thing to John.

John listened closely. What Sean said made sense, all of it.

"Thank you," said John. "Sara must never know. It's all in her hands now. I must talk to Ben. Ben can handle it from here. You are a friend, Sean, a true friend and always will be."

"Well, right now I could use a cigarette," said Sean. "I miss my cigarettes."

"I didn't know you smoked," said John. "Here, have one." John pulled out a pack of cigarettes.

"Oh God, thank you," said Sean, lighting up. "Cough, cough, cough. A little stronger than I'm used to. In our time I smoke lights, so does Sara, but there the government is trying to take cigarettes away from us, say they cause cancer. Hell, everything in our time causes cancer," laughed Sean. "Even the sun."

"Is cancer a bad thing?" asked John.

"Yes," said Sean. "But it's just a case where they need something to gripe about, so they pick on cigarettes. When cigarettes are gone, it will be something else; it always is. People always look for excuses for death. They can't seem to accept death. To them there has to be a reason. There is God's reason, our punishment handed down from God for Adam and Eve eating the forbidden fruit. I know a lot of people who die from cancer who never smoked a day in their life. I've got this weird theory that just before we're born there's three big roulette wheels. The first one we spin to determine our sex, the second determines when we die, the third determines what we die from, and from the time we're born until we die, it's our life to make of it what we can. Then when we die, we get to choose to be born again or stay. Being born again puts you in hell because they say hell is on earth, to stay is heaven. I think that our paths cross many times. I know it sounds stupid," said Sean.

"No more stupid than our spirit guides," said John.

"Well, we don't know until we die, then all our questions are answered," laughed Sean.

"Here, take the cigarettes. I must go and talk to Ben. Thank you, now I don't have to leave. I see it all now," said John, who left to talk to Ben. It was so clear. Wait till Ben hears Sara is the spirit guide. There wasn't much time to waste."

John found Ben. "Father we must talk; it's important," said John.

Ben saw the look on John's face, so they walked and talked. He told him everything Sean said, how Sara was the spirit, and why this happened. Ben listened very carefully.

"Yes, this is true, all of it," said Ben. "There's much we need to do. Sean needs all our help now. We have much to prepare for, and when Sara comes to you, what will you do?" asked Ben.

"I will do what I've always wanted to do: love her forever. It's written in the stars," smiled John.

Sara sat at the table and wrote her whole life in the book, just like she promised John. She knew it was stupid, but she wanted him to have part of her after she left, to see her life through her eyes. Then she wrote, "I love you and I always will. You will always be in my heart forever." Sara closed the book and got dressed to go get fruit to can for winter. She mixed up a chocolate chip batter. She only had to add nuts, and John had his cookies. Sean walked in smelling clean and fresh.

"You're up early," said Sean.

"I started breakfast, figured Jacob and Susan would be here soon. I cleaned the house, thought I'd get laundry done before I went to get fruit. Where did you put the canning stuff you got at the hardware store?" asked Sara.

"On a shelf in the barn," said Sean, putting his dirty clothes in the laundry. "I saw John this morning. He's coming by with some men from the nation to help me and Jacob. He says October is coming too fast, and we may not get done in time, so I'll teach them what I know." Sean did a hook with his socks into the laundry basket. "Yes, the man scores two points," cried Sean.

"You seem awfully happy this morning," said Sara.

"I am. If John brings enough men with him, I'm going to empty out Susan and Jacob's house, put all the furniture in the barn, and get their place done today. Floor, bathroom, even the kitchen sink," smiled Sean. "Tomorrow I'll do ours, then Jacob and I can cut hay for winter. We're moving in the right direction," said Sean.

"If you say so," said Sara, "But you ain't tying up this house for more than one day, I've got canning to do," warned Sara.

"I won't," said Sean.

"Did you see the pig had her piglets last night?" asked Jacob, walking in. "She had six of them."

"Six?" said Sara. "I checked on Bessy, but never thought to check on Porky. We'll have pork chops this winter," smiled Sean.

"What are you so happy about?" asked Susan, walking in.

"Seems John is coming over with some men, and they plan to have your place all done with running water," laughed Sara.

"Really?" asked Jacob, surprised.

"Yup, your place today, my place tomorrow," said Sara.

"That means we'd have time to get hay in. God, that is great," said Jacob. "No, it's fantastic."

"Or a miracle," said Susan, staring at Sara.

"Don't start, Susan. I wasn't around for this one. This is between John and Sean. If you don't behave, Junior won't get any breakfast," teased Sara.

"Okay, it's dropped," smiled Susan, sitting at the table.

Sara got up, put food on plates, and set them on the table. "You'll have to stay here today while they work on your place. I'm going with John to pick fruit. I may get the berries today and can jellies today. The fruit will keep until my house is done, then I'll can them," said

Sara. "Oh, John's going to show me where I can get nuts so we'll have nuts for baking," smiled Sara.

"Boy, we will be set for winter," said Susan.

"Have you given much thought to Christmas?" asked Sara.

"No, I haven't. Why?" asked Susan.

"Well, I thought after everything is done around here, we'd take a trip to town and get what we need. Make up a list, then we wouldn't have to go to town again till spring," said Sara.

"Yeah, you're right. We could check and see what we don't have and then we'd be set for winter. I like that," said Susan. "Riding in the wagon wouldn't be so tough carrying the baby in my arms," laughed Susan.

"How's Junior doing?" asked Sara.

"Well, Junior could be a girl," smiled Susan, "and she's moving all over the place today," smiled Susan.

"You're right," said Sara. "I'd like a girl, myself. I can make her dresses if Mommy would let me."

"Well, at the rate children grow, any help sewing is never denied," smiled Susan.

The men were talking and never heard a word the women said. Sara cleaned the dishes and washed them. She picked up the laundry basket, went over to Susan's, got the laundry washed, and all the laundry hung. The men went over to Jacob's house and moved everything in the barn. They just finished when John showed up. Sean and Jacob were shocked at the men who were with him. Sean explained how they were going to do things. First the floor, then the wall, then the sink. Sean and Jacob would run pipes; the septic tanks were ready to go. Sara and Susan sat in the kitchen.

"Thank you for showing me what to do about the curse. I got it today. I think that's why I was so moody," said Sara.

"You're not going to can with the curse are you?" asked Susan.

"Yes I was, why?" asked Sara.

"They say that if you can with the curse everything you can will spoil," said Susan, shocked that Sara didn't know this.

Sara looked shocked at such an old wives' tale. But if one can went bad, Susan would say, "I told you so." "Well, can I crush berries, make jelly, and you can?" said Sara.

"Yes, that would work just as long as you don't touch the jars," said Susan, seriously.

"We'll do it that way then," smiled Sara, trying not to laugh out loud. "The things people believe," thought Sara.

John walked in. "We brought you apples, peaches, pears. I'll show you where they are if you need more," said John. "Then we can get nuts," smiled John.

"I remembered our deal; cookies are waiting for nuts," smiled Sara. Sara grabbed a couple of burlap bags. "Let's go." John walked, and Sara followed. The fruit trees were not far from the berries; the nut trees farther. Her leg started aching.

"Need to stop a minute," said Sara. "My leg is throbbing. I don't know why, it just started."

John turned around, he saw Sara the way she looked in her other life. She was beautiful. John shook his head. "We'll stop here." John looked around him. This is where it was going to happen, right here. He must remember this spot, the moon flower had to be planted here. "How's your leg?" asked John, touching it.

"That's strange, you touch it, it stopped," said Sara. "What magic fingers," teased Sara.

"Must be," smiled John. Only John knew why it stopped.

He took Sara's hand. "Well, it's not much farther," said John.

Sara couldn't get over how her leg stopped hurting. "Strange," she thought, "but everything was strange lately." She felt like Dorothy in Oz. This wasn't Kansas either. She clicked her boots lots of times; it did no good. When she opened her eyes, she was still here, trapped in someone else's life with only a diary to guide her. And that she couldn't do right. Sara sensed John was different today. "Probably less tense, knowing I won't rape him," laughed Sara.

"What's so funny?" asked John.

"Life," said Sara, "just life."

John helped Sara gather nuts. They chose walnuts, pecans, and chestnuts. While they gathered chestnuts, Sara sang "Chestnuts roasting on an open fire."

"What's that song your singing?" asked John.

"A Christmas song. Christmas means a lot to me," said Sara.

"Oh!" said John.

"Do you celebrate Christmas?" asked Sara.

"At this time no, but I don't know about the future," said John. "We may take on many of the white man's ways. I don't know. What's Christmas like?"

"Well, we bring a pine tree in the house, we decorate it, we put pine and holly around the house, we put presents under the tree and open them Christmas morning," said Sara.

"What kind of presents?" asked John.

"Oh, things that you need, like clothes or a joke gift or something special, that says 'I love you,'" said Sara. "Santa Claus is Christmas."

"Who's Santa Claus?" asked John.

"He's a man in a red suit who makes all dreams come true," smiled Sara. "It's complicated and would take a long time to explain.

Of course, I have a lot of time, but I get the feeling you have something important to do, so I'll explain another time. I guess that should do it," said Sara.

John watched Sara. She sure felt a lot of things. He'd like to know how she did it. "You're right, I do have something to do. It won't take long," said John. "I'll take you home first."

"I can get this. I know my way back," said Sara.

"And if your leg hurts? You won't have my magic fingers," smiled John.

"You're right," said Sara.

On the way back, Sara heard many hammers at work. "I think it's nice you brought men to help Sean and Jacob. Thank you. I know they worked hard, but they never would have gotten done what they plan to have done. Thank you."

"The pleasure was all ours. You have helped us, so now we help you," said John.

All of the nation knew who Sara was and watched Sara and John walk to the house. They saw Sara the way she really looked with John beside her, the shadow of the spirit guide stood behind them. The gods were here. John was embarrassed. He knew why they watched them. Sara felt a little ill at ease with so many men staring at her. She put on her best smile and walked right by them saying, "Hello." They nodded in response and returned to work. John put the nuts down next to the fruit and left. He had to find Ben.

"It's weird how the men stare at me," said Sara.

"Why, you and John look good together; you look like you belong together," said Susan.

"Well, that will never happen. Sean is my husband and John will be leader of his people some day, and I don't figure into it anywhere, so any romantic notions you have, you cast them out with the miracle bull crap," said Sara. "Now I have to crack some nuts. I promised John some cookies for helping me. By the looks of the men out there, I'll be baking all day," laughed Sara, putting walnuts on the table.

"Can I ask you one thing, then I promise never to say anything again. Throw it out with the miracle crap," laughed Susan.

Sara put more walnuts on the table. She stood up and sighed. "Okay, as long as it ain't stupid," said Sara.

"Do you love John?" asked Susan.

Sara rolled her eyes. Susan wasn't going to give up.

"Yes, she loves John, they belong together, but she won't admit it," said Sean.

Susan's mouth dropped open. Sara's own husband saying that John and Sara belong together.

"You two are impossible," said Sara. "Would you say Sean's trying to get rid of me?" asked Sara.

Susan laughed. "You scared me. I thought Sean meant it. I'll get used to his humor some day. I've got to admit you had me going for a while, Sean."

"What are you doing here? I thought you had work to do?" asked Sara.

"I do, but I wanted to ask Susan if she wanted sink only or full cupboards," smiled Sean. "And to tease you."

"She wants full cupboards, and I don't need teasing on a PMS day, thanks to you," said Sara.

"PMS?" asked Susan.

"Bad hair day," laughed Sean.

Sara threw a towel at Sean. "Go work. Leave me alone. I've got a lot of cooking to do," said Sara.

"And lots of help," smiled Sean.

"Yeah, right," said Sara. "In your dreams."

Susan watched the two of them and didn't understand anything they were talking about.

"No, look out the window, the nation's women brought food," said Sean.

Sara look at Sean puzzled.

"Look!" said Sean.

Sara looked out the window. Women were setting up tables and placing food on them. Susan looked, then looked at Sean, then Sara.

"Miracles, I don't think I'll throw this one out," said Susan.

"You both can forget it. I happen to know that the Indian woman is a hard-working woman, who thinks highly of her men, and this is normal for them to do this. And I had nothing to do with this, so forget it," said Sara.

Susan giggled. Sean shrugged his shoulders. Sara started cracking nuts for cookies. Sean left smiling.

Sara threw nuts in the cookie dough. Susan watched Sara with a smile. Sara put spoons full of dough on cookie sheets and placed them in the oven. "Okay. Let's have it," said Sara.

"What?" asked Susan, smiling.

"That look on your face. You're bursting to tell me something, so let's have it," said Sara, sighing.

"You and Sean finally got around to it," said Susan.

"No, he wished the curse on me, and he's happy about it. And I want to kill him right now," said Sara.

"I don't care what you say, he's happy, and you're upset. Well, the first time's a little rough, but after that, it's great," said Susan.

Sara said nothing, just rolled her eyes and took the cookies out of the oven and put in some more.

"I knew it," said Susan. "I feel better now."

Sara felt like running away somewhere and crying. People were no different in this age as they were in her time, ready to talk sex. Here she's trying not to think about it, and every ten seconds it comes up. She could be just imagining it right now. Sara took the cookies out of the oven and put in some more.

"I'm going outside, it's nice out. You won't let me do anything here, so I'll go meet my neighbors," said Susan.

"Okay," said Sara. "I'll be out shortly to help."

"No, you don't help, my dear," said Ben, walking in with John following. "The women want to do this for you."

"Miracles," said Susan, going outside.

"Trapped, that's how I felt today, a caged animal. I need to be alone. I've never had people around me so much." Sara took cookies out of the oven. "Sit," said Sara to John. She poured coffee for Ben and John; set cups in front of them. Sara put a plate of hot cookies on the table. "They are better warm. Don't worry, John, your batch of cookies are over here," said Sara.

"You seem upset," said Ben. "What's wrong?"

"I've got this feeling I want to run away again," said Sara. "I don't know where I'd go or why, I just feel I need to go far away. I get this feeling like everything is closing in on me, like too many people around, like I need to be alone. My head started pounding a little time ago. Maybe I'm just tired," said Sara. "Maybe I need a nap. I don't know anymore; up-tight, heebeejeebees."

"Here," said John, standing up. "Maybe I can help: magic fingers," smiled John as he massaged Sara's shoulders, neck, and head.

"Oh God, that feels so good. You do have magic fingers," said Sara. She felt all the stress leave as John rubbed.

Ben watched carefully. He looked to see if he could see what John talked about. Ben nearly jumped when he saw the real Sara. John stood behind Sara rubbing her shoulders, his eyes closed. A warm glow seemed to surround them. An ancient Indian guide stood behind them with eagle wings spread wide. Sean walked in, he froze in the door and stared. It was the most beautiful thing he'd ever seen. If you didn't believe in God, what Sean saw right now would make anyone drop to their knees and pray. Hot tears ran down his cheeks; this was so beautiful.

Sara moved her head. "Those fingers are magic, I swear to God."

"Feel better now?" asked John, removing his hands and walking over and sitting down.

Sean wiped at his eyes, feeling foolish having seen his Sara. He cleared his throat. "They're ready for lunch," said Sean.

Sean and Ben walked out together. Sara and John walked out together. Ben asked Sean if he'd seen what Ben saw. Sean told him what he saw. "That's what I saw, and I don't believe it. I've seen it and still don't believe it."

John asked Sara if she felt like running away now.

"No," said Sara. "I'm fine. I've got cookies baked, and my promise to you was kept," teased Sara.

"You're true to your word, my princess," said John.

"Princess, what an odd thing to say," thought Sara.

Everyone sat down to eat after Sara. She was talking to John about getting some berries for jam after lunch. "I know I shouldn't harp on this canning thing, but it will keep me busy. I'll feel better knowing there's food put away for winter. Even in my other life I stored food for winter. I can a lot of food, but I buy food and store it as if it were old times," said Sara. "This is strange to a lot of people, but I get comfort knowing I can go to my pantry and it's there. I believe in a lot of the old ways."

"I see nothing wrong with the way you think," said John.

"This food is good," said Sara. "Real good."

"Yeah, it is," said Sean.

Everyone ate and talked when they finished eating. The men went back to work. The women cleaned dishes and took everything away. Susan went and lay down at Sara's. Sara went to pick berries. Sara felt comfortable being alone. It felt like being home: quiet, peaceful. She loved Jacob and Susan, but friendship got old very fast when you were together twenty-four hours a day. Everyone needed time alone. Sara understood that right now it was hard. Nothing was settled, time was limited, that early snowfall scared everyone. Poor Susan was so close to delivering that just getting up and down exhausted her. Time here was funny. It seemed to go by fast, but the days seemed long. There was so much to do, you got a lot done in a day; time wasn't broken up like in her time. There was no such thing as a nine-to-five job. You worked all day, you took time to eat, then back to work. No TV, stereo, or phones to take you away from what you were doing. Here you worked and worked hard just to survive. Nothing came easy here. You had to give our forefathers credit when they said they forged the way; they meant it.

Sean and Jacob were amazed by how much they had done. Another hour, and they would be done. That included putting the furniture back inside. It looked real fancy as far as Jacob was concerned: wood floors and ceilings, a bathroom with a tub, a slate sink, and cupboards. Also, there was some kind of fancy light Sean made for over the table that held six candles with glass globes. Sean put two candles on the wall in the bedroom, one on either side of the bed. The bathroom had candles on the wall; Sean called them scones. Jacob looked around; the place was right pretty. Susan would love this. Right now Sean and Jacob were hooking up hot water. Whoever heard of hot water? Running hot water, that is. Jacob was surprised at how little space was lost with putting a bathroom in, but the barn was 30 feet wide, which made his house 30 feet long by 16 feet wide. Sean called it a trailer, whatever that meant. Jacob didn't care, he knew he and his family would be safe for winter and warm, too. Sean ran some kind of pipe under the floor and put in registers. Damnest thing he ever saw. The heat came off the wood stove under the floor and up. He said it would keep the pipes from freezing. Sean was a smart man. Don't want heat, then close the register. Right now Jacob stood by the sink waiting for Sean to tell him to turn on the hot water. Sean built a row of cupboards on one end with cupboards over the top. Jacob told him Susan didn't need that much storage, but Sean said she'd fill it, that woman never had too many cupboards. Seemed like a waste of time and money to him.

"Okay. Jacob, turn it on," called Sara.

Jacob turned it on. At first it was cold, but damn if they didn't have hot water.

"Got it!" yelled Jacob.

Sean and John walked in. Sean tested the water in the bathroom.

"There you go, hot running water and a toilet. No more running outside," laughed Sara.

"This is nice," said John. "Real nice."

"Sean calls it a trailer," laughed Jacob. "I call it home."

It was only three o'clock in the afternoon. With this many men, Sean suggested they start his place. "We know what we're doing now. It shouldn't take too long. We've got the cupboards built. If we get the major stuff done, we're home free," said Sean.

"Slave driver," said Jacob.

"Me, look at them, they're getting everything set to go," said Sean.

John laughed. "They like your ideas; they say you are a smart man."

"How long did you plan to stay today?" asked Sean.

"Until dark, when we could work no more, why?" asked John.

"Dark! We could have my place done by then. How many men do we have, fifty?" asked Sean.

"Sixty, including the young men," said John.

"See, we could have my trailer all done by then," said Sean.

"Let's do it," said John. "Let's move everything out and do it."

Jacob shook his head and laughed. Two slave drivers. "Let's go. I'll get Susan and take her home. Wait till she sees this," said Jacob.

"Susan, you can go home now, we're done, and we're going to do Sean and Sara's place," said Jacob.

"Sara's going to be mad, she wanted to make jelly when she got back," said Susan, sitting up on her elbows.

"Well, she can make them at our house. She'll have a sink to work at, running water, even hot," smiled Jacob.

"Really?" smiled Susan.

"Yes, wait until you see how nice our home is now," Jacob smiled proudly.

"Well, help me up, and I'll see what has you smiling like that," laughed Susan.

Jacob helped Susan up. She'd gotten huge the past couple of weeks. She waddled when she walked. He knew she couldn't wait to have the baby. She kept saying she wanted to see her feet again or bend over and pick something up instead of squatting.

"Okay, close your eyes," smiled Jacob.

So Susan did, smiling. "This must really be something," she thought.

"Okay, we have a small step up here, only a couple of inches. There you go, keep your eyes closed," said Jacob as he led Susan to a spot. "Okay, open."

"Wow," cried Susan as her hands flew to her mouth. "Jacob this is beautiful. Oh, the cupboards, a floor, a real floor to sweep."

"Look at the bathroom, tub, sink, toilet, with running water, hot water, too."

"Oh, Jacob, oh, Jacob," cried Susan. "I love it, it's beautiful."

"Look, Sean put lights on the wall and ceiling. No more running outside to go to the bathroom," said Jacob, flushing the toilet. "Sean put some kind of finish on the wood that makes it shine."

"It all looks the color of honey, it's so beautiful," said Susan.

"Well, I've got to go, they're emptying out Sean and Sara's place. Their place won't take as long. We've got most of the stuff done."

Sara came back carrying berries, feeling comfortable and knowing she was going to be doing something that she knew how to do. She stopped. "What, what the—," she thought. Her stuff was outside. Berries couldn't wait to be done up. Sean promised her. "I'll kill him," Sara said to herself.

Jacob saw Sara; he knew that look. She was pissed, really pissed, so he ran up to her. "You'll have to can at our place. I thought it would be easier since we have a sink with running water, both hot and cold," smiled Jacob, taking some berries.

"A sink, running water?" smiled Sara.

"Yes, we should have you all set by tonight, too. Even have a toilet and the bathroom hooked up," smiled Jacob.

The thought of soaking in a hot tub of water changed Sara's mind. "Your place it is," smiled Sara.

So Jacob helped carry berries to his place.

"Oh, Jacob, this is beautiful," said Sara, walking in.

Jacob smiled, set the berries on the table, and left. At least Sara had calmed down.

Susan was sitting at the table smiling. "I can't get over this. This is beautiful. I never thought I'd own something this nice. Everything is the color of honey. Look, they put wood on the ceiling; it's so pretty."

Sara looked around. "They did one hell of a job. Oh look, real cupboards, a real sink, no more pans of water to dump. Now we need curtains and rugs, and we'll be set for winter," smiled Sara.

"Curtains, rugs? Sara, I never thought I'd have a home to live in for a long time, let alone curtains and rugs," laughed Susan.

"Well, I bought material to make curtains and doilies with and yarn we can make rugs out of. Let's do some canning the right way," smiled Sara. "We have running water."

"I thought you would be mad because Sean promised you that he'd do your place tomorrow," said Susan.

"Oh no, running water is more important," smiled Sara. "Sean's a doll."

Susan raised an eyebrow and didn't say a word.

"I've got to wash my hands, then we'll start," said Sara.

Sean walked in carrying boxes of canning jars, pints, just what Sara ordered. "Thought you would like these," smiled Sean.

"Sean, this is beautiful," said Sara. "You've outdone yourself on this."

"Thank you, I must admit Jacob and I never would have had this done before winter without the nation's help. I don't know what we would have done. They have sixty men helping, that's a lot of men. We'll have our place done today, a day ahead of schedule, hell months ahead of what Jacob and I could have done," said Sean. "Need anything else?"

"Sugar and pectin," said Sara.

"Okay, I'll be right back," smiled Sean.

Susan watched these two. Last night Sean sent her away; today they're the best of friends. "They made up last night," thought Susan, smiling.

"What are you smiling about?" said Sara.

"I can't believe my baby is going to be born in such a nice place," said Susan. "I never dreamed of this."

"Yeah, it's real nice," smiled Sara, taking a pail of berries off the table. "Where's your strainer and measuring cup?" asked Sara.

"Corner, over there. I don't know. The corners not there?" laughed Susan.

"Men must have put them in the cupboard," laughed Sara as she opened the cupboard doors. "Got them. The guys didn't do to bad on putting stuff away here."

"Good. I never could have gotten someone to do it," said Susan, laughing.

Sara stopped, looked at Susan; she really felt helpless. That last month was a bitch. It seemed to drag on forever. "Well, it won't be long before you will be doing things again, any time now. I know it doesn't help much, but once you have him, these past few weeks will all seem worth it. Just think: a baby, a real baby, not a doll, but a baby," smiled Sara as she washed berries and sorted through them.

Susan laughed. "You sound more excited than me. I'm having the baby."

"Well, you know, I get right into things," laughed Sara as she measured the berries in a pan and crushed them.

Sean walked in with sugar and pectin. "Here you go," smiled Sean and he left.

"Thank you," said Sara as she filled the sink with water. She shredded soap into the water with the grater. Susan watched. She was surprised. "I never thought to do that," said Susan.

"Do what?" asked Sara.

"Shred the soap? I always cut it with a knife, then you get left over chunks. That's a good idea," said Susan.

"Well, at my house I shred a bar of soap into a jar, put in some water, and just pour out the liquid. I make sure it's stirred well and set it next to the stove to keep it soft. You don't waste any soap that way," said Sara.

"Mmm, liquid soap. I like that idea," said Susan.

"When I'm done, I'll make you some," said Sara. "Only use a little, though, because it seems to be I don't know soap when it's liquid," said Sara as she put jars in the water to soak.

"Yeah, I'd like that," said Susan.

Sara measured sugar and pectin, mixed it together, put in on the stove to cook slowly, stirring while in between washing jars and lids. Sara put a huge pan of water on to boil; the jars were going in there. The first batch of jelly was done. Sara set it aside to let it cool so she could skim it. The hot jars and lids she set in front of Susan on a towel. She gave Susan the jar rubbers after she dunked them quick in boiling water. Susan filled the jars and sealed them. This was what they did until the berries were all done. Sara filled four pans with water, placed the jars in water and let them boil. Sara cleaned up the mess and put everything back where she found it. The aroma of fresh-made jelly permeated the air; the men's stomachs growled with hunger.

Ben walked in. "What are you making, it smells so good,"

"Jelly," laughed Sara. "Blackberry, blueberry, roseberry, and elderberry. Want to try some? I have blackberry and elderberry left over, fresh-baked bread."

"Talked me into it," said Ben, sitting down at the table.

Sara and Susan laughed. "That wasn't hard to do," said Sara, cutting a slice of bread, putting it on a plate. "Which kind of jelly would you like to try first?"

"Elderberry, I love elderberries," said Ben smiling.

"Elderberry it is," smiled Sara as she set a small bowl of elderberries in front of Ben with a knife.

"This is good," said Ben. "I like this real good."

Sara said, "Thank you" as she took jars out of the water and put more in. "The only jellies I won't make this year are strawberry and grape," said Sara. "Too late for strawberries, and I have no grapes. If I had peanuts, I could make peanut butter, which goes good with jelly, but that's all next year," smiled Sara.

"Will you show the women of my nation how to make these jellies and peanuts?" asked Ben.

"Sure, no problem. But you need peanuts," said Sara.

"We grow peanuts. I have peanuts. No peanut butter or jelly, but I have peanuts," smiled Ben.

"Would you like some more?" smiled Sara.

"Didn't think you would ask," smiled Ben.

Sara sat the bread on the table and jelly and said, "help yourself."

"I want some, too," said Susan. "It smells so good."

Sara cut Susan two slices of bread, and put them on a plate with a knife. Ben passed the jelly. Sara checked the jars and covered them with a towel.

"I thought I'd find you in here," laughed John.

"Jelly. Sara's jelly is so good," said Ben in between bites, "try it."

"He's always where the food is. We make jelly, don't let him fool you," laughed John.

"Not like this, try it," said Ben, handing John a slice of bread with elderberry jam on it. "Eat."

John shook his head, laughing. "Okay." He took a bite. He looked at Ben.

"Told you it was good," said Ben.

"God, this is great," said John.

"She'll teach our women how to make this. We need berries and peanuts," said Ben.

"Peanuts?" asked John.

"To make peanut butter," said Ben. "Oh, grapes, Sara needs grapes and strawberries."

Susan was on her third slice of bread. This was heaven.

"Ouch," cried Sara. She burned her hand taking out some bread. She thought she'd make bread for supper. She had six loaves made and six in the oven. Then Ben mentioned strawberries, and Sara wasn't paying attention to what she was doing and burned her hand. "Ben, you don't have to give me strawberries, you probably have just enough to get your nation through the winter. I don't want to take your food away from your people. You've been more than kind to me," said Sara.

"We had good crops this year. You teach my women what you know, and we pay you in fruits; we barter," smiled Ben.

"Barter? Barter is where you swap one thing for another. I'm not swapping anything. I'm only showing. You have been more than generous to us. You've done more than we could ever repay you for," said Sara.

"She's got you on that one," smiled John.

"No, she doesn't. We're indebted to them for saving our land, our hunting grounds, our growing fields, and our lives. That far outbeats our one day of work," said Ben.

"He's got you there," said John, reaching for more bread.

"No, he doesn't," said Sara.

"Oh, is this going to be good," smiled Susan.

"Think so?" smiled Sara.

"Think so," said John. "Sitting down."

"Yup," said Susan, spreading jelly.

"You owe us nothing, we are friends; friends help friends, friends don't take food out of someone's mouth just because he wants it," said Sara.

"But if a friend sees a friend is hungry, and his stomach is empty, he will give the friend his food," said Ben.

"But if that friend has a family of many, and the friend is one who won't accept that food knowing he is taking away from many," said Sara.

"But the friend is only one. He eats less, so if everyone gives a little, everyone gets to eat," said Ben. "Sharing is better than starving."

Sara stared at Ben for a minute. "But, if that friend takes that one thing only because he doesn't have it but has lots of other things that would keep him from starving, then that person is greedy," said Sara.

"Oh, but if that man barters what he has a lot of for what he doesn't have, then he's a smart man, and they both have some," smiled Ben.

Sara thought for a minute. "But if the only thing that friend has is knowledge, then nothing is ventured," said Sara. "The friend still has knowledge and food; the other friend has some knowledge and less food," said Sara, feeling confident she had Ben.

John and Susan were laughing.

"But the knowledge is the most important thing the friend could gain," said Ben.

"How do you figure that?" asked Sara.

"He now knows not to barter with him again," said Ben. "He has found that he's not a friend."

Sara threw her arms in the air. "You win," said Sara.

"That's why I'm chief," laughed Ben. "I always win."

John and Sara burst out laughing, tears rolled down their cheeks.

"No, you win because you're a very smart, old goat," laughed Sara.

"That, too," laughed Ben.

"You're not going to let me have the last word, are you?" asked Sara.

"Nope!" smiled Ben. "I'm chief, I always get the last word."

Sara bent over the stove, took out the last of the bread. She made it early this morning and let it rise. "You win," said Sara. "I concede."

"Thank you," smiled Ben, crossing his arms.

"What's up," asked Jacob, coming in.

"Ben and Sara are having a battle of wits," said Susan.

"Who won?" asked Jacob.

"Ben," laughed Susan.

"Good man. Nobody gets Sara," laughed Jacob.

"You behave," said Sara. "I know I can outwit you," teased Sara.

"You're right on that," smiled Jacob. "What smells so good?"

"Homemade jelly and bread," said John. "The best I've ever had."

"Well, it smells good. Everyone's stomach is growling out there," said Jacob.

"Oh, no you don't. I made this for supper," said Sara.

"But by supper the bread will be cold," smiled Jacob. "We've worked so hard we need bread. Hot bread would get us through."

"They sent you in here, didn't they?" asked Sara.

"Yes," laughed Jacob. "The smell is killing us. Please."

"Men," said Sara. She lined the bread up on trays and put jars of jellies on another tray. "Take it." Jacob passed it out the door. Men grabbed plates and passed it on. "Might as well take all the coffee. I don't have a lot of cups. You wash the cups and pass it on," said Sara.

"Thank you. You're an angel," smiled Jacob.

"Well, you tell them that was for supper, " said Sara.

"I will," said Jacob.

"I guess I could make pies for supper," said Sara.

"What kind?" asked Ben.

"I have apples, so it will have to be apple," said Sara.

"I like berry pie," said Ben.

John and Susan smiled.

"You're going to be difficult, aren't you Ben?" said Sara.

"I'm not difficult, just always right," smiled Ben.

Sara laughed. "Okay Ben, what kind?" Sara grabbed a berry pail.

"All of them," said Ben.

"All of them?" said Sara.

"Yes, all of them. I'll eat a little of each pie. I like pie, berry pie."

"I guess I can pick enough berries to have them cooked by supper," said Sara. "If I didn't like you, you would get what I made and like it," smiled Sara.

"You'll make me pies because I'm chief, and I'm always right," teased Ben.

Sara laughed.

"I'll help you," said John. "It will take less time." John grabbed two berry pails and walked with Sara to the berry patch.

Susan laughed. "I know what you're doing," said Susan.

"I'm doing! I'm sitting at the table talking to you," smiled Ben.

"No, you're trying to get John and Sara together. I happen to agree with you. They belong together. I don't know why, they just do," said Susan.

"Sometimes the gods misplace souls, souls that belong together. The only way these two souls can be happy is to become one. If they don't become one, their life could never be complete. Life is a circle; if the souls are complete, the circle grows. If a soul is misplaced, then the circle can never be formed, and life is incomplete. Then future and past generations are lost."

Susan stared at Ben as he talked. She did not understand one thing he just said. She smiled.

Ben saw the confusion. "You and Jacob are one complete soul. You bring forth a child. The circle is complete," said Ben.

"That's why Sara and Sean can't be a couple. Their souls don't belong to one another. Sean knows this, and that's why Sean sent Sara to John," said Susan.

"Yes," said Ben.

"But John and Sara didn't couple. Why wouldn't these souls know they belong together?" asked Susan.

"John was stubborn; Sean talked to him. They would come to understand.

"Now it's up to Sara. No one can choose for her. She has to decide. The future has been told. Sara is the only one who can change it," said Ben.

"I get it," said Susan. "If Sara chooses Sean, the circle dies. If she chooses John, the circle grows."

"Yes, but we can't tell her to choose or who to choose," said Ben.

"Sean went to John and told him," said Susan. "So this morning when Sean told Sara she loved John, he wasn't joking. Sara and I thought Sean was teasing her."

"What did Sara say?" asked Ben, interested.

"Sara told Sean to stop picking on her on a PMS day, that he cursed her, and Sean said PMS was a bad hair day," said Susan. "She was upset."

Ben laughed. "Sara has the curse."

"Oh!" said Susan, blushing. "Now I know why she's upset, and what they were joking about. I'm really stupid sometimes.

Ben knew Sara wouldn't come to John soon. Last night she was fertile, that's why the flower was white, a fertile virgin.

"Why can't we just push those two together?" asked Susan.

"Because the love won't be pure. The love has to be strong and full like the moon. They both have to feel the love so it will blossom like a moon flower," said Ben.

"So if they spend some time together, the love will take over," said Susan.

"Yes," said Ben.

"But if she leaves Sean and goes to John, isn't she in sin like the Bible says?" asked Susan.

"Only if the marriage was sanctified, but it's not," said Ben.

"Because Sara's still a virgin, she's married only on paper and not in the eyes of God, because she had not coupled. I understand," said Susan.

Chapter 4

JOHN AND SARA PICKED BERRIES ACROSS FROM EACH OTHER SO THEY COULD face each other and talk.

"Is your father always so stubborn?" asked Sara.

John laughed. "My father likes you," said John.

"Well, he has a funny way of showing it," said Sara. "He's stubborn."

"No, my father is chief. He gets what he wants, no question," laughed John. "You challenged, and I believe he enjoyed it. He gets you going on something because he knows you will challenge him."

"Well, I try my best," said Sara, laughing.

"Sara, may I ask you something?" asked John.

"Sure, I hope I know the answer," smiled Sara.

John thought about it for a while. He didn't want to upset Sara or have her misunderstand him. "Would you tell me in your own words how you know what you truly think about your husband, not what you think I want to hear, but what you feel in your heart?" said John. "Truth only."

"I hate him," said Sara, putting her hand down.

"Why, because he sleeps with other women?" John asked tenderly.

"That's one reason, but there are many," said Sara.

"Tell me," said John.

"I feel he took my life from me. He's self-centered, dirty, mean, and lazy," said Sara.

"I know nothing of the future. How can he take your life from you?" asked John.

"I never had a life. I went from my parents to my husband. All I did was go from cleaning, cooking, and babysitting for my parents to cooking and cleaning for my husband. I know this is what I'm supposed to do, but when you're married to a man who you can never please, what should be pleasure becomes a chore. Nothing I did was good enough. He degraded me in front of everyone by correcting everything I said or did. I'd cook a meal. It usually wasn't good enough: too hot, not done, burned. I don't care how good it was, it wasn't good enough for him. I did washing and ironing daily. He'd come home, take off his clothes, bitch and yell. I never did anything. Then he had to bowl, golf, or just go out, but the clothes he wanted to wear were dirty, so I'd have to stop what I was doing and make sure his clothes were washed and ironed. Then he'd wear something else out. Supper had to be on the table when he walked in, so I usually had a cold supper. If he yelled because the dishes were on the table too long, I didn't eat supper. No matter what I said, it was wrong. I was never allowed friends, but I had to put up with his friends and their wives. I was never allowed in the room when he had sports on. I walked in the room once during the Super Bowl. It was just to give him supper, and he threw the supper on the wall and beat me. Everything had to be scrubbed spotless. If he found one thing wrong, he'd rub my face in it to get it as clean as he liked. I'm never allowed money. I left the house twice a month to shop, so I had to get everything I needed on those two days. I was allowed so long in each store. If I spent too long in one store, he'd drag me out, yelling at me, take me home, and bitch at me all the way there. Telling me how inconsiderate I am. He always did what he wanted; everything revolved around him. He hates my family and has done everything he could to make them hate me more. He wipes snot on the wall, then makes me clean it. His underclothes smelled of perfume. They're stained with semen and shit. I have to clean it so he can go out and screw other women, then he comes home and tells me how good they screw and how ugly I am. I'm tired of being degraded. In my other life, I'm fifty years old. Fifty years of everyone degrading me. Here everyone thinks I'm the greatest thing in the world. Everyone loves my cooking. The only thing I'm lousy at in this world and mine is sex, so I decided to do without it. Is that a clear enough picture for you?" said Sara, wiping a tear from her eye.

"The only thing I miss is my children; the rest they can keep. Here my life has meaning; there my life is mean." Sara turned and walked away.

"What would you change then, just your husband or your whole life?" asked John.

"Well, we can't choose our family, but friends you can. I can't change my parents or I wouldn't be who I am. My husband would definitely go. I've been saving money so I could leave him. I know I'd get ridiculed greatly over it, but I would rather live on the streets than to live with him anymore. But you promised if I go back, you would be my husband," laughed Sara.

"I don't think I could be your husband if I had to be like him," John said seriously.

Sara laughed. "John, I wouldn't want you to be like him. I would want you to be you. I'd change nothing on you. I'd walk down the street with you. Women would have heart attacks looking at you. I could laugh at them for a change. I could go to bed with a man I love and one who loved me instead of a deal made for me," said Sara.

"Your mother bartered you away?" asked John shocked.

Sara laughed. "Yes, that is one way of looking at it. Well, now I must go make some pies; must make Chief Ben happy."

John laughed. "My father eats anything, he loves to eat."

"Well, he better be happy I'm making his favorite," laughed Sara.

Ben was gone when Sara and John got back. John set the berries on the table and went out to help Sean.

"Where's Ben?" asked John.

"Went back to his village," said Susan.

"I'll tell you, I'm looking forward to a hot bath tonight," said Sara.

"You take a bath when you have the curse?" asked Susan.

"Yes, that's when you need them the most, to keep you clean," said Sara.

Susan didn't say anything. She was always told never go near water when you had the curse. There was a lot you couldn't do. Sara believed a lot of strange things lately, but she was always right. It was like she was always a step ahead of things.

"I found some pumpkin," said Sara, coming in with jars and pie pans. "I think we have enough pans between the two of us." Sara started making pie crust and rolling it out, putting it in the lined tins. She mixed up filling and poured them in the pans. She put tops on them and baked six pies at a time on cookie sheets.

Susan watched Sara put the pies on cookie sheets. She had to ask, she just couldn't let it go. "Why the cookie sheets?"

"Oh, it catches the spills so you don't have to clean the oven, and it keeps the pie crust from burning on the bottom," smiled Sara. "Momma's secret."

"That's how she did it? Very smart on your mother's part," laughed Susan.

"If there was a way to cut time, my mother could find it," smiled Sara thinking. "Not my real mother, my dream mother." Sara was peeling apples with Susan.

"Everyone loves your jelly and bread, wait till they taste your pies, they will never leave," laughed Susan.

"Oh my, we can't have that. I can't cook like this every day," laughed Sara.

"You're making peach pie, too?" asked Susan. "That's a hard one to do."

"Oh, I'll show you an easy way," said Sara. Sara got up and checked the pies in the oven. They were done, so she set them on the counter to cool and put in more pies. "I guess they got the counters in just in time, or these pies would be all over the place," laughed Sara.

"Something smells real good," said Jacob, walking in.

"Oh no, this is for supper. You turn right around and go," said Sara, standing in front of the cupboard, arms stretched out.

"Can I go to the bathroom first," laughed Jacob.

"I don't care what you do. You're not getting the pies until supper." The apple pies made, Sara and Susan peeled peaches. Sara showed her how simple peach pie was. "Keep walking, Jacob, no tasting at all," said Sara. "Go!"

"I'm going," said Jacob. "I just wanted to tell you that we're just about done."

"Supper's in about one hour. Ben said the women are on their way; the pies are just about done, just put the last of them in the oven," said Sara.

"I'll get back to work," said Jacob.

Sara had some berries left so she made that into jelly. It more than made up for the jelly that she sent out with the bread. Tomorrow she'd can pie filling and applesauce. Maybe apple butter, too. That took eight hours to cook. Or maybe she'd do up the peaches and pears before they spoiled; apples kept longer.

"Sara, Sara," called Susan, "Sara," yelled Susan.

Sara shook her head, lost in thought, "What?" said Sara, turning around. "Oh God, not now," said Sara.

"Afraid so, junior chooses now," said Susan doubling over in pain.

"Okay, breath like this," said Sara, blowing out, pant, pant, puff.

"Why?" said Susan.

"To make sure your lungs are full of oxygen," said Sara. "Breath in deep, let it out slowly. How long have you been having pains?"

"These pains or the pains I've had throughout the day?" asked Susan.

"You've had pains all day?" asked Sara.

"Well, backaches and cramps, nothing like this," said Susan.

"Breath in deep, let out slowly; in, out, in, out," said Sara as she pulled the bedding off the bed. She pulled out sheets and towels and made the bed lightly. "In, out, in, out." Sara took a nightgown. "In, out, in, out," said Sara as she washed her hands. "In, out, in, out."

"Ahhh," Susan doubled over. Sara ran to her, she helped Susan to the bed, took off Susan's clothes, and put her nightgown on. Sara helped her lie on the bed legs up. Susan was close. "In, out, in, out," said Sara.

"Ahhh, ow, ow, oooh no," said Susan.

"That's good, we have the head, one more push we'll have the shoulders. You're doing good," said Sara. "Take a deep breath on your next pain, grab your knees and push, got it?" said Sara.

"Ow, ow, oooh," said Susan lying down.

"I've got it, we've got a boy," said Sara. She cleaned the baby's mouth and nose. The baby cried. Sara laid it on Susan's stomach; she cut the cord. The afterbirth came with a push into a bowl. Susan took the second bowl of water and cleaned up Susan. "Well, girl, we did it. I'll wash the baby off and dress him, then get Jacob. Where's the baby's clothes?"

"Shelf in the closet, right corner," said Susan.

"Got them," smiled Sara.

She flushed all the dirty water down the toilet, ran warm water in the bathroom sink, laid the baby down on the side board, and gently washed him, dressed him, and returned him to Mommy. All dirty laundry was picked up, and Susan and baby were comfortable. Sara walked over to her place. "Jacob," called Sara. "Jacob."

John, Jacob, and Sean turned around. Sara had blood on her. "It's a boy," said Sara.

"Susan had the baby?" all three men asked at once.

"Yes, a very healthy boy. I must take pies out of the oven. They are probably burned. Would you like to see your son?" asked Sara.

Sara made a plate for Susan and slipped away. Susan was sitting up in bed watching the baby sleep.

"Sara, he's so beautiful. He looks just like Jacob, brown hair and all," laughed Susan.

"I brought you some food," said Sara, "and to see how you are doing."

"I have got to go to the bathroom," said Susan.

"I'll help you, your legs will feel like rubber," said Sara.

"Rubber?" asked Susan.

"Wobbly," said Sara.

"Oh," said Susan. "I see what you mean."

"That's okay, I've got you. You may feel light-headed, but don't worry, it's your body adjusting," said Sara.

"My feet, I can see my feet," laughed Susan as she sat on the toilet slowly.

"You may have to change your pads quite often today and tomorrow, but after that it will slow down," said Sara.

"How do you know so much about having babies?" asked Susan.

"Mother told me so I wouldn't be afraid," said Sara.

"That sounds like Rachel," said Susan.

Sara wished she'd known her mother in this life. At times she sounded so nice. "Let me know when you're ready, I'll help you up," said Sara.

"My belly is like jelly, it feels so funny," laughed Susan. "Not as funny as having a baby. I wanted Jacob, but at the same time I wanted to kill him for getting me pregnant, but when you set the baby on my belly and I felt him wiggle, I was so happy. I made life, it was so fast. It was like a hundred feelings running through me at once. Somehow it all seemed worth it," smiled Susan.

Sara remembered her first time having a baby, Tom Jr. You could put up with anything. That feeling you had when the baby cried was well worth it.

"Ready?" said Susan.

Sara went into the bathroom and helped Susan up. "Can I eat at the table?" asked Susan.

"Sure, you should move around some. If you don't, you'll catch pneumonia," said Sara. She knew in the old days like now women either stayed in bed or got up, depended on the culture or belief. "Hold on to me, and we'll go slow," said Sara.

Susan sat at the table. "How long before my legs stop shaking?"

"Maybe tomorrow or the next, depends. Tomorrow you will feel a lot better," said Sara.

"Jacob told me they finished your house, and Sean had a surprise for you. What was it?" asked Susan.

"I don't know, I haven't seen it yet. With Sean it could be anything," laughed Sara.

"I know I was shocked when I saw Jacob and Sean made me a cradle. It's so beautiful," said Susan.

"Yup. Put those two together, anything can happen," said Sara. "Want some pie?" asked Sara.

"I'd like to try peach," said Susan.

"I'll see what we have. Ben's got the pies in front of him," laughed Sara.

"Ben is so funny, I love him; he's a good man," said Susan.

"He's chief and is always right," said Sara in a deep voice. "I'll be right back."

Susan laughed, "Oh, that hurts. God you got Ben down cold," said Susan.

Sara returned with some pie. "Ben is relentless. He had to tease me when I was out there," said Sara, setting the pie down. "That man is a big, cuddly bear," said Sara.

"Don't let him hear you say that," said John. "He's chief, but again you would probably get away with it, he respects you so much."

"Me? Why me?" asked Sara.

"Because you're different than any other white woman he knows," said John.

All three men said, "Yes."

"Go," said Sara. Sara went into Jacob and Susan's house for the pies. They were just starting to turn brown, so the pies were safe. The baby and Susan were fine. Jacob looked like the proud papa. Sara slipped away, went and got clean clothes, towels and soap, went up to the quarry, and washed up. It was one hell of a day. Sara sat on the rocks, dirty clothes wrapped in the towel laid next to her. Sara brushed her hair in the breeze. With the warmth of the breeze and the wetness of her hair, it formed curls. Brushing her hair seemed to have a calming effect on her. She was scared shitless delivering the baby. The only thing she knew about delivering a baby was what she saw on TV, but Susan thought Sara could do it. The baby really did the work, all you had to do was catch it.

"You did good," said Sean. "Are you okay?"

"Fine, I got washed, which helps," said Sara.

"Well, we're done with our place, and supper's ready," said Sean.

"Okay," said Sara, getting up.

Sean grabbed the basket of clothes.

"You've really done a lot today. I must admit that bread and jelly were great. It reminded me of sitting in your kitchen trying out your new recipes. You're probably the best cook in the world," said Sean.

Sara looked at Sean funny. Why was he being so nice to her? "Why are you pampering me?" asked Sara.

"I always knew you were a very hard worker. I know Tom never did much and treated you like shit, but you seem happy here. What you do here is pretty much what you do at home, isn't it?" asked Sean.

"Pretty much," said Sara.

"Well, Tom doesn't deserve you. I see how hard your life has been, and I wish I could change it for you. I just want you to know I do appreciate what you've done for me," said Sean. "It just seems everyone relies on you no matter where you go. We don't mean to take advantage of you, you just seem strong enough to handle things."

"Well, Dr. Emerson has a surprise when he comes out tomorrow," laughed Sean.

When Sara and Sean reached their home, everyone applauded Sara. She felt embarrassed, but she smiled and bowed to them. Two worlds, both the same one, yet so different. In this one, she's a hero for what she did; in the other one, she would have been a fool and criticized for it. And she didn't have to do the work, Susan did. Jacob ran up to her and hugged her. "Thank you, he's beautiful," said Jacob.

"Don't thank me, thank Susan. She did all the work," said Sara.

Ben stood up from where he sat at the head of the table and made Sara sit there. Sara started to protest. Ben said, "I'm the chief, I'm always right." So Sara sat down. John felt proud. A chief never gave up his seat, especially to a woman. This was a high honor, one Sara earned.

Sara leaned over and whispered to Ben, who sat on her left. "This is so you get closer to the pies, ain't it?"

Ben laughed. "That's right, you know me too well," said Ben.

A first-born son meant a lot to the Indians. It showed strength, wealth, power; this was all good. Tonight everyone would celebrate a new life, a new beginning in friendship. Sean and Jacob had made Susan a cradle. Now Susan and baby slept. After Sara ate, she would take Susan a plate of food and check on her and the baby. Ben was true to his word; he ate a little of each pie.

"All pies are good," said Ben. "You're a very good cook."

Every one of the men told Sara how good her pies, bread, and jelly were. They told the story of how Jacob got the bread. Sara watched and listened. Everything ever done here was praised whether it be big or small, it never went unnoticed. They had to. All they had was each other. Without praise or gratitude, nothing would get done. You encouraged each other to keep going, no matter what.

"He's right," laughed Susan. "This pie is great."

"Thank you," said Sara. "Why am I so different than any other white woman?" asked Sara.

"Let's see, your dress, your openness, your concern for things around you, you jump right in and give a hand, you don't whine and cry when something doesn't go the way you want, just to name a few," said John.

"Then Ben hasn't seen my temper," said Sara.

"You have a temper? Never," said Sean, laughing. He had empty pie plates in his hand.

Sara stood up, walked over to the sink, and started doing dishes. She had left a mess when Susan decided to go into labor. She washed and dried everything, put Susan's jellies away, lined up her jellies on trays, and made Sean and John carry them to her place. She gathered up her pans, set them on the table, and helped Susan to bed. "If you need me, send Jacob, I'll come right over," said Sara.

"I know you would, you've been so good to me," said Susan.

"I made up a bunch of rags for you. They're under the sink in the bathroom. They may look different than what you're used to, but you don't wash them, you throw them away. These you burn," said Sara. "I'll be over in the morning to get laundry. I'll bring breakfast. Now you rest, you'll need it."

"I am tired," Susan yawned and slid down into bed.

Sara picked up her pans and walked across the barn. There stood Jacob, Sean, and John. "What?" asked Sara.

"You have to close your eyes," said Sean.

"I'll take the pans," smiled Jacob.

"We have a surprise for you," said John. "Sean said you had a certain taste for things," laughed John.

"A what?" said Sara.

"Take a step, face toward your right, that's good, now open your eyes," said Sean.

Sara opened her eyes slowly. "Oh my God, an island with stools. Oh God, it's a place to cook things on. Oh God, that, oh that, oh thank you guys," said Sara, hugging each one of them.

"I don't know, Sean, it doesn't take much to get a hug and kiss from her," teased John.

"Pou-pah," said Sara, playfully hitting John's arm. She ran over to the island. "This is great. I love it."

"Well, we always seem to have a house full, so I made sure we had more seating. Over here is your corner nook dining set. I figured no living room, so we'd make a huge-ass kitchen," laughed Sean.

"God, I love it. Thank you," said Sara. "Oh the canning I can do!"

"Plus a little something special in the bathroom," said Sean. "Come this way. See, a shower," smiled Sean.

"A shower?" said Sara. She wanted a tub not a shower. She smiled and looked, a tub and shower head. "Oh, Sean that's great. Oh God, a linen closet. Oh, thank you guys," said Sara.

"Since our bathroom is two feet longer than Jacob's we had to put a long counter top on. I left one section open. You still have plenty of room in here," smiled Sean, looking from the bedroom out to the kitchen.

"Do Jacob and Susan have a shower?" asked Sara.

"Yes, but we figured with a baby they would need more space, so we didn't put a closet in," said Sean. "Well, I've got some animals who need tending."

Sara went right to the kitchen. Never in a million years did she think she'd have an island again. This made the stay here worth it. "I'll make coffee. You gentlemen can have a seat," smiled Sara, pointing to the stools.

"I don't want to leave Susan and the baby too long, so I'm going home for the night. Sean said he would do the chores so I could be with Susan. I told him I'd do them, but he insisted I be with Susan, so I better go be with Susan and my baby son," smiled Jacob. Jacob's smile lit up the whole room.

"Yes, you belong home," smiled Sara. "Go!"

Jacob left, smiling all the way home. "A son."

John sat down. "I'll have coffee only if you have one with me and sit at the island with me," smiled John.

"That I can do," smiled Sara, pouring two cups of coffee. She sat next to John.

"I like this island," said John. "I'm big, it gives me room."

"I love it. When I cook I can put everything right here and just start mixing," smiled Sara.

"Sara, I was so scared when you came in here and had blood on you. I thought you hurt yourself. It took awhile for it to sink into my brain that Susan had the baby. How come you didn't ask for help?" asked John.

Sara laughed. "There was no time. Susan had been in labor all day and thought they were normal aches and pains you get with being pregnant, so she said nothing. In this time, women are more tolerant of pain. In my time there are so many drugs that no one should have pain, so we tend to be less tolerant," said Sara.

"Your time has a lot of good and bad," said John.

"Yes, it's very confusing. Sometimes the people, they can be good. They can get together like we did today, but it takes a tragedy for them to do this. They're so involved in themselves and their lives they don't realize what they can do if they got together. Then some tragedy happens, they bond together and feel good helping. But once that's over with, they stop caring again. Oh, they may have made new friends, but in our time travel is easy, so people always move more away," said Sara.

"Travel is easy? How?" asked John.

"We have planes that can take you from New York to California in four hours, cars that would get you from here to Rome in ten minutes. Trains take you everywhere. There's buses, motorcycles, boats, all kinds of boats, big ones, little ones, vans, trucks, snowmobiles, jet sky bikes, jet skies for the water. Travel is easy," said Sara.

"All these things move you fast?" asked John.

"Yes, people are in a hurry to go nowhere and back," smiled Sara.

"Your lifetime sounds rushed," said John.

"It is if you let it be. We have phones. These are devices you talk into. If used right, they're good. But most people use them to gossip. You see, gossip can travel faster this way, and you don't have to leave your house. You sit at the kitchen table, make phone call after phone call, and, in a matter of minutes, you've destroyed someone's life," said Sara.

"What's the good thing this phone does?" asked John.

"Well, if someone needs help, they dial 911, and in seconds they have help. If there's a family emergency, in seconds they help you. I use the phone to order things. Usually in three days, it's delivered to my door. If someone is sick, you can still talk to them. If you miss a loved one who's moved away, you can call and talk to them. This is why Bell invented the phone for good things. But you have bad people who use it for bad things," said Sara.

"Gossip?" asked John.

"Yes," said Sara, leaving it there, thinking of the nasty phone calls she got from unknown women about Tom, or her mother calling to complain how bad Sara was. Here no phone rang, only silence.

John saw a sadness in Sara's eyes, but said nothing. Sara had been hurt so much he didn't want to bring up anything that would bring back the hurt.

"You look tired," John said softly.

"Yes, but it's a good tired," said Sara.

"There's a good tired?" asked John puzzled.

"Yes, good tired is a job well done. A bad tired is one's mind full of ghosts who won't let you sleep," said Sara.

"Yes, I understand. We all have a good tired tonight," said John.

"Yes, everyone worked hard today," smiled Sara.

"And we learned a lot: plumbing, heating, hot water, all good things," smiled John. "I was surprised when Jacob came out with the bread and jelly. We all smelled what you cooked; our stomachs wouldn't stop growling. It was awful. Ben's growled the loudest. He said you would give in to him," laughed John. "You always do."

"Ben is something else," laughed Sara.

"What am I?" asked Ben, walking in smiling. "Thought I'd see if you had any cookies and coffee."

Sara got up, walked over to Ben, gave him a big hug, and said, "You're my big teddy bear, and I needed to hug my teddy bear because I love him, even if I'm not supposed to. I get a hug, you get cookies," said Sara.

Ben hugged her. "I love your barter system, something for nothing," laughed Ben.

"Don't you start," teased Sara, walking to the pantry and taking out cookies.

Ben laughed. "You're my angel. You always have love and cookies for me."

"Please don't call me an angel, Susan already thinks everything I do is a miracle. Calling me angel will confirm her beliefs," laughed Sara.

"Okay, you're a princess," laughed Ben.

"Princess I can live with. I'm a poor one, but princess sounds good," laughed Sara, pouring Ben coffee.

"Princess," smiled Ben.

"Why do I have a sudden feeling that you're trying to pull a fast one on me, Ben Green?" said Sara.

"I don't know," Ben said smiling.

John shook his head, laughing. "You two," he said, taking a cookie.

"Haven't you had enough cookies by now John?" asked Sara.

"I didn't get any, Dad ate them," laughed John.

"They were good, too," laughed Ben.

"You have a sweet tooth, Ben," laughed Sara.

"No, you're a good cook," smiled Ben.

"How do you know. All you eat are my sweets," teased Sara, leaning against the sink.

"I ate your breakfast, I ate your stew, I ate your chicken and biscuits, liked all of it. You are a good cook. You know how to feed a man," said Ben.

"Thank you," said Sara, embarrassed. She wasn't used to all this praise. "Oh, before I forget," Sara walked over to the pantry. "This book has everything written down from now until my time. Everything that's important and causes severe changes in everyone's lives. This will guide you through the years. I wanted to make sure that you had it in case I go back to my time. I don't know what will happen to this Sean and Sara. If it's our souls that switched and we switch back, you two will have to fill this Sean and Sara in on what happened. I've been keeping a diary, so has Sean. They are always right here. You can keep them, but this Sara and Sean will have to read them, so they won't feel like we do right now," said Sara.

"How do you feel?" asked Ben.

"Confused, yet lost. Sean has done a lot of things the other Sean didn't do only because he's seen the future. Jacob and Susan can be told about us after we leave, then it may make sense to them," smiled Sara.

"Do you like it here?" asked Ben.

"I love it here. I don't miss any modern conveniences we have in our time. This is me. If I could take this and move it there, I would," smiled Sara.

"What do you love here?" asked Ben.

"John, the nation, you, the quiet, the land, the fruits, the trees, the breeze. Everything but my boots. They're 100 percent better than those other things they call ladies' footwear, but I'm used to feeling the ground I walk on. Barefoot is good, but outside you need something on your feet. These are heavy," said Sara.

"The boots are the only thing you've complained about since you've been here," laughed John.

"It's the only problems I see," smiled Sara.

"Only one thing wrong is not bad," said Ben.

"No, it's not. At home I've never been this happy. The boots I can learn to live with," smiled Sara.

"Well, we must go," said Ben. "The women of the nation will be here tomorrow. You teach them all you know about canning and cooking. We don't want it lost to us forever," Ben said laughing. "I've chosen ten women who will teach the others."

"Okay. I will write everything down as we go so no step is missed. And I have a feeling you'll be here to sample everything," laughed Sara.

"I'm the chief, I have to," laughed Ben.

John shook his head, laughing. "You should have named her Sunshine, the way you light up when you think she's going to argue with you," laughed John, reaching for the notebook. Tonight he would read it.

"Oh, there's a letter in there for Jacob and Susan. When I'm gone, I want them to know I'll still think of them as my friends. Even in the future I will remember then, always."

Ben wiped a tear. "It sounds like you're leaving us now," said Ben.

"No, but I like being prepared. I don't want to leave any hurt feelings," smiled Sara. "I don't know if I'll ever get to go back. You may never get rid of me."

"Would that be so bad?" asked Ben.

"No, I could be happy here. But could you put up with me?" laughed Sara.

"You're so wise," laughed Ben.

"You two can go at it tomorrow. Sara's tired and needs some sleep," said John.

So Ben got up and walked out with John. Sara cleared up the dishes, and looked around her kitchen. She was very pleased with her kitchen. It was getting dark out, so Sara lit the lamp, went in the bathroom, and changed her clothes. She felt a sense of home. "There was no couch to curl up on, no place to sit and relax, a couple chairs would fit on that wall," thought Sara. She cocked her head to one side, trying to picture two chairs and a stand there when Sean walked in.

"What are you thinking?" asked Sean.

"Oh, a couple chairs would look good there, and a stand in between with foot stools, something to curl up in," smiled Sara. "Maybe blue."

"Yeah, a place to rest after a hard day's work," smiled Sean.

"Well, I'm going to bed, I've had it," said Sara.

"Me, too. I've been thinking about that shower all day," laughed Sean. "I can't get over how much we got done in a day," said Sean.

"No TV, no phone, nowhere to run to, you can get a lot done," said Sara, yawning as she pulled the covers back on the bed.

"You're right," said Sean as he closed the bathroom door.

Sara climbed in bed exhausted.

Sean showered and shaved. That shower felt like heaven. He had to do some jerry-rigging to make one, but it was worth it. Sean walked into the kitchen, picked up the oil lamp, and walked over to the bed. He put out the lamp and went to bed.

John lay on his bed reading the ledger Sara had written. So much had happened, it looked so grim and bleak. But Sara had written the outcome in such a way that you felt there was a chance for mankind. That one day they would figure it out. Man has a chance if he would learn from his past mistakes, but mankind is a slow learner. God help us all if he never learns. The past and the present are the same; the only thing different is man's knowledge. If we could change the past, would the future be different or does man have to live in the past and the future to understand the present?

John read this several times. For some reason this made sense. Today was yesterday and tomorrow. One day was it all as time went on.

Every day in life was important. This fascinated John as he read everything. Sara made notes here and there. John felt what Sara felt as she wrote. Then John read about Sara's life. This was written with all her heart. The hurt and pain was all there, written for man to see. The changes she wanted in her life, her little one-line jokes. John sat up, "She loves me." He had to have one more chance to prove he loved Sara. She had to come to him this time. He wouldn't let her down this time. He would show her how much he loved her.

Chapter 5

SARA WOKE WITH THE RISING SUN. SHE WAS FALLING INTO A ROUTINE. SARA felt so rested. It had been years since she felt so rested and calm. Each day was a pleasure to which to wake up when you had a good sleep and knew you wouldn't wake up to a stressful day.

Sara made breakfast fast and took two plates over to Jacob and Susan. Jacob was in the rocking chair rocking Jacob, Jr. Sara smiled and thought how much the two looked alike. Susan slept. Sara made coffee for them. Jacob said, "Thank you."

"I put breakfast in the warmer for you," whispered Sara.

Jacob nodded. Sara tipped-toed quietly out of the house, and walked through the barn to her home. Sean had awoken and was sitting at the island drinking coffee. Sara made the bed, went back into the kitchen, got breakfast for her and Sean, and joined him at the island.

"What are you drawing now?" asked Sara.

Sean took a sip of coffee. "Well, I was thinking about what you said last night," said Sean.

"What did I say last night?" asked Sara.

"The two chairs. It's not a bad idea. Winter's coming, and there will be less to do. We can't sit in the kitchen all the time. We will need something comfortable to sit on. I was thinking if I put a wall up and blocked the bedroom off, we'd have a small area for a living room," said Sean. "What do you think?"

Sara looked past Sean to the bedroom area. "Yeah, that would work. The Christmas tree could go there, the rocker in the corner. It would look nice."

Sean laughed.

"What?" asked Sara.

"Must be October, you're talking Christmas," said Sean.

"I can't help it, it's a sickness with me. I live for Christmas," said Sara. "Jacob and Susan should have a wall, too."

"Don't change the subject. I've been watching you and living with you for four weeks now, and nobody knows you like I do, and Christmas is not your problem," said Sean.

"Not my problem, how can you say that? I live Christmas twenty-four hours a day, 365 days a year. I swear every breath I take in and let out says Christmas," said Sara.

"No, you're a giver, and you care too much," said Sean, taking a drink of coffee.

"Okay, Mr. Smarty Pants, what do I give and what do I care too much for?" asked Sara.

"You give of yourself, asking nothing in return, and you care for everyone you come in contact with. I swear your heart is made of pure gold," said Sean. "I've never seen anyone as trusting as you."

"Well, look where my trusting nature got us. I had to drag you along with me. I even fucked up your life," said Sara.

"You didn't fuck up anything. I think God sent me here to guide you and watch over you. It's a job I accept willingly, plus I've learned a lot here, so don't think that you ruined my life for one second. I love it here," said Sean.

"You do? So if we don't get back, you won't hate me?" asked Sara.

"Hate you? How could I hate you? You've made me the happiest man in the world. As far as I'm concerned, this place is perfect," said Sean, smiling. "I know you love it here."

"Yes I do. The only thing I regret is that I have to leave some of this behind. Sometimes I wish this was like that TV program, you know, the one with the portal," said Sara.

"Sliders?" asked Sean.

"Yes, this big hole opens, and I stand on one side and throw everything I want to take with me in the hole," laughed Sara.

"Well, I hope it's nothing big. It could kill us when it fell on us," laughed Sean.

"Well, I would love to take the stove," laughed Sara.

"The stove?" asked Sean.

"Yes, I know it's not electric, but you can put six pies in the oven. The ovens at home are so small you get two pies in them. Then there's the dishes. I'd buy a set of twenty-four in the blue, use them for holidays, then about one hundred nightgowns, and ten bathrobes. Oh, the flannel sheet and quilts and…," said Sara.

"Whoa," said Sean. "By the time you got through sending all this stuff back, the portal would close and we couldn't get back," teased Sean.

"I know, it's crazy. I just want to take it back with me. It makes no sense. Material things can't make you happy. You make yourself happy, but this stuff is so comfortable," Sara said, smiling.

Sean shook his head. "You really surprise me at how much you love it here. It's not the material things you love, it's the simplicity," said Sean.

"You may think so because I've never been into material things, but the flannel here is heaven," said Sara.

"Whatever. That's a woman's thing," said Sean.

Jacob walked in, followed by John.

Jacob carried dishes. John carried baskets of berries. Both set them on the island. Sara poured coffee for them both, put the dishes in the sink, and took the laundry out to wash. Now she could wash in the tub. Kneeling would be a bitch, but soon Susan would be back on her feet and she'd only have Sean and her laundry that she could wash in the kitchen sink. "Life goes on," thought Sara.

When Sara came back out of the bathroom, Sean and Jacob were gone. John sat at the island alone. His mind kept going over everything he read last night. It was so much to handle, he gave it to Ben to read and keep. Now he had to make Sara love him.

"I'll be right back, I've got to hang these out to dry," said Sara.

"Here, let me carry this out," said John. "You work too much."

"Here all the time I thought I was lazy and didn't do enough," laughed Sara.

"Lazy, you? Never. You're always doing something," said John as he set the basket on the ground.

"Remember that spot I ran to when I ran away?" asked Sara.

"Yeah, what about it?" asked John.

Sara shook out a sheet and hung it on the line. "Well, there was a scent that was pleasing. I'd like to get some of those flowers. I'd like to dry them so I could make some decorations for my home. It would smell like summer all winter, and it would keep me from getting cabin fever. I thought sometime we could get some. I don't remember where it was. I ran to what?" asked Sara.

John had crossed his arms and was listening to Sara talk. He had a strange look on his face. "I was wondering if you ever stopped thinking of things to do," said John.

"No, there's always something to do," smiled Sara.

"After you teach our women today, I'll take you there. Soon you'll know where everything is, and you won't need me," said John.

"I'll always need you," said Sara. "I just don't want to interfere with your responsibilities."

"You're my responsibility," said John.

"I'm what? Who put you in charge of me?" said Sara, standing in front of John, who was looking up at him.

"My father, the chief," smiled John.

"Pray tell, when did this happen?" asked Sara. "And why did he send you to watch me?"

"This morning. Ben wants me to learn everything I can from you so I can become a good leader for my people. This future is shaky," said John.

"Okay, Ben is right again," said Sara. "I will teach you everything I know. I could do worse. At least I get the better end of this barter," laughed Sara.

"How do you figure that?" smiled John.

"Because I have you all to myself for as long as I want," smiled Sara.

"This pleases you?" John asked, smiling.

"Maybe," said Sara. "Depends on how good a student you are. If you're a bad student, this could take a long time, maybe more time than I have since I don't know how long I have. One day may not be long enough," said Sara.

"Oh, but you may have longer than one day," said John.

"This is true, but I don't know what you want to learn. What I learned took me a lifetime. This won't be easy. Can you live up to my standards?" said Sara.

John looked down at Sara, who was still standing in front of him. "I can live up to any standard you set, princess," John said smiling.

"Oh, my standard is high. You're going to wish you were chief. You will be pumped so full of information, your brain will hurt," said Sara, staring at John.

John smiled calmly. "Is that a challenge?" asked John.

"Yes! Now where would you like to begin?" asked Sara.

"Well, Sean said we were going to invest in the stock market. He explained everything to me, but I don't understand where we're going to get the type of money he's talking about," said John.

"Me," said Sara, bending and picking up the laundry basket.

"You, where'd you get that kind of money?" asked John.

"Let's go inside," said Sara. Sara walked inside. John followed.

"Is this some big secret?" asked John.

"Don't worry, the money is not stolen, it's mine," said Sara.

"I didn't mean that it was," said John. "You're acting like nobody is supposed to know about this."

"They're not, not even Sean," said Sara. "Do you understand me?"

"Yes," said John, curious.

"I've been saving money for a long time. Every time I got money as a gift or a little left over from groceries, coupon savings, things like that. I managed to save ten thousand dollars. I kept it in my Bible for years, then I bought this hope chest. I found a hidden place in it, so I put the money in there. Well, the money is still there, only in today's currency, so we'll use that to invest," said Sara.

"If Sean knows about the money, why can't I say anything?" asked John.

"Because I told Sean it was in case of an emergency, but he doesn't know how much I actually have. I was planning to leave Tom. That money I saved was to leave him. I don't want Sean to know I'm planning to leave Tom. I don't want anybody involved in this but me," said Sara.

"If it's for your freedom from Tom, why use it?" said John, sitting at the island.

"Believe me when I say this, my life doesn't matter. I put up with him for thirty-two years, I'm used to him now. I can do more good this way. Your nation needs it," said Sara.

"We can't take your money," said John. "We'll find a way."

"Yes you can, and you may find a way 150 years from now, but you can do it now. Believe me, if you think about it, one versus thousands, the thousands win. I'll be all right, I can find a way. I couldn't live with myself knowing I could have done something and didn't," said Sara. "I'll be fine. There are shelters I can go to. I didn't want to do it that way, but it is probably the best way. They have shrinks there, and my attitude sucks so maybe they can help," said Sara.

"Shrinks?" asked John.

"Doctors who treat crazy people like me," said Sara.

"You're not crazy," said John.

"No, but I'm bitter. I have low self-esteem, I'm abused, I feel useless all from a mother who hated me because I was the first born, and I wasn't a son. I was an ugly girl, useless, so she married me off to a man she knew would abuse me because she thought I deserved it. Somehow I ended up here. I find out I'm not such a bad person, but if I don't help you, then I feel bad here, too. I know you don't understand me because I'm not making sense, but to me it makes sense. I need to do this," said Sara.

"I do understand," said John. "You need to feel you belong somewhere, that someone wants you."

Sara stared at John. "Yes, that's how I feel, but no one wants me, and I live in two times. That alone would get me a shrink," laughed Sara.

"But do you need a shrink if you know the problem?" asked John.

"Probably not, but I wanted you to see I will be all right," said Sara. "I'll go check Susan and be right back."

"Okay," said John, pouring coffee.

Sara watched John pour coffee. Somehow it felt so right, like he belonged there.

"Susan," called Sara, walking in.

"Over here in the kitchen," said Susan.

"Wow! You look great, up and about, too," laughed Sara.

"I feel good. Jacob slept all night," said Susan. "I just finished feeding him."

"Well, don't do too much too fast, okay? I came over to check on you two and to pick up for you, see if you need anything, and here you are up and about. That's just great," smiled Sara as she walked over and made the bed. "I guess Jacob and Sean went out to cut hay."

"I don't think so, they took the wagon," said Susan.

"They must have gone to Rome then. Sean decided to put a wall up to block the bedroom off. Or they are using the wagon for hay. Sean didn't say. Those two are full of surprises," laughed Sara.

"Jacob told me about your surprise, it sounds nice," said Susan.

"It is. I have no living room like you, but I don't have children like you. My place works for me, like yours works for you," said Sara. "Need anything?"

"Something to do," said Susan. "I was restless in bed, now I'm restless up. You've kept everything up, and now I have nothing to do," laughed Susan.

"I've got that yarn I bought, the knitting needles or crochet hooks. If you want to use it, you're more than welcome," said Sara. "I bought them for both of us."

"Yes, I can knit," smiled Susan.

"I'll get it. I'll be right back," smiled Sara. She left, went to her home, grabbed the knitting needles and four colors of yarn, told John she'd be right back, and went back to Susan's.

"I didn't know what color, so I grabbed a couple of each." laughed Sara. "If you need more, let me know. I'll bring you lunch. I've got to go, the women will be here soon."

"Oh, we'll be fine. I can sit in my rocker and knit. If I need you, I'll call," laughed Susan. "I promise, go."

"Okay. Can I sneak a peak at Jacob, Jr. first?" smiled Sara.

"You don't have to ask, God, with everything you've done for me," said Susan.

"Oh, I'd never touch a sleeping baby," said Sara.

"He's not sleeping; he's so good, so alert," said Susan.

Sara picked up Jacob. "He is. It's like he knows me. The boy is going to be smart, Susan, very smart," said Sara.

"I thought I was crazy at first. I thought something was wrong, but he just seems smart," said Sara.

"Well, you're not crazy," said Sara, kissing Jacob. "Well, I'll see you later, Sara has to go, sweetheart."

"Huh, that's Aunt Sara," said Susan. "I know we can't choose family, but in this case you've earned the right to be family," smiled Susan.

"Ooh, Aunt Sara, I like that. How about you, big fellow? Oh God, I swear to God he just smiled at me," said Sara.

"Why not, he loves you," said Susan.

Sara laid Jacob down, hot tears stung her eyes. Somebody loved her. "I have to go," said Sara. She left, Susan never seeing her tears. John saw the tears when she walked in.

"Something wrong?" asked John.

Sara shook her head no, wiping the tears.

"Something made you cry," said John.

"T…t…t…the baby loves me," said Sara.

John got up and hugged Sara. "Of course he does, what's not to love? You're the sweetest, kindest person alive," said John. God, if only he had loved her that night, she fit right in his arms perfect, like she was made just for him.

Sara drew in a deep breath. She smelled John. It felt so right here. She never felt more love and comfort then she did in those arms. She stepped back, wiped the tears, and walked to the kitchen.

"I should have gotten you pregnant," said John.

"What!" said Sara, turning around.

"I was wrong about that night. You need a child," said John.

"Now you decide you were wrong?" said Sara. "It's nice to know they play head games here, too."

"Head games?" asked John.

"First one thing, then another to confuse you," said Sara.

"No, no head games. I was right, loving you once wouldn't be enough for me. Getting you pregnant would have been easy. You don't deserve to be treated like a lady of ill repute, you deserve more. You need to be treated like the lady you are. There are two ways to love a woman. What was it you called it, 'wham bam, thank you, ma'am.' "Or you love her slowly and deeply forever. Trust me, you are not the first, you've never known the second. You have no idea how a man can make a woman feel," said John.

"Look, I was married thirty-two years. I think I know what a man can do," said Sara.

"No you don't. Tom never loved you. You were a stop between women. What you think is love is wrong. Love is the most beautiful thing in the world. When you love someone, you grow, you don't sit in a house tucked away from the world waiting for permission to be taken out and played with," said John.

Sara stared at John from across the kitchen. John walked over to the island and sat down. Hot tears stung Sara's eyes. John's words were like arrows straight to her heart. "I…I…I was just a toy to him, something for him to take out and play with whenever he wanted. If he wanted to beat me, he beat me. If he wanted to love me, he loved me. It was all a fucking game to him. I'll kill him. I will fucking kill him," cried Sara.

"No you won't," said Sean, walking in.

"Why not? I earned the right to do it. As a matter of fact, I think my marriage papers say after thirty years I have a legal right to kill him if I want. And I'm going to exercise that right," said Sara hotly.

"Sara, I think Tom hired those men to kill you," said Sean.

"He what?" asked Sara.

"Think about it. Tom's getting ready to retire. He's in debt up to his eyeballs," said Sean, pouring coffee.

"I warned him not to take that loan out on the house. I begged him not to. It was paid for, but he needed that funny truck and wanted to pay off all those credit cards he had," said Sara, "and put money in the bank."

"Oh, see, that's where Tom was very smart. It took me awhile to figure it out. The house is in your name, and your name only. If you die, he gets the house free and clear. He would be debt-free and rich," said Sean.

"Rich?" asked Sara.

"That insurance policy he took out. It had a wrongful death closure. If you were killed, he got three million dollars. So now he's debt-free, owns a house, is rich, retired, and ready to marry one of his young ladies," said Sean.

"Okay, I can see how that would look like he had me killed, but I don't think he would," said Sara.

"Oh yes he would. Do you remember what the robbers kept asking you? I do," said Sean. "It haunted me for a long time."

"Where's the money?" asked Sara.

"Yes, he was insistent there was money because he was told there was money. Tom found your money you saved. Those men were going to take that money as payment for killing you. Remember they looked in the hope chest and said it wasn't there? They didn't know about that secret storage place so they trashed the place looking for it. You were going to pay for being killed. Don't you find it strange they knew when you would be alone? If Laura wasn't sick, I wouldn't have been there, so I witnessed it all. Old Tom got his money's worth," laughed Sean.

"What do you mean?" asked Sara.

"Well, for years Tom has tried to prove you and I were having an affair. If he played his cards right, he'd say I killed you in a jealous rage. The cops prove this, and he doesn't have to pay the killers because the cops proved I killed you. He keeps the ten thousand," said Sean.

"Oh God, the money, I left the money in the hiding place," said Sara, running to the chest.

"I took the money out," said Sean. "Tom will go nuts. The killers will want their money. Tom's going to think they got the money. I left him a little note," laughed Sean.

"A note?" asked Sara.

"Yeah," laughed Sean. "It said, 'You're fucked.'"

"Oh, no!" laughed Sara.

"Well, if this thing works the way we think it is, ol' Tom's going to think someone's after him," laughed Sean. "The funny part is that if Tom shows the police the note, they can't trace it. It's from the 1800s written in quill pen," laughed Sean. "Thought I'd drop ol' Tom another note in a couple of days just in case he checks again, then he'll think someone's watching him and is sneaking in the house leaving him notes. I thought we'd try a little blackmail," laughed Sean.

"What do you mean?" asked Sara.

"Well, if this thing works right, I think ol' Tom should pay his dues," laughed Sean. "The way I see it, we're not dead. And when we go back, you'll need money for a divorce. Since ol' Tommy boy is going to jail, you need money to live like a queen. If we invest it for you, have the Indians hold it for you until you get back, I think you will have it. Ol' Tommy boy gets his just reward. I think we should ask for ten thousand dollars, just what he was going to take from you, then there's a record. He drew ten thousand dollars out of the bank. We either haven't been found yet or we're in a coma. Either way we can't do anything there, but we can from here. Confucius says, 'Best crime is no be there.' Best way to solve a crime is no be there when we wake up in our time. We tell them we heard the men talking, and they said Tom hired them," said Sean. "We'll be questioned by police separately. We both tell the same story, then Tommy boy gets checked into jail," said Sean.

"May I make a suggestion?" said John.

"Sure," said Sean.

"We're setting a trap, right?" asked John.

"Yeah, why?" asked Sean.

"Well, we're at a disadvantage, because it hasn't happened yet. Is there any way we can track this man ahead of time, a way to prove this man talked to these men?"

"Yeah, we can trace phone calls, videotape his movements, trace bank accounts, but we don't know what's going to happen, so we can't do anything to stop it," said Sean.

"But Indians listen to stories told by ancestors. We do what our ancestors say. If we had dates, times, places, we could get this done and get the two who shot you," said John.

"Yeah, but if we don't get money from Tom, he would walk, tapes or no tapes. There's laws, the laws protect the criminal; a good lawyer, a well chosen jury, he walks, goes home and beats Sara until she's dead," said Sean.

"Well, we'll sit down and figure out every angle and form a plan," said John. "We can't take a chance here. Some secret place will help us," said John. "We need to be intelligent here. We have to beat him at his own game."

"Later guys, the women are here, and that means no men in my kitchen," laughed Sara. "Go!"

Sean picked up on Sara's cue. "I like that, her kitchen," said Sean, setting his cup down. "Kicking us out, I don't believe it."

"Get," Sara said, teasing.

"I'm going," laughed Sean. John and Sean left.

The women of the nation giggled as Sean and John left.

"Men," said Sara. "I know you women probably do a form of canning. I don't know what Ben's up to, but I will show you how to do this. John brought me some strawberries, so we'll start with them. I wrote everything down step by step. I also wrote down how to can peaches and pears. Apple butter is a long process; applesauce is easy. And apple pie filling is easy to do. I also wrote down recipes of Ben's favorite cookies and pie crust then pie filling. I have a stove to cook with. I don't know how you cook. I won't insult your intelligence with my stupidity. You women can adjust this to how you live. I'm still trying to adjust to how I'm living," smiled Sara.

"We have stoves," smiled Summer.

"I should have asked you how to operate this thing when I started cooking," laughed Sara.

Everyone laughed. They all loved Sara. She was right there to help them. It was like part of her was part of them. Sara accepted their way with no questions.

Sean and John walked to Jacob and Susan's. Susan was knitting; Jacob was holding the baby. He smiled when Sean and John walked in. "Best thing that can happen to a man is a child," smiled Jacob.

"Must be," said Sean. "Nobody could wipe that smile off your face if they tried," laughed Sean.

Susan smiled softly. Jacob was sure a proud papa.

Jacob laid the baby down in his cradle gently. "Ready to work some more?" asked Jacob.

"Have no choice," said John. "Sara kicked us out."

"Sounds like Sara," laughed Susan.

Jacob, Sean, and John left. Jacob and Sean had cut down hay in the early morning. Now it needed thrashing before it could go in the barn. As they walked, Sean told them about putting up a wall for the bedroom and getting furniture for the living room. This would mean taking a trip to Rome and not telling the women about the furniture, so they would be surprised.

"Well, we do need feed," said Jacob. "I figured out how much they eat, so we could get enough for the winter. We're not out, but we will fall short of a winter's supply," said Jacob.

"Well, we've got six piglets, the cow will calf soon, we're letting the eggs hatch instead of eating them right now, and we didn't figure on all the new additions, so we better figure over that in case of a long winter," smiled Sean.

"Did all that, and allowed extra for the chickens. Just in case we ended up with more than we figured," said Jacob.

The three men arrived at the field that Sean and Jacob had cut down. John stared. It seemed like rather an odd place to cut.

Sean saw the puzzled look on John's face.

"We cut this field because this is where the fruit trees will go. We'll plant this fall. I ordered the trees. They will be here soon. With the creek so close by, we will be able to run irrigation pipes under the ground, so on hot dry summers we don't have to worry about watering. It will be done automatically," said Sean.

"Ah," said John. "Won't the winter kill the seedlings?" asked John. "They are small, the roots tender."

"Yes, but they are dormant, so planting in the fall and mulching will allow them to develop strong roots in the spring, giving a strong start. Come spring we can plant berry fields," said Sean. "If we keep along the stream, we should have good luck. Jacob's land runs at the end, north and south. The field is east and west, so they have sunlight all day," said Sean.

John nodded. This was well thought out.

"I've worked on plans for Jacob's house. I think it is more than applicable. A road will run up to it, curve around, come down the other side of the fields to our home. To the left of Jacob's home will be a barn. He will have his own stock. The winters can be bad, so Jacob must have his own farm to feed his family," said Sean, picking up a pitch fork.

John picked up a pitch fork. "Jacob can drive the wagon; we'll load it," smiled John.

"Better put on the leather gloves, your hands will blister," smiled Sean.

Chapter 6

BEEP...BEEP...BEEP.

"Susan, oh honey, I just heard," said Laura.

"Laura," cried Susan, running over to Laura's open arms. "I don't know what to do. I called John, he's on his way. He doesn't know Dad's been arrested." Sob-sob-sob.

"Susan, it's going to be okay. Sit down, talk to me," said Laura.

"Sniff, sniff. The police came this morning. They took Dad out in cuffs. He hired those men to kill Mom." Sniff, sniff. Laura handed Susan a Kleenex. Blow. "Dad had the whole thing set up. Detective Peters sat me at the kitchen table and told me that Daddy paid them ten thousand dollars to kill Mom because there's a three million dollar insurance policy on Mom. He was going to kill mom and marry his girlfriend. She's been arrested for plotting the whole thing. Sean wasn't supposed to be there. Oh Laura, this is awful. I'm worried about myself, how's Sean?" asked Susan.

"Sean's," Laura paused and choked back the lump in her throat. "Sean's been upgraded to stable. He lost a lot of blood. The bullet missed all major things. All he needs now is time. How's your mother?" asked Laura.

"She has a concussion. One bullet broke the main bone in her leg. They put a pin in it. The second bullet went through the breast and lung, it chipped a breast bone. The jaw was broken. It's wired. She has two broken back teeth, her face is swollen and bruised. The doctors said she'll live. It will all take time. They suggested counseling for her, said that it was a traumatic experience. The nurse told me to talk to her, that she can hear me. I didn't know what to say, I can't look at her with all those bruises, and her leg hanging like that so I brought that old diary she was reading. I thought I'd read it to her. Do you think she'd mind if I didn't look at her?" said Susan.

"Honey, your mother would understand. She'd love you to read that diary," said Laura, looking at Sara's leg in the air. "Did your mother get cut, too?" asked Laura.

"No, why?" asked Susan.

"Her leg has a cut the shape of a moon," said Laura.

"That's Mother's birth mark," said Susan.

"That's a strange mark," said Laura. "Well, I'm going to sit with Sean. The nurses are probably through bathing him. I can't believe they kicked me out."

"They have rules; they kicked me out, too," said Susan.

Laura turned to go, then stopped. "Susan, can I ask you something?"

"Sure, Laura, anything," said Susan.

"How did they figure your father was behind this?" asked Laura.

"Dad went to a real estate agent and put the house up for sale after the first of the year," said Susan.

"How did that make him guilty? Everyone puts houses up for sale," said Laura.

"Daddy did it November 13. He told the real estate agent he was a widower and hadn't gotten a death certificate yet to clear the house in his name. So with what the two guys that did this said, and the ten thousand dollars Dad drew out of the bank, he hanged himself. The police said they had a lot more. I didn't want to hear it," said Susan. "If he hated my mother so much, why didn't he just leave? He didn't have to try to kill her," sobbed Susan.

"Money, money is evil. I ain't seen it bring out the good in anyone. Maybe money is our modern-day satan. Seems no matter how much you have, it ain't enough," said Laura. "You can't live without it, it rules us; we don't rule it. And some people become obsessed with it to the point they will kill for it."

"I never thought once that Dad hated Mom," said Susan.

"Hate and love are only the opposite sides of a coin," said Laura.

"Well, you better go be with Sean. Tell him I'm sorry," said Susan.

"Never say you're sorry for something you didn't do. None of this is your fault," said Laura.

"I feel so guilty. I feel like I should have seen this coming. I should have been there," said Susan.

"Susan, nobody saw this coming, so don't blame yourself," said Laura.

"Susan, oh God, Susan," said John, running in.

"John, thank God. John it's awful," cried Susan, running to her brother.

"The police said Dad did this," said John, choking back a huge lump in his throat.

Laura slipped by John and Susan. They needed to be alone.

Susan cried on John's shoulder. She always teased him because he was so tall with large shoulders. With shoulders like that, women will always be crying on them. She never dreamed she'd be one of them. Right now her brother's strong arms and big shoulders gave her comfort. They kept out the big, bad wolf. John and Susan had strong Indian features. Long, blue-black hair, large brown eyes, smooth cream-colored skin. Both looked like their mother. John calmed Susan. Her tears fell silently now; all you could hear was the bleep...bleep of the heart machine. John tried to swallow the lump that grew in his throat. The police met him at the airport, drove him here, and explained everything on the way. They told him his mother looked worse than it was, but fear had a hold of his heart and was squeezing real tight. He knew he had to walk over there and look at his mother. The police didn't paint a pretty picture. Hot tears stuck in the corner of his eyes. If there was anyone who didn't deserve to be hurt, that was Sara. She bothered no one, and now she lay fighting for her life. John stepped back from Susan.

"The police said they had to cut Mom's hair?" asked John.

"Not all of it. She'd had thirty stitches. Those men threw Mom and Sean in the garage. It looks like Mom was shoved into the steel beam. It broke her jaw, bruised her face, and cut her head open," said Susan. "She can get it styled later, but it's got to be cut short."

John drew a deep breath and let it out slowly. "It's now or never." He walked slowly toward Sara. Each foot felt like it weight one thousand pounds. John saw the cast in the air, wires hung out. Slowly Sara's still form loomed before him. The only thing he could think was "Thank God she's in a coma."

"Mother, it's John. I'm here." He licked his lips with his tongue. It didn't help, his mouth was dry. "Mom, I love you." John sat down in the chair next to the bed. "Julie couldn't come right now, but she'll be here in two days with the kids. We'll be staying until after New Year's Day. She's driving up. She has a ton of Christmas presents. She made boxes of homemade candy: peanut brittle, bon bons, tortes, caramel popcorn, chocolate-covered cherries, and chocolate creams. She's been making candy for a month. You will be surprised at how good she's gotten at it," said John.

Susan stood at the foot of the bed, hugging the diary and listening to John talk.

Knock, knock. "John I hate to bother you. I'm Detective Peters, could we get some coffee?"

John looked at the man in the doorway, then to Susan. He didn't want to talk to anyone but his mother. His stomach was sick. John looked at his mother, then at the police detective.

"It's okay, John, I've got the diary to read to Mom," said Susan, walking over and putting a hand on his shoulder.

John shook his head yes, rose slowly out of his chair, and kissed his mother on the forehead gently. "I love you Mom," whispered John, then he walked to the detective; they left. Susan sat down, she gently opened the leather-bound diary. There was a white satin ribbon marking where Sara had left off. The pages were yellowed and fragile. Susan read aloud.

"October 1860."

"The nation's women have gone. We had a great time canning. I went to check on Susan and Jacob, they were napping, so I didn't bother them. I put Susan's share of canned goods away. I made several trips back and forth. I suspect Ben will be here soon, right after he tries his peanut butter. Summer loved it. They taught me how to dry foods and make jerky. October has been a very warm month. This has helped us to get settled. Jacob, Sean, and John worked the fields. The barn oft is almost full of hay.

"Then Dr. Emerson came. He said Susan and Jacob are doing fine, that Jacob was a big boy for such a small woman. Ben came around suppertime. I knew he would; he loves to eat. He loves peanut butter and jelly sandwiches. Ben loves anything that is food. The nights grow shorter, so I sew by candlelight. I'm making curtains tomorrow. I go with John to gather flowers to dry to make sachets and decorations. The rooms are beautiful but need something on the walls. Tonight I will sleep well.

"John and I went to the field of flowers. Jacob and Sean went to Rome. I gave him a list of things to get. I was hoping to go along, but there is so much to do before winter hits. Today was cooler. For the first time I had to wear a coat. Susan and Jacob grow stronger each day. I know she was counting on going to Rome but maybe next week. I told her to make a list. It's hard to travel by wagon, especially with a newborn. Ben stayed with Susan. Ben calls me princess all the time now. I know he's up to something. I started teaching John today. Ben sat in too, saying he's the chief and is always right. He only wanted the peanut butter cookies I made. The day has warmed, but you can smell fall in the air.

"Sean and Jacob returned from Rome around 3:00 P.M. Sean was furious, and Jacob couldn't stop laughing long enough to tell me what was wrong. Seems those two hundred fruit trees turned out to be two thousand. Ben said he'd bring the men of the nation by tomorrow to plant the trees. I offered to help. Ben said I should stay home and bake cookies and watch Susan and the baby. I get really mad at Ben sometimes, and we argue. This was one of those times. Ben always makes me stay at the house. I like it outside. I end up giving in to Ben because he's always right. Tonight is colder, but we're warm.

"Sean and Jacob bought some living room furniture when they were in town. Susan's is green velvet; mine is blue. I'm glad I made all the curtains white. Susan doesn't know I made her curtains yet. I was waiting for rods. Tonight after supper we went to Jacob and Susan's and hung curtains. The pounding of nails didn't wake little Jacob at all. Susan showed me the sweater set she made little Jacob. She does good work; he will be warm this winter. We talked for a while, then Sean and I went home. I started an afghan tonight for Susan for Christmas. Jacob and little Jacob's presents I'll get next week when I go to Rome. After the trees are planted, Jacob and Sean are putting up the bedroom walls."

Susan turned the pages slowly. "They were all in here: Mom, Sean, Susan, John, no wonder Mother was so intrigued with this diary," Susan thought.

"I've settled into a pretty good routine. I made breakfast for all of us, I take Jacob and Susan theirs and pick up the dirty laundry, wash it and hang it out to dry. I teach John and Ben what I know. John is a quick learner. Ben, I think, is teasing me to see if I'll get mad and argue with him. The men of the nation came early this morning so the men are in the field. Washing little Jacob's clothes is a pleasure, they're so little. Someday I will have a child. Since the nights grow shorter, less can be done outside so Jacob and Sean work in the barn. Bessy should calf soon; the piglets are growing fast. The chickens are starting to lay less, but Jacob says this is normal. Soon there will be baby chicks running around. There's one rooster I'd love to kill, he keeps pecking at me. The turkeys grow big, their eggs have hatched. They're a stupid bird, but come Thanksgiving they will taste great. I churned some butter today, enough for us, Jacob, and Susan. When I took the butter to Susan, she said she was going to forget to do this stuff if I didn't let her start doing something, so I agreed to let her start taking care of her household. It's been two weeks since Jacob was born. Now I will have time on my hands. I just don't know if I can handle that. I don't want time to think. When I came back from Susan's, I felt lost. I decided to start making Christmas decorations. I made little Jacob a teddy bear for Christmas. For Ben I decided to make cookies and sweet breads for him. John, I don't know. He shows no interest in anything other than knowledge. I love the Oneida Indians; they are good people, always ready to lend a hand. I have learned as much from them as I have taught them.

"The trees got planted and covered. Sean says that's good because tonight it looks like frost. I made supper for the two of us. It felt strange making so little after all the canning. After supper Sean and Jacob worked some more in the barn. I guess they finished what had to be done because they brought the animals in. Each day brings us closer to winter. I fear our first winter here. I know we're in a valley and are protected some, but with each winter comes uncertainty.

"Today Jacob and John put up the bedroom walls; Susan's first then mine. Susan came here, then I went there for a while. I got restless, I needed to walk. I know this winter will be rough on me if I don't get out. I picked some apples. I think Ben called them 'pippin.' I made cider and doughnuts. I have learned now to write down my recipes. Ben will ask for it anyway. I know Ben is trying to teach me something, he gets upset with me sometimes. He always makes me do what I don't want to do. Our biggest argument is my wandering off by myself, so I try to go when Ben won't be there, but he always finds me. I have noticed that the nation has a system for everything they do. I've grown to love them a lot. There is a perfect order among them. Seems like I'm the only one giving Ben gray hair. He seems to think I should stay home, but my soul is restless. It's like I'm searching for something, but I just don't know what. I found some grapevines today. I will talk to Ben tomorrow to see if I may cut some. He'll probably say yes and send John with me to protect me, from what I don't know.

"Sean came in and said it's getting cold out, but it's warm in here. The two wood stoves in the barn keep it warm. Ben and John stopped by. I offered them cider and doughnuts. This time John gave me a lecture about wandering off. I broke down and cried. I threw all three of them a curve; they couldn't understand why I was so upset. I told them I wasn't allowed to do anything. Then Ben told me there were soldiers in the area and they feared for my well-being, so I agreed not to wander off anymore. I gave him the recipes he asked for.

"The sun is out today. I opened my windows and aired out our home. I've started braiding my hair so I can put it up with pins. That way I can go chop wood to work off some energy. Ben and John won't come by in daylight anymore, only in the darkness of night, too many soldiers around. They think I'm Sean's young son with a hat on my head and men's clothing. I probably look like a little kid. The soldiers leave next week. Seems the president is passing through. I don't know, they made me feel restless, so I stay inside. Susan won't go out at all, I don't blame her with her blonde hair and blue eyes. They would rape her. It's a shame that we have to fear our own kind. We were always told the Indians were the bad guys. That's how wrong people are about one another. I started making rugs today. It takes a lot of concentration; it keeps my mind off what is going on around me. I fear for Ben and John. I don't care what kind of treaty they have with the government. It takes only one soldier to see an Indian here for them to think we're under attack, then all hell will break loose. I could never live with myself if something happened to anyone in the nation because of me. Sean promises to talk to Ben and John for me. I would do it myself, but Ben would only argue with me. This is one argument I don't want to lose. Jacob and Sean cleaned the barn and chimneys. I don't think I'm doing too bad on my rugs for my first try. I crocheted a mat, then tied off loops of yarn. It makes the rug warm. I'm going to make a design on the one for the living room. I'm doing it blue and white to match the couch, then I'm making throw pillows to match made out of cotton calico. The feed bags come in cotton calico material with the feed we've been using. Susan and I have gotten piles of free material. It helps us greatly since we won't be able to go to Rome until the soldiers leave. Susan came over today with Jacob. She asked me how come my home smelled so fresh and clean. She seemed surprised that I opened my windows daily, even if for a few minutes. Susan said she didn't dare. She was afraid of Jacob getting sick or the soldiers hearing a baby cry. She said her house needed a good spring cleaning even though it was fall, so I offered to watch Jacob while she spring cleaned. She said okay and disappeared. She came back three hours later smiling. She said she felt better breathing some fresh air. Jacob and Sean beat rugs for her and hung out laundry. We've been drying some clothes in the barn, but then they smell like the barn. I don't mind the smell of hay, it's the other smell that gets to you. Jacob and Sean have been good about keeping the barn clean, and the animals out whenever possible. They've been spreading the manure in the field where they're going to plant all the berries. Sean is getting into this farming thing. Susan was happy that I watched Jacob while she aired the house out and asked me if I couldn't do it a couple of times a week for her. I told her I'd love to. I'd watch Jacob whenever she needed me. After she left I washed windows and bed linen. I beat the pillows then hung them on the line. I had Sean and Jacob beat the mattress and put in on the line to air. It seems less like a prison here with the bedroom wall in. We have a really cute living room; it's not big. I didn't think two chairs and a couch would fit, but it's really nice. We don't have any end tables or coffee tables. I would not want to seem too pushy. Sean has been more than generous to me. He works so hard, I feel useless locked away here. I haven't written in awhile. The soldiers have left, the president didn't stop in Rome. He stopped in Utica.

"John told me a beautiful story today. In the winter of 1777–78 George Washington and his troops were starving at Valley Forge. The Oneida nation took corn to the starving troops. Polly Cooper stayed behind to show the troops how to prepare it properly. Polly turned down money for her services, so the Washingtons presented Polly a shawl from Martha Washington. These people are such great people. There are so many stories; all oral passed down from generation to generation. I will always stand proudly next to them.

"John brought grapevines. He said I should use willow. I didn't know what he was talking about. John will send Summer, she's the best basket weaver they have. They call her that because she teaches so easy.

"We went to Rome today. It felt good to get out. We ate out and shopped. It may be the end of October but I did my Christmas shopping. I have it done. I bought all the food I would need to cook a large meal and stocked up on dry stuff. I bought a lot of muslin and lace. I found a beautiful sweater for John. There's a little shop here that local women make things and put them in there to sell. I bought quite a few things there. This will probably be our last trip to Rome until spring. They have a lovely soap shop, so I bought some. Then we went to the candle shop. We bought some more, a lot more to get us through the winter. Normally you would have one candle for the house, but Sean made all those lights, and they all took candles. I found some small candles for Christmas decorations. Susan bought a lot of things. I found some corduroy to make into pants for me with a vest. I have some good calico to make a blouse to match, so I have an outfit for Christmas. I bought Sean some clothes. I just didn't know what else to get him. I hope the holiday turns out as good as I've planned."

John had stopped in the doorway and listened to Susan read the diary. It sent chills up his spine. It always did when Susan read; she read with such passion.

"What are you reading?" asked John.

"That diary Mom found in her hope chest. We're in here, all of us," said Susan.

"Woman, you are so sentimental. If you ever stopped to think logically, your brain would hurt."

"Screw you," said Susan. "What did detective Peters want?"

"Dad confessed. There will be no trial. He'll be arraigned before the judge: sixteen years to life, and two counts of murder. They had so much on him that if he didn't confess, he would have gotten the death penalty. They had tapes and phone messages. Sean saved Mom's life. He jumped in front of the bullet that was meant for Mom's head."

"Oh, my God," cried Susan. "If Sean wasn't there, Dad would have gotten away with murder."

"Afraid so. We never would have known about it at all," said John.

"How did they ever get videos and tapes?" asked Susan.

"Seems Dad and Bambi were at the casino Ruby Room eating when a waitress named Summer overheard them talking about it. She told her boss, who went to check out what Summer said. He found it was true. He went to the nation's police, who had Dad followed," said John.

Susan stared at John. She thought, "Summer?" This was even too much for her brain to handle. Susan looked at Sara then at John. She needed to think. How many people had the name Summer? "I'm hungry. Mom's resting, why don't we get supper? The food isn't the best, but it's edible," said Susan.

"Why don't I go out and get something and bring it back?" said John. "You can read to Mom. I know she'd like that."

"Okay," said Susan. "I'll get my keys, the truck's parked right out front."

"Burgers, fries, chocolate shake still your favorite?" asked John.

"Is there any other kind of food?" laughed Susan, handing John her keys and some money.

"I would have bought my sis supper," said John.

"I know, you buy the next time," said Susan. "I promise you, if you buy, it won't be burgers and fries," teased Susan.

"You only love me only for my money," teased John.

"That's right, now I'm going to read to Mom. Sean's next door, tell him what the detective said," said Susan.

"Yeah, I'd like to thank Sean," said John.

"Go," smiled Susan as she walked over to sit next to Sara.

John walked next door.

Susan started to read:

"I got what I could find for colds and flu. There's not much here. Anything for first aid is worse. I'm doing the best I can, so little to work with. I still found no bras and panties that were decent. The boots hurt my feet.

"It started to rain when we got back from Rome. I thanked God it held off until we got back. If we'd gotten wet, we would have been very ill with so little to work with. I fear the worst for the winter. The rain has made the temperature drop quickly. We're warm in the house.

"I wish I had found something to make angels with for the Christmas tree. There's just nothing here."

Susan lowered the diary and looked at Sara. "I may be emotional, sentimental, whatever you want, but I ain't stupid. I know this is you. I don't know how or why, but this is you and you're trying to tell me something. What? Mmm. Today is December 2. If you're on the same time schedule, let's see, December...." Susan read to herself.

"It's so cold, everyone is very sick. I'm the only one who can walk around. I'm tending to everyone plus the animals. Everyone's fever is so high I have nothing to give them, nothing to clean with to kill germs. Ben left some medicine they use, but I fear death is imminent. I will probably be the last to die. Little Jacob is so ill, I fear he's dehydrated. I have nothing to give him."

"Susan? John just told me. I'm so sorry," said Laura.

"Laura, Laura....look, you know me, you know I'm not crazy. I've never done anything irrational in my life, have I?" asked Susan.

"No, why?" asked Laura.

"I don't have time to explain. I will explain after. Your brother is still a doctor?" asked Susan.

"Ben? Yes, why?" asked Laura.

"I need penicillin for four adults and one child. Will he write me a prescription?" asked Susan.

"It's unusual, but I can ask," said Laura.

"Make up any names he wants. I'm paying cash," said Susan.

"What's up?" asked Laura.

"Get the prescriptions, then read these twenty pages back from the bookmark. It will give you chills," said Susan. "We have no time to waste."

Laura looked at Susan puzzled.

"Don't tell John. He thinks I'm crazy. What kind of cigarettes does Sean smoke?" asked Susan.

"Marlboro regular, why? He can't smoke," said Laura.

"No, I know that, but I think, no I know, how to save Mom and Sean. You may think I'm stupid and this whole thing bizarre. Read the diary. I need Ben to call in the prescription, please. Tell me what name they're under. I'll go when John gets back, just read."

"Okay," said Laura, doubtful. "I'll call Ben."

Susan went back and sat next to Sara. "Mom, hang in here. I hear what you're saying. I love you, Mom," said Susan.

"Burger and fries," said John, walking in. He paused, the sight of his mother shocked him again. What if she didn't live? The thought terrified John.

"Here's a chair. Sit so we can eat," said Susan.

"When did you eat last?" asked John.

"Yesterday, breakfast. I got the phone call around noon yesterday. I've been here since. An occasional coffee, bathroom break. Oh yes, I got called to Mom's house when they arrested Dad. I called you when I got called. It's been crazy," said Susan.

"I'm sorry, I should have been there," said John.

"How did you know this was going to happen?" asked Susan, biting into her hamburger.

"Of course not. I didn't know they didn't love each other," said John.

"Then you couldn't be there, could you?" said Susan.

"No, but if I hadn't moved away, you wouldn't have handled all this alone," said John between bites.

"Look, your job took you away. You have to go where the money is; you have a family," said Susan.

"Well, you do too yet, you're here with Mom. Where's Patrick anyway?" asked John.

"Patrick stayed with me through surgery and part of the night. We decided on advice of the police that Patrick take the kids to his mother's. She said she'd watch them for us," said Susan.

"Why did the police advise you to move your family?" asked John.

"Well, they didn't know all the facts, and if it was a gripe against the family, we might be in danger," said Susan.

"God, you've been through all kinds of hell," said John.

"Nothing compared to Mom," said Susan, looking at Sara.

"Have you had any sleep?" asked John.

"No, I look at Mom and I'm afraid to sleep unless I miss a movement, anything," Susan said sadly.

"Well, why don't you go home, take a hot bath, and get some rest? I'll call you. You're going to need all the rest you can get right now. When Mom comes home, she'll need all the help we can give her," said John.

Laura called Susan gently.

"Sure Laura," said Susan standing up. "I'll be right back." Susan walked over to Laura.

"I read this; I believe you. My brother gave me a hard time. He's afraid he'd lose his license, but I wore him down. It's at the Wal-Mart pharmacy under the name Susan Keller. Good luck," said Laura.

"This is just between you and me," said Susan. "Everyone else will think we are stupid."

"Stupid or not, somehow this diary has Sean and Sara, really all of us," said Laura, whispering.

"Thank you, I thought it was just me. I think I'm on the right track," whispered Susan. "As strange as it sounds, anything is possible. Who knows, maybe that weird stuff on TV really happens."

"I've got something for you. It's a hundred dollars, buy what you can with it," said Laura.

"I've got it covered. I made a list, thank you anyway. You know my mother wouldn't take your money either. Let me do this. I'll feel less guilty for what my father did," said Susan.

"You're not your father. Take this and buy some little extra things. Don't forget, there's things we have here they don't have. Susan can't breast feed on penicillin. You'll need Similac to feed the baby, lighters, flashlight batteries, take it," said Laura.

"Okay, anything to help them. I see what you mean. I look close when I shop. I hope this works," said Susan.

"It will," said Laura, hugging Susan, then leaving.

"What was that all about?" asked John.

"Sean's been taking off critical," smiled Susan.

"Thank God. You go get some rest," said John.

"I'll do just that," smiled Susan. She kissed Sara then John. "It's going to be all right, you watch," said Susan, wiping at tears.

"Sure it will," said John. "We can beat this."

Chapter 7

"I CAN'T BELIEVE THIS RAIN," SAID SARA. "AT LEAST IT WAITED UNTIL WE GOT back from Rome and unloaded."

"So am I," said Sean, pouring coffee. "Would you like a cup?"

"Yes, coffee sounds good," said Sara, turning away from the window, "but what sounds better is getting this dress off. I'm glad this is our last trip to Rome for a while. I hate wearing all these clothes. My nightgown will take care of that."

Sean shook his head.

"You're to be liberated. I swear there's layers of clothes here, no room to breath. It takes two hours to do up all the buttons and ties," laughed Sara. "Three hours to undo them because you have no breath left to do it."

"Well, go change. I'll get us something to go with coffee," said Sean.

"That sounds good," smiled Sara.

"Oh, by the way, your cowboy boots go with your dress nicely," laughed Sean.

"Well I don't care if they do or not, I'm not wearing those other things," said Sara, laughing as she walked toward the bedroom to change.

Sean found the goodies they bought while in town. "What I wouldn't give for some fast food right now," Sean thought. "I'm tired of eating good food, even pasta," dreamed Sean.

"There, that feels better," smiled Sara, walking in the living room. She stopped. "What's wrong Sean?"

"Thinking about fast food, even spaghetti. This good food is going to kill me," laughed Sean.

"I know, I've felt the same. I've been trying my best, but can't come close, maybe because it's all frozen solid and our food is fresh. Maybe it's all the additives. I don't know," said Sara.

"That's probably why people died young in this time, too much good living. At least we have additives in our food to help us live longer in a rotten world," laughed Sean.

"Well, we need the additives to fight all the pollution," laughed Sara, sitting at the island.

"Some baked goods, princess?" smiled Sean.

"Why does Ben call me that?" asked Sara, reaching for a tart.

"I don't know, he probably has a reason," said Sean. "God, listen to the rain on the tin roof. It has a quieting effect, doesn't it?" asked Sean.

"Oh yeah. I used to stay at my grandmother's house. I slept in the upstairs bedroom. She had a tin roof; God I slept so good," said Sara. "Then you could see Paul Revere riding his horse out the window."

"I know what horse you mean. The one on Revere copper brass. Remember when they shut it off? God, so many people were devastated they had to turn it back on," laughed Sean.

"Yeah, they've taken so much away from us remolding Rome, we wouldn't part with our horse," said Sara.

"The fort was a joke," said Sean.

"I don't know, I went to it, they live there. I thought it was nice," said Sara.

"You would like that old shit. We lost a lot in business when they put it in," said Sean.

"No, what ruined Rome is when they took out the American corner and the trolley car, remember that?" laughed Sara.

"Oh God, yes, candy land, Mohigan market, Wards, the bus station," said Sean, "and the tobacco store on James Street."

"Yup. On Dominick Street they had Banks, Grants, Marksons. Now we have a Wal-Mart and Kmart way on the other end of town," said Sara.

"The Strand and Capital theaters. We could go to the movies for twenty-five cents, stay there all day, watch cartoons, newsreels, and feed our faces until we were sick, all for twenty-five cents," laughed Sean.

"Now you can't go to the movies without spending twenty-five dollars," said Sara.

"You know, we could put some of this stuff away and get comfortable in the living room," said Sean.

"Yes, we could," said Sara. "I might as well help while I still can. You and Jacob have been so busy in the barn," said Sara, getting up and picking up some bundles and heading toward the bedroom.

"I shouldn't have suggested," laughed Sean.

"Sean, Sean," yelled Sara.

Sean dropped his packages and ran into the bedroom, grabbed Sara's boot, "Where is he?" asked Sean.

"Who?" asked Sara.

"The spider. That's why you yelled, right?" asked Sean.

Sara started laughing. "No, put the boot down, you look stupid."

"Well, you had that spider scream in your voice," said Sean. "I didn't want you to get phobic on me again. What did you yell for then?" asked Sean.

"We have a letter from Susan and Laura," said Sara.

"Wha…at? No way," said Sean.

"Look, there's stuff in here. Help me get it out then we'll read these. Susan's smart," said Sara, pulling a plastic bag out. "How did she get it in here?" That's how I knew something was in there, something was sticking out of the wood. I've got to take some stuff out so I can get the bag out. It must ran across the whole bottom." Sara stuck her hand in and pulled things out and set them on the floor. "She's got everything but the kitchen sink in here," laughed Sara.

"How did Susan and Laura figure it out?" asked Sean.

"I'm sure it's in the letter. Help me get this stuff out," said Sara.

"Stand back," said Sean. "Let me in there."

"What are you going to do I'm not doing?" said Sara.

"Rip the hole bigger," said Sean.

"No! It may lose whatever it has in it," said Sara. "Don't you want to send Laura a note?"

"Okay, maybe if we tip it something will fall out," said Sean.

"Yeah, that's a good idea. I don't know what's stopping the bag."

Sean tipped the chest; Sara pulled something out without looking to see what it was, just dropping it on the floor. Finally the bag gave way with Sara falling on the floor. Sean laughed at her as he set the chest back on the floor.

"Glad you find it so funny," said Sara. "It hurt."

"Sorry, let's see what we've got here," said Sean. "Cigarettes, oh God, cigarettes for me and you. Toothpaste, toothbrushes, razors, deodorant, shampoo, pills?, bras, panties, sneakers, Kotex pads, first aid stuff, cleaners, mouthwash, lighters, newspapers, photos, batteries, wrapping paper, some kind of craft stuff you probably wanted, baby stuff, tape, pens, a small flashlight," laughed Sara.

"Sneakers?" asked Sara "Bras, panties?"

"There's other stuff on the floor, but I'm more interested in what's in the bag, why it got stuck," said Sean.

Sara looked in the bag and smiled, "You wouldn't believe me if I told you. You look," said Sara. "No, sit down and close your eyes."

"It better be good," said Sean, sitting down closing his eyes.

"Oh, it is," said Sara, waving something under his nose.

"French fries!" said Sean opening his eyes and reaching for the fries. Sara pulled out hamburgers, french fries, Pepsi, and bags of Ziploc bags with spaghetti sauce with meatballs and sausage, a box of spaghetti, two cans of tuna fish, a squeeze jar of mayonnaise, and more medical stuff. Sara handed Sean a Pepsi.

"We'll eat and read out letters," said Sara. "You first."

Sean nodded, enjoying his french fries, washing it down with Pepsi. "Susan's smart; she super-sized," laughed Sean, opening his letter and reading.

"Dear Sean: Susan came to me with a bizarre story. I believed her. I don't know why. I will now if it's true if you answer this letter. I love you. You and Sara are both in a coma. Susan was reading Sara's diary. She seems to think you're trapped there in this time. The police have arrested Tom; he confessed. It's all in the papers. My mom's watching the kids. I sit next to you day and night waiting for you to open your eyes. I don't know the date in your time; here it's December 3. Please find a way home soon. You need anything, tell me. We can't get anything large in the door. It seems the chest has a false bottom that runs across the whole bottom. Love, Laura."

Sean looked at Sara. "One of our days in our time is two months our time, so we have something to work on," said Sean. "At least we're alive. Now you."

Sara wiped her hands on her nightgown.

"Dear Mom: I love you. The date here is December 3. The diary says you're all sick. I had Laura's brother Ben give me a prescription for penicillin for all of you and liquid for the baby. He doesn't know why I wanted it. I got a lot of stuff for colds and flu, like Tylenol. I gave you bandages, tapes, small packages of Kleenex. I couldn't fit the box of Kotex in, so they had to be laid flat. Sorry your sneakers wouldn't fit in, so I put your canvas deck shoes in. I hope the food wasn't spoiled. There's antibiotic cleaners. They're small, but that's all I could fit in there. I tried to get what I thought you might need. The stuff is there to make angels for you and Susan. I sent pictures of everyone, and I took pictures of the casino, gas stations, and the new reservation. There's a book on Oneida Indian history, I thought Ben and John would like these. John's here. He thinks I'm crazy. He doesn't know I'm doing this. You're in pretty in bad shape here. Your leg's in a cast, your jaw is wired, your face bruised badly. You're in a coma; maybe it's for the best. Detective Peters said Sean saved your life by jumping in front of the bullet. You both will be fine as long as you stay alive in where you are. If you tell me what you need, I will try and find a away to send it to you. Dad's going to jail for two second-degree murder charges, fifteen to life each. Why didn't you tell me Dad was so mean to you? John is as upset as I am that you felt you couldn't come to us. We would have protected you. John blames himself for not being here for you. Laura came over. We cleaned the house from top to bottom, and put all the decorations back the way you had them. Julie will be with the kids for Christmas. We'd like you home for Christmas. Love, Susan."

"Well, one thing is for sure, Susan's got her mother's brains," said Sean. "She never said the note I wrote was there in case Tom found it."

"Well, we have to write them back. There's only two things I can think of to ask for," said Sara.

"What's that?" asked Sean.

"Suture kit with Novocaine and Pepsi," said Sara.

"Let me put the sauce in a pan, then we'll go through this stuff and organize it. We have to be careful," said Sara. "I hope you know I'm in worse shape than Susan said," remarked Sara, standing up.

"How do you figure that? She painted a pretty grim picture as it was," said Sean.

"That's why," said Sara. "It's a grim picture, and if I'm in a coma and she said it's for the best, then I'm in bad shape and she doesn't want to tell me."

Sean looked at Sara. "You got all that out of the letter? You women have a strange way of communicating."

Sara left and returned. "We don't have a strange way of communicating, it's just what we don't say is as important as what we do say," said Sara.

"I did not understand anything you just said," said Sean.

Sara sat down on the floor, crossed her legs Indian style, looked at Sean, thought, then said, "You know what? I'm going to teach you all about women, starting with what I just said. We'll be locked in for winter, so I'll show you how much men are wrong about women."

"You really believe you can teach me about women?" laughed Sean.

"Yes as soon as you get rid of that attitude you just developed," said Sara.

"Attitude, what attitude?" laughed Sean.

"The one where you think with your dick and not your brain," said Sara. "The one where you think all you have to do is fuck to prove you're a superior being because you have two heads. I got news for you men. You use the wrong head to think with when it comes to women. They think of sex when they think of women because that's all men think we are good for is sex and housework, a place to satisfy your urges and keep your castle clean so you can be king."

Sean stared at Sara. He was taken back by what she said. Sara never spoke like that. "I'm surprised you think of me like that. I always thought I was very liberated in my thinking," said Sean.

Sara sighed. "Look, all I'm saying is at the mere mention of the word women, men get defensive," said Sara.

"Well, you women, so to speak, are the ones who want to rush men to the altar and have babies," said Sean.

Sara paused, thought, then said, "You know you're right. Us women are the problem. How foolish of us to think that as virgins we give up our maiden head to the man we love that he should marry us. Hell, what's in being a virgin anyway? It's just one little thing that's in the way of men making us women. When his job is done, he can go on to the next one. We're the ones who carry the baby, suffer stretch marks, swollen feet, backaches, labor, then get stuck caring for them until they leave the house. Then men think we look awful, so they head for some young thing who will make them a piece of trash. Heaven forbid if one night you come to bed and want sex, and we have a headache. We have no right to have feelings, just so long as your second head doesn't get a headache. It's always you, you, you," said Sara, standing up. "You're right, I can't teach you one damn thing about women. You know it all." Sara turned and walked out of the bedroom into the kitchen, poured coffee, and sat at the island.

Sean shook his head, reached for a pack of cigarettes and lighter. "Damn it," he said heading for the kitchen. It was dark and Sean fell over some packages. "Ow," he yelled. Sean fell two more times trying to reach the kitchen.

"Need a little light?" Sara said sarcastically.

"How the hell do you walk around this place in the dark without killing yourself?" asked Sean.

Sara lit a candle. "If you cleaned this place as much as I have, you would know where things were," said Sara.

Sean lowered the ceiling light and lit it. A warm glow cast the island. "I brought a peace offering. I promise to learn if you'll teach me. Some of what you said was true." Sara lit a cigarette. "Okay, all of what you said was true, but not about all." Sara blew out smoke. "Okay, we're bastards," said Sean.

"Well, we're off to a good start," said Sara. "Now if we can go back to why I said I'm worse off than Susan said is that Susan highlighted the bad things. There's probably other little things that she didn't want to tell me because that might upset me more."

"Well, I thought you sounded in bad shape compared to me. What could be worse than Susan described?" asked Sean.

"She said my face was bruised. Maybe those guys cut my face up so I couldn't be recognized," said Sara. "Maybe they raped me; maybe they cut my breast, anything to insult me," said Sara. "My jaw is broken. Maybe they wanted a blow job and I refused, so they broke my jaw. Men are mean to women, anything to leave their mark that they have been there."

Sean was shocked. He didn't know why Sara was right. Men like that were capable of anything. "What do you remember about what happened?" asked Sean.

"At this point, not much," said Sara. "They destroyed my house looking for money. I remember being tied up, duct tape put on my mouth, being struck several times, you falling in front of me when the gun went off. I remember how loud it sounded. I remember cold, lots of pain, and I thought I heard a siren, but then thought the sound was in my head like I had a lot of pain in my head. That's it," said Sara.

Fear ran through Sean. Was Sara shot in the head? Is that why Susan said it's best she's in a coma? If she woke up she'd be a vegetable. "What are we guessing for? Susan sent us the papers, lets see what happened," said Sean.

"Yes, I'll get them," said Sara, getting up and running into the bedroom. She ran back to the island. "There's two here, December 1 and December 2," said Sara. "Which one you want?"

"What are you two doing?" said John, opening the door and walking in; Ben followed.

Sara jumped and screamed, grabbing her chest. "You scared the shit out of me," laughed Sara.

"Why, we knocked," asked John.

"Coffee? I've got goodies, Ben," smiled Sara.

"Sounds good," said Ben, smiling.

Sara got up to get coffee and goodies for everyone.

"Susan, Sara's daughter figured out about the secret place. She sent us some things. She even sent things for you two," smiled Sean.

"Us?" asked John, surprised. "She knows us?"

"Yes, I wrote about you two all the time in my diary," said Sara. "I'll be right back." Sara went and got the book and photos. "This book is all about your heritage and leaders right through our time. The photos are a future thing. Here's the casino you guys run in our time. Here's your future reservation, and this is your culture center where your heritage is on display for the public to see," said Sara.

"We own all this?" asked Ben. "And these pictures are?"

"This is me and ol' Tom. This is Susan and her husband, two kids; this is John, his wife and two kids; this is Sean and his wife and kids."

Ben reached for the picture of John and his family. This was his grandson, the spitting image of his John. He passed it on to John, who was surprised to see himself staring back at him. He handed it to Sean. "What do you think?" asked John. Sean did a double-take. "Holy shit!" was all he said.

"What's wrong?" asked Sara.

"Nothing," said all three men at once. Sara couldn't see it.

"May I keep these?" asked Ben.

"Sure, if you want them," said Sara.

"I would like them to remember you by when you go back."

"Yeah, but I don't look like that here," said Sara.

"No, you are beautiful," said John.

"Beautiful?" laughed Sara.

"Very beautiful," said John, staring at the picture.

"We'll get your eyes checked tomorrow," teased Sara.

"Why I know what I see," said John.

"Okay, calm down. Do you want to see what Susan and Laura sent?" asked Sara.

"Yes," said Ben, getting up.

"We haven't gone through it all yet, but I'll explain what it is," said Sara as they walked in the bedroom.

Sara was explaining things as she went along and was explaining first aid things when John picked up a Kotex. "Big bandage," said John. Sean snickered, "This is a bandage," asked John.

"In a way, yes," said Sara. "It's what a women uses when she has the curse."

John threw the Kotex to the floor. "They have bandages for everything," said John.

"Sara, look, a camera. One of those throw-away kind. Let's get some pictures."

"What's this?" asked Ben, holding up the french fry container.

Sara laughed. "You would find food. French fries and hamburgers are what we eat a lot of in my time. It's called fast food," said Sara.

"Smells good," said Ben.

"It is," said Sara. "I'll see if Susan can send some more for you to try. I don't know how this is working."

"What else is in the chest?" asked John.

"Nothing, why?" asked Sara.

Sean looked. "There's something in there, a piece of green plastic is sticking out again. What do we have, a mess of things they're sending us?"

Sara crawled over to the chest. There it was, a green trash bag, so she opened the door. It had stuff in it, so she started puling stuff out, not seeing what she was pulling out. Ben had found the flashlight and was turning it off and on. "This I like," said Ben. Sara finally got everything out of the chest. "Well, Ben, here is a hamburger and french fries for you two," smiled Sara.

"Smells good," said Ben.

"Well, let's see what we have, two more letters, cold cuts, potato chips, popcorn, oh look, Christmas lights," said Sara.

"That's novel, light and no electricity," laughed Sean.

"They run on batteries," said Sara.

"More baby stuff, medical supplies, personal care products. Oh Sean, cookies, marshmallow cookies, hot chocolate, Fluff and soda, more spaghetti sauce and spaghetti, needles, Novocaine, suture kits, God, everything is here, even salad dressing, mustard, ketchup and bread," laughed Sara.

"Oh God, I can have a sandwich," said Sean.

"You can't be hungry, you just had a burger and fries," said Sara.

"Yeah, but when you don't have this stuff in a while, when you do get it you want to eat it all at once," said Sean.

"You're probably right. This stuff won't keep without a refrigerator," said Sara.

"I like hamburgers and french fries," said Ben.

"Here, have a Pepsi; this is the best," Sara popped the ring on the soda and handed Ben and John one.

"It feels funny in your mouth and throat," said John.

"It's carbonated," said Sean.

"Carbonated?" asked John.

"A future thing," smiled Sara.

"You say the future is bad, yet everything I've seen is good," said Ben.

"That's because you've been introduced to fast food," teased Sara.

Ben laughed. "You may be right, but all this stuff for medical is unbelievable."

"Yes, medical is way beyond anything here, but the world is so polluted that the medical profession can't keep up with all the new medical problems that arise. They call them doomsday viruses," said Sara.

"Doomsday?" asked John.

"Doomsday is what they call something that will change the world as we know it. Viruses kill millions of people. Asteroids kill millions of people, volcanoes, earthquakes, tidal waves, hurricanes, tornadoes, bombs, wars. You know I've got a couple books that I'll write Susan and ask her to send. You can keep them; they will help you understand," said Sara. "Let's go into the kitchen."

Everybody went back to the kitchen. Sara grabbed the two letters, some paper, and pens. Sean grabbed the food and camera. Ben still had the flashlight; John still had Sara's picture. Everyone went to the island. Sara poured coffee for everyone. She sat at the counter and started to write. Doomsday book and book on wars.

"What are you doing?" asked Sean.

"I wrote those two books down so I wouldn't forget. Oh yeah, our financial world," said Sara. "Now the notes. Ben, this one is for you; one for me."

"Dear Mom: Sorry about sending stuff so soon, Jacob's here. He wants to know what's going on. I told him, but he wanted to see for himself, typical. His interest in this is driving me nuts. He says that at the time period you're at, if you could vaccinate Ben's nation, you could save a lot of lives: Yours, Sean's, Jacob's, Susan's, and little Jacob's. Soon a massive influenza will strike followed by measles and smallpox. He wants to help if you will let him. It's all in liquid form, you only have to give them drops, but it's very important because this winter is the worst of all; many people die. I'm even surprised he believes us, and doesn't think we are nuts. Love Susan."

Ben smiled as he read his letter. Susan opened it by saying, "Hi grandpa Ben." This, Ben didn't read to Sara. He only said Susan was smart like her mother. "She says I should do what Jacob says so you explain what this vaccine stuff is," said Ben.

"Doomsday!" said John. "We'll do it. What needs to be done?" asked John.

"Vaccine is where you get, how to explain," said Sara. "It's something you put in your body that prevents you from getting diseases that kill you. Some people may get a little sick from it when they get it, but you don't die. And if you aren't vaccinated and you get sick, you will die," said Sara. "What I need to know is how many adults eighteen years and older and how many children three to eighteen years old and how many babies, and how many pregnant women?" Sara handed John a piece of paper and a pen.

"Where's the ink well?" asked John.

"Oh, the ink's inside," said Sean, taking the end cap off and scribbling on the paper.

"Nice, I like that," smiled John, writing.

"Well, we knew this winter sucks," said Sara.

"Sucks?" asked Ben.

"It's going to be a bad winter, really bad," said Sara, "so prepare like you've never prepared."

"Like what?" asked John, sliding Sara the piece of paper.

"Lots of food and wood, lots of blankets. You may not be able to get out to hunt long stretches with no meat could mean starvation."

"We kill no more than we can eat," said John.

"Fine, catch the deer, put them in a fence, and kill them as you need them. I don't care, but you will need to eat, and if you don't get out to hunt, you don't eat," said Sara.

"We are the men of the nation. We always provide for women and children," said John.

"I didn't say you didn't provide for your people, but if the snow is too deep the deer get snowbound and starve to death, then you have no food," said Sara.

"You are wise," said Ben. "These winters do happen, but we get by."

"Get by is not good enough," said Sara. "You need to keep your strength. There's a lot we have to go through yet. We may lose touch all winter. I will worry all winter after you."

"Well, these vaccines and plenty of food will give you peace of mind," said Ben.

"Yes," said Sara.

"The princess had spoken," said Ben. "We will listen. Now we leave," smiled Ben. "We'll see you in the morning." Ben took his gifts and left; John followed silently.

"Well, let's read the paper and arrange all the stuff in the bedroom. If we work together, it won't take long," said Sean.

Sara opened her marshmallow cookies. "How many times I wished for one of these cookies since I've been here," laughed Sara. "Oh look, I've been shot twice, severe head lacerations. I had surgery on my leg, my lung, and my head; I was severely beaten; I'm a mess," said Sara. "You're in good shape, though."

Sean felt sick to his stomach. What if they cut Sara's face up?

"What's that look for?" said Sara.

"I didn't protect you too well," said Sean.

"What?" laughed Sara. "I'd be dead if it wasn't for you. My wounds will heal, my life can never be replaced. Let's go through the stuff, write our letters, then put the stuff we bought away, take pictures of this place, and show them how we live. I know they want pictures of Ben, John, and us. Those you've taken we'll send with the letters."

"I was hoping to sleep sometime tonight," laughed Sean.

"Funny, you're the one who said it wouldn't take us long. I want to sleep, too. That rain on the tin roof is making me sleepy," yawned Sara.

"Well, we better get busy," said Sean, heading for the bedroom.

Sara followed. She just really didn't want to do this. The slow beat of the rain on the roof had relaxed her to the point of laziness.

Sean was right, it didn't take long to put things away. Sara cleaned the kitchen and put things away. Sean took pictures. He had one left, so he went outside and took one of the barn. Sara set a piece of paper out for Sean and one for her. Sara thought carefully, "This would probably be the most important letter she has ever written in her life."

"Dear Susan and Laura: I can't describe what it's like here. To me this is a dream world, perfect in every way. Here I can be what I'm not there. Here I'm beautiful with long, red hair and green eyes. Here I'm married to Sean. I still remain a virgin, and afraid I love John. It's like God gave me a break from reality so I could find who I am. I love all of you, and miss you all very much. I don't think I can return until I do one thing. And I don't know what that one thing is. I think my heart knows, but my brain hasn't sorted it out yet. For all I know this is a dream. Seems everyone here has the same name as there, let alone a magic hope chest with a secret place. The only thing I can't tell you is when I'll wake up. I'll have one hell of a story to tell.

There's a list from John of how many people there are in his tribe. I added us at the bottom. I hope you don't expect me to give shots. I enclosed a list of things I need. You must be careful what you send, we have no refrigerator here. Pastas and noodles are good. Sean was happy to see fast food, cold cuts, and white bread. He's tired of eating healthy. The cigarettes were great. I'm sending you both something. One for each of you from time to time. I may send things though. You get two sets of pictures made up, keep one, send one. Ben's keeping them. Go to my lawyer and start my divorce proceedings. The papers are signed, and it is paid for. The house and everything in the house is in my name, always has been. I may look stupid, but I'm not. Take everything of your father's out of my house. There are boxes upstairs with his name on them. Take your father's stuff and load it all in the truck, drive it to Aunt Carol's, and tell her she can have it all. The bills are paid to date. I have my own checking account with your name on it. Susan, you pay bills as they come along, there should be enough for a couple of months. Taxes are due January, please pay them. You should be getting them soon. The checkbook is in my purse; refills are in the stand next to my bed. Here November has just started, and I'm trying to plan Thanksgiving dinner and Christmas. There's so little to work with. I feed the turkeys a lot, so they're big and juicy. I might be able to make a couple of small salads with the mayonnaise you sent. There's no cranberry sauce. It's tough because you can't just hop in the car and run to the corner store. A trip to Rome is an all-day thing. And time is so precious here, you only make that trip once a month. Now that winter is upon us, we won't go at all. Could you send some banana bread and orange bread? We have no source of potassium and vitamin C. I've canned a lot of foods, but not many vegetables; no cabbage anywhere for cabbage salad. Pineapple is not even heard of. I guess that there's a little good in both worlds. Here it's beauty and quiet; there it's medicine and healthy food.

If I didn't miss my family so much, I would choose to live here forever. There's such an inner peace here, but in a dream world there's always an inner peace, a place to hide and heal your wounds. I sit here feeling I don't want to go back to hurt and pain, knowing I must. Each day I learn more about myself, and I've found I'm not such a bad person, no matter what I look like. Inside I'm the most beautiful person you would ever want to meet, that's my beauty. Love, Mom."

"Dear Laura: I miss you. I love you and the kids. Thanks for everything you sent. Sara yelled at me today. She thinks I'm a male chauvinist pig and plans to teach me how women think. I laughed at her. I shouldn't have done that. She's twice as head-strong here as she was at home. I figured out how to get back, but I can't tell Sara because she has to go to John on her own out of love. Why this hope chest works, I don't know. There should be enough money in the bank for six months. Tell Spencer to take over while I'm in the hospital. He knows what to do. Take another three thousand dollars out of the bank for Christmas. I used what I had to set this place up. I'm sending the land deal along with this letter. Take it to Sara's lawyer; it's important. Sara is owed a lot of money. Take some of that money and pay her house off. Leave the rest in the bank. I want decent briefs and longjohns. Buy a couple of presents for Sara from me. Send them through wrapped. I don't know what to get her. She needs something under the tree to open Christmas morning, maybe a lot of little things. I don't know, you decide. A good can opener would be nice. We have tuna fish and no opener. I've learned a lot about construction here. Things I can use at home in my business. So this has been a learning experience for me. I can't wait to get back home to you and the kids. I'll send more letters in time. One of your days is two months here, break it down. Love, Sean."

Sara and Sean folded their letters. They put everything they wanted into a green plastic bag that Susan sent, squeezed it all into the hole, closed the lid, and went to bed. Sara fell asleep right away. Sean lay on the bed looking up at the ceiling, listening to the rain until soft beats lulled him to sleep. A deep, restful sleep.

Chapter 8

SUSAN OPENED THE LID CAREFULLY. JACOB AND LAURA WAITED PATIENTLY. "There's something there," said Susan.

"Damn!" said Jacob.

"Get it out, let's see," said Laura.

"Some letters and a nightgown?" Susan said puzzled.

"Your letter, my letter, a list. I don't know what this is," said Susan.

"It's a deed," said Jacob.

"A deed?" asked Susan.

"Sean says it has to go to Sara's lawyer. She's owed a lot of money and to pay off the house and put the rest in the bank?" said Laura.

"Damn!" said Jacob.

"Is that all you can say?" asked Laura.

"Yes, I'm in shock," said Jacob.

"Well, being in shock ain't going to save those people. Sean says one of our days is two of their months," said Laura.

"Well, let's get this stuff together now. We don't have one second to lose. Jacob, come on let's get a move on," said Susan.

"Huh? Yes, let's go," said Jacob.

Everyone went their own way like a treasure hunt. "The lawyer could wait until morning," thought Susan as she drove into Price Chopper. "Here I have time to get things done; there they have no time."

Laura went to Wal-Mart to get what Sean wanted, buying small, nice things for Sara, a couple of gifts for Sean and can openers.

Jacob went to his office and took what he needed: swabs, vaccines, an air gun, rubber gloves. Everything he bagged separately. He would write the instructions at Sara's house.

Laura, Jacob, and Susan pulled in the driveway at the same time. All rushed in with their parcels. Laura wrapped, Jacob wrote instructions, Susan got out the books. They were small, paperback. Susan saw a couple more that she thought Ben would like. Mom would be surprised at what Sara had bought. It would take about three passes to get this stuff there. Everyone wrote a letter. They sent the medical stuff through first.

Sean rose first the next morning. He checked the chest; something was there, so he took it out carefully. He read the letters, then made coffee and woke Sara. "Some stuff came through. The medical supplies from Jacob, there's some letters. We'll check again in a few minutes. They're sending things through as fast as they can right now," said Sean.

Sara sat up sleepy-eyed. Sean handed her coffee. She sipped, blinked her eyes and blinked again as everything Sean said tried to register in her brain.

"Letters!" said Sara.

"Yes, here, they sent the medical right through with instructions. Looks like we're going to the nation today," smiled Sean.

"The rain stopped?" asked Sara, lighting a cigarette.

"Yes, but it's real cold out, cold enough to snow so dress warm," said Sean.

"Sean, do you ever feel or think this is all a dream?" asked Sara, getting up.

"I try not to think about it. I try to prepare a safe place for us," said Sean.

"You've done a good job. I feel comfort and warmth here," Sara said as she butted her cigarette out. "When I get back, I'm quitting smoking."

"You quit smoking, that's worth going back to see," laughed Sean.

"If we get back," said Sara.

Sean looked at Sara. "You seem a little blue. What's wrong?" asked Sean.

"Anything and everything," said Sara.

Sean stretched out on the bed. "Tell me," said Sean. "I'm your best friend."

"How can I tell you when I don't know?" said Sara.

"Sounds like you're in love," said Sean.

"You're full of yourself thinking I'm falling in love with you," snipped Sara.

"I didn't say or even think it was me," said Sean, getting up and walking over to the chest. "We have some more stuff."

Sara threw her pillow at Sean, hitting him in the back of the head.

"What did you do that for?" yelled Sean.

"Seemed right," laughed Sara. "Made me feel better."

"If you feel better, help me here. Susan's got it packed again," said Sean.

"I didn't ask for that much, a couple of books, Pepsi, nothing much. It must be what you asked Laura for," said Sara.

"I didn't ask for much," said Sean. "Just help me."

"Okay, tilt. I'll pull stuff out." So Sara started pulling stuff out. When it was empty, Sean set it back down. "Presents for you and me: can opener, canned goods, fresh fruits, a couple more Pepsis, gave me muffins. Want some? Two for you, two for me. The hash browns you can have," said Sara, sitting Indian style on the floor. Sean sat on the bed. Sara handed him breakfast. He took a couple of bites.

"What's in the cans?" asked Sean.

"I think Susan and Laura are sending us Thanksgiving and Christmas dinner or what they can," smiled Sara, reading Jacob's letter. "Jacob says there's an air gun in there and tells me how to load it. He says it should take more than an hour to inoculate everyone, that includes drops. It seems the gun works on batteries. Oh great, he wants me to give smallpox shots. He says it's easy; he's got a time schedule here, a couple of days in between for pneumonia and influenza. We have to keep it cool, but not frozen. He says I can use the air gun for it all. He sent us swabs, rubber gloves, a few samples and what they're for. They can be stored room temperature. Looks like I'm a doctor," said Sara. "Why not in a dream world? I can do anything. Everyone wants to be a hero."

"Sara, I'm worried about you. Please talk to me," said Sean.

"Why, so you can laugh in my face?" said Sara.

"Sara, I wouldn't do that. I'm in this with you," said Sean. "Another package. Help me unload."

Sara pulled things out, not saying anything. When she was done, she sat back on the floor.

"Why don't you take a nice hot bath, and I'll put this stuff away," said Sean. "We're running out of room on the floor."

Sara got up slowly. "A hot bath will do me good. I'm in love with John." Sara closed the bathroom door.

Sean smiled. "It's about time. John loves you, too," said Sean, putting cans in a plastic bag.

The bathroom door flew open. "He what?" asked Sara.

"I said he loves you, too," said Sean.

"How do you know this?" asked Sara.

"He told me," said Sean, carrying a bag into the kitchen. Sara followed him.

"Why didn't you tell me?" said Sara, yelling.

"None of my business," said Sean. "That's between you two."

"Why didn't he say anything?" asked Sara.

"He's not allowed to, he's the future chief. You have to go to him, it's the law, then they see if you're worthy of him, then they plan a wedding," said Sean, smiling and setting the bag on the island.

"How do you know this?" asked Sara.

"Ben told me. But you two have to know that you love each other," said Sean, bending down to put cans away.

"How do we do that?" said Sara.

"Think Sara. How does a man and a woman prove they love each other?" said Sean.

"I don't know," said Sara.

Sean stood up, looked at Sara. She didn't know, how could she? She'd never been in love or loved. "Okay, I'll teach you about love between men and women from our view. You teach me about love between men and women from a woman's point, deal?" asked Sean.

"Deal," smiled Sara. "I'm taking a bath, you've got stuff to put away."

"Thanks!" teased Sean.

"Any time," smiled Sara as she walked in the bathroom.

Sean heard water running and Sara humming. She was happy and that made Sean happy because Sara was headed in the right direction. Sean picked up the last of the cans and carried the plastic bag to the kitchen. "There's not much room left in the cupboard," thought Sean. "They're acting like we don't eat." The last of the cans put away, Sean went to the bedroom, checked the chest, and there was something else there. "I'll have to tell them to stop. Maybe not," thought Sean, pulling out BVDs and longjohns, books, and canned goods. The books he knew were for Ben. Sara came out towel-drying her hair. "More stuff?" she asked.

"Ben's books and underwear for me. The wool was killing my skin," laughed Sean.

"Oh," said Sara, raising an eyebrow, "and you made fun of my clothing. Look how nice I look not all squashed in?" smiled Sara.

Sean almost forgot Sara's shape. A white shirt and jeans did little to hide her beauty. "Well I must admit, futures made great progress," teased Sean. "I'm taking a shower. Your turn to put stuff away. They just keep sending things like we're desolate," laughed Sean.

"Maybe they think we are, that this won't last forever, and if we get stuck here, they will feel better knowing they tried to help," said Sara.

Sean stopped in the doorway of the bathroom. "I never looked at it that way, but I'm a man. From a woman's point of view, it's logical. From my point of view, I'd say it's excessive," said Sean.

"My God, Sean, you actually stopped and looked at both sides. Maybe there's hope for you yet," laughed Sara.

"Women!" said Sean, closing the door.

Sara stripped the bed. Everything was getting washed. On the floor lay fabric softener. How fluffy would this stuff get with fabric softener! It was sunny and windy, a good day to wash clothes, curtains, rugs. "It is only about seven in the morning, I'll probably get everything washed and on the line before Ben and John got here," she thought. Sara looked out the window—mud everywhere. "Falls are here," she thought. Sara jumped when she heard a knock on the door and opened the door for Jacob.

"Hi Jacob, come in," said Sara.

"I brought some milk and to check and see if you two were all right. Susan saw a man outside late last night. I told her she was crazy, but she insisted."

"She wasn't crazy," said Sean, walking in the room. "A man was there, came up from Albany," said Sean.

Sara looked puzzled.

"Albany, why?" asked Jacob.

"Seems a lot of sickness in Albany is headed this way. He went to tell Dr. Emerson, who laughed in his face. Seems some fancy hospital down Albany way made a vaccine to stop the sickness and Dr. Emerson wanted no part of it, so he told him to save the damn Indians John sent here. We're going to give everyone shots today. You and Susan, me, Sara, little Jacob. Albany lost 75 percent of their population. The 25 percent that lived got these shots," said Sean.

"Jesus, 75 percent dead, that's thousands of people," said Jacob.

"Yup, it's a killer, so Sara and I agreed to inoculate us and the Indians. Sara offered him coffee, but he couldn't stay. He wanted to hit as many towns as he could. A lot of towns won't take it, so this winter could be bad."

"I'll get Susan and the baby. I'm taking no chances," said Jacob. "I'll be right back." Jacob ran across the barn for Susan and the baby and to apologize for calling her crazy.

"Smooth move," said Sara, filling the sink with warm water.

"He set it up for me. I thought I saw Susan in the window last night, and I knew we would have to lie to get them to do it, but fear is the best way," said Sean.

"But you didn't lie, a lot of people are dying," said Sara, putting sheets in the water and turning it off.

"Well, let's get stuff ready," said Sean.

Jacob kissed Susan and apologized for calling her crazy, then told her everything Sean told him. Fear ran through her body and came out in a cry. She grabbed Jacob and said, "We're getting shots now." She passed Jacob to his father, grabbed a quilt, and threw it over the baby. They ran through the barn to Sean and Sara's home. Sara sat at the island, a piece of paper in front of her, bottles lined up, and alcohol swabs.

"I'm giving Sean the shots first. If he dies, we don't take it," said Sara.

"Oh, no!" said Susan.

"Susan, I'm joking. I'm going to show you how easy it is. I've got the instructions in front of me," smiled Sara. "Relax, they wouldn't have sent that man around if it wasn't easy."

Sean took off his shirt. Sara wiped the right arm, held the gun, and it went pop. Sara wiped off his arm and covered it with a bandage, then went to Sean's left arm, changed bottles, and shot Sean's left arm. "This one will scab; don't pick or scratch it, you'll end up with an awful scar." Sean held out his tongue, and Sara put drops on it. Sean swallowed. "Some people will feel a little sick. It's just your body adjusting. If you feel too sick, come and get me, I have medication for it. In two days, you get two more shots. Who's next?" asked Sara. In ten minutes everyone had their shots. "Now remember don't touch the scab, it will come off by itself. Well, we're done. Now later today Sean and I are going to the nation and giving them all shots. There's a couple I can't give shots to, they are ready to deliver, so I'll do them after the babies come, which is only a couple of days away."

"You can't take this if you're pregnant," asked Susan.

"Yes, but these two woman fear it will put them into labor early, and their children will be born with no souls, so I'll honor their request," said Sara.

"Yes, we all have our beliefs," smiled Susan. "I'll never regret getting these shots."

"Nor will I," said Sara. "Want coffee?"

"No, I'm doing laundry, not too many good drying days left," said Susan.

"Yes, I'm doing the same thing, I thought I'd air the place out while we're at the nation. I'm afraid winter's here. I expect to wake up any night and see snow," said Sara.

"I've had that feeling, too, so I'm scrubbing and washing. Can't be too clean this time of year, not with all this illness headed this way. I'm glad I'm scrubbing," said Susan.

"You know Mom gave me some cleaner that killed germs, all kinds. I think I've got some left. I'll share it with you, wash walls and everything, even the baby's stuff," said Sara. Sara took a jar down from the cupboard and went into the bedroom, poured Lysol out of a bottle into the jar. Sara looked around, a bar of anti-bacterial soap. "Ah, here's a jar," Sara poured anti-bacterial dish soap in it, then went back to the kitchen. "This is the cleaner, you don't need much. This should last you awhile. Wash your dishes with this one and your hands with the bar soap. They all kill germs, and you don't need much. Mom was a firm believer that all doorknobs and pails carried the most germs. Toilets need to be washed down a lot," smiled Sara.

"Well, if your mother used it, it's good enough for me. Your mother knew know to fight a lot of things when it came to sickness. I don't know how many people she cured. I remember her saying, 'Use a hankie when you cough and sneeze. Nobody else wants your sickness,'" laughed Susan.

"One of many of her lessons," smiled Sara.

"Well, I've got cleaning to do. I'll see you later, thanks for the cleaners. I'll get supper tonight for all of us. You come over," said Susan.

"Well, I cooked up a surprise. I was going to have you over," laughed Sara.

"Yours is all cooked?" asked Susan.

"Yes," said Sara.

"Well, I guess we eat here then," laughed Susan. "Tomorrow, my place."

"Okay," said Sara.

"Bye." Jacob, Susan, and the baby went home.

Sara did the laundry, cleaned the house, and opened windows. Sean took another bag of stuff out of the chest. He put it away. Everything was washed with Lysol. Sara was bringing in the dry laundry when John and Ben came.

"Just in time, you two. I'm just finishing up," smiled Sara.

"Well, we're ready, so let's go," said Ben.

Sean carried everything in a pillow case, even Ben's books. Sean and Sara followed Ben and John. The song, "He Ain't Heavy He's My Brother," kept playing in Sean's head. He didn't know why. Sara was trying to keep the butterflies down. She felt like she was running into doom. She didn't know why. She felt ill at ease. They came into a clearing, and people were lined and waiting. "So many." thought Sara.

Sara explained how it was going to work. No one questioned her. They just walked up, and got their shots and drops. Sara changed batteries twice. When she finished, everyone went about their task.

"Everyone's so busy," said Sara to Ben.

"Well, it going to be such a bad winter, we are putting extra work in so we're ready. Here everyone works hard," said Ben.

"And here all along I thought you didn't like women working," teased Sara.

"Only princess who doesn't have fear," said Ben, laughing.

"Oh, I see, you don't think I'm streetwise," said Sara.

"Streetwise?" asked Ben.

"It's a saying in the future for kids who live on the street. They know the bad guys, the good guys, where the drugs and guns are, what pimps are the best ones to work for. They know how to spot a cop, and who's easy to get money from, when and where to steal," said Sara.

"Oh, no you are not streetwise, your heart is too good, too trusting, too loving," said Ben.

Sara and Ben were walking through the nation while they talked.

"Ben, can I ask you something?" asked Sara.

"Sounds serious," said Ben.

"It is," said Sara.

"Then ask your question," said Ben.

Sara slid her hands in her coat pocket. Sara sighed. "Ben, would you think it wrong of me if I fell in love with John? If it's against your laws, I will walk away and say nothing. I respect you and your people and would do nothing that hurt you. I seek your advice on this matter. Whatever you advise, I will do."

"My advice? How can I advise you if you don't know if you love John or not?" said Ben.

"Oh, I love him, but John's going to be chief one day, and I would do nothing that would interfere with that. He's going to be a good leader," said Sara.

"Well, I think it's about time you realized you love John," smiled Ben. "Now you have to let your heart tell you what's right for you. It breaks no law whom John chooses to marry. The times change, we try to keep our ways," said Ben.

"Ben, I'm not Indian. This must break some law," said Sara.

"What law?" asked Ben.

"I don't know, now I'm really confused," said Sara.

"That's because you think with your head and not your heart," said Ben. "Stop thinking, start feeling," said Ben. "You get less headaches that way."

Sara laughed. "I'll try, but in my other life all I had was my brains. Here they're worth nothing. So much for education," said Sara.

"You ready to go?" asked Sean.

"Sure, I'll see you Ben. I'll be back in two days and finish giving shots, and we'll be all set," said Sara.

"I'll see you when you come back. There's a lot to do here, so I'll be busy here," said Ben. "It will snow soon."

"Well, if you need me, send someone for me," said Sara.

"I will, princess. See you in two days," said Ben.

Sean and Sara walked home.

"Are you sure you got everyone?" asked Sean.

"Yes, why?" asked Sara.

"We have extra bottles," said Sean.

"I think Jacob sent extra in case some broke," said Sara.

"Oh, so if we wanted, we could give shots to other people?" said Sean.

"Who? You going to play God and choose who in Rome should be shots and who won't?" said Sara.

"No," said Sean. "I'm must thinking if someone found out, would you give it to them?"

"I'd give it out until it was gone," said Sara.

"No you won't," said Sean. "You would put us at risk."

"Oh," said Sara, "you're right, I wasn't thinking. I'll send it back."

"Yes, then we won't have any," said Sean.

"Well we're home," smiled Sara. "More work, got to finish cleaning."

"Yeah, I'm working in the barn," said Sean.

Sean and Sara walked in their home. "Smells fresh and clean, but it's colder than hell in here, close the windows," said Sara.

They closed the windows. Sean cleaned out the kitchen stove and started a warm fire. "I don't know what to do with these ashes," said Sean.

"You are joking," said Sara.

"No, why, you know what to do with them," asked Sean.

"That's the best fertilizer you can have. Throw it on the ground on the side, I plan to put a garden there, that's why I'm saving coffee grounds. Thick layers of ash, coffee grounds, and manure will make the soil rich come spring," said Sara.

"You mean that, don't you?" said Sean.

"Yes I do it at home all the time," said Sara.

Sean snickered. "I thought you had some great secret formula that made your garden grow so good," said Sean.

"All you had to do was ask," laughed Sara. "This place warms up good."

"Well, after today you don't be able to open windows. Jacob and I are putting on storms," said Sean.

"Great, it's going to smell awful in here come spring."

"No, I don't think so. I think it got enough fresh air today for the rest of the year," laughed Sean.

"Funny," said Sara, taking the basket of clean clothes off the island and walking into the bedroom. Sara looked at the chest. Why not look? She did and there was Sean. "Can you help me a second?" called Sara.

"Sure," said Sean, walking in the bedroom.

"Close the door," said Sara.

Sean closed the door. "Not again, aren't you women ever satisfied. This is going to be the last for a while. It can't keep going on like this, we need a break."

"Please, once more, I promise I'll stop it," said Sara.

Jacob backed out the door just as quietly as he came in, a smile on his face. He walked in his house smiling.

"What's got you?" asked Susan.

"I went over to Sean's to see if he was ready to put up windows. I think I better take a coffee break," laughed Jacob.

"Oh," smiled Susan.

"This place smells real clean," said Jacob.

"It does, doesn't it?" said Susan. "There were probably thousands of germs crawling around waiting to attack."

"Well at least Sean was smart enough to take that medicine. Come spring I don't know how many people will have passed on. We don't know who took the medicine and who didn't. I would never say anything against Doc, but he was wrong. So many will die, whole families," said Jacob.

"Well, Doc did what he thought best. Now he has to live with his choice. When he sees it was a bad one, he'll live in his own hell. We must never say a word. A man should never be reminded of his mistakes, lest he make them again," said Susan.

Knock, knock. "Jacob, ready for those windows?" asked Sean, walking in.

Jacob looked at Susan. "Sure, I was just at your place. I thought you and Sara were busy," said Jacob.

"She upset me. I'm constantly moving the bed so she can clean it. She's afraid of spiders, so I have to move the furniture so she can clean it."

"If she puts cedar chips around, the spiders won't come around. They don't like the smell," said Susan.

"Thank you, I will tell her. She drives me nuts with this spider thing," smiled Sean. "She's seen one since we've been here. She goes crazy when she sees one, then it takes me two hours to calm her down. Damn thing was so small I couldn't see it to kill it right away," laughed Sean. "What are you doing with your ashes from the stove?" asked Sean.

"Spreading them on the side of the house for a garden," said Jacob.

"So are we. I was thinking maybe we should mark how big the garden will be and put the manure on it in the winter," said Sean.

"Yeah, that would work great," smiled Jacob. "Won't have to haul to the field. Bessy will deliver any time today, she's ready. I checked her a little while ago."

"Well, let's get to those windows before we get side-tracked again," said Sean.

"Sure," said Jacob.

"This place looks great, Susan," said Sean.

"Thank you," smiled Susan.

Sara wrote a note telling them to slow up on what they are sending, "We have no more room to put anything," then sent back what vaccine she didn't use. In two days she'd give the last shot. Right now she had to find a place to put this stuff, soups, crackers, corned beef, some Christmas stuff. After that was done, Sara washed everything down with Lysol, sprayed the bed and pillows with Lysol and made the bed, then scrubbed the bathroom and from there to clean the living room, ending in the kitchen where she stirred the sauce and started the water boiling for spaghetti. She set the table, then ironed the curtains and hung them up. She waved to Sean and Jacob as they met at each side of the window. Satisfied the house was clean, Sara checked to make sure nothing incriminating was out. She poured Pepsi in a pitcher so it didn't look bad, then put Italian bread on the cutting board and placed it on the table where Sean sat. Sara broke up a one pound box of angel hair in the boiling water and threw the box in the stove to burn. She just closed the lid when Susan walked in.

"Something smells good," smiled Susan, closing the door.

"Hi Sooze, this is that Italian dish I was telling you about," said Sara.

"Oh spaghetti, I remember your mom learned how to make it when she went to Italy," said Susan.

"That's the one. All those tomatoes I bought, this is it," smiled Sara. Sara couldn't remember telling Susan about it.

"I had it once at your mother's, but yours smells better," said Susan.

"Thank you, I made a few changes. I hope it's as good as you remembered," said Sara, pouring the spaghetti in a colander and rinsing it.

"It smells better than I remembered," laughed Susan. "My house smells so clean, even Jacob noticed, that's a miracle."

"What's a miracle?" said Sean, walking in.

"That you two are on time for supper," laughed Susan.

Sara put the pasta in a bowl, set it on the table, then poured sauce in a bowl, set that on the table followed by a tossed salad.

"Smells good," said Jacob.

"Wash your hands, Jacob, you know the rules," said Susan.

"Yes dear," smiled Jacob, "just as soon as Sean's done."

"There's room for two, go!" said Susan.

"Okay," smiled Jacob. "All I do now is wash my hands. Next she'll want to check behind my ears like Mom did," teased Jacob.

Sara set the pitcher of Pepsi on the table. "Seems to me that's all men want is mothering," laughed Sara. "Laundry, cooking, cleaning, more cooking."

"Okay," smiled Sean. "We understand you two spoil us rotten."

"Whoa, be still my heart," teased Sara. "He admits we spoil him."

"I understand you don't like spiders," said Jacob.

"What, Sean complained again because I make him move things so I can clean?" laughed Sara.

"No, I was going to tell you cedar chips keep them away. Susan doesn't like them either," said Jacob, sitting down.

Sean said a prayer, followed by an Amen and then he sliced the bread, and it was fresh. After everyone was fed and unable to move, Jacob and Susan agreed it was a very good meal.

"My arm was sore for a while after those shots," said Jacob.

"Everybody's was," said Sean. "Sara's was probably the worst because she had to hold it in one position to give everyone else the shot," said Jacob.

"Yeah, how did it go?" asked Susan.

"Good. They were all fired up when we got there. They're really busy getting ready for winter. I guess it's supposed to be real bad," said Sara.

"Really?" asked Jacob.

"Yeah, we had better make sure we have twice as much wood as we figured to heat with, maybe build some kind of fence for wind," said Sean.

"That's probably not a bad idea, but what kind of fence and where?" asked Jacob.

"That's a good question. Northwest winds are probably the worst," said Sean.

"Yes, they are the coldest," said Jacob.

"I don't know what to do," said Sean, leaning on the table. "What do you suggest?" asked Sean. "It's kind of late for heavy work, so what to do."

"Well, Susan and I have a little money. We could go to Rome, just buy the wood," said Jacob.

"I have a better idea. We'll go to Rome, and I'll buy the wood. You and Susan save your money. We'll leave early. I think I remembered seeing something wood, picket wood," said Sean.

"Yes, they had some picket fencing," said Jacob.

"Not fencing. I don't want it small like a fence. I want it tall. We can enclose all around both houses with a gate that leaves both barn doors open," said Sean.

"Yeah, I see what you mean. That would work and wouldn't take too long to put on,' said Jacob. "Good idea. To Rome in the morning then."

"You need help with dishes?" said Susan, getting up.

"I've got help with the dishes," said Sara. "Jacob's waking up," smiled Sara.

Susan looked toward the couch. "So he is. It's feeding time, bath, and then to bed," said Susan.

"Well, you take him home and tuck him in; the more he sleeps the faster he'll grow," said Sara.

"Please, I can hardly lift him as it is," laughed Susan. "Thanks for supper," said Susan as she put on her shawl.

"That's a nice shawl. It looks nice and warm," said Sara.

"Thank you, I made it, and it is warm, real warm," said Susan, picking up Jacob. "I'll tuck the little guy in here like this, and we're both warm. Huh, big guy?"

Jacob cried. "Oh boy is he hungry," laughed Susan.

"Well, I'll see you tomorrow," said Sara. "You take care till then." Sara heard Jacob scream all the way across the barn... 'He wanted supper." Sara watched until they were inside, then closed the door. Sean was clearing dishes when Sara turned around. "I was only joking when I said you would help me with dishes," said Sara.

"I don't mind, you've been on the go all day. I sat around and watched. The only thing I did today was windows, fed a few animals," said Sean. "You've been on your feet all day."

"Thank you for helping then. I'm going to do dishes, take a shower, get my nightgown on, and crochet for a while, then go to bed and sleep forever," laughed Sara.

Sean and Sara just finished dishes when Jacob came in.

"What's wrong?" asked Sean.

"Bessy, you got to see this. I don't even believe it," said Jacob.

Sean grabbed his coat and went with Jacob.

"How many do you see?" asked Sean.

"Three?"

"She had three?" asked Sean.

"Yes, one male, two females. I ain't ever seen anything like it in my lifetime," said Jacob. "I knew she was close, so I checked. I never expected this."

"They're all healthy, no problems?" asked Sean.

"None, none at all," said Jacob.

"Well, we have two cows a piece, and a bull to keep them pregnant," laughed Sean.

Jacob crossed his arms. "Susan says you're angels. Now I want to hear your side and now," said Jacob.

Sean sighed. "Walk with me, we'll measure for fencing. You won't believe me anyway," said Sean. "You'll think we're nuts."

"Try me," said Jacob.

They went outside. Sean talked; Jacob listened. He told him everything. "That's all of it, now tell me I'm crazy," said Sean.

"I don't think you're crazy. It all makes sense now," said Jacob. "These shots will save a lot of people who would have died, wouldn't they," asked Jacob.

"Yes," said Sean doubtful. "The nation was almost wiped out completely. The sickness that's coming is bad. The winter is horrible. Ben was going to tell you this when we returned, so you could help Sean and Sara adjust to their lives, their new lives," Sean said sadly.

"I knew there was something different, but I couldn't put my finger on it. Does Sara know what she has to do?" asked Jacob.

"No, and she can't be told. She has to do it on her own," said Sean.

Jacob laughed. "At least I don't feel so stupid now. I was beginning to think you've become a genius, yet everything was the basics from where you came from. A lot of things we have most people don't know about, do they?" asked Jacob.

"No, but I figured since I had the knowledge, why waste it? Why be uncomfortable?" said Sean.

"Why did you choose Susan and I to save?" asked Jacob.

"I don't know, something told me to. Who knows what your offspring could be, maybe even president, one who would actually do something," said Sean. "Sara's upset. When we go back she'll miss you guys. She has no friends back home except me. She's been so happy having a girlfriend to talk to, to do things with. Well probably my wife now, they're getting close."

"Can I tell Susan, she would stop calling you angels?" laughed Jacob.

"Sure, if she'd believe you. Hell, I'm living it and don't believe it," said Sean.

"Oh, she'll believe it, and after I'm done telling her, you better have coffee on because she'll be right over wanting to know everything," laughed Jacob.

"Well I better put coffee on, and let Sara know that you two know now. I don't know how she'll react, so give me a little time," laughed Sean.

Sara came out of the bedroom drying her hair. “Mmm, I smell coffee, and it smells good.”

“Sit down, I’ll pour you some,” smiled Sean. He took a deep breath, let it out and said, “I told Jacob everything, want cream?” All in one breath.

“You what?” yelled Sara.

Susan came running in. “Sara you poor thing, why didn’t you tell me? God how scared you must feel,” cried Susan, hugging Sara.

“It’s strange, I can’t explain it,” said Sara.

Jacob walked in carrying the baby, who was asleep and laid him on the couch. “You better try or none of us will get any sleep,” laughed Jacob.

“Maybe it’s best I show you,” said Sara. Sara walked in the bedroom and came back carrying two newspapers. “This is where it started,” said Sara. “This is a picture of me in my time; this is Sean.”

“You’re really beautiful,” said Susan. “Says here you went to several colleges.”

“It sounds more grandeur than it is. It was night school, and I had to go to different schools to get what I wanted,” laughed Sara.

“This man is?” said Susan, pointing to a picture.

“That man is my husband who hired someone to kill me,” said Sara.

“Bastard,” said Susan as she read. “Says there Sean saved your life by jumping in front of the bullet. Now you’re both in a coma. What’s a coma?” asked Susan.

“A really deep sleep,” said Sara.

“Okay, so when you wake up, you won’t be here anymore, but the real Sean and Sara will be here, is that how it works?” asked Susan.

“I’m assuming that’s how it works,” said Sara.

“I understand you keep in touch with your daughter and Sean’s wife who’s brother is a doctor, who sent the medicine to you to help us live?” asked Susan.

“Yes, this is weird. Wait a minute, I have letters, some I haven’t read,” said Sara. Sara went in, got letters, and came back to the kitchen. “These I’ve read; these I got before I left.”

“Oh, my God,” cried Sara.

“What?” asked Sean.

Sara held up the letter for Sean to read. “Holy shit, look and see if they sent anything else,” said Sean.

Sara, Sean, Jacob, and Susan ran to the bedroom. “Something is there, let’s see what.” Sara started pulling stuff out. Two letters and a newspaper. Sara left the stuff on the floor, and everyone went into the kitchen.

“What’s wrong?” asked Susan.

"My husband was killed by a Mr. Smithers. Sean this means changes are beginning," said Sara. "Look, we're on pages one, two, and three. Maybe we've done too much," said Sara.

Susan was confused. "Why, what's wrong?" said Susan.

Sara read the article out loud.

"Hey, you guys are famous people," said Susan.

"We weren't when we left," said Sara. "Says here Mr. Smithers walked up to Tom and shot him four times while the crowd cheered him on, then shot himself. Seems Mr. Smithers was out on bail for shooting us, so the man who shot us, Tom, then killed himself. Mr. Smithers confessed and was granted immunity for confessing. He would have been a free man," said Sean. "A note later found said Mr. Smithers regretted what he had done and said that neither man should be allowed to live for any reason. Later Mr. George was found murdered by Mr. Smithers, who said what they had done was unjust, that Mrs. Valentine was too nice of a person to have done to her what was done. May God forgive us all. He knew they would get away with it," said Sara. "Well, I don't have to worry about the divorce. Susan wants to know what to do with Tom's remains. I better send a letter. There's a will that tells her everything. Says here John's happy Dad's dead, he wanted to kill him himself. Susan has to make John understands this," said Sara.

"Have Jacob talk to him; he can make him understand," said Sean.

"Good idea," said Sara, writing as fast as she could.

Jacob and Susan just watched Sara and Sean and would ask questions later.

Susan read, Sara went and put the note in the bag, and closed the lid. "This is so strange," said Sara as she walked back into the kitchen.

"What's strange?" asked Susan.

"This whole dream, the chest, all of it, it seems so real," said Sara.

"Look, you probably don't want to hear this, but you were here for a reason. All I read is good. Maybe the bad guys lose on this; the good guys win. Maybe God got tired of bad and wanted some good, and he used you to do it. Look at the people you've saved; they're good people. The wagon train, us, the Indians, and yourselves. None of us are bad people. Mr. Smithers could be a descendent of Mr. Smithers, whose ass you saved by buying this land. We are real; this is no dream," said Susan.

"You make it sound so simple," said Sara.

"It is, you said it, life is simple. It's mankind who makes it hard," said Susan.

"You're right, I mean you knew I wasn't Sara right from the beginning, but you did help me through some tough times," said Sara. "I just wish I could be with my children right now; they need me."

"Susan and John are adults, they can handle it," said Sean.

"I'm worried about John," said Sara. "I'll get the stuff sent and bring it out."

"I'll help," said Susan, getting up. "I'd love to see some stuff from the future," laughed Susan.

"Oh, we've got a lot of things from the future," laughed Sean. "They don't stop sending."

Sara looked at Sean. "I didn't ask for this," said Sara, walking into the bedroom. Susan followed.

Sara grabbed the green plastic bag and threw things in the bag. "I'll show you everything tomorrow while the men are in Rome," said Sara.

"May I?" asked Susan, looking at the chest.

"Sure, I don't know if there's anything there this fast," said Sara.

"How do you know?" asked Susan.

"Susan usually leaves a tab or something out," said Sara.

"Like this?" asked Susan.

"Yes, just like that," said Sara. "Let's see, damn it's full. Here I'll pull it out. You stuff it in that bag," said Sara.

"Okay," Sara pulled and tugged and out came Pampers and a letter. Sara kept pulling out Pampers. Finally the bag came free.

"What's these?" asked Susan.

"Pampers, throw-away diapers," said Sara.

"Throw-away diapers? You don't wash diapers in the future?" asked Susan.

"Nope. Throw them out, burn them, whatever," said Sara.

"I think I like that," smiled Susan.

"Well, let's put the Pampers in the bag, they're yours for the baby. Don't tell John I told them to send them. We'll probably get more. I think they're having fun sending us stuff," laughed Sara.

Sara and Susan came back into the kitchen. Susan left the diapers in the living room. "I've got another letter," said Sara.

"Now what?" asked Sean.

"I don't know, I've got to read it," said Sara agitated. "You act like this is my fault. I didn't start this, they did," yelled Sara, putting the bag on the island.

"What's your problem?" asked Sean.

"I'm tired of you bitching at me. I've got enough fucking problems without you on my back," yelled Sara.

"What problems?" asked Sean.

"Oh, I don't know, let's see. I'm at death's door, my husband hired someone to kill me, then someone killed him. My children don't know what to do, and John's happy he's dead, he was planning to kill him. And I'm stuck here listening to you bitch at me because they are trying to get help the only way they know. Other than that, everything is hunky-dory," yelled Sara.

"Okay, I'll back off. I'm sorry," said Sean. "Read the letter."

"It's from John. Jacob talked to him, and he just needs to hear from me," said Sara.

Sara grabbed a sheet of paper, wrote John a letter, and said, "I love you very much my, baby boy. I miss you. I wish I could be with you, but I can't right now, so be my man. Love, Mom." Sara put it in the chest and hoped John was waiting. She walked back to the kitchen, she was tired, had a headache. It was too much for one day.

"Sara, look, I'm really sorry. I know this is tough on you, you've always been there for your kids, but they have to grow up some time," said Sean.

"They are grown up. They're just in shock and can't think clearly," said Sara.

"How about some more coffee," asked Jacob.

"Yes, and we have goodies," smiled Sean.

"Future goodies," said Susan.

"Yes, but let's see what we've got in this bag," said Sean, trying to be chipper and not mentioning Sara being upset.

"Sara, the pictures are back," said Sean, smiling. "There's a note from Susan. 'God, what a hunk John is, can I have him?'"

Sara laughed. "That's Susan, she probably thinks I can put him in the hole, and he'll flash home to her," said Sara.

"I can just picture John around Susan and Laura, poor man wouldn't stand a chance," laughed Sean.

Susan laughed. "In our time things are different. Women are bolder, very bold. They find a man that's to their liking, heaven help him. They do everything but rape the poor man," said Sara.

"Sometimes they do that," laughed Sean.

"This is acceptable behavior?" asked Susan.

"If you could see the people of the future, they would scare you," said Sara.

"Oh, more goodies, chocolate-covered Oreos, white chocolate-covered Oreos, peanut butter cookies, marshmallow candies, a box of Russell Stover candies, chocolate-covered cherries, Christmas candies, more stuff for Christmas cooking, little tea breads, some tea, baby wipes, these must be for Susan," said Sara. "Give me that box of candy," said Sara.

"What box of candy?" teased Sean.

"The one you stuffed under your arm," said Sara.

"Jacob, Susan, I would like you to meet Sara, the chocoholic. Russell Stover candies. She eats them right down. No, woofs them down," teased Sean.

"Candy," said Sara. "Please."

"Here you said the magic word," smiled Sean. "Watch this, she grabs a knife, opens like an expert."

Sara grabbed a piece and passed it around, then opened the cookies. "You wouldn't believe the size of our grocery stores in the future. Bigger than this whole barn," said Sara, eating a marshmallow cookie.

Jacob and Susan tasted everything. "The people may be strange, but the food is good," laughed Jacob.

"What are baby wipes?" asked Susan.

"To wash hands, face, and bottoms, then throw out, throw away wash clothes," said Sara. "Throw-away or recyclable," said Sara. "You wouldn't believe the trash problems we have."

"If you throw everything away, I can," said Susan.

"Oh, the Pampers don't need pins, they stick on," said Sara.

"I stick them on little Jacob?" asked Susan.

"No, look," said Sara, getting a Pamper. "These tabs stick to the front like this, then unstick to take off; no pins to hurt the baby."

"That's a nice idea," said Susan.

"There's plastic on the outside so the outside clothes stays dry," said Sara.

"They thought of everything. We were going to die weren't we?" asked Susan.

Sara took in a deep breath, let is out. "Yes, December 2," said Sara. "You may still get sick, but I have medicine for it, so I'm prepared. They, Sara, didn't write in her diary what we all had, but so many people will die this year. Jacob, millions die all across America. It's going to be real bad."

"You saved us twice now. Why, you didn't know us?" said Susan.

"I needed a friend, and you showed up," said Sara. "I don't know what your future holds for you. I just hope I haven't ruined your life."

"How could you ruin my life by saving it?" asked Susan.

"The future sucks. Maybe by saving your life I created a living hell for you," said Sara.

"Sara, I have more now than I thought I'd ever have. What Sean and Jacob are planning is far more than either of us ever thought we'd have. No you didn't ruin our lives, you gave us a life worth living," said Susan. "Hell, I have hot running water; nobody else does. This place will be in tip-top shape come spring. We plant our gardens, build our homes. The only thing I regret is not having you as a friend forever," said Susan.

"The real Sean and Sara will be so confused when we return. They have no idea of what's going on, none," said Sara.

"We'll tell them they were sick and we've been taking care of them and built all this for them," said Susan.

"Just as long as they believe you. The Indians know about the market. There will always be money, check with Ben or John. They have a list of things that change the world, the good and the bad. I've taught them what I know, but they have taught me far more," said Sara.

"Well, we're going. You look awfully tired. Sleep in tomorrow, and I'll talk to you in the morning," said Susan. Susan took the baby wipes and put them in the bag of Pampers. Jacob picked up the baby, who slept through everything.

"The baby is soaked," said Jacob.

"Not any more," smiled Susan. "When he gets home, he'll be put in Pampers. Night guys."

Sara waved good night and started picking up the kitchen.

Sara reached for a coffee cup; Sean reached for Sara's hand. "Sara, I'm really sorry for yelling at you. I know it's not your fault," said Sean.

"What's not my fault? We're here because my husband hated me enough to want me dead. My children keep sending me things because it's the only way they know how to keep in touch with the only parent they have. What part is not my fault? The way I see it, it's all my fault. My husband, my kids, my life," said Sara.

"No," said Sean. "You're the victim in this. You didn't ask for any of this. If I had married you, none of this would have happened," said Sean.

"You, marry me?" asked Sara.

"Yes, I wanted to, but I didn't know how to ask. When I came back you were married and had one child and expecting another. It devastated me, so I married Laura and swore to protect you my whole life," said Sean.

"Well look where that got you," said Sara.

"I don't regret it," said Sean, "not one second of it. My life is worthless if I hadn't known you."

"Sean that's sweet, but my life sucks, it always has. You vowing to protect me has only put stress on you. Please don't take this wrong, you sound like my husband, and I hate that. My husband yelled at me whenever he was around. He never knew me at all. I just got tired of hearing it, so I ended up saying nothing, not going anywhere. I hated life altogether. My children had grown up, married, and left. I felt loneliness set in, which opened me to more abuse from Tom. He never hit me in front of the kids, but he'd throw me. If I got hurt, he'd say I fell. A lot of times he'd walk by and push me. He always told me how useless I was. Everything that happened to him was my fault. I started feeling good about myself here, and you start yelling at me for something I have no control over and all the feelings come rushing over me again, the criticism, the hate, and the fear. You have no idea what it feels like to have your husband correct everything you say. Every time I said something, people called me a liar and storyteller. It doesn't feel good knowing what you're saying is true, and your husband has to step in and say that's not true, this is the way it is. And when you ask a question and you don't know the answer, you ask someone, and he says to ignore her. I know or watch everything I do so closely that you become so self-conscience you feel stupid, and you know he's going to embarrass you in front of everyone, so he can feel like a man. No, my life is hell. You have no idea of my hell," said Sara, walking away. "I'm going to bed, I have a massive headache. Good night."

Sean made hot chocolate, put fluff in it, carried it in the bedroom. Sara was crying. Sean handed her the hot chocolate and went in the bathroom. He took Tylenol and hand cream off the shelf in the linen closet. Sean went back in the bedroom. "Take these, and take your nightgown off," said Sean.

"What!" asked a startled Sara.

Sean held up the hand cream. "Back rub," said Sean. "Helps headaches, it does."

"It does?" smiled Sara.

"Best cure," smiled Sean.

Sara took the Tylenol, then took her nightgown off, and lay on the bed. Sean started to massage Sara's back, neck, arms, and legs. She was tense; Sean felt it in each muscle. He said nothing but kept massaging. It would take a long time to work the stress out. It was deep in Sara's muscles, some really huge knots.

"Can't I take a break and drink my hot chocolate before it gets cold?" asked Sara.

"Sure," said Sean, standing up straight. He walked over to the chest. He opened it, sure enough something was there. He took it out: a few little things and a letter for both of them. "This one's for you," said Sean, handing it to Sara.

Sean opened his; it was from Susan. "John's accepted this, he sent Mom a letter. Jacob said to keep the extra vaccine. He made a list of names he wants you to vaccinate, something about them being geniuses that died who would have changed Rome: doctors, one had a cure for cancer. I know it sounds like you're playing God, but you're not. These people can benefit mankind. We won't send any more newspapers. Mom's so rich she may go into shock. I took the will and deed to the lawyer. Dad had two insurance policies on himself. One at work for one hundred and fifty thousand dollars, double indemnity, if he was shot. How's that for a kick in the ass? Also, a wrongful death policy for five million dollars. Everything goes to Mom because the will was set up that way. If Mom died, Dad got everything. The deed has blown a hole in everything here. The deed is set up in such a way the Indians own a lot. Mom owns a lot. Everything is topsy turvy. John's in shock. I told him John's his father. He said this whole thing is going so fast that it's making our heads spin. You can't keep up with the phone calls. Laura's been great, she sends her love. The kids are great, they drew you some pictures. They're in the bag. Mom's healing really good. The doctors think it's from years of vitamins and organic foods. She always kept herself physically fit. Mom's room is loaded with flowers. People keep praying for her. The paper printed Mom's whole life, her years of abuse that led to her being marked for death, that's what the paper called it. You know them, and there are titles with movies. I don't know who told them the story. I know it wasn't us because we never knew. The lawyer said he could find out. I told him to let it go, it's already been told. You'll never change people's minds now, it's all been out. Bambi attempted suicide. I don't know how or how she is. Sorry about all the stuff we keep sending, it's just so cool. Laura and I are having a ball. John sat next to the chest waiting for Mom to answer. It came so quick he was surprised. We're saving all this stuff. Laura says you and Mom won't believe it wasn't a dream, so we have been keeping things you send us. Laura said you probably worked yourself in a dither over us sending you stuff, so this time we sent you your mechanical drawing stuff with drawing paper. She said it would sooth your feathers. That and the fact your business is doing so well. Everyone feels that you're such a hero that you are an honest man, so everyone wants your business. They say it's about time this town had a hero. The fact that a man put his life on the line for a woman has sparked the "knight-in-shining-armor" syndrome. Women demand, men open doors, send flowers, act like human beings. Laura and John are treated like royalty. We're gobbling it up like the Thanksgiving turkey. Well I'll close everything for now, but I'll keep you informed of any changes as they occur. Love, Susan, Laura, and John."

"Sara," said Sean, turning around. She'd put her nightgown on and was sound asleep, the letter in her hand. Sean covered Sara and took the letter from Sara's hand; he read it. "Mom, I love you, John." She just needed to know John was okay. Nothing he could have done wouldn't have done as much as those three words from John.

Sean read his list of names, then the letter. The word cancer kept leaping out at him. He always thought the rumors were just that, rumors. Seems this doctor made up come concoction in his kitchen, cured a lot of cancer with it. He refused to write it down because he said the world wasn't ready for it. He said that doctors would charge too much for the treatment, and people would pay it to live. "But it couldn't be true," thought Sean as he cleaned the kitchen. The man's a doctor, he had to share what he knew, didn't he? His oath said so." Sean always thought that is someone found a cure for something, they would want to share it, to get recognized for their accomplishment. Hell, the way they rip people off in our time, maybe the doctor wasn't so stupid. Sean blew out the candles and went to bed. He didn't care what Susan said, he did feel like he was playing God. He felt better knowing Jacob and Susan knew. They were putting pressure on Sara and him without realizing it. All this miracle and angel stuff could stop now.

Chapter 9

JOHN SAT AT THE KITCHEN TABLE DRINKING COFFEE, STARING AT SUSAN AND Laura. He was tired, shocked. He'd finally moved from the chest in the bedroom. He wore black jeans, a white pocket T-shirt, and a five o'clock shadow.

Susan and Laura sat across from each other talking. A knock came at the door. "Come in," yelled Susan.

"Don't do that," yelled John, slamming his fist on the table. "Mom did it, look where she is. You get up and answer the door," said John, getting up and walking to the door.

Susan and Laura were startled. Susan got up, got a dish cloth, and wiped up the coffee spills.

"These two men need to talk to us," said John.

Susan and Laura looked to see two huge Indians standing there. "Wow!" said Susan. "What are two guys like you doing here?"

"We're your bodyguards and limo drivers. Your mother is so worried about you two. Our chief thinks we should protect you. We took the liberty of paying for the funeral. I'm George Keller, this is Brian Rood, the Bear Clan that Ben and John came from," said George.

"You know all about this?" asked John.

"Yes," said George. "Oral tradition keeps the spirit alive."

"Please sit down," said Laura. "I'll get some coffee."

"Thank you," said George. "Our leader thought it best we step in a little early. This is your mother's diary she kept. She worried about you all very much. She wanted to be with you and missed you all the time, so our chief thought her diary would help you."

"You...you...you know when mother's coming back, don't you?" asked Susan.

"About, yes," said Brian. "She'll be home for Christmas; Sean, too."

Hot tears stung everyone's eyes. "They're going to make it," sobbed Laura.

"Yes, they make it, and our chief felt you would feel better if you knew," said George.

"Well, yes it helps," said John.

"What I don't understand is how John Red Feather is our father," asked John. "Susan and Laura have tried to explain, but it's stupid, it's really stupid," said John.

"Well, you get your coats, come with us, we will explain along the way. We know you will find what we say strange, so we decided to prove it to you, then you will believe what you see with your own eyes," said Brian.

"You can prove all this?" This I'm not missing," said John, grabbing his coat.

"Me, neither," cried Susan and Laura, running to the coat closet.

All five people got in the limo. Brian knocked on the window, and the driver drove away.

"Your mother and Sean were the most unselfish people there ever were. Sara was stubborn, Sean restless, but together they changed a lot of lives, so you don't have to think your mother cruel for staying where she is. She would rather be here with you, but she did so much in the 1800s that helped so many people, she was needed there," said Brian.

"That doesn't tell me how John's our father," said John.

"Sometimes people belong together, the stars mated them for life. You won't believe this, but John and Sara sent these two. Somehow the souls were misplaced in time. Sara went back in time to her soulmate, carried John's seed through the years, and you two were born. Sounds stupid to you, I know, but before you doubt what we tell you, we want to show you something, so hold your mouths," said George.

"We're here," said Brian.

"Where?" asked John.

"This is what Sean and Sara built," said Brian.

"What? The place really exists, it's still standing?" said John.

"Come," said George.

"This whole area is just the way Sean and Sara left it. This is the barn where it started. This is where Sean and Sara lived," said George, opening a door.

"Wow, this is nice," said Susan. "Look at the work here."

"There, across the way, is where Jacob and Susan lived," said Brian, walking across the barn. He opened the door, and everyone walked in. "This is just unbelievable," said Laura. "It's so beautiful."

"Sean did what he could to make it comfortable," said George.

"What was that huge log cabin we passed right there?" asked John.

"That was the home Sean built for Sara, but they never got to use it. The real Sean and Sara lived there." Brian unlocked the door, and they walked in.

"Holy shit," cried John. "This is exactly how Mom wanted her house to look, everything."

"Oh God," cried Susan. "Look at these walls. Look, real log walls inside, carved archways. Look a fireplace, just like she wanted, an open staircase. Susan, look at the kitchen," called Laura.

"Oh God, just the way she always wanted. Mom would have loved to live here; everything is perfect. Porches, she always wanted porches," said Susan.

"I don't think you understand," said Brian.

"What don't we understand, everything is true. Sean built this for my mother, who never got to live here. She would have loved to live here," said John.

"John, your mother owns all this. There's 1300 acres here," said Brian.

"What?" asked John, turning around facing Brian.

"Yes, there's a lot more," said Brian.

"There's more? But I thought the real Sean and Sara lived here, that makes it theirs."

"No, Sean set it up so your mother always owned this. The real Sean and Sara didn't like it here, so everything went to us and Jacob, who kept it all up for your mother. Come, we'll show you the rest."

"There's more?" asked Laura.

"Much more. Sara's a very rich woman. Sean owns just as much," said Brian.

"No," said Laura holding up her hand and shaking her head trying to understand. "You're telling me my husband is rich?" asked Laura.

"Yes, very rich. You have a home here. You all do," said Brian.

"You're telling us we have homes here just like this?" asked John.

"No, bigger," said Brian.

"Bigger?" cried Laura.

"Follow me," said Brian.

In shock and stunned at all this news, John, Susan, and Laura followed Brian and George. "This is the quarry your mother talks about." Then Brian walked a small stone path. "This is where John and your mother met. These are the headstones for Jacob and Susan and their four children, Jacob Jr., Sara, Laura, and Sean."

"Oh, my God," cried Susan. Even Laura and John wiped away tears. Susan swallowed a huge lump. "It's winter, what are these white flowers?" asked Susan.,

"Moon flowers. They have never been white, a leaf of the moon flower cut your mother's leg. It left a moon-shaped scar on her leg. A flower bloomed on the leaf. It was white. Ben planted it here. Sara was a pure virgin, and the future princess. This is the only place in the world the white moon flower grows," said Brian, walking back down the path.

"Princess?" questioned John. "What princess?"

"The name of your mother's company," said George.

"Whoa, stop right there. My mother owns a company?" asked John.

"Well, actually you all do, but your mother's the corporate CEO. We work for her," said Brian, opening the door.

"As a matter of fact, this limo belongs to your mother," said George.

"Okay, you had me going there for a while," laughed John. "But if my mother owned a company and limos, we would have known about it."

"How?" asked Brian.

"She would have told us," said John.

"What's that mean?" asked Brian.

"Has it occurred to you yet that Sean and Sara are in a coma, living in the 1800s, changing history, so people around here could have a better life? They haven't seen the end results of what they have done yet?" said Brian.

"Oh," said John.

Brian knocked on the window. The limo started moving. "These are the fields that Sean and Jacob planted. Here are your fruit and nut trees; these are the berries. It has an underground watering system that's a self-feed. We helped John and Jacob plant all this," said Brian.

"What's that huge log cabin there?" asked Laura.

Brian knocked on the window; the limo stopped. "This is a twenty-seven car garage. We keep all the latest equipment there. Nothing is outdated. Sean insisted that if we built anything, it had to be made out of logs to keep with the landscape. Everything has been modernized. We have electricity, but it's all underground. Over here is where we grow vegetables," said Brian.

"So we own a produce business," asked John.

"Yes, all organically grown," smiled George.

"This is unbelievable," said John.

They got back in the limo and drove on. "This house coming up is Sean's. There's a barn with horses, the best money can buy. This was supposed to be a Christmas surprise for you and the kids, but we decided all of you needed to see this now."

"Oh, my God!" cried Laura. "It's huge."

Brian knocked on the window; the limo stopped, and everyone got out.

"Talk about porches," laughed John.

"Each home has been updated through the years. They all have swimming pools, large yards with play areas for children. Even forts all built out of logs," said George.

"God, it's huge. How do I find time to clean it all?" said Laura.

"You don't. Every home has maids," said George. "Next week professional decorators come in and will decorate for the holidays. It's quite some display that we have planned."

Laura wiped at tears. "It's all ready to move into?"

"Yes, Sean left explicit details as to the type of furniture you liked. You have a family room and four fireplaces. The family room has a baby grand."

"Piano, we were told you played and were teaching your children," said George.

"Laura, your home is perfect," said Susan.

"Now we'll look at Susan and John's homes," said Brian.

"But I don't live here. I have a job out of town," said John.

"Well, Sean thought since you're vice president of the company and make three hundred thousand dollars a year, you may want to move back," said George. "Your mother would never tell you, but she misses you a lot. Here's your home John."

John sat with his mouth open, staring at George.

Susan closed her mouth. "Move your ass, VP," smiled Susan.

John moved, but in numb shock. "Now yours and Susan's homes were built this summer. The blueprints were left by Sean and were followed exactly. All the things you and your wife like are in here. We were told you're into physical fitness, so you have your own gym complete with sauna. Since you're vice president of the company, you will probably entertain a lot, so your rooms are large, there's a formal dining room that seats twenty-four. You also have four fireplaces," said George. "Oh, you all have new trucks, too."

John couldn't say one word.

"Well kid, you made big time," laughed Susan, slapping John on the back.

"Each bedroom in every house has it's own bathroom and walk-in closets, all new appliances," said Brian.

Susan guided a shocked John to the limo. "I didn't think Sean knew me that well," said John.

"Sean is a wise man. He helped a lot of people and I mean a lot. He went through the list of people Jacob sent him to give shots to. He talked to them all. He never gave them the shots if they were bad people. Believe us, they were taking money under false pretenses. John and Jacob talked to a lot of people that day. They played God, they found good people and gave them shots. What they did was the best thing they could do. That doctor who was supposed to have a cure for cancer was using some kind of acid mixture to scar people to make them believe he cured cancer," said Brian.

"Oh, my God," cried Susan. "How awful."

"Yes, everyone on Jacob's list did something awful to hurt people. He said Jacob would hate him when he got back, but he didn't care. He did what was right. This is your home Susan. We were told you liked old-fashioned things but done with class. Sean said you were a sexy lady," said Brian.

"Oh, oh, oh, double doors, etched glass, porches, oh," said Susan.

"Calm down, Sis, you haven't gotten out of the car yet," laughed John.

Susan hit him. "Shut up," said Susan, getting out of the car and running up the steps to look at the doors.

Brian unlocked the doors, and swung them open to a huge foyer with open staircase. "Oh God," Susan cried deeply. "Is this real marble on this floor?" cried Susan.

"Yes," said Brian. "Real crystal on the chandelier."

Susan looked up. "Oh my God, look at that."

"You have six bedrooms, a library, sewing room, family room, living room, dining room, kitchen, breakfast nook..." Brian never finished. Susan ran through the house, so he talked to John and Laura. "Each house has a game room, laundry, work shop. I hope you all like your new houses," said Brian. Susan ran through. "Unbelievable," was all she said after she checked everything out; they left.

On the way home, Laura, John, and Susan didn't say a word.

"The upkeep on the homes is taken out of company money. The electric, phone, and cable are paid for by the company," said Brian.

"Is that legal?" asked John.

"Yes, the company was established in 1861. It was written in such a way that the homes were to be kept up by the company since you live on company property. This law goes on from generation to generation. All schooling is paid for by a college fund set up in 1861, so that the Indians and the two families involved are well taken care of," said Brian.

"What's that?" asked Laura.

"That's Sara's garden," said Brian, knocking on the window. The limo stopped. "That field is full of the flowers that Sara loved so much. The pine trees are special. It's her favorite because that's what John smelled like. This field is where Sara picked the flowers to decorate her home with. It remains the same today as it was then. Ben wished it to be that way." Susan rolled down the window with a touch of a button. "God, smell that? You can smell that pine, it's so great," said Susan.

"Yes, your homes have these pines around them to act as a wind break," said George. "John ordered that done."

"Did John ever become chief?" asked John.

"For a while, yes, but he turned it back to Ben; his heart belonged to Sara forever," said George.

"Did John live a long life?" asked John.

"Yes he did. Now look at you, the spitting image of your father. You know those pictures you sent your mother? Ben kept them close to him. He was so proud of his grandchildren and great-grandchildren, he threatened to come back and haunt us if we didn't properly take care of you," smiled George.

John smiled. "For some reason I believe that. Grandfather would do just that. God, this is so beautiful here, it's like it's untouched by time. What's missing? It's, I don't know, maybe like Mom said, a dream world."

"What's not here is roads, lights, signs, telephone poles, noise; it's just the way your mother loved it," said George.

"I can see why," said John.

"Now we must shop," said George.

"Shop, for what?" asked Susan.

"There's a list of things your mother wished she'd had. Susan left us a list, so we will buy them and send them to her," said Brian.

"Oh good, I like watching things disappear like magic," said Susan.

Brian laughed. "We know Sean yelled at Sara once because he thought Sara was ordering stuff. Your letter made him apologize to her, something he did little of. Sara was very head-strong. She drove Ben nuts. Those two loved to match wits."

"Sounds like mother," John said, smiling. "She could stand her ground with the best of them if she knew she was right."

The limo stopped at the mall. They got out and went shopping. Two hours later, they were home sending things through.

John sat at the table with George and Brian. "This whole thing seems, I don't know, bizarre. That doesn't even describe it. There's nothing to describe it. You can't tell anyone, they would lock you up and throw away the key. I feel better having you come here, explain it, then show us, even if I don't understand it. I know those two aren't crazy now, that they actually are having fun regardless of how stupid it seems. God, listen to me, talking about it; it doesn't even make sense," said John.

"None of this makes any sense to you because you see with blind eyes, hear with deaf ears, and feel with a black soul. Until you set your black soul free into the night sky, the pure soul can never be freed to shine bright," said George.

"Some ritual thing?" asked John. "Coffee is done, want some?"

"Yes!" said George and Brian.

George waited for John to sit down.

"There's no ritual, everything is either black or white, no in-between. With a black soul you see only dark things; with a white soul you see brightness. It's what you choose to see. If the soul is black, all you will see is despair; with a white soul there is hope. Anyone can have a white soul; anyone can be happy. It's what they choose," said George.

"So what you're saying is my dark soul gives me an attitude that makes bad things happen to me, but if I rid myself of this black soul, I'd be happier," said John.

"Yes!" said George.

"Yeah, right," said John.

"Your mother has worried over you all her life. She always protected you. Did you ever ask yourself why?" George asked puzzled.

"I know why, because Mom always felt I wouldn't feel loved after Susan came," said John.

"No!" said George. "Because you always had to do things the hard way. You wouldn't listen and didn't believe what you saw with your own two eyes."

John didn't say anything, he didn't have to. It pretty much described him to a tee. John sipped his coffee.

"Your mother has cleared a path in life for you, don't be foolish, take that path and set the black soul free. Enjoy life," said George.

"You make it sound easy," said John.

"It is, the work is done. Now set the black soul free, enjoy the rest of your life," said George.

"Read this," said Brian. "Your mother's diary; she's in there. We have things to tend to. The nation's police will keep watch on the house." Brian and George left John. John looked at the diary and poured more coffee. He looked at the diary, picked it up, and went upstairs to his room to read.

Chapter 10

"SEAN AND JACOB WENT TO ROME TODAY EARLY. THEY CAME BACK EARLY and started the fencing. Susan came over. I showed her everything that Susan and Laura sent, then showed her John's letter. My son loves me, he's never said that before. If I never get home, I'll die happy here knowing both my children love me."

John lay on his bed. "I told her I love her," thought John. He sipped and thought. He couldn't think of one time he actually said it. Mom always said, "I love you," but he never said it. John rolled on his side to read.

Susan left; she didn't stay long. "I've had such a headache on the left side of my head. I take Tylenol, but it doesn't help. Today I seem to have aches and pains in weird places. My leg feels like someone drove a nail through it. My chest and shoulder aches, so I'm going to lie down."

John read this twice. Mom described all the injuries she has here. Sara was in pain, and everyone figured because she was in a coma, she couldn't feel.

"John, Laura and I are going to the hospital," yelled Susan.

"Susan come here," yelled John.

"Now what?" said Susan, stomping up the stairs.

John read her what he just read. "Give Mom some Tylenol. She's in pain, you have to do it. The hospital will think you're crazy," said John.

"Sure, I'll get some liquid," said Susan.

"Thanks," said John.

"We sent all that stuff through to Mom," said Susan.

John started reading. "Mmm," was all he said.

"I tried to lie down, but it hurt too much, so I looked to see if there was anything from the kids. They sent quite a few things. Things I didn't dare ask for because they cost too much money. I've got everything put away. I feel lonely today. I know I could go and be with Susan and little Jacob, but I want to be with John. Every nerve in my body longs to be with him, but I can't take John's being chief of his people away from him. I'm going to try and lie down again; I feel sleepy. Good night, my babies."

"Sara, are you all right?" asked Susan.

"Yeah, why?" asked Sara.

"Well, you slept all day yesterday and most of today," said Sean.

"What?" asked Sara, sitting up. "I've got to give the last of the shots."

"I did that," said Sean. "You seemed so peaceful I didn't want to bother you. You were dead to the world."

"Well, my headache's gone," smiled Sara.

"I'm surprised you don't have a headache from sleeping so long," laughed Sean.

"No, I actually feel good," laughed Sara. "Must be I needed the sleep."

"Yeah, I guess so," said Sean. "You need your shot, and I'm done."

"Did you start the fence?" asked Sara, holding out her arm.

"The fences are up," said Sean, giving Sara a shot. "You never heard us hammering?" asked Sean.

"Not once. Like I said, I was really sleeping," said Sara.

"Come on, I got supper," said Sean.

"Food sounds good," said Sara. "What we having?"

"Kentucky Fried Chicken," smiled Sean.

"The kids sent more stuff through," laughed Sara.

"Yeah, they're having a ball," laughed Sean.

"Tell me you have cabbage salad to go with it," said Sara.

"Oh, we got the works," laughed Sean. "Susan sent some Twinkies through, so she could say she knew a Twinkie that had a shelf life over a hundred years. John sent roses for you."

"Those two. Anything to horse around," laughed Sara, sitting at the island. "Paper plates, how great. No dishes, but fuel for the fire. Oh God, this tastes good."

"Yeah, Jacob and Susan liked theirs, the kids sent stuff for them and Ben," said Sean. "Susan's the one who said let you sleep."

"Tell her thank you, I seem a lot better for it," smiled Sara around bites of food. "I'm famished," said Sara.

"I'd be too if I slept over twenty-four hours," laughed Sean.

"Well, I always catnap a lot when it's chicken. I love chicken." said Sara.

"I do, too. Ben and John got it pretty well set up over there," said Sean.

"They're ready for the snow and winter," said Sara.

"They better be, it's been snowing all day," laughed Sean. "I figured the kids have sent us enough food that we'll never have to cook again," said Sean.

"Sean, you're really bad," said Sara. "It's nice and warm in here."

"Yeah, those fences cut down on the wind whipping through here," said Sean.

"It's windy out?" asked Sara.

"Real windy. We had extra wood, so we made a snow fence in front of the barn doors. Now they don't leak. I wouldn't want to lose those calves," said Sean.

"How are they doing?" asked Sara.

"Good. I picked up some hams when we were in town," said Sean.

"Some?" questioned Sara.

"Six. Thought one a piece for Christmas, one a piece for Easter, then ham slices for breakfast," said Sean. "Breakfast sausage would have been good for pancakes. The kids sent some. Jacob and I made a makeshift freezer so we could freeze things; works good," laughed Sean.

"A freezer. What's in this freezer?" asked Sara.

"Meats, rolls, bread, juices, french fries, vegetables, cold cuts, I can't remember everything. It was like they went to the frozen food section and started buying," laughed Sean. "Then went through the meat department. They sent freezer paper, tape, markers."

"What is this doing for Jacob and Susan? They won't have this stuff when we leave," said Sara.

"This is true," said Sean, reaching for more chicken, "but they will always remember this and what's to come. This is high society to them; to us also, right now."

"Yeah, but those kids are spending a lot of money to play with this. I hope it doesn't back up on them and they end up with no money for Christmas," said Sara.

"I don't think that's a problem," smiled Sean. "When have Susan and Laura ever paid an outrageous amount for anything?" asked Sean.

"Never. If they're real smart they're sending stuff from out of the house," said Sara.

"They probably are," said Sean. "That's probably where it's coming from."

"That's probably where it's all coming from," laughed Sara. "The rate those two are sending things, they wouldn't have time to shop and play with their new toy."

"They sent toilet paper through," laughed Sean.

"Real toilet paper?" said Sara. "Not that awful stuff we have?"

"Nope, the real thing. They squashed it in there." laughed Sean.

"John says our rooms are full of flowers. These he sent you are from the president," said Sean.

"Cough, cough. The president of the United States sent me flowers? Why?" asked Sara. "I don't know him."

"I guess we're in the papers all across the United States. You know, when you hit the big time, everyone gets on the band wagon," said Sean. "I don't know."

"What the hell makes me so special?" asked Sara.

"How the hell do I know," said Sean. "I got flowers, too. I'm only your neighbor. Next thing you know, Leno will be cracking jokes about us."

"I doubt that very much. He might about Tom. Tom deserves it, but we're nobodies, not worth the jokes. You have to really be famous for him to make jokes about or people won't know who he's joking about," said Sara.

"Oh, the kids sent us some games and cards," said Sean, "and you some paperbacks to read. Something about tomatoes love carrots, moon sign planting, whatever."

"Great," said Sara. "I can plant my garden."

(Diary 1860). "Time is going so fast, tomorrow is Thanksgiving. I've been cooking for days. I invited Ben, John, Jacob, Susan, and Jr. I've tried cooking for two, it's so hard. The freezer is working good, if you want to call it that. It's made of wood, has four sides, top and bottom, sits outside in the cold. If you want anything, you better make list and make one trip. It's such a bitter cold your skin freezes the minute the wind hits it. The turkeys have been cut and ready to go in the oven. Sean had to do it; I couldn't. As stupid as they are and as mean as they are, they look at you with those big, brown eyes, go 'gobble, gobble,' and I ran. Sean's been teasing me all day about it, tells me I'm not the tough old broad I pretend to be. I had him save the feathers. I'll make Sean a feather pillow to sleep on, see how mean I can be.

"Thanksgiving dinner went well. Everyone showed up. It was good to see Ben and John, especially John. I swear to God that man gets better looking each time I see him.

"The snow is getting high. Sean and Jacob went out and made a huge wall of snow all around this place. It's really high. It looks like a castle wall, but the wind has been so bad, it's helped a lot. It's not in the houses that the wind bothers me, it's in the barn. It seeps in, and Sean and Jacob don't want to lose the animals. Sean says come spring he's building new doors for the barn. The doors are where the wind is coming in. If I know Sean, he won't wait. He'll get out the wood and start making doors. I've noticed Sean will put up with something for just so long, then he does something about it. He's been fighting the doors two days; one more ought to do it.

"Today Sean and Jacob built new doors. They are nice and solid. What upset Sean is that he went out and the door had blown open, and the barn was full of snow so he built new doors. Knew he would. I started decorating for Christmas today. I have my gifts all done and wrapped. I gave Susan the angel I made for her tree-top. She cried about how beautiful it was. I took over some Christmas decorations I made for the tree and around the house. I get so excited about Christmas. I don't know why. I don't have all the fancy things I have back home; it's just the spirit in me. I made some cute things for the tree out of the craft stuff that Susan and Laura sent. I made a tree skirt for me and Susan with matching pillows since the kitchen and living room are one room. I made placemats and chair pads to match. I don't need to walk in the winter, the tredle sewing machine is enough work out for anyone's legs. Now I know why they went to electric. Susan thinks I go overboard for Christmas. She says it's just another day. I think I can change her mind.

"She has no idea that today Susan sent a nativity set through for us. John sent precut slats and a staple gun, and staples that I put together and will take to her Christmas Eve. I know right where to put it.

"I've learned to relax here. I hear from the kids once a day, which helps me a lot. I worry so much about them. John is always on my mind. There's so much for him to handle right now, but hearing from him helps a lot.

"Today Jacob sliced his leg open. I don't know what him and Sean are working on, but Jacob needed eight stitches. Sean brought him here. Susan sat Jacob in a chair and took out a needle and thread and was going to stitch away. Sean got sick to his stomach thinking about pain. He stopped Susan and brought them here, so I showed Susan how to clean a wound, then numbed it and used a suture kit to sew it. I did my best to stress the importance of keeping it clean. I put triple antibiotic ointment on it and a dry dressing with tape. Poor Jacob didn't know what to think. He kept telling Sean he needed whisky for the pain. Sean didn't understand what he meant by pain. I did the first stitch, and Jacob got ready to yell. But when he felt nothing, he looked shocked. He said he likes future medicine.

(December 1, 1986) We're having a party today. We're celebrating being alive. I baked a cake. Susan's making ice cream. In Sara's journal we were all dying today. We're healthy and happy. Jacob's stitches are coming along well. The baby is getting so big. John stopped in for a while. He said he was in Rome. He didn't stay too long. People are sick everywhere; coffins sit stacked outside homes, so people die, they take a coffin, put the body in, and carry it away. They paint the name on the coffin. Some lady sent Sean a rum cake with a letter. I don't know what that was about, but John came bearing gifts from some people in town. He says they owe Sean for saving them and their families. John looks so good. He smells good, just like those pine trees. We talked for a while. I didn't want to keep him here too long, the weather is awful. Of course, if I'd kept him here a little longer, he would have been snowed in. I know that sounds awful, but I feel so alive when he's around. I can't explain it, I actually blush when he's near. I can't believe I'm falling in love for the first time in my life. I could spend my life with him, no problems at all. The man has no defects at all. Big muscled arms and chest, real nice ass, strong legs, long, black hair down to his waist. It blows gentle in the breeze. Moonlight shines off his hair, his eyes, large brown, and doe-like, full lips, lips I like to keep kissing."

"Mother!" cried John out loud shifting, on his bed.

"When I look at John, all those years of hell with Tom fade away like they were never there, like I read about them in a book. To feel this much life inside is like a fire burning, burning like the memory of our kiss at the quarry. That kiss will last me the rest of my life. That kiss was what set me free. I look into the night sky, I think of John, the blackness of the night is his hair blowing in the breeze. The stars are that twinkle he has in his dark eyes. John will be in my heart forever.

"Our party went well, we had a good time. The ice cream was great. Susan made Jacob chop ice out of the pond to make it with. Poor man took an hour to warm up. Jacob Jr. loves cake and ice cream. We put some on our fingers and gave him a taste.

"John stopped in today. Some of the women made us gifts to thank us. They were little things. I thought they would look good on the tree. John says it's getting harder and harder to come here. The snow is too deep, too hard to walk in. A horse could never travel in it, so I gave him the presents I had for him and Ben. I had a bag of things for him to give the women of the nation and candy canes for the children. I sent cookies for the men. I gave John a hug, told him to be careful going back. I didn't want to let him go. I wanted to keep him there. Then John kissed me. He said mistletoe meant you had to kiss or bad luck would come. I didn't want John to stop kissing me, but I have no right to love such a wonderful man. I would ruin his life like I have everyone else's.

"The wind blows so hard it whistles. The snow wall is higher than our house, and it blows snow over the top. I can't imagine how deep the snow is, but we're warm in here. The barn is warm. It was a smart idea Sean had by having the doors from our home open to the barn. We can get back and forth without having to worry about snow and wind. Sean and Jacob work every day in the barn. God only knows what those two find to do. Susan's busy with the baby and baking. I'm busy baking and sewing. I scrubbed and cleaned this place with Lysol today, then opened the door a crack for a change of air. It's getting close to Christmas; it's only seven days away. I doubt we'll have a tree, we couldn't get out if we tried. The weather is too bad to try. Sean and Jacob wanted to, but Susan and I said no. It's foolish to freeze to death over a tree.

"Sean and I teach each other about men and women and how they think. We've played some board games. Sean's out for blood on these games. I think we've come to a pretty good understanding of one another. We can sit down and talk openly about our feelings about being here. I can live with it as long as my kids let me know they're okay. The only argument Sean and I have is over my children. He says if I didn't try to protect them so much, I'd have time falling in love with John.

"How can I fall in love with John? I already love him. You can't fall in love with someone you love. But if I love John, I could lose my children. My children and grandchildren are more important to me than me loving someone. John and Susan need me. Sean can't see it. He says they are adults now and don't need Mommy around their neck. This hurts me when Sean yells at me about it, so I come in the bedroom and sulk, which is what I'm doing right now."

"You done pouting," asked Sean, standing in the bedroom doorway.

"I'm not pouting," said Sara, throwing down the diary and pen.

"Sara, I'm only telling you—"

"Stop Sean, stop right there. You listen, to me and you listen good, okay? I can't fall in love with John. I love John already. I can't love him anymore than I do. This isn't about my children. I'm a woman, Sean, a woman who needs John, but I can't walk up to the man and say I love you than rape him. I don't know how to be a frilly, fancy woman; I'm me. I can't trap the man into loving me, then end up ruining his life by leaving him. You don't understand. I love John so much I have to set him free. How would you like it if you loved a woman so much your whole body throbbed twenty-four hours a day from wanting her? How do you think you would feel and she'd feel knowing this, knowing you had to hurt someone to love them? Ooh, you're so fucking thick-headed, you would think it was all right," said Sara, running into the bathroom slamming the door.

John had heard enough. Now he must take over. He set the tree down, tapped Sean on the shoulder, made a jester with his finger, then whispered in Sean's ear. Sean nodded. He went over to the bathroom door and knocked.

"Go away," yelled Sara.

"Fine, I just think you should talk to John about it, and let the man decide what he wants," said Sean as he walked away. He picked up the tree and went to the barn and made a stand for the tree. Jacob came out to do the same.

"Sara's yelling again, I hear," laughed Jacob.

"Yes, if those two don't get together soon, I'm going to kill myself," laughed Sean.

"Damn nice of him to bring us trees. Keeps a pretty close eye on Sara, don't he?" smiled Sean.

Knock, knock.

"Go away, it's not open for discussion anymore," yelled Sara.

John kicked the door in. "I say it is, and I say come June you will be my wife. That's the end of it." Sara's mouth fell open. John grabbed her and kissed her just like he did at the quarry. "That I take as a 'yes,' so it's done, you're my wife. I will tell Ben; he will make the arrangements."

"Don't I have something to say here?" asked Sara.

"No, you agreed to marry me, that's the end. We will tell the others now," said John, trying to sound upset. He had all he could do to keep from laughing.

Sara went to say something, but John was gone. John called to Sean and Jacob. "Tell Susan to come here."

Jacob shrugged his shoulder. "He probably killed her," laughed Jacob.

"I wouldn't blame him," laughed Sean. "I've come close."

Jacob, Susan, and Sean came in the house.

"Sara has agreed to be my wife. We will wed in June," said John.

"She agreed?" asked Sean.

"Yeah, after I busted the door down. I tried to be nice, but she was being herself," said John.

Sean looked; the door lay on the floor. He tried not to laugh. "Congratulations," said Sean.

"I'll need it," said John. "I'm going to live in the white man's world now," John winked at Sean.

"Oh no, you're not walking away from your people," said Sara.

"I'm not walking away, I'm helping them," said John.

"Helping them?" Sara asked puzzled.

"If I brought you there, we'd be at war in a week with that temper," laughed John. "We're peaceful people."

"Look, I haven't agreed to anything," said Sara.

"Oh, yes you did. She tried to rape me in the bathroom," smiled John.

"I did no such thing," said Sara.

"Then why am I bleeding where your hands were around my neck?" asked John.

"Oh my God, I dug you," cried Sara.

"See, she admits it, she insults me as future chief," said John.

"You can't be chief and live in the white man's world," said Sara. "Who told you that?" I'll be chief, and I'll do what is right for my people," said John.

"Take your coat and shirt off, and let me look at that," said Sara.

"She's good with stitches; you don't feel them," said Jacob.

"Good, I need stitches," said John. "I cut my leg with an ax."

"Oh my God, you're all blood," cried Sara.

"Well, it did stop. If you had opened the door when I knocked, I wouldn't have had to kick it in and it wouldn't have started bleeding again."

Sara went into the bathroom, picked up the door, set it aside, then opened the closet, took out what she needed, and walked back to the kitchen. She cut John's jeans up the leg. "This is bad," said Sara. She shaved the hair off and gave John a shot of Novocaine. She cleaned it well with surgical scrub, then put twelve stitches in John's leg and put triple antibiotic ointment on it, dry dressing, and tape. Then she looked at John's neck.

"You shouldn't worry about my neck, my leg needs stitching first," said John.

"I put twelve stitches in your leg already," said Sara. "Now hold still while I look at your neck." Sara put peroxide on John's neck.

"How could you stitch my leg and I feel nothing, that's impossible," said John.

"Well look, it's done," said Sara.

John looked down, then at Sara. "Can I pick a wife or what?" laughed John. "How did she do that?" asked John.

"She worked in a doctor's office for a while," said Sean. "Jacob said she'd make a good nurse, but she quit, don't know why."

"Because Jacob raped me," said Sara. "End of discussion.

Sean's face fell; everyone stared at Sara. Sara kept working on John's neck, not thinking about what she said.

Anger ran through Sean. He was going to kill Jacob when he got home. No wonder all those people's names were bad people. Jacob was evil. John felt a rage run through him he never knew existed.

"I didn't think I dug this like this," said Sara. "You need stitches here, too. Were you attacked by something," asked Sara.

"Yeah, a tree," laughed John.

Sara had John take off his shirt; she cleaned and stitched.

"You can't travel in this weather with all these stitches. You'll have to stay here for a couple of days," said Sara.

"Can I stay until after Christmas? That's what I came for. It's only four days away. I thought if I brought a tree you would say yes," smiled John.

"Well, if Ben knows you're here and will be here until Christmas, you might as well stay. I can keep an eye on it," said Sara as she finished on John's neck.

"What do you want to keep an eye on? You've got my shirt, cut my pants, my boots are by the door. Not much exposed right now," John teased.

Sara blushed and looked at John. "I'll get you some clothes to put on." Sara went in the bedroom and took out a set of sweats and clean socks. John's were all blood. She set them on the bed. John walked in. "You can wear these," said Sara and left.

Jacob, Susan, and Sean watched Sara as she cleaned up the mess she made sewing up John. Then she washed her hands and the island with anti-bacterial soap, made coffee, set out cups, then realized that nobody was at the island. Everyone was staring at Sara.

"What?" asked Sara.

"When did Jacob rape you," asked Sean.

"How did you find out?" Sara asked puzzled.

"That doesn't matter," said Sean. "When did it happen?"

"I don't want to talk about it," said Sara.

"Well, you're going to," said Sean. "This is when you started staying home wasn't it?" asked Sean.

"About then, yes," said Sara. "You don't need to know. It is going to cause family problems for you, so forget it. I've learned to live with it. It doesn't matter anymore; it's old," said Sara.

"No, it's not old. I want to know. I won't get any sleep till you tell me," said Sean.

"Jacob called me in and said Terry called in sick. I went in when I got there. No one was there but Jacob but I didn't know that. I went down back just like usual, put on my white gown, and there was Jacob. I didn't think anything was unusual. He always came out back for coffee. The next thing I knew I was on the floor, and he was on top of me. I fought, but he sprayed something in my face. I couldn't move, everything seemed so far away. When he finished, he laughed at me and walked away. It took me another ten minutes to be able to move. I went home, cleaned up, and never went back. It took me a long time to accept that I didn't do anything wrong. I went to work, that was my crime between Tom beating me that week and the rape. I was pretty sore and didn't want anyone around. Do you want more gruesome details as to what he did exactly? I had nightmares for years because I realized all my husband did was rape me when he wanted sex. I don't want to have the dreams again, so drop it," yelled Sara.

"Okay," said Sean. "We would like coffee. How about some goodies to celebrate?"

"You only want to get into the goodies," said Sara.

"Boy, these are nice. What did you call them?" asked John.

"Sweats," said Sean.

"Sweats, I like that," said John, comfortable. John heard all and wanted to kill Jacob. He would tell Ben. Ben would handle this. John reached in his coat pocket until he felt a box he took out. "I'm so glad Sara has agreed to be my wife. Ben will be so happy," smiled John.

"Oh, I just bet he will," said Sara.

"Sara may I hug you?" asked John.

"Permission to hug me?" asked Sara.

"Okay," said John, pulling Sara close to him. He took the diamond out of the box, kissed one hand, then the other. When he held up Sara's hand, there was the diamond ring.

"Oh, my God," cried Sara shaking.

"One carat stone, six prongs, I guess right?" asked John.

"Oh yeah, right on the money," laughed Sara. "You really wanted to marry me then?"

"I wouldn't have asked if I didn't," said John. "You kept fighting me."

"That's what I do best," said Sara.

"Here, here," said Sean, holding up his coffee mug. "She finally admits it."

Susan and Jacob held up their cups and smiled. Jacob Jr. slept on the couch.

"Well, I have a door to fix, and a tree to bring in," laughed Sean.

"I'll help," said John. "I'm responsible for both."

Susan sat down at the island with Sara. "John loves you so much. You'll be so happy. Sean will build you a nice home to live in."

"Just the way I want it," said Sara.

"What made you finally say yes?" asked Susan.

"He kissed me. I've never felt like that in my life," said Sara.

"Then it's true love?" smiled Susan.

"June is too far away. What if I'm not here?" said Sara.

"I've got a feeling you will be. Time will fly by, so much to do and get ready for," said Susan. "Where will you get married?"

"Outside, definitely outside," smiled Sara. "I want God to see I'm finally happy."

"I think he knows," said Susan.

"We better put Jacob on the bed. He moves so much now, he's going to fall, and the guys will be bringing in the tree, probably the tree that cut up John," said Sara.

"I can't believe he got trees for us. We tell our men no, and he gets them. I bet it's because he wanted to propose," smiled Susan.

Sara laughed. "You got to admit, his proposal was different. Kicks a door down, says we're getting married," said Sara.

Susan put Jacob on the bed, and covered him with a quilt, then went back to the kitchen. "He really kicked the door in, didn't he," laughed Susan.

"Yup, that's probably why I said yes," laughed Sara.

"Because he kicked the door in," Susan asked, puzzled.

"No, because I knew he wouldn't take 'no' for an answer," laughed Sara. "I looked at the door, then his massive body in the doorway, and I knew nothing would stop him from marrying me."

"You two belong together. I've never known anyone who actually belonged together," said Susan.

"Would you be my maid of honor?" asked Sara.

"Oh, I'd love nothing better," said Susan. "But I think I'm pregnant," said Susan.

"So, what's that got to do with anything?" asked Sara.

"I'll be huge and ugly," said Susan. "It will ruin your wedding."

"How?" Sara asked puzzled.

"You know, I won't be slim and pretty like everyone else," said Susan.

"I didn't ask you to be in my wedding because you're slim and pretty. I asked you because the maid of honor should be your best friend, and you're my best friend," said Sara. "We can make you a nice dress so you're comfortable. So will you be my maid of honor?" asked Sara.

Susan started crying. "Yes," she said.

"Did I say something wrong or hurt you?" asked Sara.

"No, I just can't believe how nice you are," said Susan. "A wedding is a woman's blessed day. They want it perfect, and you don't care," laughed Susan.

"Susan, I only think that a wedding is no good unless you have your friends with you. That's a perfect wedding. I was thinking of asking Summer because John will ask Jacob and Sean," said Sara.

"I like Summer, too. She's so nice," said Susan.

"Well then, the wedding's all planned," said Sara. "We can get on with other things."

"Whoa, it's not that simple," said Susan.

"What else is there, a bride and groom and wedding party, held outdoors, that's it," said Sara.

"What about guests, food, things like that? said Susan.

"Us, the nation, cold cuts, salads, done," smiled Sara.

"In other words, simple," laughed Susan.

"Yup," smiled Sara. "Think I should put out Christmas cookies since they're putting up the Christmas tree?" asked Sara.

"I think they would be disappointed if you didn't. You've got everyone so wound up about Christmas, we can't stand it," laughed Susan.

"Okay, cookies it is," smiled Sara. Sara smelled the tree before they brought it in. "Blue spruce," said Sara.

"What?" asked Susan.

"The tree is blue spruce," said Sara. "I love blue spruce."

"You smelled the tree?" asked Susan as she helped with cookies.

"Oh yeah, anything to do with outdoors I smell," said Sara.

"I suppose you smell the wind, too," teased Susan.

"Yes, the winds tells me where flowers are, where fruit trees are, where berries are, where pines are, and it tells me when it's going to snow, and what type of rain to expect," said Sara.

"What type of rain to expect?" asked Susan.

"Yes, a little rain smells musty with a warm smell; a heavy cleaning rain is a fresh clean scent. This rain washes plants and trees of dust and pollen so they release fresh air," said Sara.

"You're right, I know what you're talking about. I never thought about it. I just took it for granted. Rain is rain, but they are different," said Susan. "Is this something you learned in the future?" asked Susan.

"No, I think it's in my blood. In my time, I'm half Indian. My mother was full-blooded; my father English," said Sara, putting cookies away. "I think my Indian side is aware of what's around me."

"What's the English side do?" asked Susan.

"Makes me stubborn, and, believe me, you don't want a stubborn Indian around," laughed Sara.

"Maybe that's why you love John so much, he's stubborn," said Susan.

"No, I love John because he's one hell of a man," laughed Sara.

"I noticed," blushed Susan.

"I was so involved with what I was doing, I didn't realize how much I had taken off him," laughed Sara.

"How could you not notice that body?" said Susan, blushing.

"Susan, sounds like you're turning into a nineties woman," laughed Sara. "I may be rubbing off on you too much."

"I don't think so. I look at it as education," said Susan.

"What are those guys doing?" asked Sara. "They should have been done by now."

"Close your eyes, both of you," said Sean.

"Oh God, Sean, it's just a tree," said Sara.

"Close your eyes. You don't know what it looks like," said Sean. "Where do you want it?"

"That corner," said Sara, pointing to the right of the living room.

"Okay, close your eyes," said Sean. "Now."

"Okay," yelled Sara, closing her eyes and putting her hands over them. Susan did the same.

Sara and Susan giggled when they heard all the commotion.

"Okay, open them," said Sean.

"Oh, my God," yelled both girls at once. The tree had lights.

"How did you get the lights to work?" asked Sara. "Where'd you get the lights?"

"Well, when you told me about the lights, Susan sent some that run on batteries. I got the idea, so I sent John a letter and told him what I wanted, and he sent it to me. Watch this." The lights twinkled and played Christmas songs.

"Oh Sara, that's beautiful, no wonder you love Christmas so much. Look at all the nice things," said Susan. "All those white lights."

"Your tree lights up, too. Only you have colored lights," said Sean.

"Colored lights?" asked Susan.

"Yes, it's set up, go look," said Sean.

Susan ran out of the house and into hers. "Oh God, how beautiful," cried Susan. She ran back to Sara's, over to Sean, and kissed him. "Thank you. I love my tree."

Everyone laughed at Susan's excitement. She was like a child.

"Oh, I love Christmas," said Susan.

"It's not here yet," said Sara.

"Might as well be; this is great," said Susan.

"I've got cookies," laughed Sara.

The men walked over to the island. Susan stared at the lights and hummed to the music. "Sounds like we need eggnog," said Sean.

"Eggnog?" smiled Susan.

"This isn't homemade, this is from the future. It's great. They only make it Thanksgiving through New Year's. It's from a dairy nearby called Byrne. It's the best. I keep it in the barn; it's s-o-o-o-o good," said Sara.

"I'll get it," said Sean. "I've got to get it, right?"

"You're learning, good," laughed Sara. "When you get home, Laura will be surprised at how much you've learned."

"That or she'll hate me," laughed Sean, going into the barn.

"Sara, tell me what Christmas is like in your time," said Susan, sitting at the island.

"Lights and decorations everywhere. Streets, stores, malls, and homes. We have electric and animated decorations. I have two Santa Clauses, angels, Mrs. Santa Claus, Charles Dickens' characters, bears, elves, dolls, mmmm."

"She has so many christmas decorations she starts putting them up the day after Thanksgiving and finishes Christmas Eve," laughed Sean, walking in. "She has horses, sleighs. Anything that looks like Christmas, Sara has it. Sara lives and breaths Christmas twenty-four hours a day, 365 days a year. She shops all year long, and never gets one present from anyone. She buys her own Christmas presents, wraps them up, and opens them Christmas morning and acts surprised," laughed Sean. "Nobody gives Sara presents. She didn't get an engagement ring and had to buy her own wedding ring."

"That's awful," said Susan.

"Not really. In order to get a present, first somebody has to care for you. Since nobody cared enough to think of me, I just don't get presents," said Sara.

"That's still awful," said Susan.

"No, what's awful is the money she spends on all these people who don't give her anything," said Sean.

"You buy people presents for Christmas who don't like you or who don't give you anything?" Susan asked shocked.

"Okay, I'll say this once and once only. I refuse to sink to their level. If they're assholes, it doesn't mean I have to be. I buy gifts knowing I won't get anything, so I'm not disappointed. The reason I buy my own Christmas presents is because one year when everyone came over to open presents, I didn't have any to open. My grandson cried because Santa Claus didn't leave me any presents. He cried for two hours. He thought Santa was mean," said Sara.

"That poor child. What did you do?" asked Susan.

"I told him grandma was bad because she swore, and swearing is a bad thing, and grandma promised Santa Claus she would be good next year so I could get lots of presents," said Sara.

"How did he take the explanation?" asked Susan.

"Well, I got a lecture from him on how bad words are and shouldn't be said," laughed Sara.

"How cute, how old was he?" asked Susan.

"Three, now he's nine," said Sara. "Time flies."

"Think he'll ever swear?" laughed Susan.

"Not as long as there's a Santa Claus," laughed Sara. "Here's your eggnog, Merry Christmas," said Sara.

"Merry Christmas," everyone cheered.

"This is great, but I'm taking little Jacob home and putting him to bed for the night, then I'm decorating my tree," said Susan, "my lighted tree."

"I think I'll decorate mine, too," said Sara.

"I've got a door to fix," said John.

"I've got a cow to milk," said Jacob.

"I'll help John," said Sean.

Everyone went their way. Sara brought out a couple of boxes with decorations in them. She was careful with color and over decorating. She'd hang a few pieces, step back, look and study, lost in thought of Christmas past. The children, the way they grouped everything in one area. And she'd explain how less was more in decorating, then move things around and show the children how nice it looked when each decoration could shine by itself, like a star in the night sky. Susan became a professional decorator, naming her business, "Less Is More." She was good at what she did, with Christmas being her specialty. Susan held her mother's passion for Christmas. There wasn't much money in Rome, so Susan's business was lean until Christmas. Sara helped Susan at Christmas. She'd start making floral arrangements in June for Christmas. Sara loved it, but Tom hated anything lying around.

"Hell," thought Sara as she put the last decoration on the tree. Tom always complained if Sara had something lying around or what he called lying around. The house could be spotless, and Sara would have a ball of yarn, a pack of cigarettes, a knitting needle or spool of thread around and Tom would have a shit fit. Sara could live there, but nothing of hers could be out to say I live here, too.

"That really looks nice, Sara," said Sean, walking in the room.

"Thank you. I only have to put the angel on top and it's done," said Sara.

"I can help with this," said John, lifting Sara by the waist so she could reach the top. Sara laughed. This isn't quite what she expected, but she placed the angel on top of the tree. John set her back down. "How's that?" asked John.

"Good," laughed Sara.

"That is a real nice tree," said John.

"Well, I love it. It's probably the best I ever had. There's a little of everyone on the tree, that's what makes it so beautiful. Oh! The tree skirt. There it's decorated from top to bottom," said Sara. "It even smells good in here. Thank you for my tree, John. I love it; it's perfect."

"You're welcome, princess," smiled John.

"There are some cookies left," said Sara as she walked in the bedroom.

"None as sweet as my bride-to-be," teased John.

Sara looked at her ring on her finger. She knew John had it sent through, so the children must know. Sara took a pillow and blanket out of the chest. Something was in there, so she took it out. It was a letter for Sean and her. She took the pillow and quilt to the living room. "We have a letter," said Sara.

"Oh! I hope it wasn't sitting there too long. I didn't think to check today," said Sean.

"I don't think so. I put the quilt away this afternoon around 2:00," said Sara, opening her letter and reading. "Susan and Laura want to try something," said Sara. "What, I don't know. With these two you never know, I've given up trying. Susan says that it's Laura's idea, but Laura won't take credit for it unless it works. This should prove to be interesting."

"Well, Laura says it works. I got some work to do. I don't know if I like the sound of that. John came up with it to make it easy for me. Sara and Susan added to it, so all three of them were in on this one," said Sean.

"We're in trouble then," laughed Sara.

"This time I agree," laughed Sean.

"Susan's business is doing well. She had to hire more people. She's doing a lot of mail order business, that's great," smiled Sara. "She went online, maybe that's what she needed. "I'm happy for her. John quit his job and is moving back home. He's been offered a new job at three hundred thousand dollars a year. He wants to know if he and his family can stay at my house for a couple of weeks until his stuff arrives. Why would he ask?" said Sara, looking up.

"Maybe because he's a grown man with a family. Maybe, just maybe, he's trying to tell you he's grown up and would like to be treated like one. It's time to set him free, Sara. Tell him 'yes,' that's all you have to do. He'll do the rest."

Sara stared at Sean. She knew deep in her heart he was right. If she didn't set him free now, he'd never be free. If she never returned home, he'd never be free. If she stayed here she had John, she'd never be lonely. John would be lonely the rest of his life trying to find the freedom she never gave him because she couldn't let go. Sara walked over to the island, opened a drawer, took out pen and paper and wrote.

"Dear John: Yes, you have my permission for you and your family to stay at my home as long as you need, until your furniture arrives. Congratulations on your new job. Tell Suzie I said congratulations on her business. There's a couple of things I'd like, but I must tell you I'm engaged to John and in June a wedding is planned. I would like a fancy wedding since I didn't have one the first time, so after Christmas I'll probably have Laura and Susan send me swatches of material. I haven't asked her yet, and Susan, who is maid of honor and will be with child, so their dresses will be empire waist line. I only wish I could get that one wedding dress I loved so much. But that's impossible. Fourteen thousand dollars for a wedding gown is way too much. I'll need gifts for the men and women in the bridal party. I'll have to think on it. What I need now is a clock, two photo albums, those disposable cameras. I'd like to take pictures of Christmas and the baby. I'd also like some photos of you and your family, Susan and her family, and Laura and her family. I'd like to make photo albums for Susan and Ben for Christmas. I'd need batting, glue, and nylon mesh. Susan and Laura can get them. I need two nice pictures of me without Tom in them. I hope you have a Merry Christmas. I also would like some blanket sleepers for little Jacob for Christmas, size 1; he's big. Then after Christmas when they go on sale, have Susan buy me some in pink and blue in various sizes, so Susan has them as the children age, and "Twas the Night Before Christmas" book, a nice one, one that Susan can keep, a few toys for the baby, a snow suit, size 1. There's money in the bank. Just leave enough for food and next month's bills. There should be about two thousand dollars; taxes are due. I'll write later. I send my love. Love, Mom."

Sara folded the letter, walked in the bedroom, and screamed.

Sean and John were running. Sean led the way, saying spider, but stopped dead in his tracks, "What the, how did they do that?"

"I don't know," said Sara, looking at a hope chest full of goodies. "Look at all the Christmas toys."

"Yeah, all automatic. How do you propose to run them?" asked Sean.

"I don't know. The children probably did this to see if they could," said Sara. "I'll unload it." Sara knelt down; there was one of everything. "What's this? It has your name on it, it's from John. It's not awfully big, but it's quite heavy," said Sara.

"Here, I'll get it," said Sean.

Sara moved aside while Sean lifted the box. Underneath were four car batteries. "All right, John," Sean opened the box and smiled. "Power tools, plugs, wire, thank you," said Sean.

"Why, you can't use them," said Sara.

"Want to bet. How would you like electricity?" asked Sean.

"Yeah, right," laughed Sara.

John was looking at some paperwork that was in the box. "Your son's a genius," smiled Sean. "Let's get this out, we've got more things coming through."

"You've lost your bloody mind," said Sara.

"No, you have a brilliant son," smiled Sean as he lifted things out of the hope chest.

"Whatever you say." Sara worked on one side; Sean on the other. John didn't know what to do, so he watched Sara open the door, took out a few things, then put her letter in and closed everything. She'd never seen Sean this excited. Sara separated everything that came through into hers and Susan's. John helped Sara carry Susan's stuff to Susan's house. Sara set her stuff down and told Jacob that Sean needed help. He was losing his mind, so Jacob and John went to see Sean.

"What's this stuff?" said Susan.

"These are some of the fancy toys I told you we had in our time. Somehow the kids found a way to send bigger things through. Sean's all excited now. What I've done is this: there are eight things. I gave you four; I kept four. If you don't like any of these, you can swap with the ones I have. When I go, you can have all eight. I don't think the other Sara would understand. I don't fully understand," said Sara.

"All I know is you keep giving me presents," said Susan.

"Presents? I made this for you," said Sara. "I know you'll like this."

Susan opened it carefully. There were small square cubes of hay, then a slatted house and a bunch of things wrapped in some kind of paper. Susan unwrapped them slowly, each little figure more beautiful than the next. Hot tears stung Susan's eyes as the nativity set unfolded itself out of each piece of paper. "Th…th…this is the most beautiful thing I've ever seen. Thank you, this will be my most prized possession I'll ever own in my life. You are the best friend I'll ever know. I'll miss you greatly when you're gone," sobbed Susan.

"I'll miss you. You're the only friend I've ever had," said Sara.

"Surely you joke," said Susan.

"No, I'm afraid not," said Sara. "I wish I were, just like I wish I understood all this. I gave up on trying. Maybe I came here just to find a friend, and I couldn't find a better one," said Sara.

"Or you ran out of people to buy gifts for," laughed Susan.

"That, too," joked Sara.

"I can never repay you for all that you've done for us," said Susan.

"Susan, you owe me nothing," said Sara. "You have no idea how much your friendship has meant to me. All this stuff means nothing to me. In time it all fades and becomes trash; friendship is forever. Ours will be for two hundred years," laughed Sara.

"This is never to be trash," said Susan, looking at the nativity set. "This is forever."

"Well, I think we're in for some surprises. Sean says we're going to have electricity. This should prove to be interesting. Sean said my son, John, is a genius. God only knows what he's come up with. All I know is I've never seen Sean this excited, so I'd say Sean, John, and Jacob will be busy the next few days, which helps. The men won't be underfoot while I finish up for Christmas," said Sara.

"I know what you mean. I have a few things I've got to get done," said Susan.

"Need help with anything?" asked Sara.

"No, I've got it just about done," smiled Susan.

"Well, if you need anything, let me know, okay?" smiled Sara. "I'm going home to see what this is all about. They better not be making too big of a mess there. I'll kill them all," laughed Sara.

Susan laughed. "The sad part is, I can see you doing it."

"So can I," laughed Sara. "Well, if those kids of mine send anything tonight for us, I'll bring it over in the morning. I want to sit in the chair and stare at my tree. It took a nation of people to decorate it, so I'm going to enjoy it," laughed Sara.

"It took one person to make mine, and I'll enjoy it for years to come. Every year when I take this set out, I will remember this Christmas, the christmas a friend made me believe in Santa Claus," laughed Susan.

"You be careful of that man, you never know what surprises he has for you," laughed Sara. "Well, I'll see you tomorrow. I love your tree."

"Thank you, I'll see you tomorrow," smiled Susan.

Sara walked home knowing there was no way she'd be able to get into her nightgown, which she knew was calling her. It would have to wait. Seeing Sean happy was worth it. Sara closed the door behind her. "What the?" There were boxes everywhere. She couldn't curl up in the chair as she'd planned. Her shoulders slumped, "Damn," she thought and went in the kitchen. She didn't really want to eat, but what else was there? "God what I wouldn't give for a cold glass of pasteurized milk. Raw milk just wasn't cutting it. Maybe I should have asked for one bottle of milk, ice cold," she thought. She'd drink it right down. "Wish in one hand and shit in the other," thought Sara as she took a glass out of the cupboard. "Cold wins," she thought.

"Sean told me to give you this," said Jacob. "Sean said he figured about now you could use it." Jacob set a brown paper bag on the island.

"Please be milk," thought Sara. "Thank you Jacob. Jacob, what's in those boxes?" asked Sara.

"Small refrigerators, small generators, some power stuff. I don't understand," said Jacob.

"Really, refrigerators? How did they get them through?" asked Sara.

"One at a time," Jacob said seriously.

"Oh," said Sara, trying not to laugh. "How stupid of me," thought Sara.

"The bedroom is full of stuff. You want to look?" asked Jacob.

"No, I'll look later," said Sara, walking over to the island. "Please be milk," she thought. Sara looked in the bag, then looked up.

"You don't want it," asked Jacob.

"No, it's just what I wanted. I was just thinking, sometimes you get what you wish for," smiled Sara.

"That's okay, if it's a good wish," smiled Jacob as he walked in the bedroom.

Sara took out the milk and marshmallow cookies. Sara was folding the bag when she saw the letter. She emptied the bag on the island. One letter. So she sat at the island, drank milk, ate cookies, and read the letter. "Tell Daddy we said hi," Sara laughed. "Susan had to write this," thought Sara. "We need to know dress sizes and shoe sizes of all you women, so we can hunt for sale items for the wedding. What took you so long to say 'yes?'" Sara looked around the living room.

She knew she should feel happy about all this stuff, but it didn't seem right to her. Sara viewed it as ruination of mankind. She had no complaints the way they were living. The refrigerators were small, kind of cute in a way. Sara poured the milk. Any way you look at it, Sara wasn't a nineties woman. But she wasn't a true 1800s woman either. "I don't belong anywhere," thought Sara. You can't take a little of this and a little of that and make your own world. You lived in the one you had, if your family couldn't choose them either. Sara drank the last of her milk then worked her way to the couch and lay down. "Maybe things would look better tomorrow morning. Hell, this could be a dream within a dream. Who knows anymore," thought Sara as she closed her eyes, "who knows?"

"Well, that's the last of it," said Sean. "Everything is cleaned out of here, stacked in the barn. A really good job, guys, now Sara can't complain we made a mess. She will be surprised to see what John sent us. I think it's great he came up with this idea. This will save us hours of time when we start building. Look, she's sound asleep, she never heard us move everything out," said Sean. "She always pushes herself until she crashes, then when she sleeps, she looks like a child. You hate to wake her, but if you don't, she gets mad."

"I may not have heard you move everything out, but I sure hear your jaws flapping," said Sara, sitting up. "I thought I'd sleep on the couch and let you two men have the bed." Sara stood up, "but I'm taking a shower and getting my nightgown on."

"I'm sleeping on the floor. I have my bed roll," said John. "I don't plan to disrupt this household."

"You won't be comfortable on the floor," said Sara.

"Why not?" I sleep on the ground," John said smiling.

"Okay, you want to sleep on the floor, go ahead. I've learned when you're ready to argue, I'm too tired, so argue with yourself, I'm getting ready for bed."

Sara went into the bedroom, grabbed a nightgown off the shelf, and headed for the bathroom without saying another word.

"I don't know if I like her when she's not ready to argue," said John.

Sean laughed. "Enjoy this, you won't have too many moments like this. She always wants to argue about something."

John laughed. "Good, that's what I love the most about her."

"Well, I'm going home," said Jacob. "Susan's probably waiting for me. I may be only a barn away, but she still worries."

"Thanks for the help, I'll see you in the morning," said Sean. "I'm putting wood on the stove and going to bed myself." Sean left to clean out the bottom grates of the wood stove and put them in a metal kettle. He did this a couple of times until the wood stove was good and clean, then added more wood, banked it good and tight, then went into the kitchen and cleaned that stove and banked it. The wind blew heavy. Sean heard it whistling when he was in the barn. John came out and got his bed roll. Now he lay on the floor. "You can take a shower if you would like. The water's hot," said Sean.

"I thought I'd wait till morning, see what Sara thinks about these stitches before I get them wet," said John.

"God, I forgot all about them. Here I am making you lift all this heavy stuff that could have torn them open. I wasn't thinking," said Sean.

"Would you be my best man?" asked John.

"This would sound stupid to anyone. I'm giving my wife to you in marriage, and now you're asking me to be best man," laughed Sean, sitting on the sofa.

"Will you?" asked John.

"Sure, it's so strange," said Sean.

"What is?" said John, putting his hands under his head and staring at the ceiling.

"How is this thing going to work?" said Sean. "That's if I'm right. If you're marrying my wife, which makes it bigamy," Sean sighed. "I don't know what to do about Jacob," said Sean.

"Well, I thought I'd ask Jacob to stand up, too," said John.

"Not that Jacob, my brother-in-law, Jacob, the one who raped Sara. God, all the signs were there, and I didn't see them," said Sean.

"Signs?" questioned John.

"Withdrawing, no friends, wanting to be alone, low self-esteem, not sleeping, jumpy, and nervous," said Sean. "If Jacob was here now, I'd kill him, brother-in-law or not. That bastard has probably done this before and will do it again if he's not stopped. Fucker needs a bullet right between the eyes, and I'd like to be the one to do it," said Sean.

"Doesn't he have a family?" asked John.

"A wife, no children, which is probably good. He probably thinks incest is proper. Fucker needs to die," said Sean. "I'd spray that shit in his face like he did to Sara. I'd tell him why I'm going to kill him, let him feel the fear Sara felt when she couldn't do anything. I'd type up a suicide note. Or course, I'd make sure I had on rubber gloves, surgical boots, scrubs, hat, and mask. No traces of any kind, then I'd take the gun out of his desk, put it in his hand, put it in his mouth, and pull the fucking trigger," laughed Sean. "The whole time I'll enjoy seeing his fucking brains spatter all over the wall," said Sean.

"Wouldn't someone hear you?" asked John.

"Nope, it's his office; one whole fucking building," smiled Sean.

"Where'd you park your car?" asked John.

"Hospital parking lot," said Sean.

"Why?" asked John.

"I'd have an alibi. I'm seeing Sara, who's in a coma, plus I can put the scrub greens in the hospital laundry," said Sean.

"Why?" asked John.

"Because I'd have to take them from the hospital for two reasons: one, if I go see Sara early, I've already got my alibi. I would have been seen by everyone; two, if I take the greens from the hospital, I can put them back so everything counts up at the hospital. Now the greens with Jacob's blood is being sent to the hospital laundry."

"But how do you get out of Sara's room without being seen?" asked John.

"The greens. Everyone will think that I'm a doctor. Of course, I can't put the booties on until I'm at Jacob's office. All anyone will see is Jacob going into his office. We're the same height and build," said Sean.

"Why can't you put the booties on until you're at Jacob's?" asked John.

"Footprints. The booties will cover them," said Sean.

"You really thought this through," said John.

"That's all I think about. I never once thought I could kill someone, yet all I've done all night is plan to kill him," said Sean.

"I guess so," said John. "Sounds like you thought of everything."

"Oh, I'd miss something," said Sean. "I'd get caught."

"Not if you didn't do it," smiled John.

"Huh, oh yeah, just think about it," laughed Sean. "Well, I'm going to bed."

"You forgot one thing," said John.

"What's that?" asked Sean.

"Your brother-in-law should have greens on if he was seen wearing them," said John.

"Wow, I didn't think of that, pretty good. Can't you imagine what would be going through his mind as you dressed him in greens, and he couldn't move to fight you?" smiled Sean. "It's perfect. I only wish I could do it. He tried to get me to give the vaccine to some people in Rome who were supposed to be good people. Jacob and I checked around; they were bad people. One was supposed to be a doctor who had a cure for cancer. He was a big fake," said Sean.

"So what did you do?" asked John.

"Gave it to some good people," smiled Sean.

"Good man," said John. "Why suicide for Jacob?"

"Because the doctors have the highest rate of anybody. It wouldn't be questioned. Oh, there is one other thing I missed," said Sean.

"What's that?" asked John.

"He'd have to be in his real office," said Sean.

"Real office?" questioned John, turning to look at Sean.

"Yeah, that bastard has two offices. One is for patients he doesn't want to see, see he's not in. The second is a broom closet with a hidden door. Then his office where he sits hidden away. He's probably pissed so many people off, he needs to hide, the bastard," said Sean.

"That's like the rabbit that hides from the fox, goes in one hole and comes out the other. Pretty smart," said John," but also to your advantage."

"How do you figure that?" asked Sean.

"Well, if no one knows about his real office, then he must have killed himself," said John. "Would his wife be taken care of?"

"And the only one who knows about his real office is his nurse. I don't think even his wife knows. From what I'm told, there's a huge life insurance policy which includes suicide. Jacob pays dearly for the policy. Everything he has is covered like this, he told me once. If he didn't pay so much for the policy, he'd be rich, but he has to carry it. It's the law for doctors because you never know which doctor is going to up and pop himself. Suicide insurance is hard to get, then you pay dearly for it," said Sean. "Most doctors pay for it for years and never use it."

"The people of your time pay a lot for insurance?" asked John.

"God, yes. Our homes are insured, our cars, our life, our health; you name it, you insure it," said Sean.

"Why?" asked John.

"Well, if you lose it, then you're covered to get new stuff or if someone decides it is easy to get money by suing you, you've got it covered," said Sean.

"Strange time you live in," said John. "This suing thing, it's done a lot?"

"Yes, it's quick money. You have professionals who do it for a living then the poor bastard who really gets hurt ends up with shit because he doesn't know how the system works. Believe me, if you know how the system works in our time, you'll never have to work a day in your life," said Sean.

"There's a lot of these people?" asked John.

"Yes, our elderly are shit on all their lives. They work their whole lives paying into the system and get shit in return. They're expected to live on five thousand dollars a year or less, that's shit. If they had no bills to pay, it would take them six years just so they can pay fucking taxes and insurance. We have a food stamp program, but the elderly aren't given very much to buy food with. Some don't even qualify because they make five to ten dollars a month too much. We really shit on our elderly. When they don't know what to do with them, they dump them in nursing homes and the government takes everything they've worked their whole life for a way from them. It's sick, it really is," said Sean.

"Our elderly are respected and taken care of. We include them in everything we do. We listen to their stories, so we may learn, for they are wise. When we hunt and fish, we hunt and fish for them, too. Everyone is treated the same. We don't throw our elderly out with the trash and take what they own," said John.

"I wish they would do that for our elderly, but the government always has its excuses," said Sean. "Right now it's the baby boomers."

"Baby boomers?" asked John.

"We had a war, lots of people were killed. Men came home from war and got everything in sight pregnant. Population explosion means baby boomers. Now they're reaching retirement age, and government is pissed off that they have to pay off some of that money we paid in. It might affect their paycheck, so they keep raising the retirement age so they don't have to pay off and their high-paying jobs are safe," said Sean. "It's called 'fucking the people.' Maybe the Constitution should read, 'how to fuck the people,' instead of 'we the people,' laughed Sean.

"Isn't there a way these elderly people could find a way to make a living for themselves?" asked John.

"Oh, there used to be in my youth. We called them mom and pop stores. In the 90s you have to be politically correct, so not to insult someone, so they are called cottage industries. But government has imposed so much regulation on these through taxes and insurances that cottage industries are almost extinct. This is all designed so big business and big stores can take over, so that little old lady who sits in her chair and crochets, because she loves to, can't sell what she makes. People don't have the money to pay that little old lady what it cost her to make the afghan. It may be better quality because it's homemade, but big business and big stores will sell it for so little that this little old lady over here can't even buy half the yarn for the afghan that the store sells it for. So they sell it for ten dollars and this little old lady sells it for sixty dollars, which is cheap, probably the cost of the yarn? People with little money say I can buy six of these for the price of one of these. They are going to buy the six," said Sean.

"What happens to the afghan the little old lady made?" asked John.

"When it's done, she lovingly folds it and puts it away. Then when she dies, her kids come along, have a garage sale, now knowing the value of the afghan, put a sign on it, sells it for ten dollars," said Sean.

"But she worked so hard and paid so much for it. Why would her children do this?" asked John.

"Because they see it as junk. They want to get rid of it, so they sell it because the only thing that matters is money. You can't do anything without money. If anyone tells you money won't change them, they're a fucking liar. Money changes everything. You watch the changes around here. You know what brought those changes about? Money, not manual labor. Money bought the toys needed to make our lives simple. We have a saying in our time that pretty much puts things in perspective," said Sean.

"What's that?" asked John.

"The difference between men and boys is the price of their toys. It's all about money, nothing more, nothing less," said Sean.

"This sounds sad," said John.

"It is, but somebody set the rules to this game. I know it wasn't me. All I can do is try and keep my head above water so I can play the game. It's either sink or swim, and if you choose to swim, you better be one good fucking swimmer to beat the next guy," said Sean. "Money is the name of the game."

"It's a shame that money comes first and not the people," said John.

"Yes, it is, but there's nothing you can do about it, so you work your ass off to try and get as much money as you can, hoping one day you've saved enough to retire on, but the only retirement I see in my future involves a dirt blanket," said Sean.

"Dirt blanket?" asked John.

"Death, my friend. Six feet under with no more problems," said Sean. "Now I'm really going to bed," said Sean, standing up.

"Good night," said John.

"Good night," said Sean.

"Money's the key to the future," thought John as he went to sleep.

Sean climbed into bed, doubtful he could sleep. He thought of John's plan to get electricity. "Damn smart idea," said Sean as he closed his eyes.

Chapter 11

THE NEXT MORNING SEAN GOT UP EARLY; HE COULDN'T WAIT TO GET STARTED. Sean showered and walked into the living room, saw John sitting in a chair. "I'm about to make breakfast. I'll put coffee on," said Sean. "You're early."

"I couldn't sleep. My mind was so full of questions with no answers. I didn't know what to do," said John.

"Well, I'll get breakfast, you ask questions, I'll answer them if I can," Sean stopped. "How come you look so cold?" Isn't it warm enough in here for you?" asked Sean.

"In here it's warm," said John. "Out there it's cold."

"You were outside, why?" asked Sean as he made coffee.

"I thought the answer was out there," said John.

"What answer?" asked Sean baffled. "No, let's start at the beginning. Why did you go outside?"

"To work," John said seriously.

"To work on what?" asked Sean.

"Electricity," said John.

Sean poured coffee. "What did you do that involves electricity?" said Sean.

"I turned the outhouses into electric houses," said John. "That's what you wanted, wasn't it?"

"You worked outside all night?" asked Sean.

"Yes, I couldn't sleep, so I took those plans that John sent, went out to the outhouses, took out the things you sit on and put the white stuff in the ditch, then made floors and shelves," said John. "I couldn't sleep, so I worked."

Sean shook his head as he sliced bacon. "Anything else you did while I slept away? You could have gotten me up. I would have helped," said Sean.

"I didn't have to, Jacob helped, he couldn't sleep either. We dug that ditch you wanted; the ground was frozen solid," said John.

Sean shook his head laughing. "So I can pretty much say you two have most of the work done because you couldn't sleep?" said Sean.

"Yes, that sounds about right," said John, sipping coffee.

Sean flipped the eggs and bacon, checked the toast in the oven. He could never get it right with that toaster thing that Sara bought. "So you two worked the night shift, and I'm working the day shift," said Sean.

"Night shift?" asked John.

"That's what it's called in our time," said Sara, walking in. "We have three shifts: night shift, day shift, and afternoon shift. This is so business can keep going twenty-four hours a day, never having to stop. That smells good," said Sara.

"Jacob and I are working day shift, too," said John.

"Oh, overtime; overtime pay around here sucks," teased Sara as she set three plates on the island.

"Overtime is where you get paid time-and-a-half for working your ass off, so the government can take half of it in taxes," laughed Sara.

"Why work then if the government takes half?" asked John.

"Because the other half is what puts food on your table," said Sean.

"Oh, but what happens to the other money you make?" asked John.

"That pays the bills that keep the roof over your head and the clothes on your back and pays for the car you need to go to work in," said Sean.

"It's so complicated in the future," said John.

"Not really. There's only one way to make an honest living. That's to work and work hard," said Sean.

"And the not-so-honest?" asked John.

"Oh, the not-so-honest. There you have an assortment to choose from. Whatever your specialty is: rob, cheat, steal, kill, social services, and sue, that's the big one," smiled Sean.

"You forgot the one who robs people of their homes and money because of religion and the sure thing," added Sara. "Robbing and stealing are the same thing, Sean."

"You do have an assortment to choose from. What's that you say, 'fucked up?'" said John.

"That's it," said Sean. "We'll make him a 90s man yet."

"He'll never be a New Yorker until he gets attitude. No, a New York driver with attitude, then you're a 90s man," laughed Sara.

"This New York driver is a good thing?" asked John.

"Let me do it," said Sara, jumping up, pulling the stool out. "We will pretend that this stool is the car, and I'm the driver. I'm driving along and a car cuts in front of me. I hit the breaks to keep from smashing into this guy. This is what you say: 'You fucking idiot, haven't you heard of directional signals? Where did you get your license, in a Cracker Jack box? You stupid idiot," Sara was yelling. "Then you do like this. This is called flipping them the bird. Now the guy in front of you is pissed off, he flips you the bird and hits the brakes. You hit your brakes, but you still bump into him because he has no brake lights. He jumps out of his car holding his neck like this. He walks over to your car and says 'You fucking asshole, couldn't you see I was stopped? Who the fuck taught you to drive, your fucking grandmother? It figures, it's a fucking woman driver who's as blind as a bat.' Then I jump out of my car like this and say, 'You're the fucking asshole who doesn't know what directional signals are for and don't have any fucking brake lights.' Then he said, 'I had fucking brake lights; you broke them when you ran into the ass end of me, and if you weren't so fucking blind, you would see I had my directional lights on. Now I've got fucking whiplash because you're so fucking stupid, you don't watch where you're driving. I'm suing your fucking ass.' 'No, I'm suing your fucking ass, you stupid asshole.' Then the police come, take names, phone numbers, addresses, insurances, licenses, registrations, and plate numbers. They talked to both of you and then the cop comes up to me and gives me a ticket because I couldn't keep my car under control. Our insurances pay for our damages because of no-fault and my insurance goes up because I got the ticket," said Sara.

"But it wasn't your fault?" said John.

"I know that and you know that, but I got the ticket, so my insurance goes up. He caused it and probably ended up out of work for a long time and with a new car. Fair, no it's not fair. But his story was more believable than the truth. The truth is dull and boring, but an elaborate story always wins," said Sara. "So this man gets to go his merry way and keeps right on going too because the police said he was right and I'm wrong. Then one day this man kills someone with his car and everyone says he was such a good driver. We don't understand. Well, you try telling the family of the dead person he's a good driver. They lost a loved one because this man was allowed to get away with it until someone died. This man will look at the judge innocently and say, 'I don't know how it happened.' The bad part is he doesn't; he was never stopped from doing what he was doing," sighed Sara. She got up, picked up the stool and put it back next to the island. "You can't say the police were wrong, and you can't say the man was wrong. So far as he was concerned, he was a good driver. He drove that way all his life until someone died for his mistake."

"I don't think I want to become this type of New York driver," said John.

"Well, then you'll become a victim like me, cop an attitude, or you're out of the game. Truth doesn't count when an accident's involved, that's why insurance is so high," said Sara.

"There's no better way?" asked John.

"Nope, that's how it goes; the one with the best story wins," said Sara.

"I don't think I like this future too much: money rules and lies mean more than the truth," said John.

"Damn, I think he's got it now," said Sean.

"No wonder you two like it here so much," said John. "A man's word is his bond. We don't have to do bad things to one another to get along. I don't like the future at all."

"My sentiments exactly," said Sara. "But there's nothing you can do but live your life the best you can."

"You must find this shocking to see how we live helping one another like we do," said John.

"No I don't. This is what God wanted, but mankind fucked it all up," said Sara, "really made a big mess of it all, and now he doesn't know how to get back what he lost because he didn't know he'd lost it until it was gone."

"This is so sad. I hope our nation never gives into the white man's ways. They don't know what they are doing," said John.

"Oh no, you're allowed to keep your ways because you are a nation," said Sara.

"That's good but what does a nation have to do with anything?" asked John.

"A lot. A nation is a group of people that has a different belief, culture who live in one area that has its own laws, but live within the laws of the whole nation, which is America, so you have a nation within a nation. You are governed by the nation you entered and must live by the rules and not the other nation," said Sara.

"I don't understand," said John.

"Okay, when you're on your land, you live by your rules; when you're on the white man's land, you live by his rules," said Sara.

"Why didn't you say that in the first place?" said John.

Sean spewed coffee all over the island laughing. "In her mind, that is what she said, but us men like a simple approach in our conversations. Women drag things out to make us feel stupid," laughed Sean.

Sara hit Sean's shoulder on the way to the sink to get the dish cloth to wipe up Sean's mess.

"All women do this?" asked John.

"Yes, some are really out there. At least you can talk to Sara and get a drift of what she's saying," laughed Sean.

"Thank you," said Sara, wiping up the mess Sean made.

"Why did she thank you?" asked John.

"Because I paid her a compliment," smiled Sean.

"No, because you made a mess," said Sara.

"You thanked him for making a mess?" asked John.

"It's called criticism, and we better leave before we get on the subject and confuse you more," laughed Sean.

"Oh, it's a 90s thing," said John.

"No, a woman thing," whispered Sean.

"I heard that Sean," said Sara.

"Ears of a hawk," said Sean.

John nodded and got up.

"Where do you think you are going?" said Sara.

Both men stopped. Neither knew to whom she was speaking.

"I want to check those stitches," said Sara as she filled the sink with dish water.

Sean wiped his brow, smiled, and slipped away.

"Can you pull up your pant leg so I can see how it looks?" asked Sara.

John tried pulling the pant leg up but the sweatpants were too tight. "It won't come up any higher," said John.

"Okay, take them off then," said Sara.

John's head flew around so fast his hair swirled. "Sara!" he cried.

Sara jumped. "What? You scared the shit out of me," said Sara.

"I can't take my pants off," said John.

"Oh, I see," said Sara. "Sorry, did you plan on taking a shower?"

"Yes, if I could. It would be nice," said John.

"Okay, follow me," said Sara.

"Let's see, underclothes, T-shirt, flannel shirt, towel, soap, and shampoo. Okay, take a shower. Take the bandages off then put all these clothes on in this pile. Call me. I'll check it out, then you can put the clothes in this pile on," said Sara.

"Okay," said John, taking one pile of clothes with him into the bathroom where he showered. While John showered, Sara dressed and made the bed. She looked at the hope chest and decided to look. It was full of baby things. Sara didn't ask for all this but she got it, so she emptied it out and found a letter. It was for Sean, so she took it to him. He was in the barn just getting ready to go out. "Sean, this is for you," said Sara.

Sean read it and laughed. "John wants to know how we like our electricity. I'll write him later," said Sean. "I've got to see how much work Jacob and John did last night. By the looks of it, quite a bit."

"John's taking a shower. I'll check his stitches and then you can have him," said Sara. "I'm going to check on him now. I'm freezing, so I'm leaving you. If you're crazy enough to work in this cold, go ahead." Sara ran back into the house. She didn't care how warm John and Jacob thought the barn was; to her it was cold. When she went back into the bedroom, John was sitting on the bed. Sara saw the red line on his leg. "I thought it might be infected. A tree or an ax did this? These are bite marks, and now you can tell me how this happened." Sara walked in the bathroom, got bandages, peroxide, tape, and penicillin. She returned, knelt on the floor, and poured peroxide on the stitches.

"Aah!" yelled John. "What did you do?"

"It's infected, now tell me what happened," said Sara, pouring more peroxide.

"Aah! It hurts," said John.

"It should, it's a nasty infection. Now what bit you?" asked Sara.

"A wolf," said John. "He was hungry. I looked good to him. We fought; I won."

"Great, did he look crazy or foaming at the mouth?" asked Sara, pouring more peroxide on.

"No, he wasn't loco, just hungry," said John.

Sara got a glass of water. "Take this, it will help the infection. What did you do with the wolf after you killed him?" asked Sara.

"Skinned him and left him for other wolves to eat," said John, taking the pill.

"Hung him out to dry, huh?" laughed Sara, pouring on more peroxide.

"It doesn't hurt so much now. It just feels cold when you pour it on," said John.

"That's good," said Sara. Sara didn't tell John it was oozing infection. She was wiping it with sterile gauze that now lay in the pile on the floor; a rather sizable pile. The hot shower must have drawn it, and the peroxide was finishing the job. "Do you feel like you have a fever?" asked Sara.

"A fever?" questioned John.

"Warm, hot all over," said Sara.

"No, I'm cold actually," said John.

"That also could mean you have a fever, which more than likely you do. With infections, your fever could go so high it makes you cold because the air around you is lower than your body temperature and so you sweat, which makes your body feel cold," said Sara, pouring on more peroxide.

"Do you always talk so much?" said John.

"No, but I thought you would like to know that the medical profession has found that people have different kids of fevers for different things, that it may be of interest of you, so you could pass it on to the nation, so they can cure something faster by knowing the cause." Sara poured on more peroxide; it was looking a lot better. "I'm sorry if my talking bothers you," said Sara.

"No, your talking doesn't bother me. Sometimes I get the feeling you think I'm stupid, and you have to explain everything to me," said John.

"I don't think you're stupid. As a matter of fact, I think you're highly intelligent. God, you learned in two months what took me fifty years to learn. No, you're not stupid," said Sara, pouring on more peroxide. "It's just sometimes I come across something I didn't teach you, and I think it might interest you," said Sara.

John smiled. "So you're still teaching me when you talk so much?" said John.

"Yes," said Sara. She applied more peroxide. "There was nothing this time, but it never hurts to be sure. Do you feel better now?" asked Sara.

"Yes, I'm not cold anymore," said John. "Surprised this infection did this to me?"

"Yes, that's what I was trying to explain because sometimes these infections are inside where you can't see, and it's good to know this," said Sara, putting on a dry bandage.

"Yes I can see that," smiled John, looking down at Sara for the first time. "What's that?" asked John, pointing to the pile of gauze on the floor.

"That's the infection I just took out of your leg," said Sara. "This took it out before you got sick and died from it," said Sara, standing up and stretching her cramped legs.

"We have a populace we make for infection, but it takes days. This just took minutes," said John, holding up the brown bottle.

"If you would like I can have Susan send some through for you, and you can have it for the nation," said Sara. "Just don't let it freeze."

"Sure, if it's not trouble," said John.

"Oh, Susan and Laura love sending stuff. They are always looking for something to send, it might as well be something good. I'll tell them medical stuff for the nation."

"What's this stuff?" asked John.

"I asked for some things for Susan's body. This wasn't it, but they'll probably get around to it," said Sara. "I better check, I already know there's more stuff. I must admit I'm getting a little tired of this," said Sara.

"Why?" asked John.

"Well," said Sara, cleaning up the bandages on the floor and cleaning it with Lysol, "it just makes all of this seem more like a dream or a Walt Disney movie, a hope chest that goes forward in time, I might as well jump in and travel," said Sara.

"Who says it can't be done? Maybe you're here to do good," said John.

"That good stuff is bullshit, too," said Sara. "If I've learned anything from life, it's that one person can't change the world, and you can't fight city hall. I don't care who you are, you'll never win," said Sara, opening the hope chest and taking things out. "This is exactly what I'm talking about: a coffee pot, a toaster. What good is this stuff in this time. There's no electricity. You can't have any of this stuff out if strangers come. They have no fucking idea what this stuff is. In Salem they burn people at the stake for less, calling them witches. You can't disrupt time without some kind of repercussions in the future. This stuff is designed to save man time in the future. Well, it's more trouble than it's worth," said Sara. "If you take what a man does in a day's work here versus what a man does in the future, you get more done here than you do in the future. Why? Because of men and their toys." Sara closed the lid.

"Mentioning work, I better get going so we can get things moving here," smiled John.

"Yeah sure," smiled Sara, walking into the living room so John could dress. "What are they going to do when in one hundred years from now they find all this shit buried somewhere? It would be like trying to date the beginning of man. Only problem is, this shit's dated 1997, the year that hasn't arrived yet. That would set the geniuses of this world wondering what's happening," said Sara, sitting on the couch.

John dressed in a hurry; he wanted to run and hide. Sara was talking and talking, she wouldn't shut up. He kissed her on the head and ran out.

"What are you running from?" asked Sean.

"Sara, she's talking and won't shut up," said John.

"Really?" Sean asked puzzled. "Sara wasn't like that, I better check on her," said Sean. "I'll be right back." Sean ran into the house.

Sara was still talking, no one else was around.

"Sara, it's Sean. What's wrong? Do you hurt anywhere? Let's see if you've got a fever, no." Sean slapped Sara across the face.

"You fucker, what'd you hit me for?" yelled Sara.

"Sara, you've been rambling for the last your. It's the only thing I could think to do," said Sean. "I wouldn't hurt you for anything."

"Rambling about what?" asked Sara.

"Time, mark my words, you were freaking me out," said Sean. "As far as I'm concerned, you were in a galaxy far, far away, so I hit you, and you snapped out of it."

Sara looked around. There stood Jacob, Susan, little Jacob, and John. They all had worried looks on their faces.

"Oh God, I'm sorry. I don't know what happened," said Sara. "Go back to work, I'll be fine," said Sara. "Really, go."

"I'll stay," said Susan. "I was going to come over anyway, go. Sara and I will get lunch. We'll eat here, go," said Susan. The men left.

"Hey, the kids sent some stuff for you, I really should say for the baby," said Sara.

"Oh, what kind of stuff?" asked Susan, watching Sara carefully.

"Come, I'll show you. This is a small play pen or portable bed. This is a swing, this is a walker, this is a high chair, these are all educational toys, a stroller, coffee pot, toaster for you, some clothes. I didn't ask for this stuff, I asked for some sleepers. They might be here now, let's look," said Sara.

"Pampers are the best things yet," said Susan.

"Wait until you see sleepers. Oh, here go some clothes, let's see, onesies. These are great. There we go, sleepers, slipper socks, Pampers, see they sent the good stuff last. Sheets, plastic bottles, bottle brushes, nipples, caps." Sara was putting things out and setting them on the floor. "Please don't think me a terrible person, but I got the clothes for Jacob for Christmas. Look, jeans, flannel shirts, snow suit."

Susan was shocked at the stuff Sara had for the baby.

"Sneakers, boots, rattles, Christmas presents for John, Sean, Susan, Jacob Jr., and lunch," said Sara.

Susan looked. There was nothing else. No Christmas presents for Sara. "Do you think I could send a letter through?" asked Susan.

"Sure, I'll get you a pen and paper," said Sara. "They would love to hear from you."

"Maybe they won't," thought Susan, "but it's about time somebody did something for Sara. They weren't going to," thought Susan.

"I'd like to thank them for all they've done for us," she said.

"I'll put the subs in the kitchen for lunch," said Sara.

Susan wrote:

"Dear Susan, John, and Laura: Could you please send some things for your mother for Christmas. It would be a nice thought on your part since there are no stores here for her to buy her own Christmas presents. You sent everyone else presents, but your own mother, that is rather rude. Thank you for our presents; we need nothing else. Your mother misses you all a lot, and something from you could help her a lot right now. She's depressed and confused, so please find it in your hearts to think of your mother. Love, Susan."

Susan folded the note. Sara came in. "Where do I put this now?" asked Susan.

"Here, I'll show you. Right here. Close the lid and whenever they look, they will get it. I know what this is, it's pandora's box," laughed Sara.

"I don't understand," said Susan.

"Well, I've been trying to put this whole dream into perspective. I think I've got it now. John is my knight in shining armor, tall, dark and handsome. You, Jacob, and the baby are the friends I never had. This world is perfect, the way I always dreamed. Sean is my protector. The hope chest is pandora's box. Every time I open it, a little more of 1990s seeps in until my dream world is gone, then I wake up in the 90s, then I'll be okay. There, I feel better. I know what's happening now, it's all logical, and I can live with it. The thing with the hope chest won't bother me anymore. Now I know what's going on," said Sara.

"Let's put the Portacrib together, that will be easy. We'll set it up in the living room." Sara picked up the carry case. "Watch this, this snaps out, take the crib out, push on the center like this, lock the sides like this, take the case, put it in here, there your mattress pad. Put one of these crib sheets in like this and you have a crib, a place for him to play or sleep."

"That's nice. All this stuff folds up like this?" asked Susan.

"Sure does. Saves on space, easy storage. The stroller folds like an umbrella. It's really neat how everything folds and stores right out of the way so if you have no room, it's great," said Susan happily.

Susan wasn't sure about Sara's happiness. It seemed too happy, was the only way Susan could put it. Susan had seen people do this before and they were taken away.

"What kind of soup should we fix for supper?" asked Sara. "Tomato, that goes with anything. Two cans should be enough," said Sara.

"Sara stop it!" yelled Susan. "What's wrong?"

"I'm going stir crazy. I need some fresh air. I feel like running, but there's nowhere to run," said Sara.

"Look, you dress up warm, run back and forth out front. I'll make soup, go," said Susan.

"Yes, I could do this, run this hyperactivity out. I need to do this, I can do this. That's a good idea," said Sara.

"Go," said Susan. "Do it now." Susan pushed Sara.

"Okay, I'm going, you talked me into it, out of here." Sara dressed warm very fast. The thought of running pleased her. She was out the door and through the barn door. The wall of snow kept the wind out. Running back and forth, breathing in and out. God, this feels good. Sara ran faster and faster as her feet make a track in the snow. Sara ran around and around; she ran until there was no energy left with which to run. Sara leaned over, put her hands on her knees, kept breathing in and out until she was breathing normal, then she walked inside. "Oh God Susan, that was heaven. I feel great. I've got to do that more often," said Sara.

"Well I'm glad you've calmed down," said Susan.

"I know, I can't be cooped up too long. My blood needs fresh air; I need fresh air," said Sara.

"Well, tell the men that lunch is ready. That will give you fresh air," laughed Susan.

"Smells good," said Sara as she went to get the men. She went outside to find they weren't there. She checked both outhouses. Nobody had been here in a while. The tracks were snow-covered. The only tracks were hers, so Sara went back into the barn. "Don't panic, check Susan's house," thought Sara. Sara walked into Susan's house, there was no one here. She checked all three rooms, no one. Sara ran to her house. "I can't find them, they're not outside, they're not at your house, they're not here, they're nowhere," said Sara. "Did someone take them?"

"Calm down, they can't be far. They wouldn't leave without telling us where they were going?" said Susan.

"Well, something smells good," said Sean.

"You son of a bitch," said Sara, hitting Sean. "Where have you been? I've been looking all over for you guys. I thought someone took you guys."

"Calm down, we were in the loft running wire," said Sean. "It's all right."

"Why didn't you answer when I called?" asked Sara.

"Maybe because we didn't hear you. Believe me, if someone tried to take me there would be blood everywhere. I'm not going without a fight," said Sean, smiling.

"That's not funny," said Sara. "I thought something happened to you guys. I didn't hear any noise at all."

"There isn't any when you're running wire. You might hear hammering when we put staples in, but with so much hay it probably deadened the sound. Look nobody wants us, okay? Let's eat, we're starved."

"Next time I'll check the loft," said Sara, walking to the island.

"We're all done up there. We're ready to put in plugs," smiled Sean. "I thought we'd put two plugs in each of the rooms, that should be enough, and one in the bathroom," smiled Sean. "A plug on either side of the sink. John got six GFI plugs, which was smart. We should have Susan's place done by tonight. At the rate we're moving, maybe ours. We've got all the tough stuff done at Susan's. Now all we do is connect. These two guys had most of the hard stuff done last night. If they had gotten me up, we'd be done by tonight," laughed Sean.

"Well, one of us had to sleep," laughed Jacob. "You were so excited. You got so excited that you slept, and we couldn't. You've done so much for us that I think it's high time we did something for you. We may not know a lot, but what we do know we can do well," said Jacob, sitting at the table.

"All I know is you did one hell of a job setting up those outhouses," said Sean, sitting at the table.

"We've had a good teacher," said John.

Sara put a pill in front of John. "Take this," said Sara.

"Why, I feel fine now?" said John.

"Take it," said Sara.

"Yes ma'am," said John.

"John told me about the infection and how you got rid of it and explained about fevers," said Sean.

"Did he tell you I drove him nuts rambling?" said Sara.

"No, we all knew you were rambling," said Sean, staring at Sara.

"Right, I forgot," said Sara. "I ran outside for a while and Susan made lunch. I feel better now. Of course, I was upset not finding you guys, but other than that, I'm fine. I need something to do. I can't sit like this; it's driving me crazy. Men do this; women do this. I'm not used to that. I'm used to doing whatever I want," said Sara. "This is just bullshit as far as I'm concerned."

Sean stared at Sara. "She's right, she came from a world where men and women worked side by side. Sara knew how to do things around a house, just as good as any man. Hell, she helped him a lot of times. She loved it. Sara, after lunch how about running wire for this place? I know you can do it," said Sean.

"Encased wire?" asked Sara, sitting up straight, her interest renewed.

"Yes, encased wire," smiled Sean.

"Where's your incoming line?" asked Sara excited.

John and Jacob looked at Sean like he was crazy.

"Bathroom wall," said Sean. "To the left of the sink. Want to do it? I got power tools with battery packs," smiled Sean.

"Yes, yes, yes," said Sara, jumping up and doing a little dance. "Finally I get to do something I can do," said Sara.

"Well, you better eat if you're working for me. I don't allow long lunches," laughed Sean.

"Yes sir," said Sara, smiling.

After lunch Sean, Jacob, and John brought in wire, plugs, and casings. They thought Sean was crazy but wouldn't tell him so until he got to Susan's place.

"You're nuts letting Sara do men's work," said John.

"Why? In our world women work with men, and they do things just as good as men, that's what Sara's used to. You may not like it, but when you take a well-educated, hard-working woman like Sara, put her in a world when her only job is to be a woman, she will go crazy. She rambled, got confused. Her mind and body are used to doing things. She can't sit around like she has without losing her mind," said Sean.

"Sara can really do this?" asked John.

"Yes, Sara can do a lot of things. I bet if she put her mind to it, she could build a house. It may take her a little longer than a man, but I can guarantee that house will be well built. The sad part is, no matter how dirty or hard the work, she'll love every second of it," said Sean.

"God forgive, what am I marrying?" laughed John.

"One hell of a woman," said Sean.

"A woman who's a man," said John.

"If that's how you feel, maybe you shouldn't marry Sara," said Sean.

Jacob froze up to this point. He wasn't paying much attention. Now they had his whole attention.

"What do you mean? I thought you approved of me marrying Sara?" said John.

"I did until I found out that your male ego was in danger because Sara can do things men can," said Sean.

"My what? I feel no danger from Sara," said John.

"Yes you do. Your male pride is threatened by the fact Sara can do male things. You've got this stupid notion that Sara should do just women things. Well, Sara's not like that, okay? Sara doesn't think she's better than you because she can do things you do. She doesn't pretend to, she doesn't feel threatened by you. However, she does take pride in being able to work next to you. In her eyes, you will always be man, never woman, man," said Sean.

"No, I just think a woman should be taken care of," said John.

Sean laughed. "Let me tell you something. You may think you're taking care of her, but she's really taking care of you," said Sean.

"What do you mean?" asked John.

"Okay, let's see, you're the man, your job is to provide food, clothing, and shelter, right?" asked Sean.

"Yes," John smiled proudly.

"But you see you don't really. You kill a deer, a buffalo, whatever you bring back to camp, but the woman skins the kill, tans the hide, then makes the clothes you wear, then cuts the meat, cooks your meals, makes jerky for the winter out of it. Then with dried hides and skin, she makes the teepee you sleep in and the blankets you sleep on and cover your ass when it's cold. She gathers berries and plants and puts them aside so you have food for winter and medicine when you need it. Then she gathers the twigs that starts the fire that cooks the meal that you eat. Now you tell 'em where you provided anything," said Sean.

"You put it that way, it sounds like I don't do anything," said John.

"It's not just you, the white man is just as guilty. We ask our women to go West, but most of the time women lose. She leaves her family behind, follows her loved one into danger, bearing children along the way. Cleaning our clothes, cooking our meals, burying what children that don't make it along the way, sometimes losing her husband because she believes in him and the life she thinks we can give them. Things get tough on the trail. What do they leave behind? Her possessions. We would never think to give up any of our stuff. Our stuff is what will forge our new life on the frontier. Her possessions are trivial to us, but you know what, she does it because she loves you. She'll stand right by your side even if she has to give up her life doing it. Women have always done men things, we just never noticed. We were too full of ourselves to see it," said Sean.

"You're right," said John. "It kind of takes your breath away when you see you're not what you thought you were."

"Damn right it does. Let me tell you, women got really pissed off and now in the 90s they're paying us back. Women work and can make a home as good as any man. If you don't follow the rules, your ass is out in the street. Women won't put up with the shit we get away with here. If you're hungry and she's had a hard day, she'll tell you to get it yourself," laughed Sean. "She's probably right because she's working to buy all the new toys that are out there that you can't live without," said Sean. "And if we're not careful, they will wipe us out. They don't even need us in the 90s to have a baby."

"What!" John and Jacob cried.

"It's true, men donate sperm to a sperm bank. It's frozen. A woman walks in, chooses what kind of father she would like for her baby, gets artificially inseminated, and has a baby," said Sean.

"We really created a mess, didn't we?" asked John.

"We sure did. We created war, went and fought them like men to prove we were the best, left woman to fend for herself and she survived, found out she could, and it's been uphill ever since," said Sean. "We forced women into it because we were too busy being men doing men things. Now in the 90s we're pissed off at them. We shouldn't be, we forced them into it. You've got some men who are male chauvinists who think they're men by beating their women into submission, but that's not working anymore. Now they're striking back. There was one woman who cut a man's penis off. Women are starting to kill the men who abuse them. They would rather rot in jail than put up with the abuse. Sometimes men abuse women so badly they scar them for life or kill them. I know it sounds awful, but some of these men deserve it, like the abuse Sara had all her life. Tom needed killing," said Sean.

"Well," said John, shaking his head. "If Sara wants to do what I thought was men's work, let her. I better learn how to help her."

"You just did," smiled Sean.

"How? I didn't do anything," said John.

"Yes you did. You just let Sara be who she is," said Sean.

"That's all it takes?" asked John baffled.

"That's all," smiled Sean. "Believe me, you let Sara be who she is, she'll let you be who you are, and you two will end up working together and have a great life together," said Sean.

"This is all women want?" asked John.

"That and a couple other small things," said Sean.

"What are they?" asked John.

"To be respected and by respect I mean no abuse, verbal or hitting, but helping hand from time to time around the house," said Sean.

"Like what?" asked John.

"A hand cooking meals, doing dishes, carrying laundry, picking up after we made a mess, this is a big one with women. Feeding or changing the baby, watching the baby while she takes a nap or a bath," said Sean.

"Say we do this, what do we get for helping?" asked John.

"Some of the most incredible sex you'll ever have. She won't feel tired, she'll feel ready to please," said Sean.

"That's hard to believe. Susan's so uptight it's impossible," said Jacob.

"You're doing it wrong then," said Sean.

"There are ways?" asked Jacob.

John laughed. "There are ways," said John. "I'll tell you while we work."

Sean went to another area to work while John explained some things to Jacob. Every now and then he'd hear Jacob really cry.

"Okay Susan, pull," said Sara. "Okay, stop."

"I think I'm getting the hang of this," laughed Susan, coming in the bathroom. "I love wearing jeans and shirts," smiled Susan.

"Comfortable, aren't they? They give you freedom. Got to do something about those boots. Let's trace your foot, send it to the kids, and have them get you sneakers, ones with good arch support, you're pregnant," said Sara, covering the wire with casing. "Sean must have some ceiling lights. He shows a couple here, one for the bathroom, one for the kitchen. Okay, we'll take this board and this board off," said Sara.

"Why?" asked Susan, looking where Sara pointed.

"I think we can hide this wide from the switch to the light, then run a wire down the wall to a plug in the living room. See this wall can have the switch box and plugs recessed in it. Since the wood runs the long way on the ceiling, we can run across to the kitchen, then down, back up, then down, then all along this side and down to a plug here," said Sara.

"Sean doesn't show that here," said Susan.

"I know, but we can't do it the way Sean wants. It's too hard for us. The only thing that counts is the end results are the same. Besides, this is quicker," laughed Sara.

"Okay, what you say. Let's do it," smiled Susan.

Five hours later Sara was finishing up. The baby had eaten four times, changed three and was now sleeping in his sleepers in his crib.

"Can I check the chest?" asked Susan.

"Go ahead, the kids said they were sending supper since we were working so hard," laughed Sara. "I told them chicken with lots of mashed potatoes and gravy, cole slaw, corn on the cob, Pepsi, and cake."

"That's all," laughed Susan.

"Well, I thought we'd be starved by the time it got here," said Sara.

"Aren't you going to put all this wood back?" asked Susan, lifting the lid to the chest. There was indeed food, but presents for Sara is what made her happy. She took them out and put them under the bed. She'd find a way to put them under the tree later. "There's food here, a letter for me, and a couple white boxes," said Susan, walking into the living room, showing Sara the boxes.

"Sneakers," cried Sara. "They must have sent you some, try them on. They have good arches, they will be good for your back."

Susan sat on the couch, took off her boots, put on the sneakers, and fell in love with them. "They feel so good; they fit good, too," laughed Susan. "Now I know why you wanted your sneakers. They make you bounce."

"I never thought of it that way, but I guess they do," laughed Sara.

Both women were laughing when the men walked in to eat. On the island sat Kentucky Fried Chicken, lots of it. Jacob was taken aback to see jeans and shirt on Susan. The shirt was tied in a knot at her waist, her long blond hair pulled back in a pony tail. There was something sexy in the way she looked.

Sean looked at what Sara and Susan had done. "You trying to show off?" teased Sean.

"No, why?" asked Sara.

"Your work looks better than mine," laughed Sean.

"Only because I had to stop and think how to do mine," laughed Sara.

"Well, after supper we'll finish up. Susan's place is done. They have power. We set the refrigerator on the counter with the coffee pot and toaster. No more candles, unless we want them," smiled Sean. "John was brilliant on this one."

John was surprised how Sara was her old self. All she needed was to be who she was. She asked nothing more, and it made her happy to feel like she'd done something.

Sara and Susan set out plates and glasses. Sean took out silverware. Jacob and John helped set out the food.

Susan watched Jacob. "I'll be damned," she thought, there was something sexy about him helping in the kitchen. Tonight they all sat at the table and talked after dinner. Everyone cleaned up. "Susan was so bouncy," thought Jacob. Susan looked good.

Sara and Susan carried the things the kids sent for the baby over to Susan's, and put what had to be put together. It didn't take long, they just snapped together then folded flat for storage. The Pampers Susan put under the bed; the clothes they put in what Sara called a dressing table that folded up. After all this was done, Sara showed Susan how to use the coffee maker and toaster, then put milk, butter, and eggs in the refrigerator. "This keeps it cold," said Sara.

Susan was more interested in how the lights turned on and off. "This is really great. You have a lot of these in the 90?" asked Susan.

"Yes," said Sara. "Way too many."

"What do you mean?" asked Susan.

"Some places have so many lights, you can't see the night sky," said Sara.

"I don't think I'd like that," said Susan.

"I don't," said Sara. "Now when you're not in a room, turn the lights off. The bulbs get hot and little Jacob can burn himself, so only use them when necessary. I see John has plug covers over the plug. Use them. If Jacob sticks something in there, he can kill himself."

"Oh my," said Susan. "I'll keep them covered."

"Where's those Christmas toys I gave you?" asked Sara.

"Here, you mean we can plug them in and they work?" smiled Susan.

"Yup, watch." Sara took Santa out of his box, plugged him in. "This little thing here, you turn it and he turns on. Push this button, you get music," said Sara.

"Oh, I like that. He's so cute," said Susan.

"Never touch anything electric with hands, it can kill you, so be very careful," said Sara.

"Okay," said Susan. "Well, let's see how the men are doing at your place."

"One more thing, the kitchen light is also a fan. This turns the fan on, like this. You have different settings. This one turns the lights on. Now this one you have a night light, this casts a soft light, like this, or a bright light, like this," said Sara. "Never get near the blades when they're going around, they will get you."

"This is all dangerous stuff, ain't it?" asked Susan.

"Yes, it's not to be played with," said Sara. "Respect it and it will respect you." Sara felt that she'd explained everything to Susan well enough that she'd be careful around it, so they went to her house. Little Jacob was having a ball with his new toys. He had the cutest laugh. It was a deep, hardy laugh. It made Sara laugh hearing it. Jacob was looking up at the toy Susan had hung on the side of the crib. He'd hit it with his hand, it made a noise, and he would laugh. The men laughed as little Jacob laughed. They would replace all the wood Sara and Susan took down. The plugs were all covered, the bathroom light in, and the kitchen fan lay in pieces as Sean installed it. There were lamps on in the living room.

"Where'd the stands come from?" asked Sara. "Kids send them through?"

Sean laughed. "No, I made them for you for Christmas, but you needed them now to set the lamps on," said Sean.

"Thank you, I love them," said Sara. "We needed them, but I didn't want to bother you with such a trivial thing. You've done so much."

"Thank you, I didn't think you noticed," teased Sean. "We have stands next to our bed, too. Finally, a place to put things," laughed Sean.

"Well, everything makes sense but that corner stand," said Sara.

"I needed some extra storage, didn't think you would mind if it was hidden like that," smiled Sean.

"No, it looks cute there," said Sara.

"Well hit the switch, let's see how it works," said Sean.

Sara hit the switch. "And we have light," smiled Sara.

Sara went in the kitchen and made coffee. The men went and cleaned up their tools and took them to the barn. They were gone for a while, so Sara and Susan had coffee. They sat at the island and talked. Jacob giggled in the background.

"I can't believe how easy it is, a switch, a plug," said Susan.

"You should see all the electric toys we have for the kitchen, it's unreal. Blender mixers, bread machines, grills, microwave ovens. With a microwave oven you have a meal in minutes," said Sara.

"I like the refrigerator," said Susan. "Cold milk sounds good."

"I love cold milk, but in our time they pasteurize it, mix the cream right in it. I can drink a whole quart in one setting. They try to sell you 2 percent or skim milk. They say it's healthier for you. I ain't buying that shit. If God wanted me to drink that stuff, he would have made it that way. I won't eat or drink stuff that mankind says is new and improved. All they did is add chemicals. I totally refuse to drink chlorinated water. All that shit is is rat poison, so I know that ain't good for you. They can do all they want, just as long as it doesn't involve me," said Sara. "Well, it's time for the kids to send things through. Want to see what they sent?" asked Sara.

"Sure, it's fun," laughed Susan.

"Yeah, as long as it doesn't involve work like today," laughed Sara as they walked into the bedroom. "You open it, the thrill is gone for me," said Sara.

"Sure," smiled Susan. "Presents for you and me," said Susan.

"Me? Presents for me?" Sara knelt down next to Susan. "I better put the presents under the tree. I have them all over, including under the bed," said Sara.

"I'll help," said Susan. There were three brown bags that Sara sat on the island. She'd go through them after. There was a letter for Sean and John. The men returned just as Sara and Susan finished putting presents under the tree.

"Can we open them now?" teased Sean.

"No," said Sara. "You have a letter on the island; you too John," said Sara. "I don't know what's in the bags, I haven't checked, so if you want, you go ahead," said Sara. "I'm helping Susan take her presents home."

"We'll do that," said Sean. "Susan can get the baby, and we'll take that stuff over for you."

"Okay, I get to check the goodies," said Sara. "I'll see you tomorrow then Susan," said Sara.

"Sure, see you tomorrow. Your cooking tomorrow, aren't you?" asked Susan.

"Yup, we'll have a small Christmas Eve dinner here," smiled Sara. "See you about 6:00, is that good?"

"Yeah, we should be through wiring the barn by then. Putting in three lights, that's not much," said Sean.

"Six then," said Sara.

The men and Susan left. Sara went through her bags. "Boy were they in for a treat tomorrow," thought Sara. Milk was the only thing Sara cared about. She seemed to drink a lot of it lately. The men returned. "Well, I'm taking a hot bath and getting my nightgown on. The kids sent chips and dips for tonight. They must think it's our Christmas Eve," said Sara as she walked through.

Sara closed the bathroom door, ran water, put in bubble bath, and got in. Sean ran into the living room. "Okay, let's go," whispered Sean. All three men went in the barn and came back with three packages. They undid them and set them up and were sitting at the island when Sara walked in.

Sara started laughing, she couldn't stop.

"What's wrong?" asked Sean smiling.

"A TV, that's really stupid. What channels do you expect to get, snow and more snow?" said Sara.

"Ah, I thought we'd watch Christmas shows," said Sean. "You see, we also have a VCR and about thirty movies," smiled Sean.

"Well, as long as you don't expect to get TV stations, you're safe with movies, so the chips and dips were for tonight," said Sara.

"Yup, Susan's got a TV and about thirty movies, so we should be set through winter," smiled Sean.

"If we ain't, I'm sure the kids will send more," said Sara. "Thank you men for my power, my TV, and my hot water. You better send some chips and dip with Pepsi home with Jacob, so they can sit back and enjoy."'

"Susan was taking a bath after she got Jacob settled, but she's excited to see what the future's like," said Jacob.

"Well, remember this is movies. These are stunts, nobody dies or really gets hurt, so don't let Susan get scared," said Sara.

"Sean told us to watch "Miracle of 34th Street," the one you like. It will break us in slowly. He sent some in the order to watch them," said Jacob.

"That's a good movie to watch," said Sara. "What are we watching?" asked Sara.

"Something we both got for Christmas, movies, the same," said Sean, picking up his letter.

Sara got out a bag to put chips and dip in for Jacob; he left. John and Sean read their letters while Sara got the dip and chips ready. Jacob came in with a six pack of Pepsi.

"I was told you like these," said Jacob.

Sara turned around. "Ice cubes, a tray of ice cubes. Where'd you get these?" said Sara.

"The freezer. Sean made them this morning," said Jacob.

"Thank you guys, this is great, ice cubes for my soda, very 90s," laughed Sara. "Maybe too '90s," said Sara, walking into the living room, setting chips on the table with dip. She walked back and brought soda in with a glass of ice cubes for her. Sara sat on the couch, picked her legs up, and stretched out. "You two ready?" I am," called Sara.

"Sure," said Sean, grabbing the remote off the island. They swapped letters to read. "Jacob was found dead, suicide," said Laura. There was a typed letter; it wasn't nice. Sara needs to drink more milk, so tomorrow they will send more plus vitamins. That was the extent of the letters." John and Sean sat in the chairs. Sean started the movie. John was mesmerized by the picture before him. He wasn't sure what to think, but he knew he liked it. They watched two movies that night. The second was National Lampoon's "Christmas Vacation." John laughed like he'd never laughed before. These movies could make you laugh or cry.

After the movies, Sara picked up. She poured herself a tall glass of milk, walked over to the couch and had a cigarette. She hadn't had one in a while but felt like one now. "Well, John what do you think of the 90s?" asked Sara.

"This TV thing is pretty good," said John. "I like it. I can see why you don't get too much done. The time flew by watching it," said John.

"Some people sit in front on the TV all day watching program after program," said Sara.

"Program?" asked John.

"Talk shows, news, soap operas, sitcoms, these we call programs, and there's a lot of them. There's all kinds of sport programs for men to watch. There are educational programs, kids programs that include cartoons; there are programs on sex, too," said Sara.

"No," said John.

Sean laughed. "You wouldn't believe some of the stuff on TV."

Sara finished her milk. "I'm going to bed. If I know John, he sent you a dirty movie to watch. I won't embarrass you two by watching it with you. I'll watch it with Susan when you two aren't around," laughed Sara. "Good night guys, enjoy. Just don't shock John too much." Sara snuggled down in bed. She fell asleep in no time. It felt good to do something.

Sean and John sat at the island in the kitchen out of earshot of Sara.

"It figures that Jacob would kill himself to save me the pleasure. I don't know what Laura meant by things being a mess. I don't know if she was talking the suicide or the note. I'll write Laura a letter. I'll tell her I need to know why she thinks things are a mess, have her tell me all she knows," said Sean.

"What do they mean that Sara needs more milk and vitamins?" asked John.

"She probably is having a hard time with something at the hospital, so we'll have to have them explain better. I know Sara wasn't drinking too much of the raw milk. Maybe we should make a list of things to send, things to give her strength, things she's not getting here. That plus vitamins should give her strength. That could be why she's so depressed here." Sean got out a pen and paper. He wrote Laura a letter telling her he was so sorry about Jacob, and he wanted Laura to tell everything she knew and that if she needed money, to cash a bond. Then he explained how Sara has been uptight and depressed, then made list of things he'd like sent for her. "It's very important we build her strength," signed Sean.

"Think this will work?" asked John.

Sean thought, then wrote down a few more things. "Now it will," smiled Sean.

"What's the stuff you wrote down?" asked John.

"Christmas Eve dinner and supper. All Sara has to do is cook, it's all prepared," said Sean. "It will be there in the morning. I'll put it in there now. Do you want to take your shower first?" asked Sean.

"No, I'll take mine in the morning when Sara can check my leg. I wouldn't dream of doing it without her permission. She made me take three pills today. I don't know what for," said John. "I'm going to bed."

"Okay, I'll put this in the chest, then take my shower. Tomorrow's work isn't much," said Sean. "Maybe we'll watch 'The Santa Clause or Jingle All The Way,' That's what we would call a real good movie, funny and touching. Good night my friend."

"Good night," said John, laying out his bed roll. John lay down and was soon asleep.

Chapter 12

SEAN GOT UP EARLY. HE HAD A RESTLESS NIGHT. HE WORRIED ABOUT LAURA, the kids, and Sara. He felt helpless; he couldn't help either one right now, so he got up and checked the chest. The things he ordered were there. He took it all out and found a letter. This is what he needed. Sean carried the packages to the kitchen and made a pot of coffee. He poured a cup, went to the island, sat down, and opened the letter. There were six pages; Sean started reading. He felt better and better as he read. Jacob killed himself for the love of a woman who dumped him. Jacob's wife now had lots of money, so she said fuck him. Jacob's parents were upset, but Laura was handling it okay. Jacob was being cremated, no calling hours. He'll be buried in the spring. Sara needed vitamins and milk to keep her strength up here because she's read that Sara's on TV, and Susan feels it's not enough and doesn't want to take any chances. She read that Sara's coming down with a cold, so she wants her to take extra C. "Everything is fine, just enjoy Christmas there. You will both be home in time for Christmas here, so we're planning a big to do about it." Sean felt relaxed. He burned the letter in the sink. Sara couldn't see this. After it all burned away, Sean washed the ashes down the drain. Sean looked out the window. Snow, lots of it coming down. Feeling better, Sean went back to bed. A little sleep is better than none. Everyone slept in. Sara got up first at 11:30. She was shocked to see everyone in bed. She went in the kitchen, started breakfast, and made fresh coffee. She was setting the table for breakfast when Sean and John got up.

"Figures we all slept in on the day we've got a lot to do," laughed Sara.

"You don't have a lot to do. I had Laura send you things so you wouldn't have to work too hard today. Susan's worried, she read in the diary you got a cold, so she sent a bunch of vitamins and lots of homogenized milk to drink, so please do it and make her feel better," said Sean.

"Sure, is it okay if I make a couple of pies?" teased Sara.

"Sure, but take the vitamins and write Susan and tell her you're taking them," said Sean.

"Do I dare look and see what you ordered?" teased Sara.

"Sure, because I know your holiday meals. I had Laura make potato salad and cabbage pineapple. Susan made macaroni salad and sent lasagna and meat platters with rolls. The ham and turkey are on their way through. Baked beans and dinner rolls and sandwich bread, did I miss anything?" said Sean.

"No," laughed Sara. "You got it. I've got cookies and candy, so all I have to do is a couple of pies, so I'm ahead of schedule. Not bad for just getting up," laughed Sara, sitting down at the table.

"Jacob killed himself. Laura said he was in his office."

"Well, I feel sad for Laura. She's probably very upset, but it couldn't have happened to a nicer guy," said Sara very bitterly.

"Laura's not upset," said Sean. "I guess he killed himself over some woman, and you know how Laura feels about that kind of stuff."

"I know," sighed Sara. "That's why I never said anything about what he did to me. She would have killed him. She would have ended up in jail, and she was pregnant with Sean Jr. I would have been dragged through the mud. My kids didn't need that. Tom would have loved it. No, walking away was the best thing to do," said Sara.

John and Sean said nothing. They thought over what Sara said and knew she was right, so they ate. Sara finished her breakfast.

"What's Jacob's wife think?" asked Sara.

"I guess she told Laura she'll laugh all the way to the bank.'

"Good for her," said Sara, taking a sip of coffee, then swallowing a handful of vitamins and washed them down with more coffee.

"Susan sent all those vitamins to take?" laughed Sean.

Sara laughed. "Instead of a good multivitamin, she sent individual ones. If it's a cold, I would be taking Vitamin C and zinc, but Susan wanted to cover everything," laughed Sara. "Susan always went a little overboard, but you saw me take them. I'll take more later," said Sara.

"Can't you take too much in vitamins?" asked Sean.

"These are all water soluble, meaning what my body doesn't need it flushes out when I go to the bathroom," said Sara.

"They come like that?" questioned Sean.

"Some do, yes," said Sara, lighting a cigarette.

John didn't say anything, he just listened, drank his coffee, and smoked.

"Speaking of pills, here's yours, John," said Sara, getting the pill bottle off the island, shaking one pill in the cup. "How's that leg feel today?" asked Sara.

"Good, it doesn't throb like yesterday, and I'm not cold with fever. I slept like a baby for twelve hours. I've never slept that long," said John.

"That's good, thought you would need the sleep to fight the infection," said Sara.

"I didn't take a shower last night. I didn't know if I should until you looked at it," said John.

"I'll get you clean clothes, and you can take a shower whenever you want. I'll show you where the bandages are and you can put them on yourself today. I will look at it, but I'm sure we've got it under control now," said Sara. "John you seem quiet, is something wrong?"

"I'm puzzled why I slept so long. I can't see how I did that. I've never done that before at all, sick or not sick," said John.

"Okay, John you had a blood infection. That's why you had a streak running up your leg. A blood infection is serious, very serious. It can kill you, so I gave you the only antibiotic I have. It gets into the blood and kills all the infection. Sometimes it will make you sleep because your body uses less energy while you sleep. So by sleeping, the antibiotic gets a jump start on healing, so then you feel better faster," said Sara.

"I won't sleep like that all the time?" asked John.

"No, you'll be back to your old self today," said Sara.

"Good, I thought I would do this all the time and I can't do that. I have to be alert," said John. "To sleep is lazy and can cost many lives."

"Yes, but if you're sick, sleep is good. The body can heal itself. As a matter of fact, take some vitamin E and B-12. This will help get you going, and you'll see that you're not going to sleep all the time," said Sara, putting pills in front of John.

"What do these do?" asked John, looking down at the pills.

"Men," sighed Sara. "Always think you're out to get them."

Sean snickered.

"You shut up," said Sara. "This one, vitamin E, will make you heal quicker; this one, B-12, will build your blood to help get rid of the infection," said Sara.

"I should take these then?" asked John. "These are good for me?"

"Take the God damn pills before I shove them down your throat," said Sara. "You act like I'm trying to kill you for Christ's sake."

"I'd take them," said Sean around his coffee cup smiling.

John took the pills, and washed them down with coffee.

"Happy?" said John.

"Yes. Men, why is it so hard for you to believe something'is good for you?" said Sara.

"Years of poisoning from irate women," laughed Sean, sitting down his coffee cup.

"You're not helping, Sean. I don't think it's funny. I just took the same pills he did," said Sara.

"This is true John, she took them first. Now remember this always, let the woman take the first bite. If she lives, it's not poison," Sean said laughing.

"I don't think that's funny at all Sean," said Sara.

"I do," John said, laughing.

"You would, you're a male," said Sara. "Male bonding in all." Sara got up, got out clean clothes for John, and set them on the bed. She planned to do laundry today. Those sheets were going on the line come hell or high water. They may freeze, but they would smell fresh. "What I wouldn't give to open a window for a while or to have a vacuum cleaner, the Phanthom," thought Sara. It cleans air and everything and would cut right down on her workload. Vacuum the bed, clean all that dead skin and spores right out of there. "Wish in one hand and shit in the other," thought Sara.

"You know what Susan and I could use is a vacuum cleaner, that Phanthom one that cleans the air and everything," said Sara. "Think the kids could get us one?"

John grabbed a sheet of paper. "Let's see, anything else?" asked John.

"A handheld blender. I could whip my pies up then. I guess that's it," said Sara, "unless they can fit a washer and dryer in there," laughed Sara.

Sean laughed. "Let's put it down with, 'ha ha,' after it. We've never joked back and forth," said Sean. "Better tell Susan you took your pills."

"Okay," said Sara, walking over and writing a few lines. Even a dryer would help, 'ha ha.'

"Well, the other stuff should be here so let's mail our letter," said Sean, "and pick up our mail." Three people went to what Sean would call from now on the 'mailbox.' There was the food, a real fancy platter of cookies, meat and rolls, and a letter for Sean. Sean read the letter after all the goodies were in the kitchen.

"Seems that they have an abundance of food. People are sending all kinds of food because of the situation, two funerals and two hospital patients. They want to know if they send food through if we can get it to the nation," said Sean. "Says your kitchen is so full of food they're stacking it on the floor and don't know what else to do with it. They sent as much as they could to the shelter."

"I don't know, John, think you could get through?" asked Sean. "We could made a sled of sorts," said Sean.

"What about the lights," asked John.

"Jacob and I can put in three lights. We already have it wired, so that's no problem," said Sean.

"Sure, I'll take it to the nation. Tell them it's from Santa Claus," laughed John.

"Okay, back to the mailbox," said Sean, opening the lid. There were wrapped presents.

"Tell them no more presents; we have no more room," said Sara.

Sean scribbled "no more presents, no room," and sent it out. John took a shower. Sean found some wood to make a sled. Jacob came out. Sean explained what was going on, and Jacob got rope and a tarp, then helped Sean put sides on the sled. Sara dressed John's leg; it was fine. She showed him where everything was. John dressed warmly. Sara started pulling trays of food out of the mailbox. She laughed at the thought.

She opened and closed the lid for a half hour until the last time there were the vacuum cleaner and blender. John helped Sara take them out, then closed the lid and then John, Sara, and Jacob started carrying out platters of food. Soon John was on his way with snow shoes and sled. Sara kissed him. Sean and Jacob put the vacuum cleaner together and took one to Susan. She showed her how it worked. Sara had her sheets on the outside line. "It wasn't too cold out, just snowing, so maybe the sheets would dry quickly," thought Sara as she hung up the rest of the laundry. Sean and Jacob had the barn door open, so Sara left her door to the house open. "This place needs fresh air," said Sara as she vacuumed. Everything was cleaned and polished, vacuuming done, and food was set on the shelf in the barn. Sara started the pies. She made cream pies and cheese cake, and apple, pumpkin, and blackberry pies. The aroma filled the house and barn. Soon the Christmas Eve party would begin. Sara looked at the clock: five o'clock. She prayed John was back in time. In the summer it took only a half hour, but Sara didn't know what the world looked like on the other side of the wall. Sara took the sheets off the line. "Nice and fluffy, full of fresh air," thought Sara as she sniffed them. Sara made the bed. It was a fresh smell from being on the line. Sara looked around and was pleased at how clean and fresh it smelled and looked, then heard a commotion outside, so she ran out. John was carrying Ben in. "He's sick, high fever," said John. He laid Ben on the couch.

"Any cuts, sores, anything like that?" asked Sara.

"No, Summer says he's coughing and high fever," said John

"Okay, we'll give him a bath to bring down the fever." Sara ran into the bathroom, ran a tub of warm water, set out towel, wash cloth, soap, and shampoo, then ran back into the living room. "When you take him in the bathroom, I want you to wash him and keep washing him. Wash his hair three times and keep rinsing. Do not put these clothes back on him. I'll give you fresh clothes. You give me his clothes. I'll wash them and disinfect them to kill the germs. After the fever breaks, dry him off. Bring him here, we'll give him pills and he'll start feeling better in no time," said Sara.

John looked at her questioningly, but he did it. She seems to know what she was doing, so John scrubbed his father and kept pouring water over him. John noticed Ben's fever was getting less and less, so he kept washing Ben. Sara had washed Ben's clothes and hung them out to dry, sprayed the couch with Lysol, and the room with Lysol. John came running out. "Ben is coughing up green stuff," said John worried.

"Good, he needed to get it out. When he's done, stand him up, give him a hot shower. Make sure you pull the plug. Let Ben cough all that up. Make sure he's washed and cleaned good, then rinse in a hot shower, dry him off, dress him, and bring him out here. I'll have him feeling better in no time," said Sara.

John ran back in the bathroom and did exactly as Sara said to do. Ben did look better. John carried Ben to the couch. Sara gave him pills and vitamins, cough syrup, and Gatorade. She poured more Gatorade. "You make sure he drinks this. I'll scrub the bathroom so we don't catch his cold. Use these Kleenex to clean the phlem and mucus he'll bring up. His lungs are full of it. Once it comes up, he'll be fine," said Sara.

Ben started coughing. Sara caught the phlem in the Kleenex. "See, this is what has to come out." John got sick and ran outside.

"Oh well," laughed Sara as she threw the Kleenex in a plastic bag. "It's you and me, Ben. Come on, bring it up." Sara patted Ben's back. He coughed and coughed. Sara kept catching phlem and pulling it out until there was nothing but a good, clear cough. Ben's fever was gone. Ben took in a deep breath and opened his eyes.

"Sara!" said Ben, surprised.

"Feel better?" smiled Sara.

"What am I doing here?' Ben asked, looking around.

"You were sick. John brought you, and I made you feel better," smiled Sara.

"My princess," smiled Ben. "How did I get so sick? I had the shots."

"I think that you had a cold. Someone put something on your chest that opened it for infection. You were so full of phlem you couldn't breath, so we had to get it out," smiled Sara. "Never put anything on your chest."

Sara went and got a pillow and quilt for Ben. "Your chest will be sore from coughing, and your back will be sore where we hit on it to bring up the phlem. We're having a Christmas party tonight, so I have to get ready. Sean and John have to take a shower, too. The party will be at seven o'clock, sleep until then," said Sara.

"John brought me here, where is he?" asked Ben.

"Helping Jacob and Sean. So much has changed in the last four days," said Sara. "Now sleep, you can talk later."

"One question," said Ben.

"One," said Sara, looking at Ben

"Are you marrying John?" asked Ben.

"Yes. Now you sleep, we'll talk later," said Sara.

Ben pulled the quilt up to his chin, smiled, and fell asleep. Sara cleaned all around Ben, took the plastic bag of Kleenex, tied it off and threw it in the trash, scrubbed the bathroom with Lysol, took a hot shower, put on clean clothes, put her clothes in a plastic bag, and sprayed with Lysol.

John had stood outside listening to Sara and Ben talk. She never told Ben that John ran away and couldn't care for his father. Now as John looked down at Ben, he looked so good. Awhile ago he looked at death's door, gasping to breath. Now he slept like a baby, his color was back. Sara walked in the room.

"John, take a shower. Wash good, I set clean clothes out for you," smiled Sara.

John looked at Sara. "He's better, he sleeps well," said John.

"Yes, he'll be all right," smiled Sara.

John walked up to Sara and pulled her in the bedroom. "Why didn't you tell Ben I couldn't take care of him?" asked John.

"You think I'm the only one who can do what I did?" said Sara. "I'm one in a million, that's why I was a good nurse, that stuff doesn't bother me. Some of your best doctors can't handle it. It's nothing major. Now take a shower, put your clothes in that plastic bag in the bathroom," smiled Sara.

"Why, I took a shower this morning?" said John.

"Fine, get sick like your father. His germs are crawling all over your clothes and body," said Sara.

"I'll take my shower," said John. He went into the bathroom and took a shower. Sara sent a note to Susan. "We need some presents for Ben. Same size clothes as John." He's here and sick was all Sara said. Now she was setting the island for a party. Sean came in. Sara told him to take a good, hot shower and to put his old clothes in the plastic bag. She had clean clothes on the bed for him. Sara sprayed the trash, tied it off, and set it outside to freeze any germs. John and Sean were done with their showers, so Sara sprayed the bag with Lysol, tied it off, and set it aside to be washed later. Sara scrubbed the bathroom one more time. "That should end that," thought Sara, walking through the bedroom spraying Lysol on everything. She didn't want to take any chances. "Jacob killed himself, so any assistance from him was gone. Now she'd have to do it the only way she knew how, sterilize," thought Sara.

When Sara walked in the living room, Ben was sitting up. Sara got more Gatorade. "I want you to drink this. You may not like it, but it's got electrolytes in it to keep you from dehydrating," said Sara. "When is the last time you ate?" asked Sara.

"Three, four days," said Ben. "I was sick when John left," said Ben.

"Why did you let me go then?" asked John.

"So I could have Sara for a daughter-in-law," said Ben, smiling.

"You put the nation aside and let me go so you could have a daughter-in-law? You risked everything for that?" asked John.

"Yes," smiled Ben.

Sara made chicken broth for Ben and put it in a bowl on a plate with crackers. She set it before Ben. "Eat this, you need something in your stomach before you eat," said Sara.

Ben said, "Thank you," broke the crackers in the broth, and ate, realizing for the first time he was starving. He ate with the appetite of a bear. Ben's stomach growled.

"Excuse me," said Ben. "I didn't realize how hungry I was."

"Well, we have plenty of food," said Sara. "But don't eat too much at once, your stomach hasn't had any food in a while. We don't need you getting stomach cramps," said Sara.

"Agreed," said Ben. "I was really sick wasn't I?" asked Ben.

"Yes, but my teddy bear is back," teased Sara.

"Merry Christmas," called Jacob and Susan, walking in.

"Merry Christmas," called Sara, picking up Ben's dishes. "I hope you're hungry," smiled Sara.

"Sure are," said Susan, setting down her Christmas presents. Jacob held his son and a swing. "Susan, set up the swing and put Jacob in it." He'd been bathed, fed, and ready to sleep. The swing lulled him to sleep.

Everyone started to eat. Sara made Ben up a plate, a little of everything, poured him some Pepsi, and set it on the table for Ben to eat. "Eat slowly, let your stomach get used to having food in it. I've got pies and cookies for dessert," said Sara.

"Thank you princess," smiled Ben. "I'll eat what I can."

"Well, don't worry if you can't eat everything, you eat just what tastes good to you now. You'll eat better tomorrow," said Sara.

"Tomorrow, I'm going home," said Ben.

"That's what you think," said Sara.

"The nation needs food; we must hunt," said Ben

"I sent a lot of food to the nation, so you don't have to do anything. John took it to them in a sled, that's how much food we sent. You're getting strong, then you're going home. Until then everything is taken care of. You ask John how much food was sent. But I do know you're not leaving, so get the idea out of your head," said Sara.

"She's right, Ben. I took enough food for at least four days. Whole hams, turkey platters of meat, rolls, salads, lots of food. I told them it came from Santa Claus. Platters of cookies, breads. Summer would see that it was passed around properly, then soups can be made to last a couple more days. Summer sent you here. I'm to keep you till you can travel. One or two days won't hurt you," said John.

"But the nation is without a chief," said Ben.

"No, the nation has a chief, he's just not there. Summer will send someone if you're needed. So what is not being done?" asked John.

"Sara's got me on this one, hasn't she?" whispered Ben.

"Yup, you would be wise to stay," smiled John. "You can discuss the wedding with her. So you lose no time in the nation's affairs," said John.

"That's a way out of this for me," whispered Ben. "So I can still win."

John laughed. That's all Ben worried about, winning over Sara. Those two would go at it until the wedding.

Sara went into the bedroom and checked the chest. Ben's presents were there. She took them out; there was a letter. Sara read it quickly, called John into the bedroom, and handed him the note. A severe storm would hit December 29. A lot of the nation's people would starve. The kids wanted to send food for them. They asked how much they would need and what they needed. "Well, meat, potatoes, vegetables. I can make a trip tonight, maybe a couple tomorrow, maybe even four, four for a couple of days could get them enough. It says we're snowed in for four months. We have some food, but not enough for four months. With no way out, that's a long time. Will Ben be able to travel by then?" asked John.

"Yes," said Sara. "I'll write a list, and they can send it. We'll get it there." Sara wrote a list. She included oatmeal, flour, beans, noodles, juices, family packs of food from the frozen section. "You send it, we'll get it there. Ben's feeling a lot better. I don't want Ben to know about this. I don't want to say I told you so. Let him think he handled it, not me," said Sara. "I would never want to hurt Ben," Sara put the note in the mailbox. John kissed her.

"Oh," said Sean.

"I thought something was wrong. Getting kissed is not bad. Just getting presents," smiled Sara. She pulled out presents for Susan, Jacob, John, Sean, Ben, and little Jacob, who had his over to his house already. She handed the presents to John and Sean to carry. Sara made coffee, cleaned up the dishes, and set out pies and cookies. Ben hadn't eaten much. He was more interested in the lights that had no flame, the mirror in the corner. Sara asked Ben if he wanted coffee and pie.

"Why did you put a black mirror on the stand? Why don't your lights have a flame?" asked Ben puzzled.

"That's a TV where you can watch movies. This is electricity that you turn on like this," said Sara, hitting a switch.

Ben jumped. "I don't like it," said Ben.

"Well, I'll have Sean explain it to you. You might find you like it," smiled Sara. "Would you like coffee? I have pies and cookies."

"Only coffee," said Ben.

Sara felt Ben's head; warm but not bad. She got him a couple of Tylenol. "Here, take these. Your fever's coming back," said Sara.

"Okay," said Ben, looking at the lamp.

Sara poured Ben coffee. Sean talked to Ben about electricity.

"He's afraid," said Sara, handing him Ben's coffee.

Sara cut pie and passed them around and added Cool-Whip on top. She watched Sean talk to Ben. He seemed to understand better.

"Ben said he'd try a piece of cheesecake," said Sean.

Sara put cherries on top with Cool-Whip and took it to Ben. He ate slowly. Sara passed out presents to everyone. She knew John and Ben both had gotten bathrobes. It seemed like a stupid gift. But if they were sleeping and showering here, they needed bathrobes. Sara gave Sean the same as Jacob. Sara watched everyone open their presents. She was happy.

Susan stood up and passed out her presents. Sara was surprised to get a present. She thanked Susan. The men had all gotten hats, scarves, and gloves handmade by Susan. Sara started crying when she saw a shawl handmade by Susan. It was so beautiful. Sara's hands shook as she ran her hands over the stitching. "Susan, I love it," cried Sara as she lifted the shawl out of the wrapping paper and swung it around her shoulders. "Oh, so perfect," said Sara as she wrapped it tight around herself.

Susan almost cried at watching Sara's tears of joy as she became wrapped in the shawl. Everyone's eyes were on Sara. She never noticed. She twirled in the shawl. She was like a child in a candy store. Sean never saw Sara show such emotion, so he knew she really loved her shawl.

Everyone thanked everyone for their gifts. Ben had on his robe and lay on the couch. Sara and Susan cleaned everything, washed dishes, and put them away. Sara thanked Susan over and over for her shawl. Sara was working on a big surprise for Susan for making her the most beautiful gift she's ever gotten. Sara was sending it home. There was no way she was leaving this behind. Susan and Jacob went home. Little Jacob never woke up once, not even when Sara kissed him goodnight. It was only nine o'clock. Sara put Ben's gifts under the tree. She opened the mailbox. She and John pulled out bags of meats. Sara explained how it could be frozen and kept for months. "It's not what you're used to, but it's good and you can survive, and you get food in your stomachs." John loaded the sled. Sara closed the mailbox lid, waited, then opened it. She unloaded more meats; meats were the most important.

Sean explained electricity to Ben, how the TV and VCR worked and what movies were. Sara and John had the sleigh so full, John feared it wouldn't move in the snow. He had a backpack on that held more meats. John walked away at 10:00 P.M. Sara sat down with Ben and Sean and watched "The Santa Clause" movie. Ben decided that TV and electricity weren't so bad. He laughed and cried, never missing John. John returned around midnight as the movie was ending. Sara made him hot chocolate. John explained how Summer was going to set the food between the nation. He explained how to make a freezer out of snow and how to thaw the meat. Summer would ready the camp. Men would build a wall of snow, just as Jacob and Sean did. Summer understood that Ben would be here two days, then John and Ben would return before the storm.

Everyone went to bed to rise early. Everyone opened their many presents. Sara made breakfast. Sean and John made another sled. Sara kept pulling food out of the mailbox. Sean and John loaded their sleighs, both dressed in their carharts and warm clothing. They went to the nation. They unloaded and returned. Sara cooked lunch. Jacob made another sleigh. He was going the next time. Jacob told Sara John should have him go. He would have gone on this trip. The penicillin was helping Ben. He slept without coughing now. Sara served lunch and started Christmas dinner. The men loaded their sleighs and left after lunch to return for dinner. After dinner they left again, to return at nine, exhausted and cold. The meat, potatoes, and vegetables were all delivered. They made a lot of good time with three men doing this. Tomorrow they would leave early with dried goods. There were lots of dried goods: noodles, beans, macaroni, oatmeal, rice, juices, fresh fruit, and flour. This trip tomorrow was the last. If the storm came early, they were ready. Tomorrow night John would take Ben home in the sleigh with their Christmas presents and Ben's cough syrup and penicillin. Sara wouldn't see them until spring. She accepted this. Sean could do all he wanted to make this like home; the real world lay beyond those barn doors. Out there it was the 1800s, untamed, raw, and real. Sean could look the other way all he wanted. Sara never stopped believing what went on around her.

Sara covered Ben with a quilt. Why did mankind have to hate one another because of race? The nation were the nicest people she had ever met. What would it take to make mankind stop hating? One person alone couldn't do it. Man had to be taught how to stop hating since they were taught to hate in the first place. "The world would be so much better without hate," thought Sara as she dressed for bed. She laughed thinking how hard it would be. Explaining to parents that the racism their parents drilled in their head was wrong, they had to forget everything they learned and teach their children to love mankind. "Talk about an uproar," laughed Sara. "The Civil War would be nothing. Don't piss off the parents," thought Sara as she went to bed. They had enough problems without being told everything they taught was all wrong. Who had time to learn the truth? We were all the same, except the color of one's skin. Sure, each race had their own beliefs, but what people saw first was color. The rest didn't matter; the color said it all. Each race fought to prove it was superior, but all the same life to each race meant the same life. Sara fell asleep.

She woke early, made breakfast, and sent the men on their way.

Ben took a shower. Sara laid out his clothes she'd washed and ironed.

Ben talked about the wedding. Sara made it simple for him outside the nation, us, in June. Ben accepted for Summer to be in the wedding. Sara would make the gowns. The children wanted to send the food. Sara cleaned the house and did the laundry while she talked to Ben. Ben wanted to know where the men were. Sara told him they were making a path to take Ben home. Sara milked the cow and cleaned the barn these past three days. Now she cleaned the wood stoves and spread the ashes where the gardens would be. Feeding the animals was the easy part of all of it. Sara's back was killing her as she sat at the island talking to Ben.

"Why must the men do this now?" asked Ben.

"Because you want to go home, and remember that big storm's coming," smiled Sara.

"The future is very confusing, isn't it?" asked Ben.

"Yes, but you keep it simple, it's less confusing," said Sara.

"What makes life simple in your time?" asked Ben.

"Money," said Sara.

"You and Sean talk as though that's the only thing that matters in life," said Ben.

"It is," sighed Sara. "I look around here and see how Sean has tried to bring the 90s here. It doesn't belong here. It takes away from the beauty of it all," said Sara.

"You don't like electric," asked Ben.

"Oh, electric is good, the conveniences that come with it are good, but in this place and time it just doesn't belong. When all this stuff falls apart, it's trash, then what do you do with it? It will rot somewhere, ruining the environment. This is what I don't like. No one here knows how to fix it if it breaks, so you end up with trash," said Sara.

"Trash concerns you?" asked Ben.

"Yes, trash is what ruins our soil in the future so we can't grow food. It contaminates our water so we can't drink it," said Sara. "The two things you need to survive is being ruined because of our trash," said Sara.

"Yes, I can see why trash could be a problem when it ruins the two main things man needs to survive is threatened," said Ben.

"It's not just mankind that pays; wildlife is paying to the point of extinction," said Sara.

"Wildlife?" said Ben, surprised.

"Yes. In the future those beautiful feathers you use, you can't use them unless the government says so. You can't even pick them up in the woods or off a dead animal because you face fines and jail time. The bald eagle is the national bird and almost went extinct," said Sara.

"This is not good," said Ben.

"No, that's why Sean's been buying more land when he goes to Rome. He feels if he could make a wildlife preserve, it may help a little," said Sara.

"You don't know for sure," said Ben.

"I don't know, man gets hungry, has a family to feed. He'll kill to feed them. Tough times lie ahead. If you have a refuse for animals, all you've done is put them in one area where they would be easier to kill. Most people are greedy. One deer wouldn't be enough. It could lead to the slaughter of thousands of animals, many left to rot," said Sara.

"Yes, I see what you mean, just like the buffalo that were slaughtered and left to die," said Ben. "You are wise, princess."

"Wise, no," said Sara, getting up and pouring more coffee for her and Ben. "I'm wise here because I've seen the end result where I live. In my time, I know nothing. The knowledge that's out there is far more than one human being could ever learn. No, I'm afraid what I know is your basic education. It's just what the government wants you to know."

"Why would the government care what you know?" asked Ben.

"So they can control you," said Sara. "Most of what you learn in grade school is basic and half-truths. When you go to college, you learn that what was taught to you earlier was all wrong, so you have to learn it all over again. Not everyone goes to college; not everyone finishes high school. One in five people can read. Out of the four left, three don't pick up a book and read it, so you're left with 1 percent of the people. Those people are your professional people, the ones who put up a stink if you touch anything of theirs, so the government bows down to them. Why not, they control most of the money in the world. So who pays the other 99 percent? Who thought education wasn't worth the time? The government can control this 99 percent by feeding it tidbits from time to time. When people get too upset about one cause and the government feels it can't win, they throw a cause to them to fight for and they think they're doing something good," said Sara.

"Cause?" asked Ben.

"Well, right now the biggest cause is cigarettes. The people are so riled up about second-hand smoke, the real issues are overlooked," said Sara.

"What are the real issues?" asked Ben.

"Drugs, guns, rape, murder, pollution, ozone layer, terrorism, racism, starvation, wars, improper education, AIDS, just to name a few. This whole thing is blown so far out of proportion it's unreal. Every now and then you'll see a little piece in the paper about it. Not a big piece, but enough to let John Q Public think the government is hard at work, but there will be all kinds of pages on how the battle of cigarette smoking is being fought and won. This gives that 99 percent a sense of do-goodness. They think they're making a change, when all the time the real issues are getting out of control so bad that when mankind finally wakes up, it will be too late," said Sara.

"So the government lets the people control the simple things, so they feel that they are making a difference, when the government really doesn't care one way or the other just so long as they don't have to deal with the issues that are really hurting mankind," said Ben.

"That's it," said Sara. "If that 99 percent knew what was going on, you would have a mess on your hands. They don't, so why bother? That's why I hated leaving my house. I hate what I see. Rome is ruined, it's a ghost town. We had a base. The president took it out because we didn't vote for him, so he used his power to destroy our town. Clinton was pissed off because Rome didn't vote for him. He refused to stop in our town and give a speech, but when the president needed us, we came through. We were the first ones to stand by him. This way is all wrong because we have the right to our opinion. We voted because it was our right to do so. The president has no right to destroy a town because he's pissed off. The first time I voted for him; the second I didn't. I will not be controlled through fear," said Sara.

"You vote?" asked Ben.

"Yes, women gain the right to vote," said Sara. "Why not, at the rate men are going, all that will be left is women," laughed Sara.

"There will always be man but what shape he will be in is the mystery," laughed Ben.

Sara got up and started lunch. "Ben, would you make me a promise?" asked Sara.

"Will it be an easy promise to keep?" asked Ben.

"Probably not. I don't know why I ask, I just don't want this land ruined. Don't let them ruin it. There should be one place on earth that stays the same," said Sara.

"You ask a lot, my princess. If this future is the way you say, it will be very hard to keep progress away," said Ben.

"I know," said Sara. "But you once asked me what I wanted for myself, this is it. I want to be able to walk this ground in my time and have it all still be as pure and virginal as it is now," said Sara.

"You really love it here, don't you?" asked Ben.

"Yes, more than you'll ever know," said Sara. "This place is what God wanted; it shouldn't be changed."

"I can only give you this, I will try," said Ben.

"That's enough for me," smiled Sara. She set food in front of Ben. "You must eat, your appetite has been so little it worries me."

"I'm fine," said Ben. "I worry about the nation."

"Why?" asked Sara.

"I fear I've made a mistake that may cost us lives," said Ben.

"What mistake?" asked Sara.

"The food is not enough for my people," said Ben. "The winter is too long."

Sara put her hand on Ben's. "Don't worry Ben. You being the chief and the wisest, you've already seen to it," said Sara.

"I have?" asked Ben.

"Yes, you sent John, Sean, and Jacob these past three days to the nation with food. You had snow walls built, you had freezers built to store the food," smiled Sara.

"I did. When did I do all this?" asked Ben.

"While you lay on my couch getting better," smiled Sara.

Ben put his other hand over Sara's. "I have a wise daughter-in-law," said Ben. "This is more than money, your love of my son."

"I love John very much. I've never known love like this. Each day it grows but so does my fear," said Sara.

"My child, what fear could you have?" asked Ben.

"That I don't deserve John's love, I'm not good enough for the nation. I fear I could harm them instead of helping them," said Sara sadly.

"My son chose the woman he loves. The nation knows this is good. It is good for everyone, the gods say so, so you take your fears and cast them to the wind, let the wind cleanse you so your spirit is light and free," said Ben, "free to love and be loved. I know John loves you. You're all he talks about," laughed Ben.

Sara blushed, then smiled. She felt a warmth grow inside.

"How did John propose?" asked Ben.

Sara laughed. "Kicked the door down, told me we were getting married, and kissed me," said Sara.

"Sounds like John," laughed Ben.

Sara got up and started supper. She'd sent lunch with the men, but she knew they would be home for supper. "John has stitches in his leg and neck. They need to be cut. They must be cut right or it would be done for nothing," said Sara.

"You explain and I will see that it's done right," said Ben. "What happened?"

"A wolf attacked him. Don't worry, the wolf wasn't loco, only hungry," said Sara. "I gave him medicine to be safe. I'm not going to lose the man I love after I've traveled this far in time to find him," laughed Sara.

Ben laughed. "No, I guess you wouldn't."

As Sara set the table for dinner, sadness filled her heart. After dinner John would be gone for months. What if the old Sara was back, what if she never got to marry John?

"Those fears are showing," said Ben. "Believe me, you will marry John."

Sara turned around, hot tears laid on her eyelids. They slid silently down her cheeks. "I hope so. It seems when I get close to happiness, it gets yanked away, like I have no right to it," said Sara.

"This time the happiness is all yours to keep forever," said Ben.

"I wish I could believe that. You don't know how much I want to believe that," said Sara.

"God is trying to make a correction in your life. Not many people get blessed like you. Stop worrying, he knows what he is doing," said Ben.

Sara wiped at the tears. "I would love to believe that," smiled Sara. "But right now this is all a dream. I'm in a coma there when I come to I'm faced with more problems than you'll ever know. I probably have to sell everything I own just to pay my hospital bill. I'll end up in a dinky apartment somewhere for the elderly. Real great life I have," said Sara.

"Don't worry about the future. You'll miss out on enjoying the present," said Ben.

"You're right," said Sara.

Sean and John walked in cold and hungry. "Smells good," said John.

"Cooked all day for you," teased Sara.

"Well I better eat a lot if you worked that hard," teased John.

"Yeah, like men need an excuse to eat," laughed Sara.

Supper was eaten with idle chit chat, never mentioning John and Ben's departure. Sara cleared away the dishes, set them in to soak, and packed Ben and John some food in case they had to stop. It was snowing. Sara looked at the snow falling and packed more food. "Rather be safe than sorry," she thought. John was taking Ben back by sleigh. "He is still weak," Sara thought carefully as she packed for them. On the sleigh she put a tarp, then under John's bedding she put a pillow down for Ben and a quilt to cover him. Two packed bags, it was enough. She went back inside and gave John Ben's medicine. "You're set to go," smiled Sara.

"I need one thing," said John.

"What, I'll get it," said Sara.

"No, I'll get it," said John, grabbing Sara and kissing her.

Sara was left speechless.

"That has to last me for a while," smiled John.

"Even a lifetime," smiled Sara. "I love you."

"I love you," said John.

Sara smiled, walked to the sink, and started washing dishes. John and Ben left. The snow was falling heavy, but there was wind which made traveling slow, but steady. John knew he'd have to stop. Ben was getting cold, but he'd like to get as close as he could to the nation. Less travel in the morning, but John stopped. He couldn't take a chance with Ben's life. He'd find a place to settle down for the night. They set up camp, which to John's surprise Sara had everything pretty well covered. All he had to do was supply a fire. John and Ben talked for a while as they ate some of the food Sara packed. There was enough for two more meals. "She sure packed enough. The best is the tarp that made a home to keep us out of the cold. Food, clothing, and a roof," thought John as he fell asleep.

Ben slept soundly on the sleigh. Sara's afghan folded in half, half under him and half over his back to the fire. John slept flat on his back on his bed roll.

Sean slept deeply; Sara tossed and turned. She worried for Ben and John. Did she pack everything, food, dry clothing, tent, blankets, shovel, medicine, plenty of liquid, ax, matches? Over and over, she thought, was it enough?

Come morning Sara had a headache and backache. Sean got breakfast and told Sara she looked like shit. Sara said she felt like shit. Sean gave her some Tylenol PM and sent her back to bed. She slept three days, her body raged with fever. Sean couldn't bring the fever down. Sean worried Sara was going to die. The third day, the fever left as fast as it came. It left Sara weakened. She was in bed for a month, refusing to get up. Susan, Jacob, and Sean worried about Sara. Susan said Sara was dying of a broken heart, but Jacob and Sean disagreed. "It was some kind of virus," said Sean. One day Sara got upset at being treated in a third party sense, so she got up. She walked around in a daze. She did what she had to. The last time she went near the mailbox was the day John left, but she noticed new things around. She didn't say a word, let them have their fun. She didn't blame her either. It was all new to her. Maybe Sean could learn something about the future from it. It wasn't good for Susan to sit in front of the TV all day. She changed into a 90s woman, and Sara changed into a 1800s woman. Sure Sara still dressed in blue jeans and shirts with sneakers, but her heart and soul was with the 1800s. Sara felt like she belonged nowhere. Now it just depressed her because it had gotten so out of hand.

Sara looked around, it was clean. She made a sandwich, grabbed a Pepsi out of the refrigerator, went through her books the kids sent her for Christmas. She found one that looked half-way decent, went in the bedroom, sat on the bed, and read.

Chapter 13

"ARE YOU CRAZY?" ASKED BEN, HELPING A FROZEN SEAN INTO HIS HOME.

"John found Sean, brought him here. I didn't know what else to do," said John.

"It's Sara," said Sean.

"Sit," said Ben. "What's wrong with Sara?"

"After you left, she got really sick. For three days she had a high fever, but we pulled her through, then she was in bed for a month. Now she mopes around," said Sean. "I say it's a virus; Susan says it's a broken heart over John. Jacob agrees with me. I've done everything humanly possible, but I will go get John."

"I see," said Ben. "You're all wrong."

"What!" asked Sean.

"You really don't see it, do you?" asked Ben.

"See what?" asked Sean.

"You've ruined Sara's life," said Ben.

"I ruined Sara's life. How did I ruin her life" I've given her everything," said Sean.

"There's your answer," said Ben.

"My brain must be frozen because I don't know what you're talking about," said Sean.

"I bet since we left, you had a lot more toys sent," said Ben.

"Toys, meaning the electric things to make our life easier?" said Sean.

"Yes, they bother Sara," said Ben. "Did you see how happy Sara was over the shawl Susan gave her, but Christmas morning she wasn't so happy," said Ben.

"Yes, so what?" said Sean.

"Sara lives her life simply: food, clothing, roof over her head. You took a very large step when you put electricity in. Did Sara ask you to put it in?" asked Ben.

"No, John thought of it. He sent it forward. I surprised Sara with the toys. She helped wire four plugs and lights," said Sean.

"When Sara wired, did she know she was wiring for all the toys, as you call them?" asked Ben.

"No, she thought it was for lights," said Sean.

"I see, did she ask for these toys?" asked Ben.

"No, well one thing, a vacuum cleaner. The rest of the stuff was a surprise. It was to help her so she didn't have to work so hard," said Sean.

"Do you remember how happy she was when she first saw her new home?" asked Ben.

"Just about as happy as that shawl Susan made," smiled Sean.

"And you keep changing things, and every time you change things, Sara gets farther away. Sara doesn't like the 90s, so why are you trying to make this the 90s? Sara feels trapped. You order food when you want, Sara doesn't cook anymore, she cleans but feels useless. You've taken everything away from her, so she feels so low and useless, why get out of bed if you have nothing to do?" said Ben.

"I'm making her world here miserable," Sean said sadly.

"Have Susan and Jacob been around since you gave them their electric toys? I know you're always playing with them. You think this stuff is great, Sara sees it as trash. She told me that. I didn't understand what she meant right away. When we left to come home we had to stop. Sara packed us the basics, food, clothing, and shelter. She keeps telling us that's all that matters, and she's right. Everything else gets in the way. We lose touch with one another. That's what Sara's talking about. The price you pay for your toys is what they cost you in the end," said Ben.

"What's that supposed to mean?" asked Sean.

"Look what you lose by playing with your toys: money, time, freedom, friendships, families. You think about it," said Ben.

"Damn! Now what do I do?" asked Sean.

"I think you know what to do," said Ben. "It wouldn't hurt if you paid more attention to what Sara does. It seems to me that you take her for granted. She milks the cow, feeds the animals, does the housework and laundry. She does this every day you aren't around. I've noticed you just assume she'll do it without being told she did a good job or 'thank you.' You walk in, eat, then watch TV. Sara is a gentle human being, it's easy to take advantage of her. All she thinks about is pleasing; she does it without thinking," said Ben.

"Does what?" asked Sean.

"She gets coffee, she pours you one, she gets something to eat, she gets you something to eat. It's natural for her to put everyone before herself, so you end up taking advantage of her. She's too nice; nice people get overlooked," said Ben.

Sean ran his hands through his hair. "God, I thought I was doing so good," said Sean.

"You were," said Ben. "Sara told me to watch and see all the changes that would take place once the electricity was going. She said to watch closely and never forget that money made it all possible. She was right. No good came of it."

"I guess you're right," said Sean. "How could I be so wrong?"

"Because you really don't know Sara as well as you think you do," said Ben. "I don't think anyone does."

"Why?" asked Sean.

"Sara's smart, very smart. She doesn't see things the way everyone else does. Sara sees the beauty that's around her. To her life is simple, so everyone thinks she's simple and easy to ignore, but this is what makes her the wisest of all," said Ben.

"The wisest?" questioned Sean.

"Sara always knows what's around her because she takes the time to stop and look, but when she looks, she learns, too. That's what makes her wise," said Ben.

"Sara's always needed to learn. She's the one who came up with the way to heat the hot water," said Sean. "Oh," Sean paused, acting like it just sunk into his brain. Now he knew what Ben had been trying to say. "I took Sara's ability to learn away. I made everything modern so there was nothing to learn. God, I shut her down when I did that. I didn't give her a reason to get up. I took everything she loved from her," said Sean.

"She's been like this since we left. That's almost two moons," said Ben.

"Two months sounds around right. She looks awful. She's lost a lot of weight. She has no strength. Sara doesn't sleep well. I don't know when she took a bath last. I know she worries about you and John, not knowing if you made it back or not," said Sean.

"John, take Paint and take Sean home, spend a couple days there, Sara needs you," said Ben.

"Paint?" asked Sean.

"My best horse. He will get you through. Give Sara my gift, she will like it," smiled Ben.

"Yes," said John and left only to return ten minutes later. "Ready Sean?" asked John.

"Let's go!" said Sean. "Thank you, Ben."

'Thank you for trusting me enough to come to me," smiled Ben.

"Any time, my friend," said Sean.

Sean and John arrived at the house just as Sara stepped out of the shower. She'd changed the sheets on the bed, the first time in two months, but she had no choice. She'd spilled coffee everywhere. Sara had to turn the mattress. She wiped up as much as she could. Sara felt a little better and was just going to bed when she thought she heard John's voice. "I have to be mistaken," thought Sara as she started pulling the covers back.

"May I come in and see my princess?" smiled John.

Sara looked up to see John standing in the doorway. She didn't bother to go around the bed. She ran over the top of it. "John! My God, John, what are you doing here?" asked Sara, throwing her arms around him.

"I guess I was missed," teased John. "I have two reasons for being here. First, I missed you. Second, Ben made you a gift for helping us. He says he never wants to hear you complain again," laughed John.

"I don't complain," said Sara, snuggling closer to John, breathing in the deep smells of him.

"There is one thing you complain about," said John.

"Oh, what's that?" said Sara, stepping back and looking up at John.

"Close your eyes," smiled John. "Ben would insist."

"Okay," smiled Sara, closing her eyes.

John help up his hand. "Okay, open your eyes."

"Oh, oh, moccasin boots. Oh John, they're beautiful. I don't know what I did to deserve them. They're so soft, so warm," said Sara.

"This is so when you walk, you can feel the ground under your feet," said John.

Sara hugged John. She didn't want to talk. She just wanted to hold him and smell him.

John felt Sara's thinness through her nightgown. She was very thin. He felt all the bones in her body. "I've come to spend a few days, if you don't mind," said John, smiling.

"Mind, no that would be great. How about some coffee?" asked Sara.

"Well, it looks like you were getting ready for bed. If you're tired, we can talk in the morning," said John.

"No, I could use some coffee. How are you and Ben faring going back after Christmas?" asked Sara, walking toward the kitchen.

John's stomach churned as Sara walked past him. It was a slow, fragile walk. There were deep, dark circles beneath her eyes. The thinness of her shrunken face made her eyes deeper and bigger. Sara had lost more than a little weight. John was sick to think Sean waited so long to come for help. The white man could be stupid sometimes, this was one of them. John now blamed himself for not coming sooner. John sat at the island and told Sara all about their trip home and how Ben couldn't stop talking about how she thought of everything. "I must admit I was baffled at first when I saw a small shovel and ax. I couldn't understand what you wanted me to do with them. Then Ben got up, I saw the tarp." John laughed like he laughed when he'd seen the tarp.

"What?" asked Sara. "What's so funny?"

"Do you know how long it's been since our people made teepees? I almost forgot, my generation never used them. You should have seen Ben. He was right in his glory, telling me the old ways. He hadn't been able to tell that in years, but with Christmas presents, the food packed, and our teepee, we couldn't have been in better shape. Ben was so happy to be able to live the old way," laughed John.

"Did you have enough food and drinks?" asked Sara, pouring coffee for them.

John laughed. "We were there two days, not because we had to. I think Ben was faking it, saying he was too weak to move, but we still had food left when we got home. And I think we both gained weight. I think that's why Ben made you the boots. You gave him some good memories of old times. He tells it over and over at the fires."

Sara smiled. "Ah, the good life. I can almost see Ben pretending to be weak. That one is sly as a fox at times," laughed Sara. "Anything to get his way."

"You know Father so well," laughed John.

"Want something to eat?" asked Sara

"Sure, if you eat with me. I don't like eating alone," said John.

"Actually I'm getting hungry," said Sara as she got up to cook.

Sean had put Paint in the barn, fed him, and bedded him down, then went to Jacob and Susan's. Sean told them what Ben told him, and that John came back with him. Susan was happy John was here, but as she made coffee she thought what Sean had said. She'd turned into a greedy fool just like Sara described the people of the 90s. Susan felt awful. How easily she was led astray. Sara gave everything she had and Susan kept taking until there was nothing left of Sara to give. It ate away at her like a cancer, almost killing her. Now Susan understood greed. It was an infectious desire, silently spreading, killing everything in its way until whoever had the most in the end wins. Hot tears flowed down Susan's cheeks. "God it's awful. It kills everything good and decent, even people. Oh Sara, can you ever forgive me?" thought Susan.

"God, this is good," said John.

"I know, I can't stop eating," said Sara. "It's only ham and eggs, but I must have been starved," laughed Sara, eating more.

"Sara, tonight I want to sleep with you. I've taken a vow not to touch you until we wed. But I need to lie with you, hold you. I won't ask anything more of you. I know it is wrong of me to ask, but if I could hold you while I sleep, I can stop my heart from racing. It has not stopped racing since I left here. June seems so far away," said John.

Sara blushed. "I would love nothing more than to sleep with you, but I don't know if I can control myself." Sara's blush deepened. "I must confess all I think about and more is being your wife, in every sense of the word," said Sara.

"My feeling for you deepens, knowing you feel as I do. I'm a man of strength. I can control a situation," said John.

Sara thought carefully as she looked at John. Ever since she met this man, the only thing of her mind was going to bed with him. Now they were engaged to be married. All her fantasies were soon to be realized. Now he wanted to sleep with her and expected her not to react to his body lying next to hers. Sara was a woman of moral standings but temptation of this magnitude was beyond anyone's reasoning. "John, I don't think you understand the feelings I have for you. I honestly don't know if I can keep my hands off your body," said Sara, blushing.

"I will be strong for both of us then. I can see that if we don't move the wedding up, we may not be able to control what races through our blood," said John.

"We can't do that, Ben said June," said Sara.

"Ben hasn't set a time. Ben is thinking on it. When he chose the time, we wed," said John. "I promise not to touch you. I'm a man of honor."

"Okay, I will sleep with you under one condition," said Sara.

"That is?" asked John.

"You keep John Henry corralled up tight," said Sara.

"John Henry?" asked John puzzled.

"That certain part of your body that doesn't see much daylight," said Sara.

"Oh!" said John, laughing. "Manhood."

"Yes, manhood," said Sara, blushing.

"It's a deal," said John. "Shall we go to bed then?"

"Yes, I could use some sleep and cuddling, more cuddling than anything," laughed Sara, standing up.

"You're easy," laughed John.

"That's what you think. This will be the toughest thing I've ever done in my life," laughed Sara. "Keeping my hands off you is like locking a child in a candy store and saying don't touch. But you know what? I respect you enough to trust you. That beats love any time," said Sara, walking in the bedroom.

John followed. He knew Sara wouldn't push him. Tonight they sleep; tomorrow was another day. Sara climbed in her side of the bed, John got in the other side and rolled on his side. Sara turned out the light and snuggled in John's arms and fell asleep.

Sean came home, saw the closed door, John's rolled sleeping bag in the chair. Don't blow it, John, we're too lose. Sean threw the sleeping bag on the floor. Might as well sleep, won't know till morning if John blew it. Sean was surprised at how comfortable the bed roll was. "Smells good, too," thought Sean as he fell asleep.

Sean woke in the morning to the smell of coffee and bacon. He heard eggs frying and Sara humming. Sean sat up. John walked in the room wet from a shower, smoking a cigarette. Sean took in a deep breath, let it out slowly. "He blew it," thought Sean.

"Morning Sean, great morning," smiled John as he walked pass Sean toward Sara. He took her in his arms and kissed her. Sara cuddled next to John.

Sean buried his head in his hands. They blew it. Nobody acted like that without taking the final step. It was all his fault. He blew it with Sara, he tried to fix it. He brought John here, and now it was all for nothing, thought Sean.

"Coffee, Sean?" asked John, handing Sean a cup. "Get that look off your face, nothing happened. I'm not stupid."

Sean breathed for the first time since he woke up ad heard Sara singing. "What did you do to make her so happy?" asked Sean.

"Held her, talked to her, and ate with her," said John.

"Breakfast!" called Sara.

Sean handed John his cup and got up, looked at Sara, and felt sick. God, she was thin. The T-shirt that was tight now hung. The jeans that were painted on now were baggy. "God, Sara, how much weight did you lose?" asked Sean, walking in the kitchen.

"I don't know. I didn't know I'd lost weight until I got dressed. I may have lost twenty pounds, I really don't know," said Sara.

Sean and John sat at the island to eat breakfast. Sara set a plate in front of Sean, his stomach churned. "Sara's hands and arms are so thin, God she looks like the Grim Reaper," thought Sean. "Thank you," mumbled Sean. God he did this to her. "God forgive me," prayed Sean.

"Sara, I've got Paint with me, he's good in snow. How about we go for a ride?" You could pack a lunch, and we could ride around and see all the snow," said John.

"God, that would be great. The sun is out, looks like it will be a great day. Only one thing, I have some laundry to do," said Sara.

"Dress warm," said Sean.

Sara looked surprised. "Yes, Daddy," giggled Sara.

"It's not funny. You have been sick, you could catch pneumonia. If John wasn't taking you, I wouldn't let you go," said Sean.

"I thank you for trusting me," said John. "But I think that if Sara was still sick, she would be smart enough to say no."

"Whoa, right there. I can see where this is headed," said Sara. "Man against man. I won't have that. Sean, you're my best friend in the whole world. I love John. I'm going to marry John. I'm free in both of my lives. In one life I'm young; in my other life I'm old and wise. In both lives I've learned a lot. John is whom I chose to live my life with for how ever long I have here. When I return to my other life, I will cherish my memories here with John. This will last me the rest of my life in my other life. You have been a friend in both times, so I'm telling you this because you are my friend, don't fuck with my life. It's mine to live the way I choose. I choose to be happy for once in my life. This is the only time I will ever get to be happy and I'm taking it, so back off," said Sara.

John snickered. Sean stared wide-eyed and shocked.

"I would wipe that smile off your face, John, because now it's your turn. Sean is my friend even though he is a pain in the ass and should be respected for being my friend. When I leave here, I will go back with this man and have to put up with his bullshit the rest of my life, so when you feel it necessary to belittle the man, just remember I'm going to be the one who has to put up with all this bullshit after you two part company. So you take that male shit and throw it out the window. Sean, I didn't have sex with John. John, I've never had sex with Sean. So as to who has the biggest prick, I wouldn't know, but I will tell you this, I think you're both pricks and would like to thank you both for ruining my day. You two used the wrong head to think with today," said Sara, walking away slamming the bedroom door behind her.

Sean and John watched Sara leave the kitchen and slam the door. They then looked down at their John Henrys, then looked up at each other and laughed.

"Sara's back," said Sean. "Good job, ol' boy," laughed Sean, slapping John on the shoulder.

"Thank you, my friend, glad to be of service," smiled John.

"Ain't nobody can tell a man off like Sara," said Sean, lifting his coffee cup and taking a drink.

"Guess not," said John. "Couldn't get a word in there if we wanted. Did you notice how her voice kept getting higher and higher the madder she got?" laughed John, taking a drink of coffee.

Sean got up and cleared the dishes. "It feels so good to have Sara back. Now I've got work to do, so you get stuck washing dishes since I cleared them. It would be a great service to me if you could talk Sara into going for a ride," said Sean.

"Do you think if I wash the dishes Sara will change her mind and ride with me?" said John.

"Oh, after she calms down she'll ride with you, but if you do the dishes that will be less Sara will have to do, so you both can leave while you still can enjoy the day," said Sean.

"Now I see your point. She'll stall all she can while she stews over her blowout with us," laughed John.

"That's it," smiled Sean. "Sara's right, you learn quickly."

"Is this bundled up warm enough for the two of you or should I put on more?" said Sara.

John and Sean turned around. Sara had on so many clothes. She had put Sean's sweats on over the clothes she had on. She looked like an over-stuffed bear. She had all she could do to walk.

"I don't know, John, maybe a couple of more layers so if she falls off, the horse she can bounce right back on again," laughed Sean.

"You're mean, Sean, really mean. You're just like Tom. First you treat me like a child, then criticize when I do exactly what you told me to do. Do you think I'll ever be old enough for you to think I might now what I'm doing?" yelled Sara. She turned around, waddled back in the bedroom, and slammed the door.

"I think it's safe to say she's still pissed off at us," said Sean, turning around and looking at John.

John had this puzzled look on his face.

Sean stopped laughing. "It's a joke," said Sean.

"Joke, then why was Sara crying? Don't jokes make you laugh?" asked John.

"Crying?" Sean never looked at Sara's face, all he'd seen was all the clothes.

"Oh shit!" yelled Sean. Sara was serious. He walked over to the bedroom door, knocked on it. "Sara, I'm sorry, I thought you were horsing around like you always do. I didn't think you were serious. Damn it, Sara, I wouldn't hurt you. If anyone got hurt, it's me. You said I was just like Tom, that hurts, I hate him. I don't want to be put in the same category as Tom. He's an asshole. A dead asshole, but still an asshole."

"What's the matter, Sean, don't you like being criticized and compared to other people?" asked Sara as she took her clothes off.

"No I don't, it feels degrading," said Sean.

"Well, ain't that too fucking bad," said Sara. "Poor Sean felt degraded for a few seconds. Now you know how I feel all the time. What is it, okay for men to degrade women and we have to take it, but let a woman degrade a man once, he gets pissed off? So you assholes retaliate by degrading women more. It's not one-sided Sean. Why are men such assholes?" asked Sara.

Sean sat on the floor with his back to the door. John went into the kitchen to do dishes. This was between Sara and Sean, so he stepped away.

"Assholes, I guess we're assholes because it's the only thing we do best. Sure we have jobs, families, friends, but being assholes, that takes years of grooming. It's passed down from generation to generation, father to son, each generation adding to it until we become professional assholes. If it wasn't for women, we wouldn't be assholes," said Sean.

"Women have nothing to do with men being assholes," said Sara.

"I beg to differ with you. Women are always on such an emotional roller-coaster, we can't keep up. We're never sure if what we do will lead to getting our ass chewed out or kissed to death. We just don't understand women, and they don't understand us. We try. I mean you see some flowers, you think 'Gee, my wife would love them,' so you buy them, have them sent so it's a surprise. You get home, she's crying and you get accused of doing something wrong, so you buy them candy to make up for being a thoughtless asshole. They throw the candy at you, saying you think I'm fat. You don't give them presents, then you're a thoughtless asshole. If they are pregnant, forget it altogether. You come home from work. you throw your hat in the door, if it comes back out all chewed up, you better get back in the car and go out and eat supper. You keep this up until it's safe. Do you know how many hats I went through when Laura was pregnant with Sean Jr. Hell, Sara, they couldn't make them fast enough."

Sara giggled.

"Then they want to kill us in the delivery room. Hell it's not our fault, it's Eve's. She's the one who had women cursed. Why did God put that fucking tree there anyway?" asked Sean.

"You know what teething is?" asked Sara, opening the door.

"Ten percent," said Sean, looking up at Sara from the floor where he fell. "Ten percent of your earnings to be exact," said Sean, rubbing his head.

"God doesn't want your money. What's he going to do with it? The church wants your money. When God made Eden for Adam and Eve, there was no money. God told Adam and Eve they could eat of everything in the garden, but the one tree.

"That was God's tree," laughed Sean

"Yes, why can't God have a tree?" asked Sara.

"He can have anything he wants, he's God. But why this one tree?" asked Sean.

"You really don't get it, do you? Has the church got you that screwed up in the head you don't know? Don't you ever read your Bible?" asked Sara.

"Why should I read the Bible? I hear it every Sunday in church," said Sean.

"No, you hear what they want you to hear. And it's very obvious they are not telling you everything, or you would know why that tree was there," said Sara.

"And you know why?" snickered Sean.

"Yes, when God created man and woman he gave them a place to live. It had everything they needed to live a perfect life: perfect weather, perfect food, the perfect couple. God told them they could have whatever they wanted out of the garden, but not to eat of one tree. God wasn't being mean, God was testing their loyalty. God simply said it was his tree. Now God came and walked in the garden with Adam and Eve," said Sara.

"Yeah so," said Sean.

"That tree was God's 10 percent," said Sara. "He gave them everything. He only asked for his 10 percent. What's God guilty of asking for his 10 percent, mankind had 90 percent. Who's the greedy party here? So God liked the fruit of this one tree. He walked and talked with Adam and Eve, heaven forgive him for asking for 10 percent. God never asked for money; not once did God take money. The money was for the clergy. God asked for 10 percent of a flock. Ten percent of the food grown, this went to clergy to feed them for doing his work. Not once did God say I want your money. Jesus even said it when he asked the man in church who he thought would go to heaven. The lady who put a penny in the offering dish or the man who put in a lot of money? The man replied, 'the man.' Jesus said, 'no, he could afford to give the money, to him money meant nothing, but the woman put the only money she had in the offering. Her offering meant more to God. It was made in love,'" said Sara. "People can't see greed."

"So how do you figure greed started all this?" asked Sean.

"Because Lucifer knew that man had greed, and he tempted them with their one flaw. Greed played on it and won," said Sara.

"But why didn't God tell Adam and Eve it was his 10 percent?" asked Sean.

"Lucifer got there first. He knew he had to, so he chose the woman, not because he thought she was easier to work with but because he knew that God talked to Adam. Eve was newly born, she was in awe of everything she saw. She didn't know that animals didn't talk, so she believed what the serpent said, then tells Adam, who, in turn, took a bite. Their eyes weren't opened that day like the serpent promised. Instead, that bite of fruit was evil and now their pure souls were tainted with evil. And that evil is what God saw. He knew it for what it was. He cast it out of heaven and now it was with them. God cast them from the garden, but not before cursing woman and the serpent," said Sara. "It's my firm belief if Eve had been around as long as Adam, she would have known better. But we are reminded once a month about sin. We have to work harder and longer than men to prove ourselves worthy. As long as there's men and women, we will be looked upon as stupid and less superior than man because of Eve's mistake. We didn't do it, yet we pay the price for it twenty-four hours a day, 365 days a year. And the same shit goes on today that went on back then. Women are left in the dark, told shit, and when we do something stupid, we're yelled at and punished, but we didn't know because we weren't told. But if it pleases man to yell at us, then he does so. Then we get so fucked up, our emotions take over. We end up so fucking confused we don't know why, and you men just think about yourselves. 'Oh, poor me,' you cry. You try putting up with the bullshit we put up with."

"Wow, that's pretty heavy shit," said Sean. "You got this out of the Bible?"

"Yes and drew my own opinion on it. A lot of people will disagree, but that's their right. But greed and ignorance is what started it all. God gave us a chance to redeem ourselves through Jesus Christ. But we have to go to him, he won't come to us. I can't say as I blame him too much," said Sara. "He gave us a perfect world to live in; we fucked it up. Then he gave us his only begotten son, and we crucified him. Real great children we turned out to be. Very ungrateful if you ask me. But no matter what, he still loves us. Pretty unselfish on his part, but he gave us the right to choose him; he's there for us. We go to him in prayer. If we decide not to choose him, he's there in case you change your mind. You think about it and it will blow your mind away. He's a father, he watches you born, he watches you grow, he lets you make your choices in life whether they're good or bad. When things are tough, you know he's there. Then in death he shows you a light to guide you in a time of your worst fear. Yet people run around saying God doesn't love them. But he can't love us unless we let him. We haven't given him a reason to, either," said Sara sadly.

"Yeah, but he still does because he is our father," said Sean. "You sure the hell explained a lot more to me just now then all those men and women talks we've had. Somehow it all makes sense to me," said Sean.

John sat at the island listening. Somehow it made sense to him, and he had many gods, not just one like the white man.

"How do you know if you make the right choices?" asked Sean.

"Okay, you have two roads, one is well traveled, worn smooth. You can see forever on it. You have a second road less traveled, it's bumpy, covered with brush, but it's a straight road not curvy and winding like the first road. Which road do you choose?" asked Sara.

"The clear road," laughed Sean.

"See, that's the problem," said Sara. "Man didn't learn his mistakes, so he keeps traveling down the same road, never learning. The less traveled road is going to get you there in less time, but everyone never learned that if they took the other road they would clear the way and have a better life. In the end, it's easier."

"But the other road is already cleared," said Sean. "Everyone uses it."

"Just because everyone else does, it doesn't make it right," said Sara. "It's like the blind leading the blind. Sooner or later they will fall. But when one falls, they all fall. So the one who made the mistake made them all pay. They didn't ask for it, but they followed, so they fell. That's how it goes. Everyone thinks they have all the answers and anyone who follows will fall. When they fall, they blame the leader, but they chose to follow, so they only have themselves to blame. They were given the right to choose."

"Phew, you're blowing my fucking mind with all this," said Sean.

"It's simple. You choose the way you want to live. You can make it easy or hard," said Sara, "good or bad."

"That doesn't make any sense at all. That's really stupid," said Sean.

"Is it?" asked Sara.

"Yes," said Sean. "What makes life easy or hard, good or bad is money."

"Because you let it control you. You complicate it. You're not happy with food, clothing, shelter. No, you want the best of everything and all the toys that goes with it, so you work your ass off to get all the nice things you want. Then you don't have time for the toys. And when you finally find time, you're too fucking old to play with them. You spent your whole life enjoying nothing. You worked for nothing. Sounds like you took the well-traveled road to me," said Sara. "You played follow the leader and fell. I've got a mess to clean. You think about it." Sara went in the bedroom and cleaned and did the laundry.

John helped Sean. Sean was left speechless. How many times had he heard Sara say this and today it sunk in his thick head.

Today it sounded like riddles, but it all made sense. Sean was deep in thought.

"She's right, you know," said John, handing Sean a 2-by-4.

"Huh?" said Sean.

"Sara, she's right," said John.

"I know," said Sean. "When I go back there's going to be some changes in my life, serious changes. I think I'd better stop and smell the roses before I can't."

"What's that mean?" asked John.

"It means when I get back, I'm going to live," smiled Sean.

"Oh," said John, handing Sean another 2-by-4. "What are we doing?" asked John.

"It's a surprise for Sara," said Sean.

"I don't know, Sara doesn't seem to like your surprises. You get us both in trouble when you plan surprises," said John.

"This one is a good one," smiled Sean.

"Just do me a favor, don't tell Sara I had anything to do with it," said John. "Don't tell me what it is because I don't want to know. I'm not getting yelled at."

Sara walked by and hung up laundry. The day was really beautiful. The sun was shining. It smelled fresh and clean. It was warm. "A good day to ride," thought Sara. Sara went back inside; she left the door open for fresh air. Sara took out the vacuum cleaner and vacuumed really well. Nothing had been vacuumed in two months. "Men don't vacuum," thought Sara as she chased dust bunnies. "More like monster dust bunnies," thought Sara as she saw the size of them. Sara vacuumed, washed floors, walls, ceilings, windows, and furniture. It was two hours' hard work, but it was clean the way Sara liked. Sara left the sheets on the line while John took Sara for a ride on Paint. The snow was deep in some spots; others not. But it was beautiful. Sara wore her boots that Ben made. "This is perfect, John," said Sara.

"I thought you would like it. I love days such as these. The sun stays out longer, rises earlier, a sign that spring is near. I love spring," said John.

"I love fall," said Sara. "I love when everything is in full color, all the colors, color everywhere."

"Fall suits you," said John.

Sara snuggled in the warmth of John's arms leaning on his chest. "Why, because of the color of my hair?" asked Sara.

"No, because of your personality," said John. "Your enthusiasm, it's warm, rich, and always bursting out in full color. You're full of surprises like fall; you're special like each fall is special."

"Special?" asked Sara.

"Well, I didn't think you wanted to hear different," said John.

"Well, actually, I like different. I don't like special. In my time special is like a double-edged sword. They use special to classify people with handicaps. And when they put something on sale, they call it special. So special don't mean a whole lot in our time. As a matter of fact, words don't mean a hell of a lot in our time. They have changed the meaning so many times, nobody knows what anybody says anymore," said Sara.

"Okay. Princess, you're different," smiled John.

"Where are we going?" asked Sara, snuggling closer to John.

"A place I know, thought we'd eat lunch there and go home." smiled John.

"John, I'm cold. I put extra clothes on, but I'm still cold." said Sara.

John wrapped his coat around Sara. "She was so thin, that's why she was cold," thought John. "Feeling better?" asked John.

"Lots," giggled Sara. "How come you wore Sean's cowboy hat?" asked Sara.

"Keep the sun out of my eyes," said John.

"In my time they have sunglasses to keep the sun out," said Sara.

"That sounds like something good," said John.

"It is," said Sara. "They have all kinds. You're so nice and warm. Oh, I can see you in a pair of fitted jeans a white T-shirt with that long, black hair, black cowboy boots, a leather coat. That is what they call the hot look in my time. I wish I could take you back with me," said Sara.

"Why, first I love you and don't want to leave you; second, you would be the hottest thing in town and you would be all mine. I'd walk all over town showing you off. I'd smile sweetly and introduce my husband, but what I would be thinking is 'eat your fucking heart out,'" laughed Sara.

"I don't know if you love me or the way I look," teased John.

"Believe me, looks aren't everything. In my time it means a lot, but I know the real you and that's who I love. I've tried to hide my feelings for you and I couldn't. Believe me when I tell you this, I'm good at hiding my true feelings," said Sara.

"But you fight with Sean. Why don't you hide your feelings from him?" asked John.

"I've been fighting with Sean since I was ten years old. Most of the time, we get along. Sometimes he pisses me off and then we fight. One time I gave him a black eye. He was surprised I hit him," laughed Sara.

"What did Sean do?" asked John.

"That little creep told my mother. My mother spanked me and made me apologize to him," said Sara.

"Why did you hit Sean in the first place?" asked John.

"He called me a girl and told me girls were not allowed in his fort, so I punched him, gave him a black eye, and asked him if any girl he knew could do that," laughed Sara.

John laughed. "Now I know why Sean was surprised you didn't give him a fighting chance."

"Maybe not, but I got to go into his fort. I didn't like it, so I didn't stay," said Sara.

"After all that, all so you could see inside," laughed John.

"I didn't say it was smart. I just wanted to prove I could go in there," laughed Sara.

"Whoa boy," called John.

"What's this place?" asked Sara, looking at a small cabin.

"I found it as a small boy. Nobody ever comes here, so I've been fixing it up a little at a time. I guess you could call it my fort. You want to see it?" asked John.

"Sure," smiled Sara. "Is it warm in there?"

"Will be in no time," said John. "It has a nice fireplace. Come on, boy." Paint went forward.

John started the fire; he was right, it warmed up quickly. The cabin had a table, a bed, and a fireplace. Sara looked around. You could see where John repaired the cabin. He did a good job. The cabin was spotless, not that there was much to clean.

"We have to use chucks of wood for stools. I haven't made chairs yet," said John.

"That's okay. I love this. Did you make the bed and table?" asked Sara, sitting down at the table.

"Yes, it's made out of black cherry," said John, putting lunch on the table.

Sara looked out the window next to the table. It was the only window in this one-room cabin. Paint was tethered to a tree with a bag of oats to eat. Sara smiled. "Why does Ben call his horse Paint? He's black," Sara giggled. "All black."

"My father has a sense of humor. He says the white man thinks all our horses are multicolored, so if he named the horse Paint, the white man, seeing he's old, would think it was a painted horse," laughed John.

"Ben is funny, he makes me laugh. I hope it's not an insult to your people because I love your people very much. I know I tease Ben a lot, but he teases me, so I'm gong to give it right back to him. Ben is very smart, a good leader," said Sara.

"My father lives to tease you or argue with you. When you go back to your time, my father will miss you the most out of all of us. He just loves everything about you. I think he loves you so much because you're different than anyone he' ever met," said John.

"No, Ben loves me because I'm stubborn," laughed Sara.

"That, too," said John, passing a plate of food to Sara. "But he loves you for a lot of reasons. 'You're smart, loving, kind, caring, and a good cook," said John. "You're a lot of things, Ben sees this and respects you for it."

"Well, Ben sees more in me than I do," said Sara, taking a bite of food.

"We never see ourselves for what we are, we only see our faults," said John.

"That's a smart thing to say," said Sara. "Look at you, you're perfect in every way, and you expect me to believe you think you have faults."

"You see me as perfect; I see me as a very large man. I'm taller than most of my people. My arms and legs are larger than anyone. My nose is too small. I feel different than my people," said John.

Sara wiped at her mouth with a napkin. "In my time people spend a lot of money at gyms to look the way you do, and I mean a lot of money. It's called being physically fit. We don't have a lot of people who look like you. Those who do are looked at with awe. You would be thought of by many of my people as the perfect human being. There's even women who work very hard to look like you do. You even have nice buns," said Sara.

"Buns?" asked John puzzled.

"Ass," said Sara. "They say the bigger the buns, the bigger the pump power."

"Pump power?" asked John.

Sara stood up, held out her hands, made a movement with her hips and said, "Pump baby pump," and turned bright red.

John started laughing. He understood what Sara meant now, but that's not why he was laughing. Sara's napkin was in her belt and when she moved took on a rather bad movement of its own.

Sara looked where John was looking and turned so red it looked purple. "Oh my God," cried Sara, sitting down, hiding her face in her hands.

John laughed. "Pump power is good for just about anything," laughed John. "You must have good buns, too."

Sara knew right then and there she'd never live it down, no matter how many generations she lived. John's laugher didn't help, so his laughter filled the small cabin. Sara was never so embarrassed in her whole life. She swore to God she heard Paint laugh, too.

"Maybe your pump power is better than mine," said John as he broke into a new round of laughter.

"Nope, I'm not going to live this one down," thought Sara

John got up, walked over to Sara, pulled her up from the table, and kissed her. "I can guarantee you on our wedding night I'll have a lot of pump power, good enough for the whole night," said John. "My John Henry is looking forward to our wedding night. He's waited a long time for our wedding night," said John.

Sara ran her hands across John's shoulders down his arms and back up. The smell of him, the feel of him brought an ache deep within her, a feeling she knew only John could stop. "John, we can't stay here any longer," said Sara, laying her head against his chest.

"Don't you like my fort?" asked John. "I thought we would spend our honeymoon here."

"The cabin is fine. I love it. It's you, my body wants you. God how I want you. I want you to pick me up, carry me to the bed, and make love to me." Sara ran her fragile hands across John's chest. She could feel his power through his shirt. She slowly raised her head to stare in John's eyes.

John saw a look he'd never seen before in Sara's eyes, pure raw lust. He grabbed her arms, pulled her close and kissed her, a deep, probing kiss that set Sara's body aflame with desire. She couldn't get close enough to him. Her breathing was labored as her head fell backwards. John trailed kisses down her neck. Sara's body melted at John's hot kisses, lost in passion as Sara screamed. "Yes! Now my love, take me."

John stopped, looked in Sara's green eyes, aflame with desire. "My God what am I doing?" thought John. "Sara, we have to go, we can't stay, you're right. A few more seconds it would be ruined. Sara we can't do this, believe me, right now I'm doing everything I can to keep this from happening. We can't do this, not here, not now," said John.

"Why not, we'll be married in a couple of months. Being a virgin on my wedding night is no big deal," said Sara.

"To our nation it is," said John. "Especially for a future chief. I'll get Paint ready."

John stepped outside and took a deep breath of cold air. He let it out slowly. His body shook, not from the cold, but from desire. "My God, I almost screwed up. If this was the sample of my wedding night, I'm in for one hell of a night," thought John.

Sara was mad, not at John, but at herself. Never in her life had she acted like that. "Hell," thought Sara. "I've never felt like that in my life." Sara threw the plates on the table in the pillowcase. She felt waves of desire run through her body. "Holy shit, what's my wedding night going to be like? I'll probably screw the poor guy to death," laughed Sara as a vision of John lying on the bed and her on top trying for one more time. "I'm sick," said Sara to the pillowcase she held up. "Do you realize by my antics I almost made it so John and I couldn't marry? The love of my life, and I almost blew it." Sara checked the fireplace. The one log that John put on was almost burned out, so she poked and spread out the ashes so they would be fine when they left.

John came in. "Paint's ready," said John as he threw snow on the fire. It sizzled and went out. John watched, thinking, "I know how you feel."

"I…I…I'm sorry John. I didn't mean to tempt you like that. I don't know what comes over me. When I'm with you I can't control my feeling," said Sara.

"It wasn't just you," said John, picking up the pillowcase. "I was there, too. And I feel the same way you do. I've never desired a woman, never, yet you are all I think of. I know now I can't control my desire for you. Together we're dangerous. I almost ruined everything, so from now on, we can't be alone. I don't want to ruin our chances of being together," said John.

"I agree," said Sara. "We'll never be alone again, not until our wedding night."

"Then we can pick up where we left off," said John.

"That will be my pleasure," smiled Sara. "Let's get out of here right now."

"My buns turning you on?" laughed John.

Sara stepped outside. "It's more than your buns," said Sara.

John and Sara left in a hurry. Paint was up to a good ride. There wasn't much snow. Sara needed the cold wind to douse the hot flame that burned deep within her. Paint slowed as the snow got deeper.

"John, who owns the cabin?" asked Sara.

"You do now, it's on the land you bought," said John. "Why?"

"Well, I thought I'd make a few things to decorate it for our wedding night," said Sara.

"That would be nice. I know it's not a big place, but what we need it for there's lots of room," laughed John.

Sara blushed as she snuggled into John.

"Cold?" asked John.

"Yes," said Sara.

John wrapped his coat around Sara. She snuggled in next to him. "Nice and warm. How come your coat's so big?" asked Sara.

"It's the only one I could find for my height and size, so I had to settle for a lot of extra room," laughed John.

"I can fix it for you, so you don't have all this extra room," said Sara.

"Then where would you fit?" asked John, smiling.

"I thought we weren't supposed to be this close?" asked Sara.

"Not now," said John. "But in the near future I kind of like the idea of the two of us snuggled together in this," laughed John. "But if you don't want to, we could fix it."

"What if I'm pregnant? Then three of us can't fit in here. Then you've still got a big coat," said Sara.

"You counting on me getting you pregnant?" asked John.

"Oh, yes, several times," said Sara.

"So you want lots of children?" laughed John.

"Yes. But not right away. I want to play with you for a while, a lot!" giggled Sara.

"Mmm, sounds good to me," laughed John. "But if we play a lot your chances of getting pregnant are higher," said John.

"Well, then we better play a lot in your fort right away," giggled Sara.

"I think that can be arranged," laughed John as he pulled Paint to a halt in front of Sara's house. Sean was outside.

John got down, helped Sara down. "What's wrong?" asked John.

"We have no water. For some reason we have no pump power." said Sean, looking at the well.

"Must not have good buns," laughed John.

"Huh!" said Sean, looking up. "Oh yeah," laughed Sean. "Good one."

Sara turned bright red and ran inside.

"What's wrong with Sara?" asked Sean.

"I almost blew it. We can't be left alone," said John. "Not for one second."

"Who stopped, you or her?" asked Sean.

"Me," said John. "She wasn't going to stop. I can't believe how close we came. If she hadn't screamed yes, take me now, it would have been too late," said John, shaking his head. "Too close."

"Well, you stopped," said Sean.

"Yeah, but you weren't there, you didn't see the look I saw in Sara's eyes. It was pure, raw lust, and I got lost in it. That look is a look a man waits his whole life for. I had to walk away," said John.

"You didn't have to," said Sean. "You chose to. What did you tell Sara?"

"Lots of things. That the future chief must marry a virgin, that Ben may set the wedding date sooner, he hasn't said yet, that we can't be alone until we're married," said John.

"She took all this with no problem?" asked Sean.

"No, she agreed, but not before apologizing to me for tempting me," said John.

"Sara tempted you. I can't buy that. Sara's not like that," said Sean, looking at the pump.

"You don't know Sara very well," said John, kicking the well.

"What the hell you do that for?" asked Sean.

John kicked again. "Probably frozen. Try it now," said John.

"Yeah right," laughed Sean as he turned the faucet on. Water sputtered and started running out. "I never would have thought it was frozen. We buried it deep."

"You got water in the house, right?" asked John.

"Yeah," said Sean.

"Then follow your own rules; check the simple things first. You haven't used it since it snowed. It's cold out, it's frozen," said John.

"I've been here for an hour thinking it was a problem in the well," laughed Sean.

"Sean, where is everything?" asked Sara, running out to the yard. "All our stuff is gone. I went to make coffee, no coffee pot, went to get milk, no refrigerator. What's going on?" asked Sara.

"There's no TV or VCR, either. We only have electric lights," said Sean, turning and walking past Sara. "Follow me." Sara followed. "The coffee pot and electric appliances are under the cupboard next to the stove. On the end of the sink this cupboard opens, it hides the refrigerator, so everything looks just the way it did when we moved in. There's a cabinet wall in the barn, everything is stored there, so if you want it, you have it. No more 90s showing here, except one thing. There's a scale in the bathroom. You're to weigh yourself and start putting weight on. There are health drinks in the refrigerator. You're to drink them in between meals. The kids sent this stuff. You've lost twenty-six pounds in your other life. Doctors are worried. There's a letter on the table from the kids. I think it's time you answered them. There's some packages on the bed from Susan and Laura. I was told not to look, so I'm assuming it's the material for the wedding dress," said Sean.

Sara looked at the letter. "I've lost twenty-six pounds. This isn't good," said Sara. "I only weigh one hundred and ten pounds to begin with. That means I weight what, eighty-four pounds. God, that's awful."

"Yes. If you don't take care of yourself here, you will die there. Now I know that a lot of this has been my fault. I fucked everything up by trying to bring the 90s here. I'm trying my best. Now you have to try your best. I promise not to do anything without your permission. No more surprises. I've got a lot to do. I almost ruined everything. I sat in front of the TV and became what I hated the most: a couch potato. Now I've really got to make up for lost time. Please forgive me," said Sean.

"You're forgiven. I know you thought it's what I wanted, and you thought you were doing what was best, but I like it the way it is now. So I will eat, gain weight, and get ready for my wedding," smiled Sara.

"That's all I ask," said Sean.

"Buns," said John. "Sara needs buns."

Sara turned red and looked down at the floor, her hair falling around her face to cover her blush.

"Buns?" asked Sean.

Yes, those ones with the chocolate on top and cream in the center. The buns she likes so much," said John.

Sean laughed. "Doughnuts, yes, we have doughnuts the kids sent. That will help you gain weight, bread."

Sara turned redder and redder. Everything Sean said played into John's hands.

"Yes, being bread it can get one fat in a hurry," laughed John. "It has to be a special bread, very potent, lots of, how you say it, nuts and cream," said John.

Sean was on to it now. Sara wasn't looking at either man for love or money, so she walked over to the cupboard and took out the coffee pot and made coffee.

"Loaded with lots of butter, made with the thickest cream. Oh, cream in coffee helps the bread," said Sean. "Something about making it rise."

"Pea-nut butter is good, too," said John, smirking.

"You need the buns to get things pumping, though," snickered Sean.

John lost it, as a vision of Sara in the cabin came to mind. He leaned on the island as sounds of laughter came out.

"That's it!" said Sara, turning around. "John, you told him, didn't you?"

John shook his head no but couldn't stop laughing.

"Tell me what?" asked Sean. Sean looked at John then Sara. "Ahhh, that has to be good. Tell me," said Sean.

"You didn't tell him?" asked Sara.

John shook his head no, trying to stop laughing but couldn't.

Sean looked at John. "This must really be good," said Sean. "That man doesn't laugh like this for nothing. What did you do, Sara?" said Sean.

"Fuck you!" said Sara.

"Oooh, this is real good," teased Sean. "It deserves a 'fuck you.' What could you have done to bring a man the size of John to his knees with laughter. He can't tell me, but you can," said Sean

"I ain't telling you nothing," said Sara.

"Oh you will," said Sean. "Or you can't come to my fort and play."

John couldn't handle this. He sat on a stool and held his sides bent over laughing, gasping for air to breath.

"Mmmm, you and John played in the fort didn't you?" smiled Sean.

"No," said Sara. "Nothing happened."

"John Henry wouldn't come out to play, tied up too tight to get away," said Sean.

John was going to die laughing, this he could guarantee. Now he gasped for air, slamming his hand on the island top. "Tucked in was more like it," thought John.

"No," said Sara. "John Henry has nothing to do with this."

"Okay, let's go back over the conversation." Sean went over it in his head. "This guy didn't start laughing until I said you need the buns to get things pumping," said Sean.

"I explained to John what women say about the bigger the buns, the bigger the pump power. He keeps laughing over it. I don't know why he thinks it's so funny. When we came to the house, you said you have no pump power. He said you needed bigger buns. I don't know why this man finds this so funny," said Sara.

"Yes, he did say that, so you really didn't do anything?" asked Sean.

"No," said Sara. "Look, even John's shaking his head no."

Sean looked at John.

"Damn, I thought it was going to be something good," said Sean.

Sara poured coffee, took out doughnuts, put them on a plate and set them on the island, and put coffee out for Sean and John, thankful Sean found out nothing. Sara pulled a stool around to her side and sat down and opened her letter. She read it.

"Mother: I read your diary. The snow is all done, no more snow. You and John will soon wed in June. Ben wants you wed in May. You will wed among apple blossoms and flowers. There will be no time for you to make wedding gowns, so we took the liberty of buying gowns. I only hope they meet with your expectations. The gown you wanted was gone. I hope you like this one as much as you did the other ones. Some of the nation's men came, they paid for Dad's and Jacob's funeral. The dresses are made to the measurements Susan sent. The shoes go to the diagrams that Susan sent. The nation paid for this. They said the gown had to be very special for the princess. I think this thing costs a lot of money. I've never seen anything like it. I told Laura I think your tiara is real diamonds. We would like to get your permission to send a camcorder with tapes for Sean to take pictures of the wedding. We would love to see you in this gown. The bridal flowers are in the large, long box. This wedding must mean a lot to the nation; no money was spared here. You will see. They pop in here and say send this to your mother. And if you saw the size of these guys, you would know why I say, 'Yes sir." John won't even say no. They're given us protection. They arrive every day in a huge limo and take us to the hospital. You've been taken out of ICU and put in a private room, the best there is. Two Indians stand outside your door at all times. They're bigger yet. I've got a real strong feeling nobody messes with them either. They don't talk much. They just tell us what we have to do. This wedding is very important. I don't know why, but it's a major event in their lives. Love, Susan."

Sara looked at John. "He's going to be mine. But what's so important about me that the nation needs to protect me in both lives? What have I got to give them?" thought Sara. She slid the letter to John for him to read and took a doughnut. "Better start gaining weight," said Sara. "I've got a wedding to attend." John read the letter and slid it to Sean to read.

Sean read the letter and looked at Sara and John.

"We don't have a hell of a lot of time to get ready for this wedding. Men must be taught to build homes, plant these fields. If the sun stays warm like this, we may be able to plant in March. If the ground is not too wet. It's obvious, Ben has chosen the when and where. Now I must work three times harder. I lost two months lying around. If the wedding is the first part of May instead of the end of June, that's two full months lost there," said Sean.

"What do you have to do?" asked Sara.

"Make blueprints for four special homes and about ten regular homes. That includes plumbing and electric so they can be updated as time goes by," said Sean. "Make cement blocks, cut logs, and wood. There's no way we can be done in time," said Sean.

"Yes there is," said Sara. "I didn't think I'd ever say this. Have John send chainsaws, cement, gas, oil, whatever you need. Set up a small sawmill. You have generators. Get everything you need. Get it cut and ready to go before the snow melts. Nobody will be here right away to see you working. Set up where you want to build and work from there. I can draw the blueprints for the ten houses; You do four. I don't want to get involved in special, that means details. We could get plastic and insulation from the kids, nontoxic paint, too," said Sara.

"Yes, we can do this. We'll be so busy we won't be able to think, but we can do this," said Sean. "If we get the men of the nation, we could really get this thing going, be done for the wedding. Oh, go check your dress, see if it's suitable for you, then write the kids, we're going to be busy," said Sean.

"The nation will help," said John.

Sara went to check on the gowns. Her hands shook as she lifted her wedding gown. "Holy shit," cried Sara. "Pearls, rhinestones, lace, bead work out of this world." Sara put it on. "Holy shit," cried Sara. "Sean, can you come here a minute?" called Sara. "Not John, just you."

"Must be she wants to show me the dress. You can't see it until the wedding, pal," said Sean, getting up and walking into the bedroom.

"Holy shit," cried Sean. "Don't move, stay there." Sean ran out of the house over to Susan's, came back with Susan, and they ran into the bedroom. Susan froze.

"Ugh, oh my God, Sara it's the most beautiful thing I've ever seen. What are these?" asked Susan, pointing.

"Sequins, pearls, rhinestones," said Sara. "But look at the veil." Sara set it on her head. It sure to hell looked like real diamonds to Sean.

"Sara, you look beautiful," said Susan.

"Look, the shoes have rhinestones on them," said Sara. "Yours is on the bed. I don't even know the colors of yours and Summer's dresses. I was surprised to see this."

"Sara you're beautiful. God you look like a princess. No take that back, you're a queen. You've moved to the head of the class on this one. I better go so you two can go through this stuff and try it on. We'd better get moving now, time will fly," laughed Sean as he closed the door.

"Something wrong?" asked John.

"Susan, oh Susan, it's beautiful, look at this, I've never seen a pink like this. The color suits you, try it on. You can use the bathroom," said Sara, taking her veil off and setting it in its box, smoothing it out. She took her dress off, hung it on the padded hanger, put it in the plastic bag and zipped it shut, then got dressed. She carefully wiped the shoes off and was putting them in their box when Susan came out of the bathroom. She was crying.

"Susan, what's wrong?" asked Sara.

"I can't believe how beautiful this is. I've never felt this beautiful. The material is so beautiful," sobbed Susan.

"Well, this is supposed to be the most beautiful day of my life," said Sara. "So why shouldn't my girls feel like I do? That dress color we call mauve. I was hoping for teal green, but this has all been prearranged. Does your dress feel comfortable?"

"Yes, there's so much room for my baby," laughed Susan. "How did they do that?"

"It's callcd an cmpirc waist linc. It comcs undcr thc bust and flows out. It hides babies and wide hips," smiled Sara. "There's a lot of wide hippy ladies in my time, and a lot of pregnant brides."

"Women are pregnant when they get married?" asked Susan.

"Yes, and a lot of women are pregnant without any husbands. Most of them are young kids, thirteen years old to seventeen years old. It's sad, but the government is trying to stop it by giving sex education classes," said Sara.

"Sex education classes. They teach sex in school?" asked Susan.

"Yes, parents aren't telling their children about sex, so they turn to their peers, who know less than we do. So everyone ends up having unsafe sex, getting pregnant and sexually transmitted diseases. Some even kill, so the government stepped in and is trying to educate the kids when they're still teenagers so they can learn there is a better way, so they're allowed to be children and have fun instead of babies," said Sara.

"My mother didn't tell my anything. My wedding was a total surprise. I had no idea what to expect or what to do. Jacob was a doll. He explained everything to me and how it worked," said Susan.

"My mother didn't tell me anything either. If she had, I would have known that the abuse I took during sex was really rape. Seems that was the only thing that turned him on," said Sara.

"How awful," said Susan. "I don't think John will be a bad lover. I think you hit the jackpot when you got John."

"I know," said Sara.

Susan panicked. "You and John didn't do it, did you?" asked Susan.

"No, but we came close. We've agreed not to be alone again until our wedding night," said Sara.

"Who stopped?" asked Susan.

"John. I'm afraid I'm the one who started it. I feel awful, but for some reason I can't keep my hands off him. I'm not like this in my other life. I'm quiet and withdrawn. I would never do what I did today," said Sara.

Susan laughed. "Sara, you're in love, really in love. Don't you know what that does to your emotions?" asked Susan.

"I don't know what it does. All I do know is I can't think right. In my other life I always said if anything happened to my husband, I'd never marry again. One man in my life was enough for me. Now my husband in my other life was a very good-looking man. He tried to have me killed. I live; he dies. I'm free, so what do I do? I run into a good-looking man, fall in love, and try to rape him. Real strong I am, standing by my words," said Sara.

"Sara, you and John belong together and you didn't run into his arms. You fought longer than anyone I ever saw. I don't think if I was single and in love like you and John are, I could deny my feelings like you, especially knowing everything you do. Sorry, but John would have been stripped and bedded five minutes after I met him," said Susan.

"Susan," laughed Sara. "Now we're respectable women."

"Yeah, we know a good thing when we see it. We don't waste any time claiming what's ours. Respectable, but not stupid," said Susan, going in the bathroom to change.

Sara looked at the box with flowers. She opened it. She didn't want to venture too far into this type of conversation with Susan. Everyone seemed to think Sara had all the answers. Well, she didn't, and she was still a human being with emotions running wild right now. What difference did it make of what she knew in her other life? She was still prone to making mistakes.

"Are these our flowers?" asked Susan.

"Yes, they're what we call silk flowers," said Sara.

"They're beautiful, which is which?"

"The real big one is mine, the next one is yours, then Summer's," said Sara. Sara looked at Susan. "I don't know what the men are wearing, there's only two boutonnieres. John must have something to wear. In my time men wear a tux, here I don't know."

"What's a tux?" asked Susan.

"A fancy suit, a real fancy suit," said Sara. "Makes any man look good." Sara didn't dare think of John in a tux. "Susan, where I'm going you'll have to take all this stuff and keep it hidden from the real Sean and Sara. That's why I get upset when the kids send stuff through. I don't want too much stuff around that you and Jacob have to move. I don't know how or when we're going back and then everything is dumped in your laps. You're stuck cleaning up after us. Then you're got to come up with some story to tell Sean and Sara, why they can't remember anything. I'm dumping so much on you," said Sara.

"Don't worry. Sean and Jacob have it all worked out. Everything is taken care of. We worked everything out while you were sick. It's all written down and everything organized," said Susan. "I'm changing my clothes."

"That's me," said Sara, closing the flower box. "I always think I'm the only one who can handle things. There are capable people out there."

"You know, I wish I had a whole closet of fancy dresses like this," said Susan, walking in the bedroom.

"Be careful what you wish for, you're liable to get it," laughed Sara.

"Well, that wish wasn't a bad one," said Susan.

"No, but I always wish for a million bucks. I think that's a better wish," laughed Sara. "Ever since my father told me that, I've always wished for a million bucks."

"Why?" asked Susan.

"I just guess with a million dollars it would take care of anything I ever wanted, so why wish small?" laughed Sara. "But Dad told me a lot of things. Wish in one hand and shit in the other, see what gets full first. Mmmm, the grass grows greener over the septic tank, but if you remember what's in the septic tank, then you concord life. It's all just a bunch of shit," laughed Sara. "So with a million dollars I could get someone to take care of that shit."

Susan laughed. "I like that, you thought this through a lot."

"Ever since I was a little girl and realized you can't do anything without money, no matter what you did or where you went, the only thing that meant anything was money. It talked louder than any words I've heard," said Sara.

"I always thought you were against money?" asked Susan.

"I am," said Sara, "but I'm no fool, either. Money solves a lot of problems but it also creates as many as it solves. Money changes people. People always say I'd stay the same ol' me if I had money. It's bullshit, all of it. They buy and own things they would never have without it. They change, they don't think they do, but they do," said Sara, putting the flowers in the closet.

"Okay, let's say you had a million dollars. What would you do first?" asked Susan.

"That's easy, buy a lot of land, build a log cabin, and live in it. No outside world around me. Just me and nature. That's all I've ever wanted out of life," said Sara.

"You really mean that, don't you?" asked Susan.

"Yes, I want to take a small part of this world and save it. Leave it the way God wanted," said Sara. "I know it sounds stupid, but that's how I feel."

"What I don't understand is you're always giving. You believe in God, you're very understanding of everyone around you, but you don't seem happy. I don't mean it in an awful way, it's just all around you. You make everyone happy. You make things nice for everyone else, but you as a person, you're—I don't know how to define it. You laugh, joke, and tease, but there's something that's there you can't see. You feel a sadness about you," said Susan. "You kind of go along. I don't know how to put it."

"Sad, lonely, entrusting," said Sara.

"No, lack of enthusiasm. Most women would go crazy marrying John. The beautiful dress, flowers, you don't respond to it like anyone else would," said Susan.

Sara sat on the bed. "Well to me this is a dream. The perfect man, the perfect wedding, the perfect friends, everything I do is perfect. I can't believe John and I will actually marry. I'm waiting for someone to come along with a huge needle and stick it in my dream world, then I'm thrown back into the real world, a world I hate. I'm on edge all the time waiting for the bubble to burst. Then it's all gone. The hurt I feel every day wondering if I'll ever see John again. It's awful. I finally found a man to love, the man of my dreams, and it has to be a man who doesn't exist, a man made up in my dreams, a man I will never have. This is why I'm like I am. My whole life has been look, but don't touch, you're not good enough to touch. That's why I can't believe any of this," said Sara.

"Sara, this is real. You are marrying John," said Susan.

"Watch, something will happen and it will all be taken away from me. It always does. I've worked hard my whole life. When I thought I'd finally got somewhere, it was all taken away and I start over and over, going nowhere. I was never meant to be happy. I was chosen to work my ass off for life with no reward at all," said Sara.

"Well, you keep feeling the way you do and you won't enjoy your honeymoon or wedding," said Susan.

"Listen, if today was a sample of my honeymoon, I'll enjoy it," laughed Sara. "Then I'll know happiness, but getting to the honeymoon is going to be a long, long road for me. If I keep busy and not think about it, I might make it. If I think about it, it will drive me crazy."

"Okay, I'll handle the wedding stuff, you forget about it. Keep busy. We'll get you to the church on time," laughed Susan.

"That's a deal," said Sara. "Just don't go crazy on me. I'll let you read Susan's letter and you'll understand. Want coffee?" asked Sara. "Oh, you can take your dress and stuff home. There's a plastic bag to hang it up."

"Yes to coffee," said Susan. "I'll put my stuff in the living room until I leave. What about Summer's?"

"I'll send it back with John. I don't know if he'll stay much longer. We can't be alone," said Sara. "He has to talk to Ben. These next couple of months are going to be crazy. We're building your home and barn and my home. We'd like to get some started for the Indians, but God, a couple months isn't much time."

"Why not? The men of the wagon train built this barn in two days," said Susan.

"Yeah, that was a barn. A house is a lot different. More detailed. Sean says he can do it, and I believe he can. He's a good carpenter at home, so I'll go along with what he says. He's making a list for the kids so everything is going to go crazy for a while," said Sara.

"Sean says it can be done, I believe him," said Susan.

"What choice do we have?" laughed Sara, getting up and starting for the kitchen, then stopping. "Oh, John found a cabin in the woods where we'll spend our honeymoon. I want to fix it up, scrub it good, air it out. It has a bed and table, nothing else. I thought if I decorated it, it might make it feel more like this is going to happen. Know what I mean?" asked Sara.

"Sure," said Susan. "You need to make it feel special so you can believe this is really going to happen and it's real.'

"Yup," said Sara, walking to the kitchen and pouring coffee for her and Susan.

"What's it like?" asked Susan.

"It's not as big as this place. When you walk in, there's a huge fireplace to the right, a bed to the left, a table with one window by the table. Everything is wood except the fireplace, which is stone," said Sara.

"Sounds small and cozy. When you want to do to it?" asked Susan.

"Well, John's going to make two chairs for the table," said Sara. John looked up from the table at mention of his name. Sean and John moved to the table so Sean could make up his list. John watched him, and Sean explained what it was about. "So I thought I would get a stand for each side of the bed. We'll need lamps. I don't know if I want kerosene lamps or candle lamps. Maybe candle on each side of the bed and a kerosene lamp on the table. We'll need some kind of light," said Sara.

"Why?" asked Susan.

John smiled. He knew he didn't need light.

"What do you mean why? I need light to get us food to eat. I've already lost too much weight. Now I have to eat several times a day to gain it back. I don't want to get sick on my honeymoon, too. These last couple of months have been a big toil on my body. I don't think John wants to put up with what I put you guys through," said Sara.

"Okay, one candle and we set food outside your door so you don't have to cook. How's that?" asked Susan.

John smiled and turned back to watch Sean.

"I'm going overboard again. See, I try to think that I have to do everything. I don't know why I do that. I lose track of what I'm supposed to be doing, ravishing my husband's body," said Sara.

John and Sean laughed. "We can hear you, Sara," said Sean.

Sara turned bright red.

Susan giggled.

"Sorry," said Sara.

"No need to apologize," said Sean. "I just thought I'd tell you we can hear you before you got too graphic," smiled Sean, looking at Sara. "Although I don't think John minds listening. You don't need a light. We'll supply food, room service if you would like and coffee. John needs to know that he can't talk to you until you've had two cups of coffee. She'll chew your head off."

Sara threw a towel at Sean. He moved to the right a little and it hit the wall.

"She throws things, too, so the less you have around, the more you're likely to survive," teased Sean.

"A woman with spirit, I like that," teased John.

Susan giggled.

"Men!" cried Sara.

"Better get used to us. There's going to be a lot of us around for a while," laughed Sean.

"Oh God, help me," teased Sara.

"Well, I better get home before Jacob starts pulling his hair out," laughed Susan. "Every time Jacob moves, Jacob follows him with his eyes and if Jacob gets out of his sight, Jacob cries."

"Somebody loves their daddy," laughed Sara.

"Too much," laughed Susan. "I feel left out. I'll see you tomorrow."

"Thanks Susan. Kiss little Jacob for me," said Sara.

"Sure, he'll love that," said Susan as she left, dress box under arm.

Sara poured another cup of coffee, sat at the island, opened a drawer, and took out graph paper, pencil, and ruler. She started drawing outhouses. Sara loved doing this. She could see each room finished and decorated in her mind. She always got lost in her own world; nothing else mattered. She fell in love with designing when Sean came to her with some blueprints he'd had drawn up for his home. Something just like this or this or this should be here. She was never sure what it was, but Sean was impressed and said, "yes you're right." The rest was history. She helped Sean with blueprints. He called her a natural. Sara found she loved it.

Sean poured two cups of coffee. Sean started toward the table when he saw what Sara was doing. He stopped to look at the papers she'd stacked in front of her. She never knew Sara was there or took the stack of papers. Never heard him talk. "John, look at these, Sara shocks me every time she does this," said Sean.

"What's that?" asked John.

"She gets out graph paper, draws out floor plans, then makes blueprints. These are fabulous. Sara, I love these," said Sean. "She doesn't hear me, she gets into this designing thing so much, nothing else matters. It's like she's in a trance."

"She really can't hear can she?" laughed John.

"Nope, she'll draw up a pile of plans, tell me to pick the ones I like, then she does full blucprints for me. In one week she'll have it done. I've never seen anyone who can do blueprints like Sara can. She really gets into it," laughed Sean.

"What do you do with the blueprints you don't use?" asked John.

"I've got them in my office for future use. I get some people looking for something different. I pull out Sara's plans. I have as yet to run into anyone who wanted to change anything on her designs. She could make a lot of money doing this and she won't," said Sean.

"Why not, if she's good at it?" asked John.

"That's why. She's too good and it's too easy for her, so she doesn't like it," said Sean. "She can't believe she has a rare gift. To her it's boring, so her talent gets wasted."

"Oh, I've seen people who have talent. So I know what you're talking about. There's no challenge there for them, so they let their talent go," said John. "We have a man who's a beautiful artist. To him, sitting down and drawing is nothing. He sees things that no one else sees. When he draws, his work looks so real, yet he chooses not to draw," said John.

"Maybe he'll paint me a picture," said Sara, drinking coffee.

"You heard us talking?" questioned John.

"Yes, I choose not to get into a conversation with Sean as to why I don't get into this. I have two good reasons not to get into this, and one very good reason why I'm so good at it," said Sara.

"This ought to be good," said Sean. "Let's hear it."

"One, I'm a woman, and a woman in a man's field doesn't stand a chance, I don't care what time period it is. If anyone knew a woman did this, they would tear it apart and find fault with it just because I am a woman.

"Two, I don't have a shingle. I could go to college four years to get one, but I'm afraid that college offers no good classes on architecture because they don't know what they are talking about. They don't know the first thing about houses."

"Okay, that's two good reasons, but why are you so good at it?" asked Sean.

"Because I'm a housewife," said Sara.

"What's that got to do with anything?" asked Sean.

"It's got everything to do with it. I'm home cooking, cleaning, doing laundry, trying to find a place to put this or that, so I know where the problems are in a home. I don't try to design a house for beauty. I design a house to live in; a house that's easy to clean, low maintenance, and has storage, a place to put things. I don't decorate the house when I design it. I decorate the house after it's done the way it's supposed to be. Less is more. A woman should be able to decorate a house, then achieve a whole new look simply by changing curtains and rugs. This way you get a whole new look at minimal expense. That's why less is more," said Sara. "I'd much rather live in a good, sound home that I decorate with furniture than some fancy home. That ain't worth shit, but it looks good," said Sara.

"So you're saying it's cheaper in the long run to put money into a home built solid than a house designed for beauty? I don't understand your thinking here," said Sean. "They're both wood."

"Yes, they are," said Sara. "But the fancy house has a better chance of falling apart because the stress points in its design. A home built simple but solid will stand time. Look at some of the homes in our area. How many times do you see an older home being repaired versus the new one?" asked Sara.

Sean thought carefully. A lot of homes built in the 1800s were still standing strong. Occasionally a new roof night be put on or someone redesigns the inside. The new homes were constantly having something done to them. "Okay, you're right, but what's the difference?" asked Sean.

"In the 1800s man designed homes to last. They had no architecture. They figured out what they needed, and they built it to last. In our time, no thought goes into a home. People outgrow a home, they sell it, move to a bigger home. They do this because owning a home is a sound investment. They're always going to get more out of it than they invested, so the cheaper and faster you build them, the more money you make and it all boils down to money, something there wasn't a lot of in the 1800s. They couldn't afford to make mistakes. In our time if you make a mistake, you level it, build over or move on. You've got a bunch of men and women out there who went to college to learn nothing more than fancy design. They don't care if the house lasts. They don't have to live in it. Look at Florida, where all those homes were destroyed. One man's house remained standing. He designed and built that house himself. Who got blamed? The contractors, not the architect. Who got sued? The contractor. They only went by designs drawn by the professional with the shingle. That's why I don't want a shingle. I won't be classified in that group," said Sara. "I can design them, you build them, I don't care. For me I love this, but I can't go out there and rip the people off. I can't, it's not me. I know better, so it's my way or no way," said Sara.

"I know you well enough that you won't change your mind. So you design and I'll build," said Sean. "These are great, I love this one you call Sara."

Sara giggled. "I don't name the house. "That's my home, that's the one I want you to build," said Sara.

"Oh, but is it big enough?" asked Sean. "It looks small."

"Believe me it's far from small. Three bedrooms, three-and-a-half baths, living room, dining room, kitchen, breakfast nook, pantry, sewing room, walk-in closets, there's more than enough room. Oh, an open staircase. I always wanted one of those."

"If it's what you want, then you've got it,' smiled Sean.

"This one is Jacob and Susan's. I know you wanted to design mine and theirs but since I did the ten, I threw these two in as a bonus," smiled Sara.

"This is great, they will love this," said Sean.

"Yes, it is them isn't it?" said Sara. "Well, I'm going to bed, it's been a long day. Good night guys.'

"Good night," Sean and John called, not looking up. John was lost in what Sean was saying. Sean explained why Sara did this or that. John decided he liked the way Sara did things.

Sean heard the shower going and looked at John. "Tell me about this cabin you found," said Sean.

John studied the drawings. "It's not big. You two own it; it's on your land. I showed it to Sara, thought we would honeymoon in it. Why?" asked John.

"Well, Sara said you were working on it. I thought if I lent a hand, you would get it done faster. I've got a couple days here since Sara designed two of my homes," said Sean. "What's wrong with it?"

"Right now I'm working on the roof, it leaks," said John, putting the paper down.

"Is it as big as this place?" asked Sean.

"No, why?" asked John.

"I might have enough tin left over to do the roof," said Sean.

"That would work, save time trying to make shingles for the roof. I fixed the holes, so it doesn't leak and was going to start making shingles but your way is faster and easier," said John.

"Anything else wrong with it?" asked Sean.

"I really don't know. I came upon it by accident. It looked good and solid, but the roof was awful, nothing like what we put on here. So I took the old roof off, saved the nails or what I could save, put a new roof on right now. It's just bare wood, but it keeps the weather out," said John. "Why?"

"Any running water nearby?" asked Sean.

"Oh no! We're not changing anything. Sara loves it just the way it is," said John. "She's not yelling at me."

"I thought you would like a toilet and sink, nothing more," said Sean. "But if you want to keep running outside on your honeymoon, that's fine with me."

"Sean, you and I both know what's going to happen, we don't need a bathroom," said John.

"Yeah, you're right, Sara would get pissed off at me," said Sean. "A piss pot and a picture of water is all you need, but if I'm wrong, you're shit out of luck," said Sean.

John thought carefully. Sean was right, what if this wasn't the way it was going to happen? "Talk to Sara," said John.

"Talk to Sara about what?" asked Sara walking in the living room.

"Sean wants to put a bathroom in the cabin," said John. "I said no, but he made a good argument, so I said to talk to you. I'm not getting yelled at."

Sara went over the cabin in her head. Then walked over to the island and wrapped a towel around her head. "There's no real room in the cabin, see, it's like this." Sara drew up plans. "You've got a bed, fireplace, table. If you moved the table by the fireplace, you would have room here for a bathroom, but then you lose the only window you have. The front of the house faces east, so when you come up to it by the trail it's south. That's where the window is. If you had a window on the east side here by the bed and a door with a window, you might be able to get away with it because you have a covered porch here on the east side that runs the whole length here. For some reason, whoever built it didn't like the view on the east side. Maybe they couldn't afford a window."

"Or," said Sean, "only one person built it. See how everything is centered? The window, the door, the fireplace? Looks like one person built it and couldn't afford to waste time with windows, all the cutting and stuff."

"This is probably true because the side walls can't be more than six feet. The height is in the ceiling like a small cathedral ceiling, not more than two feet. Over here where the bed sits the floor is all rotted wood. I think it's where the roof leaked. Other than that, it's in good shape. John did real good putting the roof on. You can see where he added trusses for support. Whoever built this wasn't too sure on truss work, so I don't know how sound the floor is to support the weight of a bathroom," said Sara.

John was impressed that Sara noticed his work and said he did a good job. How she saw everything else he didn't know "How did you remember everything in the cabin?" asked John.

"Because she's the best," said Sean. "She's probably got it all decorated and color coordinated," laughed Sean.

"I do," said Sara. "But you have to consider two things here. How long are we going to be here? Overnight. It's not worth all the work. A few days maybe, but is it worth the lost time to do the work involved? You'll have to take up the old flooring, put in a good floor then put in a new floor. What's under there I don't know. But you could end up with more trouble than it's worth."

"Or we'd end up with a place for people who get lost in the woods. You know the ones," said Sean. "A safe place to stay in a storm, a getaway cabin, a lot of things," said Sean.

"Well, if that's what you plan, then fix it. Just remember you could be getting yourself into a lot of trouble here. Everything looks easy on paper. On paper you can say 'oops' and erase. With work, you can't do that. Oops don't work," said Sara.

John listened, then said. "What gets lost in the woods?"

"Snowmobilers who run out of gas. Some dumb fool who thinks he'd go for a walk not knowing anything about hiking," said Sean.

"People do these things?" asked John.

"All the time. So maybe it's not such a bad idea to fix it up. It might save some poor fool's life," said Sean. "What size would you say this is?"

"Not as big as this," said John.

"Fourteen feet by eighteen feet at the most," said Sara.

John looked at Sara. "How would you know that?" he asked.

"I told you she has already got it decorated," laughed Sean. "How big a window here and what size door?" asked Sean.

John looked at Sara.

"What's everyone looking at me for?" asked Sara.

"We're waiting for an answer," said John.

"Oh, you want me to pick a size," said Sara.

"Thirty-two by forty-nine and one-half for the window, thirty-six-inch door," said Sara. "At least that."

"I figured a twenty-inch wreath so it's thirty-six inches. Let's see." Sara drew out the cabin. "Yup, thirty-six inches is good, but a thirty-four-inch-by-forty-nine and one half window would be better. See what it does with light. You would have more light. A bathroom here like this and you're set."

"What size window is the bathroom window, maybe thirty inches wide? Why?" asked Sara.

"I just wondered if it would get enough light," said Sean.

"I think there's more than enough light there. It's not a very big room. Well, it's long, maybe too long. See, you can't do much because the window is centered. If you didn't have the window here," Sara picked up a pencil. "Okay, let's see this. I could have a better idea." She started erasing. She looked, moving her hand back and forth. "You don't need much," murmured Sara.

"Watch this," said Sean. "She'll cut down on our work. I love it when she does that."

"If you did this, put this here, left that there. Okay, this is what we can do. Since the floor's where the bed is, it's rotted. We can put the bed on the other side. Just take this part of the floor up. put in floor joint here, bathroom here, then this window we had there, move it here. Then you have constant light for this section. Then put a small window or no window in the bathroom," said Sara. "So you're looking at maybe eight feet of flooring to replace versus the floor. Two walls; one long, one short. Two doors, one bathroom; and one storage closet. I wouldn't put a window in the bathroom. What I would do is put a ceiling floor here. I know it's not very high, but if you needed storage, you would have it. You could go up it from the storage closet or a loft," said Sara. "No, you don't have good height for it. Get this," Sara erased, taking another piece of paper and drawing on it. She sat at the stool. "Yes, I like this better. See what we have?" Sara showed John and Sean.

"Where did you learn to do this?" asked Sean.

"Do what?" asked Sara.

"You just did an artist rendition of what the cabin would look like finished," said Sean. "Where did you learn to do this?"

"First, that's no artwork. Second, it's how I see it. It's my mind's eye. Third, I didn't learn how to do anything. That's just my doodling," said Sara. "Now I'm going to bed. Good night."

Sean reached for Sara's hand. He knew when not to push her. "If you get time on the other houses could you do some doodling for me? What your mind's eye sees?" asked Sean.

"Sure if you want me to. Do you want them in color? asked Sara. "I'll need colored pencils, all colors," said Sara.

"We can have the kids send them, thank you," smiled Sean. "Good night." He let go of her hand."

"Good night," said Sara and she left.

"You didn't know Sara could do this?" asked John.

"No, but with work like this, I could have one hell of a business if people saw stuff like this. Sometimes not too often, but sometimes Sara shocks me. This is one of those times," said Sean. "She's a natural when it comes to design."

"Well if this is what that cabin looks like after we're done, it's one fancy place," said John.

"Look at it. This is what Sara was talking about. It's simple, very simple. The furniture and decorations make it look elaborate. Nothing we do will compare to the set up of this place. Look, take this stuff away and you have nothing. One room, see?" said Sean.

"You're right, it's just a room. How did she do that?" asked John.

"I don't know. I wished I did," said Sean.

"What was it she said, 'less is more'?" said John.

"Well if less is more, that's an understatement. Do you know how many women would love this as a bedroom? It has a bathroom, walk-in closet, fireplace. Put two chairs and a round table in front of it and you've got every woman's dream. Not too big to clean, but big enough to chase hubby around," laughed Sean. "This alone could make me rich."

"Women love this stuff?" asked John. "Even Sara?"

"I don't know what Sara loves other than you. She's so tight-lipped it's hard to say," said Sean. "I know just about everything she hates, though."

"How can you know what she hates and not know what she loves?" asked John.

"Because the only time she says anything is to say I don't like it," laughed Sean.

"Oh," said John, getting up and taking his bed roll off the chair and spreading it on the floor. "So if Sara says she loves something, she means it?" asked John, lying down.

"If Sara says she loves something, she definitely means it, but she very rarely says it. That's why I know she loves you. She says it over and over and over," said Sean, turning to the lights. "Why do you have doubts?" asked Sean.

"Doubts?" About what?" asked John.

"Sara's feelings? said Sean.

"Oh God, no. I just know why with you she hates things, with me she loves everything," said John.

"It's because here she's in love, there she doesn't feel love," said Sean lying on the couch. He then got up and got a pillow and blanket and lay back on the couch.

"You're not sleeping in bed?" asked John.

"Look, you and Sara may find nothing wrong with me sleeping on the bed, but I find it awkward," said Sean. "If it was my future wife and a man was sleeping on the bed, I'd kill him. I don't care if I know they are not doing anything or not."

"Whatever, it's your sleep loss not mine," said John. "Do you think I'm doing the right thing by Sara?" asked John.

"What do you mean?" asked Sean, hitting his pillow with his hand.

"If Sara's happy here and not happy there, and this thing works the way you think it will work, are we doing the right thing by her? Then what happens if it doesn't work? What if she married the wrong man?" said John.

"First off, I'm right and you know it. Ben knows it. You've seen the pictures; you know I'm right. As for marrying the wrong man, Sara has never thought of me as a husband or lover. We're nothing more than friends, real good friends. We grew up together and have known each other almost our whole lives. I say almost because we don't remember when we were babies. Are we doing the right thing? Sara has two children and four grandchildren who need her," said Sean.

"You're right, I'm being selfish. I wonder if I can love enough in one night to last us both a lifetime," said John, rolling over.

Sean stared at John's back. This is one hell of a mess. He'd never known a man who loved a woman like John loved Sara. This was going to be toughest on him. He was going to be the biggest loser in all this. He'd lose Sara and his kids. Sean felt like shit. He'd spent his life protecting Sara. Now he had to hurt his best friend to save her. "You'll do fine," said Sean.

"Everyone puts too much faith in me. There's a lot of pressure on me. It may sound easy to everyone, but there's a hurt deep in my heart. It's causing a darkness. I will never love anyone like I love Sara. No one can take the darkness from my heart, except Sara. But I love her enough to set her free. I will do what is required, then spend the rest of my life remembering," said John.

"I know it sucks. I feel like shit. I'm losing the best friend I've ever had. You've become a very good friend, and I will think of you a lot. I will tell John and Susan what a great father they had. If I know Susan, she'll drive me nuts with questions. She always has; she's a lot like Sara. Not just looks, her mind, her walk, her attitude. She's so much like Sara it's scary. John, he's the spitting image of you, in looks; that's where it ends. John's always took the tough road in life. Sara did her best to help him, but he always did the opposite. I think of Tom. He taught John to hate his mother. As hard as she tried, John just wouldn't get close to her. Sara felt responsible for him, she said it was all her fault, so she protected him, overprotected him. Really she loved John so much," said Sean.

John rolled over. "How can he not love Sara, especially after she gave birth to him? Sounds like he needs a swift kick. Is he close to his mother now?" asked John.

"No, he moved away. Nearly killed Sara. She cried for a month. Ol' Tom kept throwing it in her face, that she was a horrible mother. She went into a severe depression, worse then she went into here. The doctors put her on Valium. She bloated up She looked awful. John never left a forwarding address or phone number. I think Susan talked John into calling Sara. She accepted the fact she'd lost John. Then John called, said he'd be home for Christmas. She went crazy decorating, cooking, and cleaning. Only thing is, Sara got shot before she got to see him," said Sean.

"John must feel like shit right now," said John.

"I don't know. Susan said John's come around, but I think he's got a lot to deal with right now. He's trying his best, but he's probably so confused right now he won't know which way is up. It's a bitch knowing your father is a killer, the man you trusted and believed. The only person who loves you is fighting for her life. That's the person you walked away from. I wouldn't want to be in John's shoes right now," said Sean.

"Me either," said John. "Good night."

"Good night," said Sean.

Chapter 14

JOHN SAT ON THE EDGE ON HIS OLD BED. HE LOOKED AT HIS MOTHER'S DIARY. He felt sick to his stomach. During the day he'd read Sara's diary to his mother, then came home and read his mother's. He told Brian he wanted to write his mother and tell her to stay where she is. He didn't deserve her as a mother. Brian talked him out of it. John felt that his mother finally found happiness and deserved to keep it. She was giving up everything she ever wanted in life to be with her children. Why, she spent her whole life in hell so they would be a family. John sat on the bed and stared at the ceiling. "She gave up so much so we could be a loving family," thought John. "How many times did she say, 'honey I love you' and hug him. All the time. John blinked at the tears in his eyes. He'd always had everything he'd ever wanted, but what price did his mother have to pay for him to have it? A beating here, a rape there. She never said one fucking word, just gave him what he wanted and said, "Here honey I love you." He'd take it and run, never saying "thank you" or "I love you." He didn't have time for such foolishness. Now he prayed that he could say it just once.

Susan got whatever she wanted. She was daddy's little girl. John believed that his whole life, but Mom paid the price for Susan, too. His father hated them both. No matter what he'd done to please his father, it wouldn't have been good enough. So to get back at his father, he shit on the only person who really loved him. Once again his mother was going to prove how much she loved her children by losing the only love she'd ever known. He didn't deserve that kind of love, unconditional love. Nobody deserved a mother like Sara, least of all him. John sat up on the bed, picked up the diary, and started reading.

Knock, knock.

"Come in," called John.

"John, Brian and George want to talk to you," said Susan.

"I'll be right there," said John.

"No, they're here," said Susan, shrugging her shoulder.

"Send them in then," said John, setting the diary down.

Susan let them in. They waited for Susan to leave. They heard the footsteps on the stairs before they spoke.

"Brian has told me that you want to write your mother and tell her to say where she is. He also told me he told you not to do that," said George.

"Yes," said John.

"I must admit you've been a tough one to deal with. You have to do everything the hard way. I was hoping if you would read your mother's diary, you would understand a little better, but you seem to have a knack for blinding the issues, so we decided to talk to you, hoping you won't do anything foolish, hoping you'll listen to what we have to say. What we're about to tell you is between the three of us. No one else is to know. I don't expect you to understand our ways of doing things. We'll tell you everything, then you can ask questions. No one is to know what we talked about in this room. Do you understand?" asked George.

"Yes," said John, pointing to two chairs. "Please sit." Their bigness made John feel small and useless, so Brian and George sat.

George started talking. Brian and John listened. John asked questions, Brian and George answered. John paced; Brian and George watched. Then they talked some more. One hour later, after they were sure John understood that his mother had no choice but to come back, they left. John looked at his mother's diary. Tears ran down his face. When would her pain end? All this pain for the love of a nation of people he never knew. He should have, they were his people, too. It was just one more thing he didn't have time for. Sara had tried to explain his heritage and what he had to be proud of, but his attitude kept him from paying attention. Now it was being told to him over and over. It wouldn't have to be if you found time to listen. George was right, John did everything the hard way. John picked up the diary. He couldn't blame his mother, she tried. She tried her best, but now he had to face the facts. He only had himself to blame. It's a tough world when reality comes up and slaps you in the face. In John's case it took several punches to make it sink in. John opened the diary and read through the tears. All he wanted right now was peace, the kind of peace only a mother's hug could give.

John set the diary back on the night stand, turned off the light, got up, and walked over to the window. He stared into the cold December sky. The new fallen snow looked blue and white against the dark sky. The coldness of the night made the stars look like they were twinkling down at you.

Knock, knock.

"Come in," called John.

"John, you awake?" called Susan. "I brought you a snack."

"Set it on the table," said John. "I'm up, I'm looking at the night sky."

"Oh," said Susan. "Are you okay?" asked Susan, setting a tray on the table.

"I'm thinking about Mom and what she told us," said John, turning around. "How did she say it? 'Take pride in who you are. The world could take whatever they wanted away from you, but your heritage. They couldn't take that from you. You were the only one who could hurt your heritage.'"

Susan didn't say anything. She knew John was hurting. There was nothing she could do. We all had demons and only you could fight them.

"I can't believe I was so fucking stupid. All I had to do was listen. Once in a while say 'thank you' and 'I love you.'" John shook his head. "I couldn't do it. The sad part, Mom still loved me. I bitched, I yelled, I kicked, then ran away and she loved me enough to let me go. Fuck!" yelled John. "Why couldn't I see how much I hurt her?" asked John.

"You make it sound like you're the only one who dumped on Mom," said Susan. "I did, too. Every time I ran into trouble I ran to Mom and had her handle it. I did a lot of things I'm not proud of. We played right into Dad's hands. I've gone over it in my head a thousand times. We can't change what happened, we can only go forward now, changing our mistakes along the way," said Susan.

John turned back to the window. "Have you read Mom's diary?" asked John.

"No," said Susan.

"Take it, I can't read any more. It hurts me. She loved John so much. A love like that is what stories are written about. Men fight wars and change history for half the love that John and Mom have. I wanted to write Mom and tell her to stay where she was. I didn't deserve to ruin her life anymore." John started crying again. "But I want her here to hug me and say 'I love you.' Just so I can say 'I love you, Mom.' How selfish is that? Taking Mom's one true love away from her, so I can say something? I had thirty years to it and couldn't do it," said John.

Hot tears ran down Susan's cheeks. "I feel the same way,' said Susan, picking up the diary. "But I know she has to come back. This diary will be all she has left of her love." Susan held the diary to her bosom. "Sometimes the written word will remind us of what we thought we forgot," said Susan.

"Believe me, Mother will never forget her love for John. In two days they will be married. Mother will know what true love is, at its entirety. She has to give it all up. No, mother will never forget John. All she has to do is look into my face and she'll remember. John's my father, a man I would have loved to know." John put his hands on the window sill. "I'll be a constant reminder to her of what she gave up to save a nation of people she never knew. How would you love to live with that the rest of your life?" asked John.

"Oh no, you don't," said Susan, setting the diary down. "His blood is in my veins, too. I feel the same as you do."

"Yeah, but you don't look like him, I do," said John.

"No, I look like Mother. Take a good look at us. We together are Mother and John. It doesn't matter if we're together or apart. When she sees us, she will be reminded of the life she lost. Her youth is gone. Now she lives through us. We're all she has of John, so don't go saying it's all on your shoulders. I'll always know what she's thinking when she looks at me," said Susan.

"What's that?" asked John.

"What it's like to be young and in love, then lose that love. So don't think you're the only one who's been dumped on a lot," said Susan.

"Maybe you're right," said John, turning around. "But Mom wouldn't say a word to us about it. All we have is her diary to read to see how she feels. Why God chose Mom to carry John's seed through life, I'll never understand. Who knows, maybe it's his way of saying he fucked up. It wasn't supposed to be that way, so he gave her a chance to love the man she was supposed to be with. I don't know why Mom chose to save the people. I don't know," said John.

"That's Mom, John. She's always helping someone. She was sent there for a reason. We'll never know, no one will ever know what Mom's done, because Mother never existed, so she gets to come home to a world she hates and a bunch of ungrateful kids. Some fucking reward for helping someone," said Susan.

"Mom's never looked for rewards," said John, looking back out the window. "Mom only wanted someone to love her."

Susan picked the diary up. "Your coffee's getting cold," she said and left.

John turned around. Susan was gone. He looked at his snack; he wasn't hungry. He took off his clothes and went to bed. It was after midnight.

One more day and Mom would marry John. One more day and his mother would be back. Sara had gained back her weight. John couldn't help but thinking how beautiful Sara looked today as he read to her out of the diary. Today at one o'clock Sara would be wheeled into surgery, the wire in her jaw removed, the pin removed from the cast. The shoulder cast was taken off yesterday. The bruised, swollen face gone. After today the only reminder that all of this ever happened would be the IV bottle that hung next to her bed. The flowers long gone, Sara's story long forgotten. The world moved to other tragedies. When Sara woke, it would be plain and simple: Two children waiting to say 'I love you.' Two big men stood outside the door to stop the world at her door.

"John, Susan," said Dr. Emerson. "Surgery went fine. The marks on your mother's leg will heal. When she's back on her feet, she can get those two teeth looked at. Now all she has to do is wake up and she can go on with her life. She will have a good life. Nothing she went through will keep her from living a good life. She healed well," smiled Dr. Emerson. "A normal life."

"A good life," said John. "Her life sucks. There's no cure for what she has to live with the rest of her life, so don't give me that bullshit, a good life, a normal life. That's a polite way of saying you did your job. The wounds my mother will bear the rest of her life aren't wounds that heal, so you stick the bullshit where the sun don't shine," said John.

Susan grabbed John's arm. "John, let go," she said.

"I can't," said John. "I can't look at her and ever think her life will be normal. It's not normal for a husband to abuse his wife then hire someone to kill her. How she suffered thirty years of abuse and no one suspected anything is beyond me. When she leaves here, she returns to a home she loved to be reminded of how she was almost killed. No, doctor, her life will never be normal again. Every night when she lies down to sleep, she will be reminded of her loneliness and the rape she went through in that bed. Now you tell me, doctor, does that sound like a normal life to you?"

"John, I know there will be some adjustments your mother will have to go through. That's why I recommend psychotherapy when your mother wakes up. But she can lead a normal life, a good life," said Dr. Emerson, putting his hands in his pockets.

"Adjustments, psychotherapy, where was your psychotherapist when mother came to you bruised? No, you can stick your adjustments and psychotherapy where the sun don't shine. My father's the one who needed the fucking shrink, not my mother. You're a doctor, you're supposed to know abuse when you see it. You don't wait until they're wheeled in here on a gurney all shot up fighting for their life. You rush in here all shocked and surprised, fix all the wounds, expecting a fucking pat on the back. You've done your job. Then you stand before me calmly and say she can live a normal life. How many fucking times did my mother come to you with bruises?" asked John.

"She always said she fell. She never said Tom hit her. I had no reason to doubt her word. If I had, I would have done something, but I didn't see a pattern to her accidents where I would call it abuse. If I had, I ever would have let her go back home," said Dr. Emerson.

"Pattern to abuse, what's that, a cop out? You want to know the pattern? She was too fucking scared to tell you. She prayed over and over you would suspect something was wrong and not send her home. My father was one sick mother fucker. She was scared to death of him. She feared for her children, but she took the abuse, so we didn't have to. So don't you tell me some shrink will make it better. Her wounds go way beyond anything we could ever imagine," said John.

"Unless a patient tells us they're being abused, there's nothing we can do," said Dr. Emerson.

"Yes, there is, but you don't want to see what's in front of you because your fear of being sued is stronger than your fear of losing a patient," said John.

"Dr. Emerson, I'm sorry for John's behavior. We've had a lot to deal with these past few days," said Susan.

"Don't apologize for me, Susan," said John, stepping in front of Dr. Emerson. "I'm right and he knows I'm right." John stared right into the doctor's eyes.

"I'm sorry you feel that way, John," said Dr. Emerson.

"No, doctor, I feel sorry for you. What's it going to take for you to admit you were wrong? How many more women will pay with their lives before you admit you could have done something?" asked John.

"What do you mean?" asked Dr. Emerson.

"My mother always told us if we don't learn from our mistakes, then we've learned nothing. How many other women come to your office claiming it was an accident, hoping and praying that since you're a professional, you might care enough to stop their abuse? What's it going to take for you to open your eyes and see abuse? How many women will die before you do something?" asked John.

Dr. Emerson turned and walked away.

"John, calm down," said Susan, touching John's arm.

"Don't touch me, Susan. Don't make an apology for me again. Never, ever do it. You understand?" said John, turning around, looking at Susan.

Susan stepped back in fear. John scared her. He never looked like this; he was really pissed. "Okay," said Susan.

"He's just as responsible for this as we are. He had the power to protect us and our mother, and he chose to look the other way. What kind of man can he be if he closes his eyes to what he sees? Do you think our mother is the only mother in this town that gets abused?" asked John.

"No, but you can't expect him to save them all," said Susan.

"No, but if he doesn't save one, what Mom went through was for nothing," said John.

"You yelled at him so he would save someone?" asked Susan shocked.

"Susan, it starts with one, then two, then three. Don't you see? Mom can save people in both times. Her heritage and her sex both were abused. Many people turn their heads choosing not to see. Everyone around here hates the Oneida Indians. This is wrong. They have done nothing to the people here. Everyone hates, but they don't know why. But the Indians are hated because they make money. They don't pay taxes and it pisses everyone off. Well they were here first, and they had a smart leader. We'd have what they have if we started choosing better leaders. We're too stupid. We put the same assholes back in office and wonder why nothing changes. The madness has to stop. That's why Mom went to help. There's a lot of good people in the world, but you have to find them. Dr. Emerson is one of those people, he just needs to know he can make a difference. Sometimes yelling is the only thing they understand. It makes them open their eyes. First they hear, then they see," said John.

"I knew you didn't hate me," said Dr. Emerson. "You're right, I was wrong. Laura sent me to get you. Sean is starting to come around. He's moving in his bed. There's multilevels of consciousness. We're never sure how long it takes, everyone is different, but he is coming out of it," said Dr. Emerson.

John and Susan ran to Sean's room. Laura was holding Sean's hand. "Why is he coming around now? I thought it was tomorrow?" asked Laura.

"Dr. Emerson said there are levels that they go through to regain consciences. Sean must be going through them. The closer it gets to the wedding the more they will wake up here. I think Sean will come to first. Mom's got to make the last step," said John.

"God," said Laura. "What your mother has to go through. I look at Sean with such longing. The waiting is horrible and it's only been a couple of weeks. I can't even begin to think what it would be like to live my life without him. Your mother has to leave the only man she'll ever love just to set things straight. I don't know if I could do that," said Laura.

"My mother has no choice," said John. "If she stays, everything she worked for there will be ruined."

"I know," said Laura. "I'm saying if it was me, I would say fuck you and stay where I was happy. Nobody gave her a reason to be happy here, but she has to walk away from happiness to save people. Why, what did they do for her?" asked Laura.

"They didn't have to do anything," said John. "She just cared enough to help, asking for nothing, losing everything."

"It's six o'clock, let's get some supper," said Susan. "We know tomorrow is our big day. We need to keep our strength up. We'll be no good to either of them if we falter now," said Susan.

"You're right," said Laura. "We can't let our nervousness get in our way now. We've come too far."

"Well, you want to eat in the snack shop or cafeteria?" asked John.

"Cafeteria," said Susan. "If they need us they can page us. We won't hear them in the snack bar. They said Mom should be back in her room by 6:30 or 7:00."

"Okay, let's go," said John.

"I thought Sara was supposed to go to surgery at one," said Laura.

"She was, they had three emergency surgeries, which set everything back," said John. "Then she finally got in three hours later."

"John yelled at Dr. Emerson," said Susan, stepping on the elevator. "John blames him for Mom being here. John said Dr. Emerson should have realized Mom was being abused, but he didn't do anything. He could have done something but he didn't. John really yelled at him."

"Good for you, John. It's about time somebody said something," said Laura, stepping off the elevator.

"You agree with John?" asked Susan shocked.

"Yes, I do. Dr. Emerson has known your mother all her life, so who would better be qualified to know your mother was being abused? He knew better," said Laura, grabbing a tray and going through the line.

"You're saying my mother didn't have to go through this because the doctor didn't do his job?" questioned Susan, following Laura in line.

"Yes, that's what I'm saying, you have a problem accepting this?" asked Laura.

"Yes. If Mom said it was an accident, how do you know it wasn't?" asked Susan.

"Susan, how many times can a woman fall and hurt herself before someone starts to think she's falling a little bit too much? How many stitches does it take before someone notices? I've thought about it a lot lately. I think Sean suspected and tried to catch Tom but couldn't. You know Sara, she wouldn't say anything. If someone cornered her and asked her, she might say something," said Laura.

"Yes, but she'd have to really be cornered," said John. "We lived there and never knew what was going on. How she kept it from us, I'll never know. She never once complained. I did some soul-searching last night. The signs were there, I just didn't see them," said John, shaking his head.

"John, you were little, you grew up with it. How were you supposed to see the signs if it was a normal part of your life?" asked Laura.

"One time I found Mom crying. I was maybe six. My mother never cried. Know where she was? On the bed. You know what she told me? She didn't feel good, but she got up and got me lunch. Dad came home for lunch, his lunch was my mother. He raped her. I thought about that time last night. Mom sat on the chair rubbing her stomach and said it was a boo-boo. Do you know how many times my mother said boo-boo to me? When I grew up, every day of my life," said John.

"John, how were you to know that boo-boo meant abuse? Boo-boo was the only way your mother knew to tell you she was hurting. You were never abused, so you had no way of knowing your mother was being abused. You knew nothing about sex, so how would you know she was being raped? You're putting too much on yourself," said Laura.

"Am I? We learned about sex and abuse in school and it went right over my head. I still didn't see it, but Dr. Emerson knew better," said John.

Susan was crying. She suddenly felt sick.

"Susan, what's wrong?" asked John.

"I saw Mom getting raped, remember? When I was five you hit me in the mouth with the ball. I ran into the bedroom. I came running back screaming, saying Daddy was hurting Mommy. Then Daddy came out and said Mommy and Daddy were only playing a game," said Susan.

"Yes, Dad spanked me for hurting you, gave you a washcloth with ice for your lips, then he left. Mom came out and calmed me down and took care of you, then she baked us cookies. It was a Saturday. I remember that day because that was the only time Dad spanked me," laughed John.

"Well, I knew Mom was being hurt. I never gave it much thought till now. I forgot all about it," said Susan.

"Susan, you were told by your father that Mommy and Daddy were playing a game. You were young. You had no reason to think your father was lying to you. He was your father," said Laura. "Looking back isn't going to change anything. We have to start going forward now. When Sean and Sara get home, we'll all sit down, talk it all over, and get on with our lives. It's the only thing we can do," said Laura.

"You're right," said John. "We'll get on with our lives or what we can of our lives. We'll all have our lives changed by this, but none will be changed like my mother's. There's nothing we can do for her."

"Maybe there is," said Laura.

"What?" asked John.

"Well, we can include her in things we do. We can have her to dinner, take her to lunch, let her babysit. You know as well as I do how much she loves kids. Look at all the things she can do that she was never allowed," said Laura.

"God, you're right. Mom's free to do anything she wants," said Susan.

"Well, we can sit here all night and make plans for Mom, but it's her life she has to live. I'm sure she'll let us know what she had planned for the rest of her life," said John. "So let's wait and see what she wants to do."

"Mom's probably back by now," said Susan.

"Yes, let's go. Before you know it, they will be kicking us out of here," said John.

"Tonight will be the longest night of my life," said Laura as she walked to the elevator.

"I know, I really don't want to go home. Time will last forever," said Susan.

"We could rent a movie, get some pizzas, not talk or think," said John.

"Yeah, I like that," said Laura. "We wouldn't be alone. Susan's husband went to his mother's house to be with the kids. We could stay at Sara's house. We wouldn't be alone, just stare and eat," said Laura, stepping off the elevator.

"Mom's back, the guards are there," said Susan.

"I'll get the movie, you two get the pizza ordered, enough for Brian and George. You know they will be there tonight," said John.

"John, there's something wrong. Look, there are doctors in Mom's room," cried Susan.

John reached the room first. Susan and Laura followed. "What's wrong?" yelled John.

"Nothing," said Dr. Emerson. "This is Dr. John Stevenson, the neurologist for your mother. She's starting to regain consciousness so I called him in to test your mother's responses. Let him tell you."

"We were afraid your mother would have some paralysis with her head trauma, so we waited till she regained some level of consciousness to test her. She's fine, her responses are all normal. This may take hours or days for her to come fully to, but she's fine. I took the stitches in her head out, so everything is good," said Dr. Stevenson.

"She's not going to have any problems later on, is she?" asked John.

"What do you mean?" asked Dr. Stevenson.

"Seizures, epilepsy, that kind of stuff you get with head trauma," said John.

"No, if she hasn't had any seizures by now, she won't. With a head trauma like your mother's there are usually no side effects. Once in awhile there is, but she would have had a seizure by now if there was any damage, so your mother is in good shape. As a matter of fact, the best I've ever seen. She's a survivor, she is. I'm looking forward to her waking up so I can talk to her. She impresses me in a coma. So I can't wait to talk to her when she's awake. She seems highly intelligent to me. From what Dr. Emerson tells me, she's one fine lady. That's rare these days," said Dr. Stevenson.

John looked at Dr. Stevenson. "It depends on what Dr. Emerson said. My mother can be a lady, but a stubborn lady. She would do nothing to hurt anyone. Her heart is pure gold," said John.

"I've been told this. There is one thing we don't understand," said Dr. Stevenson.

"What's that?" asked John.

"Your mother seems to look younger. This is impossible, we know, but she's younger looking. Maybe you would know why?" asked Dr. Stevenson.

"Mother's not smoking," said John.

"Ah, now it makes sense. Smoking will make you age; giving it up will have a reverse effect. Was she a heavy smoker?" asked Dr. Stevenson.

"Depends, it was a mood thing with her. Sometimes a pack a day, sometimes none. I figured with no smoking and all the oxygen, she's on her way to healing her body, that and all the vitamins and exercise didn't hurt her," said John.

"No, she was in good shape physically, which probably helped her more than anything. Every little we do to keep our body healthy helps," said Dr. Stevenson. "I see you're into body-building."

"Some," said John. "Haven't had much time lately, eating a lot of fast foods doesn't help, either. But in cases like this, you have no choice. I'll have a lot of catching up to do when this is all over," said John.

"Do you go to a gym?" asked Dr. Stevenson.

"No, I have my own gym in my house," said John. "You waste a lot of time and money running to a gym, then you have to work out when they're open. It wasn't worth it, so I took the money I'd spend in gym fees and gas and invested it in my own machines. If I want to work out at midnight, I can," said John.

"That's a very smart move on your part, son. I can see Sara's children are very smart, too," smiled Dr. Stevenson.

"And you, young lady, I'm told have a very good business you built from nothing. That's hard to do these days, very hard. I think my wife has bought things from your store. I think she hired you to decorate our house for Christmas. You're the shop that does that, right?" asked Dr. Stevenson.

"The only one in town," smiled Susan.

"I must say you did one hell of a job. Anyone would think I had money," laughed Dr. Stevenson.

"Thank you," smiled Susan.

"Right good family you are," said Dr. Stevenson. "I'll see you later."

Everyone said good night. Susan giggled when he left. "Did you detect some English in his voice? He looks English, tall, brown hair, blue eyes, broad shoulders, handle-bar mustache. 'Right good family,'" laughed Susan. "That means he's old."

"For a while there I thought Dr. Stevenson was trying to fix himself up with Mom," said John. "But when he said wife, I knew it was impossible. I doubt very much he's too old, maybe sixtyish."

"John, Sara does look younger," said Laura, looking at Sara.

"I know, I saw it yesterday. I thought maybe the stress of her life was finally leaving her as she approached her wedding. Maybe, just maybe, her happiness is so great there it's affecting her here," said John.

"That's probably true. Everything she did there affects here," said Laura.

"I've been watching her since yesterday. She's just glowing. I've never seen her look so beautiful," said John.

"You know now that Mom's got the stitches out. We should call down to the beauty shop and have them come up and wash her hair," said Susan.

"That's a good idea," said Laura. "When she wakes up, it would be all nice and clean and soft."

"Women," said John. "Is that all you think about, beauty shops?"

"Yes," came the reply.

Susan picked up the phone, called the nurses station. "Hello, Nurse Jane speaking."

"Yes, this is Sara Valentine's daughter. We would like a beautician to come in here and wash my mother's hair," said Susan.

"Dr. Stevenson has already ordered that. They're on their way," said Jane.

"Thank you," said Susan shocked.

"What's wrong, you look shocked?"

"I am, Dr. Stevenson already ordered a beautician. She'll be here soon. I'm surprised he'd think of such a thing."

"I don't know, he seemed like a nice enough doctor. He probably figured your mother's been through enough and wouldn't want a mess of her hair when she wakes up," said Laura.

"Listen to you two. You make him sound like a saint. He's a doctor," said John.

"So," said Susan.

"He probably had the nurse call to get Mom's hair washed so she doesn't get lice. It's not a vanity thing with him. It's medical," said John.

"John, what a horrible thing to say," said Susan.

"Why, because it's the truth? Mom's in a hospital, you pick up all kinds of things, head lice is one of them," said John.

"Oooh, the thought makes my head itch," said Laura.

"Mrs. Valentine?" asked the beautician. "I'm Natalie, I'm here to do your mother's hair and nails."

"Yes," smiled Susan. "My mother hasn't had her hair washed in a while. They took the stitches out today," said Susan.

"Oh, I remember your mother. Dr. Stevenson had me come in and cut her hair so there wouldn't be too much damage. How's she doing?" asked Natalie.

"Good, she's starting to regain conscious," said Susan. "Why did Dr. Stevenson have you cut my mother's hair?" asked Susan.

"Well, in cases like your mother's, he has us come in and style the hair so there's not much of a hair loss. We arrange it so it looks like nothing happened. In your mother's case, it was very important because she has such long hair," said Natalie.

"Dr. Stevenson had you do that for my mother?" asked John.

"Oh, not just your mother, he does it for everyone. He feels we don't need to look in a mirror and be reminded of what happened. He feels the less we're reminded, the faster we heal. And from what I've seen, it works," said Natalie.

"Mom washes her hair three times," said John.

"That's good," said Natalie. "But if you don't mind I'd like to wash it, maybe four or five times till it is clean," said Natalie.

"Sure, that's fine," said John. "I'm sick," thought John, "I'm discussing washing my mother's hair."

"I see a lot of hair has grown already. This is good," said Natalie. "She chatted away with everyone as she washed Sara's hair. "Your mother has such nice red and gold highlights in her hair," said Natalie as she blew dry Sara's hair.

John looked at Susan and Laura. "Red and gold highlights?" asked John.

"Yes, your mother has beautiful hair. There, see, you can't tell she has a scar there," smiled Natalie.

John, Susan, and Laura stared at Sara. She had highlights and you couldn't tell she had a scar. Sara's hair was brushed full of highlights. Natalie did Sara's nails and left.

"John, what's going on? Mom looks younger than me," said Susan.

"I don't know, but if I come in here tomorrow and there's a little girl there, then I'll worry," said John.

"Well, before we panic, your mother's hair was really a mess. Maybe the shampoo brought out the highlights and the fact the hair is styled may make her look younger. Remember, we've been looking at her at her worst for a few weeks," said Laura.

"You're right," said John. "We just forgot how pretty Mom is. I mean the bruised, swollen face alone scared the hell out of me. Then the hair pulled over and the scar showing. All we saw was ugly. Now she's Mom again," said John. "Mom never looked her age."

"No, she didn't," said Laura. "I always hoped I'd look as good as she did when I was her age."

"Visiting hours are over."

"Great, we finally got to see Mom the way she used to look and they're kicking us out," said John.

"I'll say goodbye to Sean, give him a kiss, then we'll get pizza. You get a movie," said Laura.

"No weird shit either, John. I don't need to be up all night scared out of my mind," said Susan.

"Still scared of boogey men?" teased John.

"Yes, I am. Only I didn't know the boogey man was my father," said Susan.

John didn't say anything. He didn't have to. Susan just said it all. Susan kissed Sara on the cheek, said "I love you, Mom" and left to meet with Laura.

John walked over to the bed, took his mother's hand, and kissed it. "That's for the princess." Then gently laid her hand down and kissed her cheek. "That's for being the greatest mom in the world. I love you. See you tomorrow," then he left to get a movie.

John got two movies, "Phenomenon" and "Jingle All the Way." Laura and Susan got three pizzas and two six-packs of Pepsi. They all arrived at Sara's house at the same time. Brian and George were there waiting. They watched both movies; they didn't talk or think. They went to bed at one-thirty exhausted and fell right to sleep. Brian and George kept watch as they slept.

Excitement filled the air; tomorrow was a big day for everyone.

Chapter 15

"NO SEAN, PLEASE DON'T LEAVE ME, NOT NOW," CRIED SARA.

"Sara, Jacob's house is done. The barn is done, the animals have all been moved to Jacob's barn. Your house is done. We've got a good start on the homes for the nation. I'm exhausted. I need to sleep. I need to sleep in a bed, that's why Jacob left the bed for me," said Sean, rubbing his neck.

"No, you're staying here, please Sean, I'm scared. I can't be alone tonight. I'm getting married in the morning," Sara started crying. "Sean, please. I've got this feeling that I will be sent back before I marry John. Sean, you know me. You know I've never been happy. John makes me happy. I don't want to lose now, not now," sobbed Sara.

"Sara, I need a bed. That couch is killing me. I can't guarantee that if I stay here we won't be sent back," said Sean.

"Don't you think I know that?" cried Sara. "Somehow I feel safe when you are close. I feel like this will happen if you sleep at Jacob's house. I won't feel the security I feel when you're close by."

"We can bring the bed here and set it up in the living room," said Sean.

"Do you know how stupid that sounds?" said Sara. "These beds are heavy. Two men couldn't lift them. All I need is for you to hurt yourself."

Sara sat on the couch and cried. "Sean, I'm scared, really scared," sobbed Sara.

Sean sat next to Sara. "You really are scared. Come on, it will be all right," said Sean, putting his arm on Sara's shoulder.

Sara shrugged her shoulder to move Sean's arm. "No it won't," said Sara. "You know it won't so don't baby me, I hate that," said Sara.

"What are you so afraid of?" asked Sean.

"Being happy. I've never been this close to being happy. It's like someone says, 'Sara Valentine, oh she has no right to be happy. We'll tease her and taunt her with happiness. We just won't let her have it.' My whole fucking life has been like this, so why should now be any different? Dangle the man of your dreams in front of your face, make her drool, then take that magic string, yank John away from me and laugh at me. How dare she think she could be in love and happy. You sit there feeling all smug. Why not, you're happy. You know happiness. I've never known love or happiness of any kind, not from my parents, my sisters, my husband, or my children. They all crucified me my whole life, so don't sit there and act like you understand because you have no fucking idea what it is to live in hell," sobbed Sara.

Sean hung his head. Sara was right, he knew it. He couldn't imagine living the life Sara led. How bad was her hell being raped and beaten by your husband over and over. He probably hoped she'd died in the process. When she didn't he hired someone to kill her. Everything that could be done to hurt someone was done to Sara. No wonder she was scared of happiness. She really believed she didn't deserve it. How could you believe in something you've never known. "Damn it," thought Sean, "she always wins." Sean stood, "Let's go to bed. You can't have red eyes on your wedding day."

"Really?" asked Sara, looking up, tears glistening off her eye lids.

"Really," smiled Sean.

"Do you think I should marry John? I mean, am I doing the right thing?" asked Sara.

"Do you love him?" asked Sean.

"You have no idea. I keep trying to hide my feelings just in case it doesn't happen, then I won't be hurt again, but I can't, they just keep popping up. This time if it doesn't happen, I don't know what I'd do. I can't live without John. I really can't," said Sara.

"Sara, I promise you, you will marry John," said Sean.

"I wish I could believe that. You don't know how much I want to. I just keep getting this funny feeling," said Sara.

"Bed, tell me your funny feeling on the way," said Sean.

"My breasts are all swollen and aches. I get these wavy things and they settle deep in my belly. It aches, throbs, in a place I don't want to mention, but it feels hot and wet. They don't go away and they're really bad when John's around. I get warm all over and my breasts do these crazy things. Then they end up really hurting," said Sara, climbing in bed.

"Sara, what does sex and desire mean to you?" asked Sean, lying on the bed.

Sara rolled over and turned the light out. "Well, sex is a lot of pain, sometimes more than others. I don't really like it. The handcuffs hurt my wrist, the rapes burn my legs, the scarf around my neck chokes me, the belt hurts a lot on your bare skin. Some of those things they put inside you hurt a lot. But it has to be done, so you do it. I really hate the belt across my breast, that hurts a lot. Desire, that's when you want something you know you can't have," said Sara.

Sean was glad the lights were off right now. Hot tears ran down his face and rested on the pillow. How could he do that to her? That twisted mother fucker. Sean wished Tom was alive so he could torture that mother fucker. "Sara, that's not sex, that is a sick twisted version of sex. Sex between a man and a woman who love each other is the most beautiful thing in the world," said Sean.

"Yeah right. You're the male, you get to beat on Laura, tie her up and do what you want. You're not on the receiving end of it," said Sara.

Tears kept falling as Sean listened. A thought came to Sean's mind. That day on the bed when he walked away. Sara really didn't know she was playing with fire. She didn't know it was sex. She really didn't know. Just like now, she didn't know what she felt was lust. "Sara I don't tie Laura up. I don't beat on Laura, that's not sex," said Sean.

"It's not?" asked Sara.

"No, it's not. Remember that day on the bed when you asked me to get you pregnant?"

"Yes, I was supposed to get pregnant that night. John or you wouldn't get me pregnant. We loused it up. You walked away, told me I didn't have the look. I still don't know what you meant by the look. All you did was kiss me," said Sara, "gave me a strange feeling."

"Sara that's how sex is supposed to be, soft, gentle, sweet, and pure," said Sean.

"Sean don't try to feed me that bullshit. I was married for thirty years," said Sara.

"Okay, don't believe me, but you're in for a real big surprise tomorrow night," said Sean, rolling over. "What you're feeling now is lust."

"Yeah, right," laughed Sara. "Lusting for pain."

"Sara, there is no pain with sex. None, well the first time being a virgin, but if it's done right, the pain lasts only seconds," said Sean.

"Look, I was a virgin for Tom. I know better, I was so sore and swollen I couldn't walk for a week. Remember, I'm the woman here. I'm on the receiving end of all this. All men do is have pleasure breaking our maiden head, so they can make us a woman," said Sara. "You don't know what it feels like."

"Yes I do," said Sean. "I felt Laura's pain. I felt it because I loved her. Women go around thinking that it is easier on the man. Well sometimes you love someone so much you feel what they feel. So don't lay that bullshit on me. Remember how you feel when John kisses you, remember how you felt in the cabin?" asked Sean.

"Yes," said Sara.

"Multiply that by a thousand and that's what sex is about," said Sean.

"Oh great," said Sara, sitting up in bed.

"Now what?" asked Sean.

"I've got something new to worry about. I was all prepared for one thing and now you tell me that it's wrong, that something else is going to happen. Thanks a lot."

Sean got up and walked to the bathroom, got four Tylenol. "PMs and a glass of water, take these," said Sean, handing them to Sara. "I need sleep. I didn't know this was going to turn into a fucking pajama party."

Sara swallowed the pills. "Sorry I'm such trouble. I thought I had things under control. You screwed it all up by saying it's wrong. Now I don't know what to do. I don't know what to expect," said Sara.

"Fireworks, please go to sleep," said Sean, lying on the bed.

"Fireworks, they bring fireworks with them? Oh God, the cabin will catch on fire. We'll burn to death. I don't know what to do with fireworks," said Sara.

"Sara, shut up!" yelled Sean. "Look, when a man and a woman get together and have sex you see fireworks, you don't bring fireworks with you. A husband and wife get together for pleasure, not pain. Both of you try to please each other, you bring pleasure to one another by touching and kissing," said Sean, his head throbbing.

"I-I-I can't touch John, I wouldn't know what to do," said Sara.

"John doesn't expect you to know, you're a virgin. John is the man, he will show you what to do. He will show you how to please him. Don't assume you have to know everything for once in your life. Let someone show you something," said Sean.

"You telling me I'm stubborn?" said Sara.

"No, what I'm telling you is for once in your life let someone do something for you. Knock down that wall you've built around your heart and let someone in there. John loves you more than life. Let him show you how much," said Sean.

"I'm tired of being hurt," said Sara.

"Sara this is the 1800s not 1997. Nobody here wants to hurt you. You're the only one who can hurt you here. You love John; John loves you. In a few short hours you're going to be husband and wife. Don't you think that it's time for that wall to come down? Enjoy what you have here. Enjoy John making you a woman, his woman. I guarantee you will have pleasure you've never known in your life. It's time for Sara to be a woman."

Sara slid down in bed. "A woman, I don't know how," said Sara.

"John will show you," said Sean.

"Maybe this honeymoon won't be so bad after all. All I have to do is enjoy. Maybe you're right, maybe this time is my time," said Sara.

Sean fell asleep.

Sara dreamed of John's kisses.

John paced outside in the moon light. It was a beautiful night. The wedding and the honeymoon played over and over in his head. It had to be the best for Sara. The absolute best, thought John.

"Drink this," said Summer. "It's chamomile tea. It will help you sleep so we can all sleep." Summer handed John the cup. "You're so nervous, don't you love Sara?"

John drank the tea, handed it back to Summer. "Thank you, yes, I love Sara more than anyone could ever know, but I feel pressure," said John. "I get one chance and one chance only to love her. That has to last us a whole lifetime," said John.

"Come with me," said Summer. Summer walked to where the wedding would take place. John followed. She walked John through the wedding step by step. "See this circle, this circle of moon flowers, this is where you and Sara will stand."

"I know that," said John.

"But did you know it's a magical circle. One flower made this circle. A circle has no beginning and no end. It goes around. When you step into that circle tomorrow and join in marriage with Sara, if your love is pure, you both are virgins, the flowers will stay white. And when you are pronounced husband and wife, and when you step out of the circle and the flowers are still white, you will love forever. This has never happened before to our nation. Tonight the flowers are out; tomorrow in the sun they will not be. When you and Sara step into this circle and hold hands, if your love is pure enough, the moon flowers will bloom in daylight, making a virginal circle around you. The gods are telling you your love for one another is never-ending, no beginning, no end," said Summer.

"And if they don't bloom, what happens?" asked John.

"Your love stays inside the circle, it ends there," said Summer.

"I don't understand," said John.

Summer walked away. John followed. "I'm your mother, I love you dearly. Sometimes you don't listen or you listen and don't hear. Your love will bloom like a flower and grow or it will stay and never grow. You sit here and think about it. I'm going to get some sleep, tomorrow is a long day."

"I'm going to bed, too. I understand," said John. "It won't matter where we are, we'll always love each other. Only we can let the love wither and die," smiled John.

Summer stopped. "You did listen to me. As for your honeymoon, you are your father's son; you will have no problems," said Summer.

"Mother!" said John.

"What, a mother can't talk to her son about such things?" laughed Summer. " I do know how you got here."

"Your boldness comes from being around Sara too much," said John.

"I happen to love my future daughter-in-law a lot. And I know for a fact you'll get two opportunities to make Sara a woman," said Summer.

"Mother, you shock me," said John.

"The truth is the truth," laughed Summer. "And I love my grandchildren very much. They're good children, they love us, never meeting us," said Summer.

"That's because Sara taught them love well," said John.

"Yes she has, and she loves you more than anything in this world. She just glows when you're around," said Summer.

"I love her just as much, but when I look at her I don't see her with red hair. I see her the way she is in her other life," said John.

"My, you do love her a lot to see what she really looks like," said Summer.

John smiled. "Good night, Mother."

"Is he all right?" asked Ben.

"I think so. I gave him tea to make him sleep. I took him to where you're to wed and explained everything to him," said Summer.

"Everything?" asked Ben.

"Everything he needed to know. I told him he was his father's son and would have no problems on his honeymoon," laughed Summer.

"Well, come here, let's see if we still have the flame we've always had," smiled Ben.

"Oh, the flame is there," smiled Summer, getting in bed next to Ben. "It's just we've never found a way to put it out; it grows stronger and stronger."

"Well, let's see how high the flame will grow," laughed Ben.

John went to bed, he felt a lot better. He would finally get some sleep. All night through his dreams he'd dream of Sara coming to him.

Sean got up at nine and yelled at Sara to get up. The wedding was in two hours. Sara rolled over and went back to sleep.

"Shit!" said Sean. He ran back into the kitchen, made coffee, ran into the bathroom. and started the tub for Sara. Ran back into the kitchen, poured a cup of coffee for Sara, and ran back in the bedroom spilling coffee along the way. "Sara, Sara." Sean pulled her up, put the cup to her mouth. "Swallow," said Sean. Sara swallowed. He gave her more. "Sara," said Sean.

"What?" asked Sara.

"Drink this, we're overslept. It's nine o'clock," said Sean.

"Shit!" said Sara, grabbing the cup and drinking.

"I started your tub water," said Sean. "I didn't put anything in it. I didn't know what you wanted in it."

"I'll do it," said Sara, jumping out of bed and running into the bathroom.

Sean ran back into the kitchen, poured two cups of coffee, one for him, one for Sara. He left his on the island, took Sara her second cup, then ran back into the kitchen and made a quick breakfast. He took Sara hers. She was making the bed. "What the fuck you doing? The girls will be here soon," said Sean. "Eat."

"I can't have the house looking awful," said Sara. "I'll eat in the tub while I soak."

"Go, I'll finish the bed," said Sean.

"I thought I was supposed to be the nervous one today," laughed Sara.

"You haven't had time to get nervous, we overslept by two hours, so go take your bath," said Sean.

"Okay," said Sara, grabbing the plate of food. Sean made the bed, mopped up the trail of coffee he spilled, cleaned the kitchen, and just finished when Summer and Susan showed up.

"You look awful," said Susan.

"We got up late. Sara kept me up late with question and question. Some were rather embarrassing. I finally gave her something to sleep, so we'd get some sleep," said Sean.

"Did you answer her questions?" asked Summer.

"The best I could. The honeymoon was rather hard to explain. What she thought it was like is not what it is like." Sean felt his face get hot. "I think I did a pretty good job. She remembers her honeymoon with Tom, but that's not the way it is. It's hard to explain what a woman should feel," said Sean.

Summer laughed. "Sean, don't be embarrassed. I had to talk to John last night myself," said Summer. "He was up most the night. I had to give him something to sleep," laughed Summer.

"We'll talk to Sara," said Susan. "If you two talk to John."

"God yes. I don't think I did too good of a job. I told her there's fireworks," said Sean. "I couldn't think how to explain it to her. All she knows is rape."

Susan laughed. "No, you didn't to it right. We'll handle it."

"We could arrange fireworks," laughed Summer.

"Sara's in the tub now. When she gets out, I'll take a shower, then go to your place."

"Sean, get your stuff, go to my house, take the shower there. We'll handle it from here on in," said Susan.

"Thank you." Sean ran in and got his stuff and left. He took the wagon Susan brought down with her. Sean saw Susan's house as a refuse. He stopped in front of Susan's house and knocked on the door. Jacob let him in.

"You look like shit, pal," said Jacob.

"Thanks, I've had one hell of a night. Sara kept us up with questions. We just got up a little while ago. I haven't had a shower. Susan told me to take one here," said Sean.

"Sure, go ahead. What the hell did Sara keep asking you questions about?" asked Jacob.

"Sex. I think I invented a new way of talking about it without saying anything," said Sean.

"What did you tell her?" laughed Jacob.

"Fireworks," said Sean. "It's the only thing I could think of. Summer and Susan said they would talk to Sara."

Jacob laughed. "That's funny. What's she going to do when there's no fireworks?"

"The girls will explain to Sara while we explain to John," said Sean.

"We what?" asked Jacob.

"We'll talk after I'm dressed," said Sean.

"Okay, I'll make coffee; you get ready. This better be good," said Jacob.

"It is," said Sean. Sean showered, shaved, and dressed. Jacob made coffee, then dressed. He was in the kitchen waiting for Sean when Sean walked in.

"Tuxes are a bitch," said Sean. "They had to send up white ones with pink cummerbunds," said Sean.

"Mine's some kind of green," said Jacob, turning around to give Sean coffee.

"Can we take this outside, I need a cigarette," said Sean.

Jacob handed Sean a dish. "Go ahead, we just can't smoke around Susan, it makes her sick to her stomach," said Jacob. "It will pass. Now tell me about this talk we're to have with John. Shit, he told me things I didn't know."

Sean lit a cigarette. "I have to explain to John that Sara's a true virgin. In her other life, she never had sexual pleasure of any kind. From what I've been told, every time she had sex there was a lot of pain involved. She was raped every time. It seems that was the way Tom liked it. I think from what the kids read in her diary, then they told me. Tom liked to tie Sara up, beat on her, then force her to do all kinds of things," said Sean.

"That bastard," said Jacob. "No man should treat a woman like that."

"Well, Sara's going to have a problem on her honeymoon because she thinks this is the way sex is supposed to be. I tried to explain sex isn't that way at all. I don't think she believed me, so I figured I better talk to John and explain it to him," said Sean

"Explain?" said John, walking in.

"How come you don't have a tux?" asked Jacob.

"This is my wedding dress. It tells our history, our heritage, our nation's colors. My mother made it for me. Tell me what?" asked John.

Jacob poured John coffee. "Sit, Sean needs to talk to you," laughed Jacob.

"Thanks," said Sean, looking at Jacob.

"If it's sex, I know, we are taught on how to please women," said John.

Sean sighed, looked at John, told him everything he had pieced together. He watched John go from a slow rage to full war.

"That bastard, how could he do that to her?" asked John.

"Well, I explained the best I could, that this was the wrong way, that sex is a very beautiful thing. Summer and Susan are talking to her now. Sara's scared now because she was prepared to make love to you the way she knew how. I told her that you would show her the right way. She thinks she won't please you. I told her you would show her what to do the whole way through, you would show her what pleases you," said Sean.

"Other words, slow," said John.

"Yes," said Sean.

"Tell him about the other thing," laughed Jacob.

"What other thing?" asked John, looking at Sean.

"Fireworks," said Sean.

"Fireworks?" questioned John.

"It's the best way I could describe orgasms," said Sean.

"Fireworks, you couldn't have found something easier for me to achieve?" asked John. "Maybe thunder and lightning? How many of these fireworks am I supposed to deliver?"

"I told her she'd lose count," said Sean.

Jacob laughed. "Good job, Sean."

"This isn't funny. You've put a lot on my shoulders," said John.

"Not really," said Sean.

"How do you figure that?" asked John.

"Sara described how she felt when she looked at you. Every time she looks at you, she has orgasms. She doesn't know what they are. She calls them wavy things settling you know where. That's just looking at you with your clothes on. When you unleash the woman in her, I think you'll be surprised," said Sean.

"This is how Sara feels about me? That's how I feel about her. There's only one thing I don't understand that has me a little on edge," said John.

"What's that?" asked Sean.

"Does Sara go back while we're making love?" If she does, then I'm right in the middle of making love to the other Sara," said John.

"I don't know. That's why there's no lights. The other Sara will think it's me. She goes to sleep and when she wakes up, I'm supposed to be there," said Sean. "Jacob will see to it that the real Sean is lying next to the real Sara."

"We're pushing our luck here. How do we know who's who?" asked John.

"We don't. Jacob has to stick close to me and watch me, that's the only way," said Sean.

"Beautiful day for a wedding," said Ben, walking in. "We'd better be going; Sara is ready. Summer has her in the bedroom. Jacob you get the buggy, pick up the women, give John, Sean, and I time to get there. Then bring the women to where I showed you; let's go," said Ben.

The men followed Ben. Sean checked twice to make sure he had the rings. Ben was doing the ceremony because he was chief. John looked at the circle and stepped inside. No moon flowers blossomed. One of the men from the nation was in charge of the camera, his name was Kelly. He also was to roll out the carpet and play the taped version of the wedding march. The carpet was rolled out. Susan walked first through the apple trees in full blossom, then Summer. The music played. John looked up and saw Sara. God, she was beautiful. She was a princess. Sara never stopped looking into John's eyes. Any thought of flowers was gone from his mind. There was just Sara. He felt his heart beating stronger and stronger as Sara walked closer. Her thighs started throbbing as she got closer to John. She didn't let it bother her. Once John took her hand, it would go away. All they saw or heard was each other and their heartbeats as they beat as one.

John held out his hand. Sara took it and stepped in the circle. She looked into John's eyes. "I love you," she said.

"I love you," said John. Everyone watched as the flowers bloomed and spread a blanket of snow white.

"Do you declare to love one another for ever?" asked Ben.

"I do," said Sara and John.

The flowers grew and spread around.

"Do you declare John to be your husband?" asked Ben.

"I do," said Sara.

"Do you declare Sara to be your wife?" asked Ben.

"I do," said John.

Sean handed Ben the rings. "These flowers are growing everywhere," he whispered.

The rings are gold, the purest thing a man and a woman can give each other. A band of gold that has no beginning, no end. Just as love should be, pure with no beginning, no end. John took a ring and slid it on Sara's finger. "With this ring I declare thee to be my wife forever," said John.

Sara took the ring Ben gave her and slid it on John's finger. "With this ring I declare thee to be my husband forever," said Sara.

The flowers had now formed a white blanket on the ground. The only place there were no flowers is where John and Sara stood.

"You may kiss your wife, my son," said Ben.

John kissed Sara. Everything around them blossomed. Sean looked around. This was really weird. He saw it and didn't believe it.

John and Sara turned around and faced everyone.

"Now I present to you Mr. and Mrs. John Feather Green."

John loving and tenderly put his hand on Sara's waist. They stepped out of the circle, walked down to the wagon. On either side of the red carpet, white flowers grew as they walked.

John helped Sara into the wagon and drove to Sara's house.

Summer was crying. Sean went to her. "What's wrong?"

"The prophecy has been fulfilled," said Summer. "I don't cry out of sadness, I cry out of happiness. This is good for our people."

"What's with all the flowers?" said Sean. "Did you see those things grow?"

"Yes," laughed Summer. "It's part of the prophecy. It means their love is pure, will last forever, and can only bring richness and happiness for our people. Sara and John's love will always be strong no matter what happens."

"Let's eat," said Ben. "We don't want to give them too much time alone right away," laughed Ben.

"No, all you're thinking about is that wedding cake," laughed Summer. "You have a sweet tooth."

Sean laughed; Sara rubbed off on Summer.

"No, my dear, every tooth in my head craves sweets, that's why I like biting you, you're the sweetest thing there is," teased Ben.

Summer shook her head and laughed. "Let's go, the food is calling him."

"I thought I heard something," joked Sean.

"I think tonight will be a busy night at the nation. Come February we'll have a lot of new ones around," laughed Ben. "The way everyone watched John and Sara, I could see a lot of emotional thoughts."

"You're probably right. Our nation hadn't had this much blessing in a long time," said Summer as they walked the path to Sara's house. They were the first to arrive. John and Sara were kissing.

"Don't waste those," teased Ben.

Sara blushed. John smiled. "I don't intend to," assured John.

"That's my boy," said Ben. "Congratulations."

"Thank you," said Sara. "I hope I do right by your nation."

"You already have my dear. You've blessed us beyond all belief," smiled Ben.

"But I've done nothing," said Sara.

"You've done more than you will know. Just take care of him; keep him in line. Every once in a while you argue with him. Long journeys of marriage can make a man forget why he married in the first place," said Ben. "Show him your spirit and the journey will be an easy one," said Ben.

Sara smiled. She didn't understand exactly what Ben meant. "I think it means a long, happy marriage," thought Sara. "I will," said Sara.

Sean didn't understand it either, but he knew that every step in life was called a journey. But Ben knew that Sara and Sean were going back today some time.

"Congratulations," said Sean. "Ben wants to eat. I think we better sit down so he can eat," whispered Sean.

"Okay," said John. "He really only wants the cake, but mother warned him, no cake till he ate something," whispered John.

"He's been eyeing that cake ever since he got here. It's so huge it took three times for all of it to come through," laughed Sara. "Let's sit, I think everyone's ready now," said Sara.

John gently put his hand on the small of Sara's back and led her to the table. They sat and were served food. Sean took a lot of pictures with a camera. They would stay here with John, so he'd always have Sara near to him. Sean toasted the bride and groom. They cut the cake, each took a bite, and talked to their guests. Sara gave Susan and Summer a gift for being in the wedding. Sara threw the flowers then changed to go to their cabin. The cabin had been ready for a couple of days. Sara was nervous as she walked out to the buckboard. She wore a white dress that Susan sent her. Underneath was a white teddy and garter with white lace stockings and white shoes. John helped her into the wagon. "Something tells me I'm going to like playing in the fort this time," whispered John.

Sara blushed. "I think I will, too," she whispered as she kissed his cheek.

John drove away; Sara was waving to everyone. They arrived at the cabin. John helped Sara out of the wagon, picked her up in his arms, carried her over the threshold, walked over to the bed, and laid her down. He sensed her nervousness.

"Before we have any kind of sexual relations, I want to talk and explain everything to you. First, I will never hurt you. I will stop at anytime you feel I hurt you."

Sara reached up, grabbed John's shirt, and pulled him down and said, "Shut up."

"So much for going slow," thought John, as he kissed Sara. "No," thought John, "slow is the only way to go." Sara was expecting fireworks, and she was going to get them. John stood up. "I am a man, I make you a woman my way," said John. "This is not going to be a rush job. I'm going to show you how it feels to be a woman. When I'm done with you, you'll be grateful you're a woman," said John. John felt Sara's nervousness in her kiss. He knew she wanted to get it over with in a hurry to end herself being scared. John took Sara's dress off slowly, savoring what lay before his eyes. He pulled the ribbon on the teddy so he could see her breast. He sucked one, then the other until they were tight little rosebuds. He kissed her full lips tenderly, then a deep probing kiss. His hand slid the teddy down and each breast was exposed. He fondled them gently, trailing kissed down her body until his mouth closed over the rose-tipped bud. His thumb rubbed across the other one. His mouth traded kisses back up Sara's body until his lips found Sara's mouth, Sara's body aflame with desire. John's hands slid the teddy down and down. His hands running across Sara's body, leaving trails of desire and want. The need in her grew beyond anything she imagined. His hands seeking, probing; his kisses probing deeper and deeper in her mouth. Her body was on fire. Her body couldn't take much more without exploring. John's hand slid down lower and lower. The ache deep within Sara needed more, much more. She didn't know what the ache was, but it grew to a burning flame. John's hand slid lower. "Oh my God," cried Sara. She grabbed John's arm as orgasms ripped through her hot throbbing body. John trailed kisses down Sara's body until it found its mark, licking one thigh than the other until it led to a deep probing kiss. Over and over her body rippled with orgasm. She withered on the bed as the waves rushed in her body, yet deep inside there was something that needed more. "What more can there be?" thought Sara. A deep throbbing grew deep within her again. The aching and throbbing grew. She wanted more. "More!" screamed Sara. John spread Sara's legs, touching her with his hand. She was wet and hot. She climaxed again. He entered her slowly. He felt another orgasm. Sara screamed more. John felt her virginity leave as he went with her orgasm. "Yes," cried Sara as she felt him deep within her. The throbbing now roared like a lion. It needed more, he waited, then started slowly until Sara moved with him. "She got her fireworks ten times over," thought John. She was warm and moist, and he had to go slow so he could enjoy the softness deep within her. Sara screamed "Yes, yes, yes," as she climaxed over and over. John felt her fire, her need for him deep in her womb. He drove harder and harder. Sara had dug her nails into John's shoulders. The pain kept him from coming. There was a flash of lightning, the clash of thunder, heavy rain hit against the cabin. John stopped, rolled over on his back, helped Sara get on top. This would have to last them both a lifetime. Sara slid John into her slowly. John ran his thumbs across Sara's breast. Bolts of electricity ran through her body, settling deep within her. Each bolt met with a deep thrust. Her body was no longer hers; it was John's. Lightning slashed all around outside. Sara stopped, looked at John. "If this is lovemaking, I want more. What else is there?" gasped Sara. John showed Sara everything. She just couldn't get enough of him. John was getting to the point he couldn't hold back any longer. He laid Sara on the bed and started all over. This time he had to release. He felt her climax and released. She felt him come deep within her. She felt its warmth, it made her have another orgasm. She screamed at such an orgasm. There were fireworks. She saw the flashing of light. She wrapped her legs around John. "Don't take him out, leave him right where he is," said Sara. "You will never take him out," said Sara.

John looked at Sara. She was serious. "Can I take it that I satisfied you?" said John.

"Oh yeah. I decided I like sex, and it stays where it is," said Sara.

"Well, they say the second time is better, and every time after that," laughed John.

"I don't care what they say, this thing ain't leaving, no way it's getting away," said Sara.

"You expect me to just keep it there forever?" laughed John.

"Yes, when it rises to the occasion, I can do what I want with it," said Sara. "I move a little like this and holy shit, feel that," said Sara.

"Yes," laughed John.

"That's my body telling your body that it belongs there, so it stays there," said Sara.

"What if I have to go to the bathroom?" asked John.

"Tough," said Sara.

"How about I carry you to the bathroom? We can take a shower together, then come back here and do it again," said John.

"Just as long as John Henry stays where he is," said Sara.

"I think I created a monster," smiled John.

"No, you made me a woman, and I'm never letting go," said Sara. She moved and cried, "My God that feels good." She moved again. She had a major orgasm that gave John a throbbing hard on. "Oh my God," cried Sara. "Did you feel that?" He just popped right up, right there inside of me."

"I sure did," said John. "Take it you're ready for round two."

"Oh yeah. I really like it that way," said Sara. "That drove me wild."

"What way was that?" asked John. "I aim to please."

So Sara showed him. John said fine and that's how they started. He never would have figured her for doggie style, but she loved it. Hell, she loved any way he did it. The second time was longer because they both enjoyed it. This time they took a shower, went into the bathroom and showered together, that is. They made love in the shower, then went to bed. This time they pulled down the covers and got in bed. John made love to her again. John was surprised Sara hadn't left him yet. Maybe Sean was wrong and John would be spending the rest of his life making love to Sara. "What a nasty life that would be," thought John, smiling. "How about something to eat?" asked John. "There are two plates of food on the table," said John.

"Okay, I'll get it," said Sara, getting out of bed. "Oh, no!" said Sara.

"What? Something wrong?" asked John.

"I can't walk," said Sara. "When I do this, I have an orgasm," said Sara.

"I'll get the plates, don't move. I have an idea," said John.

John grabbed the plates, and walked over in front of Sara. "I'm going to pick you up, and you can put John Henry where he belongs. I'll sit on the edge of the bed and we'll eat, then make love," said John.

"Okay," said Sara. "This wouldn't have happened if you left him where he belonged," said Sara.

"I didn't know that you would love sex so much," said John. John felt him grow inside of Sara. "This is unbelievable," thought John.

"I didn't know sex could be so good, but I think I got it figured out," said Sara.

"What figured out?" said John.

"Well, for every orgasm here, erases the abuse there. Every time you come inside of me, I stand a better chance of getting pregnant back there. I'd love nothing better than to have another one of your children, maybe six," said Sara. She fed John.

John coughed. "Six children, you want six of my children?" asked John.

"Yup, and you and I both know I'll be going back. When, we don't know, so we have to get all our loving while we can. It has to last us a lifetime, so if you stay inside of me, I will never forget," said Sara. "You made me a woman. I must say I was a little shocked. I didn't know that John Henry's came in sizes like yours. If I had, we never would have lasted until our wedding night," said Sara. She wiggled. "Oh my, that is so fine."

John started choking. Sara patted him on the back. "Mmm, I do like my husband's manhood," smiled Sara.

"Sara, I hope you don't go around talking such things to other women," said John.

"Honey, I won't be seeing any other women, I'm staying right here. I'm not losing one second of this for nobody," purred Sara.

Sara started eating her supper.

"Sounds like my wife wants some more of her man." John gave a thrust.

"Oh my, yes, it is fine. I will never complain," smiled Sara.

"Any way you want to start with?" asked John.

"Anything we haven't tried yet. Any way you like the best," smiled Sara.

"Well, there's a lot I know. There's a lot we haven't done. If we did everything, it could take all night," smiled John.

"Well you better start teaching me what you know. We'll try things we haven't done. We'll pick and choose what we do and don't like. I think we should take another shower and start all over," said Sara. "I don't want to leave you until we've done the things that gives us pleasure several times, then I might let you sleep a little, but you never leave my body. I will sleep on top of you if I have to."

"I don't understand, I can't sleep," said John.

"Only for a little bit. I've got a lot of erasing to do, and a lot of making up to do. You made me a woman, and I'm glad to be alive," said Sara.

"You were a woman. I only helped you blossom," said John.

"No, I never was a woman. Now I am," said Sara. "Let's shower and start all over," said Sara, putting her plate down. "Oh my, those movements do something to me."

John and Sara took a shower. He carried her back to bed and they started over. John was impressed at Sara's eagerness to please him any time he wanted. About four in the morning Sara fell asleep on top of John. She'd move in her sleep and said "Mmm."

John woke about 7:00. Sara was gone. His heart raced as he felt for her. Their one night of love was over. "I only hope I did right by you, my love," said John with a broken heart. "I love you."

Chapter 16

Sara heard voices, she moved. "Oh, that hurts," said Sara.

"Oh my God, Mom's back. Mom, it's Susan. John's here, too. I'll get the doctor."

"Sean," whispered Sara. "How's Sean? Is Sean alive?" asked Sara, then closed her eyes, hot tears ran down her cheeks, her dream was over.

Susan ran to the nurse's station. "Mom's awake." Dr. Emerson got up. "Call Dr. Stevenson." They walked to Sara's room.

John held his other's head. "Mom, I love you," cried John.

"Sean, is Sean alive?" asked Sara.

"Yes Mom, Sean's all right. Do you want me to get Sean?" asked John.

"Yes, I want him. I want to see that he's alive," said Sara.

"I'll get him," said John, running next door. "Mom's awake, she wants to see Sean. She won't believe he's alive," said John. "She's crying."

"God she's here. I'm coming," said Sean, getting out of bed. "Help me, John, I haven't got my legs yet."

John picked Sean up, carried him next door.

Dr. Emerson slowed his walk when he saw John. Sara needed to talk to Sean before he started poking at her.

"God Sean, you're really okay," cried Sara.

"You're the one who got hurt the worst. Now if you could tell John to put me down, we can talk. I don't think I was moving fast enough for him," laughed Sean.

"Sorry," said John. "Mom was crying." John set Sean in the chair.

"Leave us," said Sean.

John left. "How you feeling?" asked Sean.

"Sore, tired, empty," cried Sara.

"What do you remember?" asked Sean.

"About what?" asked Sara.

"Well, well, look who's awake," said Dr. Emerson. "Could you leave us for a little bit? I don't think you should be out of bed yet," said Dr. Emerson to Sean.

"I'm fine," said Sean, standing. "I'll be right outside," said Sean.

Sara nodded, she knew Sean was okay. She was never talking to anyone about her dream. She never would act like that in her life. Better left where it was in her dream. Sara blushed to think she even dreamed of acting like that.

"Sara, how do you feel?" asked Dr. Emerson. "Dr. Stevenson is on his way."

"Stiff, sore," said Sara. "You think I can hang my legs over the side of the bed for a couple of seconds, please?" asked Sara.

"We'll see when Dr. Stevenson gets here. Let me check you over first," said Dr. Emerson. "You were in pretty rough shape when you were brought in here. You had a lot of surgery on your head, your jaw, your shoulder, and your leg. You lost two back teeth. You can get them fixed later. Yesterday you some more surgery. We took out stitches and wires. We put a soft cast on your leg. You've been in a coma two weeks. I would like to know what you remember about what happened?" asked Dr. Emerson.

"All of it. And you want to hear all the gory details? Well we'll wait for Dr. Stevenson. I'm only telling it once, then I never want to talk about it again. Do you understand?" said Sara. "If you want to hear it over and over, you better get a tape recorder. Just get me home, so I can continue my life. I'm sure Tom has a mess and a half waiting for me. Christmas Eve is only ten days away."

"Sara, I don't mean to sound personal, but I have to tell you something. You better prepare yourself, this is bad news," said Dr. Emerson.

"Don't treat me like a child, don't talk down to me ever again. I think I've suffered enough in my lifetime that I've earned some respect. I'm divorcing my husband and starting over. I'm walking away, do you understand me, no more, I'm through," said Sara.

Susan, John, Laura, and Sean leaned on the wall outside waiting to talk to Sara. Brian and George had left, said they would be back shortly. They went to get a cup of coffee. They passed Dr. Stevenson on the way. Brian and George turned around and followed him to Sara's room. They stood on each side of the door.

"Sara, this is Dr. Stevenson. He's the neurologist that worked on you. Sara says she wants to put her legs over the bed for a while. She seems quite snippy. She told me she remembers the whole thing and said if I wanted all the gory details I'd have to wait for you and use a tape recorder. She says she's only telling it once. She wants to go home and clean her house for Christmas," laughed Dr. Emerson.

"So you're telling us our job?" asked Dr. Stevenson.

"Somebody has to. I've been through too much to start over a bunch of bullshit. You get one shot, tape it. You can go over and over it all you want; for me it's over. I want to forget it. I refuse to be treated like a child or be talked down to. I am an intelligent woman and expect to be treated like one. Now please, let me put my legs over the side. I know I'm allowed to do this. Chris checked me over and everything is normal. If I get dizzy, I will tell you. My legs feel numb, and my lower back is killing me," said Sara. "Two weeks in one position will kill anyone."

"Well, I have a tape recorder. If we set you up with the tape in front of you, do you think you can tell us what we need to know?" asked Dr. Stevenson.

"Yes, just get my legs over the side," said Sara.

Dr. Stevenson sat Sara up. She told them everything she knew, then the doctors asked her questions and she answered them. One time she got reluctant, when the same question was asked twice. "I told you I wasn't stupid, you asked me that question before. You may have rephrased it, but it's the same fucking question. The answer to question twenty is the same answer to question ten. I told you I will not answer the same question twice. Don't you dare treat me like an idiot. You act just like the press, say the same thing over and over, only it's phrased different. So if you try it again, I will say no comment to you. That way, you will understand I've already answered the question. You want to act stupid, I'll treat you stupid," said Sara.

A half hour after Dr. Stevenson walked in Sara's room, he turned the tape recorder off. "You seem as smart as I figured you would be," said Dr. Stevenson.

"How's your leg feel now?" asked Dr. Emerson.

"Yes, a lot better; my lower back still aches. A back rub will help a lot."

"What's taking them so long?" asked Susan.

"I don't know," said John worried.

Susan moved. She heard a noise, a commotion. "Oh my God." John looked quick. "You can't miss this look," said Susan. John turned and looked down the hallway. He smiled and nodded to Sean. Sean looked. "Holy shit." Laura looked up, she started crying. Walking toward them was John: Black jeans, white T-shirt, black cowboy boots, long, black hair moving as he walked toward John, Susan, Sean, and Laura. The nurses were swooning behind him. He stopped in front of Sean. "She had her fireworks, but I doubt she's ready for this," laughed John.

"How the hell did this happen?" asked Sean.

"Well, I woke up in the cabin this morning, Sara was gone. The next thing I know, these two over here came in the cabin and took me to the home we built. I'm told a million things. I'm cleaned up, brought here. How's Sara doing?" asked John.

"We don't know, the doctors are with her," said John.

"Well, I want you to know daddy's home. That your grandmother and grandfather told me to tell you they love you and are very proud of you. And I'm here to tell you there are going to be some big changes," said John.

Susan ran over and hugged John. John hugged his father. John and Susan cried. "God, Mom's finally going to be happy," said John.

Laura shook her head. "This is unbelievable," said Laura. Hot tears ran down her cheeks.

John hugged his children, nodded to Brian. Brian went into Sara's room, whispered to Dr. Stevenson. Dr. Stevenson nodded and Brian left.

"Who's that?" asked Sara.

"You better lie down," said Dr. Stevenson. Dr. Emerson smiled. "We have something to tell you, and you will be shocked."

"Are my children okay?" asked Sara.

"This time you shut up and listen," said Dr. Emerson. "We had to make a few changes in your life. I guess you would call this a debriefing," said Dr. Emerson.

"Changes?" asked Sara.

"Well, we know you know Tom arranged to have you killed. We know Tom is dead. We know you married John Red Feathers Green. We know you were given a chance at life no one ever gets, so we had to make some changes. John's their father. Tom was never your husband. John's your husband. Tom's the man who tried to kill you," said Dr. Stevenson. "There's been a lot of work here to make you John's wife."

"Why?" asked Sara. "John was a dream, and it's apparent I talk in my sleep."

"Sara, John came back with you. He's here and he's your husband," said Dr. Emerson.

"Okay, I'm still dreaming," said Sara.

"John come here," called Dr. Stevenson.

John stepped in the doorway. Sara looked, blinked, looked again. "John!" said Sara.

"Some fireworks," smiled John as he walked toward Sara.

"John!" Sara was shocked.

"Yes, Sara, I'm real. You really want six kids or just to come to my fort to play?"

"John!" cried Sara. "You came back with me." Hot tears ran down her cheeks.

"I told you I'd be here when you woke up," smiled John. "Do you still want me to be your husband?" asked John.

"Yes, oh God yes, forever," cried Sara, holding out her arms. John sat on the bed and held Sara while she cried on his shoulder. "My God, you're real." Sara ran her hands across John's chest. "How?"

"Spoken like a true Indian," laughed John.

"Still want to divorce your husband?" asked Dr. Emerson.

"No way," laughed Sara. "This one's not getting away."

"This is highly irregular, and normally we wouldn't do this, but John assures us that if we send you home with him today, that you will stay in bed at least a week. We will come to your house daily to check on you. I wouldn't want to be the one to interfere with your honeymoon. Just go easy on this guy. I understand you wore him out," laughed Dr. Emerson. "He assures me he's hired a maid and cook so you don't do anything till we say you can, understand?"

"Yes, can I have sex?" asked Sara.

"Yes, if you're careful. I'd say don't get pregnant right away, but from what John says, it may be too late." laughed Dr. Emerson.

"Well, I guess we made love enough," said Sara.

"What do you mean?" asked John.

"Remember I said for every orgasm I had I erased one bad thing here? Well, we did one hell of a job. We wiped the slate clean," laughed Sara.

"Well, we'll leave you two alone," said Dr. Stevenson. "When you're ready, let us know. You still have a few minutes." Dr. Emerson and Dr. Stevenson left and walked out into the hallway.

John looked at Dr. Stevenson. "You knew, that's why you had Mom gussied up. You've known all along. How? We never said anything to anyone," asked John.

"Ben Green was my great-great-grandfather. I grew up with the legend of this time, the stories. It's been handed down generation to generation. After John and Sara wed, Ben and Summer had another grandson. My grandmother's name was Sara. My grandmother had two children, a son named Sean and a daughter named Susan. Susan's my mother. The nation has gone through a lot of things, but nothing ever changed our lives like Sean and Sara did for us; they changed our lives so we changed theirs," said Dr. Stevenson.

"What do you mean changed their lives?" asked John,

"Since John is really nonexistent in this life, we had to make him exist, so John is legally your father, legally Sara's husband. The man who used to be your father is just a man who became infatuated with your mother. When she paid no attention to him, he tried to have her killed. Your father has been erased. John is your father, so he should have the right to his children."

"The press, the news, everyone thinks that Tom was my father," said John.

"Yes, they do and we're going to use that to our advantage. We're going to prove that Tom was so infatuated with Sara, he stalked her for years. Your father never brought anyone to the house. He never took her where they were seen together. Anyone who was at their wedding has long since passed on. And the beauty of this is Tom was so infatuated with your mother, he led everyone to believe they were married and signed everything over to your mother so she still gets to keep all the insurance money. Tom's sister agreed to all of this and took a large amount of money to back up the whole story. Tom's lover ratted him out when she found out Tom was never married and could have married her all along. The man who shot Tom isn't dead. It was a debt paid, a Mr. Ely Smith's great-great-grandson. Seems Sean and Sara turned the man's life around, and they've always wanted to repay your mother. I think we used the name Smithers and he was brought here. We were attending physicians. We pronounced Mr. Smithers dead and Mr. Smith went home. The paper should be interesting reading tonight. We gave them one hell of a story," laughed Dr. Stevenson.

"We? You knew about this all along?" asked John, looking at Dr. Emerson.

"Please don't take this wrong. When Eric came to me a couple months back with this bizarre story, I told him he was crazy. Then he showed me your mother's diary and wedding pictures. You're the spitting image of your father. I still had a hard time believing him, but I went along with him. The nation's police got to your mother's house one minute after she was shot. They tried to get there before, but your mother was off on the time. It seems the clock in your house was set ten minutes ahead. Your mother would have died. Sean took the first bullet by diving in front of her. The others were ricocheted off the floor in the garage. The nation arrested the two men. The ambulance brought your mother here. We already knew what injuries your mother had, so we wasted no time in surgery. By all rights, your mother should be dead. In the course of changing already what happened, we were able to save her so she could have a happy life. I really never knew your mother was being abused.

That's being changed as we speak. All the women in my office are being screened as we speak," said Dr. Stevenson.

"So you're telling me that if you hadn't changed what happened that day, that my mother died?" asked John.

"Yes, she did. We didn't know a bone fragment had cut an artery. Eric sent the paperwork back in time through the chest. He gave it to Brian. Brian sent it through, and we got it back the day before. If your mother had remembered the clocks were ten minutes ahead of time, she wouldn't be there at all. Ben kept everything sent through to him; it was passed down, so we knew what to do," said Dr. Stevenson.

"Mom," said Susan, clearing her throat, "always set the clocks ten minutes ahead, because Dad, or Tom, was always ten minutes late. She probably got so used to it that she didn't think about it. What happens now?"

"Well," paused Dr. Stevenson. "We're sending Sean and Sara home. Sara has to stay in bed a week. John's hired a maid and a cook. You all will go to your new homes. John, your household goods came yesterday. Your house is set up. We're flying your wife and kids in. They will be here for supper. Laura, your household goods have all been moved. Your husband and children will be there when you get home. Sean, Laura, the same for your children and their children; they will be home for supper. Sean, you can't do anything for about six weeks."

"New homes?" questioned Sean.

"Sean, you ain't going to believe it, so we better show you," laughed John.

"One other thing: Your mother is a newlywed woman. Give her some room, if you know what I mean," said Dr. Stevenson. "What is this thing about fireworks?"

Sean laughed and told the whole story.

"We've got to get them some fireworks for tonight," laughed Susan.

Brian laughed. "It's been done."

"Well, when you're ready you can go. The limos are ready," said Dr. Stevenson.

"Limos?" asked Sean.

"Let's get you dressed and home, then we can talk about it on the way. There's been a few changes."

"I guess the only thing left is what's for supper," said Susan.

"Oh, we forgot, you're all going to John and Sara's house for supper. You talk, eat, and enjoy," said Dr. Emerson. "At 6:00."

"Dr. Emerson, I think that all of us have something else on our minds right now," said John.

"What's that?" asked Dr. Emerson.

"Our spouses; it's been so long, almost a year for Sean," laughed John.

"Oh, I'll tell you all what I told your mother, but in your mother's case I think it's too late," smiled Dr. Emerson.

"Don't get pregnant," laughed Dr. Emerson.

Sean and Laura looked at each other, then at John and Susan.

"That's why she's been looking like that?" asked John.

"I'm afraid so, we assumed that you knew because you kept saying she looked so beautiful. We told the press she was pregnant and the baby's fine," said Dr. Emerson.

"A boy or a girl?" asked Susan.

"Too soon to tell. Give us a couple of months, but as they say, the rabbit died," laughed Dr. Emerson. "John and Sara want six children."

"Six more kids?" asked Susan shocked. "Isn't she too old to be having children?"

Dr. Emerson looked at John and Susan. "You haven't figured it out yet?" he asked.

"Figured what out?" asked John.

"When John came back with your mother, your mother turned the age she was when they got married. Your mother was given a new life," said Dr. Emerson. "That's why she healed so quickly. I thought you two had it all figured out. You did so well with everything else."

"Our mother is younger than us?" asked John.

"Not on paper; paper she's still fifty, but yes, your mother's younger than you," said Dr. Emerson. "She went back in time at fifty, but when she came forward, she came with John, so she stayed the same age she was when she married John. I don't know how it works, it's an Indian thing. Eric has tried to explain. I gave up trying to understand legends. Prophecy and that stuff is way out of my league. I just know facts. Fact is, your mother's test says she is twenty. Any questions?" asked Dr. Emerson.

"You've got about twenty minutes to get out of here before the press is here. My advice is to leave now," said Dr. Stevenson.

"And I thought the 1800s were strange," said Sean to Laura as he dressed. "New homes, limos, younger ages, not to mention Sara bringing a husband back," said Sean.

"You don't like me being here?" asked John.

"I don't mind you being here, it's just strange. Sara kept saying that she was dreaming in the 1800s, to me it made sense. Now we're back in 1997, and now I feel like I'm dreaming. And to Sara it makes sense. I don't know, I'm confused," said Sean.

"Don't worry, tonight at our house our tribal leader will be there to explain everything and answer all questions. We just can't tire Sara out."

"Didn't take you long to get her pregnant," said Sean.

"I tried not to, but the woman is relentless," laughed John. "You told me to go slow and, believe me, I did, but when I unleashed the woman in her, I unleashed a lot. Dr. Emerson told me it's not normal for a woman to act like that, that she will calm down," said John.

"You talked to Dr. Emerson about it?" asked Sean.

"I had to, he asked me if I felt all right or if I hurt anywhere, so I told him how I hurt in certain areas of my body. We made love for twelve hours. There were two quick showers, and a quick bite to eat. She fed me while we made love. I wasn't allowed to stop," said John.

"Twelve hours, are you fucking nuts?" asked Sean.

"Well, if I knew I was coming with Sara, I could have paced myself a little better," said John. "It's pretty tough when you know you have to cram a lifetime of love into one night. The sad part is, Sara's already talking about tonight."

Sean tried to tie his shoes with one hand. John walked over to Sean and tied his shoes.

"So what does Dr. Emerson say?" asked Sean. "Thank you."

"He gave me something for soreness and told Sara to go easy on me," said John.

"Think it will help?" asked Sean, trying to button his shirt. John buttoned it for him.

"The soreness is gone. As for Sara going easy on me, I doubt it. She still can't believe I'm here," said John.

"I went through all this, too. I can't believe you're here. I'm glad I didn't have to leave my best friend behind. I'm glad Sara finally is happy, but all this talk of sex and it's been a little long for me. I want to go home and be with my wife for a while," smiled Sean. "That is all that's on my mind right now. Let's get out of here. The press is coming," said Sean.

John opened the door; the wheelchair sat at the door. "No way, I'm not riding in one of those," said Sean.

"Thought you would say that," said John, picking Sean up and sitting him in the chair. "Hospital policy. No time to argue, the press in on the way. Laura's signing you out. Susan's signing Sara out. We're wheeling you two out of here," said John.

"Holy shit!" cried Sean when he saw the stretch limo. Sean slid in the limo smoothly, feeling the leather and velvet as he slid. John handed Sara to John and he set her down gently. John pushed the wheelchairs back inside to the nurses. Susan and Laura ran out, and got in the limo. "The press is here, go," said Susan. Brian drove away so smoothly.

Sara watched out the window as they drove by. "It looks the same but somehow different," said Sara. "This isn't the way home."

"Yes it is, Mother. Brian likes to circle around a bit to make sure no one's following us," said John. "You know how the press can be."

"Oh, yes I do. I'm sure there's a reason for everything," said Sara.

John put his arm around Sara. "You sound tired," said John.

"A little, my back aches from lying in one position," said Sara.

"Where, here?" asked John, rubbing the small of her back.

"Oh God, that feels so good," said Sara, closing her eyes.

John kept rubbing Sara's back. She leaned on him. He still smelled the same; he felt the same. She closed her eyes and snuggled into him. If this was a dream, she didn't want to wake up. Her hand held John's black leather coat lapel. He felt so strong and secure to her. She dozed.

"Mother, we're home," Susan said gently.

"Huh, oh home, yes," said Sara, sitting up. "I don't live here," said Sara.

"Yes you do. This is our home. Recognize anything?" Sara looked around.

"Oh my God, this is it, this what we had worked so hard at. Sean, look, it's the same." Sean only stared with his mouth open.

"Ben saved it for us," said John.

Sara cried. She couldn't stop; she cried so hard she shook.

"We didn't get to live in our home then, but it's here for us now," said John. "We're home." John got out, picked Sara up and walked up the stairs, carrying her over the threshold. The whole place was decorated for Christmas. John, Susan, Laura, and Sean followed. John sat Sara on the sofa, sobs racking her body. John sat next to her.

"Hey John, remember when we did this?" said Sean, rubbing the date carved in the wood.

"Sure do, my friend. Nobody but us knew why we did that," smiled John.

"I can't believe Ben kept this place," said Sean.

"Sean, Ben kept it all just the way it was. You and Sara still own all this: the land, the houses, it's all yours, just the way you left it untouched by the outside world. It was Ben's way of saying thank you. You and Laura live in Jacob and Susan's house. John and Susan have those homes you designed. It's all here. The barn in still the same with a home on each side," said John.

"Ben didn't have to do this," said Sean.

"I know, but Dad loved Sara so much he wanted to give her the only thing she ever wanted: a small piece of the world untouched by man. The trees, the berries, it's all here. Ben named this place Sara's Garden. You two have one hell of a business, rightfully named, "Princess." It has Sara's picture as a symbol," said John.

"We what?" said Sean.

"Let's get you home," said Laura. "I'll explain, we all can talk later. We're rich, very rich, so fucking rich we're richer than the rich," said Laura. "Let's go, let Sara get some rest." Laura started pushing everyone out the door.

"But I don't understand," said Sean.

"Go," said Laura. "Bye, get some rest." She closed the door.

"You want to get some rest?" asked John.

"No! I want you to make love to me. I want to know this isn't a dream. I need you to touch me, make me feel alive," said Sara.

"Where here? No here?" teased John. He stood up, leaned over, picked Sara up, and carried her to the bedroom. They made love and fell asleep. John woke to darkness. He looked at the clock. 5:00 P.M. "Shit!" yelled John. He jumped out of bed and took a quick shower and dressed.

"Sara, Sara honey. The kids will be here shortly. Time to get up," said John.

"Not until I get a kiss," teased Sara.

"Oh, no you don't. I'm not getting near the bed. I know what you want, and it's going to wait. Your kids need to see you. You'll have me the rest of your life," said John.

"You're right, I'm being a rotten mother," said Sara.

"No you're a woman with an appetite I can't fill right now. Somebody's here," said John going to the door. "Hi," smiled John. "Sara the caterers are here honey," yelled John.

"Shit!" said Sara. "John, I need a hand here," yelled Sara.

"Kitchen's in there," said John, pointing. "My wife just got out of the hospital. She has a cast, she can't get around too well. I'll be right back." John ran back to the bedroom. Sara had the cast off. "Help me into the tub so I can shower," said Sara.

"Are you sure you should?" asked John.

"Yes, soft casts are only on with an Ace bandage. I need a shower," said Sara.

John carried Sara to the bathroom and set her on the toilet, turned the shower on and helped her in the shower, then ran into the bedroom and made the bed. "Sara, you want a nightgown or clothes?" asked John.

"I'd love a nightgown, but I better wear clothes," said Sara.

John took a nightgown out. She'd be on the couch anyway. John went in the bathroom when he heard the water shut off. He helped Sara out of the shower. "I got you a nightgown, you'll be lying on the couch anyway," said John.

"I don't think it's proper, John," said Sara, wrapping her hair in a towel.

"We'll tell them you can't get your clothes over your cast," said John.

"Yes, we could, that would work," said Sara, putting on her nightgown.

"This is one of the nightgowns I sent back." Sara started feeling the material. John picked her up.

"Later, let's get the cast on," said John, setting her on the bed. Sara brushed her hair. John put the cast on. Sara explained to John how to do it. When he came to the end of the roll, there were three clasps. "What are these?" asked John.

Sara giggled. "They're clasps, they work like this." Sara fastened them. John watched, shaking his head. "Yes." He put Sara's bathrobe on, it was a pink chenille, then carried her to the living room and set her on the couch, ran to the kitchen, checked things, then ran into the bedroom and picked up the bathroom. He quickly took a pillow and quilt out of the hall closet, ran back to the living room, and covered Sara. He made her comfortable and just sat in the chair when the door busted open.

"Grandma, grandma," yelled four little kids as they ran into the living room. They all ran to Sara for their hugs. Sara hugged and kissed them all. John Jr. spoke first; he always did.

"My Daddy said some bad man tried to hurt my grandma, and the law got him and shot'em dead, pow, pow." John's sister Nicole stood next to him nodding her head yes, pow, pow.

John walked in the room laughing. "That's not quite how we explained it, now is it John? This is John III." Two of Sara's grandchildren will start school next year, Rachel and John.

Rachel leaned into Sara's face. "Is that my grandpa?" she asked.

"John Jr., Nicole, Rachel, and Ted Jr., this is your grandfather, John Green."

"Grandpa," they yelled and ran over to him. John laughed as they climbed in his lap.

"My Daddy says you're a real injun and we're real injuns, and you saved my grandma," said John Jr. Three little kids shook their heads "yes" as John III talked away to John. "Shoot any cowboys?" asked John III.

John laughed. "No, but I punched one right in the nose once," said John.

"Wow!" came the response.

"My grandpa's a hero, just like the Ninja Turtles," said Ted Jr.

Nicole kissed John's cheek. "Will you save me some day?" she asked.

"I'd save all of my babies," said John, hugging them all.

John Jr. laughed. "Okay you guys, give Grandma and Grandpa a break, okay?"

"Ah, Dad, he's an injun, he can tell us lots of stories on cowboys."

"Later," said John. "I told you they both have been on a long journey and will be tired."

"Injun," nodded Nicole.

"How about this?" said John. "Every day for the rest of your lives, you come and see Grandpa and I'll tell you a story every day for one hour."

"Yeah!" yelled the kids. They climbed down after kissing John.

They went to Sara. "Where are the toys?" asked Rachel.

"Honey, I don't know yet. Maybe Uncle John knows."

"We brought coloring books and crayons for them," said John. "Something quiet."

"You really don't expect those four to be quiet, do you?" laughed Sara.

"No, but Santa Claus is watching," smiled John.

"Okay kids, to the kitchen to color pictures for Santa Claus.'

"Yea Santa," yelled the kids following Susan.

"How you feeling, Mom?" asked John, sitting down in a chair.

"Well, body-wise I feel good, my backache is gone; mind-wise I think I'm still dreaming," said Sara.

"Well, I was going to tell you I love you, and that I've been an ass-hole for a son, but if you're still dreaming you won't believe me," said John, laughed.

"Honey, I know you love me, and you were never a bad son," said Sara.

"You don't know how close I came to writing you and telling you to stay where you were. You loved John so much, and you were finally happy. I didn't want you hurt anymore," said John. "Nobody knew John was coming back with you. I just wanted you to be happy," said John.

"That's so sweet, but what made you think I wouldn't want to be with my children?" asked Sara.

"Mom, we're not exactly the Brady Bunch here. We took and took from you. We never gave you a thing, now all this, this is unreal," said John.

"John, you kids gave me a lot; you made me laugh. I watched you grow into fine adults, you gave me grandchildren. What else is there?" asked Sara.

John looked around the room. "If I knew Tom was doing what he was doing, I would have killed the fucker," said John.

"I know," said Sara. "But you have to understand, I didn't know it was abuse. We started out that way, and I didn't know that it wasn't right. I trusted him. He was my husband. I thought he knew what was right. So let it go, it's in the past. I'm married to the right man now. I have a second chance," smiled Sara.

John shook his head. "All I can say is God loves you, and he gave you one hell of a second chance," said John.

"Yes, he did, and I'm not wasting one second of it," said Sara. "I'm living."

John laughed. "We were thinking of ways to keep you happy when you got back to help you through being hurt. When you came back, you came with a vengeance," laughed John.

"Have you ever known me to do otherwise?" laughed Sara.

"No, but this one sure is a kicker, Mom," laughed John.

"Coffee?" asked Susan, carrying a tray.

John remained silent. He felt his son handled it real well. "Where's Sean?" asked John.

"They are running a little late; the kids just got there. The driver ran into a snowstorm. Sean said about fifteen minutes," said John.

"Dad, if I asked you something personal, would you tell me the truth?" asked Susan.

"If I can," said John.

"Is it true Mom made you make love to her for twelve hours?" asked Susan.

"Susan!" said Sara. "Forgive her, John, she has my boldness."

"Yes," laughed John. "The cast has slowed her down a bit." He winked at the kids smiling.

"John, the kids don't need to know these things," said Sara, blushing.

"Why not, you almost killed me. They have a right to know you almost killed their father," teased John, smiling.

"You think that night was bad, wait until the cast comes off," teased Sara.

"Why, Mother, you made a joke and teased at the same time. I swear you're a changed woman," teased Susan. "Whatever did you do to her, John?"

"I made her a woman, my woman," said John in a deep voice, hitting his chest.

Everyone was laughing when Sean and Laura came in. "I'm afraid the trip did them in. They're sleeping," said Laura.

"Bedroom to the right has twin beds," said Susan.

"Thanks," said Laura.

"How did you know that?" asked Sara. "I don't even know what's here yet."

"Mom, I'm the only business in town that goes to the homes and decorates, remember?" smiled Susan.

"You did this?" asked Sara.

"Yeah, I think it turned out pretty nice myself," said Susan.

"I love the raffia with the red bows on the staircase, that is really nice," said Sara. "What made you think of that?"

"Wings, the TV program. You know how we taped Christmas to get ideas? That was there, and I fell in love with the idea of it," said Susan.

"I love everything. What I can't figure out is why the tree is covered," said Sara.

"You always make such a fuss over the tree, that I figured I'd wait until we all got together, then reveal it for everyone to see," said Susan.

"Well, we're here, so let's see," said Sara.

"I should have warned you, it's different. It is not what you're used to. Come on guys, I'll put the lights in, then you take the sheet off," said Susan. "Okay, on three. One, two, three." John and John took the sheet off and let it fall to the floor. A little bit of the tree showed as the sheet fell.

"Oh Susan, it's beautiful. It's the most beautiful thing I've ever seen. Where did you get such beautiful decorations?" Sara threw the quilt back and hobbled to the tree.

"Sara, you're not to be walking," said John.

"Mom doesn't hear you," teased Susan. "When it comes to a tree, there is nothing else."

"Look at these beautiful ornaments, where did you find them?" asked Sara.

"They found me," said Susan.

"How do decorations find you?" asked Sara.

"After you left, Susan would buy you ornaments for your Christmas tree. The Indians kept them safe and sound. The nation would add something to it every year. Susan lived into her eighties, and every year she bought you an angel. Some of these are worth a lot of money today. Their was a note inside. It had your name on it. I put it on the tree here," said Susan.

Sara took the note. "Back to the couch," said John, picking her up and carrying her to the couch.

The letter was yellowed and frail, so Sara opened it slowly. Read it aloud.

"Dear Sara: I still think you were an angel. I know you didn't like it, so I never said it again. So every year of my life, I will buy you an angel for Christmas. It makes me feel like a little part of you is here somehow. We know that John went back with you. I hope that this Christmas is your best ever. I do believe in Santa Claus. Love, Susan."

Hot tears stung Sara's eyes. "Sh...sh...she never forgot me," said Sara.

"No, after you left she had a girl, she named her Sara," said Susan. "Her nickname was Angel."

"Oh Susan, you made my Christmas," said Sara, looking up.

Everyone in the room wiped at tears. "What a Christmas," said Laura.

"It can't get any better than this," said Sara.

"I don't know," said John, smiling. "There's Santa Claus!"

"What's that supposed to mean. You're not planning any surprises; I hate surprises," said Sara.

"You say that but you don't mean it," said John.

"Yes I do," said Sara.

"Oh yeah, then why did you bring Dad back? I think that constitutes as a major surprise," said John.

"Oh, that little thing, that was nothing," teased Sara.

"What, Sara, our Sara joking?" teased Sean.

"Amazing ain't it?" laughed John.

Sara smiled.

"Oh my God, is that a smile I see; not on our Sara's face," teased Sean.

"Don't start, you guys," teased Sara.

"My God, John, she's a changed woman. It only took you twelve hours," laughed Sean.

Sara threw her pillow at him. He ducked. Everyone laughed.

"Throwing pillows wasn't on the list of things to do," said Dr. Stevenson, walking in and getting the pillow in the face.

"She likes to throw things," teased Sean. "A little habit she picked up in the 1800s."

"I know times were rough back then, but what enemies could you kill with a pillow?" laughed Dr. Stevenson.

"Ones with big mouths," said Sara, looking at Sean.

"Oh, I see, stuff the pillow in their mouth. That might work," laughed Dr. Stevenson. "I'm a little bit surprised to see you following my orders. I expected to see you running around doing things."

"Give me a day," said Sara.

"Wow, right to the heart with that one, took direct aim," said Dr. Stevenson.

"I'm a good shot," said Sara.

"Fireworks yes; pillows no," said Dr. Stevenson, handing Sara the pillow.

"Sorry," said Sara. "Sean deserved it."

"Well, I would say it's safe to assume you're feeling better?" asked Dr. Stevenson.

"Yes. How come you have an English accent?" asked Sara.

"English nanny forced on me as a child by my mother, who was English," said Dr. Stevenson. "How come you're so direct?"

"It's the only way to get an answer," said Susan. "Why beat around the bush? Say what you mean and be done with it."

"Aren't you afraid you might hurt someone's feelings?" asked Dr. Stevenson.

"No, if they want me to know, they will tell me. I can't see sugar-coating it; it's still the same question, still goes in the brain the same way," said Sara.

"I'm afraid you're right. No matter how much sugar you put in medicine, it's still medicine," said Dr. Stevenson.

"Exactly," said Sara.

"I'm here to check on Sara and to explain as much as I can. Now you must understand, I don't expect you to believe one word I say because it's been an Indian legend for years. I know John stands here with us now, but this is still going to be hard to swallow. As Sara says, sugar-coating won't make it any easier to digest, so I'll explain the legend. Any questions, I'll answer after." So Eric explained how a nation of people faced with extinction and a princess would come to save them. She would take the chief as a husband. They would go on a long journey, never to return. This journey would lead them to another time, to once again help the nation. That time is the year the white buffalo was born; this year the white buffalo was born. And now they're here. "Any questions?" asked Dr. Stevenson.

"John wasn't chief, Ben was," said Sara. "So what happens now?"

"I was the chief," said John. "Ben took over when he knew we were to wed. Now I know why. He knew I was coming here, that's why you had to teach me all the things you knew."

"That's what he meant by the speech he gave you about journeys on your wedding day. He knew you were going with Sara," said Sean.

"But what good can I do here? I know nothing of their ways," said John.

"See, that's why you're here. We're losing a lot of the old ways, you must help us to keep them. You will teach us what was lost," said Dr. Stevenson.

"Does John stay with me or do they take him back?" asked Sara.

"He stays here forever with you," said Dr. Stevenson.

"How did you get here?" asked Sara.

"That's a good question. The cabin was blessed and incantations said in the cabin, it was purified and free of spirits, only two pure spirits could enter the cabin, you and John. All the decorations you made were of the purest herbs and flowers that the nation had to offer, the spirit guide who brought you here. The second John took you as his wife, meaning your virginity, your blood fell on him, making you both one, so you traveled as one here. It's a little hard to swallow right now, but that's the way it had to be done, on holy ground," said Dr. Stevenson.

"But what do I have to do now?" asked Sara.

"You've already done it. You conceived on holy ground with the union of two souls being one. You will give birth to John's children. From this will come many good leaders for our nation, starting with John here," said Dr. Stevenson.

"Me?" said John. "I don't know about me, I'm really good at screwing things up."

"You only think you do, you're a lot smarter than you give yourself credit for. Look at how fast you two figured this all out. That's why John and Sara could get married so soon. We thought we'd have to send someone to show you, but you two were way ahead of us. Our translation was poor, but you did well," said Dr. Stevenson.

"It was Sara and Laura who did it," said John. "Not me."

"It doesn't matter who did what, you three worked together and did what was in the legend long before we figured it out," said Dr. Stevenson.

"Let me get this straight," said Sara. "My only participation in this whole thing is to have sex with John, bear his children?" said Sara.

"Yes, that's all," said Dr. Stevenson.

"There is good after all," said Sara.

"Mother!" cried John and Susan.

John shrugged his shoulders and said, "Fireworks."

"I understand there was thunder and lightning, too," laughed Sean.

Sara threw the pillow and hit Sean in the head.

"Gotcha," laughed Sara.

Everyone laughed.

"Legend tells us the thunder and lightning was God's accepting the union of these two. The rain was the purification of conception. And it was the only spot where it thundered and lightninged in the whole world. It's a lot to believe, but legends have their times," said Dr. Stevenson. "Any more questions?"

"Why'd I go?" asked Sean. "I don't even know how I got back."

"That's the part of this legend we couldn't figure out. You weren't supposed to go, only Sara, but like John, when you dove in front of Sara, the bullet passed through you into Sara. Your blood and her blood became one. When she passed on, she took you with her. It worked out for the best because you got everything going in the right direction. You corrected a lot of mistakes that were made while Sara was down with fever. You did a lot before Sara had any idea what was going on. You saved us years of work," said Dr. Stevenson.

"When John made Sara a woman, you passed out and hit your head. You came back first. We didn't check on John until later. I think we scared the shit out of him, but he came along. We explained to him what happened up to the point we picked him up. We brought him here, he cleaned up, and put the clothes on him that Sara wanted to see him in. Two things we weren't sure of were hat size and the leather coat. We picked a long one because it's in style. We figured if he dressed the way Sara said, it would be less frightening. We asked John a lot of questions, but all he wanted was Sara. He had to see for himself that they were really here together, so he went to the hospital and saw you guys first, then Sara."

"What happened to the real Sean and Sara?" asked Sara.

"They woke up here in the cabin. Jacob sat the night with them. The story was told just as it should be. They stayed here about a month and left. They moved to Rome. Jacob, Susan, and the children ran this whole thing through the years. Jacob's children married into the nation. Sara had the baby that this Sara was worried about, at the correct time. Sara and Sean were killed in an accident. Jacob and Susan raised their son, who became a lawyer for the nation. Everything went just as you had written in the book, Sara," said Dr. Stevenson. "Our success is due to you and no one will ever know, only in stories, which no one will believe."

"No, the success is all yours. Your nation did all the work, all I did was write a few things down," said Sara.

"Dinner is served," said a man entering the living room.

"Great, I'm hungry," said Sara, throwing back the quilt and standing up.

"Where do you think you are going?" said John, picking Sara up.

"I'm hungry," said Sara.

"For what?" whispered John as he kissed Sara.

Sara smiled. "What you got, mister?"

"How about junk food?" laughed John.

"Nah. I like solid stuff," giggled Sara.

"That's dessert," teased John as he sat Sara at the table.

"What would you like to start with?" asked Susan.

"Dessert," said Sara.

"Mother! I know what you're talking about. Now if you were like any one of us, you would have grabbed a little dessert before we got here," laughed Susan.

"I did, now I want more," said Sara.

"Well, we better hurry up and eat so we all can get some more dessert," teased Susan.

"Why, Susan, you're teasing your mother. You know it's not nice to tease Mother Nature," teased Sara.

Everyone laughed. "Got to hand it to you John, I didn't think the day would come that Sara would be this happy," said Sean.

Sara smiled. "I have a real good reason to smile, a huge reason," said Sara.

"Sara," said John. "You promised never to say anything."

Everyone started laughing. Sean spit coffee on the table.

"I was talking about us finally being a family. Besides, I didn't say anything, you did," said Sara.

"Oh," said John. "I'm new to this kind of talk. This is what you meant when something could mean two things?" asked John.

"Yes," said Sara.

"Please forgive me. I still need to learn some things," said John.

"Not much," said Sara.

Everyone laughed. "Dad, Mom's egging you on. It's better to let it go before you really hang yourself here," said John.

"Why would I hang myself?" asked John.

"It's a phrase meaning that the more you say, Mom will make you say more until you embarrass yourself on your own words," said John.

"I see, if I don't understand, then don't say anything," said John.

"Exactly," said John. "Mom was never like this, so we all have to get used to it. Mom always kind of barked at everyone before, mean, bad, no money," teased John.

"Oh, so that's why she likes barking orders, she's a dog?" said John.

Everyone starting coughing. Sara turned bright red.

"That's one I should have said nothing to, right?" asked John.

"By the look on Mother's face, I'd say yes," said John, laughing.

"My God, John, what did you two do in that cabin?" asked Sean.

"Everything," said John, taking a bite of food.

Sara was so red she was turning purple. Dr. Stevenson couldn't stop laughing.

"I don't want to know," said Sean. "We'll drop it there. We'll talk later on how men should talk. John and I will teach you when it's proper to say things and when it's not okay to say things," said Sean.

"Okay." said John as innocent as a baby with what he'd spoken. He felt no embarrassment whatsoever. He had no knowledge of what he'd said. Sara wanted to crawl somewhere and die. Dr. Stevenson was still laughing. Laura and Susan were glad the children were in the kitchen eating.

"I'm glad we're a family anyway," said Sara. "Now that everyone knows I have a stud for a husband, and I enjoy sex, maybe we can pick up and start over. I never want to hear about Tom again, ever. John's your father."

"Like father, like son," said Rachel, smiling.

John looked at Rachel. "Smiling kept you happy?" smiled John.

Rachel smiled. "Sure has."

"Okay, let's not start this again," said Sara.

"Why not?" asked Dr. Stevenson. "This is the best conversation I've ever had."

Susan looked at Ted. "Ted's pretty well endowed himself. We do want to make Dr. Stevenson's dinner something to remember," said Susan. "If Dad's comfortable talking about it, so am I," said Susan. "I was quite surprised on my honeymoon," said Susan.

"I looked at John, then at John Henry, I wanted to run," said Rachel. "He promised not to hurt me, but standing there nude scared me. Then I couldn't get enough of him after." "My mother told me on my honeymoon to expect a little prick. I looked at Sean and said, 'No way.' I didn't think something like that would fit," said Laura.

Sean, John, and Ted were bright red.

Dr. Stevenson was laughing again.

"You were all surprised on your honeymoon?" asked Sara.

"That's an understatement. We were scared," said Susan.

"I was so scared with John I thought sex was the way I had it before. Sean told me what sex was. I was so confused. Then John was so gentle with me, my fears went away. It was such pleasure, I couldn't get enough," said Sara.

"Us, too," said the girls.

"Sean made me relax. We enjoyed our first so much; I felt so much love for him, it was unreal," said Laura.

"Thank god, I thought there was something wrong with me when John took my virginity. It was like I couldn't love him enough at that moment. After that, I couldn't get enough. I thought I was a sex maniac," said Sara.

"No, we all felt that, so we must all have a loving husband," said Rachel.

"Thank you, girls, you've made me feel so much better. I was starting to feel guilty for the way I felt about John," said Sara.

"Never feel guilty about loving John, Mom. He's done so much for you. We've never seen you so happy. You need John; John needs you," said Susan.

"I won't. I just never knew something could be so beautiful. I may have overdone it on my honeymoon, but I wanted as much loving as I could get while I could. I didn't know John was coming back or I wouldn't have worn him out. I didn't even know when I was coming back. I thought that beautiful feeling we shared would have to last me a lifetime," said Sara.

"You two didn't know John was coming back either?" asked Dr. Stevenson.

"No," said Sean and Sara together.

"My God, you married a man you loved to save his people, thinking you were going to lose him?" asked Dr. Stevenson.

"Yes," said Sara.

"No wonder you were so confused," said Dr. Stevenson. "What you did goes beyond saying. You risked everything for our people. Unbelievable."

"Did I do something wrong?" asked Sara.

"No, I can't believe that as much as you loved John, you could walk away. That has got to be the most unselfish thing I've ever heard," said Dr. Stevenson.

Dishes were cleared from the table by caterers getting ready for dessert.

"I would consider it unselfish from my point of view. It was my only chance at knowing happiness. I loved John so much that having a little of him was better than having none at all. I couldn't spend the rest of my life knowing that I could have him and didn't. I fought it; God how I fought it. When he kicked the door in and stood there in the doorway, I knew I couldn't fight it any longer. He just stood there. I knew he was talking; I couldn't hear him. He just looked perfect to me at that moment. That moment I knew it was all right to love him. When he kissed me, I was happy. It was no longer my choice. When John took that step toward me, I knew he loved me as much as I loved him, that nothing in the world could stop how we felt about one another," said Sara.

"John, why did you kick the door down?" asked Dr. Stevenson.

"I knocked, she told me to go away. I got tired of Sara pushing me away, so I kicked the door down and took her in my arms and claimed her as mine. I knew she loved me from the kiss at the quarry, but she kept pushing me away. I heard Sara arguing with Sean. She said she loved me, but didn't know what to do, so I did what I thought I had to do," said John.

"Weren't you afraid she would run from you or tell you to leave?" asked Dr. Stevenson.

"She had nowhere to go, and I didn't give her time to talk. I kissed her. I wasn't going to take 'no' for an answer. I knew she loved me, that's all I needed to know," said John.

Dessert was served.

"What? I don't understand, Sara. If you loved John, why didn't you tell him?" asked Dr. Stevenson.

"Yeah, Mom, we would like to know that one," said John.

"Because Sara felt by loving John she'd hurt him," said Sean. "Love scared her, she never had it, never knew what it was, so when Sara fell in love, it scared her. She thought it was bad," said Sean.

No one said a word; they ate their dessert. The dishes were cleared, and coffee was poured.

"So love confused you," asked Dr. Stevenson.

"I thought I did something wrong. My body acted funny. I felt funny, so I thought I'd be a curse to the nation. You have to understand this is hard to explain. I couldn't accept I was in the 1800s. I couldn't accept I was beautiful. I couldn't accept that John could love me the way I look now, let alone love me at all. I never knew desire, I was so confused. One day I ran. I couldn't handle anymore. John came to find me. I begged him to make love to me. He turned me down, then the hope chest thing, it all just got to me," said Sara. "When I woke up here, I knew it was a dream. I was so hurt and alone I wanted to be left alone. Then John walked in and it all seemed right. You do have to admit I had a lot that needed explaining, and no one had any answers. This I never expected in a million years, and I hope not much more will be dumped in my lap right away. I need to get this right in my head first, going from dead to not dead, married, widowed, married, it's been a bumpy ride here. Let me enjoy my husband for a while with peace and quiet, then poor to rich, then old to young, I'll handle as I go along. There's only one question I have," asked Sara.

"What's that?" asked Dr. Stevenson.

"How far along am I?" asked Sara.

"We'll find out after Christmas. We're not sure if it's in the time period you were in or this one because one of our days equal two or three months your time. If its their time broken, a month. But you don't worry till the holidays are gone. Like you said, one thing at a time. If there's no more questions, I'm going home," said Dr. Stevenson. "Dr. Emerson will stop in tomorrow to check on you and Sean."

"I think we're all going. It's been a long day and sleep sounds good," said Sean.

"Yeah, the kids are up way past their bedtime, so they will be cranky," said John.

Everyone started moving. John carried Sara to the couch. She hugged and kissed some sleepy kids and said goodbye to everyone. The caterers cleaned and left. John started a fire in the fireplace, then turned all the lights out except the Christmas tree lights. They made love in front of the fireplace. Orange glows danced across their skin. "I love you, Sara." Then fireworks went off.

"Now what?" asked Sara.

"Looks like fireworks," said John.

"This time of year? Sean isn't going to let us forget this," said Sara.

John pulled his pants on. "I don't think Sean had anything to do with this," said John. "Look."

Sara put her nightgown on and sat up. They were pretty, so she stood up. There were hearts inside heart rings, bows, multicolored rainbows, a grand ending, then a sign lit up that said congratulations, and it was over. "The kids did this," said Sara.

"I think the nation did this. How about we go to bed and make our own fireworks?" said John.

"Sounds good to me." John carried Sara to bed, then turned the tree lights off and went to bed. Sara and John made love and fell asleep. Tomorrow they would start their new lives together.

John woke up to the smell of coffee. He looked at the clock, it read 9:30. Sara slept soundly, so John got up, showered, dressed, and followed the smell of coffee.

"Hi," said John.

"Oh, mother of God, you scared me. I'm Penny Chambers, your cook."

"John Green. Coffee smells good," said John.

"Would you like a cup, Mr. Green?" said Penny.

"Yes, call me John; my wife is not up yet," said John.

Penny poured a cup of coffee. "Poor thing needs her rest," said Penny, setting the coffee in front of John. He took a sip.

"Sara's not poor, she had a bad accident happen to her," said John.

Penny looked at John and laughed, "You're funny. You like to joke; we'll get along fine," said Penny.

John stared at Penny with a puzzled look, wondering what he said.

"You were not joking?" asked Penny.

"You must forgive me, I'm just learning English. I have a hard time understanding the meaning of things. Some words I get; it's just so many things are two-sided. You say one thing and mean another. I hope I didn't insult you," said John, sipping coffee.

"No, it's refreshing to find someone who says what they mean. I'm sixty-three years old and I grew up in a time when words meant something, so I understand your problem. Even I have a hard time understanding," said Penny. "I listen to my grandchildren talk. I have no idea at all as to what they're saying. I grew up with the English language, so you just learning it must be awful."

"My friend Sean and my son, John, have helped me with English. Now they are going to help me understand what is being said," laughed John. "I speak Onyato real well, my native tongue."

"Well, you speak English well," said Penny. "How many children do you have?" asked Penny.

"I have two children, John and Susan, four grandchildren, Ted, Rachel, John, and Nicole, and one on the way," said John.

"You look too young to have grandchildren," said Penny, pouring coffee.

"I feel too young to have grandchildren," said John. "Thank you."

"How is your wife doing? I read in the paper last night how that man stalked her for years, then hired someone to shoot her. She really went through a lot and never lost the baby. That baby is blessed by God," said Penny.

"Sara never wants that man's name mentioned in this house. She doesn't want anything mentioned about what happened at all. She wants to forget it. We moved in here yesterday. She'll never go back to the other house. We feel the baby is blessed by many gods. He's come a long journey," said John.

"Well, I don't blame her, and I'll never mention it. When is the baby due?" asked Penny.

"We're not sure. Dr. Stevenson will do tests after the holidays. He wants to get Sara back on her feet first. She's come a long way, but she's got a long way to go," said John.

"She'll be fine. She pulled through the tough part. Now the healing begins, and nothing helps healing like a new baby," said Penny. "Pick any name yet?"

"Ben if it's a boy; Summer if it's a girl," said Sara, walking in the kitchen.

"You shouldn't be walking," said John.

"No, I shouldn't be lying around. I'm already stir crazy," said Sara.

"Okay, we'll ask Dr. Stevenson what we can and can't do," said John. "This is Penny Chambers, the cook."

"Hi," said Sara.

"Hello, Mrs. Green," said Penny.

"Please call me Sara. I feel old enough without being called Mrs." laughed Sara.

"Yes, Sara," said Penny. "Want coffee?"

"Yes, please," said Sara.

"I like the names you picked for your baby," said Penny, pouring coffee. "I don't think you would want to go out today, it's nasty out there. A big storm is going to hit at about 3:00," said Penny.

"I want you home before the storm hits. I will pay you for the whole day. Don't worry, if it's still bad out tomorrow, don't come to work. I will pay you. So if the weather's bad, you're sick, anything like that, please don't think you'll lose a day's pay because you won't. John's a pretty good cook," said Sara. "You know, maybe we should see if we need anything before the storm hits. If we got snowed in, we should be prepared."

"Yes Sara, you want to check with me or should I do it?" asked Penny.

"I'm sure John wouldn't mind helping me to the kitchen. The breakfast nook is okay, but I like kitchens," said Sara.

"Me too," said Penny.

"Okay, I get what you're saying," teased John. "You need me to carry you to the kitchen."

"No, I need a hand walking to the kitchen," said Sara.

"No," said John. "You're not walking till Dr. Stevenson says so. What if you fell? You could break a leg, lose the baby. Do you want that? You would be in the hospital for a long time then," said John.

"Okay, carry me then," said Sara. "I won't argue."

John smiled. "I thought you would see it my way." He winked at Penny.

Penny smiled. "You have a lot of canned food, do you can a lot?" asked Penny.

"I can anything I get my hands on," said Sara. "What I can't can, I freeze."

"That is so unusual these days with the young folks," said Penny.

John set Sara on the island, she screamed. "John look, the stove, my stove, my wood stove. How did they get it here?"

"God, Sara don't do that," said John, sticking his finger in his ear. "You have to forgive us, we don't know what's been moved of ours yet. She screams every time she sees something. I know I'm deaf from it," smiled John.

"I understand," smiled Penny. "I was quite surprised to see this stove myself. I used the electric one, I hope that's all right," said Penny.

"My stove, " said Sara. "My stove."

"That's fine, Penny. Sara likes this one because she can bake so much in the oven, six pies or about twenty loaves of bread. Then if there's no power, she can cook and heat at the same time," said John, taking his finger out of his ear.

"That's a good idea. I live in the area, so I know the power's out all the time for one thing or another," said Penny.

"Where do you live?" asked Sara.

"A tiny apartment on Spring Road. My husband, Arnold, hates it. We pay about one hundred dollars a month plus utilities. He is retired, so he is bored. He can't do anything. But what are you going to do, Christmas is coming, no room for kids or grand kids," said Penny.

"Do you have a lot of grandchildren?" asked Sara.

"Eight and one on the way," smiled Penny.

"John, hand me the phone and that card Brian gave us," said Sara. "That is a lot of grandchildren. They need room to run and play, a place to stay over at grandma's," said Sara as she dialed the phone. "Your husband needs a garage and work shop. Hello, Brian, this is Sara."

"Yes, Sara how may I help you?" said Brian.

"I've got a couple things. Check with everyone here, make sure they are stocked up well for food, a big storm is coming our way. I'm making a list myself."

"Yes ma'am, will do," said Brian. "The second thing?"

"Is my house emptied out and cleaned?" asked Sara.

"Yes ma'am it is," said Brian.

"Okay, I want you to sell Penny Chambers my house for one dollar. I want her and her husband, Arnold, moved in before Christmas Eve. The shop is still set up, isn't it?

"Yes, the shop's still set up, but I don't think it's legal to sell the house for one dollar," said Brian.

"It's my house. If they won't let me sell it one dollar, then declare it as a Christmas present for my help. There's no closing cost, fees, taxes, nothing, and no moving charge. See what her lease reads and do what you have to. Get them into the house before Christmas Eve," said Sara.

"Yes ma'am," said Brian. "I'll come by for that list."

"Okay, Brian, thank you, you're a doll. Thanks for the fireworks too," laughed Sara.

"Oh my, Sara, we couldn't take your house," said Penny.

"Why not, I'm never going back. It has three bedrooms, a huge kitchen, the appliances are all there, including a washer and dryer, a sewing room, living room, two-and-one-half bathrooms, two-car garage, full cellar, workshop, pool, and two acres of land. My whole house is run electric with backup generators. The upstairs can be closed if you want. It cost $252 a month for electric and forty-eight dollars a month for phone. Taxes are eight hundred dollars a year for everything. I don't want it. I'll never go near it again, and it's only one mile down the road from where you live. It's everything you need for a family. I think the furniture is still there. I haven't come across anything of mine yet, except the stove. That was in storage. Insurance is two hundred fifty dollars a year. You have fruit trees, berries, and a garden."

John looked at Sara. He thought that stove had always been there. He and Sean put it in. This is one of those times he didn't understand, so he said nothing.

"But your home," said Penny.

"No it's not my home. This is my home right here. Would you rather it sat there and rotted away? It cost about $450 to $500 a month to pay for everything. Look what you're saving in money alone. Your husband can work in the shop out back. It's got all the tools for woodworking and a two-car garage; it's perfect for you."

"May I call Arnold and at least ask him? He's kind of funny. He'd feel left out if I didn't discuss it with him," said Penny.

"Sure. If he has any questions, I'll talk to him," said Sara. "We got any doughnuts?"

"Oh God, your breakfast," said Penny.

"It's okay. I need coffee, lots of coffee and doughnuts to wake up, then I can eat lunch," said Sara.

"Box of goodies in the refrigerator from some bakery," said John.

"Good, we'll eat those, make out the list, and we'll be all set," said Sara.

Penny called her husband and told him. He didn't believe her, so she handed the phone to Sara. Sara explained everything to Arnold, then told him she wasn't sure if it would cost one dollar or be free yet. Sara explained where the house was.

"I know the house, I drive by it all the time. I always wished I owned it, but this, this, are you sure you don't want it?" asked Arnold.

"Positive, plus you can be moved in before Christmas," said Sara, "at my expense."

"We have a contract here. I don't think they will let us break it," said Arnold.

"Don't worry about it, it's being handled," said Sara.

"Thank you, yes we accept," said Arnold.

"Great, want to talk to Penny?" asked Sara.

"Yes, please, thank you, thank you just doesn't seem enough," said Arnold.

"It's enough," said Sara, grabbing a third cream-filled doughnut. "Oh, I'm sending Penny home early. I don't want her traveling on bad roads. You make sure you check the weather before she comes to work," said Sara.

"Yes ma'am," said Arnold.

"I'm Sara, always call me Sara. I already feel too old for Mrs. or ma'am," laughed Sara. Sara handed the phone to Penny.

"That woman's a saint," said Arnold. "I accepted for both of us, I hope you don't mind," said Arnold. "Wait till I tell the kids. I got my dream house. I love you, bye." Arnold was so excited, he hung up.

Penny laughed. "I never saw him this excited," smiled Penny.

Sara reached for another doughnut. Penny stopped her. "Too much sugar for the baby. I'll fix something quick," said Penny.

"Sara loves cream-filled things and the raspberry ones. She eats them a lot," said John.

"Not anymore," said Penny. "I'll fix a western egg sandwich quick. Good for the baby, lots of protein."

"Protein's good. Can I have two sandwiches and the doughnuts?" smiled Sara.

"Sara, you really have picked up on that appetite," said John.

"Eating for six," said Sara.

"Six!" said John.

"Yeah, this baby and the other five I want," said Sara.

"No, you said six kids total; this is three," said John.

"Changed by mind, I want six starting with this one," laughed Sara.

"Do you know how old we'd be when they grew up?" asked John.

"About one hundred," laughed Sara. "We can do it."

Sara started writing her list. "This is all junk food," said John as he read the list.

"Of course, I already have the good stuff here," said Sara.

"How about some fresh fruit?" asked John

"That sounds good," said Sara, adding more sweets and fruits.

"Sara, that's too much goodies," said John.

"I know, but I'm craving this right now. It will pass," said Sara. "Soon I'll have morning sickness and won't be able to keep anything down, better eat while I can," said Sara. "With John I was sick for four months and had to take vitamin shots. I couldn't keep them down either," said Sara. "That was thirty years ago. You don't remember, I do. I couldn't smell food at all, so let me enjoy while I can," said Sara.

"Sara, that's a long time for morning sickness," said Penny.

"Tell me about it, those B-12 shots are horrible. I tried everything to stop it, nothing worked," said Sara.

"Here's your sandwiches; did you drink ginger tea?" asked Penny.

"I never heard of ginger tea," said Sara.

"I have some home. I shall bring it with me tomorrow. Keep it on hand. It calms the stomach from dry heaves, nausea, vomiting, it keeps you from dehydrating and supplies vitamins," said Penny. "That's all we used in my day."

"Sounds good to me," said Sara. "I lived in hell. You don't realize how many food places there are until you get morning sickness and go for a walk. I had to stop walking until it passed. Everywhere was the smell of food. I got depressed, I couldn't go outside, me, I love it outside. I ended up being hospitalized with I.V.s, which only depressed me more. It's summer and I can't get out; it is awful," said Sara.

"Well, I'll make sure you don't go through that this time," said Penny.

"Great, these sandwiches are great," said Sara.

"Really great," said John. "Now I feel like doughnuts."

"Sometimes men go through the same things their wives do when they're pregnant," said Penny. "Sometimes worst."

"I will get big, too?" asked John.

"If you eat too much," laughed Sara.

"You seem awfully happy," said John.

"I am, I got rid of my house," said Sara. "That bothered me a lot, thinking I 'd have to go back there. I feel free. It's hard to understand, I know, but all I could think of was what happened there. I don't think that was good for the baby," said Sara. "The stress of it all."

John wrote down Kentucky Fried Chicken on Sara's list.

"That sounds good, but not as good as a hot bath," said Sara.

"One hot bath coming up," said John, walking out of the kitchen into the bathroom.

"He sure loves you a lot. You don't see men taking care of their wives like that anymore," said Penny.

"Oh, it will wear off with him. Right now he's happy. I'm alive, then finding out I'm pregnant, and two lives survived. He's so happy right now, I could ask for the moon and he'd go outside and try to get it for me," laughed Sara.

"Yes, I could see where he'd be happy, but that one will never tire taking care of you. He loves you too much. You love him just as much. It's good to see someone in love. Arnold and I, we've been married forty-five years. He worked his whole life with nothing to show for it. I work here one day, and end up with more than I had my whole life. That one will never stop amazing me," said Penny. "He couldn't wait to call the children to tell them."

"How old is Arnold?" asked Sara.

"Sixty-six, retired two months ago, been driving me nuts ever since," laughed Penny.

"Well, now he'll have lots to do," said Sara. "The house is beautiful. It's just something I want to forget. Here is where I belong."

"Did you just buy this place?" asked Penny.

"No, we inherited it from John's father. I designed it for him. My two children live down the road, and John's friend, Sean. We're all Oneida Indians. Everyone gets pissed off because we live tax free," said Sara.

"Why? Not all Indians do. Arnold's 100 percent Crow; we don't live tax free," said Penny.

"You should, that's a law for New York Indians. It was a deal made a long time ago. I'd look into it because your children are one half and they qualify for that. Your land and home would be tax free. That really works out good because I'm giving the house to another Indian; different tribe, but still Indian."

"I don't have to pay taxes of any kind?" asked Penny.

"Nope, Brian will be here in a little while. I'll have him get you set up. You'll have a card that makes you tax exempt. Say you wanted a new car, you pay no taxes at all," said Sara. "That's what got everyone up in arms. The Indians, it's not our fault, we had a smart chief."

"Do you know how much money I could save in a year?" said Penny shocked.

"Yes, I do. That's money you can use for other things," said Sara.

"Arnold wants a big screen TV, now we can get one," said Penny.

"Won't have to, there's already one there with cable," said Sara.

"Oh, my goodness," said Penny.

"Bath is ready, my princess," said John as he picked Sara up.

Sara explained to John about Arnold and his kids. "They have rights that aren't being used," said Sara.

"Okay," smiled John as he undid the cast. "This looks swollen. Does it hurt a little?" asked John.

"More like a throb, it's all this lying around. I'll do it for the baby, but I don't think it's good. I'm not used to it," said Sara.

John lifted Sara into the tub of warm water and bubbles. "This feels great, thank you. I love you, John," said Sara.

"I love you, too, princess," said John as he kissed Sara. "Door bell, probably Brian."

"The list and the Arnold thing," said Sara.

"Don't worry, I can handle it," said John. "I'll be right back."

"Brian, a couple of things, come here, follow me." John walked in the kitchen. "Penny, call Dr. Emerson, the phone number's next to the phone. Tell him Sara's leg is all swollen and it doesn't look good to me," said John.

"Right away," said Penny, dialing as she talked.

"Sara okay?" asked Brian.

"I don't know, her leg doesn't look good to me. This is her grocery list. I know it's almost all junk food, but being pregnant, she has these cravings that are strange," said John. "And I'm supposed to tell you Arnold Chambers is 100 percent Indian. His rights have been violated on the tax issue. Sara would like you to help him and his children get their rights. I don't understand," said John.

"The doctor wants to know if there's any red or blue spots," asked Penny.

"Yes, it's red fading into blue around the ankle," said John.

"Oh my," said Penny. "Yes doctor, red fading to blue. Yes I'll tell him."

"The doctor is on his way, keep her foot up," said Penny.

"Okay, when she's out of the tub," said John.

"No, now!" yelled Penny.

John ran to the bathroom. "I don't feel good," said Sara.

John pulled her out of the tub, wrapped her robe around her, and ran to the bed and propped her leg up. "Feel better now?" asked John.

"Yeah, not so sickly feeling," said Sara.

Penny knocked on the door.

"Come in," called John, covering Sara with a quilt.

"I just yanked her out of the tub, she doesn't feel good," said John.

"Go, I will take over. Brian waits," said Penny.

"Thank you," said John, looking scared.

John went back out to talk to Brian. The look on John's face told him something was wrong, seriously wrong. "I've got the paperwork for the house. I had Penny sign. I'll talk to Arnold and have him sign. I'll get him set up for his rights, do the shopping and get right back here," said Brian. "If you want me to, I'll call her children."

"That's a really great idea, but if you were me, you wouldn't know how to use the phone either," said John.

"Oh God, I'm sorry, I just assumed. Here, let me do it. I'll show you how it works. I'll call, you talk," said Brian. "This must really be strange to you."

"Yes, there's a lot that's strange, but I'm learning," said John.

"Here is John's phone number. You punch those numbers here onto these numbers here, it's ringing, hear it?" said Brian, handing John the phone.

"Hello?" said John.

"John, something is wrong with Sara. Dr. Emerson's on his way," said John.

"I'll be right there," said John. "Bye." The phone went dead.

"He said he'd be here, now the phone says nothing," said John.

"Hang it up, then pick it up and dial this number," said Brian.

So John did. "It goes beep, beep," said John. "Hear?"

"That means to push this down, then say hello," said Brian.

"Hello?" said John.

"John, Sean, what's up? John said something is wrong with Sara."

"Yes her leg is swollen red and blue," said John.

"I'll be right there. John's calling Susan so you don't have to go be with Susan," said Sean. "Bye."

"Thank you, Brian, that wasn't so bad," said John.

"Glad to help. I'll help you more, right now I've got to run," said Brian.

"I understand," said John. "I've got Sara to tend to. We'll talk later."

Brian was leaving when everyone showed up. John had picked up Susan and Sean. Dr. Emerson had Dr. Stevenson with him. John had just walked away from the door when it flew open and everyone walked in stomping off snow and brushing new fallen snow off their coats.

"Sara's in the bedroom with Penny," said John.

Dr. Emerson and Dr. Stevenson went back to the bedroom. Everyone else followed John to the kitchen. Penny came in as John was pouring coffee.

"I'll do that John," said Penny. "Sit with the kids."

"How did you know they were my children?" asked John surprised.

"Could be because your son looks just like you. Your daughter looks like Sara, and the other one must be your friend Sean," said Penny. "It ain't hard to figure that one out," laughed Penny.

"No, it's probably not," laughed John. "Everyone, this is Penny; she's our cook. This morning your mother sold Penny and her husband, Arnold, the old house for the sum of one dollar," said John.

"That's great. I hope you enjoy the house," said Susan. "It's really beautiful."

"Yeah, Mom's probably so happy. She started doing flip-flops," smiled John. "I know it's a great relief to her."

"You children aren't upset over your mother's decision?" asked Mary, surprised.

"No, not at all. I know Mother. That house has been on her mind ever since the ambulance took her away. She's probably so happy, I'm surprised she didn't give it to you," said Susan. "This is where Mother belongs."

"Well, she tried to give it to them as a Christmas present," said John. "But to make it legal and binding, Sara had to sell it for one dollar. Brian was explaining it to me, and I didn't understand," said John. "Sara's going to have them all moved in before Christmas."

"That is great. You know, you could stay there tonight. As a matter of fact, I've got my keys to the place," said John, taking his keys out. I hope you have a large family, that place was made for kids. There's even a tree fort there. These three keys are to the house. House keys are red, front door, back door, and side door. These two gold keys are for the garage, and the green one is for the workshop. If you need anything explained to you, this is my card. I'd be more than glad to explain everything to you. I won't be in the office until after New Year's, but my home phone is on there. If the power goes out, there's a switch in the garage that starts the generator. The furniture, dishes; it's all there. The place has been cleaned top to bottom. The only thing it needs right now is food and people," laughed John.

"Here's my keys, too," said Susan. "Same as John's."

"Are you people always so generous and agreeable?" asked Penny.

"Oh, we have our moments, believe me," laughed Susan. "But we've grown a lot in two weeks, not to mention what we've learned is far more than anything taught to you. Family is the most important thing there is, other than a friend like Sean," smiled Susan.

"This family is going to be a pleasure to work for," said Penny, pouring coffee. She left the breakfast nook and returned with a platter of doughnuts.

Dr. Emerson walked in the room. "Who took Sara's cast off?" He looked around the room.

"I did sir," said Penny, stepping forward. "It didn't look right, it being so swollen and all. I'm the one to yell at if something wrong was done, sir."

"Actually it was a smart move. It was too tight," said Dr. Emerson. "We're taking the cast off for good. You must be Penny. Sara said you put hot and cold packs on the leg," said Dr. Emerson.

"Yes sir. Was I wrong?" asked Penny.

"No, the swelling is going down. Most people don't know to put hot and cold packs on after noting them. She might have a slight infection. I thought blood clots at first, but I'm not taking any chances. I did blood work. I'll call you with the results. I want Sara to take two aspirins, one now, one tonight, again tomorrow, one morning, and one night. Here's a prescription for antibiotics for the infection; one for the swelling. She will have to walk around," which Sara was glad to hear. "Do not let her climb stairs, anything at all. If she has pain, give her Tylenol. Dr. Stevenson is giving her a couple of shots right now. Start the prescription about four tonight. She has to take it until it's gone. She doesn't stop it when it feels better because then it's of no use to her. She has to take it all. I know Sara, she will stop taking it," said Dr. Stevenson.

"No she won't," said John. "That I can guarantee."

"I'll get the prescription for Mom," said John.

"Well, she'll be out shortly. She's really mad at us right now for giving her some shots," laughed Dr. Emerson, "so be prepared to hear all about it. I'm mean and cruel right now."

"You're a monster," said Sara. "Shots, that's all he ever does is give me shots. He's shot happy," said Sara.

"See what I mean?" laughed Dr. Emerson.

"Well you would think by now you would know how to give the damn things. They always hurt," said Sara, winking at everyone.

"No, you just don't like shots," laughed Dr. Emerson.

"But, Sara, I thought," John stopped right there.

"Oooh, Dad just got the look," laughed John.

"The look?" asked John.

"The look that means 'shut up while you're ahead' look," laughed John.

"Oh, I thought she was going to kill me," said John.

"She would have if you kept talking," laughed John.

"Will you guys stop picking on me. I'll sent you both to bed without dessert," said Sara.

"Can't Mom, Rachel already does," said John.

Everyone laughed. "Don't start, John," said Sara.

"Or what, I'll get the look? I've gotten the look so much I'm used to it now," laughed John.

"You're impossible," laughed Sara.

"I try my best, Mother, I really do," laughed John.

"Coffee, Mr. Monster?" asked Sara.

"Thought you would never ask," laughed Dr. Emerson, walking in.

Penny left, and brought back cups and coffee. Everyone chit-chatted for a while, then left. John dropped everyone off, then came back to take his father on his first-ever shopping spree. Susan and Penny sat and talked.

"You call this a mall?" asked John. "That means a small place to shop."

"This is a mini-mall," said John. "That means a small place to shop."

"This place is far from small; this is bigger than my village," said John.

"Believe me, this is small; it only has fourteen places. The other one on the other side only has seven, but they're much bigger," said John. "There's the drugstore we're going to," said John.

"They sell drugs here?" asked John, looking.

John laughed. "The good drugs. The bad drugs are sold on the streets," said John.

"Why sell the bad drugs on the streets when you can buy the good ones here?" asked John.

"I'll explain later. Now I know you're not used to this and it's going to be shock at first. I'll explain as we go. We won't talk loud so no one can hear me explaining this to you," said John.

"Why?" said John.

"We don't want anyone to know where you come from," said John.

"Look, Sean just pulled in," said John, getting out of the truck.

"I thought you could use a hand. It might be a little frightening at first," said Sean, walking over to John. "Besides, I came from the same place he did."

"Thanks, I told him I'd explain as we went along. Mom gave him the checkbook. She showed him how to write a check. He wants us to stop at the bank and get some money so he has some on him, in case he sees something he wants. She says he has to learn. Then we go to the movie place and get a couple skin flicks so she can explain different types of movies to him. This ought to be fun. We have to be back by 2:30. There's a storm coming and he wants Penny home early," said John.

"Do we dare take him in a grocery store?" asked Sean.

"He's going to have to learn sometime; we're here," said John, opening the door to the drugstore. "This way, Dad."

John followed his son. John showed his father where to hand the prescriptions over. The pharmacist said that will be about fifteen minutes. "Thank you," said John. The three men walked around the store looking. Everyone stared at John. He was so impressive it was hard not to look at him. John had picked up a basket and put a few things in the basket that was of interest to him: aftershave, shaving cream, razors, deodorant, aspirin, Tylenol. He was very selective. He looked like any normal shopper. This impressed Sean and John. Then he went back to pick up his prescription. He wrote a check, then showed his I.D. just like Sara explained, then went to the front of the store, wrote another check for his purchases, thanked the sales clerk, and walked outside. Sean and John followed.

"That went well," said John.

"Did you see the stuff in that store?" whispered John. "So much stuff. Sara told me it was going to be more than I imagined and any thought or comments shouldn't be made in a store, but that was unbelievable," said John. "I did remember to say thank you, didn't I?" asked John.

"Yes, Dad, you did really well. We'll put this stuff in the trunk. Now we'll go to the bank and get money. Mom explained everything to you, right?" asked John.

"Yes. Write a check, hand it to the lady behind the window, she'll give me money. I say 'thank you,' count my money, and leave," said John.

"That's it," smiled John. "Where'd you get a driver's license?" asked Sean.

"Brian. He said he'd teach me to drive later. I also have my Indian card. It has my picture on it. That's my second ID. You need two. Sara said to make the check out for one thousand dollars, that's ten one hundreds, so when I count my money, I have to remember ten one hundreds," said John.

"Yes, that's right," said Sean, opening the door to the bank.

John walked in like he'd been there a thousand times, made out his check, walked up to the teller, and handed her the check and two IDs.

"You're new here, aren't you?" asked the teller.

"Yes ma'am, just got married," smiled John. "Been here a couple of days. I hope my money has arrived, my associate assured me it would be here," said John.

"Let me see," smiled the teller. It came up thirty million dollars; her eyes grew large. She looked at John. "Thirty million dollars sound right?" she asked shocked.

"Yes, that's about right. There will be more deposits," said John.

John and Sean were trying not to laugh. John didn't know the teller was flirting with him and when she saw the amount in the bank account, she almost died on the spot.

She handed John the money. John counted it. "Ma'am, you gave me too much money," said John. "Please count it again. I wouldn't want what wasn't mine."

The teller counted, shocked that someone was honest enough to say something. "You're right, there's an extra one hundred dollar bill here. Thank you for your honesty. We usually don't get many honest people here. They take the money and run, then we're stuck picking up the tab. May I ask what you do?" asked the teller.

John looked at the name tag. "Sheri, my wife and I own the Princess Corporation and if more people were honest, there would be less problems today," said John.

Sheri blinked twice. She said, "Yes you're right. You have a good day now."

"You too," said John. "Thank you." He walked away, his heart beating wild in his chest. He went outside. "Did you see her? It was disgraceful the way she acted," said John Sr.

"Calm down, Dad. You better get used to it. You're a good-looking man. You're gong to get reactions like that from women all the time," said John.

"What?" said John Sr. "What are you talking about?"

"The teller was flirting with you," said John.

"That stupid look she got on her face when I told her she gave me too much money? She thought I was lying," said John Sr. "Now where?"

"Dad, that's normal, nobody believes anyone anymore. The grocery store is there," said John, pointing. "Everyone thinks everyone lies; it's a way of life."

"Well, no wonder your mother hates it here. 'You're right' is all she had to say to me after thinking I lied to her. If any more of her breast was exposed, she'd get frostbite," said John Sr.

"Believe me, Dad, she was dressed conservative. Today's clothes are made that way."

John stopped. "What's that?" asked John Sr. "That group of people."

"Those are teenagers. School's out early today. They come to the mall and hang out," said John.

"Why do they have a thing in their nose and ear with a chain?" Their clothes are falling off, their hair is red, green, purple, and pointed. Are they doing a ritual dance? What are those big, black things?" asked John Sr.

"It's called body piercing; the clothes are made that way. They dye and style their hair that way. The black boxes are radios, and, no, it's no ritual they're doing. They're just hanging out," said John.

"That kid, his mouth is pierced shut. How does he eat?" asked John Sr.

"They're earrings. You can remove them, then put them back. They pierce all parts of their body," said John.

"That man, why's he painted, is he doing a ritual?" asked John Sr.

"No, he's just tattooed his body. They take these needles with dye and inject it into the skin and it stays there forever," said John.

"This is stupid, stupid people. You ever do any of this stuff, I will kill you," said John Sr.

"Don't worry, Dad, I won't," said John as he stepped on the pad for the automatic door opener. The door slid open. John Sr. didn't say anything, just looked, but was quite surprised at the size of the store. He bought a few things, found a doll he liked for Sara, bought some goodies, then checked around and found something he'd like to try: some cheeses and cold cuts. He bought rolls and Pepsi. Sean and John grabbed a couple of carts and began shopping. They ran into Brian, who was shopping for Sara and his family. "John's here, just put Sara's stuff in with his. We'll take it home," said John.

"How's he handling this? This must be awful for him to comprehend. This morning I showed him how to use a phone, something we take for granted. It's like a major thing to him," said Brian.

"He's doing real well. Mom briefed him. There's a lot he's been shocked by, but he talks to us before he says or does anything. He's careful what he buys. He bought Mom a doll. I don't understand that. After this we're going to the video store and renting some skin flicks. Mother wants to explain something to him. If he sees it, maybe he'll understand better," said John.

"Your mother wants to show John sex, so he'll know what he's doing?" asked Brian puzzled.

"No, this isn't about sex, it's to show John what's going on and explain people who do this, so if someone comes on to him, he'll be prepared," said John.

"Oh, because we are taught young about sex. It's a good point, your mother's thinking some woman would like to grab him and he wouldn't know why. How's Sara doing?" asked Brian.

"Good, a slight infection," said John.

"Brian, how good to see you," said John Sr., walking up. "I like these baskets on wheels, that's a good thing. You buy a lot of stuff, you can't carry it, you push it," smiled John Sr.

"Dad, I told Brian to put the stuff Mom wanted in your basket, and we'll take it home. I know he wants to see Mom, but let him take his goodies home to his family first," said John.

"Sir, this is all ours, too?" asked John Sr. smiling. "I really like shopping."

"You won't," said John. "It's always the same ol' stuff. You get tired of it after awhile." John took the smaller basket out of Brian's basket and put it in John Sr.'s.

"There's a lady that gives you things to eat over there. She gave me a recipe, so I bought some stuff to make it. It was good. Want some? She gave me the plate so I took it," said John Sr.

"Dad, they're samples; you only take one," said John.

"No, she told me to take the plate. I was the only one who liked them," said John Sr. "She had these plates, nobody wanted them but me. I took just one and loved them. She said, 'Bless you son,' then gave me a plate and told me I could have it. Then there's a lady over there who has some kind of snacks. I liked it, so she gave me a recipe and the stuff to make it. I took only one like your mother told me. I have everything I need except those marshmallow cookies you sent us. Those I can't find," said John.

"They're called Pinwheels. If you look up, you'll see signs that tell you what's in the aisles, see?" said John.

"Yes, that's another food thing," said John Sr.

"Cookie aisle is right behind you," said Sean.

"Okay, I'll get my cookies and check out," smiled John Sr.

"Okay, Dad, we'll meet you at the checkout," said John.

"Okay, have fun," said John Sr. "See you later. Brian don't forget Kentucky Friend Chicken for supper with lots of potatoes and biscuits. Those corn on a stick, those are good," said John Sr., turning his cart around. "Oh, you probably need money for that, here," said John, handing Brian a one hundred dollar bill. Buy some for your family's dinner tonight. It's good for them, get us both big buckets, all breast," said John Sr.

"John, you don't have to buy my family supper tonight," said Brian.

"Yes I do. You helped Sara today. She'd only do it if I didn't," said John Sr. "Buy Pepsi to go with that; Pepsi is good. I'll see you later. Pinwheels, I love those, not many in a package though." John was gone.

"I can't let John buy supper," said Brian.

"Why not, Mom would do it when you got there. You don't know my mother too well. My mother's a giver, not a taker. It took me a long time to understand that. I always thought my mother was stupid when she did something for someone. Now I'm thirty years old; now I understand. Giving gives my mother pleasure. She never wanted much in love, only to be able to give you and George work for her now, believe me when I tell you this. Your lives will change, not because my mother has money, money never meant anything to her. Your lives will be changed just by knowing her. She's one hell of a lady. It took me thirty years to see that. I'm must glad it didn't take me all my life because then I never would have known my mother," said John.

"You have learned a lot these last couple of weeks," smiled Brian.

"I had no choice with you and George on my case," laughed John. "I'm not complaining. I'm grateful you two got through this thick head of mine. I just regret it took so long."

Sean left to check out, he was next to tears, John had grown up. He didn't think he'd live to see the day.

"Well, I've got to have Dad home to 2:30. I've got one more stop, then home. I'll probably see you later, thought I'd check on Mom before the storm hits. Those fireworks were great," smiled John. "I bet Mom loved them."

"She did, she thanked me this morning. How she knew it was me, I'll never know," laughed Brian.

"Don't worry, Mom's pretty sharp. She don't miss much," laughed John as he turned his cart around and walked away.

"That I believe," thought Brian as he watched John walk away.

John had checked out. Sean was going through the line when John Sr. came up behind Sean. The men checked out, and put their groceries in John's truck. When Brian came out, he walked up to the worst car John had ever seen and put his groceries in it, then drove away. "Was that Brian?" asked Sean.

"Yes it was, get in," said John.

"Brian has a limo," said John Sr.

"No Dad, those limos are ours. Come on, I'm following him.

John Sr. was very disgusted at the home Brian pulled into. John drove by.

"He can't live there, that's awful," said John Sr.

John turned around. "That's what I say to Dad, but he does live there. Our limo is parked in front. If Mom saw this, she'd have a shit fit. We've got to change this before Mom finds out." John looked at the clock. They still had time to get a movie. He picked up his car phone and dialed Susan's. "Sue, what are you going to do with your old house?" asked John.

"Old house, that house is only five years old. Why, do you know somebody who needs one?" asked Susan.

John explained about Brian and how Mom would feel if she found out. "I can bet George is in the same boat."

"Give him my house. It's just like Mom's, needs food and people. We can't have people who work for us living like this. Mom would be so pissed," said Susan.

"Thanks Sis, I knew you would understand. Love you, see you later," said John.

"Love you too, kid, bye," said Susan.

"George can have my house. Like Susan said, all it needs is food and people."

"Thanks, they will be in there tonight," said John.

"But he is dressed too well. I don't understand," said John Sr.

"That's the way it is today, Dad. You never know with people. That's probably the only suit he owns," said John, parking the truck. "His wages are probably so low that he can't make ends meet, just like everyone else," said John, getting out.

"But, I thought the Indians were supposed to be taking care of him," said John Sr.

"Yes, if you live on the reservation. But if you live off the reservation, you get no special treatment. He probably married a white woman, and they chose to live off the reservation. Things are bad for the nation, but like Brian's case, they suck," said John, opening the door. John walked up to the counter. "We're having bachelor party tonight, do you have about three XXX movies? I think three should cover it, don't you, Sean?" asked John.

"Yeah, with the stripper that should last us all night," said Sean.

"I know just what three you're looking for," said the clerk. He left and came back.

John pulled out his rental card, set it down, put out some money, and got his change and left. "Thank you," said John as he left.

"Enjoy," smiled the clerk as they left.

"When we get home, I'll call Brian, tell him to have George come with him. I'll go over the payroll and see how much they make a week. I know it's not much. Then I'll meet them at Mom's. We'll buy them new vehicles. What kind of company is this? Two people who put their lives on the line for us in dumps. This has got me pissed off. So I can imagine what Mom would feel," said John Sr.

"We are making it right though?" asked John.

"Yes we are," said John Sr., pulling in the driveway. "Don't say anything to Mom. I'll be right back. I want to get our books."

"I'll get the keys for my house and Susan's and meet you there," said Sean, grabbing bags of groceries, passing them to both Johns, then grabbing a couple for him to take in.

"Did you buy enough?" laughed Sara.

"There's a couple of more bags, I'll get them," said John. "Be right back, Mom."

"Sure honey," said Sara.

"I bought you something," smiled John Sr.

"Me, you bought me something?" smiled Sara. "Let me guess, candy?"

"No," smiled John, handing Sara a bag.

John walked in just in time to hear Sara scream. "Oh, John, she's beautiful."

"That's odd, never thought Mom liked dolls. This bag goes with it," smiled John, putting it down in front of Sara.

"Oh John, this is beautiful, a rocking horse. God, this is perfect; it can go on the mantel. John thank you," Sara kissed him.

"I never knew you were into dolls, Mom," said John. "That was the first thing Dad saw in the grocery store. He said it was for you. I must admit I thought Dad was buying the wrong thing at first, but I guess he knew all along," smiled John. "I've got to go, but I'll be right back. I bought groceries, so did John. We'll be back."

"Okay, honey," said Sara, setting her doll on the horse.

Sean and John left. "I never knew Mom liked dolls so much."

"Probably because she never could afford them. You should have seen the dolls she bought back in the 1800s. Three of them, real beauties. I made some doll furniture for them for her for Christmas," said Sean. "But she couldn't bring them back with her. I knew she loved those dolls," said Sean.

"That must be what those packages are that we're supposed to give her for Christmas," said John, starting the truck.

"What packages?" asked Sean.

"There's a ton of presents for Mom for Christmas from Ben, Summer, Jacob, and Susan. We got some for you, too," said John, stopping in front of Sean's house. "We love our house. Thank you," said John.

"I didn't build it, I only designed it," said Sean.

"I know, but you did one hell of a job," laughed John. "See you at Mom's."

Sean took his three bags of groceries. "See you in a few," said Sean.

John left and drove to his house, dropped off the groceries, called Brian, went through his books, "Six-fifty an hour," said John.

"Something is wrong?" asked Rachel.

"Yes, I must correct it now. I'm going to Mom's. I won't be long," said John.

"Okay, I'll hold supper till 6:00. After that you're on your own," laughed Rachel.

"It's only 3:00," laughed John. "This should take about an hour at the longest. It's cut and dry. Changes are being made."

"Oh, something serious?" asked Rachel.

"Won't be in a few minutes," said John, leaving the house. "See you in a few minutes." He took his books and then left.

When John got to Sara's place, he went inside. "I see Penny left. It's starting to get dark out there. Looks like a good one's coming," said John, sitting at the table. "I asked Dad not to say anything and let me tell you," said John.

"What's wrong?" asked Sara.

"This involves Brian and George. Some changes have to be made. These two men live in horrible homes, which will be changed tonight. They're being moved into Susan and Sean's homes. I would like your permission to buy them both new vehicles. Theirs I don't even know how they're running. They're getting paid six-fifty an hour. That's got to change. God, if they ever had to take a bullet for us at six-fifty an hour, it's awful, Mom. I saw this with my own eyes; Dad and Sean saw. These books tell me what they get paid an hour. I know you wouldn't want this. I called Brian and George here," said John.

"You're right, no one in my employment will be paid cheaply or live cheaply. What seems a good wage for what they do?" asked Sara.

"One hundred or one hundred fifty thousand dollars a year," said John. "They have families; they're our guards, it seems only fair."

"You're right, one hundred fifty thousand dollars, it will be their wage. Have Brian and George buy themselves a good four-wheel drive vehicle. Make up the difference in this year's wages when they get here. You've done well, so handle this. I will just confirm so they can't say anything," said Sara. "John, please get the door when they come. I've been sitting so long I'm numb, my ass actually hurts from those shots."

"Mom, take Tylenol, Dr. Emerson said you could," said John. "Dad bought some for you."

"I know, but I can't move to get some," said Sara. "John's been busy, and I didn't want to bother him. It sounds stupid, I know, but you weren't here. John was having so much fun putting groceries away. I didn't want to disturb him," laughed Sara.

"Should have seen him in the stores; he loves to shop," said John.

"Sure do," smiled John Sr., setting the Tylenol and a glass of water in front of Sara.

"They are here, I'll get the door and you take the pills," said John, walking to the door. Brian and George stood in front, Sean in back. "Come in, they are in the breakfast nook, I made coffee."

"Here's your Kentucky Fried Chicken," said Brian in a regretful voice.

"Why do you sound so down Brian?" asked Sara.

"You called us here to fire us, right?" said Brian.

"God no, whatever gave you that idea?" said Sara.

"I saw John follow me. George and I don't live on the reservation, so we don't qualify to work for you," said Brian.

"Yes, I followed you. Yes, we know you don't live on the reservation. Where you live is a concern to us. We brought you here to tell you that you both have been grossly misused, and we would like to correct the situation," said John.

"I don't understand," said Brian.

"We run a huge business, we can't have you living in rundown housing. I'm sure you feel it's a good place to live, but we don't feel comfortable where you live, it's not good policy for a company to treat their employees in this fashion, so we've decided to give you two homes, a raise, and new vehicles of your choice. You're not here to be fired, far from it. We want to show our appreciation. Brian, we're giving you Susan's house; George, you're being given Sean's house," said John.

"I'd like Susan's house," said George. "Sean's house is Brian's kind of place if that's all right," said George.

"Sure, you two work it out. Sean has the keys. Now you're being paid six-fifty an hour, this is not good. Your new wages will be one hundred fifty thousand dollars a year. Tomorrow you two will go and buy a four-wheel vehicle of your choice, do you understand?" said John.

Brian pulled out a chair and sat down. "I don't think I can breath. I know I couldn't have heard you right when you said one hundred fifty thousand dollars a year," said Brian.

"Yes you did, we want you in your home as soon as possible. All they need is food and people. You write a check from the company for your vehicles, I'll sign them. You will have to write in the rest, just let me know how much. I had hoped you could move into your homes tonight, but I don't know with the storm that's coming. One more thing, these checks are your wages for the rest of the year. The difference is made up of the one hundred fifty thousand dollars. Do you still think we want to fire you?" asked John.

"No, I guess not. I'm rather shocked," said Brian. "I know George is, he hasn't breathed since you mentioned our salaries. I don't understand the raise, it's so large," said Brian.

"Well, you are our two main men. You protected us. If you take these checks I wrote, you pay off any bills you might have, buy what you need, put the rest in the bank. You have new clothes, new homes, new vehicles. There will be no temptations that you could leave us for," smiled John. "We love having you two around. Is there anything wrong with that?" asked John. "You two are family to us."

"We are shocked, but not shocked enough to say we need time to think this over; we accept. If I could use your phone and the limos, we could move in tonight," smiled Brian.

"Go ahead," laughed John. "Phone's in the kitchen."

Brian walked to the kitchen and dialed his home. The clock read 3:30 P.M. "Kelly, Brian, take all the food and clothes in the house, put them in bags, put it in the limo, get the kids and Mom dressed. I'll explain when I get there. It's all good, so don't worry, just pack it in anything. No, pack all the food and clothes for two, three days," said Brian. Then Brian called April and told her to do the same thing and told them both to do it quickly, that they were on their way home.

"Okay, we'll be moved in tonight. I didn't tell our wives too much. They would be shocked like George," said Brian. "He's speechless. God, maybe I should have told them this would be the first time my wife wouldn't have something to say," laughed Brian.

Everyone laughed.

"Your wife, my wife has a certain reaction, that when she's happy that I might not live the night," laughed George. "And believe me, she's never been this happy. She'll kill me tonight, I know that for sure."

"I thought that with Sara, but I decided if I was going to die, I'd die with a smile on my face," said John Sr. "I found they can't kill you that way."

"Father, I think you're getting the hang of English," said John.

Everyone laughed.

"These are the keys to Susan's house for George. These are the keys to my house for Brian."

"These are your checks. The phones, lights, and all that are still hooked up at the houses. Tomorrow you can start changing things over," said John.

"We have call forwarding, so we'll just have them forwarded to Susan's and Sean's thank you. Thank you so much," said Brian.

"I told you my mother was a genius," said John.

"Yes you did, son, but something tells me this was all your doing. You just had to believe in yourself."

"Well, when you have two men around the size of you two, you have a tendency to listen," laughed John.

"That's all it took?" said Sara, joking.

"Mom, look at them, would you argue with them?" asked John. "I take it back, you would," laughed John.

"It's starting to snow, you better get moving," said John. "Beat the storm."

"Here's another fifty dollars, make sure George gets chicken for supper," said John.

"No, I still have enough leftover. We're fine, thank you."

"I'll see you tomorrow, thank you," said Brian, and they left.

Brian dropped George off then went home. George had money in his hand for chicken; the limo was loaded. The family waited inside. George was still shocked, and couldn't think what to say other than, "Let's go."

"Where, what's up?" asked April.

"You won't believe me, I can't believe it. Just get in the limo," said George.

George drove to Kentucky Fried Chicken and pulled in the same time as Brian. They ordered, paid, and drove to their new homes. George pulled into Susan's. "This is our new home," said George. He got out and left the family to talk while he opened the garage door. He got back in, and drove the limo in. George didn't think it would fit, but it did. George was so shocked, he never heard the flurry of questions. "Let's take everything out, eat, then I'll explain." Everyone scurried out, grabbing bags, and putting them in the house. April didn't pack much, mostly food. George carried supper in, set it on the table, took off his coat, and sat down. "This is our new home. Tomorrow I have to buy a new four-wheel drive vehicle, anyone I want, it's all paid for. I got a raise," said George.

"A raise?" said April "I thought Brian thought you two were going to be—."

"He was wrong, they love us, they consider us family," said George.

"Well, how much of a raise? A couple of dollars would help a lot," said April.

"April, sit down," said George. "You won't believe me."

"You make it sound so dramatic," laughed April. "Just tell me."

"I warned you," said George. "I now make one hundred fifty thousand dollars a year."

April blinked twice, sat down, and stared at George. "You're joking, right?" asked April.

"No, I'm not. This check is the difference for this year. We pay off all our debts, and put the rest in the bank. We have money, home, vehicle, and a new lease on life," said George, sliding the check across the table to April.

April looked at the check, then George. "You're not joking, are you? This is our home? Oh my God, George." April's hands started shaking. "My God, oh my God, we don't have anymore problems," said April.

"No we don't. In fifteen minutes our problems were over," said George.

"Does this mean I can buy new boots?" asked George Jr.

"Yes honey, we can get you both some new clothes," said April, wiping at tears.

"Why are you crying?" asked George Jr.

"Because Mommy's happy, honey, very happy. You have no idea how happy," laughed April. "What did Kelly say about this?" asked April.

"We didn't say anything to our wives, we couldn't believe it, so how did we expect you to believe it. We just showed you," said George, filling his plate.

"Let's eat then put groceries away and find your bedrooms," said April.

"Do we have to change schools?" asked George Jr.

"No, son, it's still the same school," said George.

"Cool," said George Jr.

Kelly stood staring at Brian in the kitchen, she was numb. She couldn't think of one thing to say. All the problems they had were gone. Nothing left to think about. No more bill collectors calling, no more praying the car could get through one more day, no more leaky roof and windows. The kids could get some much-needed clothes. Brian's mother seemed less a burden. She didn't have anything to yell at Kelly about. Kids ran through the house yelling "Neat, cool." She actually had a washer and dryer and a refrigerator that didn't have a stick holding it shut.

Hot tears ran down her cheeks as she stared at the dishwasher. The only dream she ever had, a dishwasher. No more red, cracked, bleeding hands from doing dishes and laundry by hand. A trash compactor, a stove. She bet all four burners worked and the oven didn't have hot spots. A freezer and pantry, a table with twelve chairs. They would be able to sit down and eat with room to spare. An island with stools. Kelly's thin body shook with sobs. Brian held her. "I know it's been tough. God only knows why you didn't leave me. I love you so much, you deserve this plus more. Now it's all behind us; hard times are over. I was thinking we've had Mom for fifteen years. I think it's time my brother accepted his responsibility and took Mother in. He's the first son. I think we need a life of our own. I'll call Terry tomorrow and make arrangements. I love you, Kelly," said Brian.

"I love you," sobbed Kelly.

"What do you say we eat now?" said Brian.

Kelly nodded.

"Kids, let's eat," called Brian. They came and sat at the table. Kelly sat down.

"Our first meal together," she thought as she helped Pearl set the table. "Thank you God," said Kelly.

"We picked out our rooms upstairs. This place is best," said Pearl, Brian's oldest daughter. "We assumed you and Grandma would sleep downstairs."

"Yes dear, we are, just as long as you're all happy," said Brian.

"Happy doesn't describe us all not having to sleep in one room. We all have our own rooms, this is really cool," said Pearl.

Brian laughed. "Real cool means you're pleased, I take it," he said.

"Sure, we put our clothes in our room, then I put Grandma's stuff in her room. Both rooms have a bathroom, so I gave her the one in the back, it's quieter for her," said Kelly. "She won't have to yell at us so much."

"Thank you, sweetheart," said Brian.

"I wouldn't yell if you would be quiet five minutes," said Pearl.

"Mother, you know the other house was too small for this family. The four kids slept in one room. You had the other bedroom, Kelly and I slept on that pull-out couch. I think the children behaved very well under those circumstances. They are kids. They play and when they play, they make noise. It's the way of life. Kelly went way beyond anything one woman should have to do to keep the clothes clean and mended. That house was spotless. You had good, solid meals three times a day. You are lucky to have a daughter-in-law who loves you so much to do this for you. Tomorrow I'm calling Terry, you're moving in with him. I don't care what you think about it. I don't need your insults anymore. I have a good wife and family. Someday you will see that," said Brian.

The kids stared at Brian. Never once has he said one thing bad to his mother. He always took her insults. Pearl was hardest on Kelly. Brian never saw what Pearl had done to Kelly. Nothing Kelly did was good enough. She always had to redo everything. Kelly never complained, she just did it. Never spoke ill of her mother-in-law. The kids were around, they saw it. How it would all end. They knew their father well enough that if he said it, he meant it.

The phone rang; everyone jumped. It broke the silence. Kelly answered it. It was April. They talked, then cried, talked some more, then said good-bye. Kelly hung up. "April's as shocked as me," was all she said.

They finished eating, then put everything away. Kelly found some dishwasher soap under the sink, put the dishes in the dishwasher, and washed them. Right at that moment, she felt like a queen.

Nothing could take that feeling away. Kelly walked from room to room, each one finer than the next. When she took her clothes in their bedroom, she cried, "A real bed." She hadn't slept in one for fifteen years. Her mother-in-law always had the bed; they had the couch. She walked out after putting everything away and helped her mother-in-law get ready for bed. She bathed her and washed her hair, then dried her off and brushed her hair dry. She put her nightgown on and helped her to bed. The night was now Kelly's. Kelly took a hot shower and put her nightgown on, went in the living room, and sat next to Brian on the couch. The kids all went to bed early, enjoying their newfound privacy.

Kelly looked at Brian. "This is all so unbelievable," said Kelly.

"This family is unbelievable. They like giving things to people. Sara gave her maid her house today," said Brian. "That shocked me, but this is going to take a long time to sink in. John, the son, did all this, I know he did because Sara never said one word. She let him handle the whole thing. I'm surprised at how fast he got things done. It couldn't have taken him a half hour total. I don't even work that fast," laughed Brian.

"Isn't he the one who gave you a hard time at first?" asked Kelly.

"Sure was. Two weeks ago today. You wouldn't know it was the same man. He said he loved us. You could have knocked me over with a feather. I couldn't breath, I sat down. George, he said nothing. He just stared with his mouth open. Then when he gave us our pay for the rest of the year—ten days or one hundred twenty five thousand dollars—I thought I had died and was in heaven," laughed Brian.

"Would you mind going to bed early, I can't wait to feel what a real bed feels like," said Kelly.

"No, I thought I've got a lot to do tomorrow, so have you. You get to pay off all our bills then do some shopping. You and the kids need new clothes. I've got a brother to deal with, a truck to buy, a house to close down. We've got a house to decorate for Christmas and new decorations to buy. John says to use the limos tomorrow, so you travel in style, my love," smiled Brian.

"Terry's going to be shocked. He hasn't spoke or written your mother in ten years. I doubt if he even knows she's still alive," said Kelly.

"He will tomorrow. I can't wait to see the look on his face when we pull in his driveway. There's a limo, truck, and a home he said I never would have. We spend as little as we can of my paycheck, we have to save every penny we can, our kids are going to college," smiled Brian.

"Well, you've got it all figured out," smiled Kelly. "I'm going to bed, the sound of that even sounds great. I know 8:30 is early, but you've got me tired thinking of all the fun I'm having tomorrow," laughed Kelly. "I know it's a tough job, but somebody has to do it," said Kelly as she left the room to go to bed.

Brian turned the lights out, locked the doors, and checked on his mother and the kids. When he got to bed, Kelly was fast asleep. He looked out the window, it was still snowing. This was going to be a Christmas to remember, lots of snow. Everyone's wish came true this year. Brian took a shower and went to bed.

The snow fell softly and quietly all night. In the morning there would be no school. Brian and George put money in the bank, and went around town and paid off every bill they had. They had the phone and electric put in their name, bought their trucks, bought Christmas decorations, new clothes, and changed their addresses. Brian called his brother and told him to come and get his mother tomorrow. Terry was given no choice. He said, "Yes." Brian told him where he lived. Tomorrow was Saturday, so his brother had no excuse not to be there. Brian bought his mother new clothes and a set of suitcases. Terry wasn't going to have anything to say about how Kelly treated their mother. Brian knew Terry wasn't pleased, but it was his responsibility and he better start being responsible. Everyone took what they wanted out of their old home and walked away. George tracked down people from school Monday morning. Brian and his kids will be picked up in front of their new homes. Brian got everything done for the houses, that meant Penny's too. George and Brian were now proud new homeowners. They picked up their new trucks the next morning. Brian got a white Ford Expedition; George got a green one. They also had the plates switched and insurance paid, everything done by three o'clock. Sara was pleased to hear everything had been done.

"Now you and George can take a vacation until after New Year's. You take and enjoy your new homes. The kids start vacation Wednesday. I want you and George to have a happy Christmas. If anything comes up, I'll let you know, but I think we should take this time to adjust to our new lives," said Sara. "I would love to meet your families sometime."

"You will," smiled Brian. "But there's something you should know. My Kelly looks just like her great-great-grandmother," said Brian.

"Is it someone I met while I was in the 1800s?" asked Sara.

"Yes, Sara is Kelly's great-great-grandmother: red hair with curls, green eyes. I had to tell you I was shocked when I saw pictures you sent back. I wouldn't want you shocked. I have four children, Brian Jr., Pearl, and twins Trey and Tere. The twins look like their mother," said Brian.

"I thought you had five or six kids," said Sara.

Well, we do if you hear my wife talk. She includes me and my mother," laughed Brian. "But my mother's leaving tomorrow. She's gong to be moving in with my brother. He's the oldest. She's supposed to be with him, tradition says so, but his wife refused. Today I gave him no choice. He hasn't spoken to Mother in ten years. That's an awful way to treat your mother. He would end up with a a lot of regret in the end, and I don't want to hear it. All he had to do was pick up the phone and call her. He couldn't do it, so I'm forcing him to do what he was supposed to do," said Brian.

"I don't blame you, Brian. When someone dies in a family, there are always regrets by some family member. You have no regrets, you're wise to see your brother will. You're doing what is right for your mother and brother. How long has your mother lived with you?" asked Sara.

"Fifteen years. Kelly and I never had a honeymoon. I lived with Mother. We bought our home knowing it was small, but we planned to add on. We went home after our wedding and Mother was there with a note from my brother pinned to her dress. Kelly quit her job, took care of my mother, had my children, and never complained. My mother has come a long way under Kelly's care. I know it wasn't easy on her. I never saw her as happy as she was last night, that was when I realized that Kelly's life was never easy. I'm a lucky man to have such a wife. So it's time I did something for her by making my brother act like a son is a start," said Brian.

"Well your wife sounds like a real fine lady, and I look forward to meeting her," said Sara. "Now go enjoy Christmas."

"Yes, ma'am. I plan to have a real fine Christmas thanks to you," said Brian and he left.

Tonight Brian was taking his family out for a steak dinner. Now he was going home to decorate for Christmas. He passed George, he was hanging lights outside. He waved. Brian waved back. Seven o'clock tomorrow morning Brian was taking George and Kelly to pick up their new trucks. It's only fair that Kelly drives the truck. She put up with that old car for so long. The kids were outside when Brian pulled in. They looked so happy it made Brian feel proud seeing his kids in new clothes. Brian smiled when he got out of the limo.

"Daddy, we got the lights ready," smiled Trey.

Brian laughed. Trey had two dimples every time he smiled. He hated them and decided not to smile anymore. Today he smiled all day long. "We got everything put away. We helped Mom put up the tree. Now she's baking cookies, so she sent us out here," said Trey.

"Well we better put up the lights then," smiled Brian.

Two hours later Brian and his kids had the whole outside decorated. Red nose and rosy cheeks, they stormed into a warm house filled with the smell of freshly baked Christmas cookies.

"A Norman Rockwell painting," thought Brian as he hung up his coat. When the pressures of everyday life were gone, you could enjoy the little things.

Kelly was cleaning up the kitchen, so they could go to supper. "One cookie, it will spoil your supper," smiled Kelly. "Want to rent a movie tonight?"

"No, we're watching 'Miracle on 34th Street' at 8:00," said Pearl.

"Oh, I forgot. Ready to go to supper?"

"Yes, we are hungry," said Tere.

"Okay, get your coats," Kelly helped Pearl get her coat on then put on her coat. The kids were already in the limo. Kelly helped Pearl get into the front. She knew the kids bothered her, so she got in the back. Kelly was going to enjoy herself. Being served things still hadn't settled in her mind. This was her life now. Kelly knew the kids were talking, but she was staring at the house. It was all lit up, it was so beautiful. When they returned, the house still looked beautiful to her. Kelly got Pearl ready for bed and tucked her in and took a shower, put on her nightgown, and made popcorn, two large bowls. The kids got out Pepsi. Everyone was dressed for bed and sitting in front of the TV when the movie came on. Kelly curled up on the couch next to Brian. She was so relaxed and comfortable she fell asleep. Brian carried her to bed. She'd been going all day, probably will be all day tomorrow, too. She had Pearl all packed, her Christmas presents bagged to go. Presents were stacked in the bedroom all wrapped waiting for Santa to put under the tree. "Kelly looked so much better," thought Brian as he covered her. The strained look she had was gone. Her hands were healing. "How could I have been so blind?" thought Brian as he turned out the bedroom light and walked into the living room. The kids had taken over the couch, so Brian sat in the chair. It was a big recliner. Brian was afraid to sit in a chair. With his size and height, he could never get comfortable, but this chair was quite comfortable. He stared at the TV but wasn't watching. He was thinking about talking to Sean about fixing up his house and selling it. There wasn't too much wrong with it. The roof needed fixing, the spot in the kid's room where it leaked needed fixing, windows, and siding. Kelly had kept the inside good. It was small, but anything he put into it he'd get back plus. The house itself was paid for fifteen years ago. He and Kelly bought it for ten thousand dollars. He and Kelly had pooled their savings to buy it. They had enough left over to get a stove and refrigerator, a table, a bedroom set, and a living room set. Kelly had insisted on a fold-out couch if company came. She said company came all right, with a note pinned to her dress. They cancelled their honeymoon and bought a TV. Brian and Kelly thought they were ahead of the game. They worked long hours not to be in debt when they started out. Kelly was going to keep her job, put all her wages away, so they could add on to the house. They wanted two more bedrooms and a garage. Kelly was on the pill, they didn't want children right away. They had talked about Kelly keeping her job at the silverware plant and hiring day care for his mother. It ended up costing them all of Kelly's paycheck plus so they sold Kelly's car, and paid off Brian's. Kelly quit her job and took care of Pearl. Taking care of Pearl wore Kelly down quick. She got sick. The doctor put her on antibiotics, which cancelled out the birth control pills, and Kelly got pregnant with Brian Jr. Instead of having a rosy glow, Kelly looked old and worn. She had a tough time with delivery. It was eighty-two hours of hard labor before Kelly had a C-section. She never screamed or carried on once. Brian sat there next to Kelly, holding her hand, feeling her agony, cursing his brother for what he'd done to them. Sure he'd call every Saturday and say "How's Mom?," talk a couple of minutes, then hang up. He never sent cards or presents. Never talked to her. Then the phone calls stopped. Kelly kept right on working with Pearl. She got Pearl walking and feeding herself. Soon she started talking. Kelly always thought Brian Jr. is what got her talking. She'd see Pearl sneak a peek at the baby. Then one day Kelly told Pearl she could pick him up if she wanted. Pearl was shocked to tears. "I can? You don't think I'd hurt him, do you?" asked Pearl.

"No, Mother, you're not old, and you won't hurt him," said Kelly.

After that Pearl always had Brian Jr., cooing and rocking him. There was nothing wrong with Pearl, she'd just shut down when her husband died. She'd felt she had become a burden to her children. "Maybe being dumped in a rocking chair with a note pinned to her dress had something to do with it," thought Brian. That still pissed him off, probably always would.

Kelly and Brian discussed Kelly going back to work. Pearl insisted she'd watch the baby. Pearl was good with Brian Jr. They had bills that were starting to pile up, so Kelly went back to work. Pearl did good with Brian Jr. They had paid off all their bills and started saving money. Maybe it was all right. Kelly bought a washer and dryer. No more trips to the laundromat. Then Brian's car died; they bought a new one. It wiped out their savings, but they weren't in debt. Two years' savings gone. Kelly worked one more year and got pregnant for Pearl. That whole year her paycheck went into the bank. Kelly, Brian, and Pearl sat down and discussed Pearl baby sitting two children and how hard it would be on Pearl. Pearl insisted she could do it. She'd had six children of her own. Kelly needed to work because her insurance would pay for her C-section. She wouldn't have a debt like they did with Brian Jr. if they could build up their savings, so they tried under one condition: That Pearl would tell them if it got too much for her. Pearl agreed. Six months after having Pearl, the elder Pearl told Kelly and Brian it was too much. Pearl cried all the time; Kelly understood. Pearl was a colic baby. So Kelly quit her job never to return a year later. She'd had the twins, a boy and girl. The doctors tied her tubes. She could only have three C-sections. The savings were gone, and everything started falling apart. Even with two jobs, Brian couldn't make enough to stay ahead of the game. Kelly never complained, not once. The kids grew out of their clothes faster than they could manufacture them. Shoes were next to impossible, seemed every month someone needed new shoes. Kelly started having lawn sales to get rid of clothes that no longer fit anyone. She'd set the money aside for new clothes. Then one year she sold a lot of household things. She didn't need all the baby stuff she'd accumulated through the years; she'd sold enough to buy two new bunkbeds for the kids. She moved Pearl to the back bedroom after she scrubbed and painted it, and put the kids in the front bedroom because it was larger. She scrubbed that room and painted it. Now the kids had room to play. Pearl wasn't happy with the new arrangement. Her room was too small and cramped, stuffy, she'd say. So the following spring Kelly sold the beds the kids used to sleep in and bought Pearl a twinbed. This seemed to please her. "She only wanted a new bed because the kids had new beds," thought Kelly. She's happy, that's all that matters. Then Pearl started complaining about the noise the kids made, so come the following spring, Kelly cleaned out the cellar and sold everything that wasn't nailed down in the cellar. She turned it into a playroom for the kids. They moved all their toys down there. Kelly made enough extra money to buy a new mattress for the couch. God, she worked so hard to keep everyone happy. During spring, Kelly planted a garden. She canned all summer and fall. Extra vegetables were sold by the roadside. She took that money to buy fruit to can. One year Kelly had a huge garden. Brian couldn't understand her logic, but she'd sold enough extra vegetables to buy a used freezer. The kids were growing and so were their appetites. Brian took up hunting; Kelly and the kids fished, anything to save money. Pearl was happy once again. She had venison and fish. "About time we had a decent meal," she'd say to Kelly. Kelly had a system for everything. Then the roof started leaking. Kelly got an estimate. They said five thousand dollars. Kelly said, "No." She only wanted the spot fixed where it leaked. They told Kelly that according to the law they had to replace the whole roof so they weren't sued. Kelly called all over and was told the same thing over and over. A week after the contractor had been there, he stopped to talk to Kelly.

"We can't fix it, but there's no reason you can't," said Joey. "I'll tell you what to do, how to do it, and it won't cost you a hundred dollars."

This intrigued Kelly, so she let Joey in. She poured him a cup of coffee, and handed him a pen and paper. He wrote it all down for her.

"Why are you doing this?" asked Kelly.

"Because every now and again you run across decent people. You're one of those people. And I wouldn't feel right not helping you. I can't guarantee it won't leak later on, but it will stop it for a while. Now if you replace this whole side, I could do it for you for about three hundred dollars, but nobody is to know I did this for you," said Joey.

Kelly got up and walked to the cupboard and took our three hundred dollars. That left her two hundred dollars for school clothes in the fall. She thought carefully, "Maybe the garden would bring in the extra." So she took a chance. She paid Joey three hundred dollars. She knew one side wouldn't leak. If the other side started, she'd worry about that when it came. Kelly and Brian helped John strip the roof. They found other holes, so Kelly took another one hundred dollars and bought wafer board to cover the other roof. It was cheaper that way. George came over and helped. He didn't like Kelly on the roof, so Kelly and the kids became the ground crew, cleaning up the mess on the ground. Kelly was glad their roof wasn't very big. They squeezed by that year, but they made it. Then the washer and dryer broke. Brian Jr. needed braces; Pearl needed glasses. Kelly refused to take the laundry to the laundromat, it cost too much. The handle broke on the refrigerator, so Kelly propped it shut with a stick of wood. Then the back part of the roof started leaking. They only repaired the one leak. Paint started peeling on the outside of the house. Kelly scraped and covered it with primer. Window sills started leaking and rotting, so Kelly covered them with plastic. Everything was falling apart; Kelly couldn't keep up. Pearl complained more and more about the kids. Bill collectors called threatening to turn off the phone and electric. It was getting all out of control. When the electric company called and said the power was being shut off, she just started crying. It was five hundred dollars and had to be paid by five o'clock. She couldn't stop crying. Right there on the phone, she cried. She looked around, the kids were running around, Pearl was yelling. She looked at the stick on the refrigerator and broke down. A new leak appeared all that day on the ceiling. Kelly couldn't stop crying. She never broke down in her life; now she couldn't stop. The house grew silent as they watched Kelly break down. The lady on the phone kept calling her name, but all she got was sobs. She called her boss over and explained what happened. She felt Kelly needed help. Her boss said, "Hang up, it's an act, they will do anything to get out of paying a bill. You better get used to it. People are liars and cheats." The young girl stood up, looked her boss in the face, and said, "You're one sick mother fucker, and I quit." She grabbed Kelly's bill, paid it, got a receipt that it was paid, and dropped it off in Kelly's mailbox. Kelly and Brian never knew who that person was. Kelly's world has fallen apart, beyond repair. She couldn't do it anymore. Brian got scared because Kelly wouldn't stop crying. He ran to get April. She came right over. Kelly still sat there crying. April sent the kids downstairs. Pearl started yelling, saying it served her right, she could have done better. April stood up and yelled at Pearl and sent her to her room. Pearl never acted like this around Brian. April made Kelly some tea. Kelly calmed down and they talked. April told her things would work out, they always do. "I just can't do it anymore, I've done all I can do. I know five hundred dollars is a lot of money, but with Mom's prescription, Brian's braces, Pearl keeps breaking her glasses. I can't make ends meet. If I had it I'd pay it, but I don't. Now I'll have no power, all our food will spoil. I've got one burner that works, an oven that has hot spots, a stick holding my refrigerator closed, a roof that leaks, kids that need new clothes and shoes every time you turn around. The car's going; it's starting to nickel and dime us to death. I've got doctor bills for the twins, allergy shots. I don't know what to do anymore. I've done all I can do."

"Mom, here's the mail," said Brian Jr. "I got it for you."

"Thank you, sweetheart," smiled Kelly as she looked at the stack of bills. That was the last thing she needed right now, but she looked anyway. Brian Jr. went back downstairs. "One hundred fifty dollar phone bill, twenty-five dollars to the doctor, one hundred dollars for Brian's braces. I only owe two hundred dollars on the gas bill and for the car one hundred dollars. Pearl's glasses are one hundred dollars. She'll break them again next month because she doesn't want to wear them, so they get broken. The electric bill, the electric bill," Kelly repeated, "has been paid, who paid it?" Kelly looked at April, she shrugged her shoulders.

"How much money would you need to get on track?" asked April.

"Way too much. We were thinking of taking a loan against the house to fix it up and pay off all the bills, then get a new car. But Brian doesn't make enough for a family of seven, so we were turned down," said Kelly. "The bank said if I had a job, we could get a load. If I had a job, we wouldn't need the loan. What hurts us is Brian's braces. Mom's pills run four hundred dollars a month, a hundred a month for new glasses for Pearl. I owe the doctor one thousand dollars for the twins' shots, I pay him twenty-five dollars a week. I owe four thousand dollars on Mom's bill, we pay one hundred dollars a month on that. If I had house payments, I don't know what I'd do. I've got all this money going out with nothing to show for it. I feel awful, I broke down, but I couldn't handle it anymore. Fifteen years of scraping to get by just took its toll, I guess."

"I wonder why," said April. "I couldn't have put up with half of what you put up with. If Pearl were my mother-in-law, she would have been out a long time ago. I wouldn't put up with it, but how much would it take to get you back to where you were?" asked April.

"I don't know, I've always been afraid to figure it out. I've got four hundred seventy-five dollars sitting right here. It would have been a thousand with the electric. I don't know who paid it. I'd love to thank them. Then Mom's pills, that's another four hundred dollars." Kelly got up, went to the cupboard, and took out her money tin; she counted it. "The kids will need one more pair of shoes before school lets out. If I planted a bigger garden, maybe I could make enough for school clothes. If Pearl would stop breaking her glasses, that's one hundred dollars a month extra I wouldn't have to pay out. Brian's braces will be paid off next, that would give me an extra hundred there I'd save. It's these bills that are killing me, the extras."

Pearl made a silent oath never to break her glasses again. She and Brian sat on the top of the stairs listening.

"We're paying out five hundred dollars a month on Pearl alone. That's what started this whole thing. Brian tried talking to his brothers and sisters. They don't want to know anything. Terry won't even return his calls. All he asked was that they all chip in a hundred a month, that's not too much. He thought it would be easy for them to do since they had such high-paying jobs. It would be extra we'd set aside for future problems; they wouldn't do it. So in teeth, eyes, and Mom, seven hundred a month is gone, before anything else."

"God, no wonder you can't get ahead," cried April. "That's a month's pay."

Kelly had dreamed of this conversation with April. It took place in February. April lent Kelly six hundred dollars to be repaid as she could. Strangely Pearl stopped breaking her glasses, she paid Brian's braces off, paid the phone bill off, bought the kids shoes, planted a huge garden, had another lawn sale, and kept the phone and electric paid. The repairs around the house could wait. They patched the back roof as much as they could. Kelly paid April back, then Kelly's eyes flew open. She looked around, it was true, all that was behind her now. She looked at the clock: 6:00 A.M. Kelly got up, made coffee, and was sitting at the table drinking a cup when Brian walked in the kitchen. Kelly poured Brian a cup of coffee, then made the bed.

They picked up George at 7:00, drove to the Ford dealers, picked up their new trucks, and drove home. In a couple of hours Terry would be here, so Kelly made breakfast. The smell of food woke everyone up. They came to the table in pajamas. After breakfast Kelly cleaned the kitchen, put the dishes in the dishwasher, dressed Pearl in her new clothes, then she went into the living room to sit. Kelly stripped her bed, put on the new bed linen she'd bought, and washed the bed linen she'd taken off Mother's bed. Kelly walked through the house, making beds and picking up, gathering laundry along the way. The house would be spotless when Terry came.

"Need a hand?" asked Brian, taking the basket.

"Brian how did you get Terry to take your Mom after all this time?" asked Kelly.

"Terry refused to talk to me, so I went to tribal counsel and explained everything to them. They, in turn, talked to Terry. I was told to call him back and tell him when to pick up his mother."

"But I thought you couldn't go to counsel because you don't live on the reservation."

"I can't, but I could go on my mother's behalf because her rights were in violation because of Terry, who does live on the reservation. So if Terry wanted to keep his rights to live on the reservation, he had to obey their laws. Their laws say Mother goes to the eldest son first, and so on down the line," said Brian.

"What would they do to Terry if he didn't live by the rules?" asked Kelly.

"First he'd be removed from his house, then the counsel would meet and decide what would be the best punishment for his crimes against his mother. I'm told those are the harshest punishment, sins against family. George told me about it. I went in March. It took them till now to decide if I was correct. They looked very closely into everything. Now if something happens to Terry, Mom would go to the next in line, which is me, but since I already did my share, it passes me to Samantha. That, you know, would cause a real uproar, but she has to do it, it's been written," said Brian.

"So your brother isn't going to be a happy camper, is he?" asked Kelly.

"I don't care if he is or not," said Brian. "I've had it with my family. I made sure the counsel knew that none of my sisters and brothers helped us financially. They are all being called before counsel on that one. I told them how she was left with a note pinned on her dress, how you took care of her, how they never called, wrote, or visited, and there was no reason. They were all within a ten-mile radius. I know when I walked out of there, they were furious. I was the only one who didn't live on the reservation who went by and met their rules. They were impressed at what we'd done," Brian said proudly. "You impressed them the most."

"Me, what did I do?" asked Kelly.

"They watched you. The most they remembered of Mom was how she got after Dad died. They saw you help her out, and how well you treated her and what a long way she'd come. Everyone around us talked very highly of you and how well behaved the children were, how clean Mother was. I guess April told them your house was so clean you could eat off the floor. She didn't know how you did it with a family of seven in a two-bedroom house. I guess April had a lot to say."

"She would," laughed Kelly, sorting clothes. "I was thinking I'd like to go back to work."

"Not now, we'll talk later. First you're getting some much needed rest," said Brian.

"Okay, just as long as that rest isn't too long," teased Kelly, walking into the kitchen.

"Terry's here," said Pearl, walking into the kitchen. "I don't think he thinks he's got the right house. He's just sitting in the car staring at the house."

"I'll get him," said Brian. He went outside and waved Terry in.

"When did you move here?" asked Terry. "The counsel said you've done well for yourself, but this is unbelievable," said Terry, walking in.

Brian was quite pissed off. He didn't think he could feel this pissed off. "Well if you had kept in contact, you would know a few things," said Brian.

"I tried calling you," smiled Terry. "Never got an answer."

"That shit might work on Mom, Terry, but don't try it on me, okay? I doubt even Mom would buy that shit, she's pretty sharp," said Brian.

"Yeah, that's what the counsel tried to feed me. I don't think it was right of you to go to the nation's counsel. You got everyone pissed off at me," said Terry.

"Well I don't really give a damn. All I wanted was one hundred dollars a month from each of you, and you all refused. You didn't even return my call. Not onc of you called, wrotc, or sent a gift to Mom," said Brian.

"Well we didn't have your new address," said Terry.

"That's bullshit and you know it. I've been here three days. I've been waiting to hear your excuses. So far all I've heard is bullshit. The phone number is still the same. I want one thing understood, I will stay in touch with Mom. I will pick her up every Sunday and take her out. I hear her complain once, see one mark on that woman or see she's not properly taken care of, I go to the counsel on her behalf. You can spread whatever shit you want around, I will hear it. I will go to counsel on behalf of my children. In other words, nobody in this family fucks with me and Mom," said Brian. "Do you understand me Terry?"

"When did you develop an attitude like that?" said Terry.

"The day I came home, found Mom sitting in a chair with a note pinned to her dress. I kept the note. I gave you fifteen years to correct it. You didn't, so I turned the note over to counsel. So you can deny whatever you want, but the truth is the truth. You can pull whatever you want, but Mom goes to Samantha next. I had my turn, counsel said so. I don't pay any of you anything. I paid more than my fair share, counsel already ruled on that," said Brian.

"You really covered your ass," said Terry.

"No, I covered Mom's. You walk in my house, you treat me and my family with respect or I'll knock you on your ass. Do you understand?" said Brian.

"Yes," said Terry.

"Go talk to Mother then," said Brian.

Terry walked in, shocked at what he saw. Outside of the fact that the house was beautiful, Kelly, the four children, and his mother sat at a huge table talking and laughing. His mother never did that. "You have four kids?" asked Terry.

"Yeah, you would know if you called once in awhile. Trey and Tere are nine years old now," said Brian.

"Twins? You do surprise me, Brian," said Terry. "Hi, Mom."

"What, I hear someone called me Mom? I thought I only had one son. Who is this man?" said Pearl.

"Okay, Mom, I was a little less than a perfect son. I made one little mistake, you going to condemn me for life?" laughed Terry.

"One mistake, you made more than one mistake. You threw me away like the trash you throw out, then you disowned me, you and your brothers and sisters," said Pearl.

"Now you know that ain't true, Mom. We all got so busy, time flew by, that's all," smiled Terry.

"So you were so busy you forgot me on holidays and my birthday. Mother's Day came and it didn't cross your mind once that you had a mother?" said Pearl.

Terry knew his mother would never forgive him, so he decided to tell the truth. "My wife, Rosemary, didn't want you around. She threatened to leave me and take my children away where I'd never see them again. I had no choice, I loved my children," said Terry.

"So why does she love me now?" asked Pearl.

"The counsel has threatened to take our house and throw us into the street, disown us, all our rights stripped away. The children would have to go to public schools and there would be no college for them," said Terry.

"Oh I see, it took you losing everything you owned to remember you had a mother," said Pearl.

"It wasn't me, it was Rosemary," said Terry.

"Aren't you the head of the house?" asked Pearl.

"Yes, I am," said Terry.

"No, I don't think you are. If you were, you would tell your wife, not your wife telling you. You know what I think? Children, leave the room," said Pearl.

The children left the room.

"No, Mother, what am I?" asked Terry.

"You're pussy-whipped. Your wife runs your life by how she fucks you. You think with the wrong head, my son. You are not a wise man. You are stupid. Did you not learn anything?" said Pearl.

"Mother!" said Terry. "When did you get so forward?"

"The day you dumped me," said Pearl.

"I didn't dump you, I moved you to Brian's house. You had a nice home," said Terry.

"Brian and Kelly gave up their bedroom for me. They slept on a couch for fifteen years. Would you have done that for me?" asked Pearl.

"You shared a room with Crystal," said Terry.

"But I've always had my own room at Brian's, no kids. And I better have one at your house or I'll send Brian to counsel on my behalf," said Pearl.

"The girls can move in together," smiled Terry.

"Does this bedroom have its own bathroom. I have my own bathroom," said Pearl.

"Well, no, only our bedroom has its own bathroom," said Terry.

"Good, that's the one I will sleep in. You're the oldest son, you wouldn't want your brother to show you up now, would you?" asked Pearl.

"Mother, now I know you never had your own bathroom. You're just trying to be difficult," said Terry.

"Come, follow me," said Pearl. "You have to pick up my luggage anyway." Terry followed Pearl to her bedroom. "This is my bedroom, this is my bathroom. Now do you think I'm looney and a liar or maybe difficult?" said Pearl, staring at Terry.

"You may have our room," said Terry, picking up some suitcases. Brian helped Terry carry the suitcases to the car. "I'm really screwed up here. Rosemary won't like this at all."

"I don't know what to tell you," said Brian. "I'll get the rest of the luggage. We have Christmas presents for Mom."

"Sure, whatever," said Terry.

"Well, you would be wise to buy her some presents. She's already counted the ones we gave her. She makes sure nobody gets more than the next," said Brian.

"She sure is in rare form, very outspoken," said Terry.

"She's as sharp as a tack, but if you'd kept in touch, she would have understood. Now she's going to make you pay, that's all I can tell you," said Brian.

"Let's get Mom, you're all loaded," said Brian. "Kelly's getting her coat on for her."

"Kelly dresses Mom?" asked Terry.

"Kelly dresses Mom, she baths her, brushes her hair, brushes her teeth, washes her clothes, sews them, irons them," said Brian. "And she keeps her on schedule for her pills."

"Rosemary has to do all that? She won't do it. I know her," said Terry.

"Well you better go to counsel, tell them they will have to kick you out and pass Mom to Samantha. I'm not being mean, just telling you the facts," said Brian.

When Brian and Terry walked in, Pearl was hugging the kids and thanking Kelly. She hugged Kelly. "Terry will pay, watch me," whispered Pearl.

"Now, I don't want you to pick me up tomorrow. I want to get settled in, so you pick me up next Sunday," said Pearl, kissing Brian.

"Well if you want to come here for Christmas dinner, you call, I'll pick you up. You're always welcome here," said Brian.

"I know I'm welcome here, but I have to take my difficult body to Terry's and make myself known. Now remember, you promised to pick me up in the limo," said Pearl.

"I will, the white one, not the black one," laughed Brian.

"You have two limos?" asked Terry.

"Don't tell him, he doesn't need to know what you have. He's being rude," said Pearl. "Get going."

"This is a schedule of how she does things, it helps," smiled Kelly.

"Thank you, Merry Christmas, we got your card. We don't send them out, Rose says it's too much trouble."

"If cards are too much trouble, what am I going to be?" asked Pearl. "Cards are once a year, I'm an everyday problem."

"Mother, you're no problem. Rose has her exercise classes she goes to. She has her hair and nails done once a week, then her massages twice a week, then yoga."

"What makes you think that she can do that stuff when I'm there?" asked Pearl.

"She does it while the girls are in school," said Terry.

"I don't go to school. She plans to leave me alone?" asked Pearl.

"Don't worry, Mother, it will work out," said Terry. "Let's go."

They left. Terry took Pearl home. He spent three hours moving things around. Rose complained a lot, but Terry ignored her. She complained while Terry worked his ass off. Rose cried, she was too tired to cook, so Terry got take-out.

Pearl just watched. She decided to make it very hard on Rose. She caused all the problems. Her attitude needed some serious changing, and she was going to be the one to change it. She'd show her just how much her fancy attitude was.

"Brian, you know Pearl's going to give Terry and Rose a hard time. She told me she would," said Kelly.

"I know, and they have it coming," laughed Brian. "Now we start enjoying ourselves. I know it's fifteen years late, but I think we've got a good start," said Brian.

"That we do, but what have you got planned for the rest of today?" asked Kelly.

"I thought we'd go to the mall in our new truck and buy a few more Christmas presents," smiled Brian.

"But I thought we were done?" said Kelly.

"Well, I made a list. I'd like my kids to have one hell of a Christmas. April's babysitter's coming for the day. They can have pizza delivered for supper. We'll come back, oh, maybe around 10:00, after the kids are in bed," said Brian.

"Just as long as you don't start spoiling the kids. I won't have that," said Kelly.

"No, just one nice Christmas is all I want," said Brian. "I promise."

Chapter 17

SARA STOOD IN THE LIVING ROOM LOOKING OUT THE WINDOW. A LIGHT SNOW was falling. Sara stared at the four houses lit up for Christmas.

"What are you doing?" asked John, walking up to Sara and hugging her.

"Enjoying the calm before the storm," smiled Sara.

"It going to storm?" asked John.

"Yup, those three houses out there will soon open, and when they do, we're going to be swamped with so much noise and excitement. You're going to enjoy having this few minutes of peace," laughed Sara.

"Ah, the children," smiled John Sr. "I must admit my grandchildren are a bundle of excitement. When I was outside with them today, all they talked about was Santa Claus," laughed John.

"That's why we have Christmas at my house. They're so wound up that if they get to open some presents Christmas Eve, they at least get some sleep tonight. We try to wear them out," laughed Sara.

"No, they will never wear out. They nearly killed me going up and down the hill today," laughed John Sr.

"Here we go, they're coming. George and Brian are here. I'm glad they came. Brian's had a hard life. George's was just like everyone else's. I hope they're happy in their new homes," said Sara as she waved out the window. The tree was laden with presents that spilled all over the room. Sara and John were excited about meeting Kelly.

The door opened with a flurry of people stomping snow on the porch. A swift wind blew in the open door, bringing with it a fresh, clean smell. Sara took a deep breath, she longed to go outside. Her leg was a lot better, but not good enough to go out in the snow with, so when someone came or went, she breathed in as much fresh air as she could. She needed it for the baby. She quit smoking for the baby. John smoked on the porch when he needed one. He didn't like the cigarettes of the 90s, you couldn't taste the tobacco. He only smoked a couple a day. Sean was surprised Sara quit. Sara told him she never smoked while she was pregnant but would wait until after. She never smoked around the children. She had her rules.

Squeals of laughter and excitement followed each and every group that came in the door. It excited Sara. Her excitement for Christmas this year was just not there. She couldn't understand why. This was the best Christmas ever. Everything was here plus, but the spirit wasn't there. She hoped it didn't show. Sara didn't want to bring anybody down. Sara thought it was because she didn't get to be to any stores this Christmas, she didn't get to cook dinner, she didn't get to decorate, she didn't get to shop. She didn't know if she'd get to go shopping the day after Christmas, which was her favorite. What the hell good is money if you can't do anything? Everybody does things for you was how Sara felt.

"Food's out there," said Sara. "It's buffet style." Introductions were made along the way. Everyone was hungry. Kid wanted presents, mothers insisted they eat first. Some sat to eat, others walked around or stood. There was plenty of room for everyone to sit, but the men seemed on edge, so they paced, walked, leaned, and talked. Women sat at a table and talked. Sara tried to sound excited and happy. She hoped she wasn't overdoing it. Kelly and April fit right into the family. Every dish cleared away, and kids ran into the living room. "Presents time." The kids all got new pajamas, bathrobes, slippers, clothes, and toys. Women got clothes and trinkets. April and Kelly got a set of crystal angels for Sara. They each were blowing a trumpet. She "oood" and "aahed," then set them on the mantel of the fireplace. They looked perfect there. Sara knew expensive when she saw it, and this was expensive. Wrapping paper was cleared away, presents stacked and put in everyone's cars. Sean and Sara were placed in a chair and presents laid out before them.

"What's this?" asked Sara.

"We don't know," said John. "All we know is that we were to give this to you Christmas Eve to open."

"Yeah, we've been going nuts trying to figure out what it was," said Susan. "Some of this stuff is heavy."

"Where did it come from?" asked Sara.

"Read the tags," said John.

Sara picked up a small package from Summer. Sara read. She opened it. It was a small pair of moccasins for the baby. "They're adorable." The next package was from Ben. "My boots," cried Sara. The next one was a teal green shawl from Susan. "You said you loved this color," was gently written. The next one was a handmade cradle for the baby. Sara went through packages after packages; two huge packages still remained. One held a letter. Sara read it, then smiled. "There are packages inside of here that I'm to hand out marked, let's see, John and Rachel, Ted and Susan, Sean and Laura, Brian and Kelly, George and April, John Jr., Nicole, Ted Jr., Rachel, Sean Jr., Kera, Brian Jr., Pearl, Trey, Tere, George Jr., Holly, Sean, John, Ted, Brian, George, John. I've got quite a few here." Sara couldn't reach down, so John helped her.

"Oh my God, quilts!" cried Susan. "All handmade quilts."

Everyone was shocked that there were presents for them. The kids even got quilts. The men had hats, gloves, and scarves. Sara opened a quilt for her, then a quilt for the baby, nightgowns, two photograph books, two diaries, heavy flannel material, calico material. "My God," laughed Sara. "Susan didn't have to do all this, look at this afghan." It was cream on the side with a teal green center. "It's huge. Two more to go from this box and you're done with it. They're from Mom and Dad," said John, smiling.

"A diary and photo albums," said Sara. She passed them around.

"John, here's a letter for you," said Laura.

"A letter?" asked John.

"Looks like a letter. It has some kind of seal on it," said Laura as she handed it to John.

"I'll read it after Sara's through opening her presents," said John. "Then I'll read it out loud."

"Well, that box is done," said Sara.

Susan started putting wrapping paper in a box; Laura helped. "This box says breakable," said John.

"After all this time, something is probably broken," said Sara.

"Depends on how it was stored," said John.

Sara opened it. It was her dolls and some Susan had added. "Oh John, my dolls, look, my dolls." There was a note attached.

"Dear Sara: I hope none of the dolls are broken. Every year I was alive, I bought you a doll. I'd look for the prettiest one. Jacob made doll furniture to go with it, just like Sean showed him. I made some fancy dresses for them, little sweaters out of scrap yarn, some have quilts. I never forgot you. You were always my dearest, sweetest friend. After you left on July 24, 1861, I had a little girl. I named her Sara Elizabeth, after you. The photo albums have pictures of the kids, and the journals were carefully written so every major event was recorded so you and John knew of our history. I was surprised Sara was born on your birthday. I guess you could say God left a little reminder for me. You made our lives great, and I hope you and John now have a great life. Tell Kelly 'hi' from great-great-grandma. John Jr. sent us a copy of our heritage to your time. I didn't do too bad. I know Kelly is a descendant of Sean and Sara's, but I raised Sean Jr., so I consider Kelly one of my own. I had a beautiful life, thanks to you. Now I'm old. Jacob died a couple of years back. Now I'm afraid that the Lord is calling me. The doctor says my heart is just plain worn out. The old coot doesn't know nothing anyway, never did. I'm not afraid to die, I always had my guardian angel around. She showed me that heaven is beautiful and that Santa Claus is real. What more is there in life? I love you, my friend. Now I must close, I'm tired. Love, Susan."

"Dear Sara; Three days after writing this letter, my mother died. It was a peaceful death. She closed her eyes, smiled, and went to sleep. The second diary is from me. I will keep it going as long as I can. I promised Mother. A day didn't go by that Mother didn't speak of you. She said friends like you, you never forget. The last thing she did was buy you a china doll. I think this is what kept her going. She died December 28, 1924. Love, Sara."

There were no dry eyes when Sara read the letter. Sara's lower lip quivered as she remembered her friend Susan. She wiped at tears and said Sean is next. Sara knew what was missing now, Susan. Sara looked at her tree, then her dolls, and knew Susan would always be with her every day until they met in heaven.

Laura and Susan wiped tears and cleaned up wrapping paper.

Sean opened his presents. There were journals kept by Jacob, flannel shirts, coats, jeans. "The good stuff," smiled Sean. "Feel the weight of this stuff," said Sean.

"One more box," said Susan.

Sean opened it. It was a handmade coat from Summer and Ben. There was a note. Sean held up the coat, it was beautiful. "I say that Ben got the albino deer, and the coat was made from it," said Sean.

"Open it, look inside," said John Sr.

"Why?" asked Sean.

"Just do it," said John.

So Sean unbuttoned it, opened it, and there lining the coat was the fur of the albino deer. Sean recognized it right away because the deer was only half white then brown. "He really got the deer," laughed Sean.

"What was it you said, 'the one that got away,'" laughed John Sr. "Ben proved it didn't get away."

"How long and hard did we try to get him?" laughed Sean.

"Too long," said John. "Ben probably waited him out. Mom probably made the coat to prove Ben got it."

"This is beautiful," said Sean, standing up and putting it on. "Fits perfectly."

"Mother was always a good judge of size," said John. "What's your letter say?"

John opened his letter.

"Dear son: There are many packages for you held in storage by the nation. We had to be selective what we sent first. There were so many, I suggest you go through them carefully. There are a lot of gifts for Sara and you, more than enough to make your house a home. I always wondered if you were upset because that night we took a walk and I explained some things to you. I didn't tell you that you would be going back with Sara. I wanted to but couldn't. Nether one of you were supposed to know. You had to do what you did by marrying Sara out of love, for no other reason. The moon flowers still grow, just as the child I carry grows. We plan to name him Sean Miles Green, for the journey that Sean made for our people. Brian is related to us; George is related to Sean and Jacob, whose son, Jacob Jr., married a future daughter I have. We named her Sara Angel Green because Sara was the angel princess who saved our people. I want you and Sara to have a good life together. You two always belonged together. Ben and I miss you, but we know you're happy. You remember to tell my great-great-grandchildren we love them very much. I love you, John, Summer."

"John: got that albino. Took a long time, but I got him. I wish you all the best, Sara will be a good wife and mother. I enjoyed her cooking. She taught the nation's women well; Sara taught everyone something. We learned that there are good and bad in all of us, it's just up to us what we want to be, good or bad. You have your own account for money. Sean arranged it before he left, something about a man being independent. Yes, Sean knew you were going back. We discussed the legend in detail. That's why the cabin was so important, something that time couldn't change. I hope you didn't give Brian and George a hard time. I love you son, Ben."

John looked up smiling.

"Well, did you?" asked Sara.

"Maybe, a little," laughed John.

"A little," said Brian. "We had to hold you down while we explained," laughed Brian.

"What did you expect? I wake up, Sara's gone, I feel all over for her, I close my eyes, prayed I did right by her, open my eyes, and these two are standing at the end of the bed. I didn't know what they were there for. I thought they wanted to kill me. My wife was gone, replaced by those two. Even you have to admit it was strange. George told me not to panic. He explained, so I swung at him. They wrestled me to the bed while they explained. I calmed down enough to get cleaned up and dressed. The only thing that made me believe them was when George said Sara's coming, too. I was taken to the hospital, asked a million questions, was checked out by Dr. Stevenson, then was allowed to see Sara. Until I saw Sara, I wouldn't believe it. I came walking down the hall, saw Sean, Laura, John, and Susan. My heart was racing; it was true. I was here with Sara. She came back for me, and I came forward for her to correct some mistakes. Now I know how Sara felt going back. It's confusing like a dream. It's not real, but it feels real, and you wait to wake up. Then we're brought here, that throws us back into the past. It's been a little confusing," said John.

"That's it!" said Sara. "That's what's been driving me nuts."

"What's driving you nuts?" asked John.

"I've had this nagging feeling that something was missing," said Sara.

"Me, too," said Sean. "What is it?"

"We've been thrown back in time. My memory keeps telling me I have to do something, something is missing. The animals, the milking, the feeding, the gathering of eggs. We got so used to it our minds keep telling us to do it," laughed Sara.

"You're right," laughed Sean. "I woke up this morning to do something, and I couldn't remember what I had to do. I thought I was going crazy," said Sean. "Seeing this place brought back all the old habits." Sean shook his head. "My mind hasn't adjusted to this time."

"You milked cows?" asked Susan, staring at Sara.

"Yeah, Sara always got most of the milk when she milked," said Sean.

"That's because I talked to them," said Sara.

Everyone laughed.

"You two talked to the cows when you milked them?" asked John. "Mother, I can't picture you milking a cow, you're so small."

"Oh, I did a lot of things. I cleaned stalls, spread manure, fed the hogs, fed the chickens and turkeys, cleaned the wood stoves, and you know what, I miss it," said Sara. "Oh, I chopped wood, too."

"Me, too," said Sean. "It had a way of making you feel like you did a real day's work."

"Go on, you're joking, right?" asked Laura.

"No I'm not, and I think I'm going to bring some animals back to this place, it needs it," said Sean.

"Horses, Daddy, can we have horses?" asked Kera.

"Yup, horses for all the kids to ride," said Sean.

"I think we'll open our barn, too, get my garden going," smiled Sara.

"You two are nuts," said Susan.

"No they're not," said John. "I agree with Sara. You two know how good it felt to work the farm. We did it because we had no choice if we were going to survive. Now we want to do it because we learned what a day's work could mean," smiled John. "It's too easy to sit around today," said John, "too easy."

"Well, I'm game," smiled John. "I'll have a go at it, but if it's not my thing, I will tell you. I know farming is hard and has long hours," said John.

"Hell, I'll give it a try," said Ted. "As long as I get to ride a horse, wear a cowboy hat, and get to say 'you all' from time to time." Everyone laughed. "Think about it, we're already farmers. It may be fruits and vegetables, but it's still farming," said Ted.

"Yea, we're getting a horse," cried Kera.

"Well it's late, we better go or Santa's going to pass right over us," said John.

"We didn't miss Santa on the radar, did we?" asked John III.

"No, but you better hurry and get your coats on or we will," smiled John.

Kids all ran for their coats yelling, "Santa's coming."

"Santa? Radar?" asked John Sr.

"Local news at eleven breaks in with a news report that a radar spotted an unidentified flying object. It shows them zooming in and Santa, his sleigh, and eight reindeer appear. They say Santa's coming and kids run and go to bed," laughed John Jr. "They are so wound up by then. When it's confirmed Santa's been spotted, the kids go to bed willingly, knowing he's coming. They fall right to sleep."

"Ready, Daddy?" said Nicole. "Come on, hurry up."

"I see what you mean," said John Sr.

Everyone gathered their presents from Susan and Jacob and put their coats on in a hurry because kids were pushing parents to hurry. "Merry Christmas" was yelled and everyone left as fast as they came. Sara and John waved out the window then cleaned up the mess. Sara made two cups of hot chocolate, sat on the couch, turned the TV on, and watched as Santa was spotted.

John laughed. "That is so cute," said John.

"What's cute about it, that's Santa Claus," said Sara.

"Yeah right," laughed John.

"Okay," said Sara. She got up, went through her packages, put out the afghan, placed the quilt at the end of the bed, and placed her dolls through the house. Then she put her nightgowns away, except one which she put on. Then she and John set out the presents they bought each other. Sara's spirit was back; she looked around, and everything looked good. She washed out the cups and put them away. They went to bed, made love, and fell asleep. Cookies and milk waited for Santa.

John Sr. heard a noise. "Thump, thump," he listened. "I'm losing my mind," laughed John. "Thump, thump," John looked up, then at Sara. "It's all this talk they filled my head with," thought John. Sara slept away. "Why didn't she hear it?" John heard a jingle; someone's in the house. John got up, put his bathrobe on, and walked slowly to the living room. There stood a man in a red velvet suit with white fur. "Sure," thought John, "Sara's pulling some kind of trick on me."

"Hello," said Santa, turning and facing John.

John jumped. He was just like Sara said he was. John nodded, he couldn't speak.

"You must tell Sara that Mrs. Santa Claus would like her recipe for these cookies. She'll know where to send it," said Santa. "Merry Christmas," And he was gone. Fine, gold sparkling things fell to the floor where he stood.

"John, something wrong?" asked Sara, rubbing her eyes.

"Sa...sa...Santa was here, I saw him, then poof, he was gone. He stood right here and talked to me," said John Sr.

"What did he want?" asked Sara.

"Mrs. Claus wants your recipe for your cookies you left out for him," said John, feeling stupid. It didn't sound right even as he said it.

"Okay," said Sara. She walked over to the kitchen, wrote down the recipe, and set it on the tree. "He'll come back over; he'll take it," said Sara. "Let's go to bed now."

"I'll be right there," said John. He needed a minute to think. He was dreaming, that's it, then the recipe sparkled and was gone. John rubbed his eyes, looked, then ran into the bedroom, shook Sara awake. "The recipe is gone," said John.

"You said Mrs. Claus wanted it, didn't you?" asked Sara, sitting up.

"Yes, but I thought you were pulling a trick on me, but I saw Santa, I saw the recipe disappear," said John.

"I keep telling everyone Santa is real. Why won't anyone believe me?" said Sara. "I saw him as a child. He came into my room and gave me a doll. Every year someone, and only one person, sees Santa. Susan saw him, I saw him, and now you saw him," said Sara.

"Santa Claus chose me to see him? said John, laughing.

"Yes, so you would believe. I know you won't believe it now, but next year the day after Thanksgiving, you will get so excited about

Christmas, you won't be able to control yourself. This excitement will pass on to others and that's how the magic of Christmas works, by what we give to others," said Sara.

"Can we open our presents now?" asked John.

"No, in the morning like everyone else," said Sara. "Now sleep."

John lay down; he tried to sleep, but he couldn't. He tossed and turned. Finally he got up, and walked into the living room. He sat in front of the tree. There were more presents there than what they put under the tree.

Sara got up that morning to find John sleeping on the floor by the tree. She laughed and shook John. "Come on, open your presents," said Sara.

"I was watching the tree, and those sparkling things appeared and another present, poof, right there, that one," said John, pointing. "To you from Mrs. Claus."

"Why did she sent me a present?" asked Sara.

John shrugged. He wanted to see what the big package was with his name on it. Sara smiled, she knew why John was chosen to see Santa: so he could find the child within him, so he'd always feel young like she did. No matter how old you were, if you kept the child in your, life could be great.

"Go ahead, start opening," smiled Sara. Sara opened hers from Mrs. Claus. A Christmas quilt. Sara smiled as she touched it and said thank you. For fifty years Sara was going to make a Christmas quilt, now her wish came true. John's was a coat like Sean's. He loved it. John's excitement made him rush through his presents. There were some toys, a remote car, a train set, some tools, and clothes. Sara's excitement was watching John. She watched him. It started with Christmas, this Christmas. From here life would be easy. The presents weren't what Santa gave Sara; Santa gave Sara John, a man who would always feel like she did about Christmas. "You know Christmas shopping starts tomorrow," said Sara.

"What time?" asked John.

"The stores open at 9:00 A.M.," said Sara.

"We'll be there at 8:30 A.M.," said John. "I like Christmas. I want to get Santa a present," said John.

Sara laughed. "Spoken like a true child."

John and Sara started shopping the next morning for Christmas. The gifts in storage were plenty. Sara passed them around, she kept the blue dish set and blue pan set. Books and ledgers for John to go through. John taught the old ways and learned the new. The barns were opened and livestock put in.

Sara had six children and lived to watch them go to college, wed, and give lots of grandchildren. She quit smoking; so did John. Sean always said he'd never live to see the day, but he did, so he quit smoking, too. Sara's garden never was touched. Every year her and John would take a day and go gather flowers for her to dry. John and Ted loved farming. Ted got to say "you all" as much as he wanted. Sara stayed inside her world as much as she could. Every spring she planted flowers at the graves of Jacob and Susan and the family. Every summer they had a huge barbecue with the descendants of Jacob and Susan, Ben, and Summer, Sean's, and Sara's. The Indian's lore was taught to all so it would go on.

Pearl passed on during her fourth year living with Terry. She'd broken Rosemary, made her get off her high horse, as Pearl put it. Terry became man of his house and had no regrets when Pearl passed on. Brian always picked up his mother on Sunday in the white limo.

Brian and George's kids went to college. Kelly finally talked Brian into letting her go back to work. It wasn't for the money, it was boredom. April worked with Kelly. Brian and Kelly finally got their honeymoon. John and Sara sent them to Hawaii after Pearl died. George and April were sent after Brian and Kelly came back. One summer John and Sara sent both families to Disney World in Florida for two weeks.

Sara and John never traveled; they loved where they were too much to leave. However, they did go for moonlights swims at the quarry and spent every anniversary in the cabin. Sara read Susan's diaries carefully. She never wanted to get lost in a diary again. John never spoke of seeing Santa, but he lived inside of him. He showed up every year right after Thanksgiving.

Sara kept the hope chest. The secret place was removed. The diaries were laid inside for future use. When someone asked about the legend, Sara read them the diaries. "The truth lies in our hearts," was all Sara would say.